ALLISON • SARIN • FLEMING • COGAR

# GIANT DAYS™

## NOT ON THE TEST EDITION

WINTER SEMESTER

BOOM! BOX™

Putterham

OVERSIZE
TEEN GRAPHIC
*Giant Days*
*V2*

**GIANT DAYS NOT ON THE TEST EDITION Volume Two, January 2018.** Published by BOOM! Box, a division of Boom Entertainment, Inc. Giant Days is ™ & © 2018 John Allison. Originally published in single magazine form as GIANT DAYS No. 9-16. ™ & © 2015, 2016 John Allison. All rights reserved. BOOM! Box™ and the BOOM! Box logo are trademarks of Boom Entertainment, Inc., registered in various countries and categories. All characters, events, and institutions depicted herein are fictional. Any similarity between any of the names, characters, persons, events, and/or institutions in this publication to actual names, characters, and persons, whether living or dead, events, and/or institutions is unintended and purely coincidental. BOOM! Box does not read or accept unsolicited submissions of ideas, stories, or artwork.

BOOM! Studios, 5670 Wilshire Boulevard, Suite 450, Los Angeles, CA 90036-5679. Printed in China. First Printing.

ISBN-13: 978-1-68415-058-8, eISBN: 978-1-61398-735-3

## This book belongs to:

Name: _____

# SHEFFIELD UNIVERSITY

## WINTER SEMESTER

# GIANT DAYS™

## NOT ON THE TEST EDITION

### WINTER SEMESTER

**CREATED & WRITTEN BY**
## JOHN ALLISON

**ILLUSTRATED BY**
## MAX SARIN

**INKS BY**
## LIZ FLEMING
(CHAPTERS 13–16)

**COLORS BY**
WHITNEY COGAR

**LETTERS BY**
JIM CAMPBELL

**COVER ART BY**
MAX SARIN

**DESIGNER**
MICHELLE ANKLEY

**EDITORS**
SHANNON WATTERS
JASMINE AMIRI

# CHAPTER
# NINE

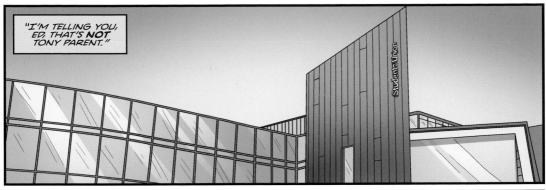

"I'M TELLING YOU, ED, THAT'S **NOT** TONY PARENT."

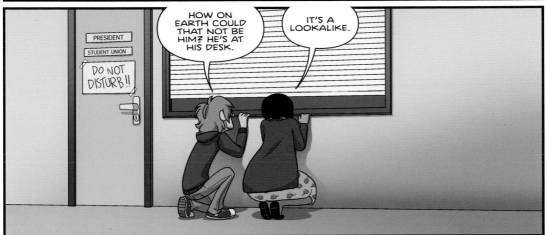

HOW ON EARTH COULD THAT NOT BE HIM? HE'S AT HIS DESK.

IT'S A LOOKALIKE.

PRESIDENT

STUDENT UNION

DO NOT DISTURB!!

HE'S THE STUDENT UNION PRESIDENT, NOT SADDAM HUSSEIN. HE DOESN'T HAVE BODY DOUBLES. **NO ONE'S TRYING TO ASSASSINATE HIM.**

I MEAN, NO ONE EXCEPT YOU, AMANDA. WHAT ARE YOU DOING?

I'M GOING TO NAME AND SHAME THIS IMPOSTER.

BUT THERE'S A **DO NOT DISTURB** SIGN!

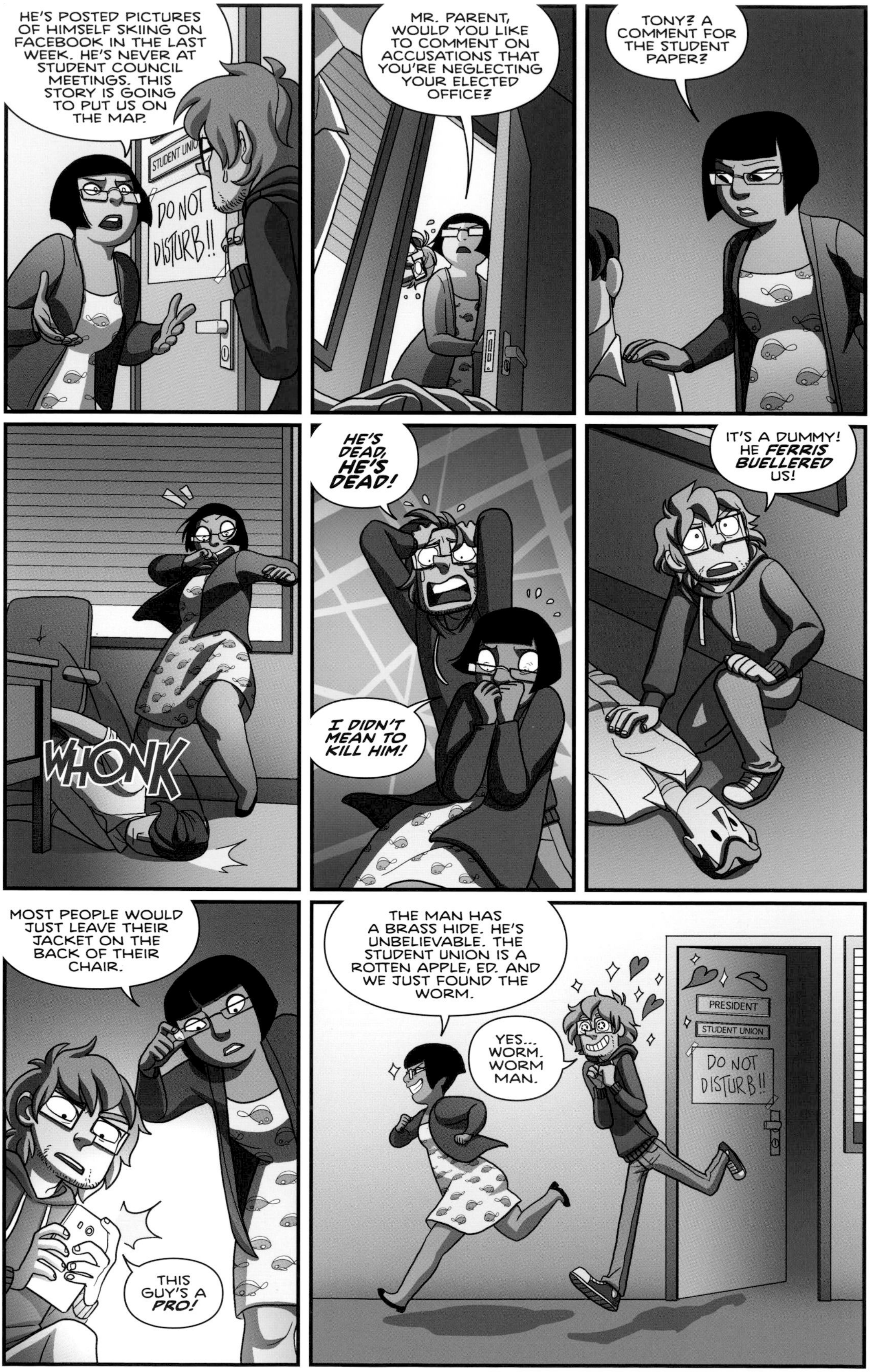
HE'S POSTED PICTURES OF HIMSELF SKIING ON FACEBOOK IN THE LAST WEEK. HE'S NEVER AT STUDENT COUNCIL MEETINGS. THIS STORY IS GOING TO PUT US ON THE MAP.
STUDENT UNION
DO NOT DISTURB!!
MR. PARENT, WOULD YOU LIKE TO COMMENT ON ACCUSATIONS THAT YOU'RE NEGLECTING YOUR ELECTED OFFICE?
TONY? A COMMENT FOR THE STUDENT PAPER?
WHONK
HE'S DEAD, HE'S DEAD!
I DIDN'T MEAN TO KILL HIM!
IT'S A DUMMY! HE FERRIS BUELLERED US!
MOST PEOPLE WOULD JUST LEAVE THEIR JACKET ON THE BACK OF THEIR CHAIR.
THIS GUY'S A PRO!
THE MAN HAS A BRASS HIDE. HE'S UNBELIEVABLE. THE STUDENT UNION IS A ROTTEN APPLE, ED. AND WE JUST FOUND THE WORM.
YES... WORM. WORM MAN.
PRESIDENT
STUDENT UNION
DO NOT DISTURB!!

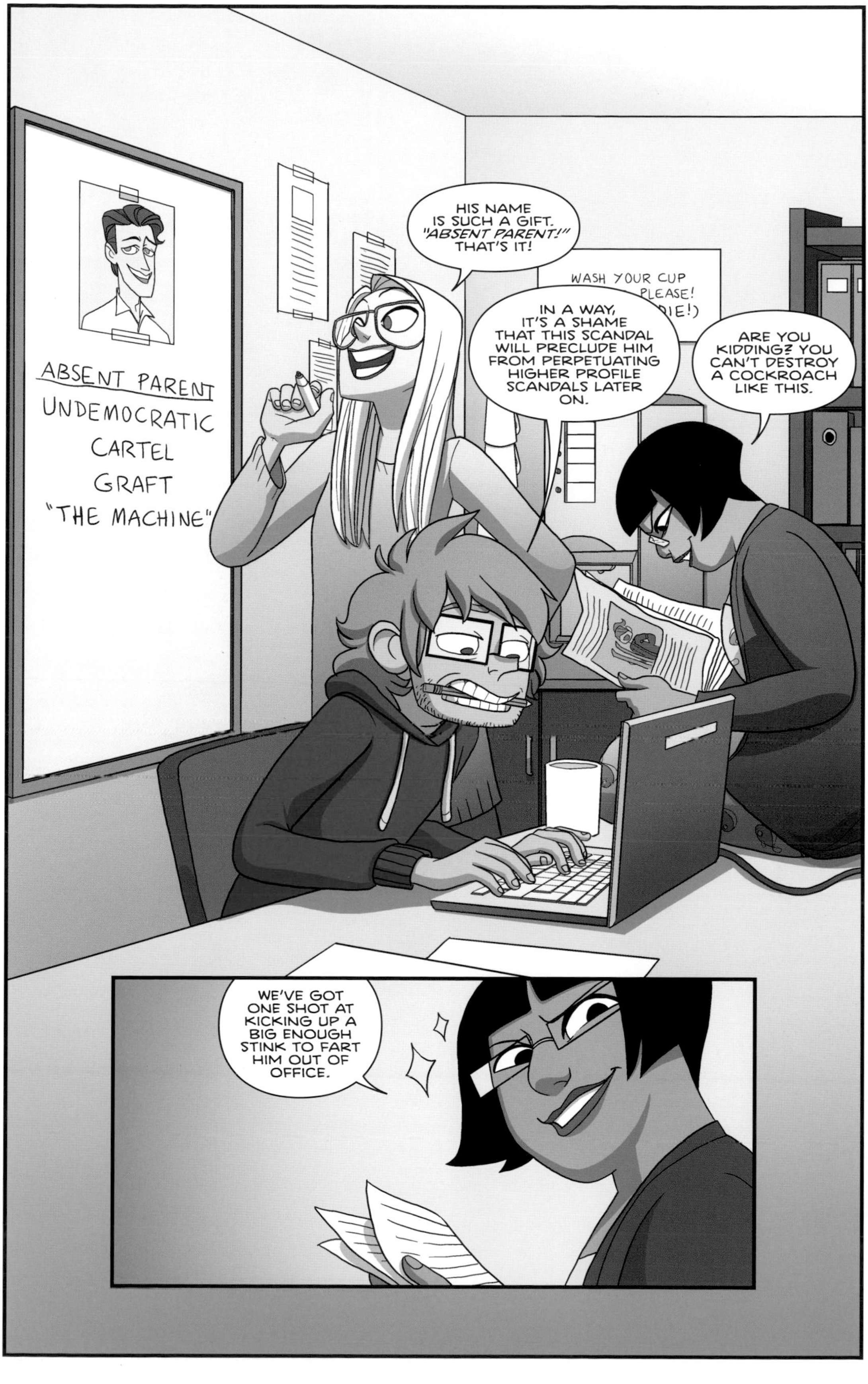
ABSENT PARENT
UNDEMOCRATIC
CARTEL
GRAFT
"THE MACHINE"
HIS NAME IS SUCH A GIFT. "ABSENT PARENT!" THAT'S IT!
WASH YOUR CUP PLEASE!
IN A WAY, IT'S A SHAME THAT THIS SCANDAL WILL PRECLUDE HIM FROM PERPETUATING HIGHER PROFILE SCANDALS LATER ON.
ARE YOU KIDDING? YOU CAN'T DESTROY A COCKROACH LIKE THIS.
WE'VE GOT ONE SHOT AT KICKING UP A BIG ENOUGH STINK TO FART HIM OUT OF OFFICE.

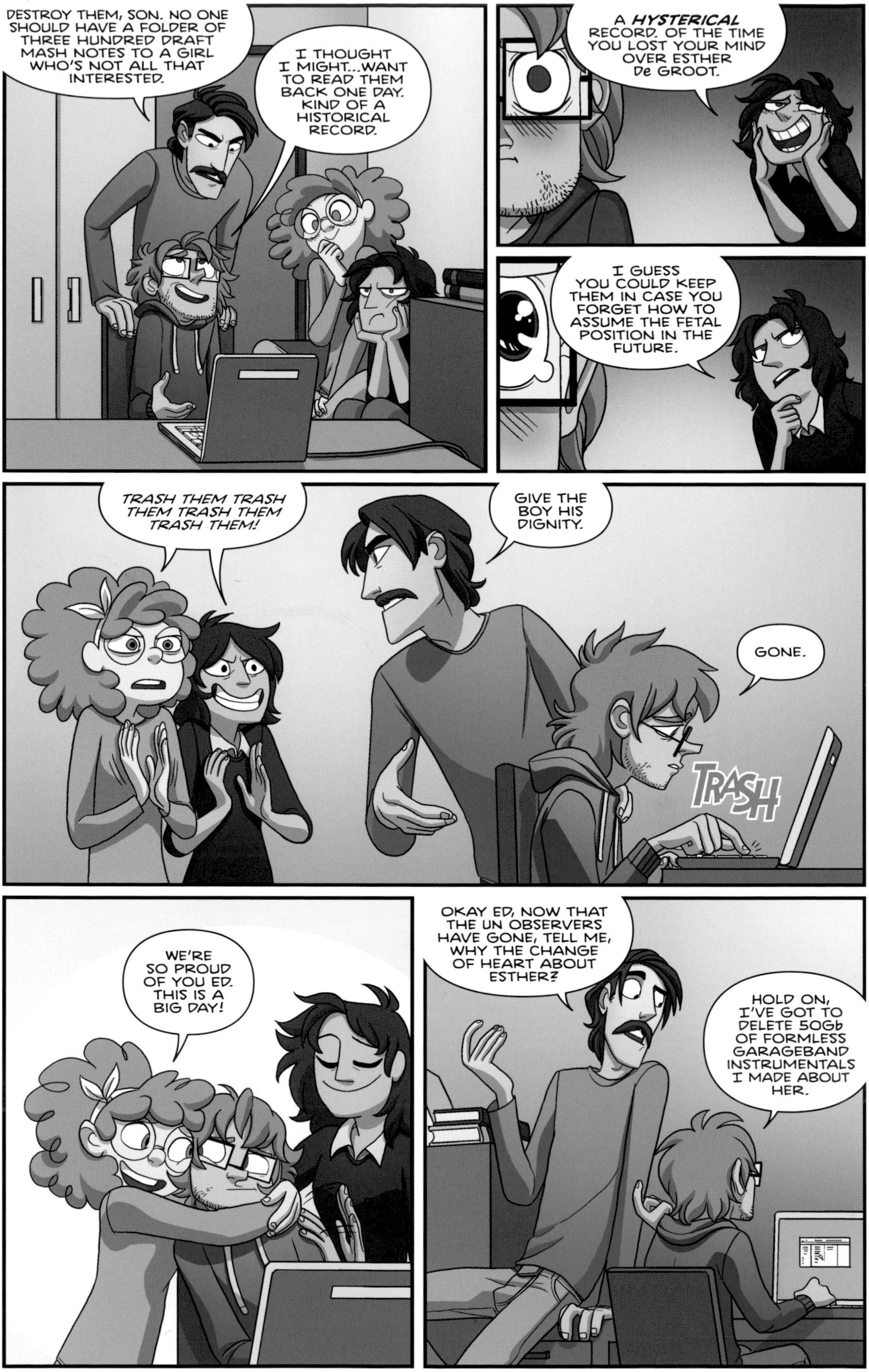
DESTROY THEM, SON. NO ONE SHOULD HAVE A FOLDER OF THREE HUNDRED DRAFT MASH NOTES TO A GIRL WHO'S NOT ALL THAT INTERESTED.
I THOUGHT I MIGHT...WANT TO READ THEM BACK ONE DAY. KIND OF A HISTORICAL RECORD.
A *HYSTERICAL* RECORD. OF THE TIME YOU LOST YOUR MIND OVER ESTHER De GROOT.
I GUESS YOU COULD KEEP THEM IN CASE YOU FORGET HOW TO ASSUME THE FETAL POSITION IN THE FUTURE.
*TRASH THEM TRASH THEM TRASH THEM TRASH THEM!*
GIVE THE BOY HIS DIGNITY.
GONE.
TRASH
WE'RE SO PROUD OF YOU ED. THIS IS A BIG DAY!
OKAY ED, NOW THAT THE UN OBSERVERS HAVE GONE, TELL ME, WHY THE CHANGE OF HEART ABOUT ESTHER?
HOLD ON, I'VE GOT TO DELETE 50Gb OF FORMLESS GARAGEBAND INSTRUMENTALS I MADE ABOUT HER.

I'M 85% CERTAIN SUSAN CAN'T HEAR US HERE.

1. PUT IN LAUNDRY (EMPTY POCKETS,

2. PUT IN WASHING POWDER/LIQUID

3. SELECT PROGRAM

4. PUT IN MONEY

5. PRESS START

6. PICK UP YOUR LAU

7. ... RE DON

THIS GOES NO FURTHER, McGRAW, BUT I'VE MET SOMEONE AT THE PIG. WE'VE GOT... *SOMETHING*... YOU KNOW?

A CONNECTION?

YEAH, I'M A BIT NERVOUS ACTUALLY. SHE'S A THIRD YEAR. A WOMAN OF THE WORLD.

6. P ...

7. BOOM! YOU ... DONE!

DO ... ES/PEOPLE - OR ANYTHING ELSE B ... WASHING MACHINES

... ASHING MACHINES

AND I'M...

...LESS WORLDLY.

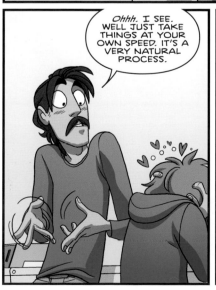

*Ohhh.* I SEE. WELL JUST TAKE THINGS AT YOUR OWN SPEED. IT'S A VERY NATURAL PROCESS.

I'M GOING BACK TO WORK ON A STORY WITH HER THIS EVENING. *JUST THE TWO OF US.*

JUST SEND ME A TEXT SO I KNOW THAT... *THE EAGLE HAS LANDED.* OTHERWISE I WON'T SLEEP.

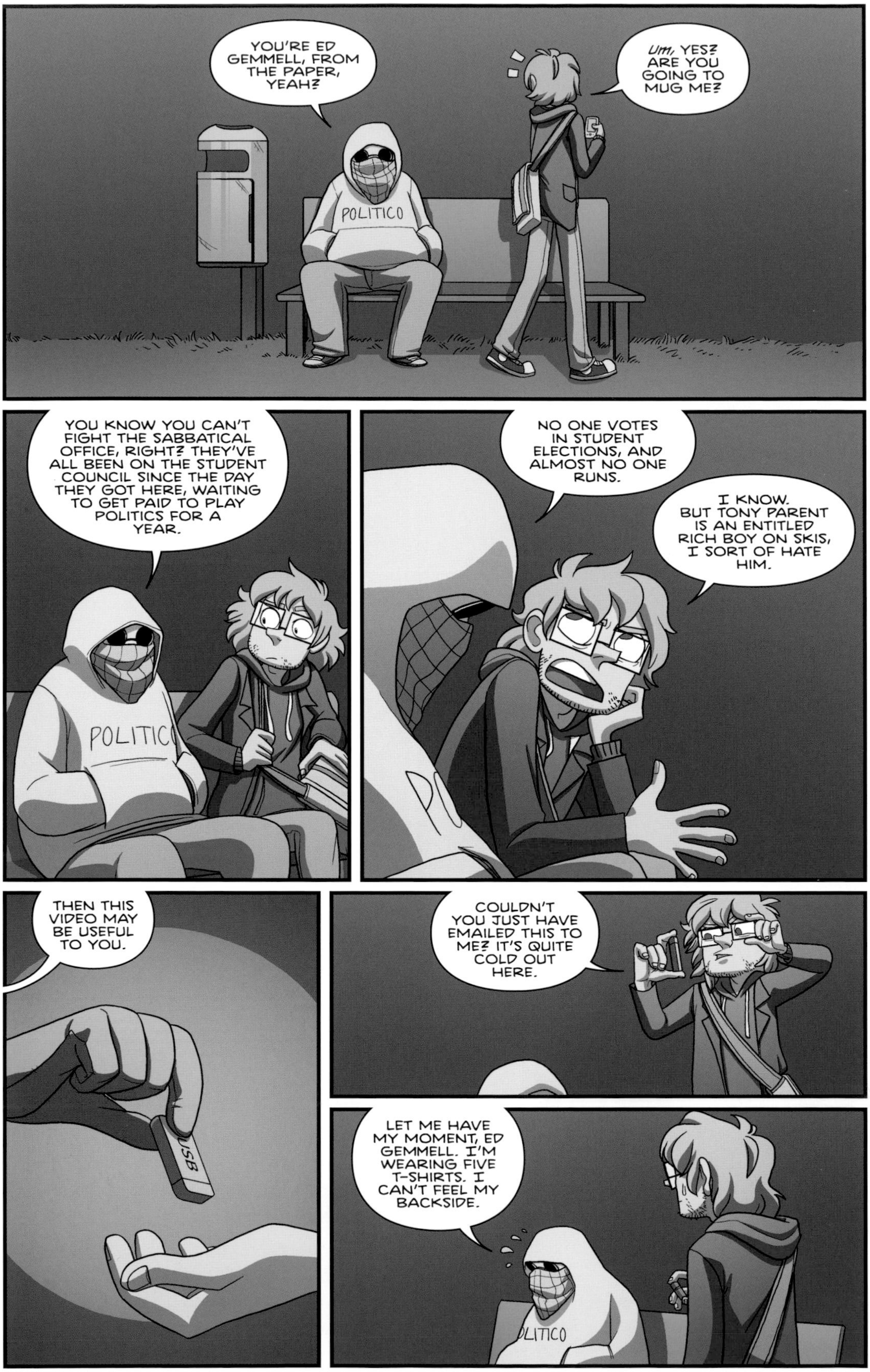
YOU'RE ED GEMMELL, FROM THE PAPER, YEAH?
Um, YES? ARE YOU GOING TO MUG ME?
POLITICO
YOU KNOW YOU CAN'T FIGHT THE SABBATICAL OFFICE, RIGHT? THEY'VE ALL BEEN ON THE STUDENT COUNCIL SINCE THE DAY THEY GOT HERE, WAITING TO GET PAID TO PLAY POLITICS FOR A YEAR.
POLITICO
NO ONE VOTES IN STUDENT ELECTIONS, AND ALMOST NO ONE RUNS.
I KNOW. BUT TONY PARENT IS AN ENTITLED RICH BOY ON SKIS, I SORT OF HATE HIM.
THEN THIS VIDEO MAY BE USEFUL TO YOU.
USB
COULDN'T YOU JUST HAVE EMAILED THIS TO ME? IT'S QUITE COLD OUT HERE.
LET ME HAVE MY MOMENT, ED GEMMELL. I'M WEARING FIVE T-SHIRTS. I CAN'T FEEL MY BACKSIDE.
OLITICO

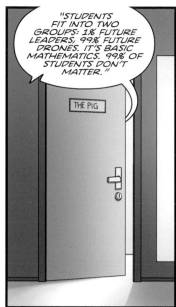

"STUDENTS FIT INTO TWO GROUPS: 1% FUTURE LEADERS, 99% FUTURE DRONES. IT'S BASIC MATHEMATICS. 99% OF STUDENTS DON'T MATTER."

THE PIG

*THE SMOKING GUN!* THIS IS HOW WE'RE GOING TO GET RID OF TONY PARENT. ED, HOW DID YOU FIND THIS?

HE'S TALKING IN A SEMINAR AT A PARTY CONFERENCE LAST YEAR. THERE ARE MAYBE THIRTY PEOPLE IN THE ROOM, BUT SOMEONE FILMED IT.

I'VE NEVER SEEN A MAN BLOW HIMSELF UP BEFORE. IT'S INCREDIBLE. LET'S WATCH IT AGAIN.

I'M SO TIRED. DO YOU WANT A CUP OF COFFEE?

YAWN

THE UNION TOOK OUR COFFEE MACHINE AWAY THIS MORNING. CUTBACKS, THEY SAID. PRETTY WEIRD.

YOU KNOW WHERE THERE'S COFFEE? MY HOUSE.

ABSENT PARENT
UNDEMOCRAT
CARTEL
GRAFT
"THE MACHINE"

DON'T WE NEED TO FINISH THIS...?

I THINK WE SHOULD *DEFINITELY* FINISH THIS.

fwump

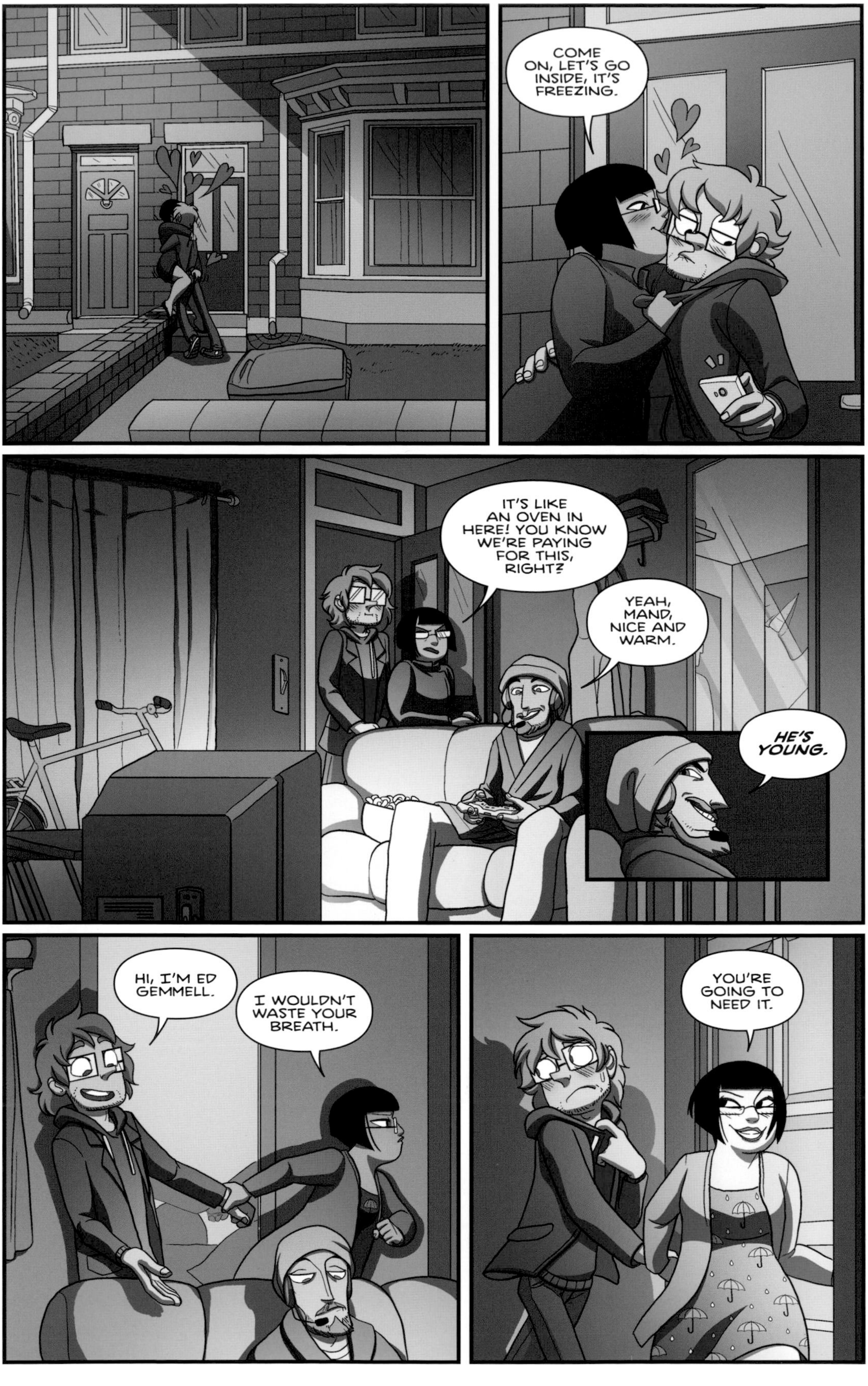
COME ON, LET'S GO INSIDE, IT'S FREEZING.
IT'S LIKE AN OVEN IN HERE! YOU KNOW WE'RE PAYING FOR THIS, RIGHT?
YEAH, MAND, NICE AND WARM.
HE'S YOUNG.
HI, I'M ED GEMMELL.
I WOULDN'T WASTE YOUR BREATH.
YOU'RE GOING TO NEED IT.

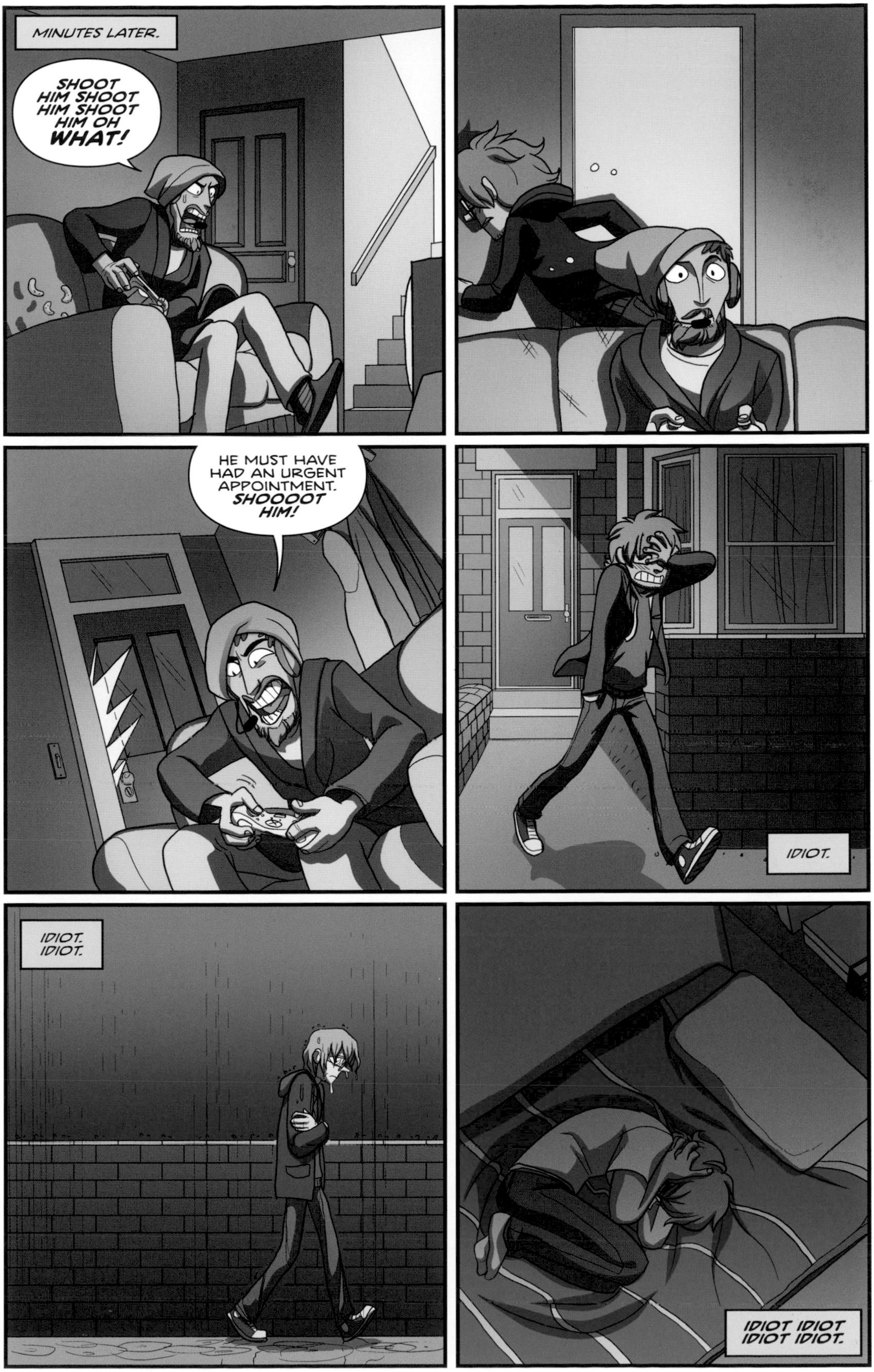
MINUTES LATER.
SHOOT HIM SHOOT HIM SHOOT HIM OH WHAT!
HE MUST HAVE HAD AN URGENT APPOINTMENT. SHOOOOT HIM!
IDIOT.
IDIOT. IDIOT.
IDIOT IDIOT IDIOT IDIOT.

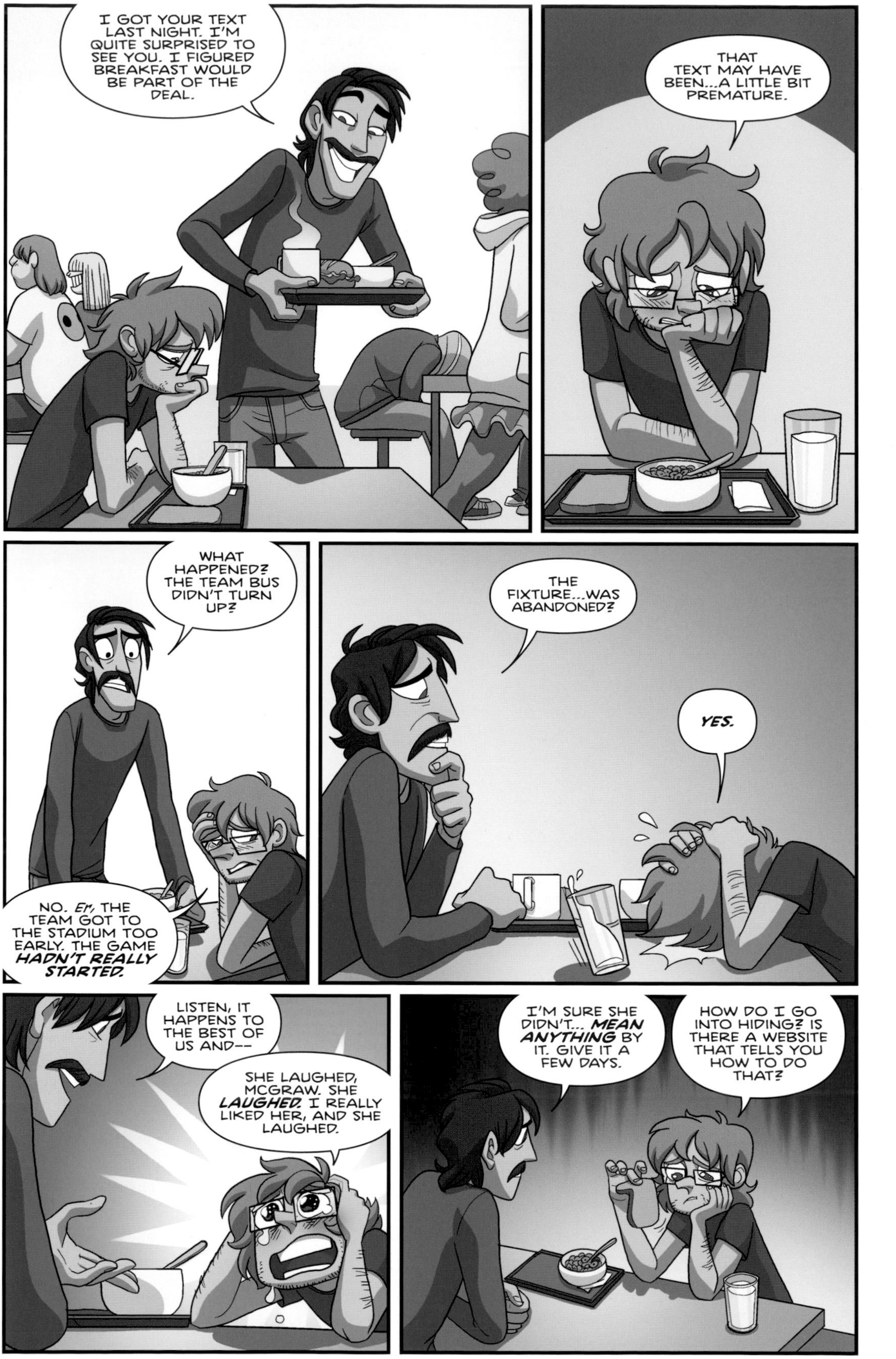
I GOT YOUR TEXT LAST NIGHT. I'M QUITE SURPRISED TO SEE YOU. I FIGURED BREAKFAST WOULD BE PART OF THE DEAL.
THAT TEXT MAY HAVE BEEN... A LITTLE BIT PREMATURE.
WHAT HAPPENED? THE TEAM BUS DIDN'T TURN UP?
NO. *ER*, THE TEAM GOT TO THE STADIUM TOO EARLY. THE GAME ***HADN'T REALLY STARTED.***
THE FIXTURE... WAS ABANDONED?
***YES.***
LISTEN, IT HAPPENS TO THE BEST OF US AND--
SHE LAUGHED, MCGRAW. SHE ***LAUGHED.*** I REALLY LIKED HER, AND SHE LAUGHED.
I'M SURE SHE DIDN'T... ***MEAN ANYTHING*** BY IT. GIVE IT A FEW DAYS.
HOW DO I GO INTO HIDING? IS THERE A WEBSITE THAT TELLS YOU HOW TO DO THAT?

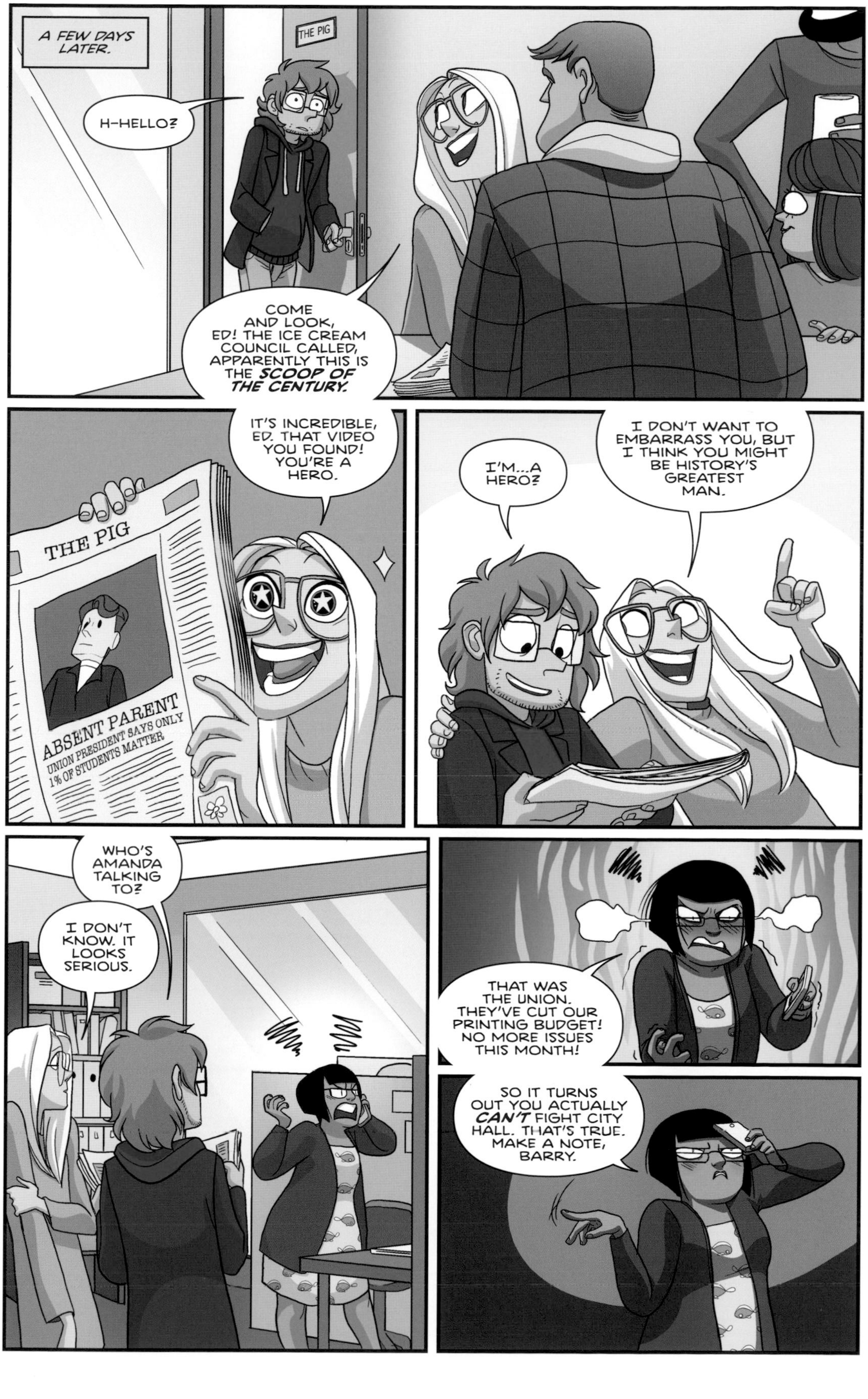

A FEW DAYS LATER.
THE PIG
H-HELLO?
COME AND LOOK, ED! THE ICE CREAM COUNCIL CALLED, APPARENTLY THIS IS THE *SCOOP OF THE CENTURY.*
IT'S INCREDIBLE, ED. THAT VIDEO YOU FOUND! YOU'RE A HERO.
THE PIG
ABSENT PARENT
UNION PRESIDENT SAYS ONLY 1% OF STUDENTS MATTER
I'M...A HERO?
I DON'T WANT TO EMBARRASS YOU, BUT I THINK YOU MIGHT BE HISTORY'S GREATEST MAN.
WHO'S AMANDA TALKING TO?
I DON'T KNOW. IT LOOKS SERIOUS.
THAT WAS THE UNION. THEY'VE CUT OUR PRINTING BUDGET! NO MORE ISSUES THIS MONTH!
SO IT TURNS OUT YOU ACTUALLY ***CAN'T*** FIGHT CITY HALL. THAT'S TRUE. MAKE A NOTE, BARRY.

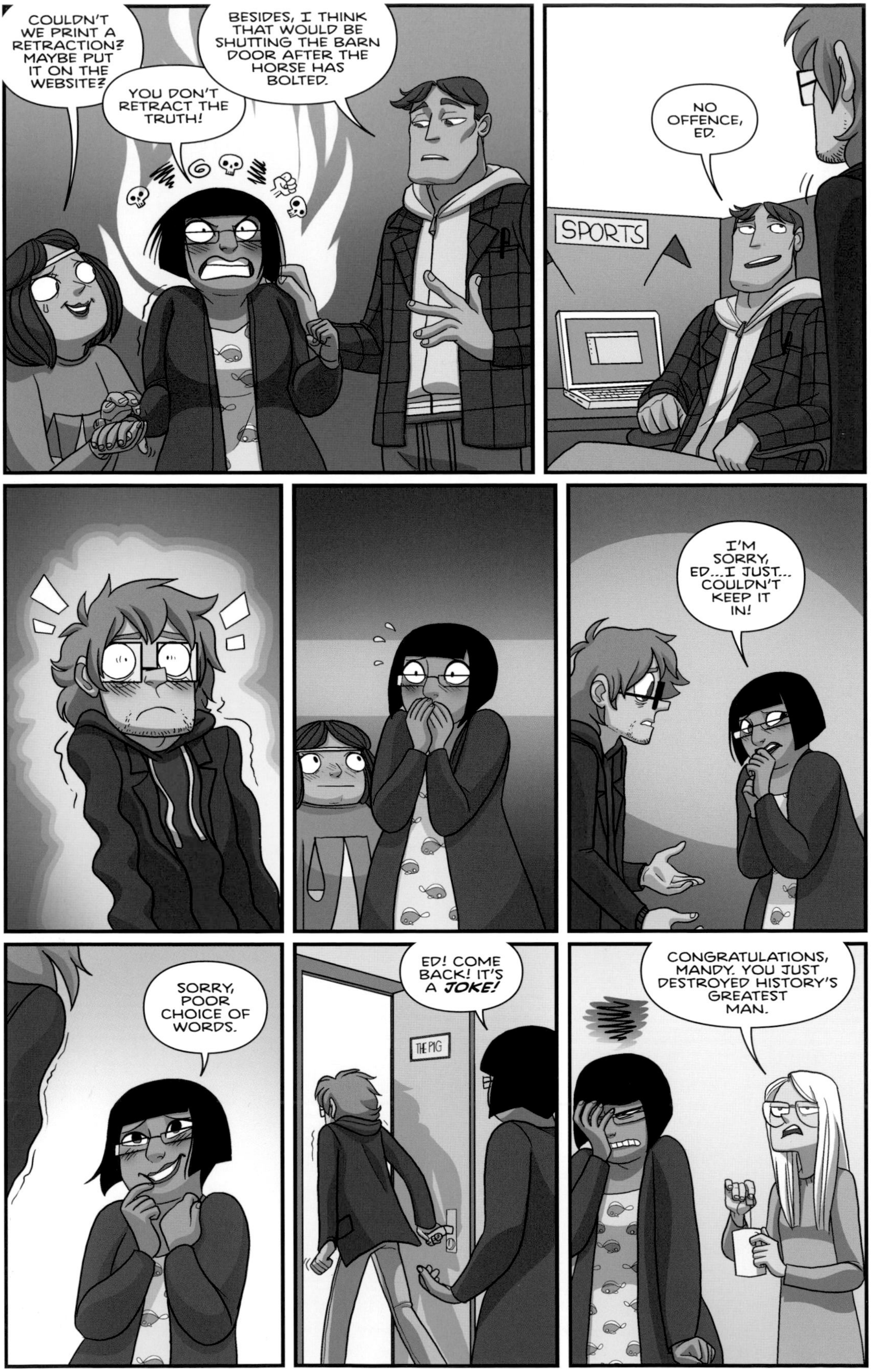
COULDN'T WE PRINT A RETRACTION? MAYBE PUT IT ON THE WEBSITE?
YOU DON'T RETRACT THE TRUTH!
BESIDES, I THINK THAT WOULD BE SHUTTING THE BARN DOOR AFTER THE HORSE HAS BOLTED.
SPORTS
NO OFFENCE, ED.
I'M SORRY, ED... I JUST... COULDN'T KEEP IT IN!
SORRY, POOR CHOICE OF WORDS.
ED! COME BACK! IT'S A *JOKE!*
THE PIG
CONGRATULATIONS, MANDY. YOU JUST DESTROYED HISTORY'S GREATEST MAN.

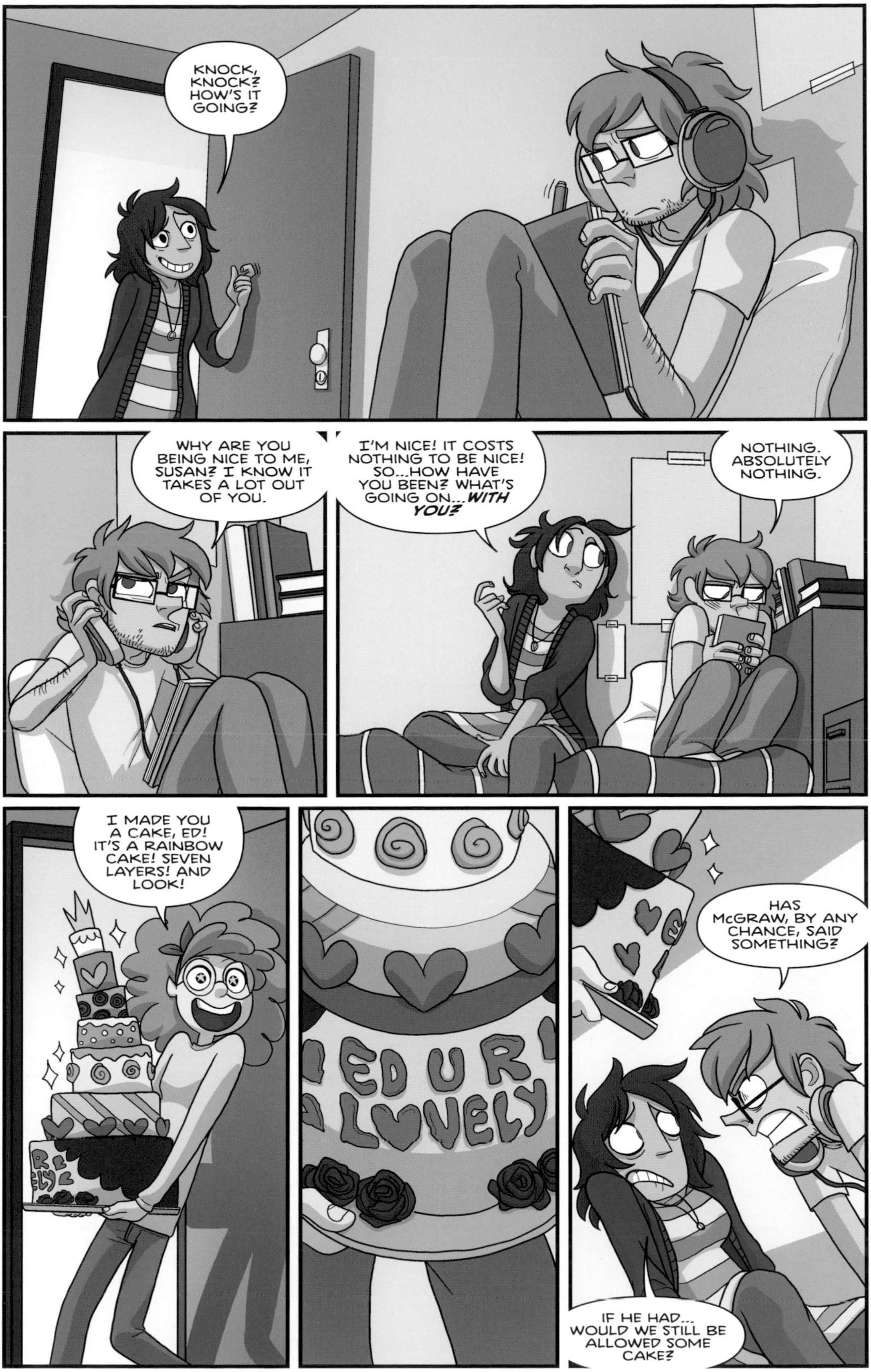
KNOCK, KNOCK? HOW'S IT GOING?
WHY ARE YOU BEING NICE TO ME, SUSAN? I KNOW IT TAKES A LOT OUT OF YOU.
I'M NICE! IT COSTS NOTHING TO BE NICE! SO...HOW HAVE YOU BEEN? WHAT'S GOING ON...WITH YOU?
NOTHING. ABSOLUTELY NOTHING.
I MADE YOU A CAKE, ED! IT'S A RAINBOW CAKE! SEVEN LAYERS! AND LOOK!
ED U R LUVELY
HAS McGRAW, BY ANY CHANCE, SAID SOMETHING?
IF HE HAD... WOULD WE STILL BE ALLOWED SOME CAKE?

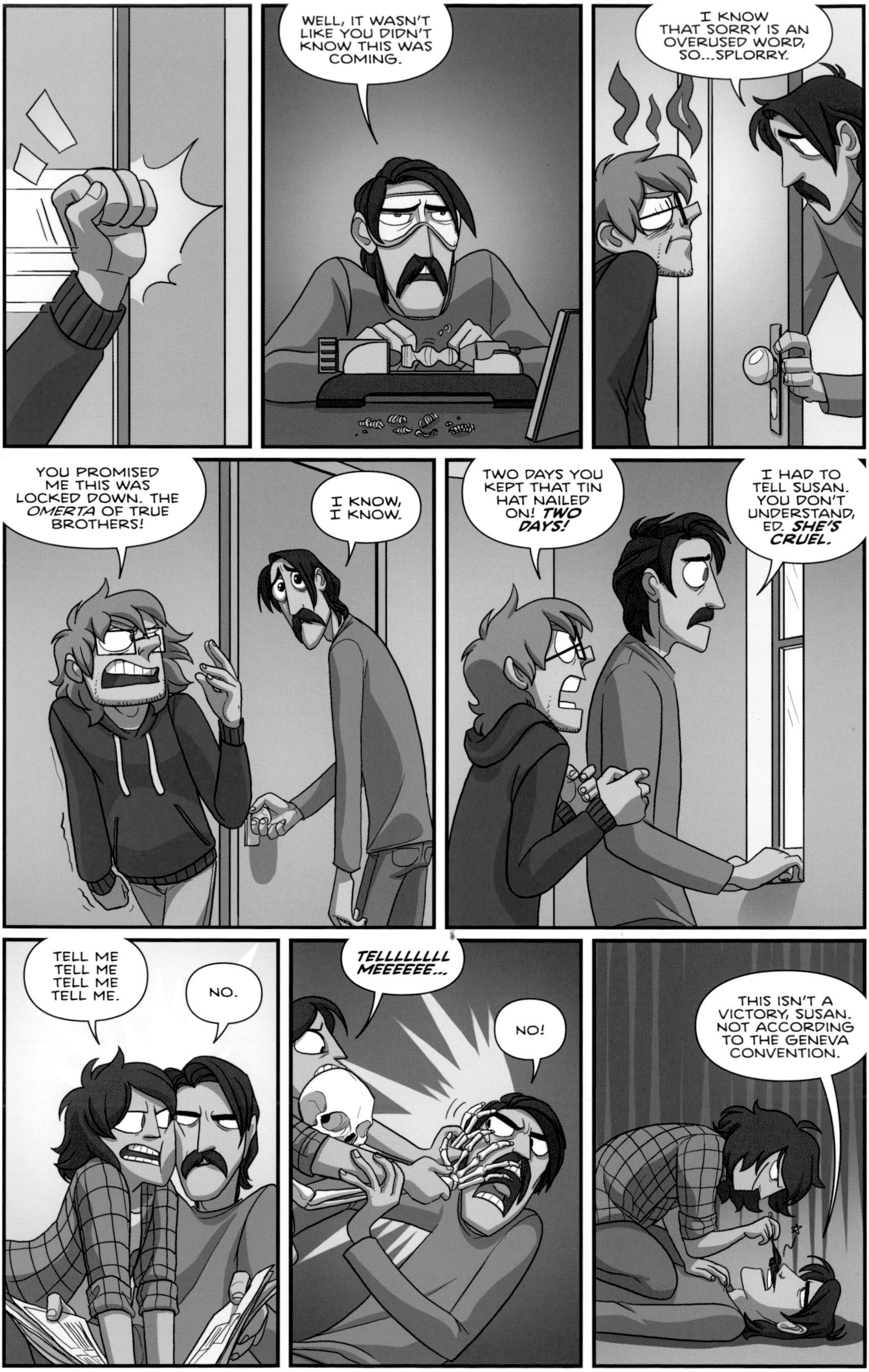
WELL, IT WASN'T LIKE YOU DIDN'T KNOW THIS WAS COMING.
I KNOW THAT SORRY IS AN OVERUSED WORD, SO...SPLORRY.
YOU PROMISED ME THIS WAS LOCKED DOWN. THE OMERTA OF TRUE BROTHERS!
I KNOW, I KNOW.
TWO DAYS YOU KEPT THAT TIN HAT NAILED ON! TWO DAYS!
I HAD TO TELL SUSAN. YOU DON'T UNDERSTAND, ED. SHE'S CRUEL.
TELL ME TELL ME TELL ME TELL ME.
NO.
TELLLLLLLLL MEEEEEE...
NO!
THIS ISN'T A VICTORY, SUSAN. NOT ACCORDING TO THE GENEVA CONVENTION.

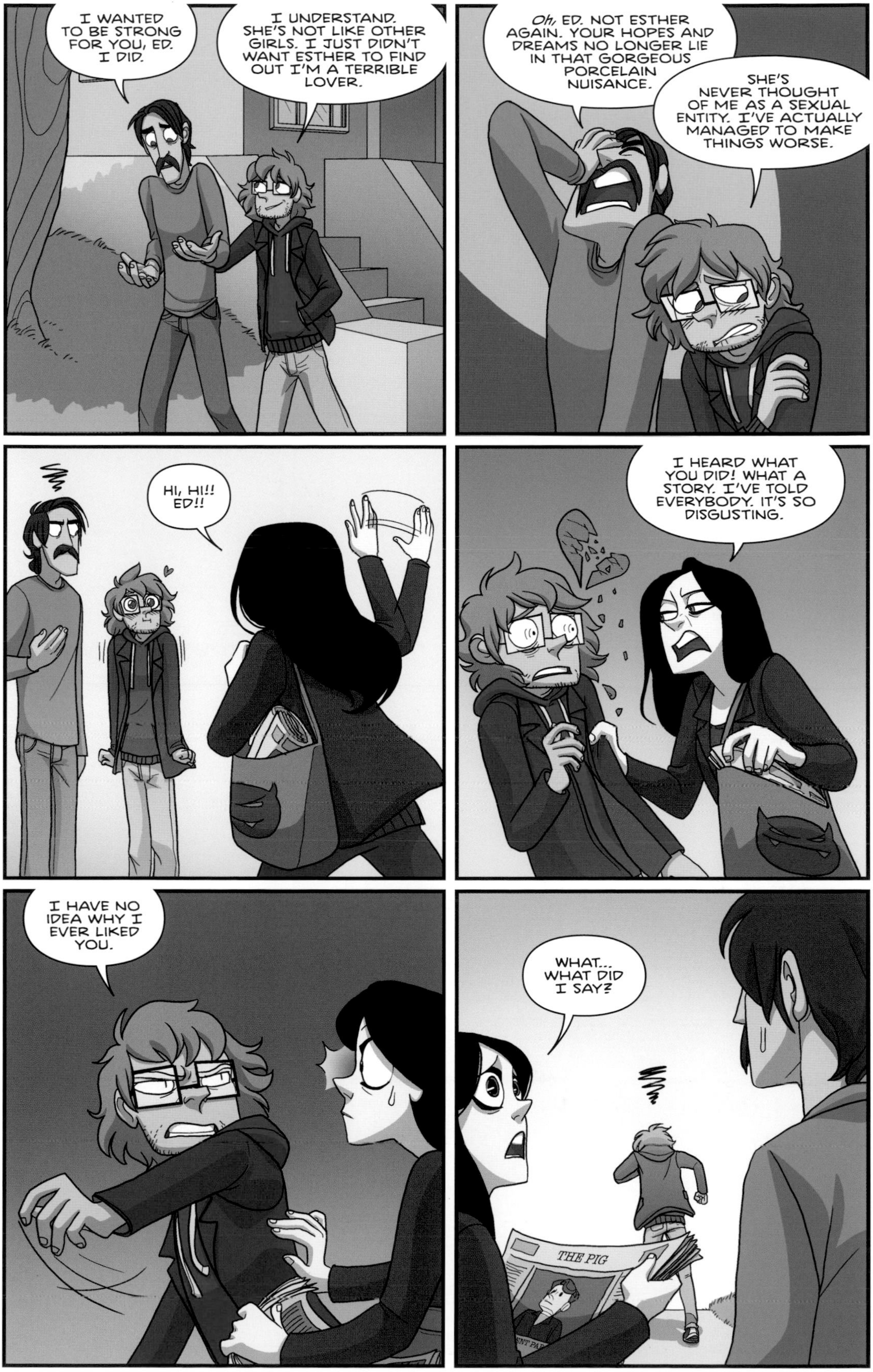
I WANTED TO BE STRONG FOR YOU, ED. I DID.
I UNDERSTAND. SHE'S NOT LIKE OTHER GIRLS. I JUST DIDN'T WANT ESTHER TO FIND OUT I'M A TERRIBLE LOVER.
*Oh,* ED. NOT ESTHER AGAIN. YOUR HOPES AND DREAMS NO LONGER LIE IN THAT GORGEOUS PORCELAIN NUISANCE.
SHE'S NEVER THOUGHT OF ME AS A SEXUAL ENTITY. I'VE ACTUALLY MANAGED TO MAKE THINGS WORSE.
HI, HI!! ED!!
I HEARD WHAT YOU DID! WHAT A STORY. I'VE TOLD EVERYBODY. IT'S SO DISGUSTING.
I HAVE NO IDEA WHY I EVER LIKED YOU.
WHAT... WHAT DID I SAY?
THE PIG

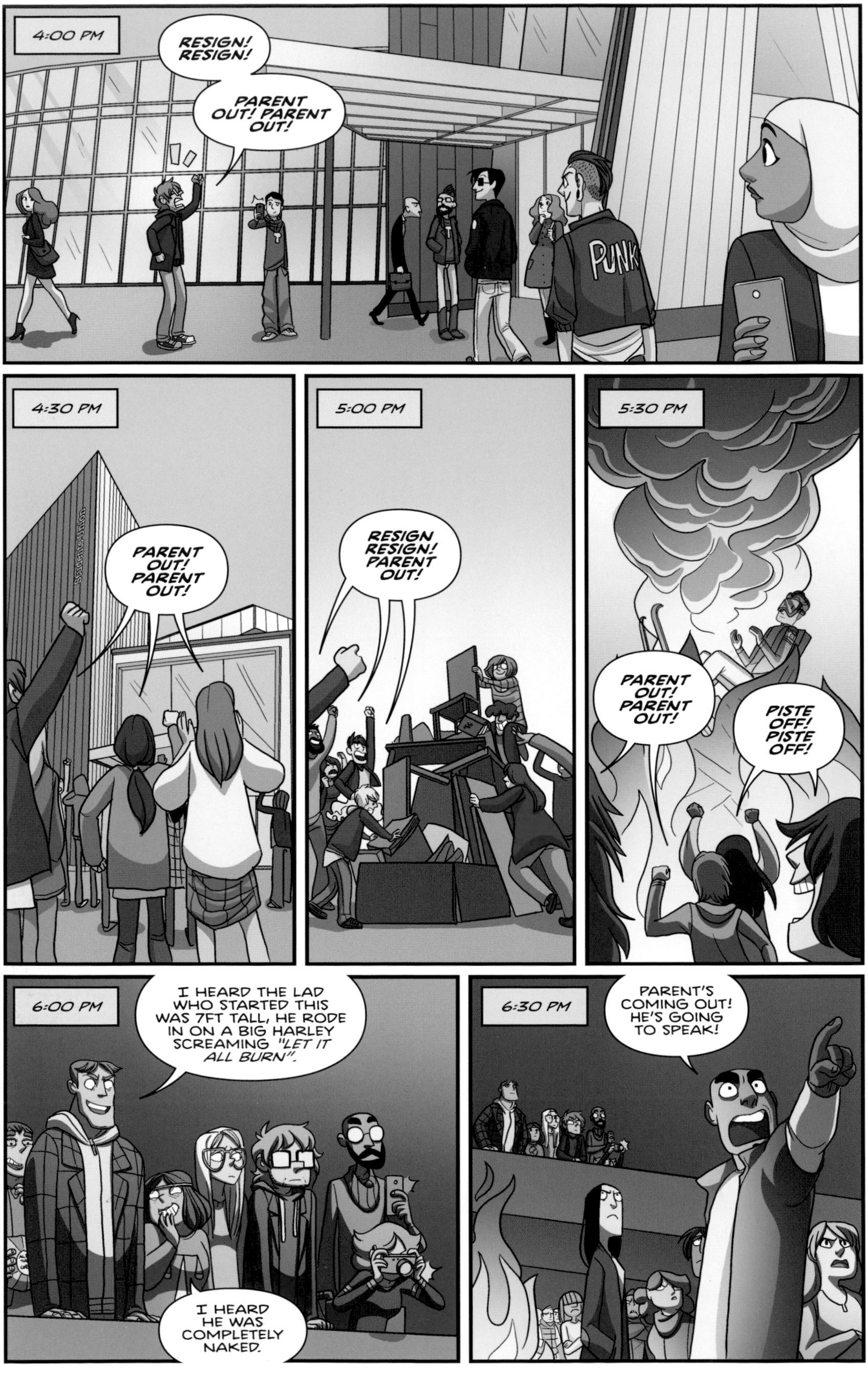
4:00 PM
RESIGN! RESIGN!
PARENT OUT! PARENT OUT!
PUNK
4:30 PM
PARENT OUT! PARENT OUT!
5:00 PM
RESIGN RESIGN! PARENT OUT!
5:30 PM
PARENT OUT! PARENT OUT!
PISTE OFF! PISTE OFF!
6:00 PM
I HEARD THE LAD WHO STARTED THIS WAS 7FT TALL, HE RODE IN ON A BIG HARLEY SCREAMING "LET IT ALL BURN".
I HEARD HE WAS COMPLETELY NAKED.
6:30 PM
PARENT'S COMING OUT! HE'S GOING TO SPEAK!

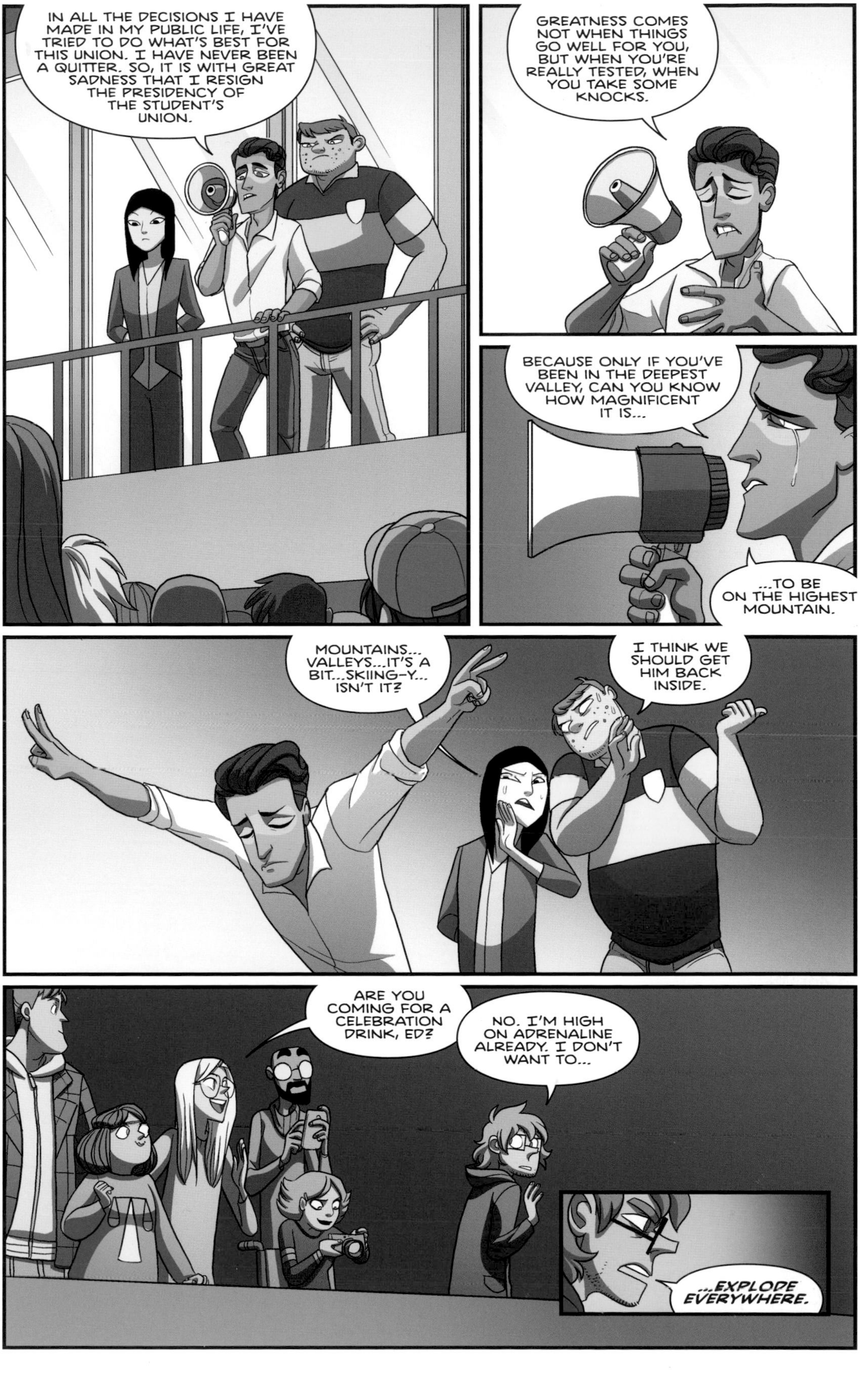
IN ALL THE DECISIONS I HAVE MADE IN MY PUBLIC LIFE, I'VE TRIED TO DO WHAT'S BEST FOR THIS UNION. I HAVE NEVER BEEN A QUITTER. SO, IT IS WITH GREAT SADNESS THAT I RESIGN THE PRESIDENCY OF THE STUDENT'S UNION.
GREATNESS COMES NOT WHEN THINGS GO WELL FOR YOU, BUT WHEN YOU'RE REALLY TESTED, WHEN YOU TAKE SOME KNOCKS.
BECAUSE ONLY IF YOU'VE BEEN IN THE DEEPEST VALLEY, CAN YOU KNOW HOW MAGNIFICENT IT IS...
...TO BE ON THE HIGHEST MOUNTAIN.
MOUNTAINS... VALLEYS...IT'S A BIT...SKIING-Y... ISN'T IT?
I THINK WE SHOULD GET HIM BACK INSIDE.
ARE YOU COMING FOR A CELEBRATION DRINK, ED?
NO. I'M HIGH ON ADRENALINE ALREADY. I DON'T WANT TO...
...EXPLODE EVERYWHERE.

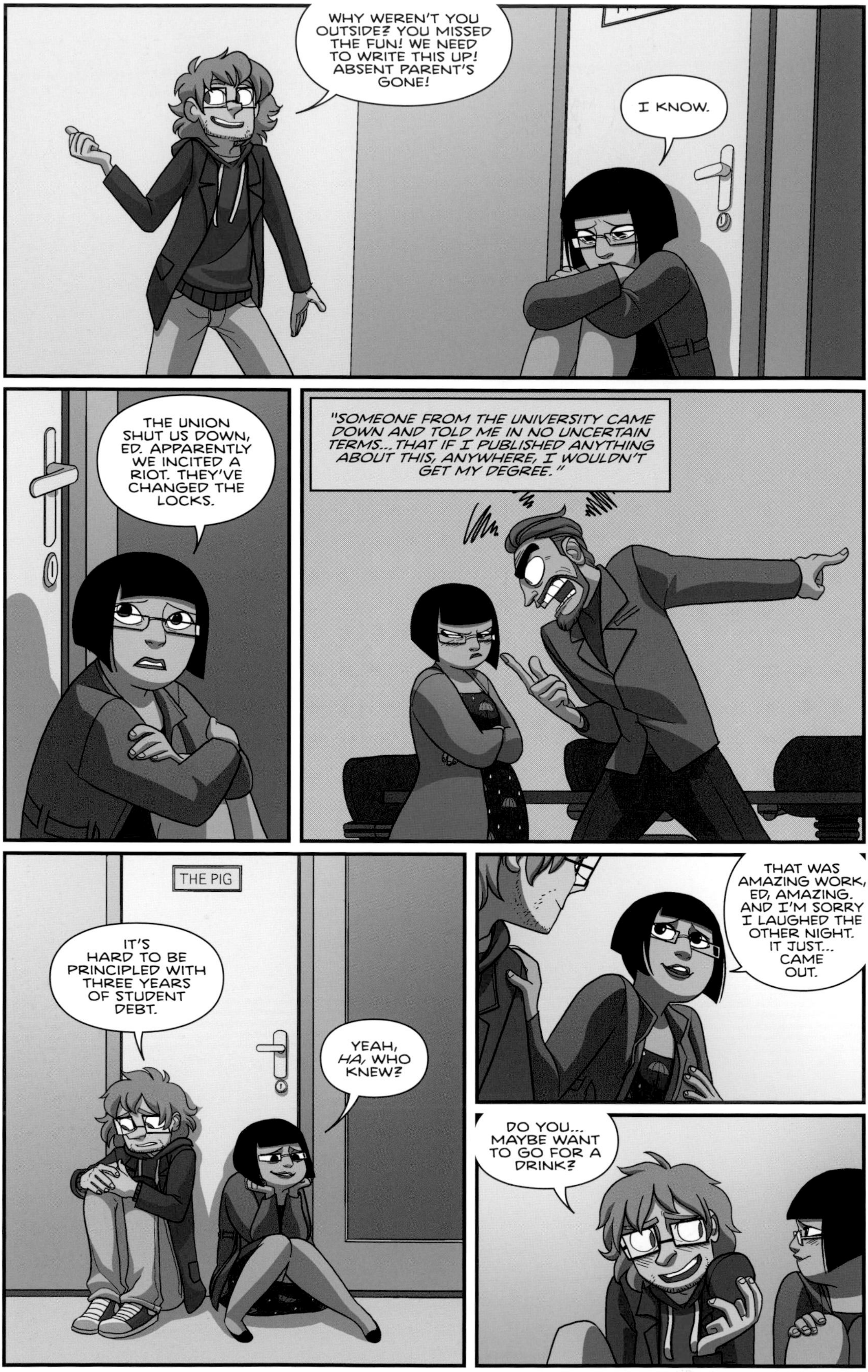
WHY WEREN'T YOU OUTSIDE? YOU MISSED THE FUN! WE NEED TO WRITE THIS UP! ABSENT PARENT'S GONE!
I KNOW.
THE UNION SHUT US DOWN, ED. APPARENTLY WE INCITED A RIOT. THEY'VE CHANGED THE LOCKS.
"SOMEONE FROM THE UNIVERSITY CAME DOWN AND TOLD ME IN NO UNCERTAIN TERMS...THAT IF I PUBLISHED ANYTHING ABOUT THIS, ANYWHERE, I WOULDN'T GET MY DEGREE."
THE PIG
IT'S HARD TO BE PRINCIPLED WITH THREE YEARS OF STUDENT DEBT.
YEAH, *HA,* WHO KNEW?
THAT WAS AMAZING WORK, ED, AMAZING. AND I'M SORRY I LAUGHED THE OTHER NIGHT. IT JUST... CAME OUT.
DO YOU... MAYBE WANT TO GO FOR A DRINK?

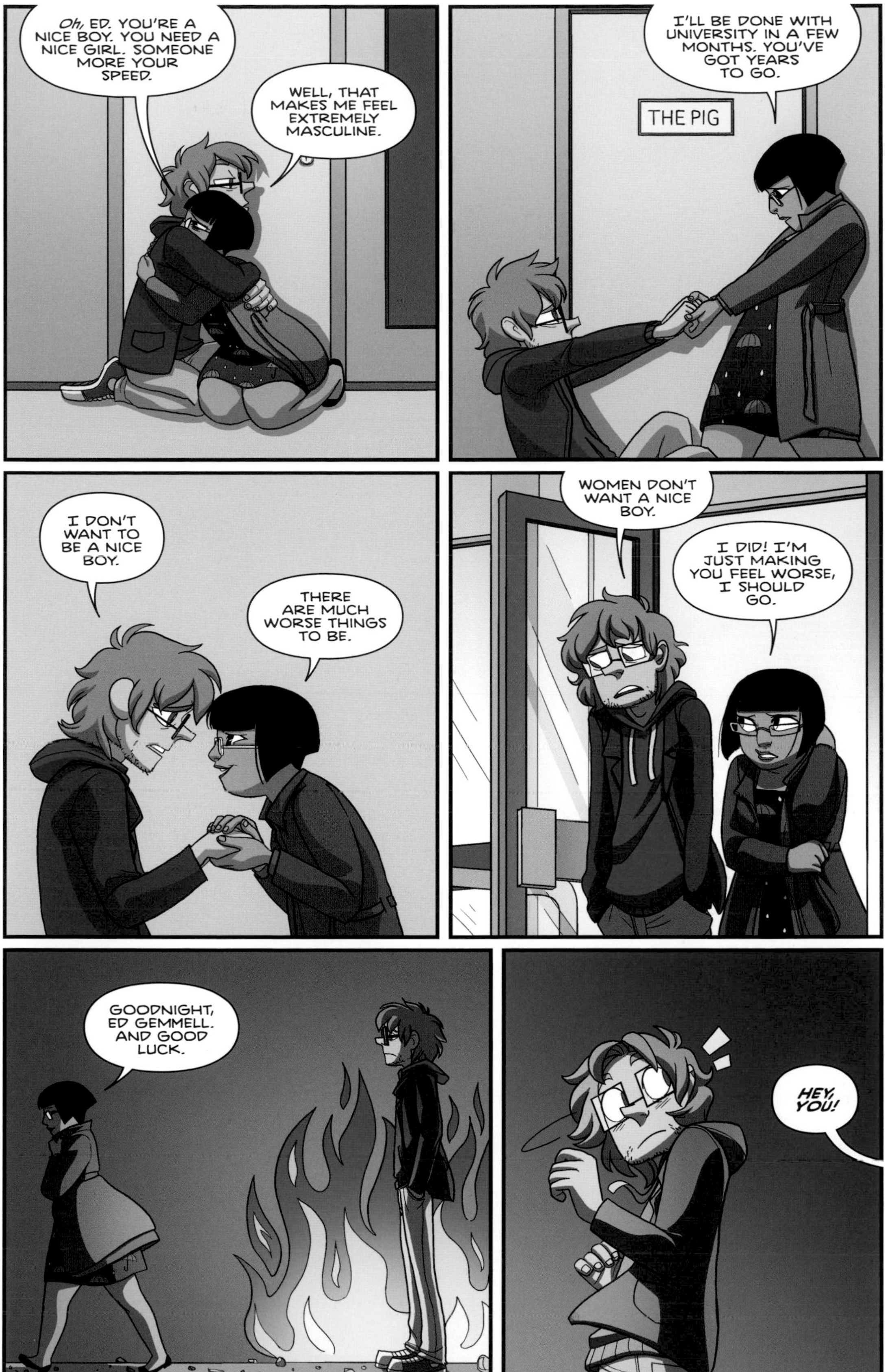
*Oh,* ED. YOU'RE A NICE BOY. YOU NEED A NICE GIRL. SOMEONE MORE YOUR SPEED.
WELL, THAT MAKES ME FEEL EXTREMELY MASCULINE.
I'LL BE DONE WITH UNIVERSITY IN A FEW MONTHS. YOU'VE GOT YEARS TO GO.
THE PIG
I DON'T WANT TO BE A NICE BOY.
THERE ARE MUCH WORSE THINGS TO BE.
WOMEN DON'T WANT A NICE BOY.
I DID! I'M JUST MAKING YOU FEEL WORSE, I SHOULD GO.
GOODNIGHT, ED GEMMELL. AND GOOD LUCK.
HEY, YOU!

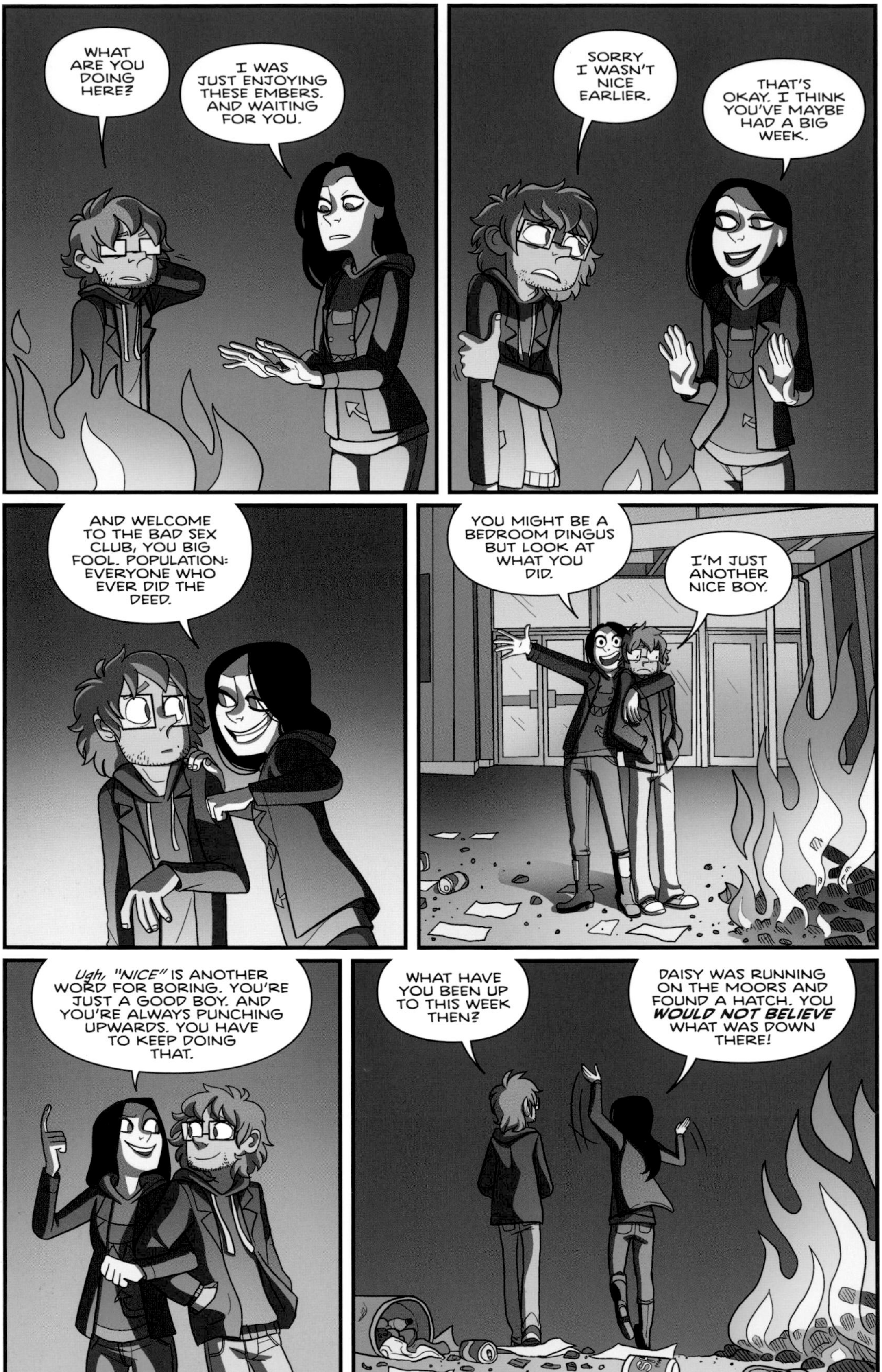
WHAT ARE YOU DOING HERE?
I WAS JUST ENJOYING THESE EMBERS. AND WAITING FOR YOU.
SORRY I WASN'T NICE EARLIER.
THAT'S OKAY. I THINK YOU'VE MAYBE HAD A BIG WEEK.
AND WELCOME TO THE BAD SEX CLUB, YOU BIG FOOL. POPULATION: EVERYONE WHO EVER DID THE DEED.
YOU MIGHT BE A BEDROOM DINGUS BUT LOOK AT WHAT YOU DID.
I'M JUST ANOTHER NICE BOY.
*Ugh*, *"NICE"* IS ANOTHER WORD FOR BORING. YOU'RE JUST A GOOD BOY. AND YOU'RE ALWAYS PUNCHING UPWARDS. YOU HAVE TO KEEP DOING THAT.
WHAT HAVE YOU BEEN UP TO THIS WEEK THEN?
DAISY WAS RUNNING ON THE MOORS AND FOUND A HATCH. YOU ***WOULD NOT BELIEVE*** WHAT WAS DOWN THERE!

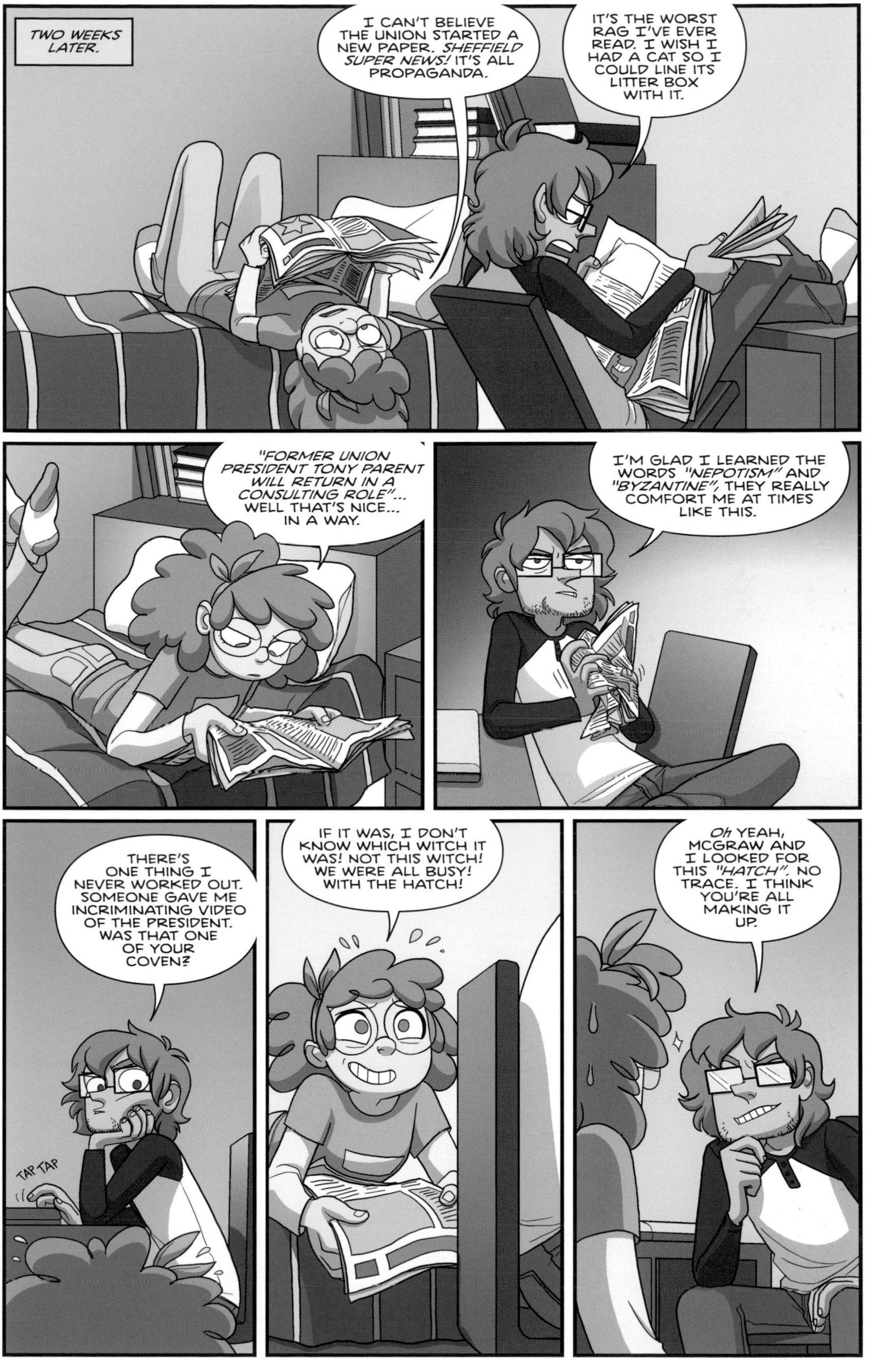
TWO WEEKS LATER.
I CAN'T BELIEVE THE UNION STARTED A NEW PAPER. *SHEFFIELD SUPER NEWS!* IT'S ALL PROPAGANDA.
IT'S THE WORST RAG I'VE EVER READ. I WISH I HAD A CAT SO I COULD LINE ITS LITTER BOX WITH IT.
*"FORMER UNION PRESIDENT TONY PARENT WILL RETURN IN A CONSULTING ROLE"*... WELL THAT'S NICE... IN A WAY.
I'M GLAD I LEARNED THE WORDS *"NEPOTISM"* AND *"BYZANTINE"*, THEY REALLY COMFORT ME AT TIMES LIKE THIS.
THERE'S ONE THING I NEVER WORKED OUT. SOMEONE GAVE ME INCRIMINATING VIDEO OF THE PRESIDENT. WAS THAT ONE OF YOUR COVEN?
TAP TAP
IF IT WAS, I DON'T KNOW WHICH WITCH IT WAS! NOT THIS WITCH! WE WERE ALL BUSY! WITH THE HATCH!
*Oh* YEAH, MCGRAW AND I LOOKED FOR THIS *"HATCH"*. NO TRACE. I THINK YOU'RE ALL MAKING IT UP.

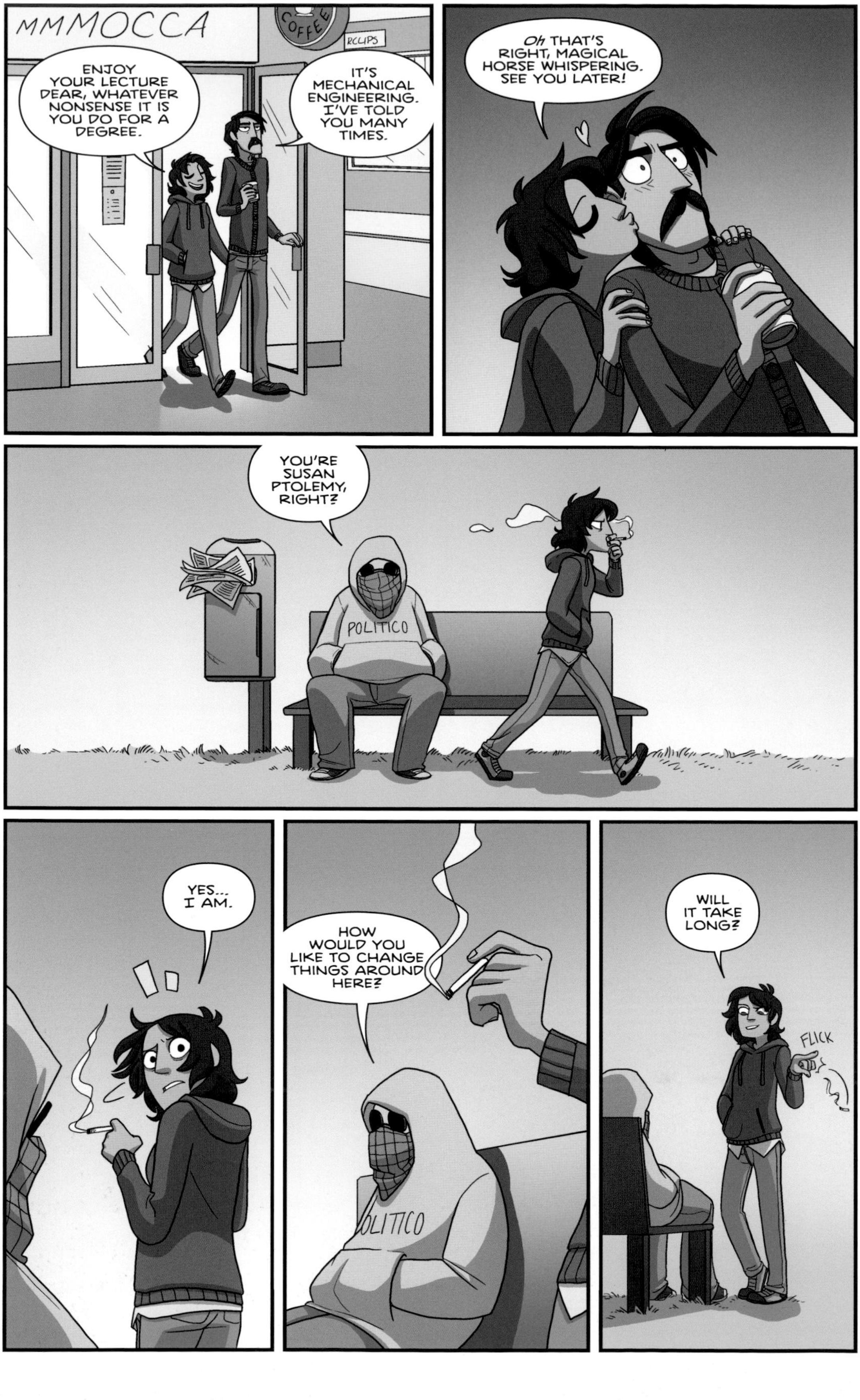
MMMOCCA
COFFEE
RCUPS
ENJOY YOUR LECTURE DEAR, WHATEVER NONSENSE IT IS YOU DO FOR A DEGREE.
IT'S MECHANICAL ENGINEERING. I'VE TOLD YOU MANY TIMES.
Oh THAT'S RIGHT, MAGICAL HORSE WHISPERING. SEE YOU LATER!
YOU'RE SUSAN PTOLEMY, RIGHT?
POLITICO
YES... I AM.
HOW WOULD YOU LIKE TO CHANGE THINGS AROUND HERE?
OLITICO
WILL IT TAKE LONG?
FLICK

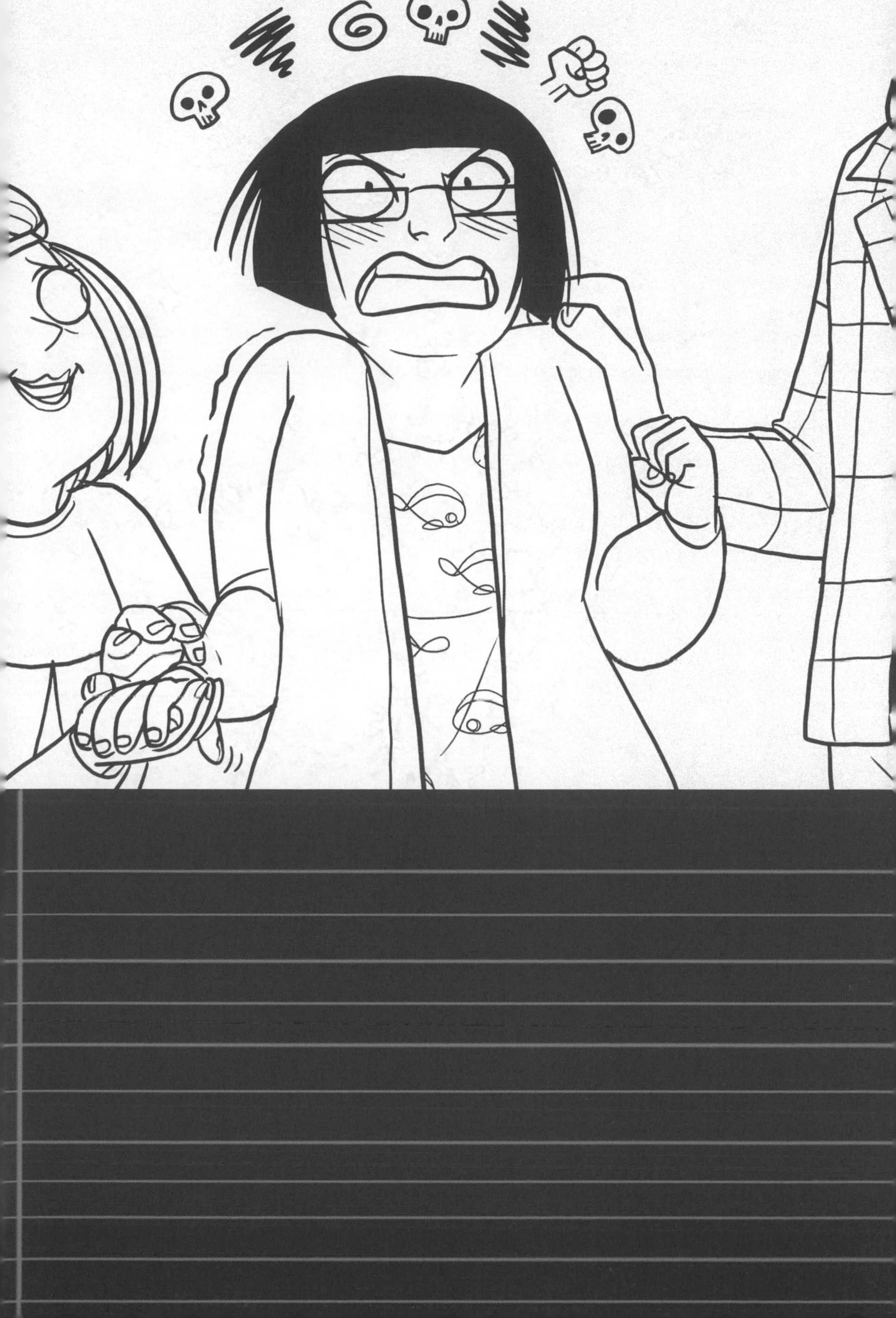

# CHAPTER TEN

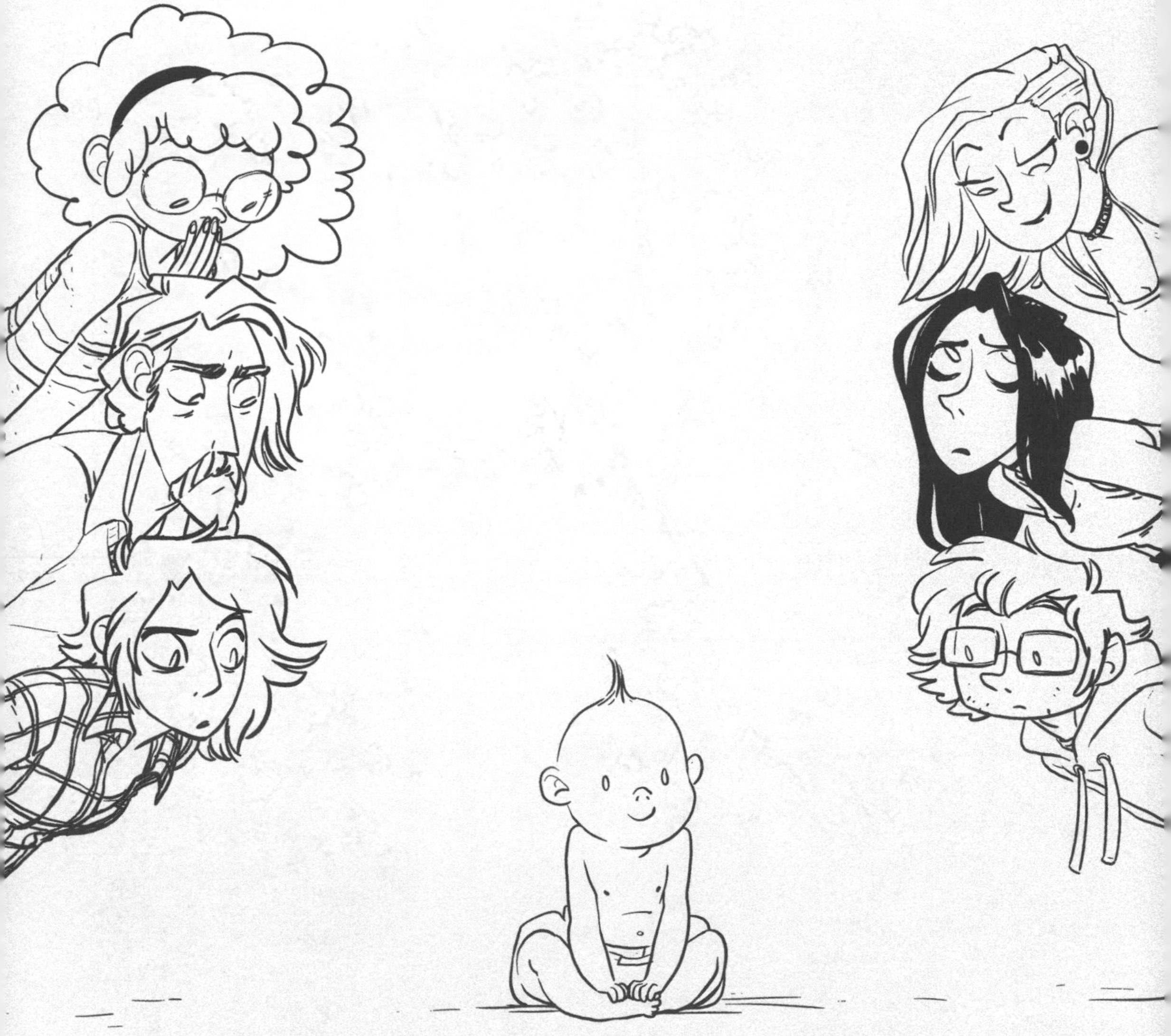

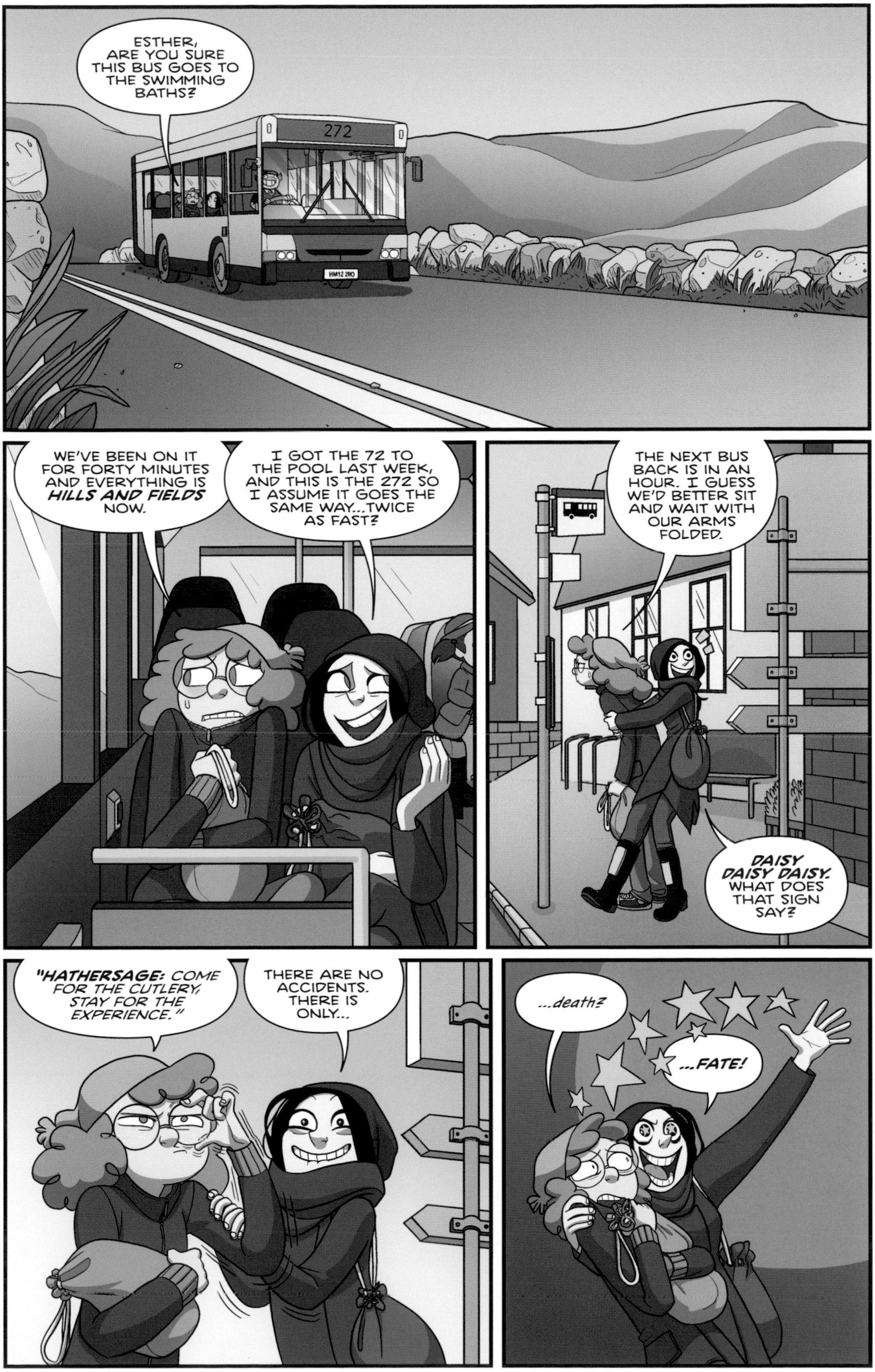
ESTHER, ARE YOU SURE THIS BUS GOES TO THE SWIMMING BATHS?
272
HM12 2RO
WE'VE BEEN ON IT FOR FORTY MINUTES AND EVERYTHING IS *HILLS AND FIELDS* NOW.
I GOT THE 72 TO THE POOL LAST WEEK, AND THIS IS THE 272 SO I ASSUME IT GOES THE SAME WAY...TWICE AS FAST?
THE NEXT BUS BACK IS IN AN HOUR. I GUESS WE'D BETTER SIT AND WAIT WITH OUR ARMS FOLDED.
*DAISY DAISY DAISY.* WHAT DOES THAT SIGN SAY?
*"HATHERSAGE:* COME FOR THE CUTLERY, STAY FOR THE EXPERIENCE."
THERE ARE NO ACCIDENTS. THERE IS ONLY...
...death?
...FATE!

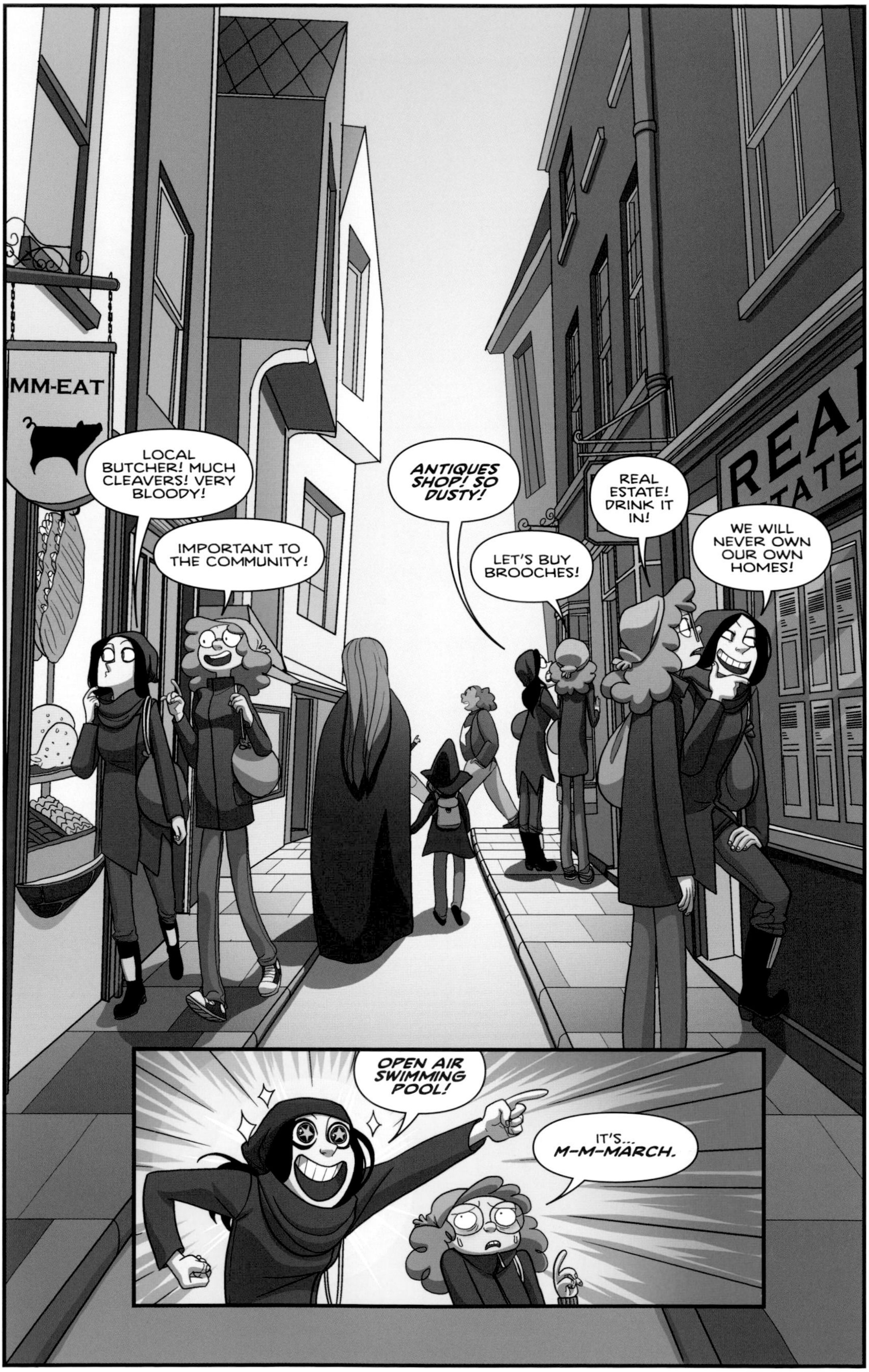
MM-EAT
LOCAL BUTCHER! MUCH CLEAVERS! VERY BLOODY!
IMPORTANT TO THE COMMUNITY!
ANTIQUES SHOP! SO DUSTY!
LET'S BUY BROOCHES!
REAL ESTATE! DRINK IT IN!
WE WILL NEVER OWN OUR OWN HOMES!
OPEN AIR SWIMMING POOL!
IT'S... M-M-MARCH.

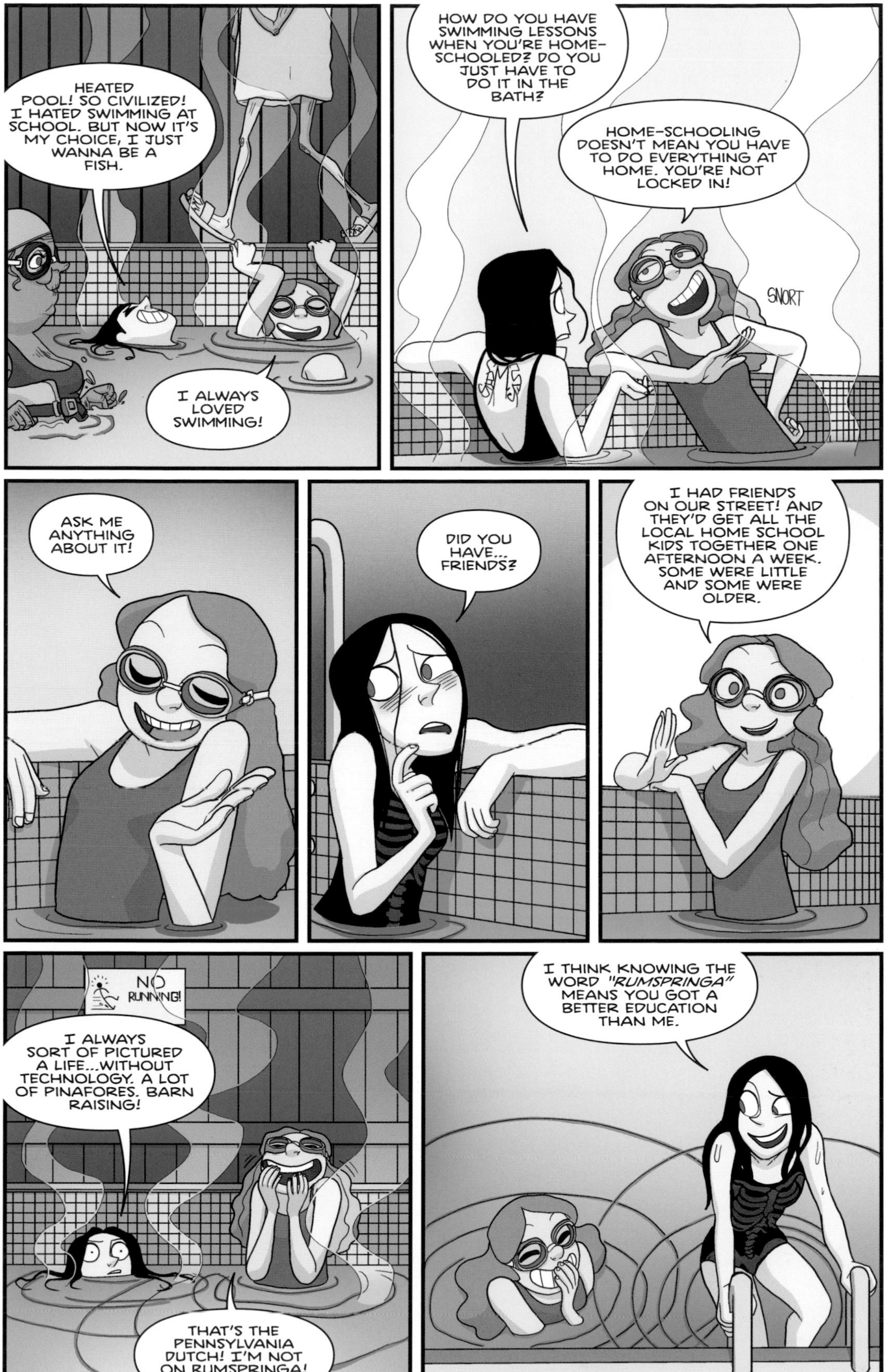
HEATED POOL! SO CIVILIZED! I HATED SWIMMING AT SCHOOL. BUT NOW IT'S MY CHOICE, I JUST WANNA BE A FISH.
I ALWAYS LOVED SWIMMING!
HOW DO YOU HAVE SWIMMING LESSONS WHEN YOU'RE HOME-SCHOOLED? DO YOU JUST HAVE TO DO IT IN THE BATH?
HOME-SCHOOLING DOESN'T MEAN YOU HAVE TO DO EVERYTHING AT HOME. YOU'RE NOT LOCKED IN!
SNORT
ASK ME ANYTHING ABOUT IT!
DID YOU HAVE... FRIENDS?
I HAD FRIENDS ON OUR STREET! AND THEY'D GET ALL THE LOCAL HOME SCHOOL KIDS TOGETHER ONE AFTERNOON A WEEK. SOME WERE LITTLE AND SOME WERE OLDER.
NO RUNNING!
I ALWAYS SORT OF PICTURED A LIFE...WITHOUT TECHNOLOGY. A LOT OF PINAFORES. BARN RAISING!
THAT'S THE PENNSYLVANIA DUTCH! I'M NOT ON RUMSPRINGA!
I THINK KNOWING THE WORD "RUMSPRINGA" MEANS YOU GOT A BETTER EDUCATION THAN ME.

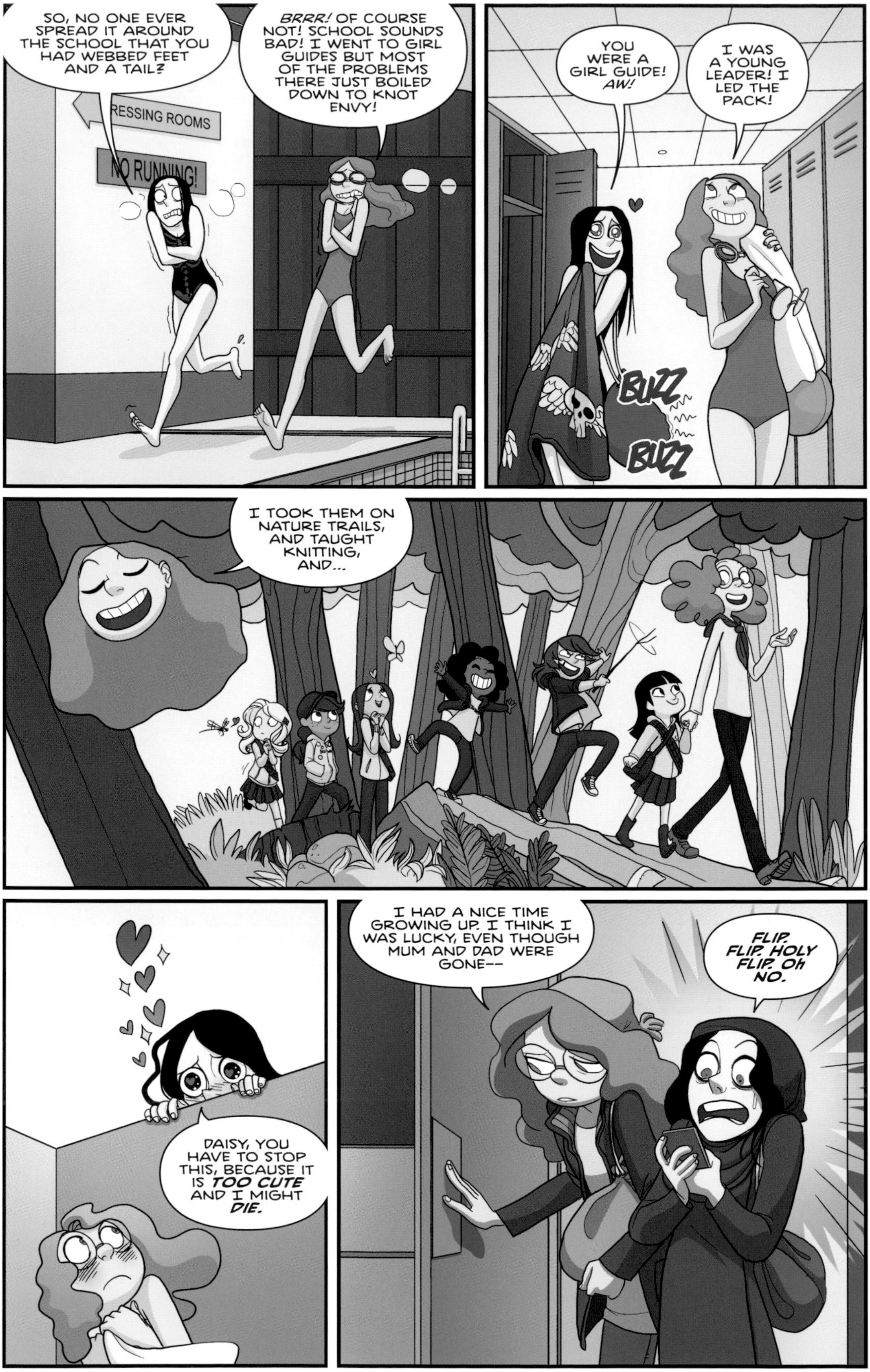
SO, NO ONE EVER SPREAD IT AROUND THE SCHOOL THAT YOU HAD WEBBED FEET AND A TAIL?
BRRR! OF COURSE NOT! SCHOOL SOUNDS BAD! I WENT TO GIRL GUIDES BUT MOST OF THE PROBLEMS THERE JUST BOILED DOWN TO KNOT ENVY!
RESSING ROOMS
NO RUNNING!
YOU WERE A GIRL GUIDE! AW!
I WAS A YOUNG LEADER! I LED THE PACK!
BUZZ
BUZZ
I TOOK THEM ON NATURE TRAILS, AND TAUGHT KNITTING, AND...
DAISY, YOU HAVE TO STOP THIS, BECAUSE IT IS TOO CUTE AND I MIGHT DIE.
I HAD A NICE TIME GROWING UP. I THINK I WAS LUCKY, EVEN THOUGH MUM AND DAD WERE GONE--
FLIP. FLIP. HOLY FLIP. Oh NO.

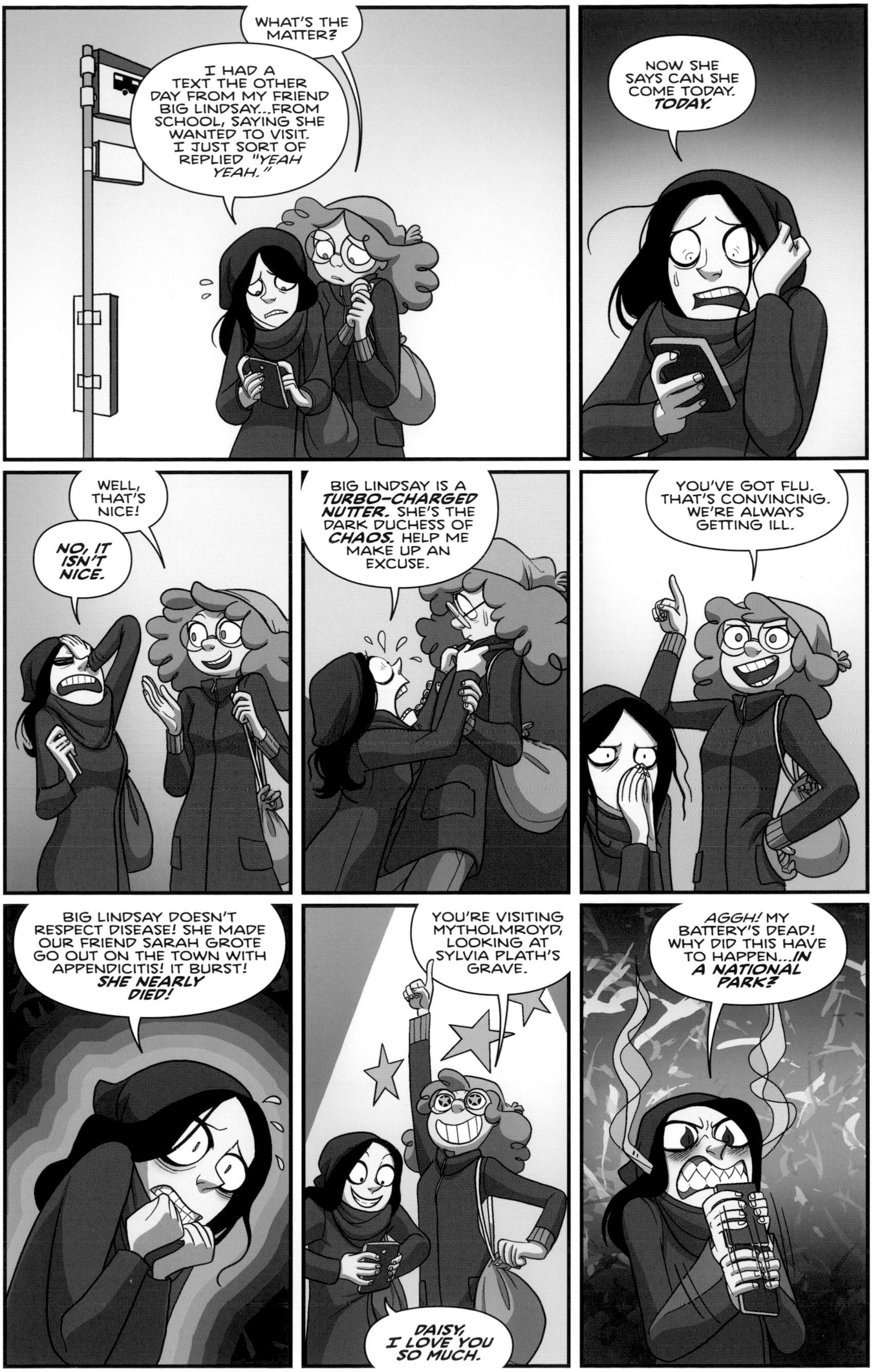
WHAT'S THE MATTER?
I HAD A TEXT THE OTHER DAY FROM MY FRIEND BIG LINDSAY...FROM SCHOOL, SAYING SHE WANTED TO VISIT. I JUST SORT OF REPLIED "YEAH YEAH."
NOW SHE SAYS CAN SHE COME TODAY. TODAY.
WELL, THAT'S NICE!
NO, IT ISN'T NICE.
BIG LINDSAY IS A TURBO-CHARGED NUTTER. SHE'S THE DARK DUCHESS OF CHAOS. HELP ME MAKE UP AN EXCUSE.
YOU'VE GOT FLU. THAT'S CONVINCING. WE'RE ALWAYS GETTING ILL.
BIG LINDSAY DOESN'T RESPECT DISEASE! SHE MADE OUR FRIEND SARAH GROTE GO OUT ON THE TOWN WITH APPENDICITIS! IT BURST! SHE NEARLY DIED!
YOU'RE VISITING MYTHOLMROYD, LOOKING AT SYLVIA PLATH'S GRAVE.
DAISY, I LOVE YOU SO MUCH.
AGGH! MY BATTERY'S DEAD! WHY DID THIS HAVE TO HAPPEN...IN A NATIONAL PARK?

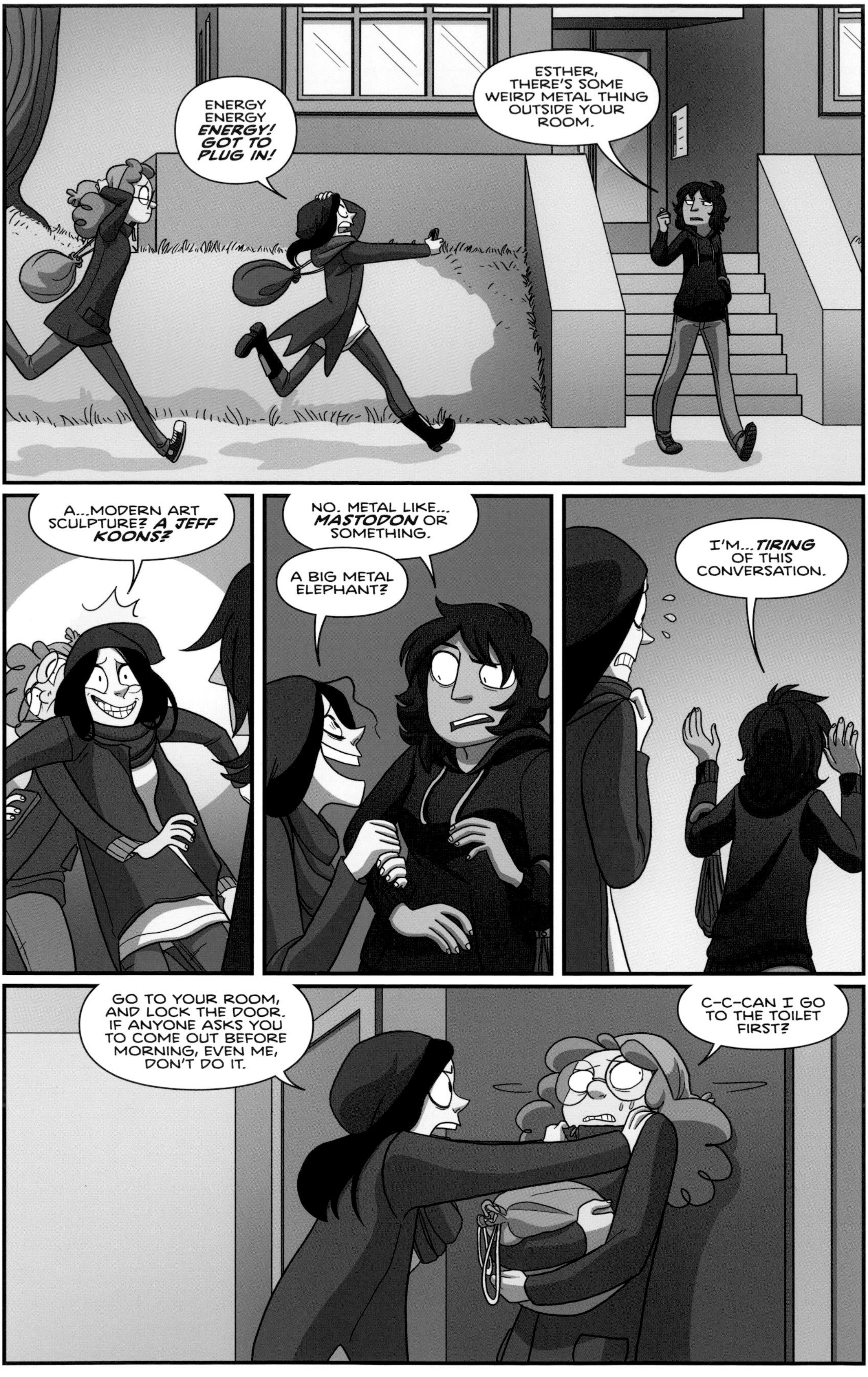
ENERGY ENERGY ENERGY! GOT TO PLUG IN!
ESTHER, THERE'S SOME WEIRD METAL THING OUTSIDE YOUR ROOM.
A...MODERN ART SCULPTURE? A JEFF KOONS?
NO. METAL LIKE... MASTODON OR SOMETHING.
A BIG METAL ELEPHANT?
I'M...TIRING OF THIS CONVERSATION.
GO TO YOUR ROOM, AND LOCK THE DOOR. IF ANYONE ASKS YOU TO COME OUT BEFORE MORNING, EVEN ME, DON'T DO IT.
C-C-CAN I GO TO THE TOILET FIRST?

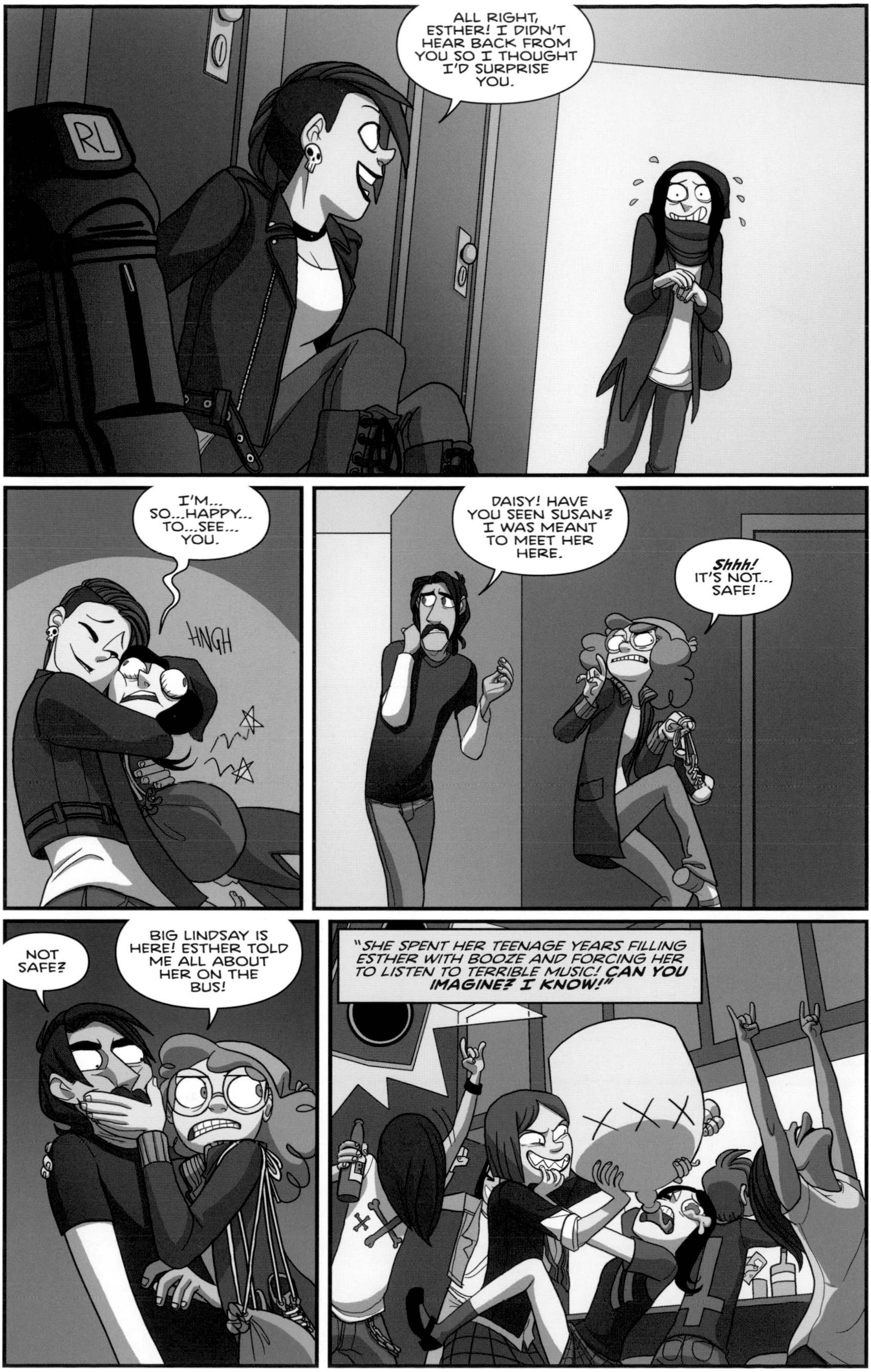
ALL RIGHT, ESTHER! I DIDN'T HEAR BACK FROM YOU SO I THOUGHT I'D SURPRISE YOU.
RL
I'M... SO...HAPPY... TO...SEE... YOU.
HNGH
DAISY! HAVE YOU SEEN SUSAN? I WAS MEANT TO MEET HER HERE.
Shhh! IT'S NOT... SAFE!
NOT SAFE?
BIG LINDSAY IS HERE! ESTHER TOLD ME ALL ABOUT HER ON THE BUS!
"SHE SPENT HER TEENAGE YEARS FILLING ESTHER WITH BOOZE AND FORCING HER TO LISTEN TO TERRIBLE MUSIC! CAN YOU IMAGINE? I KNOW!"

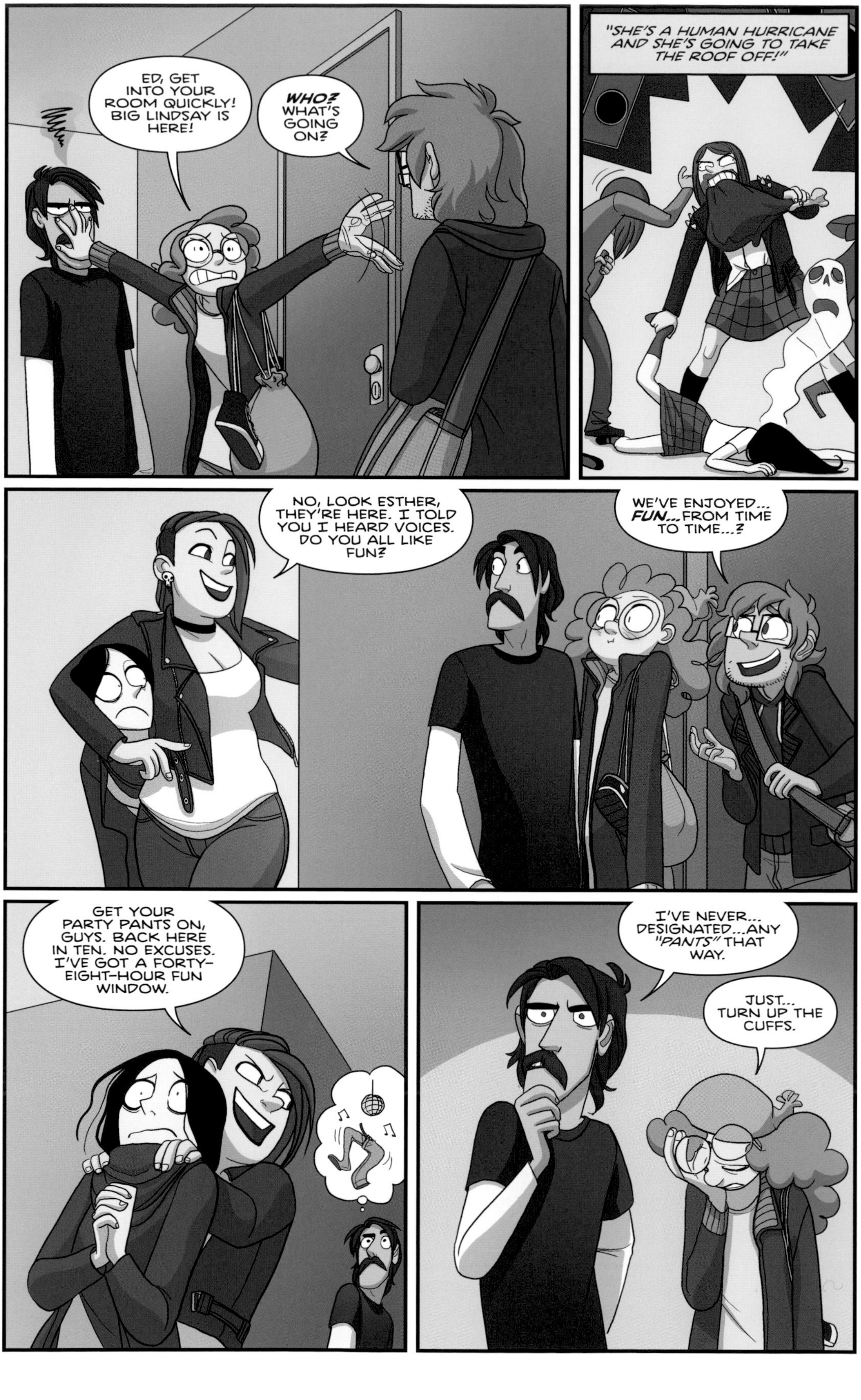
ED, GET INTO YOUR ROOM QUICKLY! BIG LINDSAY IS HERE!
WHO? WHAT'S GOING ON?
"SHE'S A HUMAN HURRICANE AND SHE'S GOING TO TAKE THE ROOF OFF!"
NO, LOOK ESTHER, THEY'RE HERE. I TOLD YOU I HEARD VOICES. DO YOU ALL LIKE FUN?
WE'VE ENJOYED... FUN... FROM TIME TO TIME...?
GET YOUR PARTY PANTS ON, GUYS. BACK HERE IN TEN. NO EXCUSES. I'VE GOT A FORTY-EIGHT-HOUR FUN WINDOW.
I'VE NEVER... DESIGNATED... ANY "PANTS" THAT WAY.
JUST... TURN UP THE CUFFS.

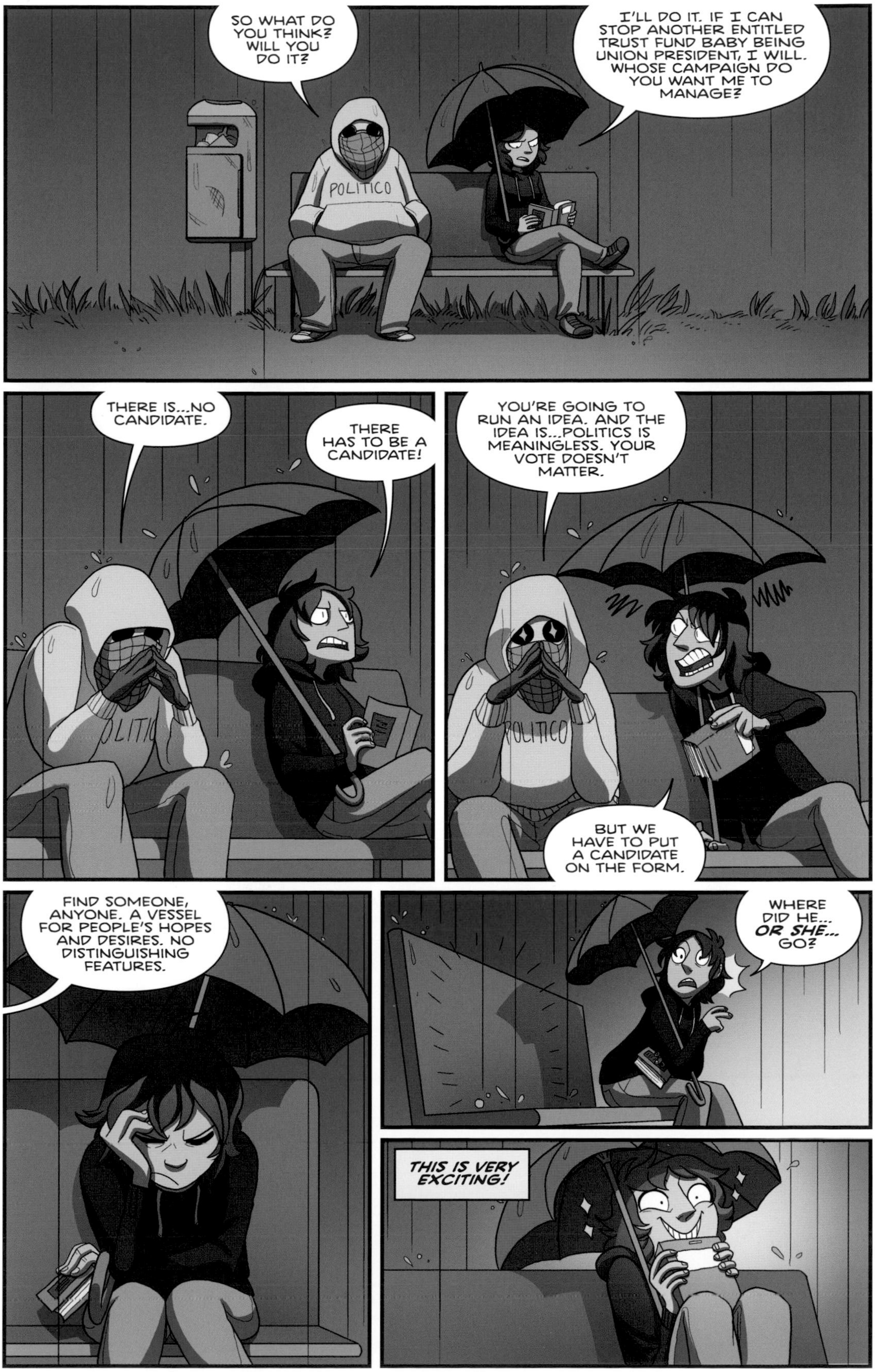
SO WHAT DO YOU THINK? WILL YOU DO IT?
I'LL DO IT. IF I CAN STOP ANOTHER ENTITLED TRUST FUND BABY BEING UNION PRESIDENT, I WILL. WHOSE CAMPAIGN DO YOU WANT ME TO MANAGE?
POLITICO
THERE IS...NO CANDIDATE.
THERE HAS TO BE A CANDIDATE!
POLITICO
YOU'RE GOING TO RUN AN IDEA. AND THE IDEA IS...POLITICS IS MEANINGLESS. YOUR VOTE DOESN'T MATTER.
POLITICO
BUT WE HAVE TO PUT A CANDIDATE ON THE FORM.
FIND SOMEONE, ANYONE. A VESSEL FOR PEOPLE'S HOPES AND DESIRES. NO DISTINGUISHING FEATURES.
WHERE DID HE... *OR SHE...* GO?
*THIS IS VERY EXCITING!*

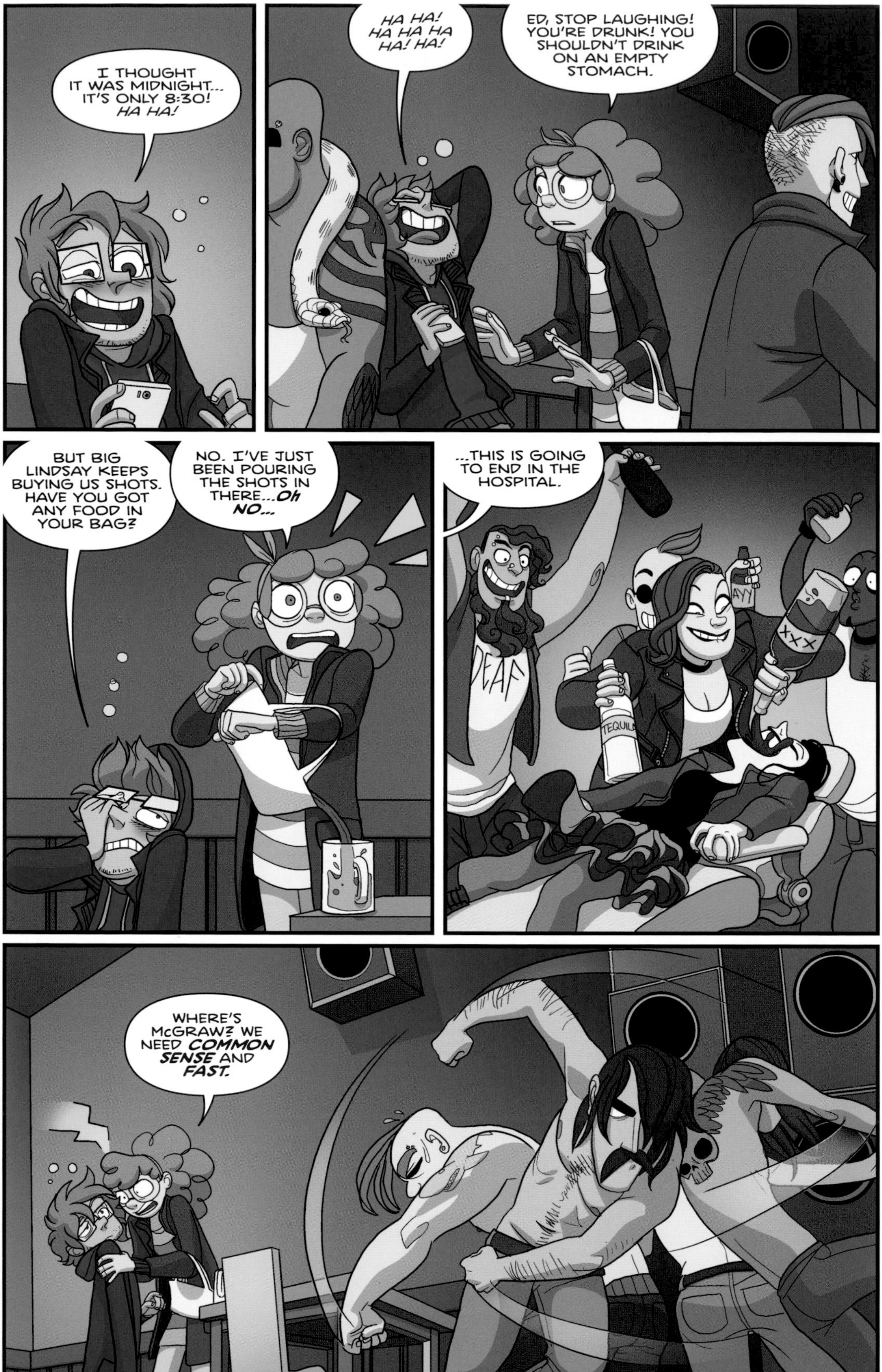
I THOUGHT IT WAS MIDNIGHT... IT'S ONLY 8:30! HA HA!
HA HA! HA HA HA HA! HA!
ED, STOP LAUGHING! YOU'RE DRUNK! YOU SHOULDN'T DRINK ON AN EMPTY STOMACH.
BUT BIG LINDSAY KEEPS BUYING US SHOTS. HAVE YOU GOT ANY FOOD IN YOUR BAG?
NO. I'VE JUST BEEN POURING THE SHOTS IN THERE...Oh NO...
...THIS IS GOING TO END IN THE HOSPITAL.
DEAF
AYY
XXX
TEQUILA
WHERE'S McGRAW? WE NEED COMMON SENSE AND FAST.

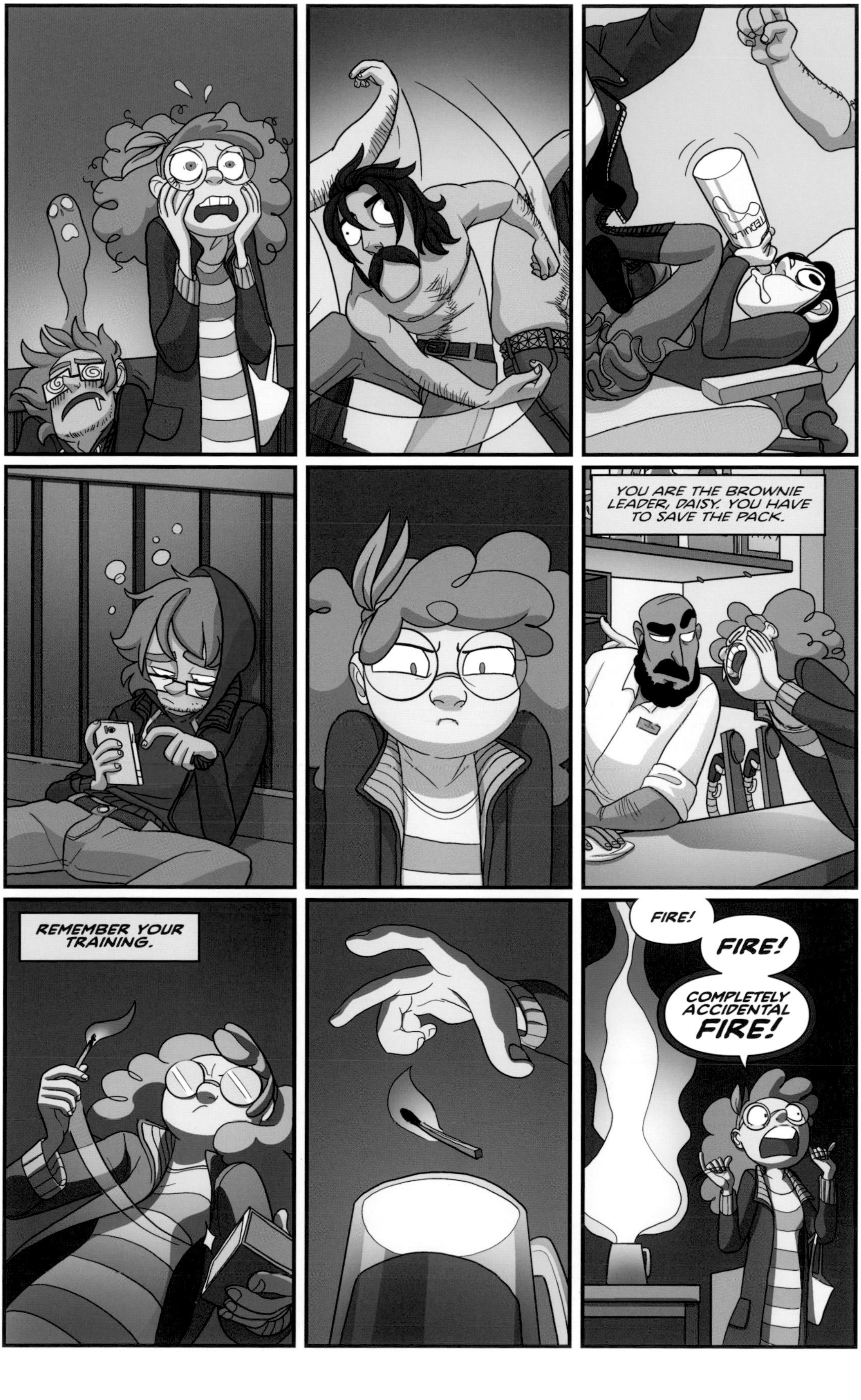
TEQUILA
YOU ARE THE BROWNIE LEADER, DAISY. YOU HAVE TO SAVE THE PACK.
REMEMBER YOUR TRAINING.
FIRE!
FIRE!
COMPLETELY ACCIDENTAL FIRE!

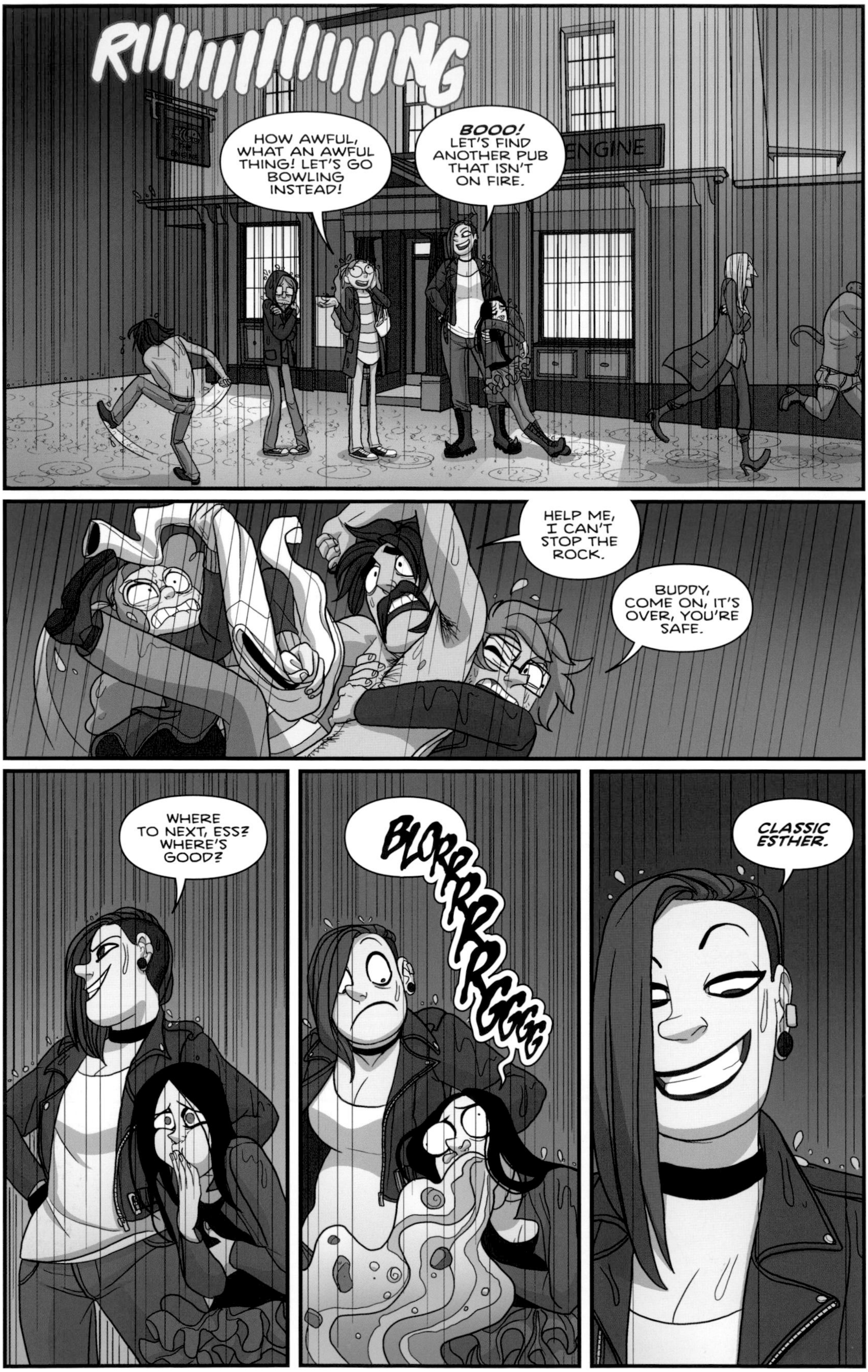
RIIIIIIIIIIIIIIING
ENGINE
HOW AWFUL, WHAT AN AWFUL THING! LET'S GO BOWLING INSTEAD!
BOOO! LET'S FIND ANOTHER PUB THAT ISN'T ON FIRE.
HELP ME, I CAN'T STOP THE ROCK.
BUDDY, COME ON, IT'S OVER, YOU'RE SAFE.
WHERE TO NEXT, ESS? WHERE'S GOOD?
BLORRRRRGGGG
CLASSIC ESTHER.

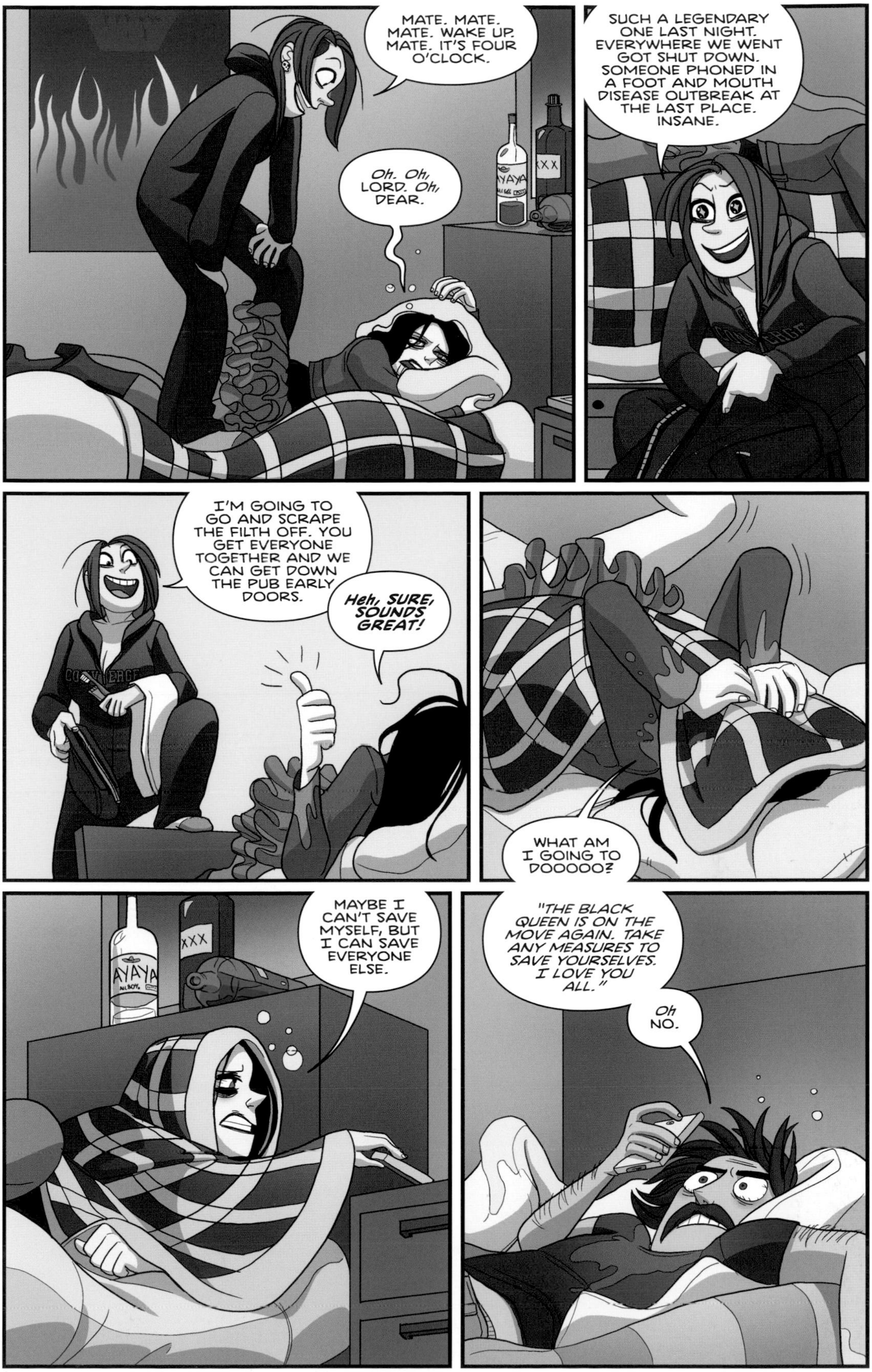
MATE. MATE. MATE. WAKE UP. MATE. IT'S FOUR O'CLOCK.
*Oh. Oh, LORD. Oh, DEAR.*
XXX
SUCH A LEGENDARY ONE LAST NIGHT. EVERYWHERE WE WENT GOT SHUT DOWN. SOMEONE PHONED IN A FOOT AND MOUTH DISEASE OUTBREAK AT THE LAST PLACE. INSANE.
I'M GOING TO GO AND SCRAPE THE FILTH OFF. YOU GET EVERYONE TOGETHER AND WE CAN GET DOWN THE PUB EARLY DOORS.
***Heh, SURE, SOUNDS GREAT!***
WHAT AM I GOING TO DOOOOO?
MAYBE I CAN'T SAVE MYSELF, BUT I CAN SAVE EVERYONE ELSE.
XXX
*"THE BLACK QUEEN IS ON THE MOVE AGAIN. TAKE ANY MEASURES TO SAVE YOURSELVES. I LOVE YOU ALL."*
*Oh* NO.

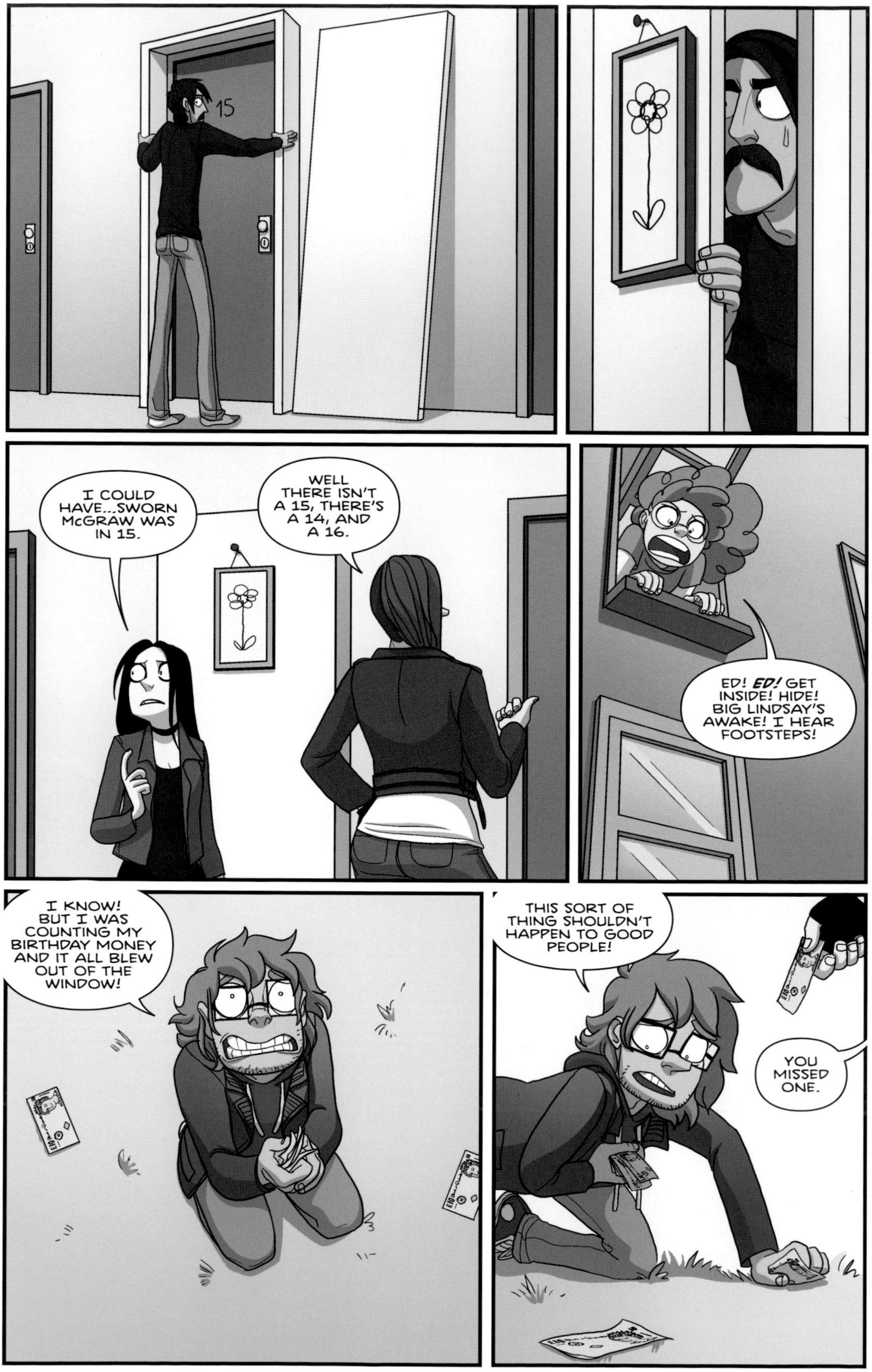
15
I COULD HAVE...SWORN McGRAW WAS IN 15.
WELL THERE ISN'T A 15, THERE'S A 14, AND A 16.
ED! ED! GET INSIDE! HIDE! BIG LINDSAY'S AWAKE! I HEAR FOOTSTEPS!
I KNOW! BUT I WAS COUNTING MY BIRTHDAY MONEY AND IT ALL BLEW OUT OF THE WINDOW!
THIS SORT OF THING SHOULDN'T HAPPEN TO GOOD PEOPLE!
YOU MISSED ONE.

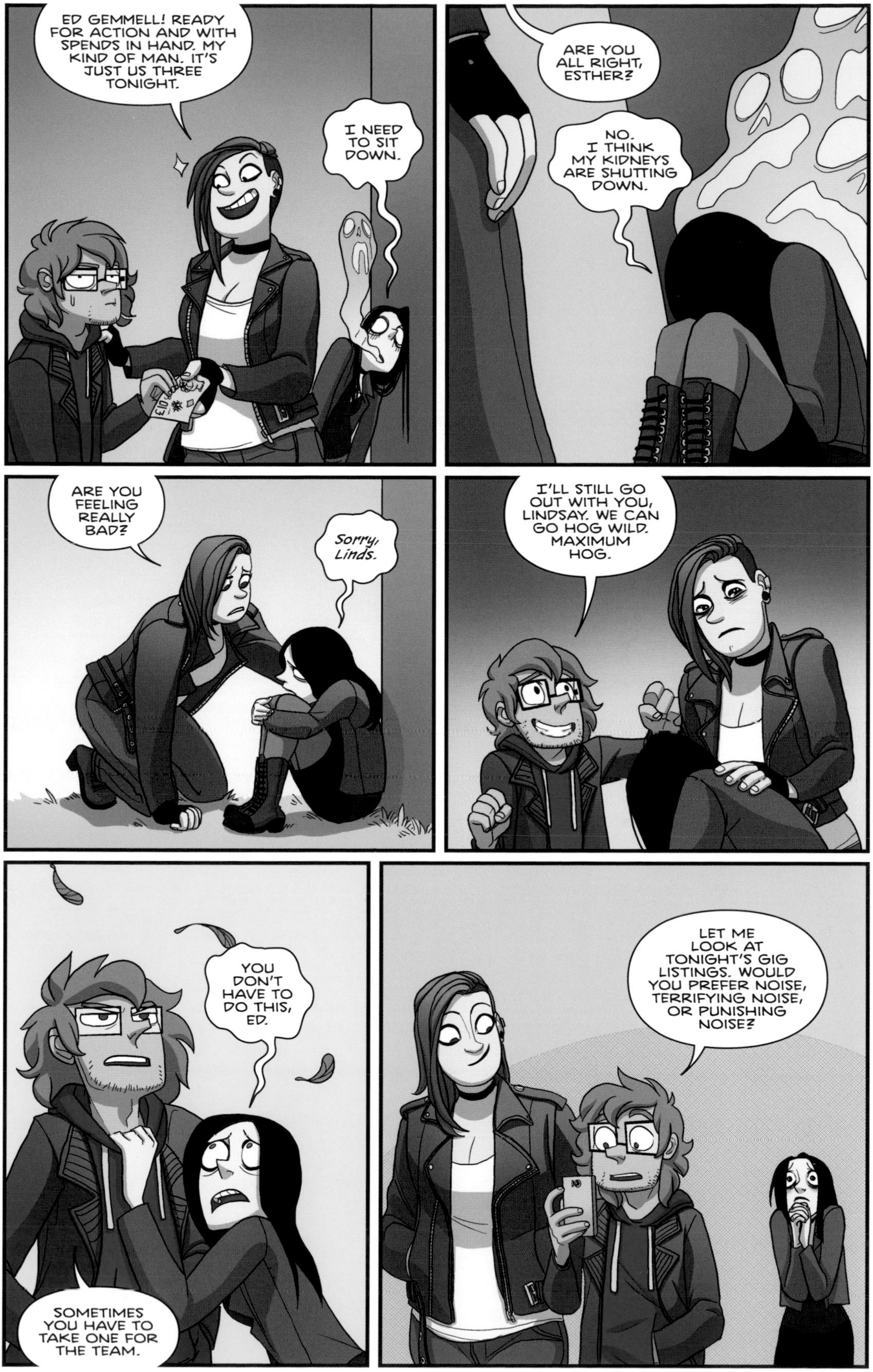
ED GEMMELL! READY FOR ACTION AND WITH SPENDS IN HAND. MY KIND OF MAN. IT'S JUST US THREE TONIGHT.
I NEED TO SIT DOWN.
ARE YOU ALL RIGHT, ESTHER?
NO. I THINK MY KIDNEYS ARE SHUTTING DOWN.
ARE YOU FEELING REALLY BAD?
*Sorry, Linds.*
I'LL STILL GO OUT WITH YOU, LINDSAY. WE CAN GO HOG WILD. MAXIMUM HOG.
YOU DON'T HAVE TO DO THIS, ED.
SOMETIMES YOU HAVE TO TAKE ONE FOR THE TEAM.
LET ME LOOK AT TONIGHT'S GIG LISTINGS. WOULD YOU PREFER NOISE, TERRIFYING NOISE, OR PUNISHING NOISE?

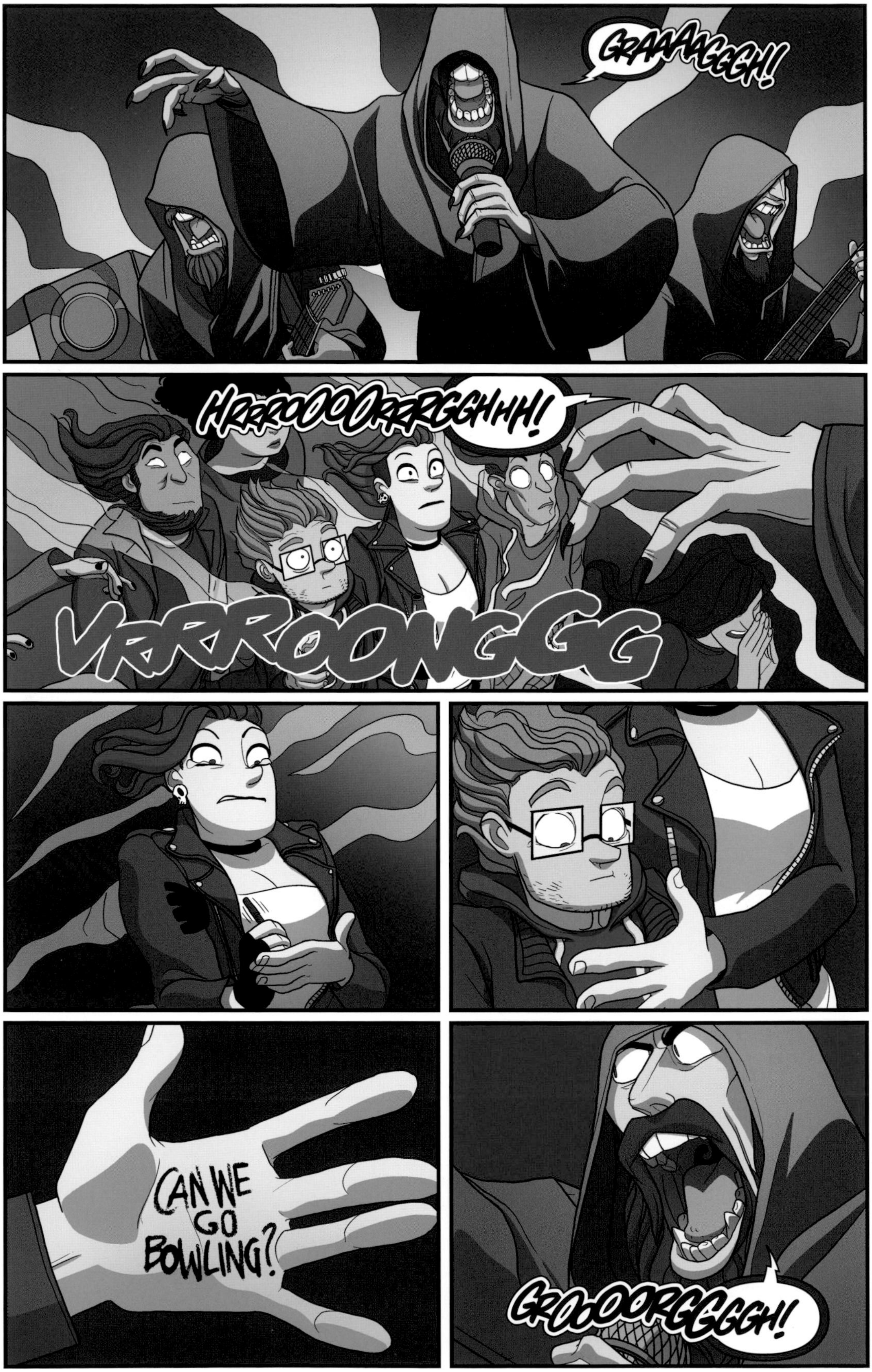
GRAAAAGGGH!
HRRROOOORRRGGHHH!
VRRROONGGG
CAN WE GO BOWLING?
GROOOORGGGGH!

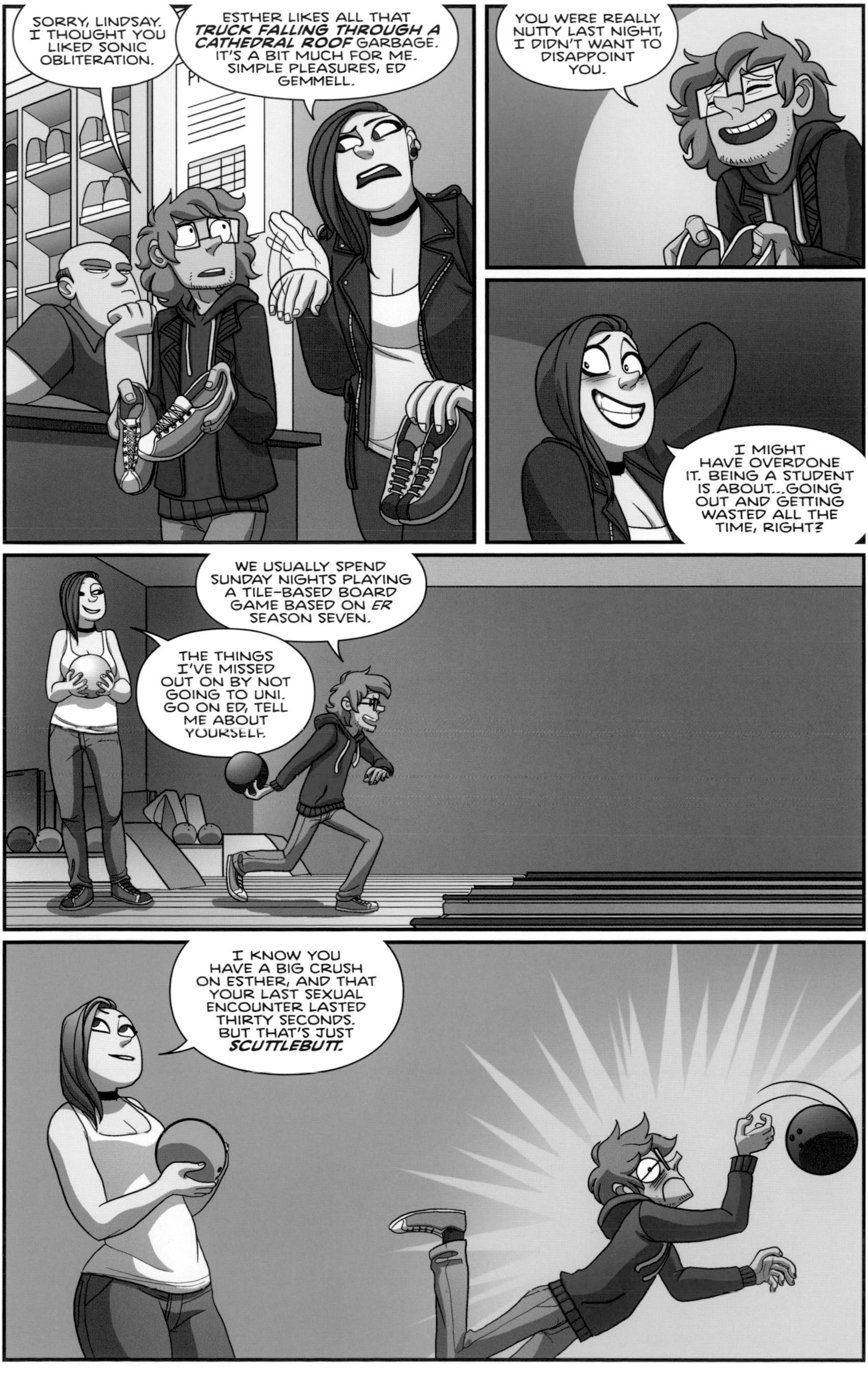
SORRY, LINDSAY. I THOUGHT YOU LIKED SONIC OBLITERATION.
ESTHER LIKES ALL THAT *TRUCK FALLING THROUGH A CATHEDRAL ROOF* GARBAGE. IT'S A BIT MUCH FOR ME. SIMPLE PLEASURES, ED GEMMELL.
YOU WERE REALLY NUTTY LAST NIGHT, I DIDN'T WANT TO DISAPPOINT YOU.
I MIGHT HAVE OVERDONE IT. BEING A STUDENT IS ABOUT...GOING OUT AND GETTING WASTED ALL THE TIME, RIGHT?
WE USUALLY SPEND SUNDAY NIGHTS PLAYING A TILE-BASED BOARD GAME BASED ON *ER* SEASON SEVEN.
THE THINGS I'VE MISSED OUT ON BY NOT GOING TO UNI. GO ON ED, TELL ME ABOUT YOURSELF.
I KNOW YOU HAVE A BIG CRUSH ON ESTHER, AND THAT YOUR LAST SEXUAL ENCOUNTER LASTED THIRTY SECONDS. BUT THAT'S JUST *SCUTTLEBUTT.*

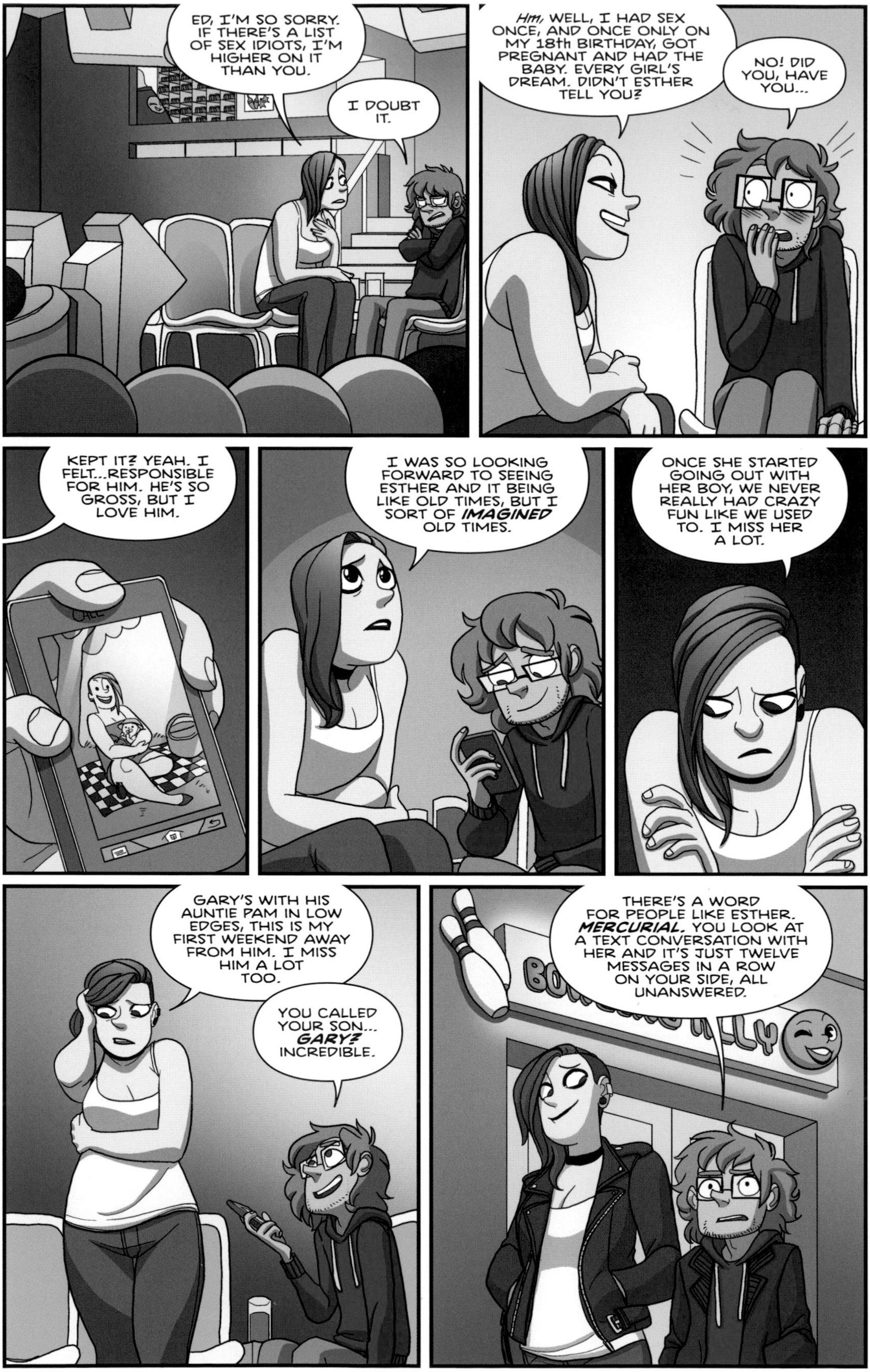
ED, I'M SO SORRY. IF THERE'S A LIST OF SEX IDIOTS, I'M HIGHER ON IT THAN YOU.
I DOUBT IT.
*HM*, WELL, I HAD SEX ONCE, AND ONCE ONLY ON MY 18th BIRTHDAY, GOT PREGNANT AND HAD THE BABY. EVERY GIRL'S DREAM. DIDN'T ESTHER TELL YOU?
NO! DID YOU, HAVE YOU...
KEPT IT? YEAH. I FELT...RESPONSIBLE FOR HIM. HE'S SO GROSS, BUT I LOVE HIM.
I WAS SO LOOKING FORWARD TO SEEING ESTHER AND IT BEING LIKE OLD TIMES, BUT I SORT OF ***IMAGINED*** OLD TIMES.
ONCE SHE STARTED GOING OUT WITH HER BOY, WE NEVER REALLY HAD CRAZY FUN LIKE WE USED TO. I MISS HER A LOT.
GARY'S WITH HIS AUNTIE PAM IN LOW EDGES, THIS IS MY FIRST WEEKEND AWAY FROM HIM. I MISS HIM A LOT TOO.
YOU CALLED YOUR SON... ***GARY?*** INCREDIBLE.
THERE'S A WORD FOR PEOPLE LIKE ESTHER. ***MERCURIAL.*** YOU LOOK AT A TEXT CONVERSATION WITH HER AND IT'S JUST TWELVE MESSAGES IN A ROW ON YOUR SIDE, ALL UNANSWERED.

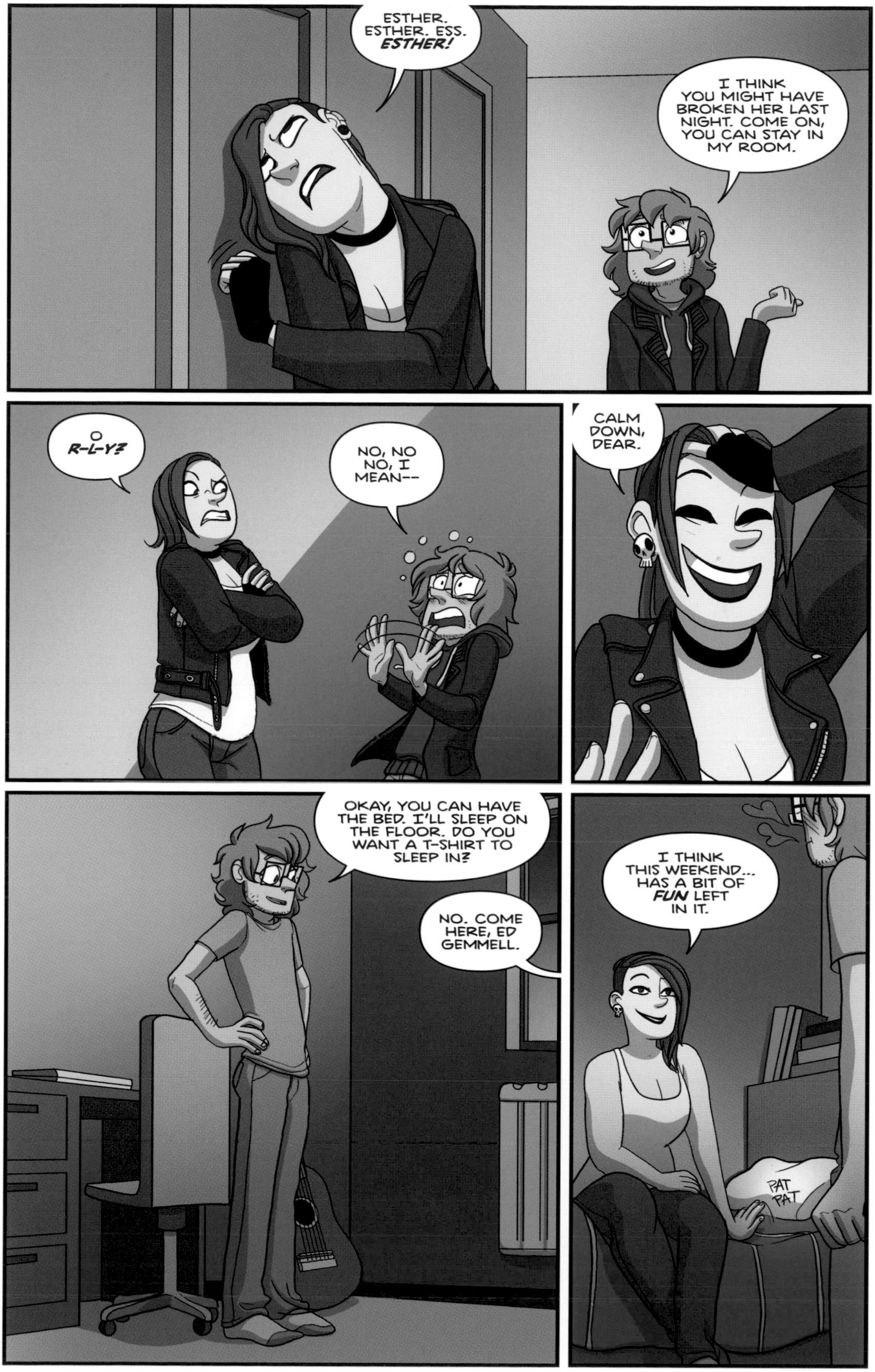
ESTHER. ESTHER. ESS. ESTHER!
I THINK YOU MIGHT HAVE BROKEN HER LAST NIGHT. COME ON, YOU CAN STAY IN MY ROOM.
O R-L-Y?
NO, NO NO, I MEAN--
CALM DOWN, DEAR.
OKAY, YOU CAN HAVE THE BED. I'LL SLEEP ON THE FLOOR. DO YOU WANT A T-SHIRT TO SLEEP IN?
NO. COME HERE, ED GEMMELL.
I THINK THIS WEEKEND... HAS A BIT OF FUN LEFT IN IT.
PAT PAT

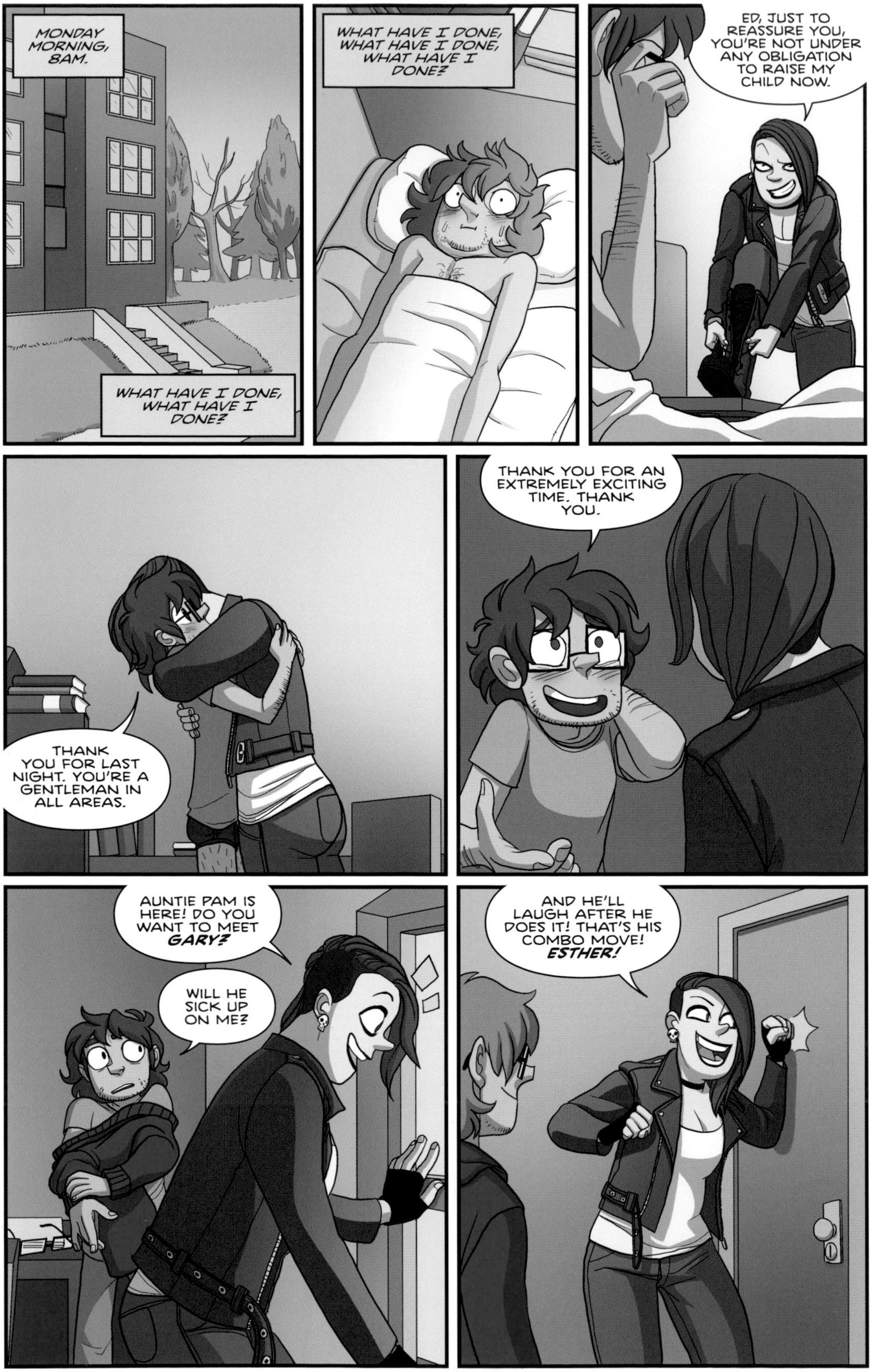
MONDAY MORNING, 8AM.
WHAT HAVE I DONE, WHAT HAVE I DONE?
WHAT HAVE I DONE, WHAT HAVE I DONE, WHAT HAVE I DONE?
ED, JUST TO REASSURE YOU, YOU'RE NOT UNDER ANY OBLIGATION TO RAISE MY CHILD NOW.
THANK YOU FOR LAST NIGHT. YOU'RE A GENTLEMAN IN ALL AREAS.
THANK YOU FOR AN EXTREMELY EXCITING TIME. THANK YOU.
AUNTIE PAM IS HERE! DO YOU WANT TO MEET **GARY?**
WILL HE SICK UP ON ME?
AND HE'LL LAUGH AFTER HE DOES IT! THAT'S HIS COMBO MOVE! **ESTHER!**

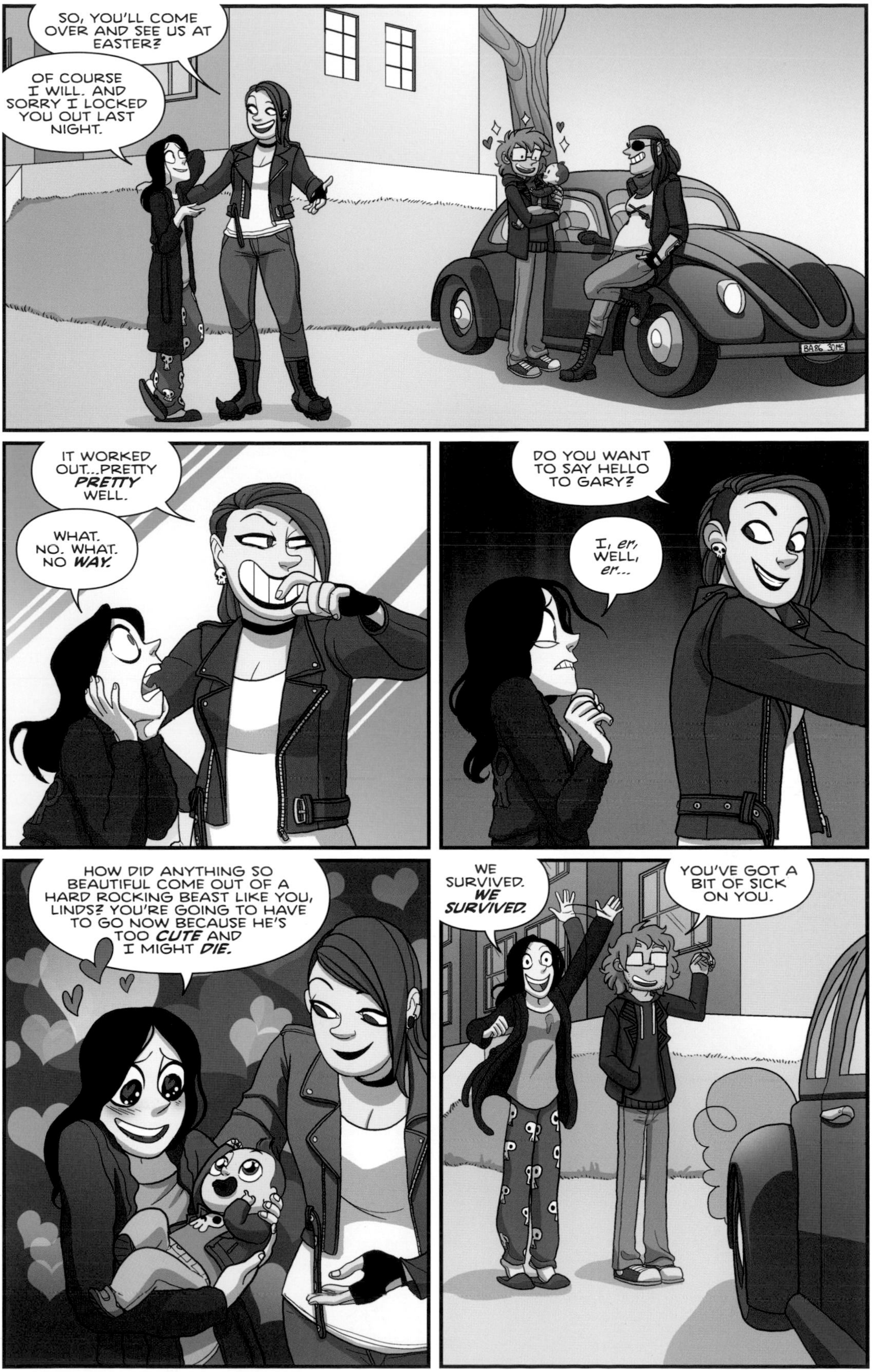
SO, YOU'LL COME OVER AND SEE US AT EASTER?
OF COURSE I WILL. AND SORRY I LOCKED YOU OUT LAST NIGHT.
IT WORKED OUT...PRETTY *PRETTY* WELL.
WHAT. NO. WHAT. NO *WAY.*
DO YOU WANT TO SAY HELLO TO GARY?
I, *er,* WELL, *er...*
HOW DID ANYTHING SO BEAUTIFUL COME OUT OF A HARD ROCKING BEAST LIKE YOU, LINDS? YOU'RE GOING TO HAVE TO GO NOW BECAUSE HE'S TOO *CUTE* AND I MIGHT *DIE.*
WE SURVIVED. *WE SURVIVED.*
YOU'VE GOT A BIT OF SICK ON YOU.

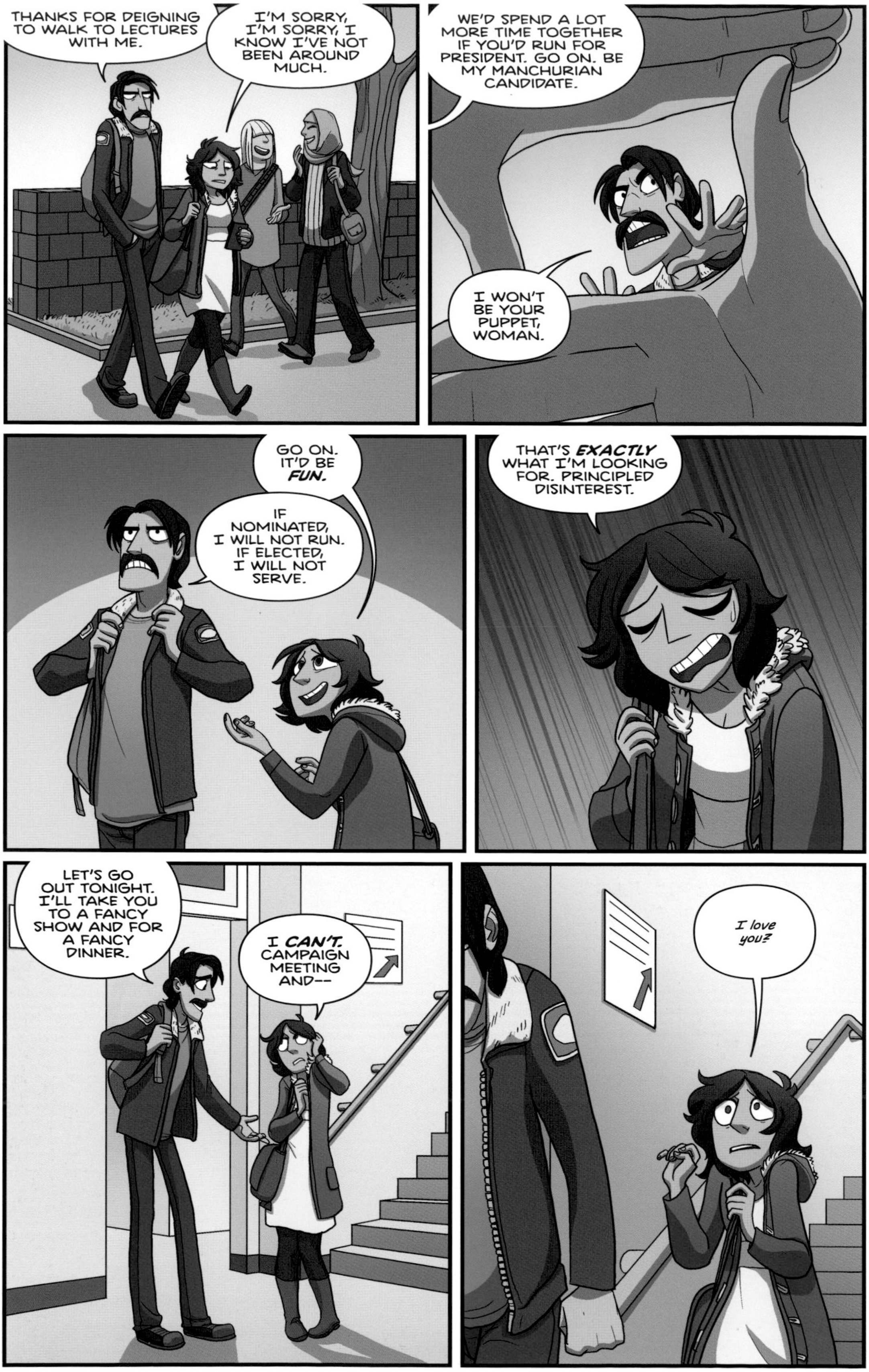
THANKS FOR DEIGNING TO WALK TO LECTURES WITH ME.
I'M SORRY, I'M SORRY, I KNOW I'VE NOT BEEN AROUND MUCH.
WE'D SPEND A LOT MORE TIME TOGETHER IF YOU'D RUN FOR PRESIDENT. GO ON. BE MY MANCHURIAN CANDIDATE.
I WON'T BE YOUR PUPPET, WOMAN.
GO ON. IT'D BE ***FUN.***
IF NOMINATED, I WILL NOT RUN. IF ELECTED, I WILL NOT SERVE.
THAT'S ***EXACTLY*** WHAT I'M LOOKING FOR. PRINCIPLED DISINTEREST.
LET'S GO OUT TONIGHT. I'LL TAKE YOU TO A FANCY SHOW AND FOR A FANCY DINNER.
I ***CAN'T.*** CAMPAIGN MEETING AND--
*I love you?*

# CHAPTER
# ELEVEN

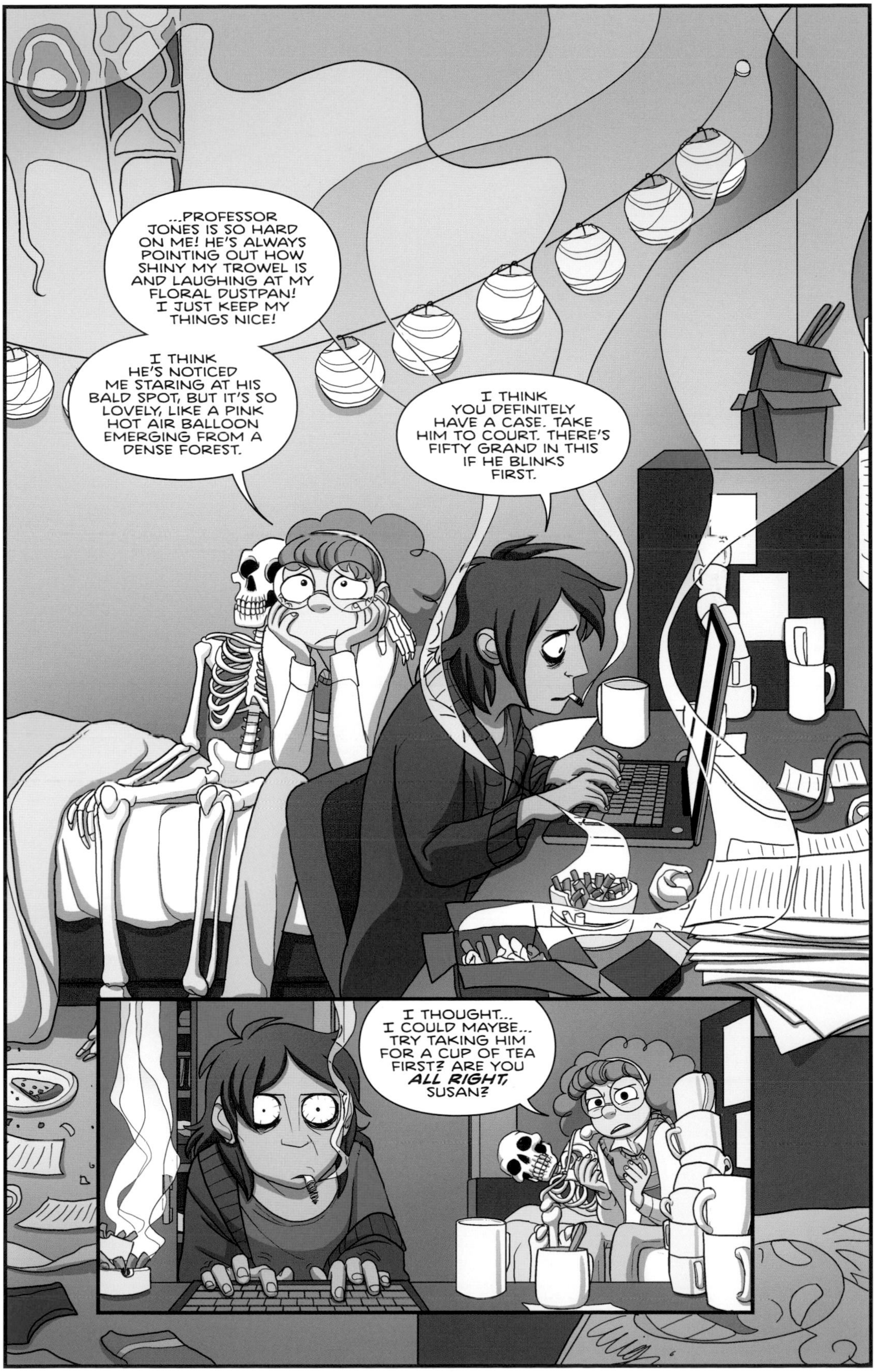
...PROFESSOR JONES IS SO HARD ON ME! HE'S ALWAYS POINTING OUT HOW SHINY MY TROWEL IS AND LAUGHING AT MY FLORAL DUSTPAN! I JUST KEEP MY THINGS NICE!
I THINK HE'S NOTICED ME STARING AT HIS BALD SPOT, BUT IT'S SO LOVELY, LIKE A PINK HOT AIR BALLOON EMERGING FROM A DENSE FOREST.
I THINK YOU DEFINITELY HAVE A CASE. TAKE HIM TO COURT. THERE'S FIFTY GRAND IN THIS IF HE BLINKS FIRST.
I THOUGHT... I COULD MAYBE... TRY TAKING HIM FOR A CUP OF TEA FIRST? ARE YOU ***ALL RIGHT,*** SUSAN?

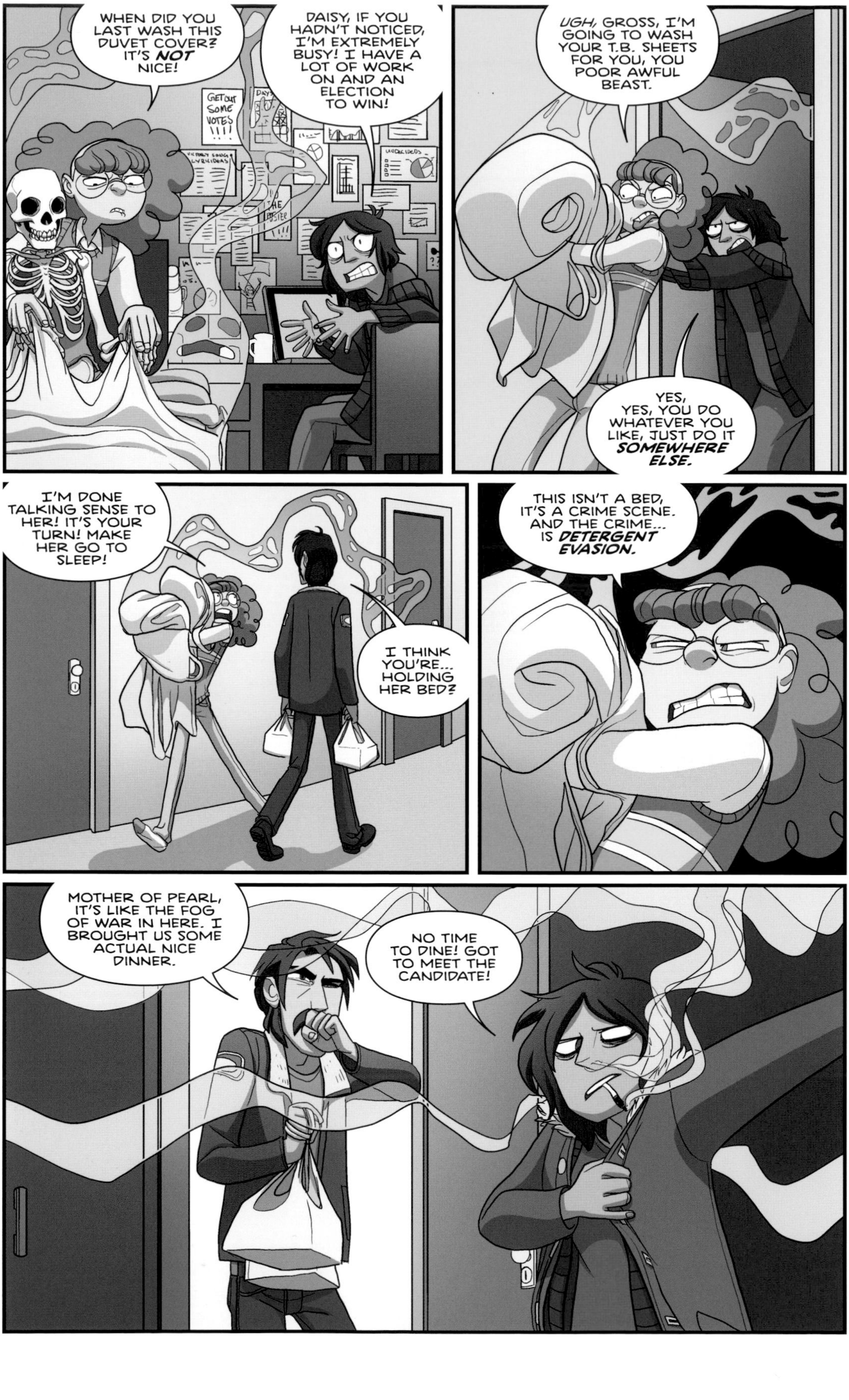
WHEN DID YOU LAST WASH THIS DUVET COVER? IT'S **NOT** NICE!
GET OUT SOME VOTES !!!!
DAISY, IF YOU HADN'T NOTICED, I'M EXTREMELY BUSY! I HAVE A LOT OF WORK ON AND AN ELECTION TO WIN!
*UGH,* GROSS, I'M GOING TO WASH YOUR T.B. SHEETS FOR YOU, YOU POOR AWFUL BEAST.
YES, YES, YOU DO WHATEVER YOU LIKE, JUST DO IT ***SOMEWHERE ELSE.***
I'M DONE TALKING SENSE TO HER! IT'S YOUR TURN! MAKE HER GO TO SLEEP!
I THINK YOU'RE... HOLDING HER BED?
THIS ISN'T A BED, IT'S A CRIME SCENE. AND THE CRIME... IS ***DETERGENT EVASION.***
MOTHER OF PEARL, IT'S LIKE THE FOG OF WAR IN HERE. I BROUGHT US SOME ACTUAL NICE DINNER.
NO TIME TO DINE! GOT TO MEET THE CANDIDATE!

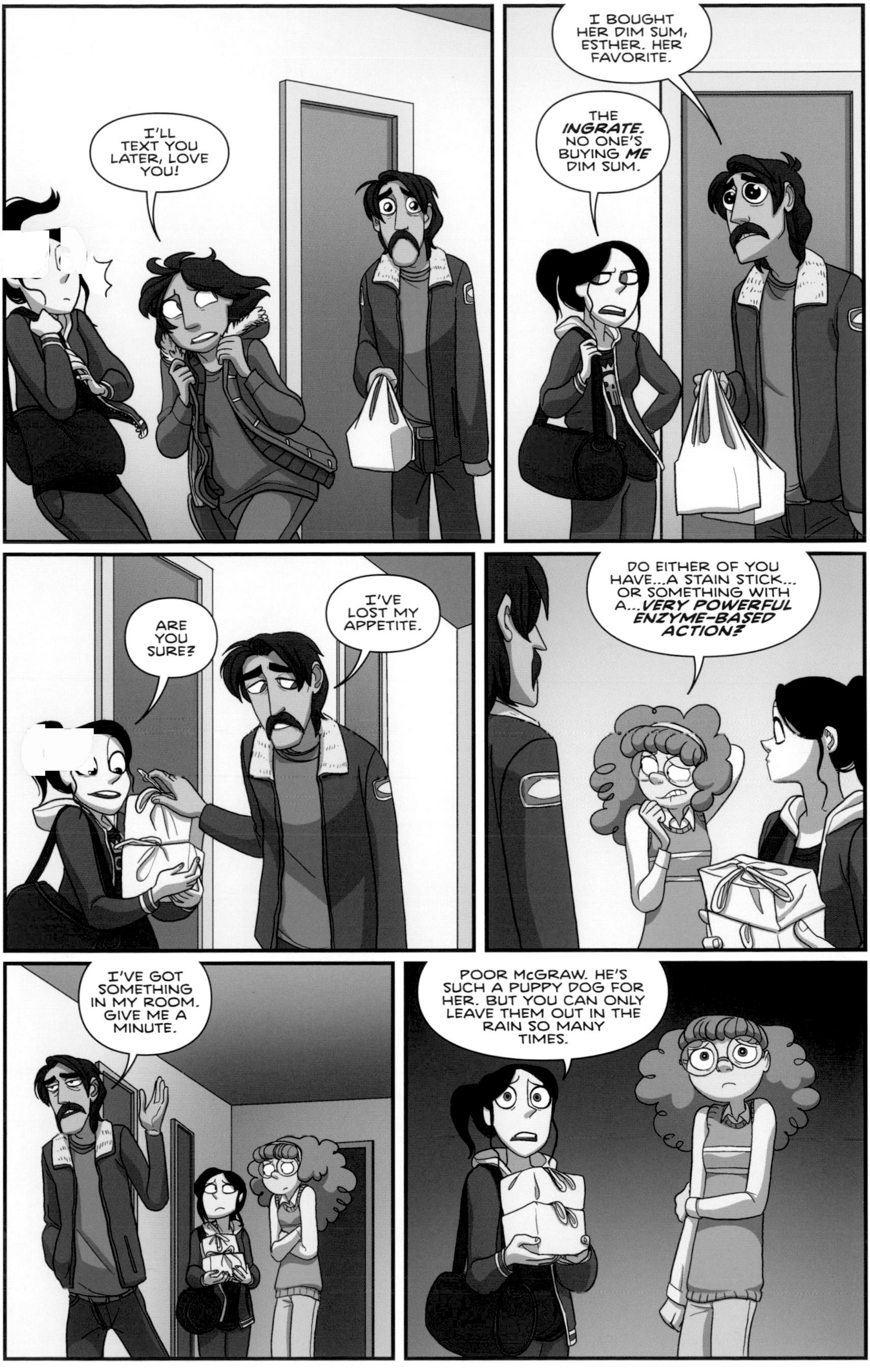
I'LL TEXT YOU LATER, LOVE YOU!
I BOUGHT HER DIM SUM, ESTHER. HER FAVORITE.
THE ***INGRATE.*** NO ONE'S BUYING ***ME*** DIM SUM.
ARE YOU SURE?
I'VE LOST MY APPETITE.
DO EITHER OF YOU HAVE...A STAIN STICK... OR SOMETHING WITH A...***VERY POWERFUL ENZYME-BASED ACTION?***
I'VE GOT SOMETHING IN MY ROOM. GIVE ME A MINUTE.
POOR McGRAW. HE'S SUCH A PUPPY DOG FOR HER. BUT YOU CAN ONLY LEAVE THEM OUT IN THE RAIN SO MANY TIMES.

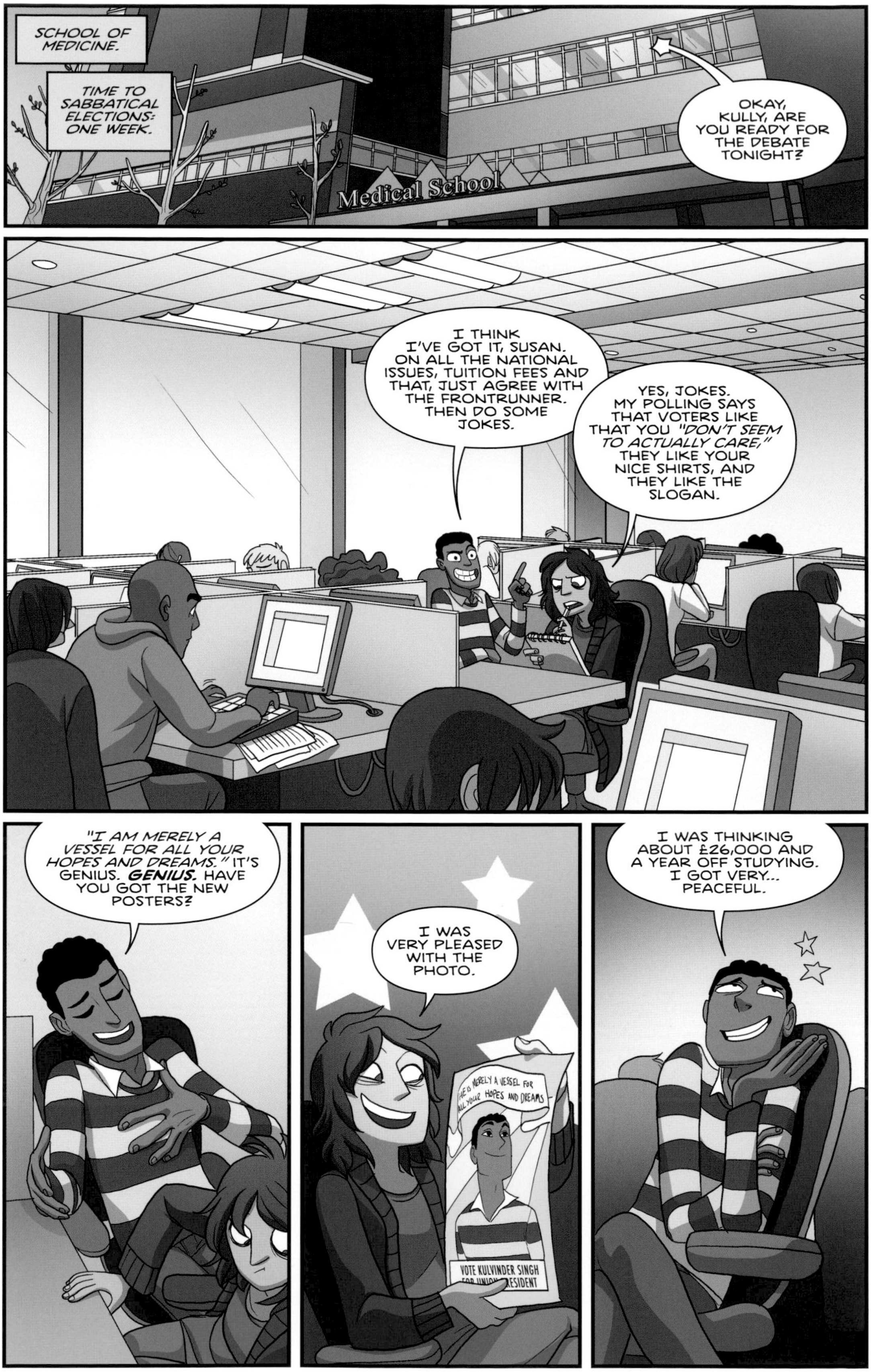
SCHOOL OF MEDICINE.
TIME TO SABBATICAL ELECTIONS: ONE WEEK.
Medical School
OKAY, KULLY, ARE YOU READY FOR THE DEBATE TONIGHT?
I THINK I'VE GOT IT, SUSAN. ON ALL THE NATIONAL ISSUES, TUITION FEES AND THAT, JUST AGREE WITH THE FRONTRUNNER. THEN DO SOME JOKES.
YES, JOKES. MY POLLING SAYS THAT VOTERS LIKE THAT YOU *"DON'T SEEM TO ACTUALLY CARE,"* THEY LIKE YOUR NICE SHIRTS, AND THEY LIKE THE SLOGAN.
*"I AM MERELY A VESSEL FOR ALL YOUR HOPES AND DREAMS."* IT'S GENIUS. ***GENIUS.*** HAVE YOU GOT THE NEW POSTERS?
I WAS VERY PLEASED WITH THE PHOTO.
HE IS MERELY A VESSEL FOR ALL YOUR HOPES AND DREAMS
VOTE KULVINDER SINGH FOR UNION PRESIDENT
I WAS THINKING ABOUT £26,000 AND A YEAR OFF STUDYING. I GOT VERY... PEACEFUL.

WE'RE NECK-TO-NECK WITH POTTER. I THINK THE FACT THAT VOTERS FIND HIM PHYSICALLY REPULSIVE IS HELPING.

HE'S OUT EVERY NIGHT THOUGH-- HE'S THE PARTY KING. HE'S LOCKED DOWN THE SPORTS VOTE.

BUT HE'S SOFT ON ISSUES THAT THE WEAK, UNCOORDINATED SECTION OF THE ELECTORATE CARE ABOUT. AND HE KEEPS SWEATING HIS HANGOVERS ONTO THEM.

MORE of the SAME

VOTE CHRIS POTTER FOR UNION PRESIDENT

SUSAN, YOU KNOW THIS IS OUR LAST COMPUTER ANATOMY LAB BEFORE YOU HAVE TO START CUTTING UP A *REAL* CADAVER NEXT WEEK.

*UGH*, I'VE DONE ALL THE EXERCISES SO MANY TIMES, DOCTOR T. I CAN'T DISSECT A SHOULDER GIRDLE AGAIN. AND I'VE BOSSED THE BRACHIAL PLEXUS. I'M READY FOR THE DEAD.

COULD YOU AND MR. SINGH TRY TO KEEP IT DOWN TO A DULL ROAR, THEN?

YOU'RE SO CONFIDENT! I'M BRICKIN' IT, SUSAN.

I'VE NOT SLEPT FOR A WEEK, BUT OTHERWISE, I CAN'T WAIT.

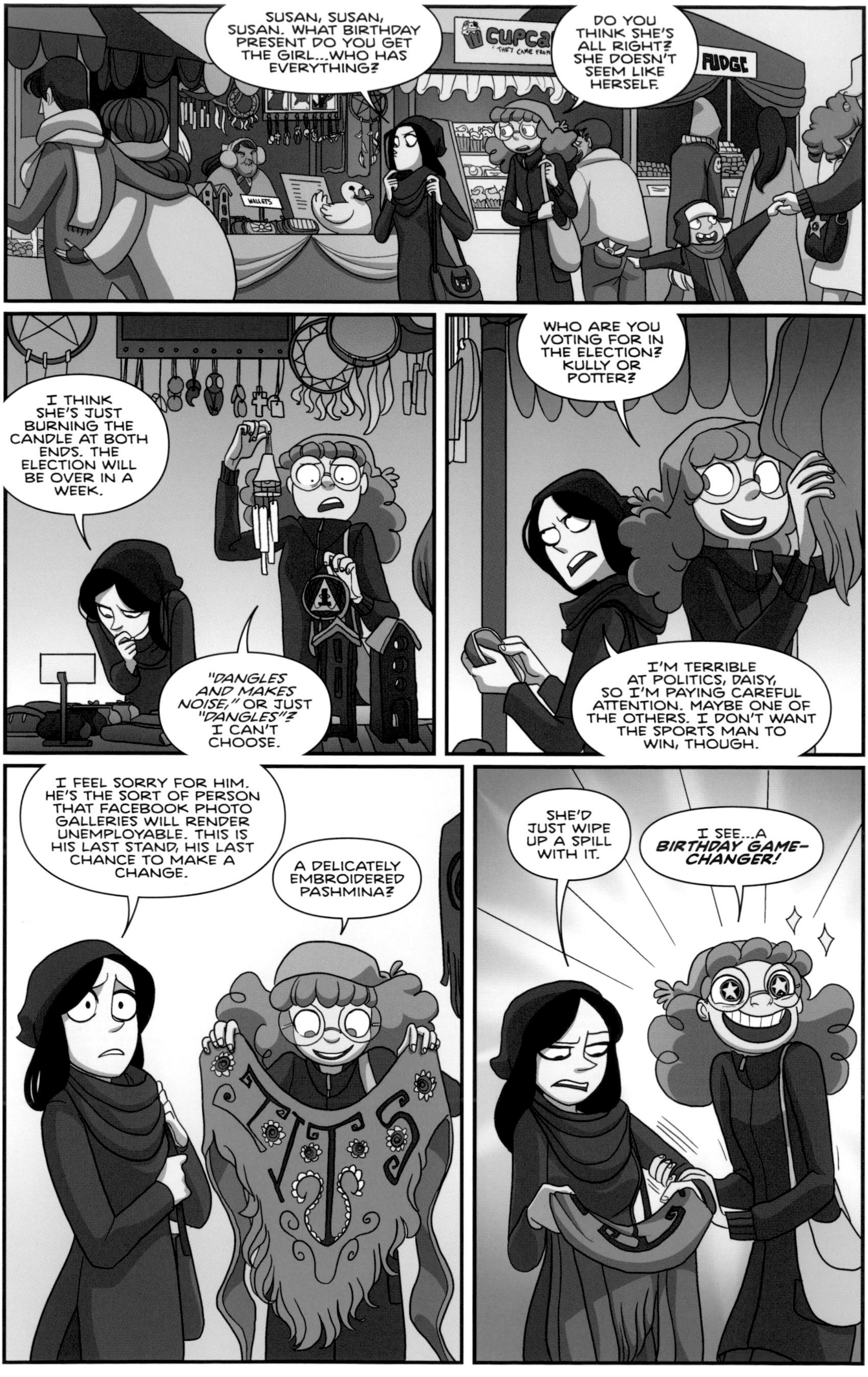
SUSAN, SUSAN, SUSAN. WHAT BIRTHDAY PRESENT DO YOU GET THE GIRL...WHO HAS EVERYTHING?
DO YOU THINK SHE'S ALL RIGHT? SHE DOESN'T SEEM LIKE HERSELF.
FUDGE
WALLETS
I THINK SHE'S JUST BURNING THE CANDLE AT BOTH ENDS. THE ELECTION WILL BE OVER IN A WEEK.
"DANGLES AND MAKES NOISE," OR JUST "DANGLES"? I CAN'T CHOOSE.
WHO ARE YOU VOTING FOR IN THE ELECTION? KULLY OR POTTER?
I'M TERRIBLE AT POLITICS, DAISY, SO I'M PAYING CAREFUL ATTENTION. MAYBE ONE OF THE OTHERS. I DON'T WANT THE SPORTS MAN TO WIN, THOUGH.
I FEEL SORRY FOR HIM. HE'S THE SORT OF PERSON THAT FACEBOOK PHOTO GALLERIES WILL RENDER UNEMPLOYABLE. THIS IS HIS LAST STAND, HIS LAST CHANCE TO MAKE A CHANGE.
A DELICATELY EMBROIDERED PASHMINA?
SHE'D JUST WIPE UP A SPILL WITH IT.
I SEE...A BIRTHDAY GAME-CHANGER!

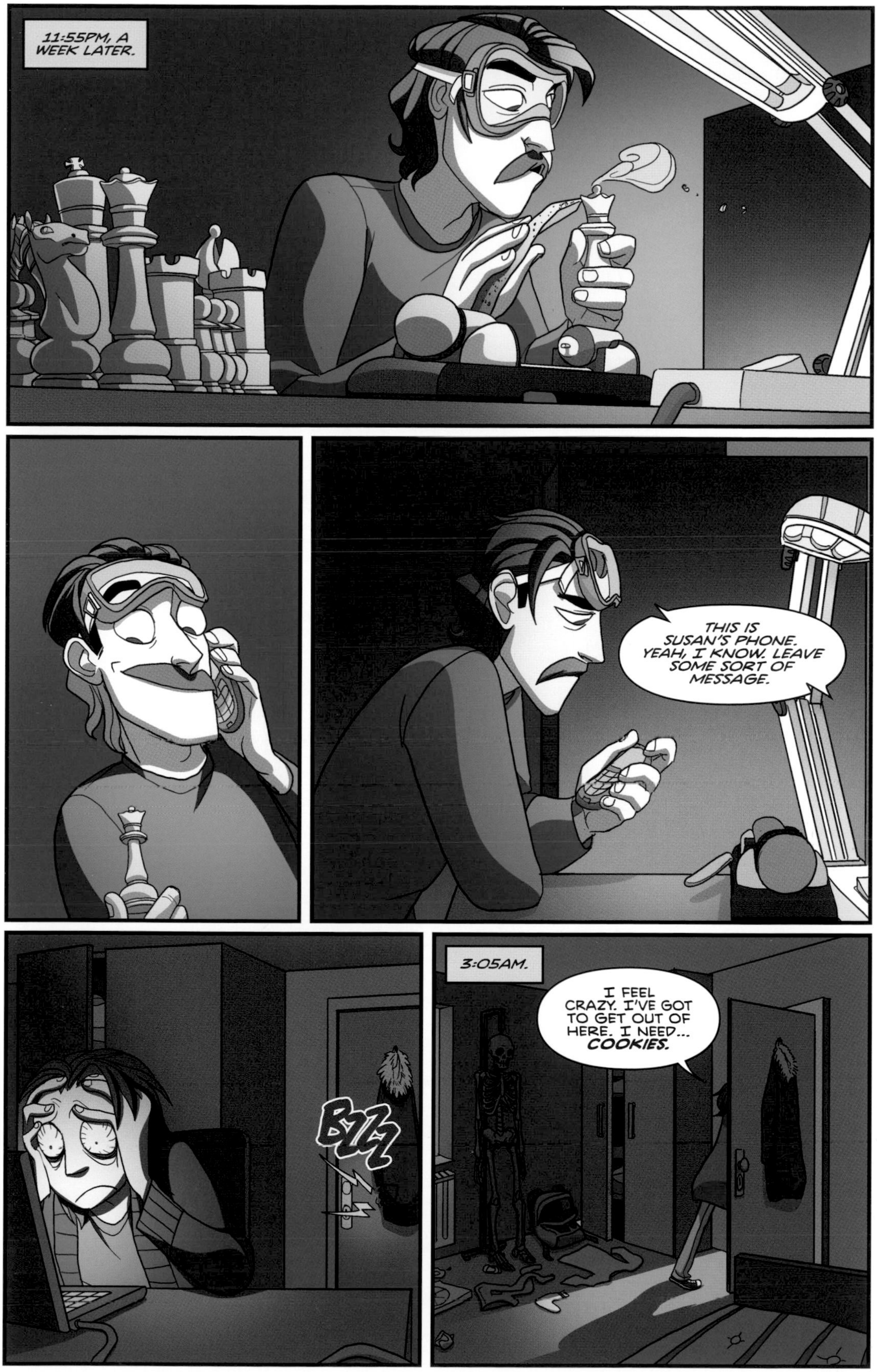
11:55PM, A WEEK LATER.
THIS IS SUSAN'S PHONE. YEAH, I KNOW. LEAVE SOME SORT OF MESSAGE.
BZZZ
3:05AM.
I FEEL CRAZY. I'VE GOT TO GET OUT OF HERE. I NEED... COOKIES.

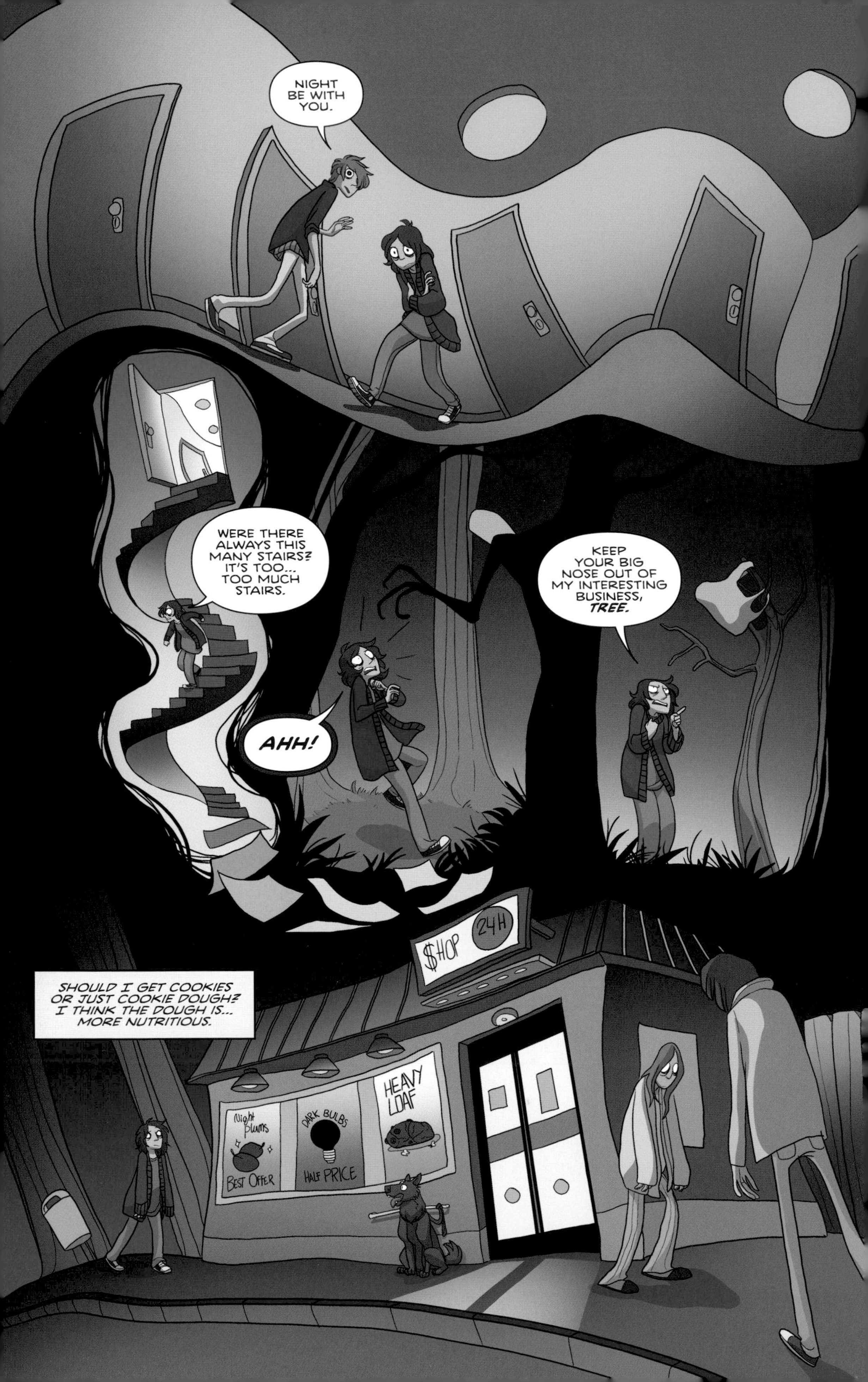
NIGHT BE WITH YOU.
WERE THERE ALWAYS THIS MANY STAIRS? IT'S TOO... TOO MUCH STAIRS.
AHH!
KEEP YOUR BIG NOSE OUT OF MY INTERESTING BUSINESS, TREE.
SHOULD I GET COOKIES OR JUST COOKIE DOUGH? I THINK THE DOUGH IS... MORE NUTRITIOUS.
$HOP 24H
Night plums
BEST OFFER
DARK BULBS
HALF PRICE
HEAVY LOAF

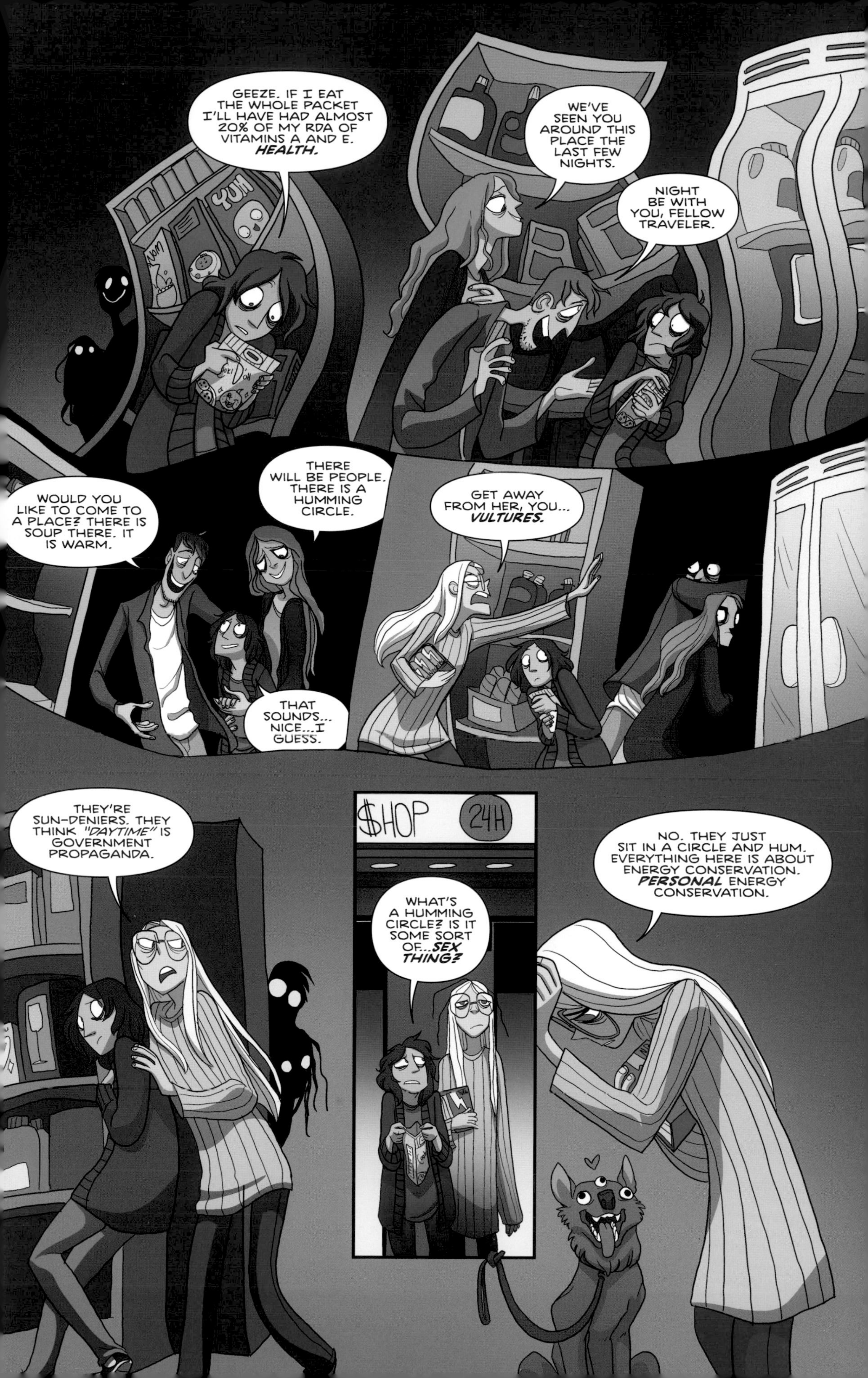
GEEZE. IF I EAT THE WHOLE PACKET I'LL HAVE HAD ALMOST 20% OF MY RDA OF VITAMINS A AND E. ***HEALTH.***
YUM
NOM
WE'VE SEEN YOU AROUND THIS PLACE THE LAST FEW NIGHTS.
NIGHT BE WITH YOU, FELLOW TRAVELER.
WOULD YOU LIKE TO COME TO A PLACE? THERE IS SOUP THERE. IT IS WARM.
THERE WILL BE PEOPLE. THERE IS A HUMMING CIRCLE.
THAT SOUNDS... NICE...I GUESS.
GET AWAY FROM HER, YOU... ***VULTURES.***
THEY'RE SUN-DENIERS. THEY THINK *"DAYTIME"* IS GOVERNMENT PROPAGANDA.
$HOP
24H
WHAT'S A HUMMING CIRCLE? IS IT SOME SORT OF...***SEX THING?***
NO. THEY JUST SIT IN A CIRCLE AND HUM. EVERYTHING HERE IS ABOUT ENERGY CONSERVATION. ***PERSONAL*** ENERGY CONSERVATION.

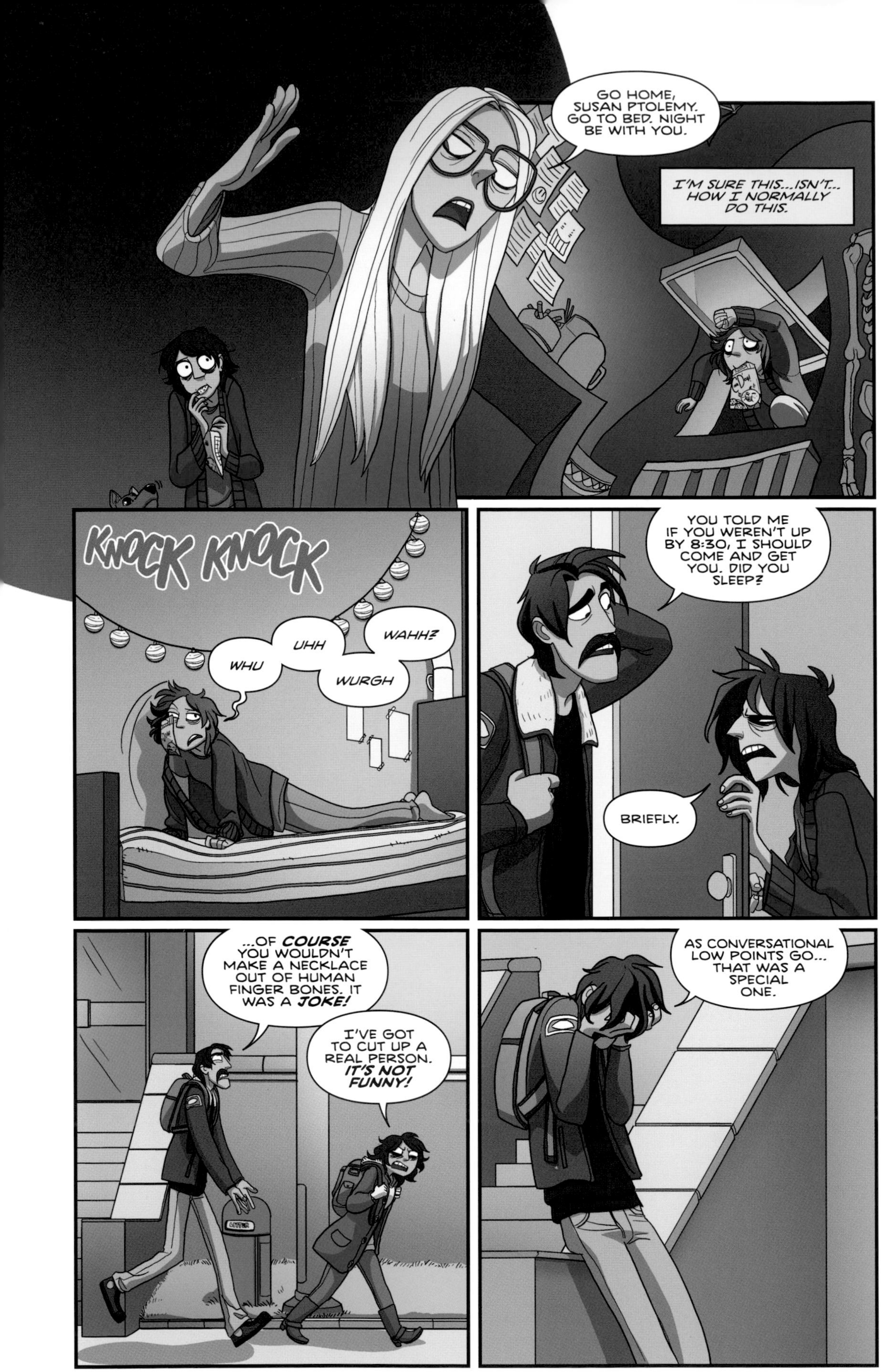
GO HOME, SUSAN PTOLEMY. GO TO BED. NIGHT BE WITH YOU.
I'M SURE THIS... ISN'T... HOW I NORMALLY DO THIS.
KNOCK KNOCK
WHU
UHH
WURGH
WAHH?
YOU TOLD ME IF YOU WEREN'T UP BY 8:30, I SHOULD COME AND GET YOU. DID YOU SLEEP?
BRIEFLY.
...OF COURSE YOU WOULDN'T MAKE A NECKLACE OUT OF HUMAN FINGER BONES. IT WAS A JOKE!
I'VE GOT TO CUT UP A REAL PERSON. IT'S NOT FUNNY!
AS CONVERSATIONAL LOW POINTS GO... THAT WAS A SPECIAL ONE.

DO YOU WANT TO MAKE THE ABDOMINAL INCISION AND GET US STARTED, SUSAN?

O-OKAY.

SO I'M JUST GOING TO...*er*...MAKE A VERTICAL INCISION AND THEN WE, *er*...CAN...

COME ON, SUSAN.

GO ON, MATE, YOU'VE GOT ALL THE HIGH SCORES IN THE COMPUTER LAB.

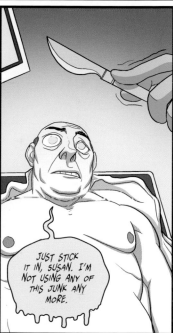

JUST STICK IT IN, SUSAN. I'M NOT USING ANY OF THIS JUNK ANY MORE.

IN TWENTY-FIVE YEARS OF MEDICINE, THAT'S THE MOST SUSTAINED SCREAM I THINK I'VE EVER HEARD. FROM A SMOKER, I CONSIDER IT EVEN MORE EXCEPTIONAL.

THANKS, DR T.

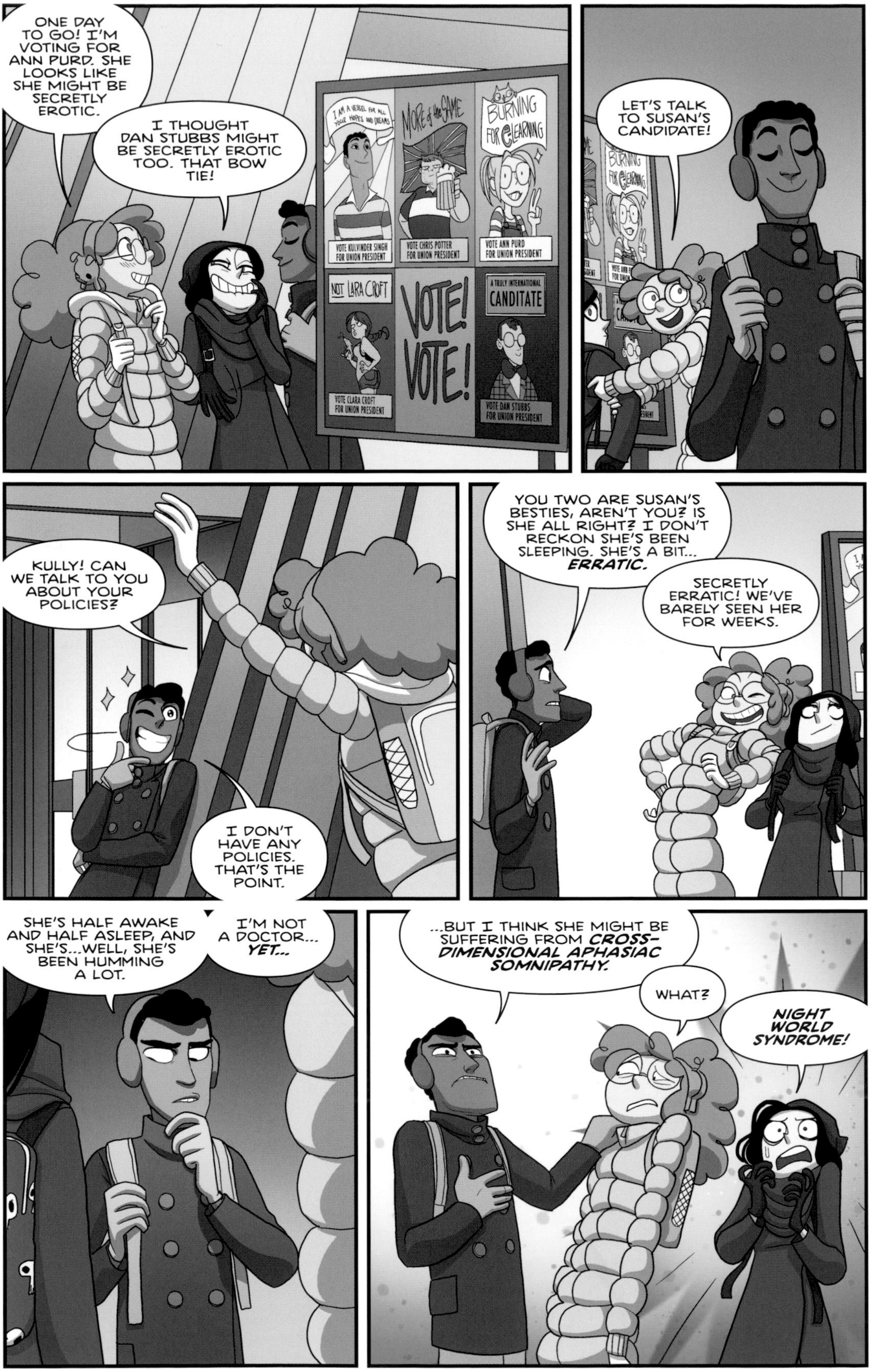
ONE DAY TO GO! I'M VOTING FOR ANN PURD. SHE LOOKS LIKE SHE MIGHT BE SECRETLY EROTIC.
I THOUGHT DAN STUBBS MIGHT BE SECRETLY EROTIC TOO. THAT BOW TIE!
I AM A VESSEL FOR ALL YOUR HOPES AND DREAMS
VOTE KULVINDER SINGH FOR UNION PRESIDENT
MORE of the SAME
VOTE CHRIS POTTER FOR UNION PRESIDENT
BURNING FOR LEARNING
VOTE ANN PURD FOR UNION PRESIDENT
NOT LARA CROFT
VOTE CLARA CROFT FOR UNION PRESIDENT
VOTE! VOTE!
A TRULY INTERNATIONAL CANDITATE
VOTE DAN STUBBS FOR UNION PRESIDENT
LET'S TALK TO SUSAN'S CANDIDATE!
KULLY! CAN WE TALK TO YOU ABOUT YOUR POLICIES?
I DON'T HAVE ANY POLICIES. THAT'S THE POINT.
YOU TWO ARE SUSAN'S BESTIES, AREN'T YOU? IS SHE ALL RIGHT? I DON'T RECKON SHE'S BEEN SLEEPING. SHE'S A BIT... *ERRATIC.*
SECRETLY ERRATIC! WE'VE BARELY SEEN HER FOR WEEKS.
SHE'S HALF AWAKE AND HALF ASLEEP, AND SHE'S...WELL, SHE'S BEEN HUMMING A LOT.
I'M NOT A DOCTOR... *YET...*
...BUT I THINK SHE MIGHT BE SUFFERING FROM *CROSS-DIMENSIONAL APHASIAC SOMNIPATHY.*
WHAT?
*NIGHT WORLD SYNDROME!*

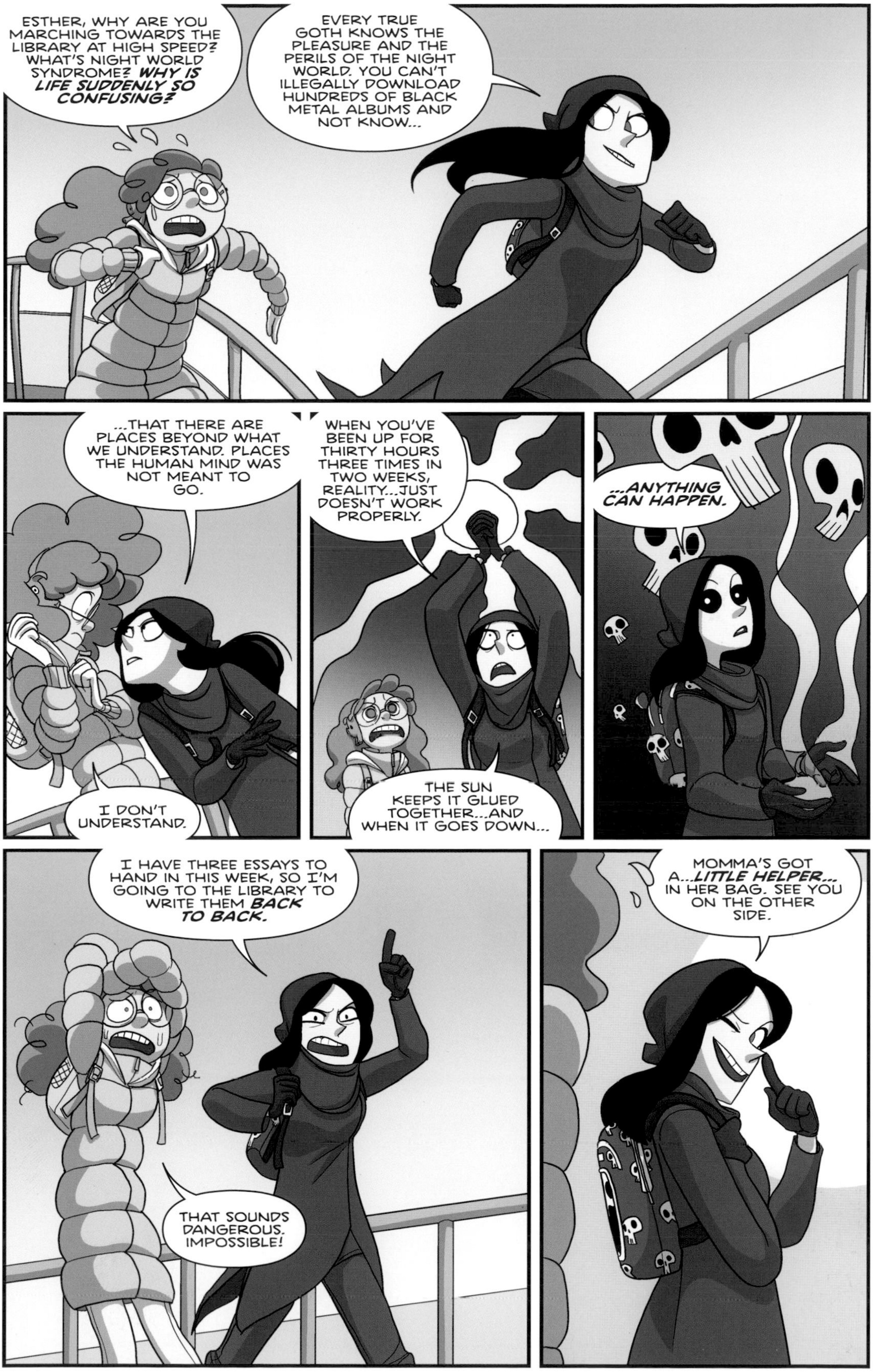
ESTHER, WHY ARE YOU MARCHING TOWARDS THE LIBRARY AT HIGH SPEED? WHAT'S NIGHT WORLD SYNDROME? ***WHY IS LIFE SUDDENLY SO CONFUSING?***
EVERY TRUE GOTH KNOWS THE PLEASURE AND THE PERILS OF THE NIGHT WORLD. YOU CAN'T ILLEGALLY DOWNLOAD HUNDREDS OF BLACK METAL ALBUMS AND NOT KNOW...
...THAT THERE ARE PLACES BEYOND WHAT WE UNDERSTAND. PLACES THE HUMAN MIND WAS NOT MEANT TO GO.
I DON'T UNDERSTAND.
WHEN YOU'VE BEEN UP FOR THIRTY HOURS THREE TIMES IN TWO WEEKS, REALITY...JUST DOESN'T WORK PROPERLY.
THE SUN KEEPS IT GLUED TOGETHER...AND WHEN IT GOES DOWN...
***...ANYTHING CAN HAPPEN.***
I HAVE THREE ESSAYS TO HAND IN THIS WEEK, SO I'M GOING TO THE LIBRARY TO WRITE THEM ***BACK TO BACK.***
THAT SOUNDS DANGEROUS. IMPOSSIBLE!
MOMMA'S GOT A...***LITTLE HELPER...*** IN HER BAG. SEE YOU ON THE OTHER SIDE.

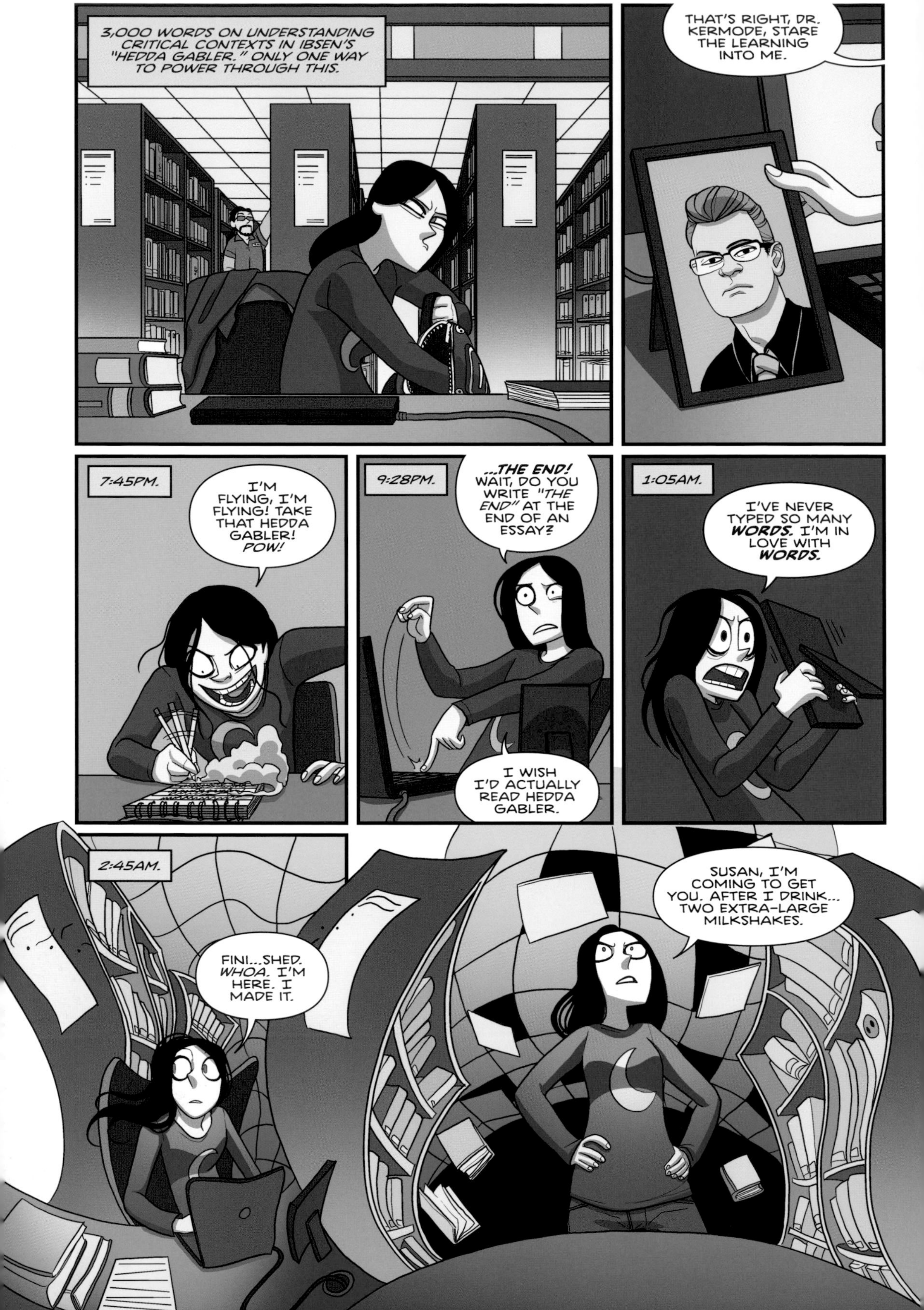
3,000 WORDS ON UNDERSTANDING CRITICAL CONTEXTS IN IBSEN'S "HEDDA GABLER." ONLY ONE WAY TO POWER THROUGH THIS.
THAT'S RIGHT, DR. KERMODE, STARE THE LEARNING INTO ME.
7:45PM.
I'M FLYING, I'M FLYING! TAKE THAT HEDDA GABLER! *POW!*
9:28PM.
***...THE END!*** WAIT, DO YOU WRITE *"THE END"* AT THE END OF AN ESSAY?
I WISH I'D ACTUALLY READ HEDDA GABLER.
1:05AM.
I'VE NEVER TYPED SO MANY ***WORDS.*** I'M IN LOVE WITH ***WORDS.***
2:45AM.
FINI...SHED. *WHOA.* I'M HERE. I MADE IT.
SUSAN, I'M COMING TO GET YOU. AFTER I DRINK... TWO EXTRA-LARGE MILKSHAKES.

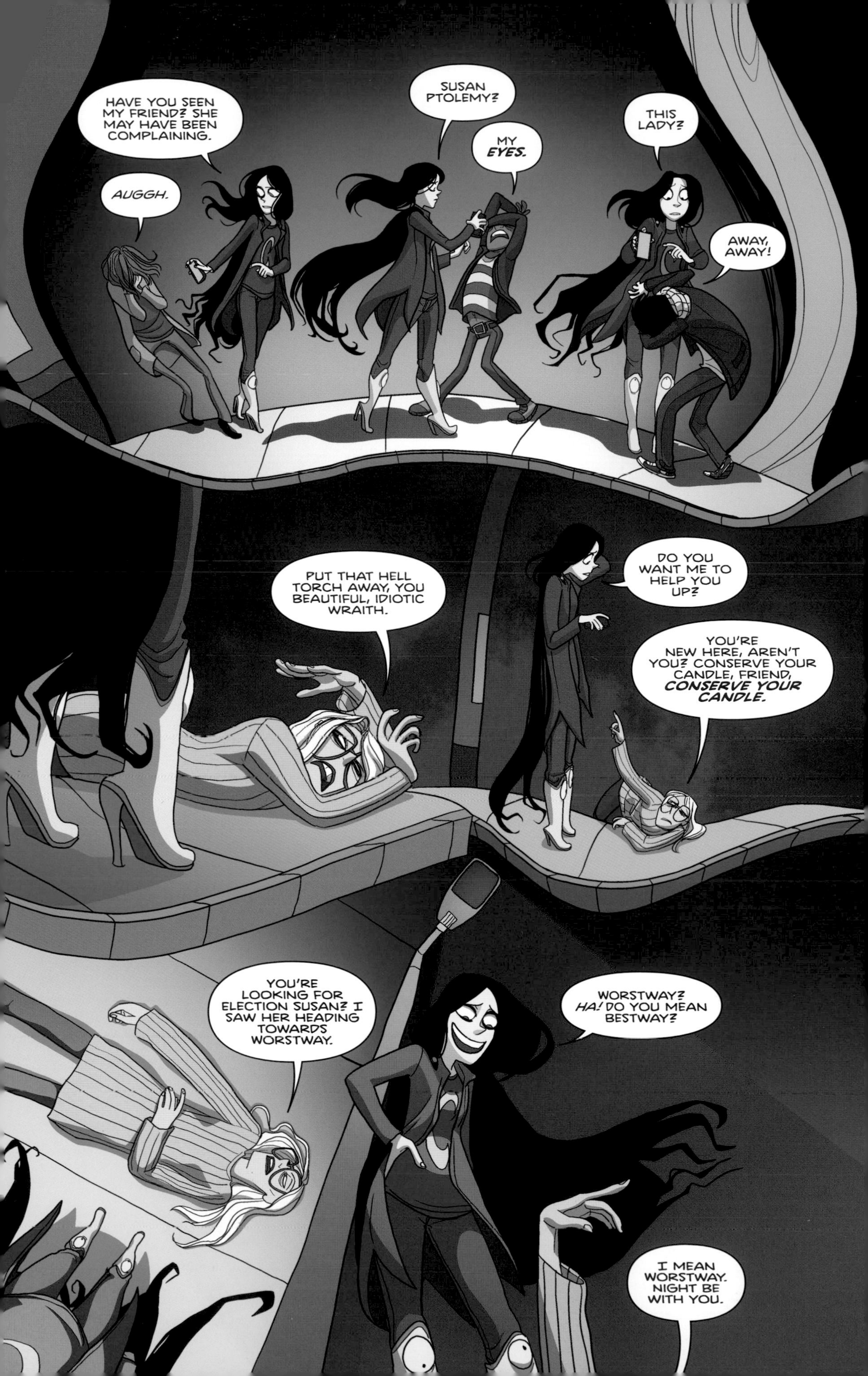
HAVE YOU SEEN MY FRIEND? SHE MAY HAVE BEEN COMPLAINING.
AUGGH.
SUSAN PTOLEMY?
MY *EYES.*
THIS LADY?
AWAY, AWAY!
PUT THAT HELL TORCH AWAY, YOU BEAUTIFUL, IDIOTIC WRAITH.
DO YOU WANT ME TO HELP YOU UP?
YOU'RE NEW HERE, AREN'T YOU? CONSERVE YOUR CANDLE, FRIEND, ***CONSERVE YOUR CANDLE.***
YOU'RE LOOKING FOR ELECTION SUSAN? I SAW HER HEADING TOWARDS WORSTWAY.
WORSTWAY? *HA!* DO YOU MEAN BESTWAY?
I MEAN WORSTWAY. NIGHT BE WITH YOU.

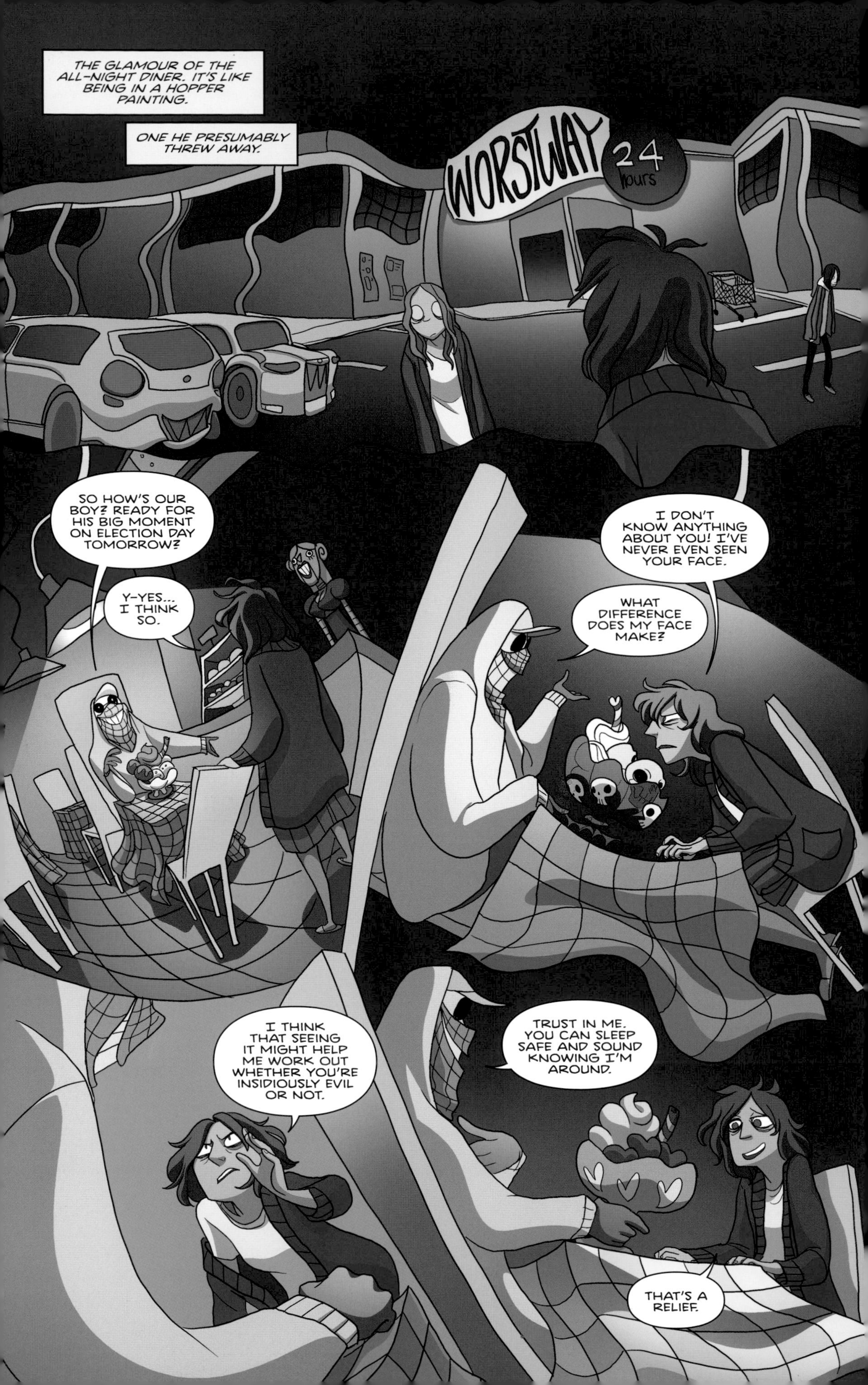
THE GLAMOUR OF THE ALL-NIGHT DINER. IT'S LIKE BEING IN A HOPPER PAINTING.
ONE HE PRESUMABLY THREW AWAY.
WORSTWAY
24 hours
SO HOW'S OUR BOY? READY FOR HIS BIG MOMENT ON ELECTION DAY TOMORROW?
Y-YES... I THINK SO.
I DON'T KNOW ANYTHING ABOUT YOU! I'VE NEVER EVEN SEEN YOUR FACE.
WHAT DIFFERENCE DOES MY FACE MAKE?
I THINK THAT SEEING IT MIGHT HELP ME WORK OUT WHETHER YOU'RE INSIDIOUSLY EVIL OR NOT.
TRUST IN ME. YOU CAN SLEEP SAFE AND SOUND KNOWING I'M AROUND.
THAT'S A RELIEF.

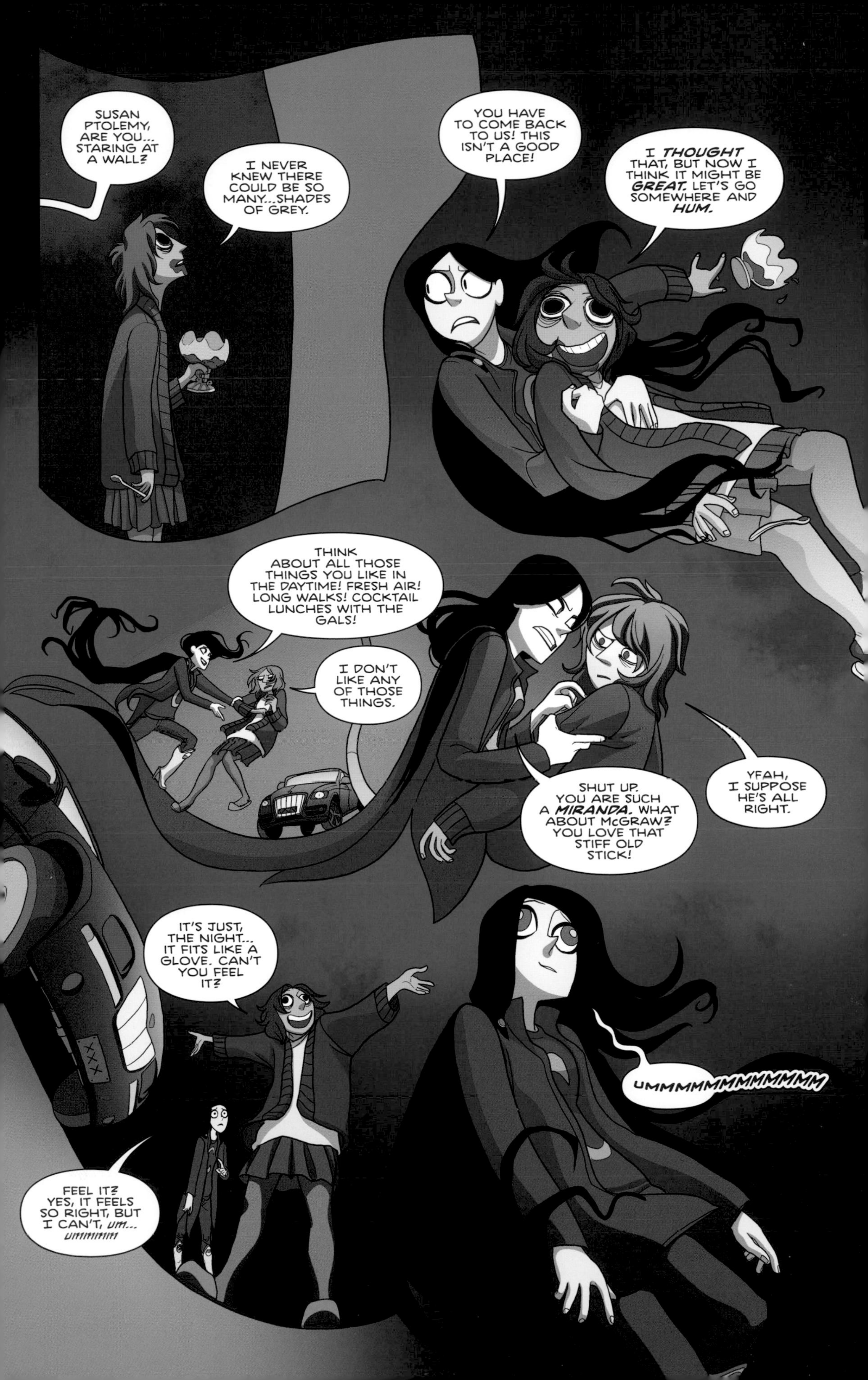
SUSAN PTOLEMY, ARE YOU... STARING AT A WALL?
I NEVER KNEW THERE COULD BE SO MANY...SHADES OF GREY.
YOU HAVE TO COME BACK TO US! THIS ISN'T A GOOD PLACE!
I *THOUGHT* THAT, BUT NOW I THINK IT MIGHT BE ***GREAT.*** LET'S GO SOMEWHERE AND ***HUM.***
THINK ABOUT ALL THOSE THINGS YOU LIKE IN THE DAYTIME! FRESH AIR! LONG WALKS! COCKTAIL LUNCHES WITH THE GALS!
I DON'T LIKE ANY OF THOSE THINGS.
SHUT UP. YOU ARE SUCH A ***MIRANDA.*** WHAT ABOUT McGRAW? YOU LOVE THAT STIFF OLD STICK!
YEAH, I SUPPOSE HE'S ALL RIGHT.
IT'S JUST, THE NIGHT... IT FITS LIKE A GLOVE. CAN'T YOU FEEL IT?
FEEL IT? YES, IT FEELS SO RIGHT, BUT I CAN'T, *UM... UMMMMMM*
UMMMMMMMMMMMM

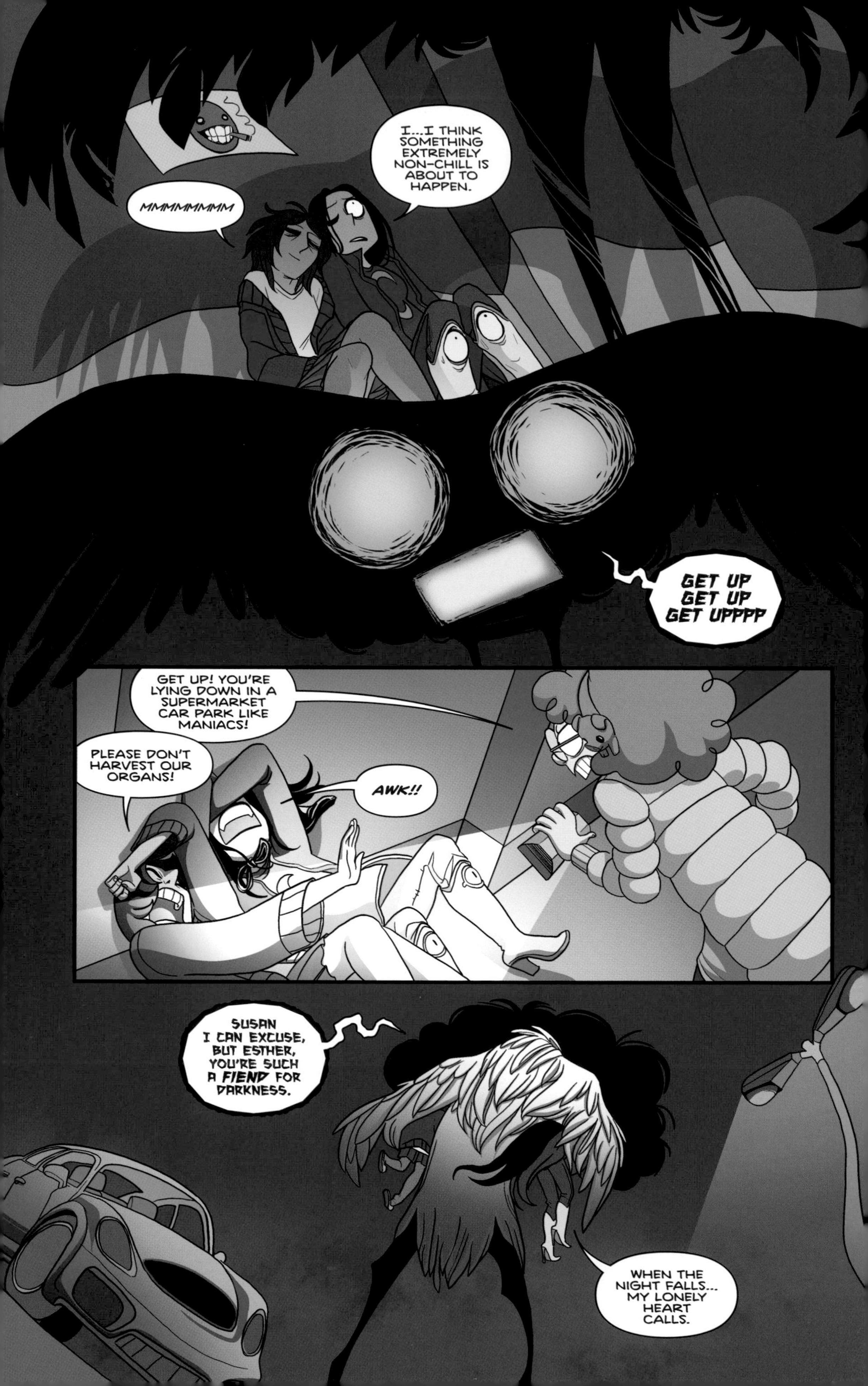
I...I THINK SOMETHING EXTREMELY NON-CHILL IS ABOUT TO HAPPEN.
MMMMMMMM
GET UP GET UP GET UPPPP
GET UP! YOU'RE LYING DOWN IN A SUPERMARKET CAR PARK LIKE MANIACS!
PLEASE DON'T HARVEST OUR ORGANS!
AWK!!
SUSAN I CAN EXCUSE, BUT ESTHER, YOU'RE SUCH A FIEND FOR DARKNESS.
WHEN THE NIGHT FALLS... MY LONELY HEART CALLS.

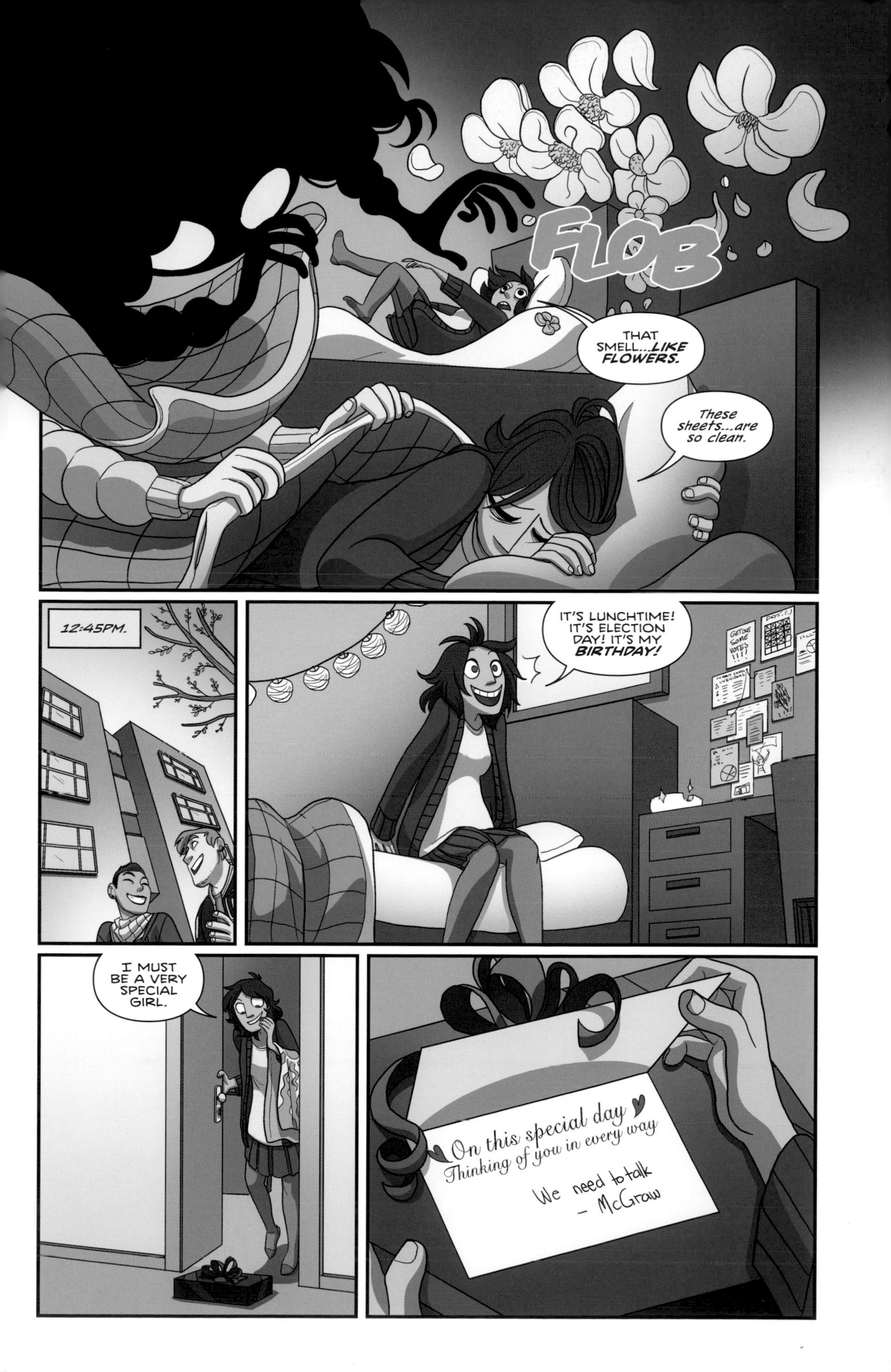
FLOB
THAT SMELL...LIKE FLOWERS.
These sheets...are so clean.
12:45PM.
IT'S LUNCHTIME! IT'S ELECTION DAY! IT'S MY BIRTHDAY!
I MUST BE A VERY SPECIAL GIRL.
On this special day
Thinking of you in every way
We need to talk
- McGraw

15

KEYS CUT

WHO WRITES 'WE NEED TO TALK' ON A *BIRTHDAY CARD?*

SAYING IT TO YOUR FACE DIDN'T SEEM TO BE WORKING.

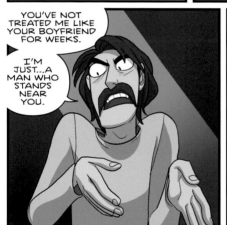

YOU'VE NOT TREATED ME LIKE YOUR BOYFRIEND FOR WEEKS.

I'M JUST...A MAN WHO STANDS NEAR YOU.

I MIGHT AS WELL BE A GHOST HAUNTING YOU.

THAT'S NOT FAIR. THINGS HAVE BEEN INSANE FOR ME, YOU KNOW THAT.

WE ALL HAVE LIVES. WE ALL HAVE THINGS TO DO. I'M JUST THE LAST THING ON YOUR LIST.

WELL *SORRY* I COULDN'T *DO YOU.*

NO, I'M SORRY. I DON'T WANT TO BE WITH YOU ANY MORE.

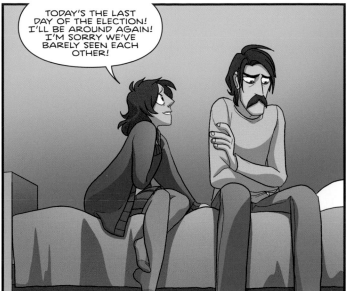

TODAY'S THE LAST DAY OF THE ELECTION! I'LL BE AROUND AGAIN! I'M SORRY WE'VE BARELY SEEN EACH OTHER!

IT'S NOT THAT I HAVEN'T SEEN YOU, IT'S THAT WHEN YOU WERE IN TROUBLE, YOU DIDN'T COME TO ME. YOU JUST LOCKED YOURSELF AWAY.

AND I CAN'T CHANGE YOUR MIND?

NO. I STILL WANT TO BE FRIENDS.

FINE. WHATEVER.

HAPPY BIRTHDAY, SUSAN!

UN-HAPPY BIRTHDAY?

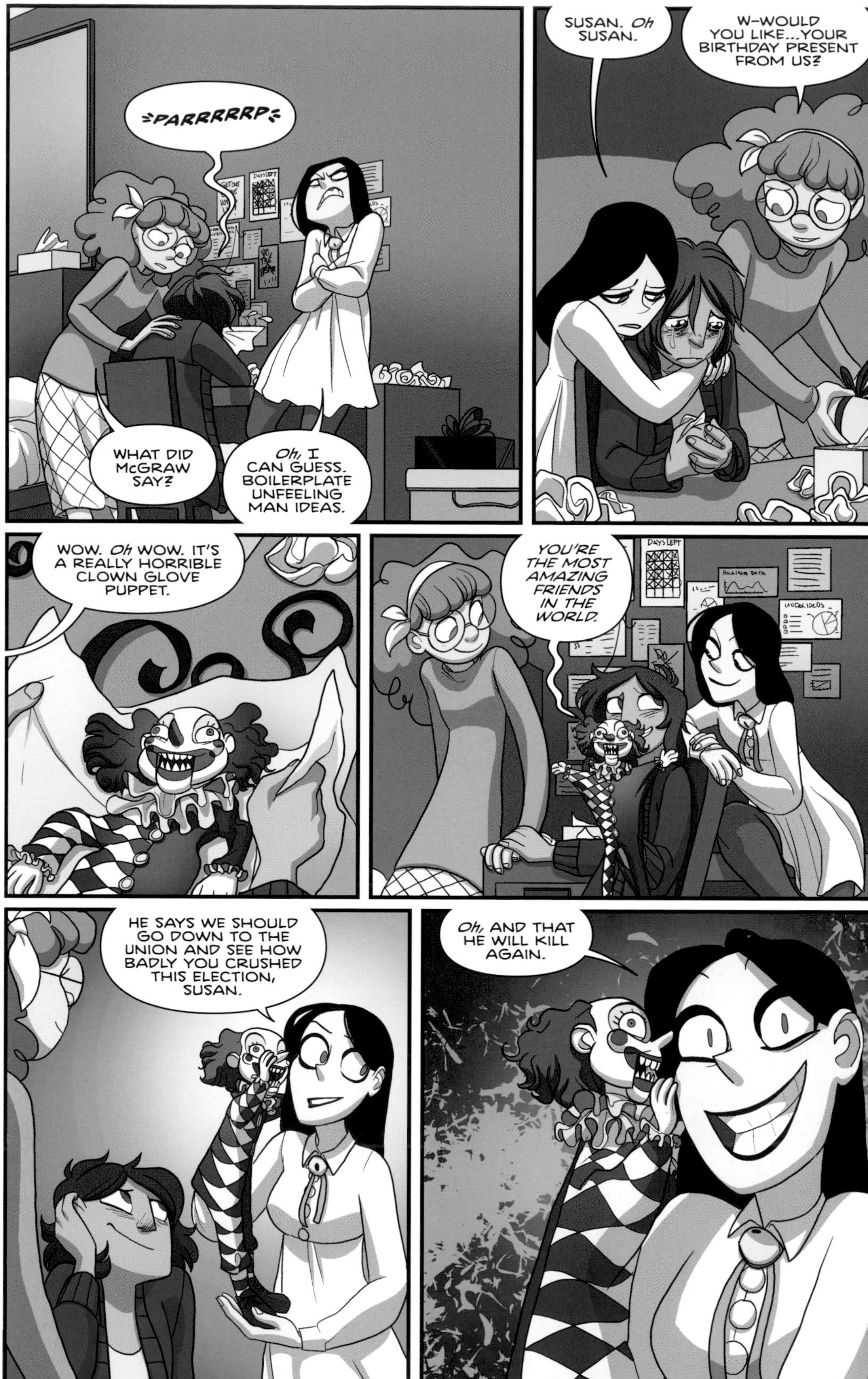
PARRRRRP
WHAT DID McGRAW SAY?
Oh, I CAN GUESS. BOILERPLATE UNFEELING MAN IDEAS.
SUSAN. Oh SUSAN.
W-WOULD YOU LIKE...YOUR BIRTHDAY PRESENT FROM US?
WOW. Oh WOW. IT'S A REALLY HORRIBLE CLOWN GLOVE PUPPET.
YOU'RE THE MOST AMAZING FRIENDS IN THE WORLD.
HE SAYS WE SHOULD GO DOWN TO THE UNION AND SEE HOW BADLY YOU CRUSHED THIS ELECTION, SUSAN.
Oh, AND THAT HE WILL KILL AGAIN.

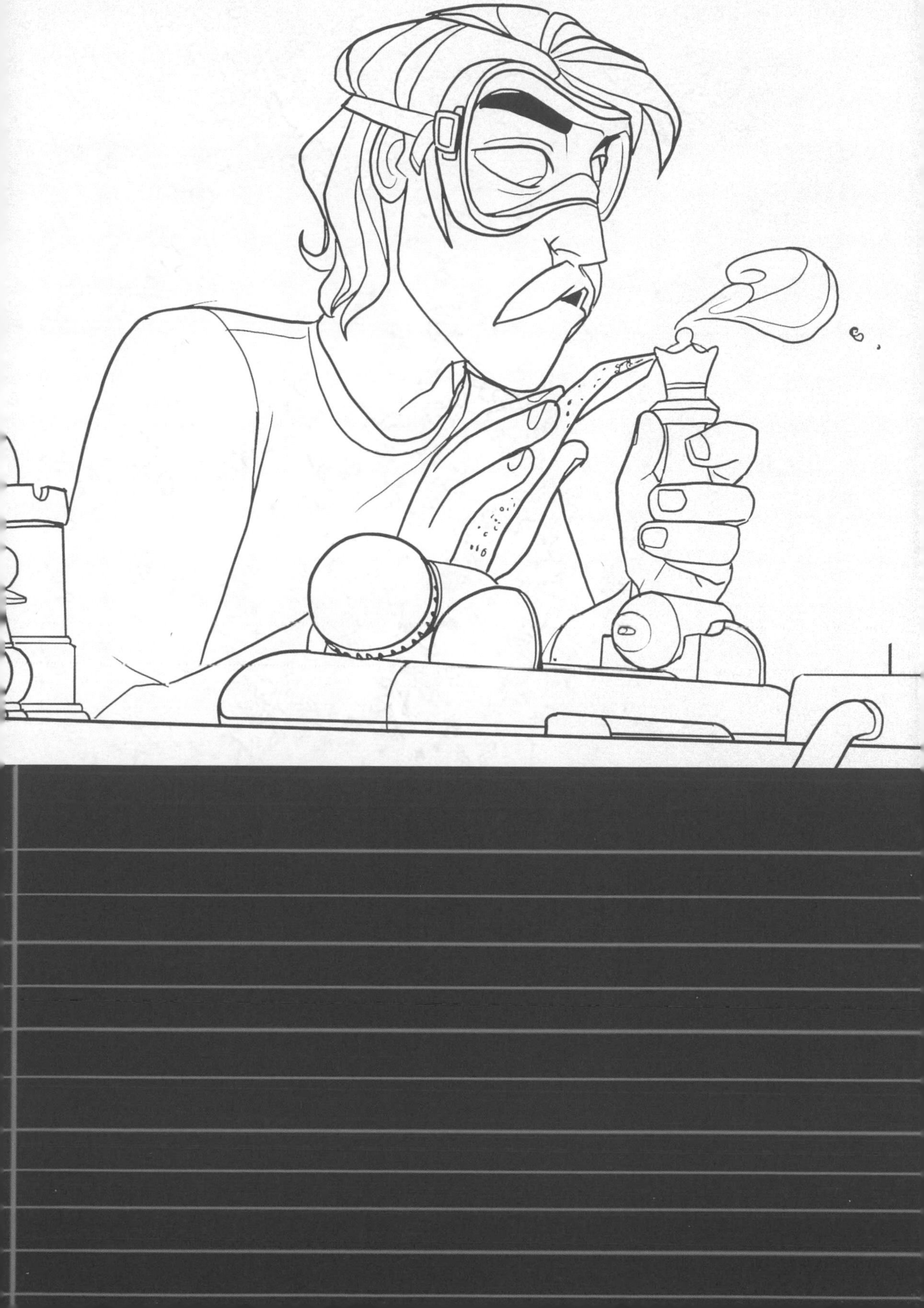

# CHAPTER
# TWELVE

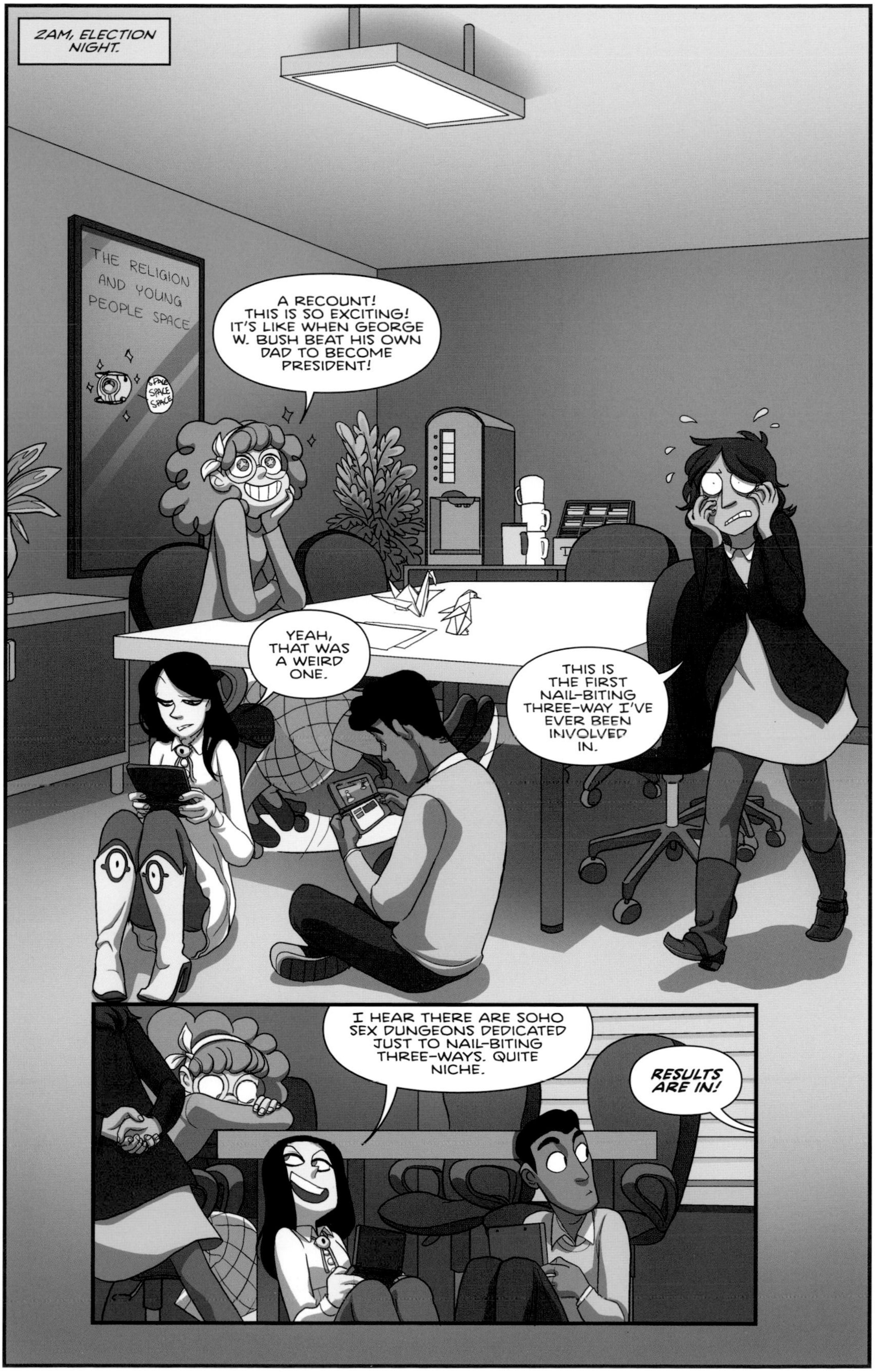
ZAM, ELECTION NIGHT.
THE RELIGION AND YOUNG PEOPLE SPACE
A RECOUNT! THIS IS SO EXCITING! IT'S LIKE WHEN GEORGE W. BUSH BEAT HIS OWN DAD TO BECOME PRESIDENT!
YEAH, THAT WAS A WEIRD ONE.
THIS IS THE FIRST NAIL-BITING THREE-WAY I'VE EVER BEEN INVOLVED IN.
I HEAR THERE ARE SOHO SEX DUNGEONS DEDICATED JUST TO NAIL-BITING THREE-WAYS. QUITE NICHE.
RESULTS ARE IN!

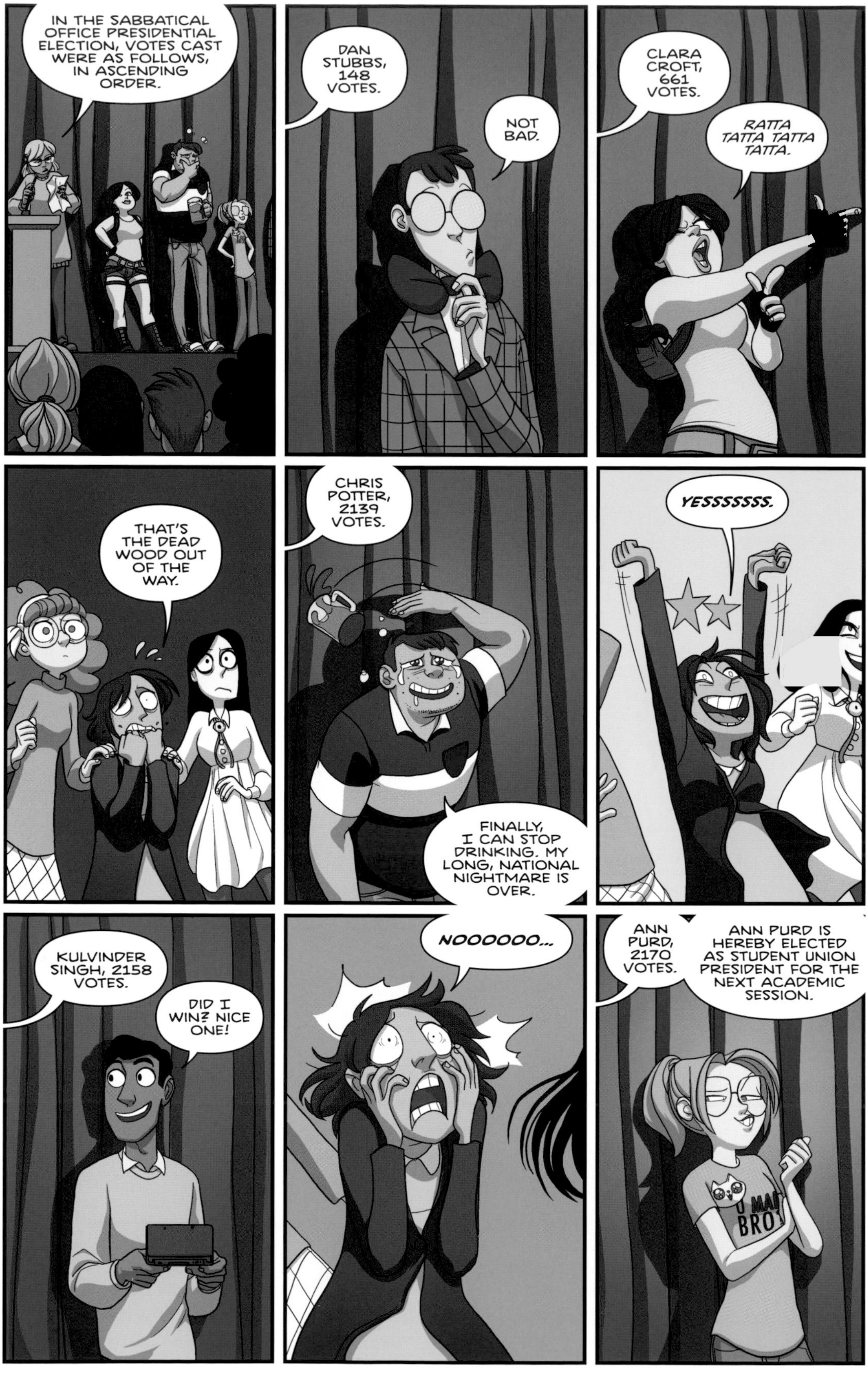
IN THE SABBATICAL OFFICE PRESIDENTIAL ELECTION, VOTES CAST WERE AS FOLLOWS, IN ASCENDING ORDER.
DAN STUBBS, 148 VOTES.
NOT BAD.
CLARA CROFT, 661 VOTES.
RATTA TATTA TATTA TATTA.
THAT'S THE DEAD WOOD OUT OF THE WAY.
CHRIS POTTER, 2139 VOTES.
FINALLY, I CAN STOP DRINKING. MY LONG, NATIONAL NIGHTMARE IS OVER.
YESSSSSSS.
KULVINDER SINGH, 2158 VOTES.
DID I WIN? NICE ONE!
NOOOOOO...
ANN PURD, 2170 VOTES.
ANN PURD IS HEREBY ELECTED AS STUDENT UNION PRESIDENT FOR THE NEXT ACADEMIC SESSION.

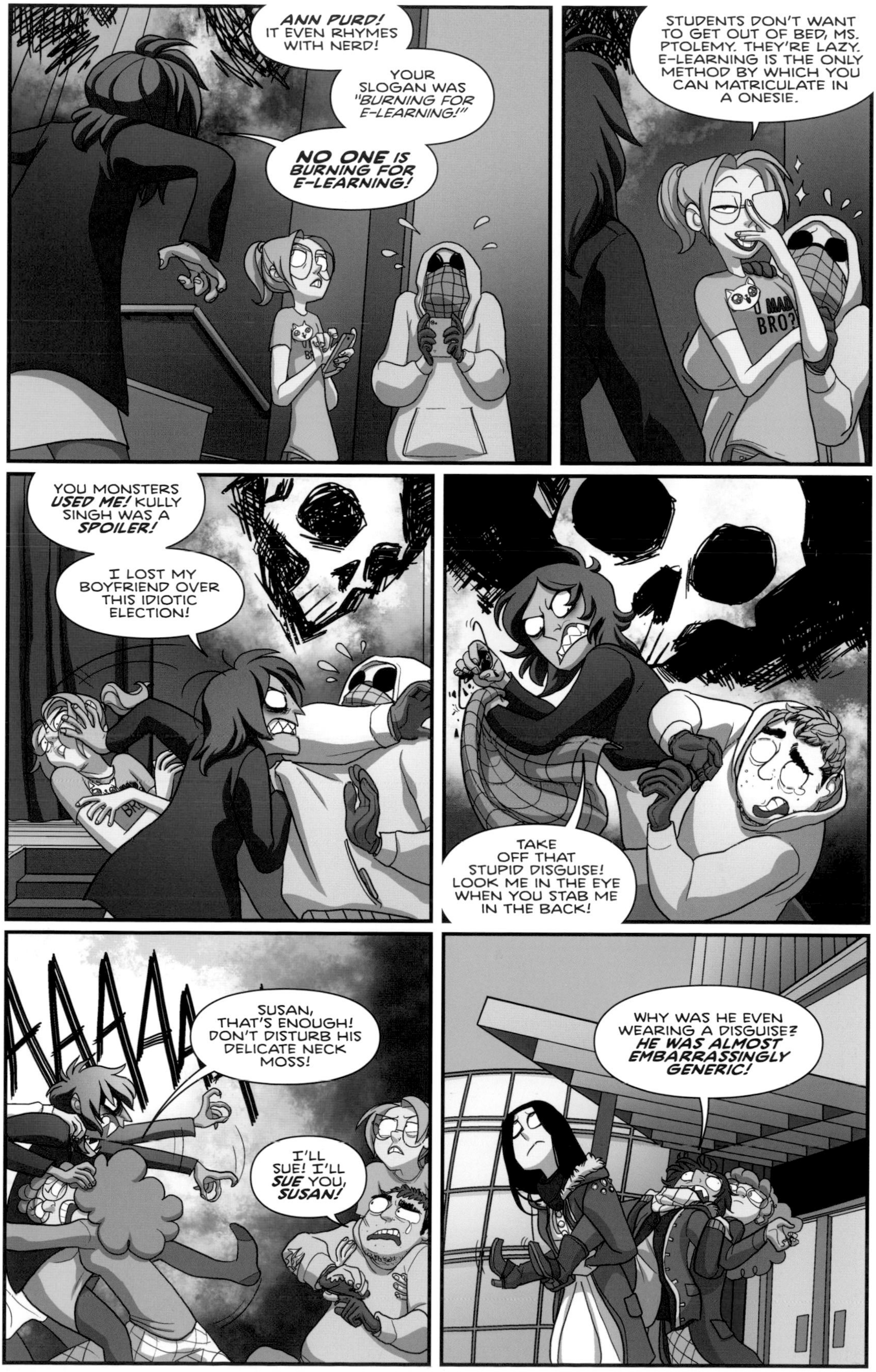
ANN PURD! IT EVEN RHYMES WITH NERD!
YOUR SLOGAN WAS "BURNING FOR E-LEARNING!"
NO ONE IS BURNING FOR E-LEARNING!
STUDENTS DON'T WANT TO GET OUT OF BED, MS. PTOLEMY. THEY'RE LAZY. E-LEARNING IS THE ONLY METHOD BY WHICH YOU CAN MATRICULATE IN A ONESIE.
U MAD BRO?
YOU MONSTERS USED ME! KULLY SINGH WAS A SPOILER!
I LOST MY BOYFRIEND OVER THIS IDIOTIC ELECTION!
TAKE OFF THAT STUPID DISGUISE! LOOK ME IN THE EYE WHEN YOU STAB ME IN THE BACK!
AAAAA
SUSAN, THAT'S ENOUGH! DON'T DISTURB HIS DELICATE NECK MOSS!
I'LL SUE! I'LL SUE YOU, SUSAN!
WHY WAS HE EVEN WEARING A DISGUISE? HE WAS ALMOST EMBARRASSINGLY GENERIC!

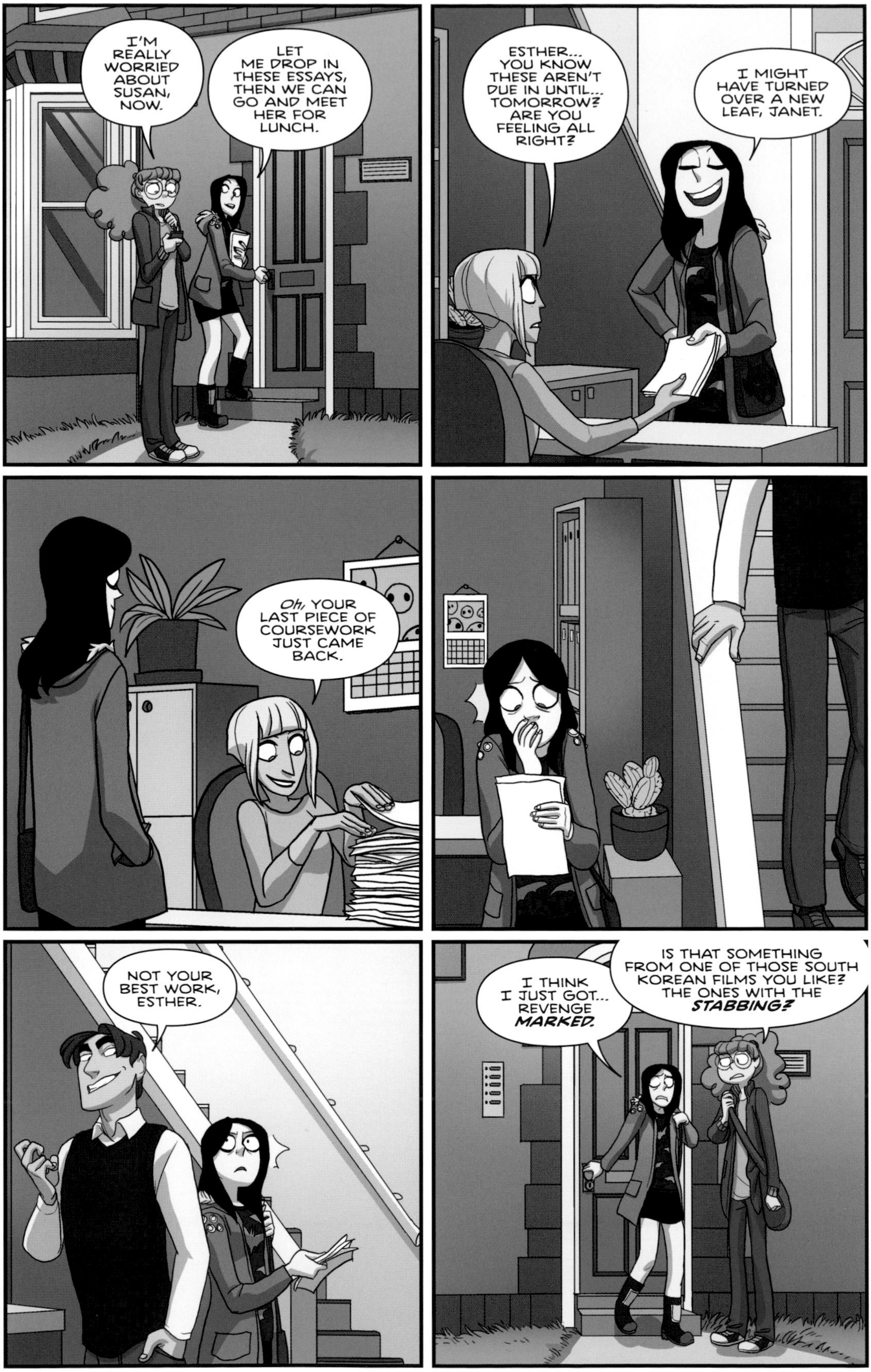

I'M REALLY WORRIED ABOUT SUSAN, NOW.
LET ME DROP IN THESE ESSAYS, THEN WE CAN GO AND MEET HER FOR LUNCH.
ESTHER... YOU KNOW THESE AREN'T DUE IN UNTIL... TOMORROW? ARE YOU FEELING ALL RIGHT?
I MIGHT HAVE TURNED OVER A NEW LEAF, JANET.
*Oh,* YOUR LAST PIECE OF COURSEWORK JUST CAME BACK.
NOT YOUR BEST WORK, ESTHER.
I THINK I JUST GOT... REVENGE ***MARKED.***
IS THAT SOMETHING FROM ONE OF THOSE SOUTH KOREAN FILMS YOU LIKE? THE ONES WITH THE ***STABBING?***

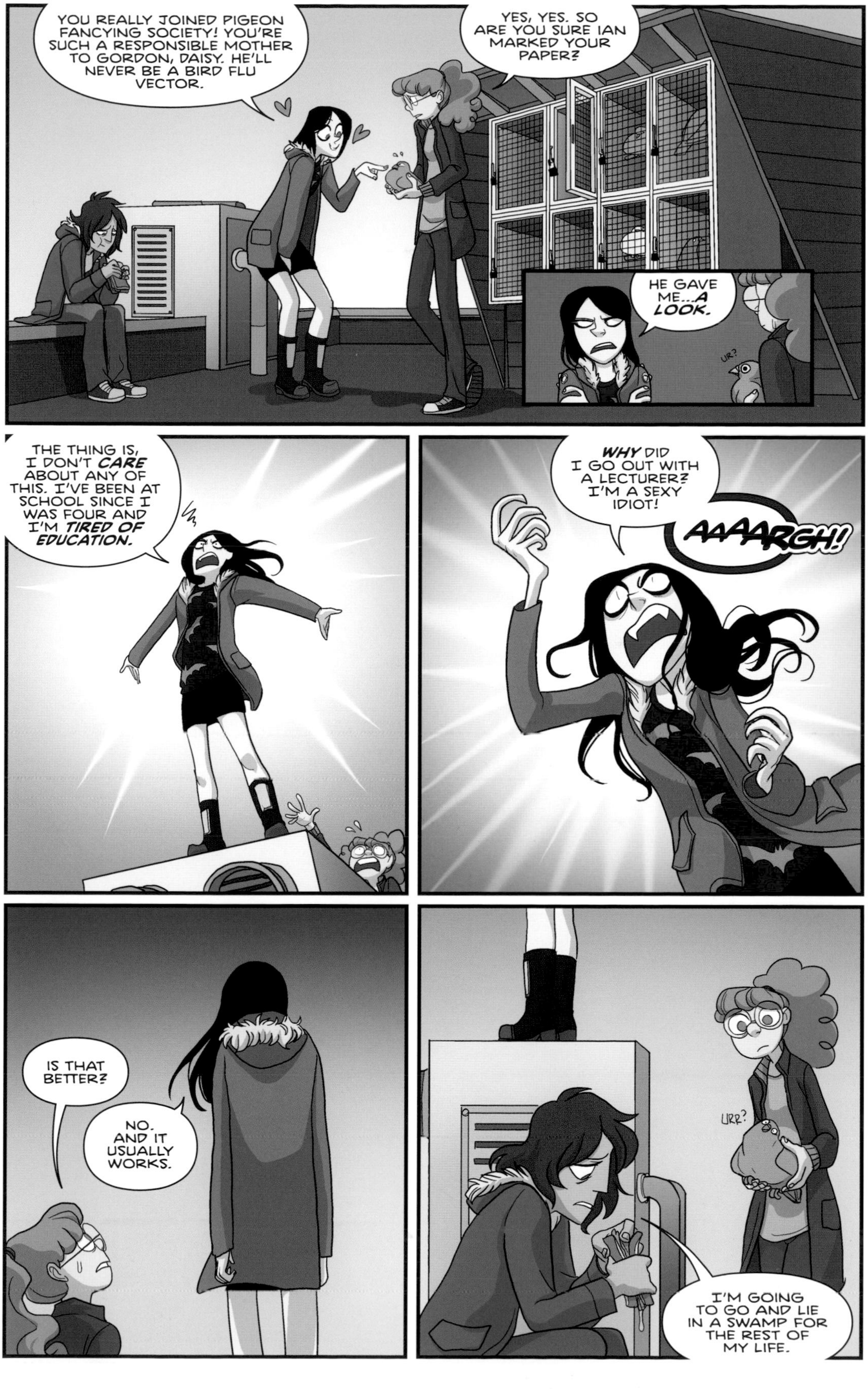
YOU REALLY JOINED PIGEON FANCYING SOCIETY! YOU'RE SUCH A RESPONSIBLE MOTHER TO GORDON, DAISY. HE'LL NEVER BE A BIRD FLU VECTOR.
YES, YES. SO ARE YOU SURE IAN MARKED YOUR PAPER?
HE GAVE ME... A LOOK.
URR?
THE THING IS, I DON'T CARE ABOUT ANY OF THIS. I'VE BEEN AT SCHOOL SINCE I WAS FOUR AND I'M TIRED OF EDUCATION.
WHY DID I GO OUT WITH A LECTURER? I'M A SEXY IDIOT!
AAAARGH!
IS THAT BETTER?
NO. AND IT USUALLY WORKS.
URR?
I'M GOING TO GO AND LIE IN A SWAMP FOR THE REST OF MY LIFE.

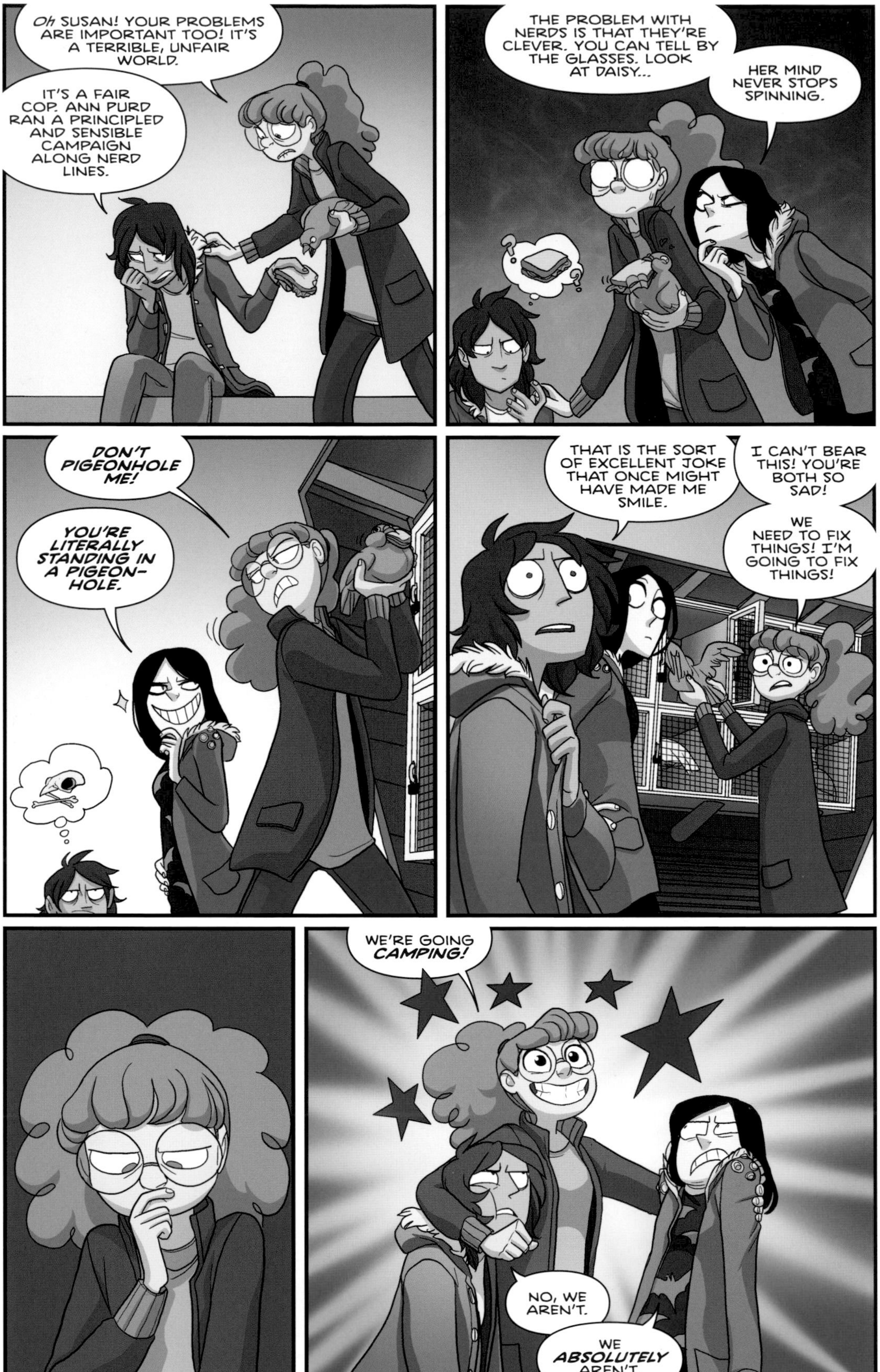
Oh SUSAN! YOUR PROBLEMS ARE IMPORTANT TOO! IT'S A TERRIBLE, UNFAIR WORLD.
IT'S A FAIR COP. ANN PURD RAN A PRINCIPLED AND SENSIBLE CAMPAIGN ALONG NERD LINES.
THE PROBLEM WITH NERDS IS THAT THEY'RE CLEVER. YOU CAN TELL BY THE GLASSES. LOOK AT DAISY...
HER MIND NEVER STOPS SPINNING.
DON'T PIGEONHOLE ME!
YOU'RE LITERALLY STANDING IN A PIGEON-HOLE.
THAT IS THE SORT OF EXCELLENT JOKE THAT ONCE MIGHT HAVE MADE ME SMILE.
I CAN'T BEAR THIS! YOU'RE BOTH SO SAD!
WE NEED TO FIX THINGS! I'M GOING TO FIX THINGS!
WE'RE GOING CAMPING!
NO, WE AREN'T.
WE ABSOLUTELY AREN'T.

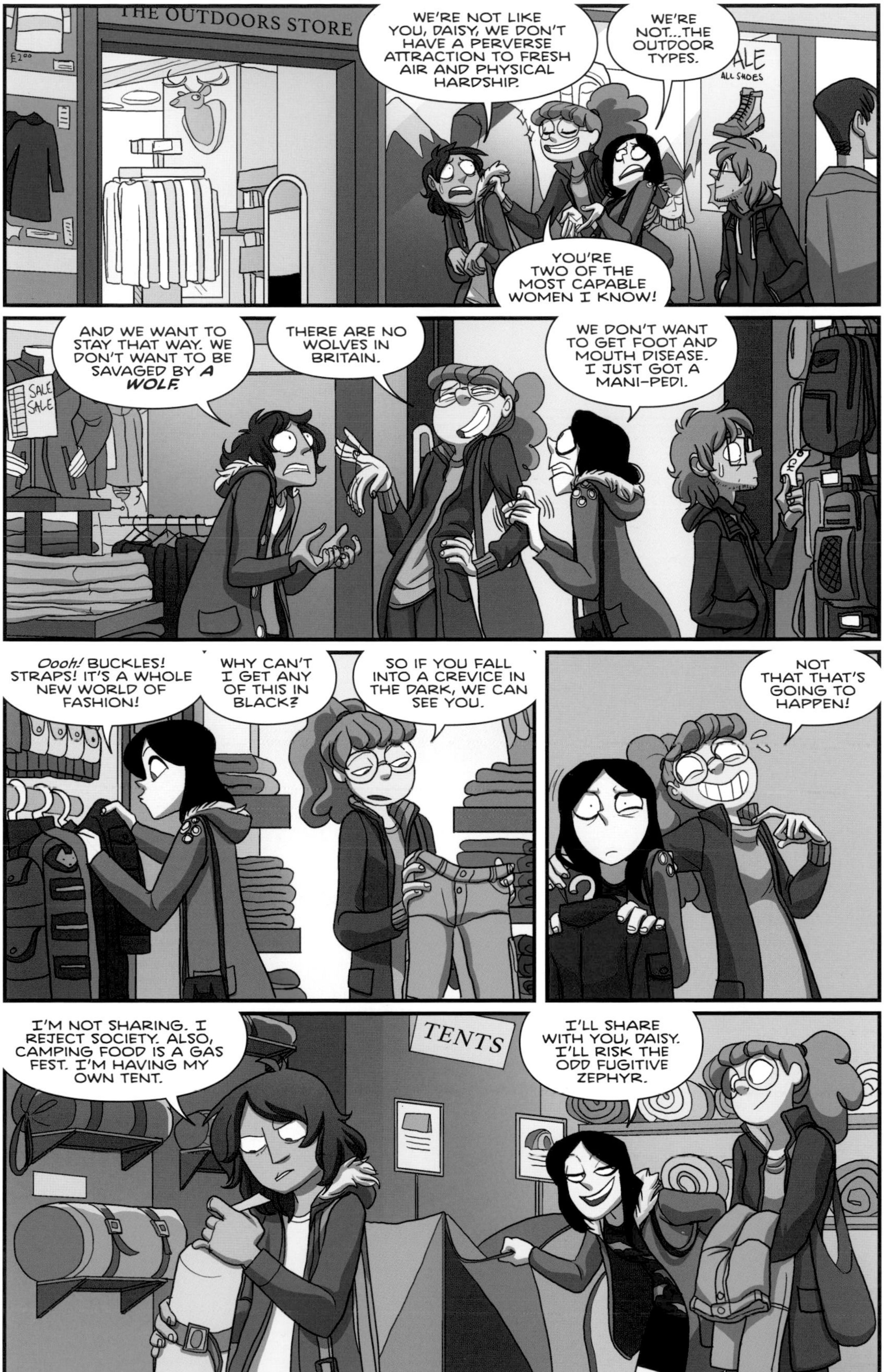
THE OUTDOORS STORE
£2.00
WE'RE NOT LIKE YOU, DAISY, WE DON'T HAVE A PERVERSE ATTRACTION TO FRESH AIR AND PHYSICAL HARDSHIP.
WE'RE NOT...THE OUTDOOR TYPES.
SALE ALL SHOES
YOU'RE TWO OF THE MOST CAPABLE WOMEN I KNOW!
AND WE WANT TO STAY THAT WAY. WE DON'T WANT TO BE SAVAGED BY *A WOLF.*
THERE ARE NO WOLVES IN BRITAIN.
WE DON'T WANT TO GET FOOT AND MOUTH DISEASE. I JUST GOT A MANI-PEDI.
SALE SALE
*Oooh!* BUCKLES! STRAPS! IT'S A WHOLE NEW WORLD OF FASHION!
WHY CAN'T I GET ANY OF THIS IN BLACK?
SO IF YOU FALL INTO A CREVICE IN THE DARK, WE CAN SEE YOU.
NOT THAT THAT'S GOING TO HAPPEN!
I'M NOT SHARING. I REJECT SOCIETY. ALSO, CAMPING FOOD IS A GAS FEST. I'M HAVING MY OWN TENT.
TENTS
I'LL SHARE WITH YOU, DAISY. I'LL RISK THE ODD FUGITIVE ZEPHYR.

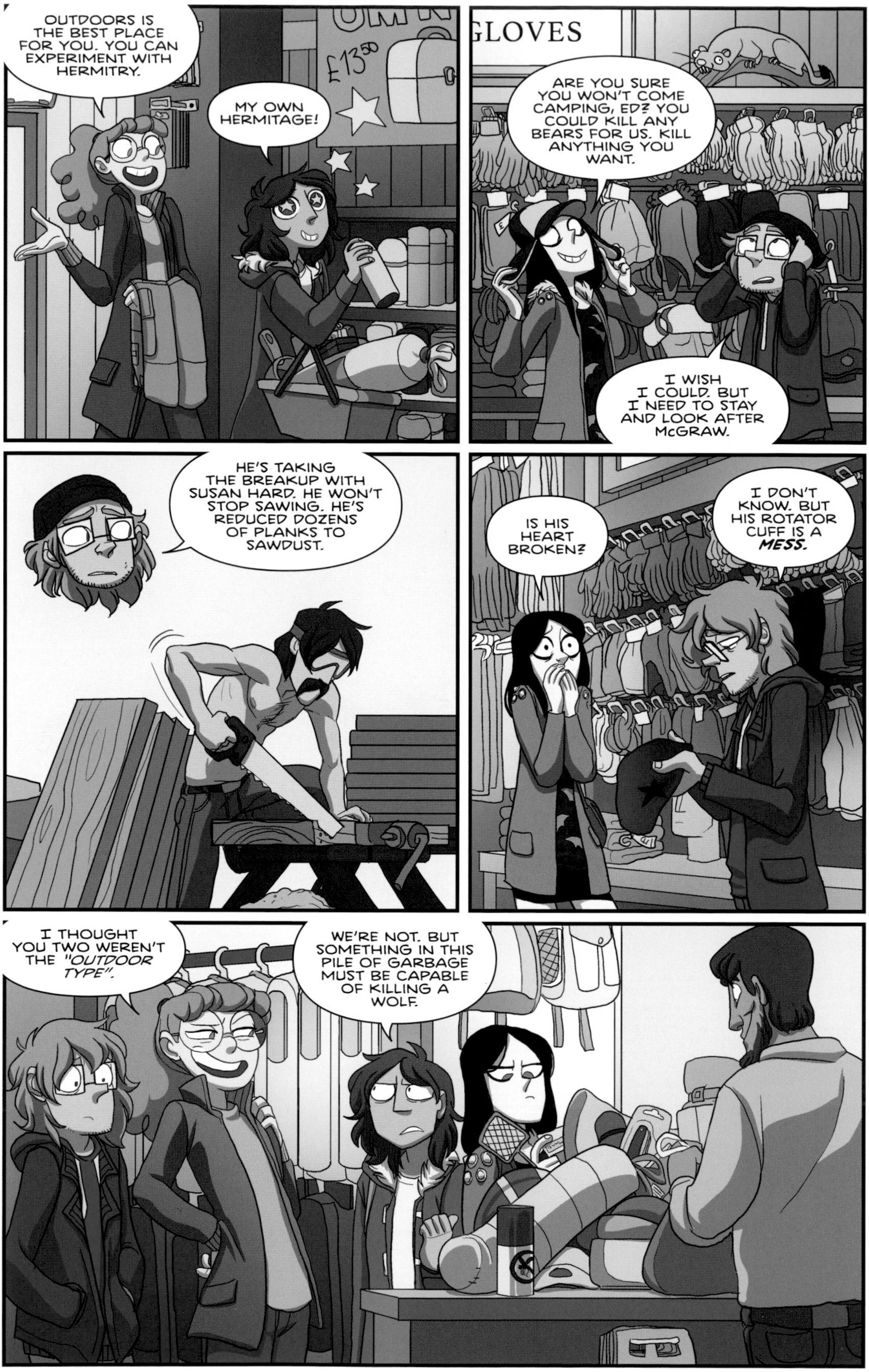
OUTDOORS IS THE BEST PLACE FOR YOU. YOU CAN EXPERIMENT WITH HERMITRY.
MY OWN HERMITAGE!
£13.50
GLOVES
ARE YOU SURE YOU WON'T COME CAMPING, ED? YOU COULD KILL ANY BEARS FOR US. KILL ANYTHING YOU WANT.
I WISH I COULD. BUT I NEED TO STAY AND LOOK AFTER McGRAW.
HE'S TAKING THE BREAKUP WITH SUSAN HARD. HE WON'T STOP SAWING. HE'S REDUCED DOZENS OF PLANKS TO SAWDUST.
IS HIS HEART BROKEN?
I DON'T KNOW. BUT HIS ROTATOR CUFF IS A ***MESS.***
I THOUGHT YOU TWO WEREN'T THE *"OUTDOOR TYPE"*.
WE'RE NOT. BUT SOMETHING IN THIS PILE OF GARBAGE MUST BE CAPABLE OF KILLING A WOLF.

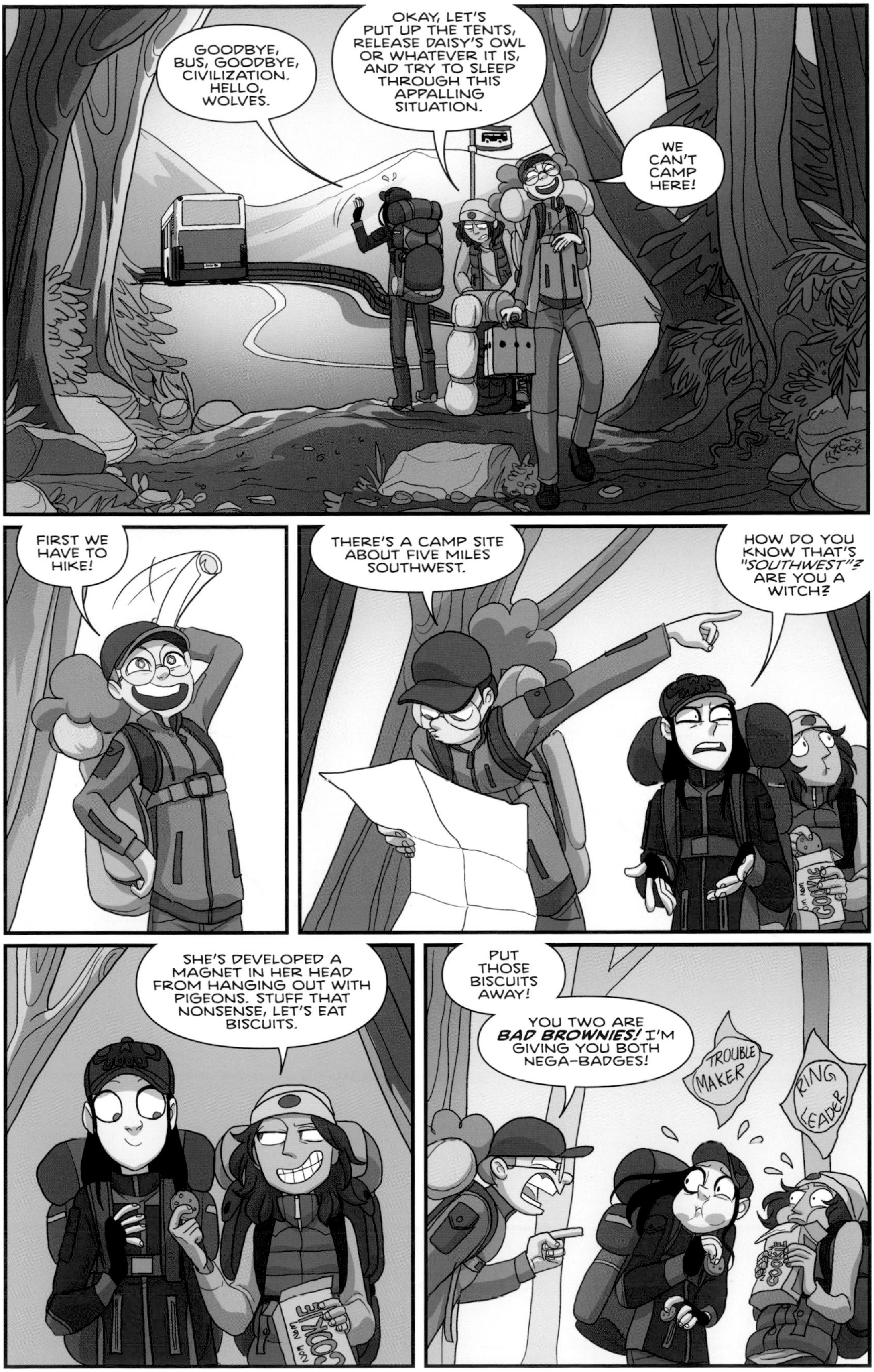
GOODBYE, BUS, GOODBYE, CIVILIZATION. HELLO, WOLVES.
OKAY, LET'S PUT UP THE TENTS, RELEASE DAISY'S OWL OR WHATEVER IT IS, AND TRY TO SLEEP THROUGH THIS APPALLING SITUATION.
WE CAN'T CAMP HERE!
FIRST WE HAVE TO HIKE!
THERE'S A CAMP SITE ABOUT FIVE MILES SOUTHWEST.
HOW DO YOU KNOW THAT'S "SOUTHWEST"? ARE YOU A WITCH?
SHE'S DEVELOPED A MAGNET IN HER HEAD FROM HANGING OUT WITH PIGEONS. STUFF THAT NONSENSE, LET'S EAT BISCUITS.
PUT THOSE BISCUITS AWAY!
YOU TWO ARE BAD BROWNIES! I'M GIVING YOU BOTH NEGA-BADGES!
TROUBLE MAKER
RING LEADER

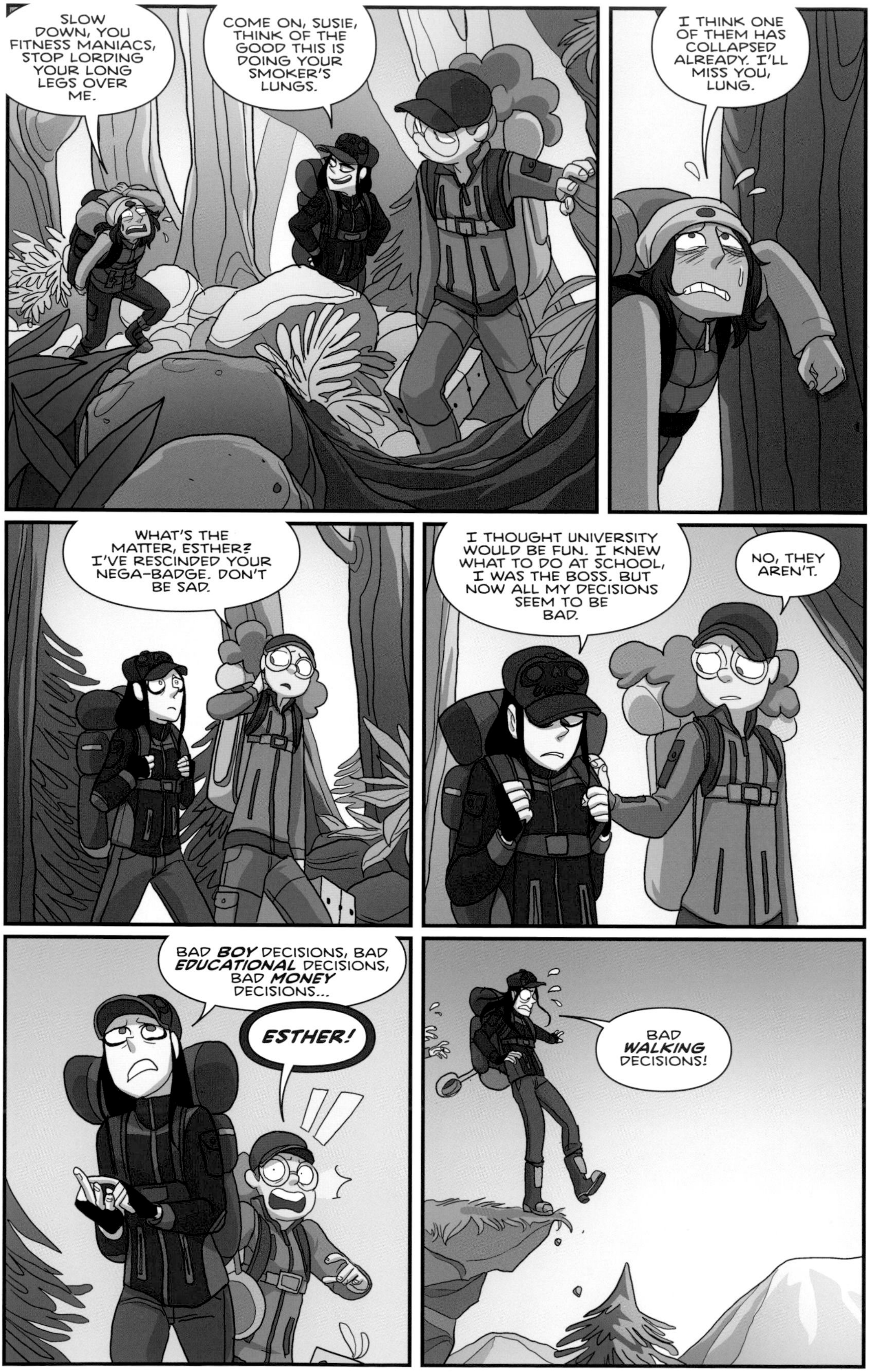
SLOW DOWN, YOU FITNESS MANIACS, STOP LORDING YOUR LONG LEGS OVER ME.
COME ON, SUSIE, THINK OF THE GOOD THIS IS DOING YOUR SMOKER'S LUNGS.
I THINK ONE OF THEM HAS COLLAPSED ALREADY. I'LL MISS YOU, LUNG.
WHAT'S THE MATTER, ESTHER? I'VE RESCINDED YOUR NEGA-BADGE. DON'T BE SAD.
I THOUGHT UNIVERSITY WOULD BE FUN. I KNEW WHAT TO DO AT SCHOOL, I WAS THE BOSS. BUT NOW ALL MY DECISIONS SEEM TO BE BAD.
NO, THEY AREN'T.
BAD BOY DECISIONS, BAD EDUCATIONAL DECISIONS, BAD MONEY DECISIONS...
ESTHER!
BAD WALKING DECISIONS!

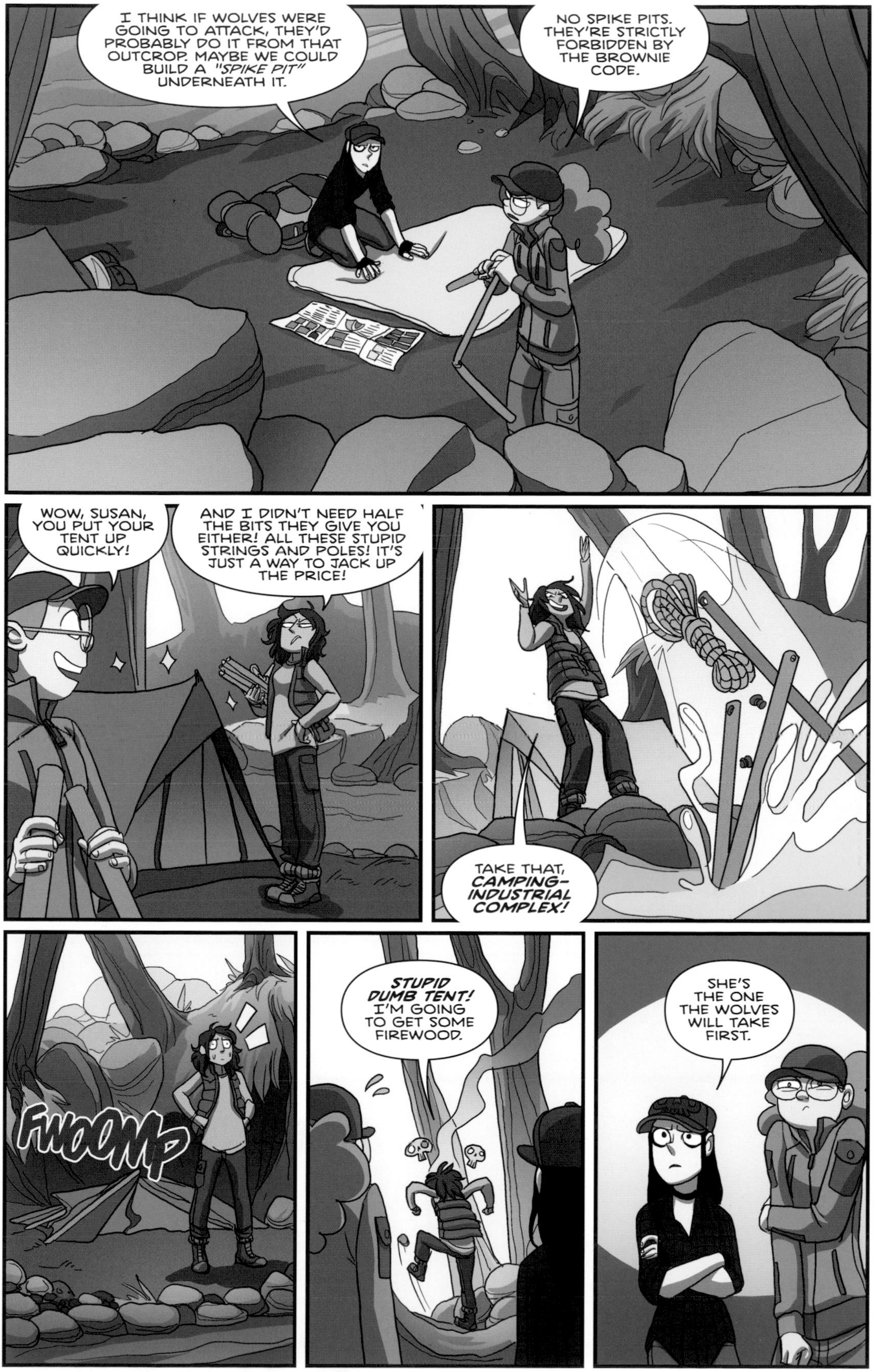
I THINK IF WOLVES WERE GOING TO ATTACK, THEY'D PROBABLY DO IT FROM THAT OUTCROP. MAYBE WE COULD BUILD A "SPIKE PIT" UNDERNEATH IT.
NO SPIKE PITS. THEY'RE STRICTLY FORBIDDEN BY THE BROWNIE CODE.
WOW, SUSAN, YOU PUT YOUR TENT UP QUICKLY!
AND I DIDN'T NEED HALF THE BITS THEY GIVE YOU EITHER! ALL THESE STUPID STRINGS AND POLES! IT'S JUST A WAY TO JACK UP THE PRICE!
TAKE THAT, CAMPING-INDUSTRIAL COMPLEX!
FWOOMP
STUPID DUMB TENT! I'M GOING TO GET SOME FIREWOOD.
SHE'S THE ONE THE WOLVES WILL TAKE FIRST.

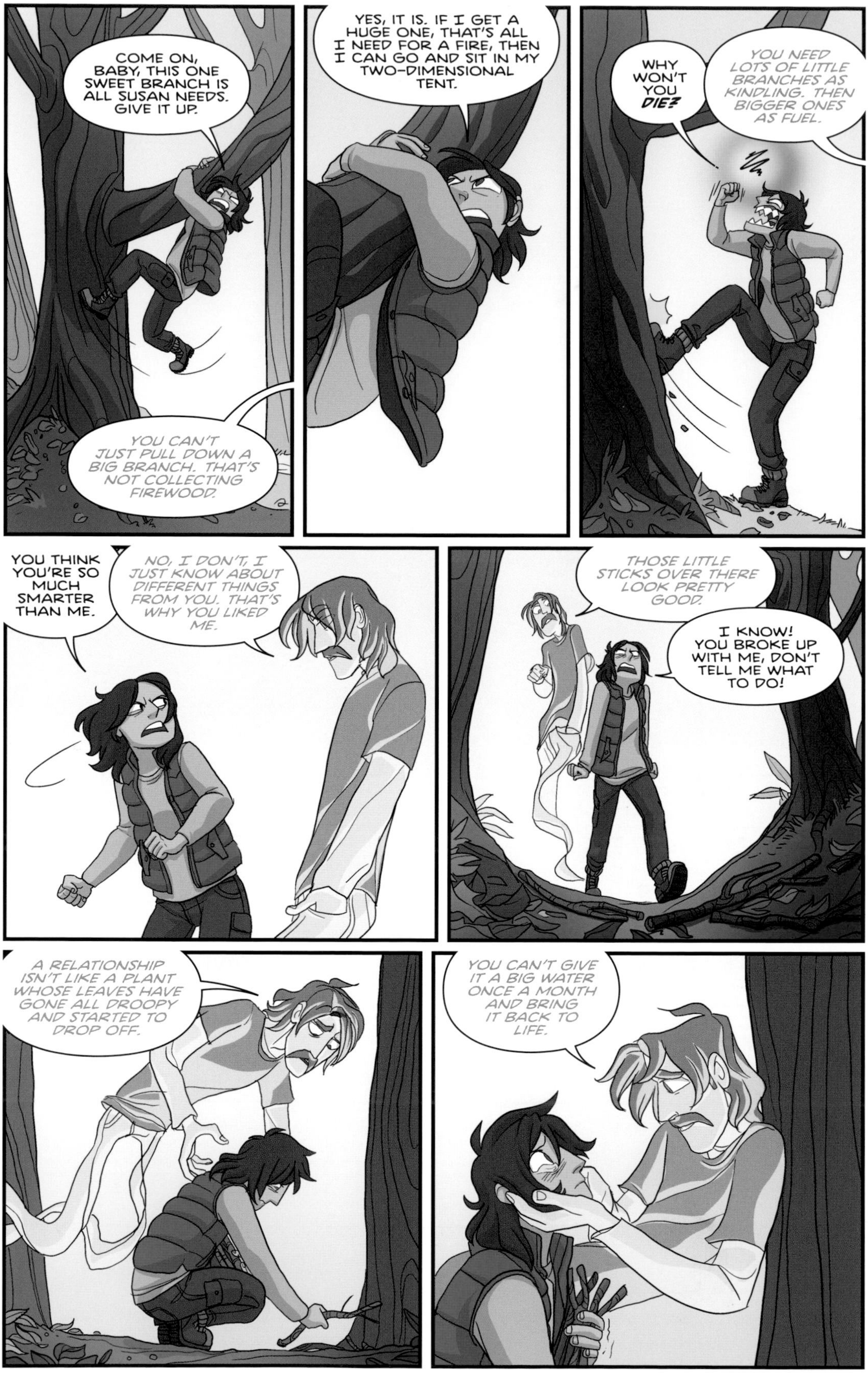
COME ON, BABY, THIS ONE SWEET BRANCH IS ALL SUSAN NEEDS. GIVE IT UP.
YOU CAN'T JUST PULL DOWN A BIG BRANCH. THAT'S NOT COLLECTING FIREWOOD.
YES, IT IS. IF I GET A HUGE ONE, THAT'S ALL I NEED FOR A FIRE, THEN I CAN GO AND SIT IN MY TWO-DIMENSIONAL TENT.
WHY WON'T YOU DIE?
YOU NEED LOTS OF LITTLE BRANCHES AS KINDLING. THEN BIGGER ONES AS FUEL.
YOU THINK YOU'RE SO MUCH SMARTER THAN ME.
NO, I DON'T, I JUST KNOW ABOUT DIFFERENT THINGS FROM YOU. THAT'S WHY YOU LIKED ME.
THOSE LITTLE STICKS OVER THERE LOOK PRETTY GOOD.
I KNOW! YOU BROKE UP WITH ME, DON'T TELL ME WHAT TO DO!
A RELATIONSHIP ISN'T LIKE A PLANT WHOSE LEAVES HAVE GONE ALL DROOPY AND STARTED TO DROP OFF.
YOU CAN'T GIVE IT A BIG WATER ONCE A MONTH AND BRING IT BACK TO LIFE.

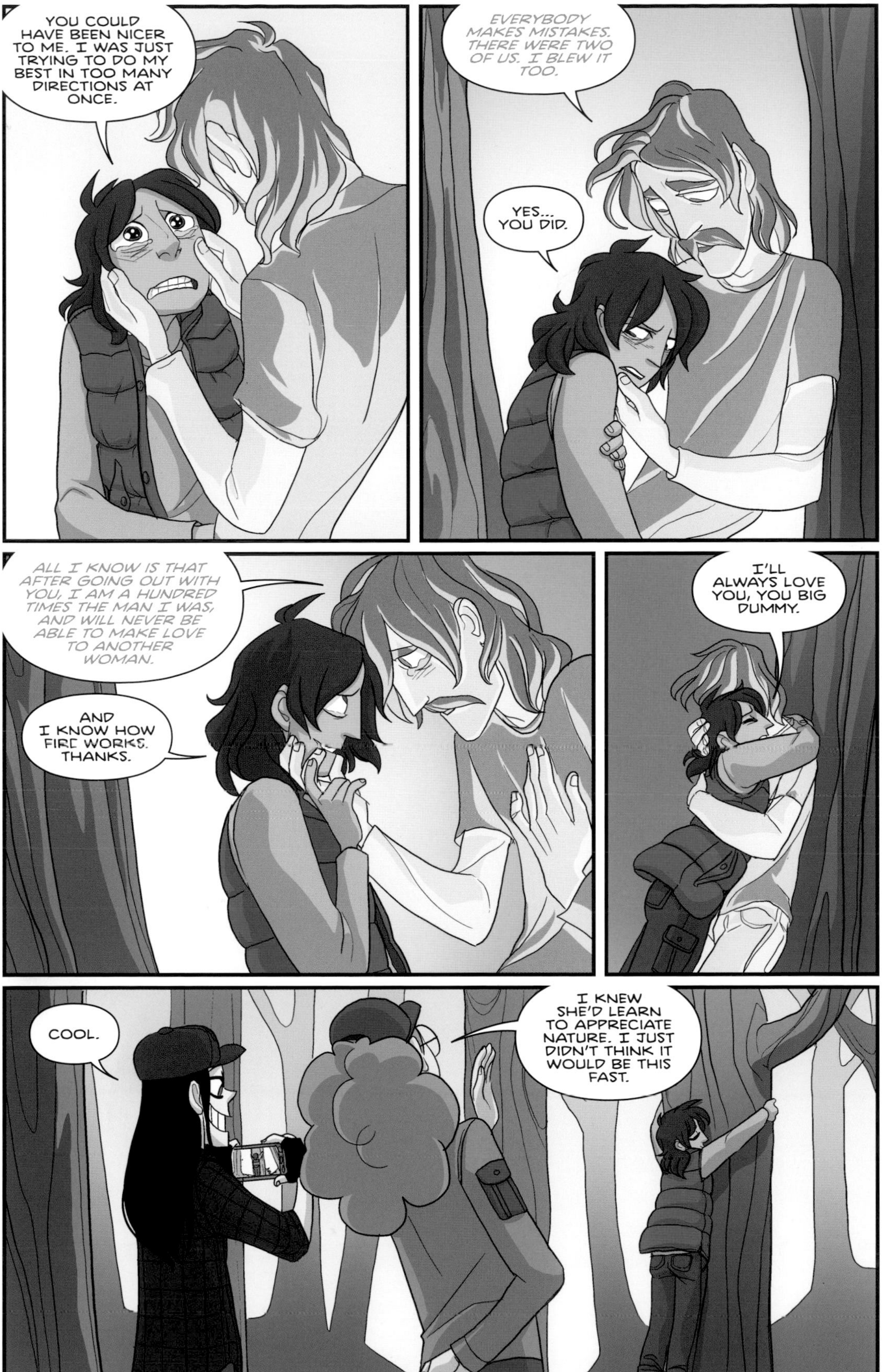
YOU COULD HAVE BEEN NICER TO ME. I WAS JUST TRYING TO DO MY BEST IN TOO MANY DIRECTIONS AT ONCE.
EVERYBODY MAKES MISTAKES. THERE WERE TWO OF US. I BLEW IT TOO.
YES... YOU DID.
ALL I KNOW IS THAT AFTER GOING OUT WITH YOU, I AM A HUNDRED TIMES THE MAN I WAS, AND WILL NEVER BE ABLE TO MAKE LOVE TO ANOTHER WOMAN.
AND I KNOW HOW FIRE WORKS. THANKS.
I'LL ALWAYS LOVE YOU, YOU BIG DUMMY.
COOL.
I KNEW SHE'D LEARN TO APPRECIATE NATURE. I JUST DIDN'T THINK IT WOULD BE THIS FAST.

MCGRAW... MATE? ARE YOU OKAY IN THERE?

click

creeeeaaaakk

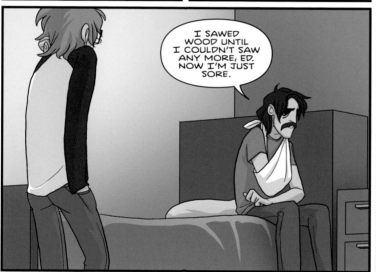

I SAWED WOOD UNTIL I COULDN'T SAW ANY MORE, ED. NOW I'M JUST SORE.

IS THAT A JOKE?

A SMALL ONE.

DO YOU WANT TO GO TO THE PUB? TO THE CINEMA? TO THE ZOO?

I'D LIKE TO VISIT A QUALIFIED PHYSIOTHERAPIST.

A *VERY NON-JUDGMENTAL* PHYSIOTHERAPIST.

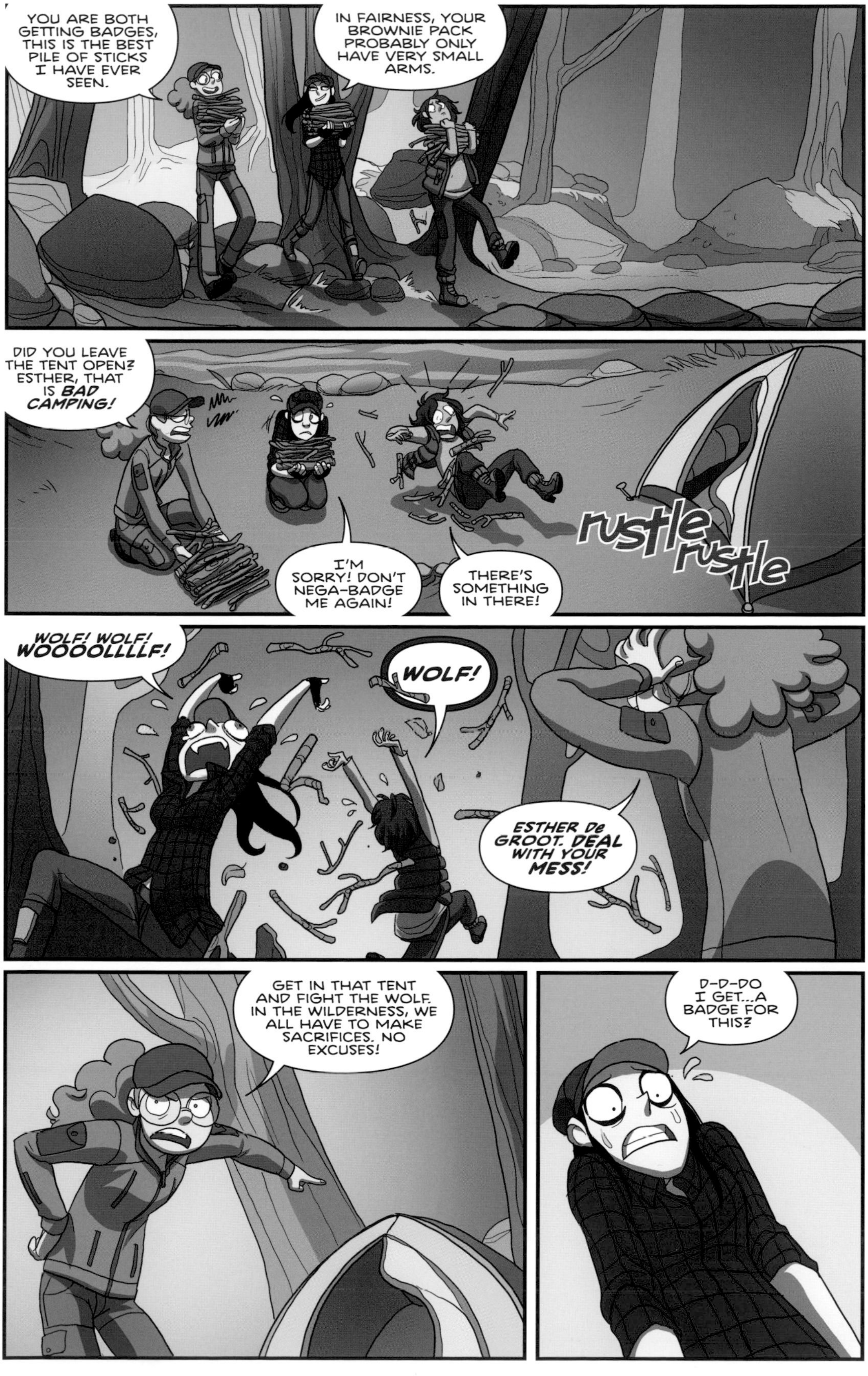
YOU ARE BOTH GETTING BADGES, THIS IS THE BEST PILE OF STICKS I HAVE EVER SEEN.
IN FAIRNESS, YOUR BROWNIE PACK PROBABLY ONLY HAVE VERY SMALL ARMS.
DID YOU LEAVE THE TENT OPEN? ESTHER, THAT IS BAD CAMPING!
I'M SORRY! DON'T NEGA-BADGE ME AGAIN!
THERE'S SOMETHING IN THERE!
rustle rustle
WOLF! WOLF! WOOOOLLLLF!
WOLF!
ESTHER De GROOT. DEAL WITH YOUR MESS!
GET IN THAT TENT AND FIGHT THE WOLF. IN THE WILDERNESS, WE ALL HAVE TO MAKE SACRIFICES. NO EXCUSES!
D-D-DO I GET...A BADGE FOR THIS?

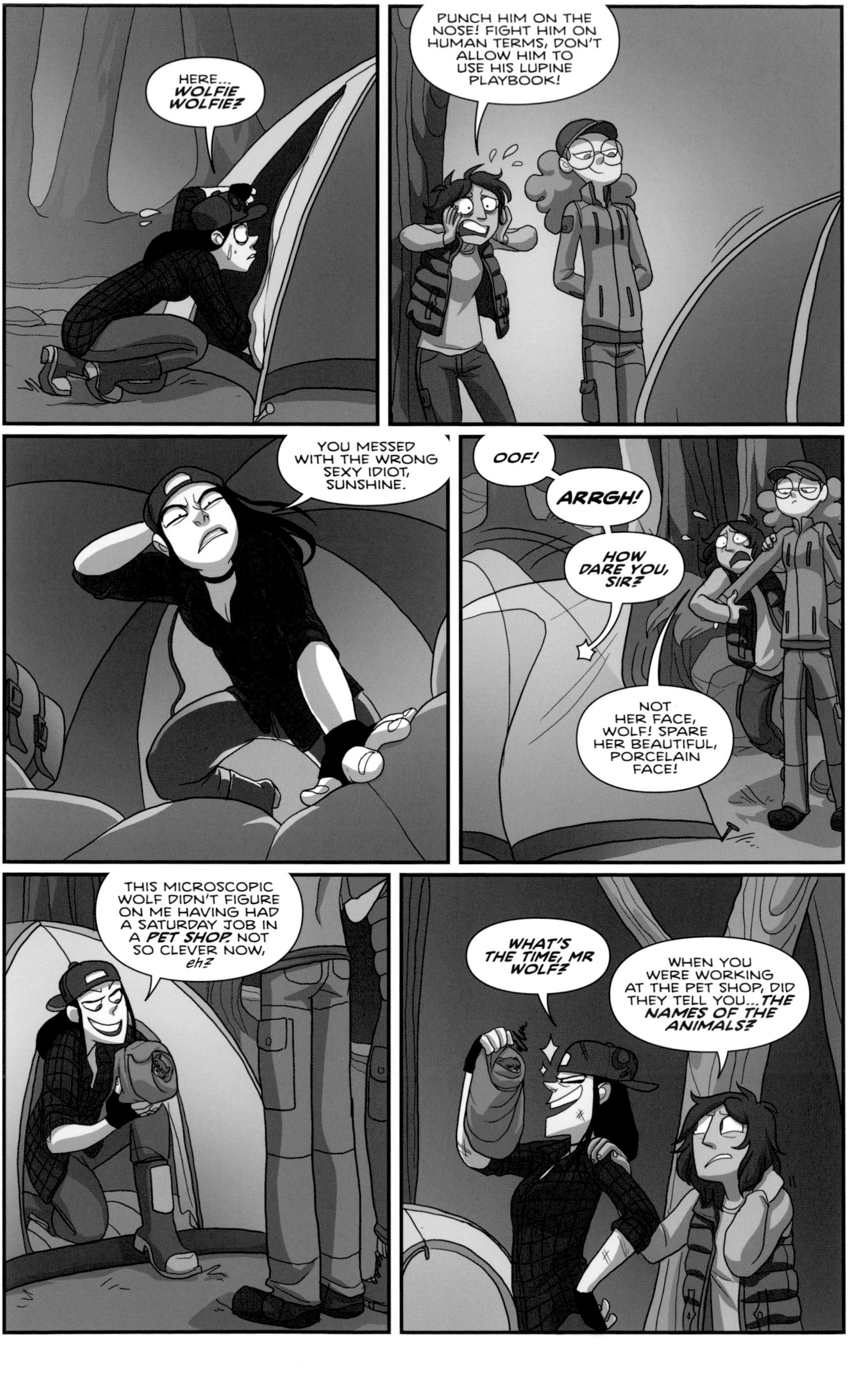
HERE... WOLFIE WOLFIE?
PUNCH HIM ON THE NOSE! FIGHT HIM ON HUMAN TERMS, DON'T ALLOW HIM TO USE HIS LUPINE PLAYBOOK!
YOU MESSED WITH THE WRONG SEXY IDIOT, SUNSHINE.
OOF!
ARRGH!
HOW DARE YOU, SIR?
NOT HER FACE, WOLF! SPARE HER BEAUTIFUL, PORCELAIN FACE!
THIS MICROSCOPIC WOLF DIDN'T FIGURE ON ME HAVING HAD A SATURDAY JOB IN A PET SHOP? NOT SO CLEVER NOW, eh?
WHAT'S THE TIME, MR WOLF?
WHEN YOU WERE WORKING AT THE PET SHOP, DID THEY TELL YOU... THE NAMES OF THE ANIMALS?

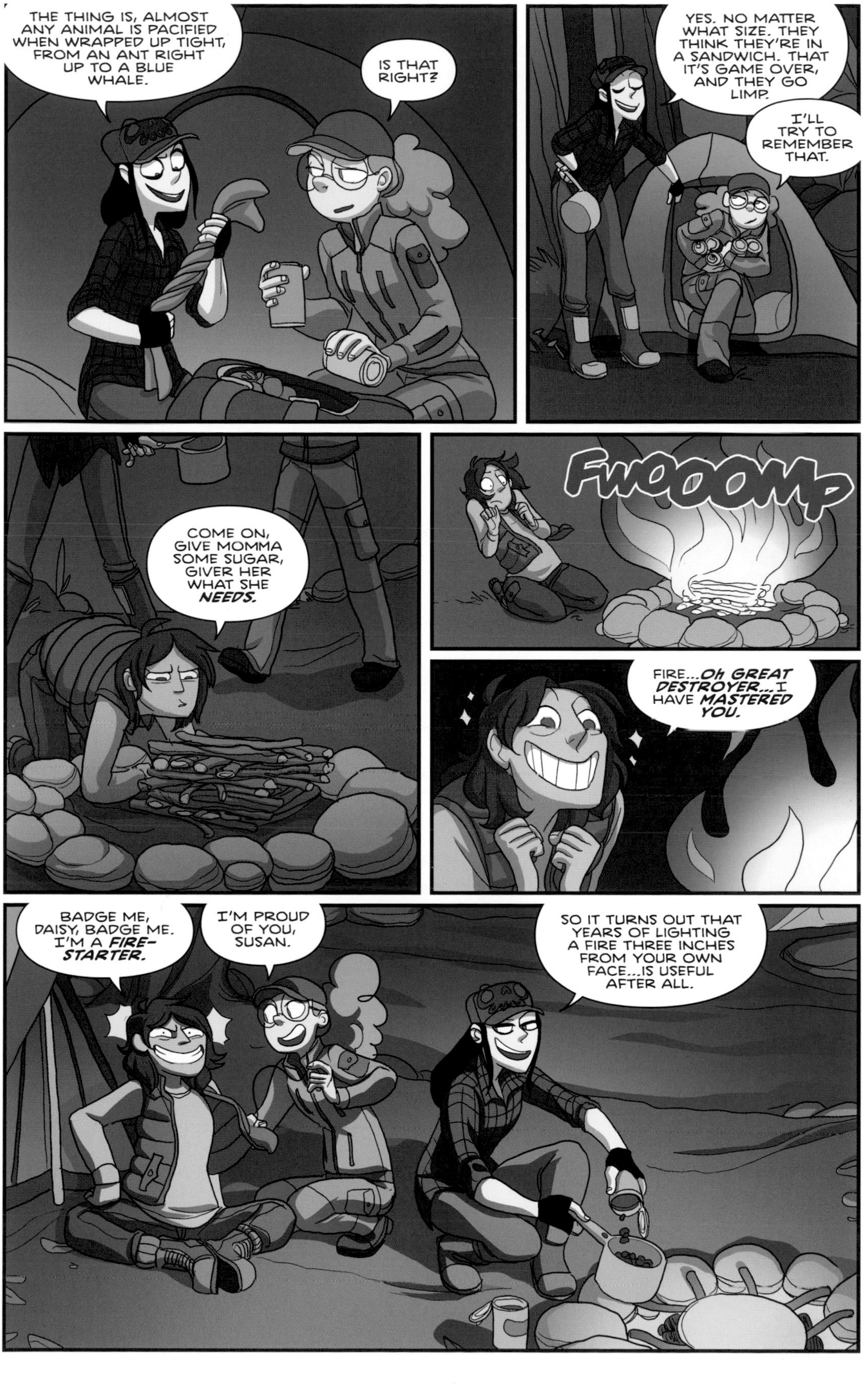
THE THING IS, ALMOST ANY ANIMAL IS PACIFIED WHEN WRAPPED UP TIGHT, FROM AN ANT RIGHT UP TO A BLUE WHALE.
IS THAT RIGHT?
YES. NO MATTER WHAT SIZE. THEY THINK THEY'RE IN A SANDWICH. THAT IT'S GAME OVER, AND THEY GO LIMP.
I'LL TRY TO REMEMBER THAT.
COME ON, GIVE MOMMA SOME SUGAR, GIVER HER WHAT SHE NEEDS.
FWOOOMP
FIRE...Oh GREAT DESTROYER...I HAVE MASTERED YOU.
BADGE ME, DAISY, BADGE ME. I'M A FIRE-STARTER.
I'M PROUD OF YOU, SUSAN.
SO IT TURNS OUT THAT YEARS OF LIGHTING A FIRE THREE INCHES FROM YOUR OWN FACE...IS USEFUL AFTER ALL.

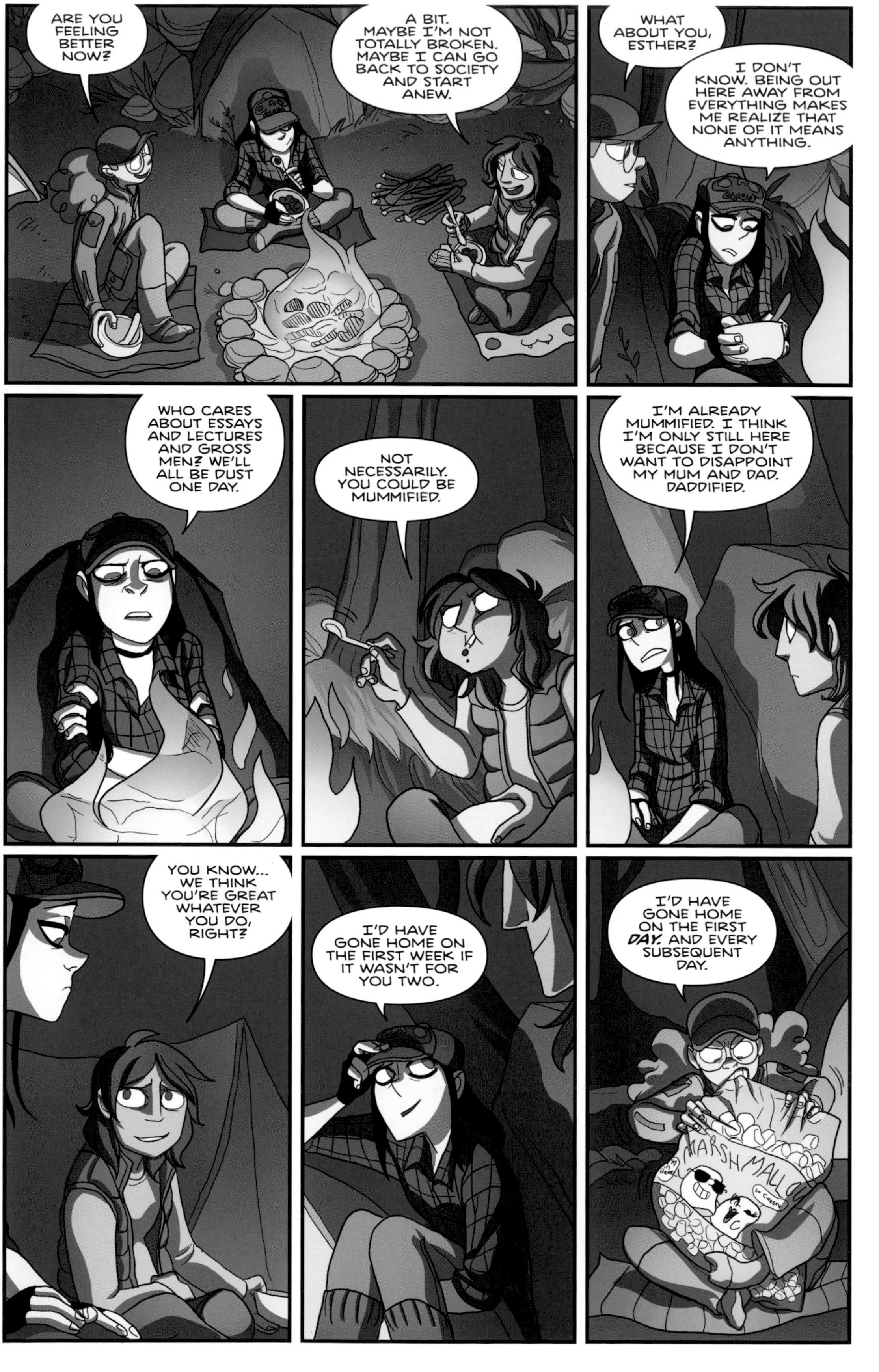
ARE YOU FEELING BETTER NOW?
A BIT. MAYBE I'M NOT TOTALLY BROKEN. MAYBE I CAN GO BACK TO SOCIETY AND START ANEW.
WHAT ABOUT YOU, ESTHER?
I DON'T KNOW. BEING OUT HERE AWAY FROM EVERYTHING MAKES ME REALIZE THAT NONE OF IT MEANS ANYTHING.
WHO CARES ABOUT ESSAYS AND LECTURES AND GROSS MEN? WE'LL ALL BE DUST ONE DAY.
NOT NECESSARILY. YOU COULD BE MUMMIFIED.
I'M ALREADY MUMMIFIED. I THINK I'M ONLY STILL HERE BECAUSE I DON'T WANT TO DISAPPOINT MY MUM AND DAD. DADDIFIED.
YOU KNOW... WE THINK YOU'RE GREAT WHATEVER YOU DO, RIGHT?
I'D HAVE GONE HOME ON THE FIRST WEEK IF IT WASN'T FOR YOU TWO.
I'D HAVE GONE HOME ON THE FIRST *DAY.* AND EVERY SUBSEQUENT DAY.

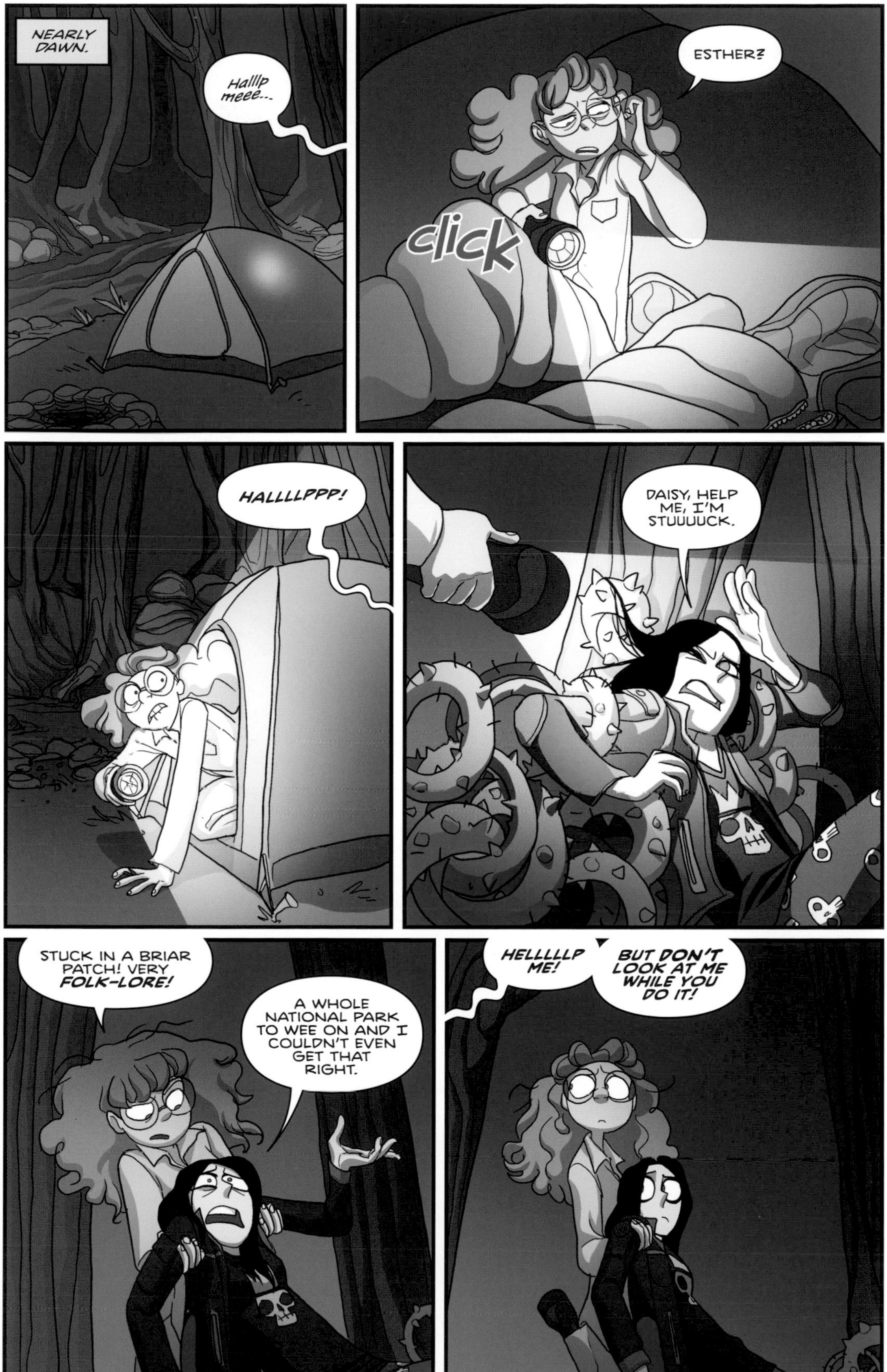
NEARLY DAWN.
Halllp meee...
ESTHER?
click
HALLLLPPP!
DAISY, HELP ME, I'M STUUUUCK.
STUCK IN A BRIAR PATCH! VERY FOLK-LORE!
A WHOLE NATIONAL PARK TO WEE ON AND I COULDN'T EVEN GET THAT RIGHT.
HELLLLLP ME!
BUT DON'T LOOK AT ME WHILE YOU DO IT!

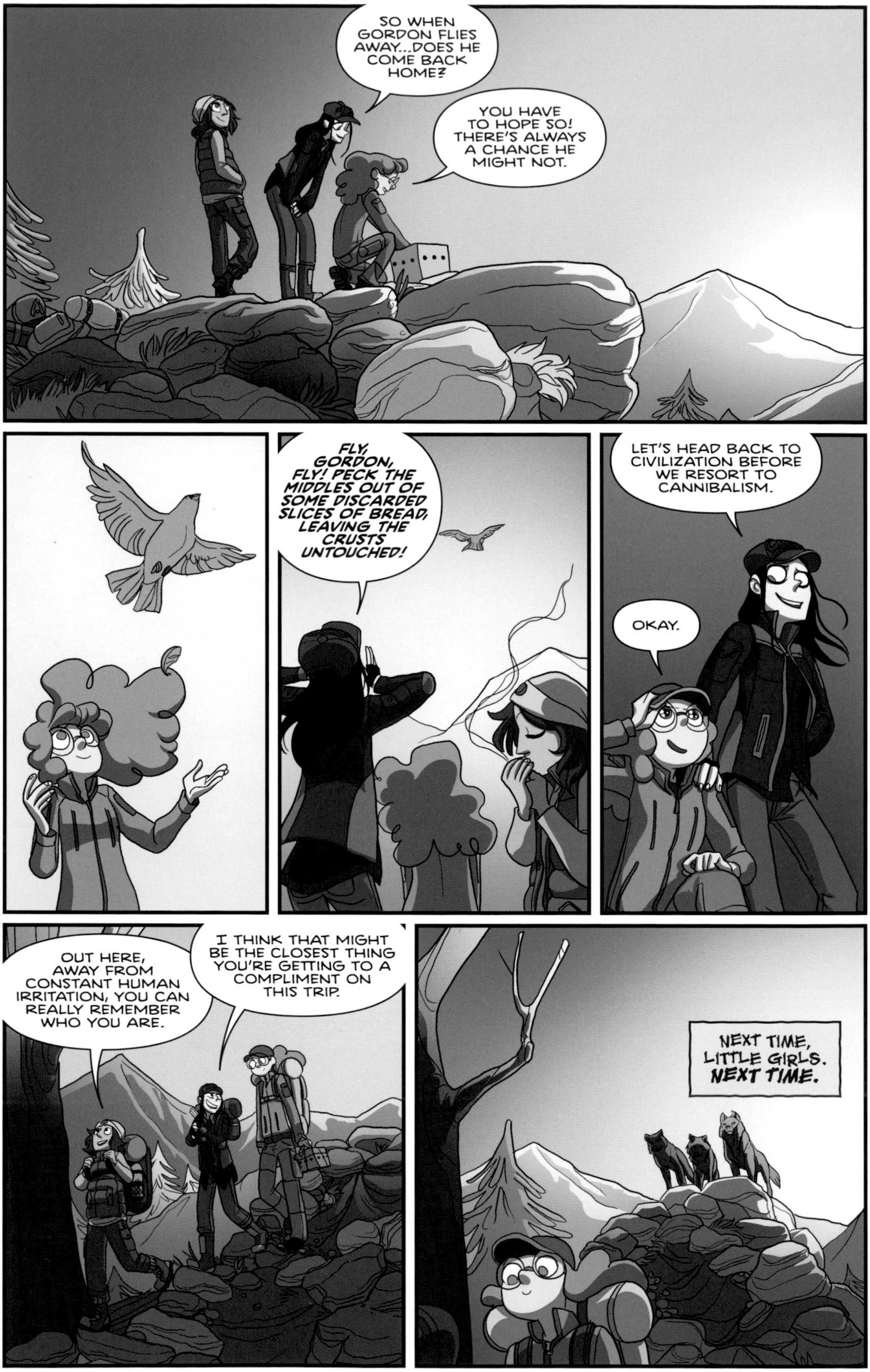

SO WHEN GORDON FLIES AWAY...DOES HE COME BACK HOME?
YOU HAVE TO HOPE SO! THERE'S ALWAYS A CHANCE HE MIGHT NOT.
FLY, GORDON, FLY! PECK THE MIDDLES OUT OF SOME DISCARDED SLICES OF BREAD, LEAVING THE CRUSTS UNTOUCHED!
LET'S HEAD BACK TO CIVILIZATION BEFORE WE RESORT TO CANNIBALISM.
OKAY.
OUT HERE, AWAY FROM CONSTANT HUMAN IRRITATION, YOU CAN REALLY REMEMBER WHO YOU ARE.
I THINK THAT MIGHT BE THE CLOSEST THING YOU'RE GETTING TO A COMPLIMENT ON THIS TRIP.
NEXT TIME, LITTLE GIRLS. NEXT TIME.

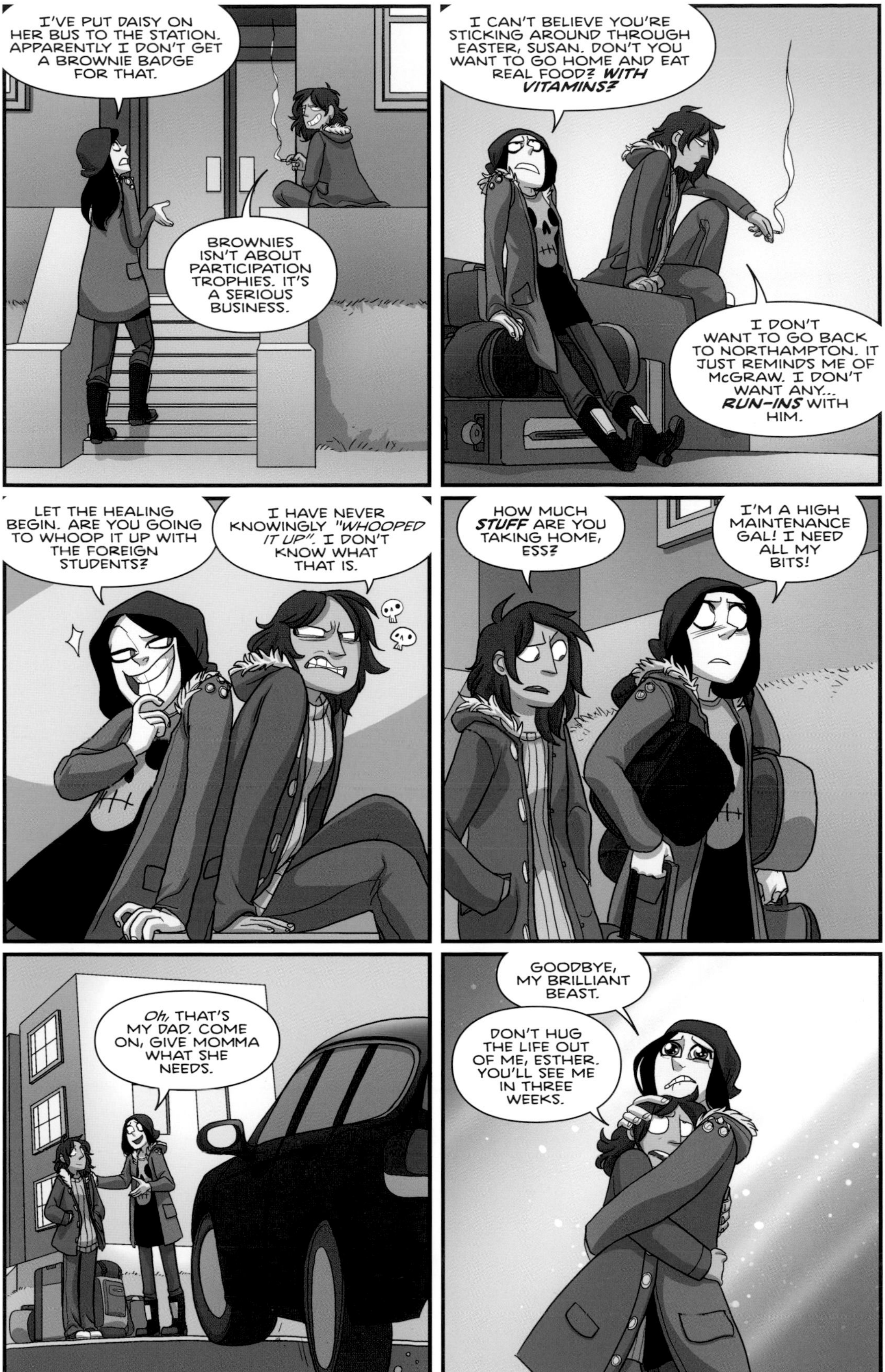
I'VE PUT DAISY ON HER BUS TO THE STATION. APPARENTLY I DON'T GET A BROWNIE BADGE FOR THAT.
BROWNIES ISN'T ABOUT PARTICIPATION TROPHIES. IT'S A SERIOUS BUSINESS.
I CAN'T BELIEVE YOU'RE STICKING AROUND THROUGH EASTER, SUSAN. DON'T YOU WANT TO GO HOME AND EAT REAL FOOD? WITH VITAMINS?
I DON'T WANT TO GO BACK TO NORTHAMPTON. IT JUST REMINDS ME OF McGRAW. I DON'T WANT ANY... RUN-INS WITH HIM.
LET THE HEALING BEGIN. ARE YOU GOING TO WHOOP IT UP WITH THE FOREIGN STUDENTS?
I HAVE NEVER KNOWINGLY "WHOOPED IT UP". I DON'T KNOW WHAT THAT IS.
HOW MUCH STUFF ARE YOU TAKING HOME, ESS?
I'M A HIGH MAINTENANCE GAL! I NEED ALL MY BITS!
Oh, THAT'S MY DAD. COME ON, GIVE MOMMA WHAT SHE NEEDS.
GOODBYE, MY BRILLIANT BEAST.
DON'T HUG THE LIFE OUT OF ME, ESTHER. YOU'LL SEE ME IN THREE WEEKS.

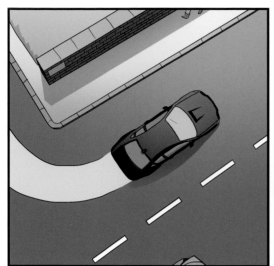

DAD, I'VE GOT...A BIT OF NEWS.

ALL I'M SAYING IS, WHY DOES EVERYTHING HAVE TO BE SO *DRAMATIC* WITH YOU?

I THOUGHT YOU'D *UNDERSTAND!*

WHAT'S ALL THIS SHOUTING ABOUT? I HOPE THIS WASN'T ANOTHER *"DISCUSSION"* ABOUT TATTOOS.

SHE SAYS SHE'S QUITTING UNIVERSITY, SHE'S NOT GOING BACK!

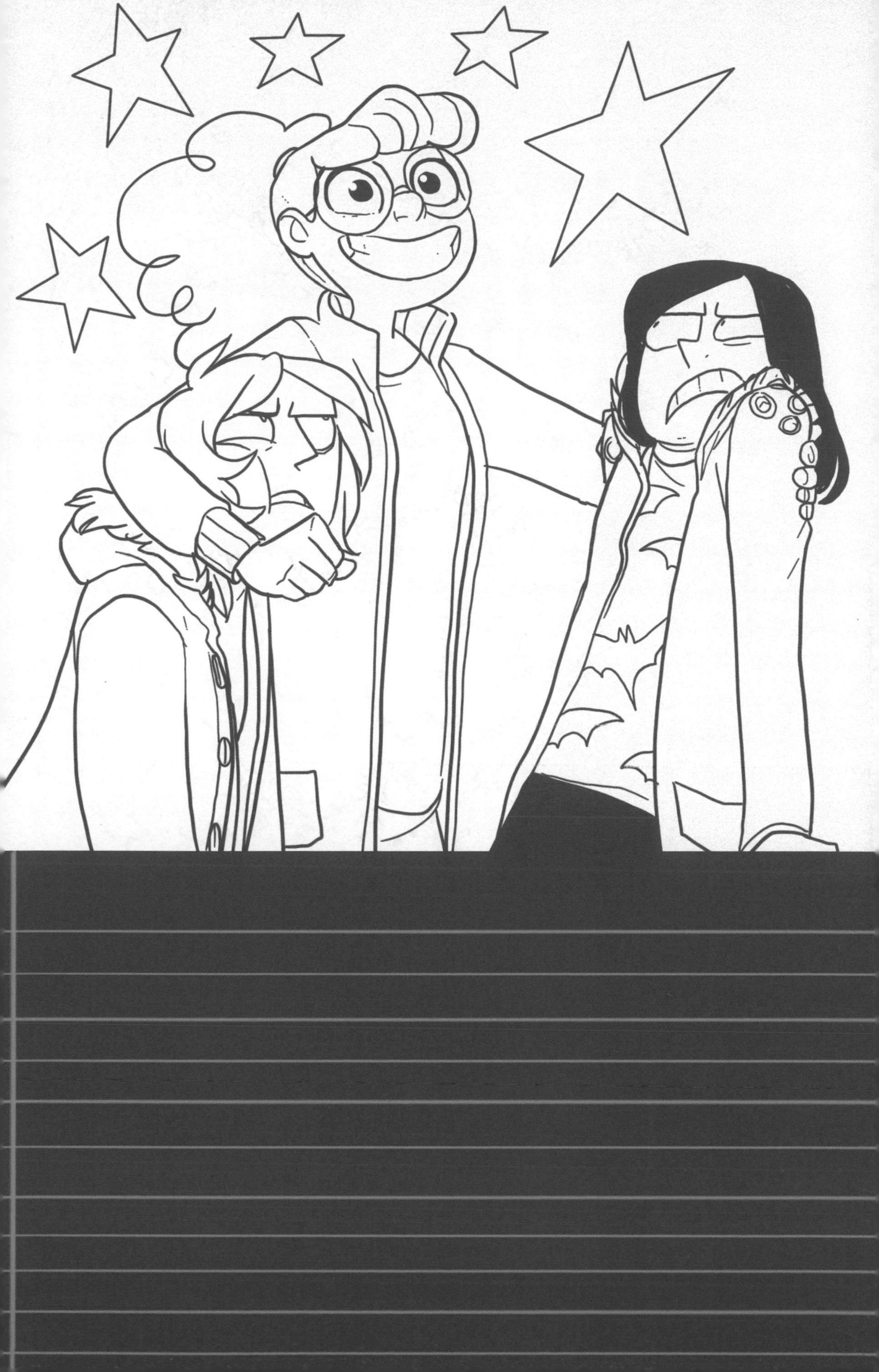

# CHAPTER
## THIRTEEN

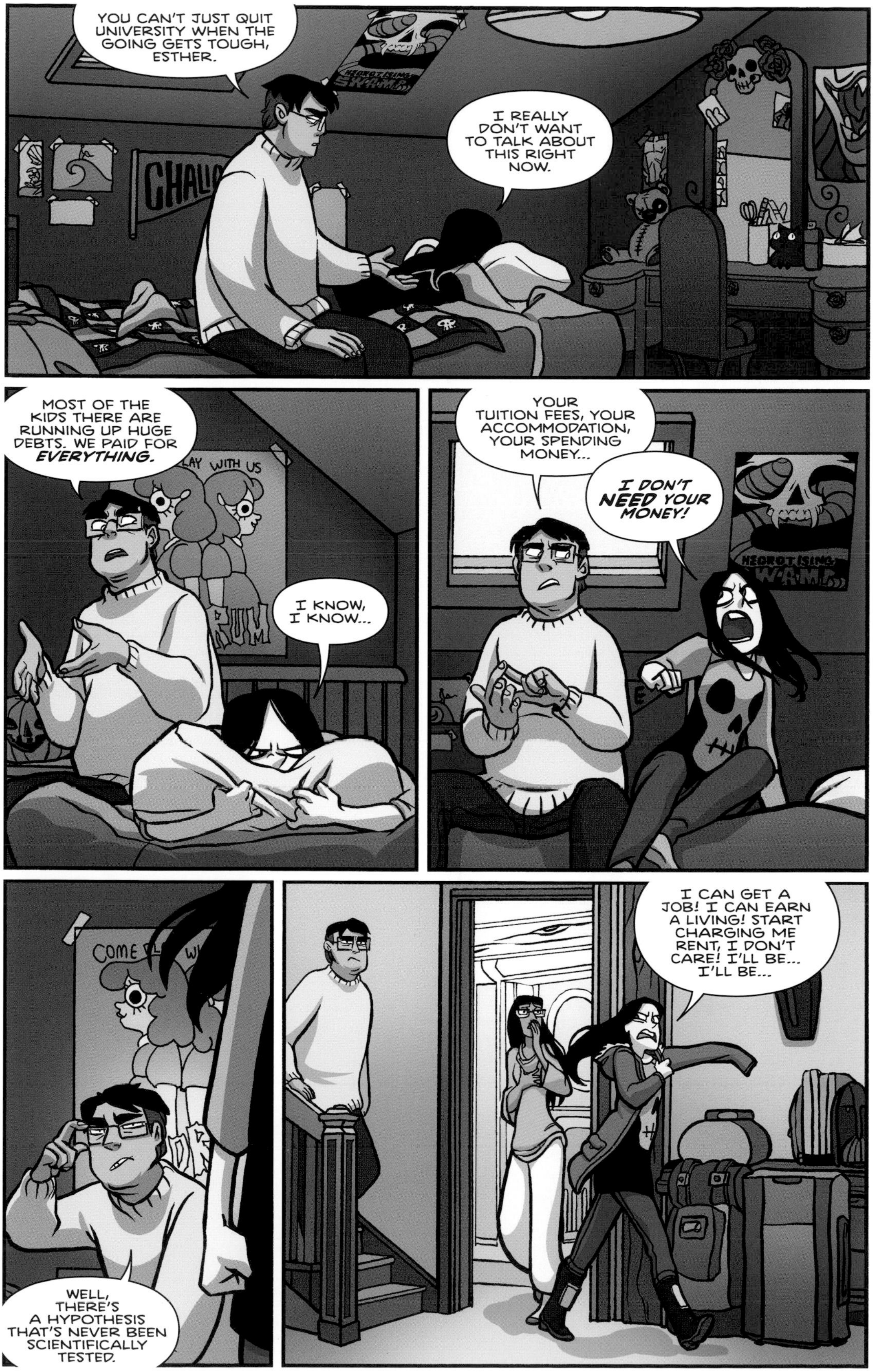
YOU CAN'T JUST QUIT UNIVERSITY WHEN THE GOING GETS TOUGH, ESTHER.
I REALLY DON'T WANT TO TALK ABOUT THIS RIGHT NOW.
MOST OF THE KIDS THERE ARE RUNNING UP HUGE DEBTS. WE PAID FOR EVERYTHING.
I KNOW, I KNOW...
YOUR TUITION FEES, YOUR ACCOMMODATION, YOUR SPENDING MONEY...
I DON'T NEED YOUR MONEY!
WELL, THERE'S A HYPOTHESIS THAT'S NEVER BEEN SCIENTIFICALLY TESTED.
I CAN GET A JOB! I CAN EARN A LIVING! START CHARGING ME RENT, I DON'T CARE! I'LL BE... I'LL BE...

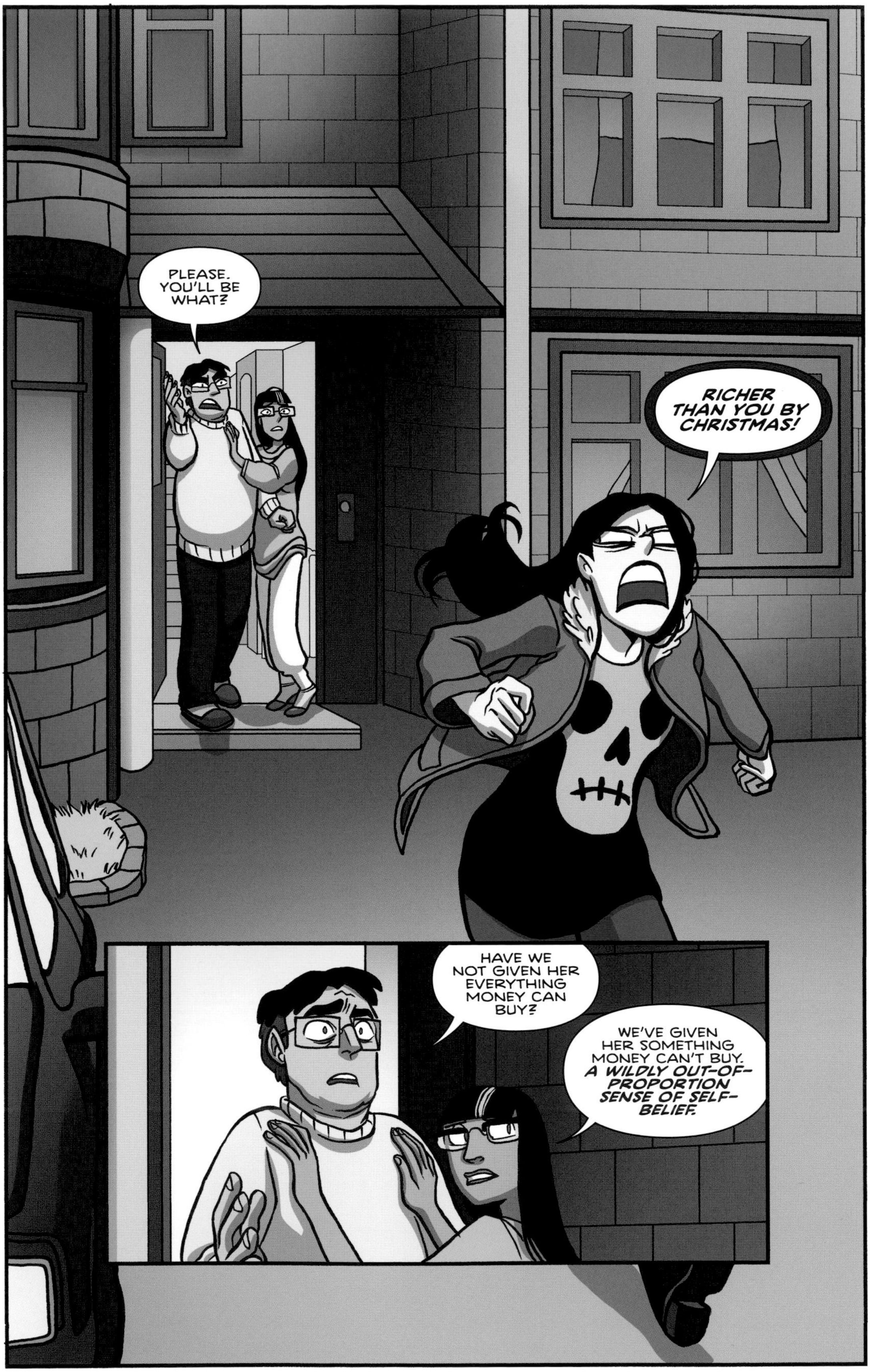
PLEASE. YOU'LL BE WHAT?
RICHER THAN YOU BY CHRISTMAS!
HAVE WE NOT GIVEN HER EVERYTHING MONEY CAN BUY?
WE'VE GIVEN HER SOMETHING MONEY CAN'T BUY. A WILDLY OUT-OF-PROPORTION SENSE OF SELF-BELIEF.

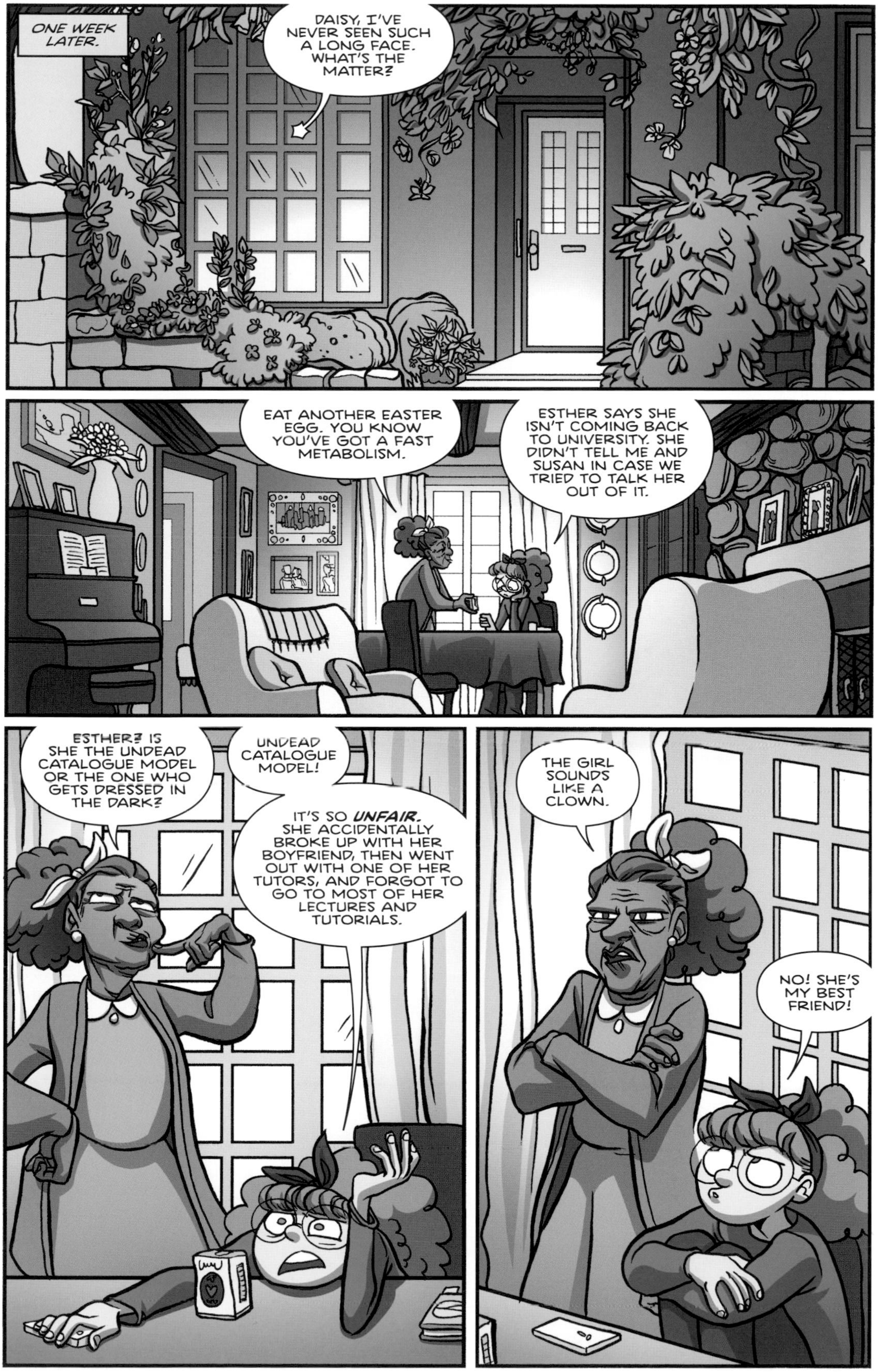
ONE WEEK LATER.
DAISY, I'VE NEVER SEEN SUCH A LONG FACE. WHAT'S THE MATTER?
EAT ANOTHER EASTER EGG. YOU KNOW YOU'VE GOT A FAST METABOLISM.
ESTHER SAYS SHE ISN'T COMING BACK TO UNIVERSITY. SHE DIDN'T TELL ME AND SUSAN IN CASE WE TRIED TO TALK HER OUT OF IT.
ESTHER? IS SHE THE UNDEAD CATALOGUE MODEL OR THE ONE WHO GETS DRESSED IN THE DARK?
UNDEAD CATALOGUE MODEL!
IT'S SO UNFAIR. SHE ACCIDENTALLY BROKE UP WITH HER BOYFRIEND, THEN WENT OUT WITH ONE OF HER TUTORS, AND FORGOT TO GO TO MOST OF HER LECTURES AND TUTORIALS.
THE GIRL SOUNDS LIKE A CLOWN.
NO! SHE'S MY BEST FRIEND!

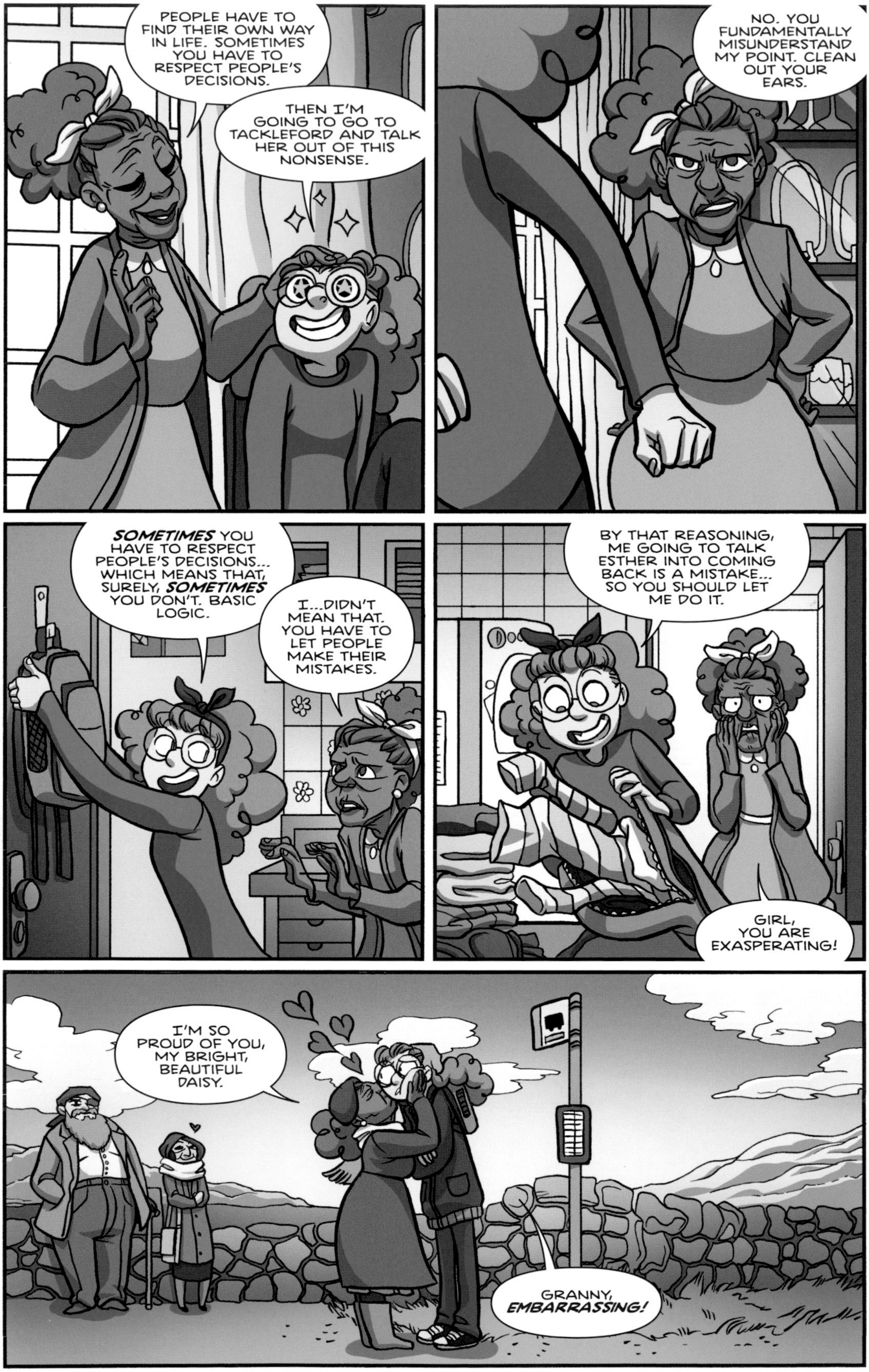

PEOPLE HAVE TO FIND THEIR OWN WAY IN LIFE. SOMETIMES YOU HAVE TO RESPECT PEOPLE'S DECISIONS.
THEN I'M GOING TO GO TO TACKLEFORD AND TALK HER OUT OF THIS NONSENSE.
NO. YOU FUNDAMENTALLY MISUNDERSTAND MY POINT. CLEAN OUT YOUR EARS.
*SOMETIMES* YOU HAVE TO RESPECT PEOPLE'S DECISIONS... WHICH MEANS THAT, SURELY, *SOMETIMES* YOU DON'T. BASIC LOGIC.
I...DIDN'T MEAN THAT. YOU HAVE TO LET PEOPLE MAKE THEIR MISTAKES.
BY THAT REASONING, ME GOING TO TALK ESTHER INTO COMING BACK IS A MISTAKE... SO YOU SHOULD LET ME DO IT.
GIRL, YOU ARE EXASPERATING!
I'M SO PROUD OF YOU, MY BRIGHT, BEAUTIFUL DAISY.
GRANNY, *EMBARRASSING!*

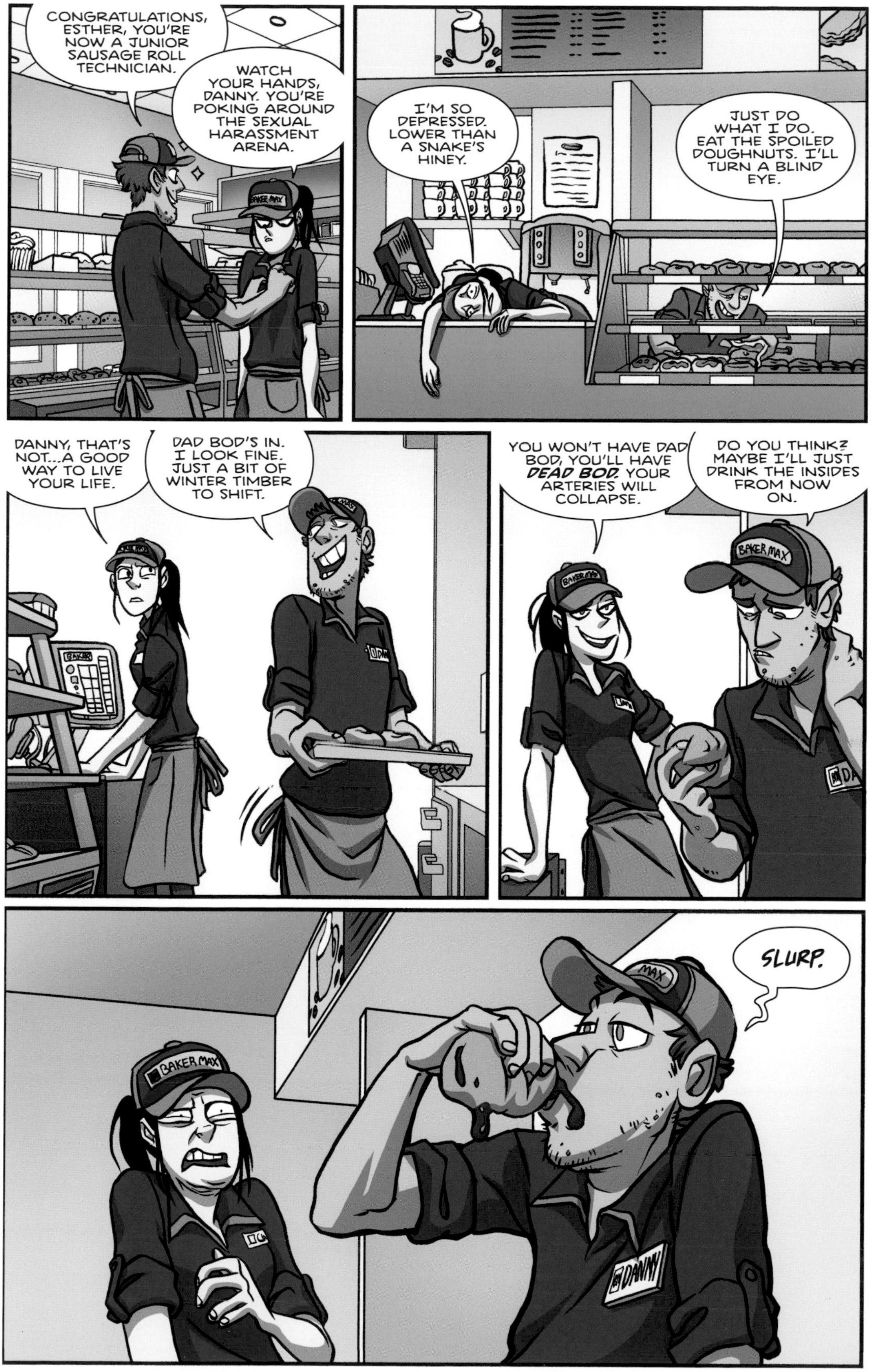
CONGRATULATIONS, ESTHER, YOU'RE NOW A JUNIOR SAUSAGE ROLL TECHNICIAN.
WATCH YOUR HANDS, DANNY. YOU'RE POKING AROUND THE SEXUAL HARASSMENT ARENA.
BAKER MAX
I'M SO DEPRESSED. LOWER THAN A SNAKE'S HINEY.
JUST DO WHAT I DO. EAT THE SPOILED DOUGHNUTS. I'LL TURN A BLIND EYE.
DANNY, THAT'S NOT...A GOOD WAY TO LIVE YOUR LIFE.
DAD BOD'S IN. I LOOK FINE. JUST A BIT OF WINTER TIMBER TO SHIFT.
YOU WON'T HAVE DAD BOD, YOU'LL HAVE DEAD BOD. YOUR ARTERIES WILL COLLAPSE.
DO YOU THINK? MAYBE I'LL JUST DRINK THE INSIDES FROM NOW ON.
BAKER MAX
SLURP.
BAKER MAX
DANNY

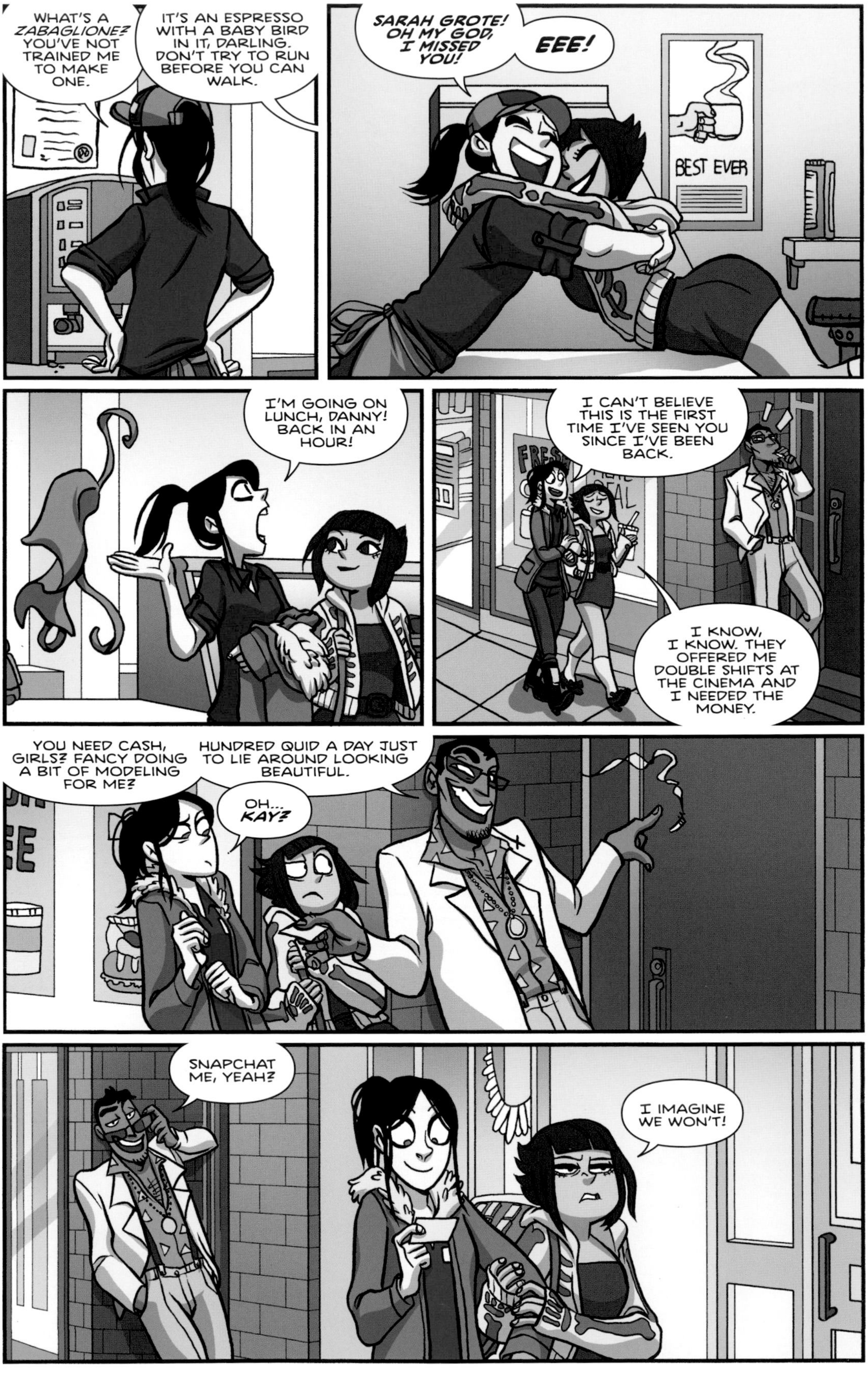
WHAT'S A ZABAGLIONE? YOU'VE NOT TRAINED ME TO MAKE ONE.
IT'S AN ESPRESSO WITH A BABY BIRD IN IT, DARLING. DON'T TRY TO RUN BEFORE YOU CAN WALK.
SARAH GROTE! OH MY GOD, I MISSED YOU!
EEE!
BEST EVER
I'M GOING ON LUNCH, DANNY! BACK IN AN HOUR!
I CAN'T BELIEVE THIS IS THE FIRST TIME I'VE SEEN YOU SINCE I'VE BEEN BACK.
I KNOW, I KNOW. THEY OFFERED ME DOUBLE SHIFTS AT THE CINEMA AND I NEEDED THE MONEY.
YOU NEED CASH, GIRLS? FANCY DOING A BIT OF MODELING FOR ME?
HUNDRED QUID A DAY JUST TO LIE AROUND LOOKING BEAUTIFUL.
OH... KAY?
SNAPCHAT ME, YEAH?
I IMAGINE WE WON'T!

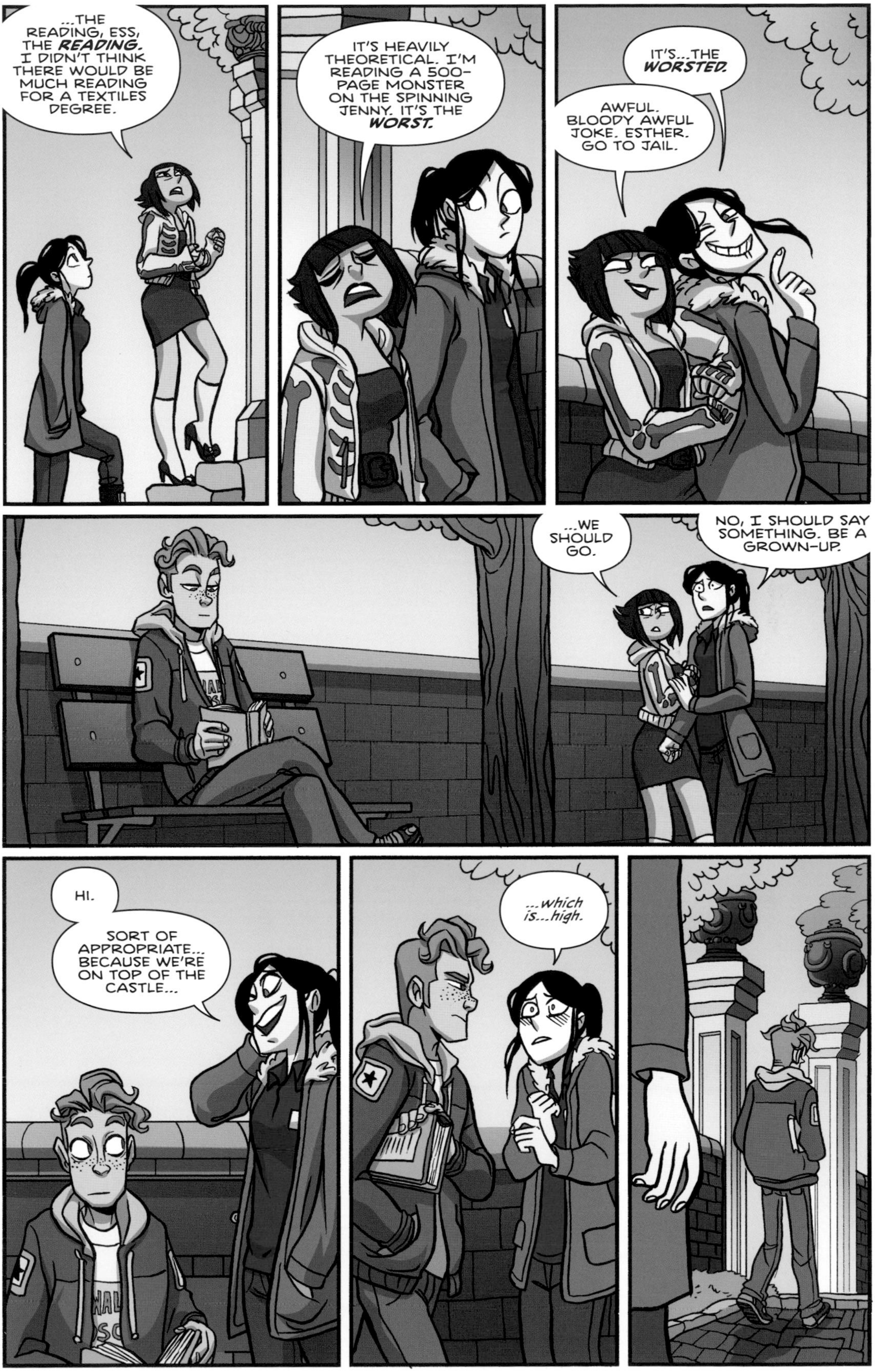
...THE READING, ESS, THE **READING.** I DIDN'T THINK THERE WOULD BE MUCH READING FOR A TEXTILES DEGREE.
IT'S HEAVILY THEORETICAL. I'M READING A 500-PAGE MONSTER ON THE SPINNING JENNY. IT'S THE **WORST.**
IT'S...THE **WORSTED.**
AWFUL. BLOODY AWFUL JOKE. ESTHER. GO TO JAIL.
...WE SHOULD GO.
NO, I SHOULD SAY SOMETHING. BE A GROWN-UP.
HI.
SORT OF APPROPRIATE... BECAUSE WE'RE ON TOP OF THE CASTLE...
*...which is...high.*

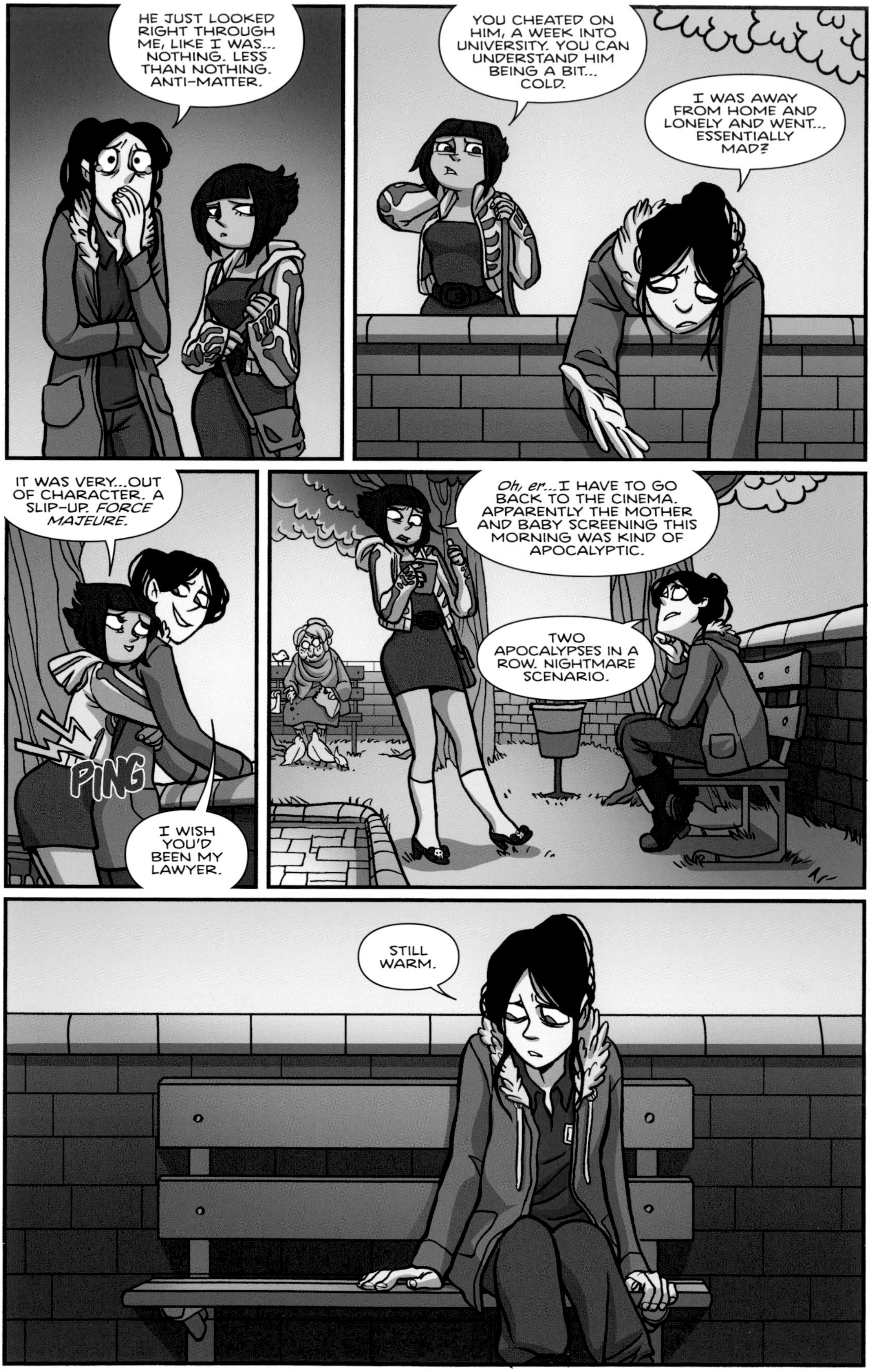
HE JUST LOOKED RIGHT THROUGH ME, LIKE I WAS... NOTHING. LESS THAN NOTHING. ANTI-MATTER.
YOU CHEATED ON HIM, A WEEK INTO UNIVERSITY. YOU CAN UNDERSTAND HIM BEING A BIT... COLD.
I WAS AWAY FROM HOME AND LONELY AND WENT... ESSENTIALLY MAD?
IT WAS VERY...OUT OF CHARACTER. A SLIP-UP. *FORCE MAJEURE.*
PING
I WISH YOU'D BEEN MY LAWYER.
*Oh, er*...I HAVE TO GO BACK TO THE CINEMA. APPARENTLY THE MOTHER AND BABY SCREENING THIS MORNING WAS KIND OF APOCALYPTIC.
TWO APOCALYPSES IN A ROW. NIGHTMARE SCENARIO.
STILL WARM.

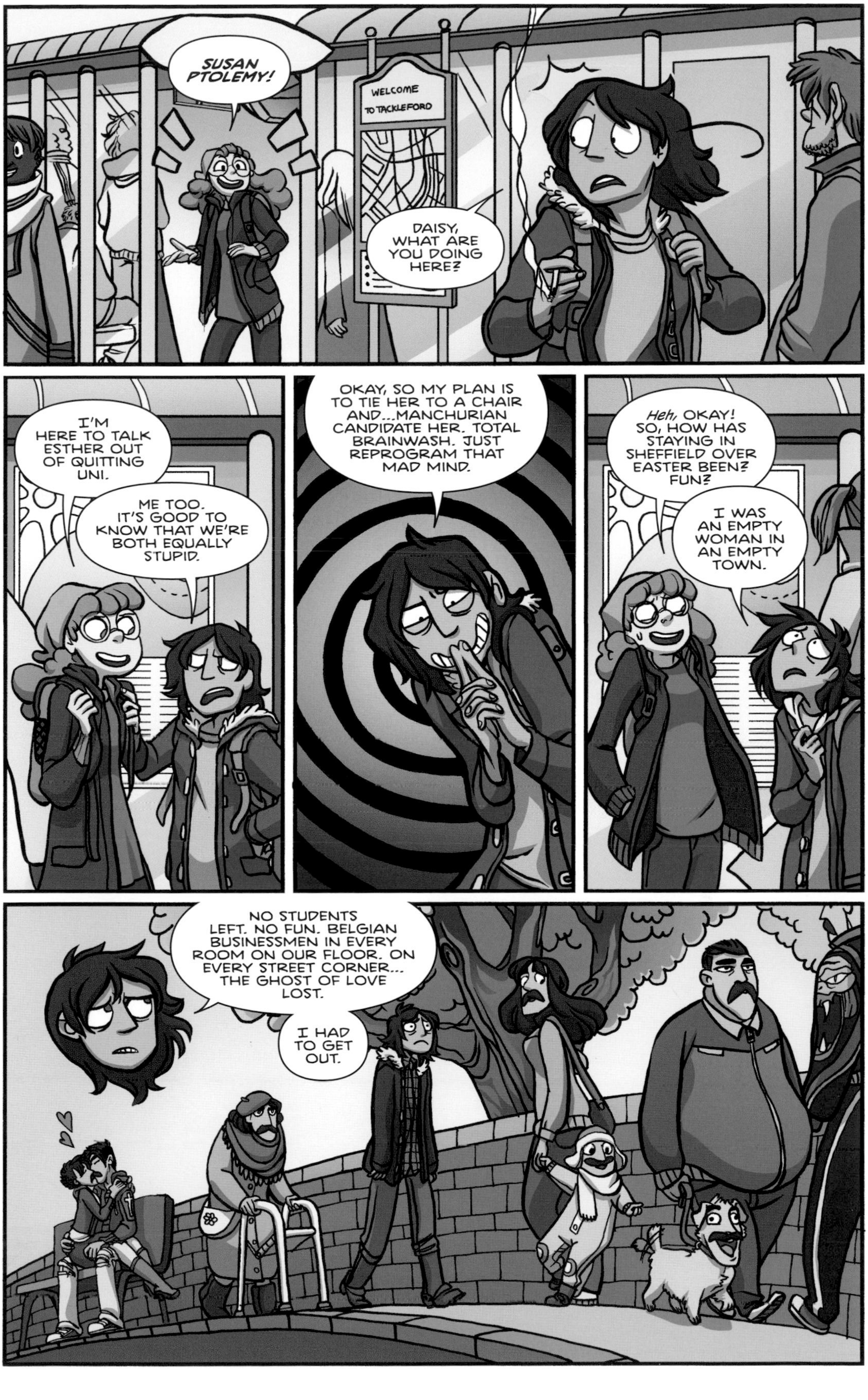
SUSAN PTOLEMY!
WELCOME TO TACKLEFORD
DAISY, WHAT ARE YOU DOING HERE?
I'M HERE TO TALK ESTHER OUT OF QUITTING UNI.
ME TOO. IT'S GOOD TO KNOW THAT WE'RE BOTH EQUALLY STUPID.
OKAY, SO MY PLAN IS TO TIE HER TO A CHAIR AND... MANCHURIAN CANDIDATE HER. TOTAL BRAINWASH. JUST REPROGRAM THAT MAD MIND.
Heh, OKAY! SO, HOW HAS STAYING IN SHEFFIELD OVER EASTER BEEN? FUN?
I WAS AN EMPTY WOMAN IN AN EMPTY TOWN.
NO STUDENTS LEFT. NO FUN. BELGIAN BUSINESSMEN IN EVERY ROOM ON OUR FLOOR. ON EVERY STREET CORNER... THE GHOST OF LOVE LOST.
I HAD TO GET OUT.

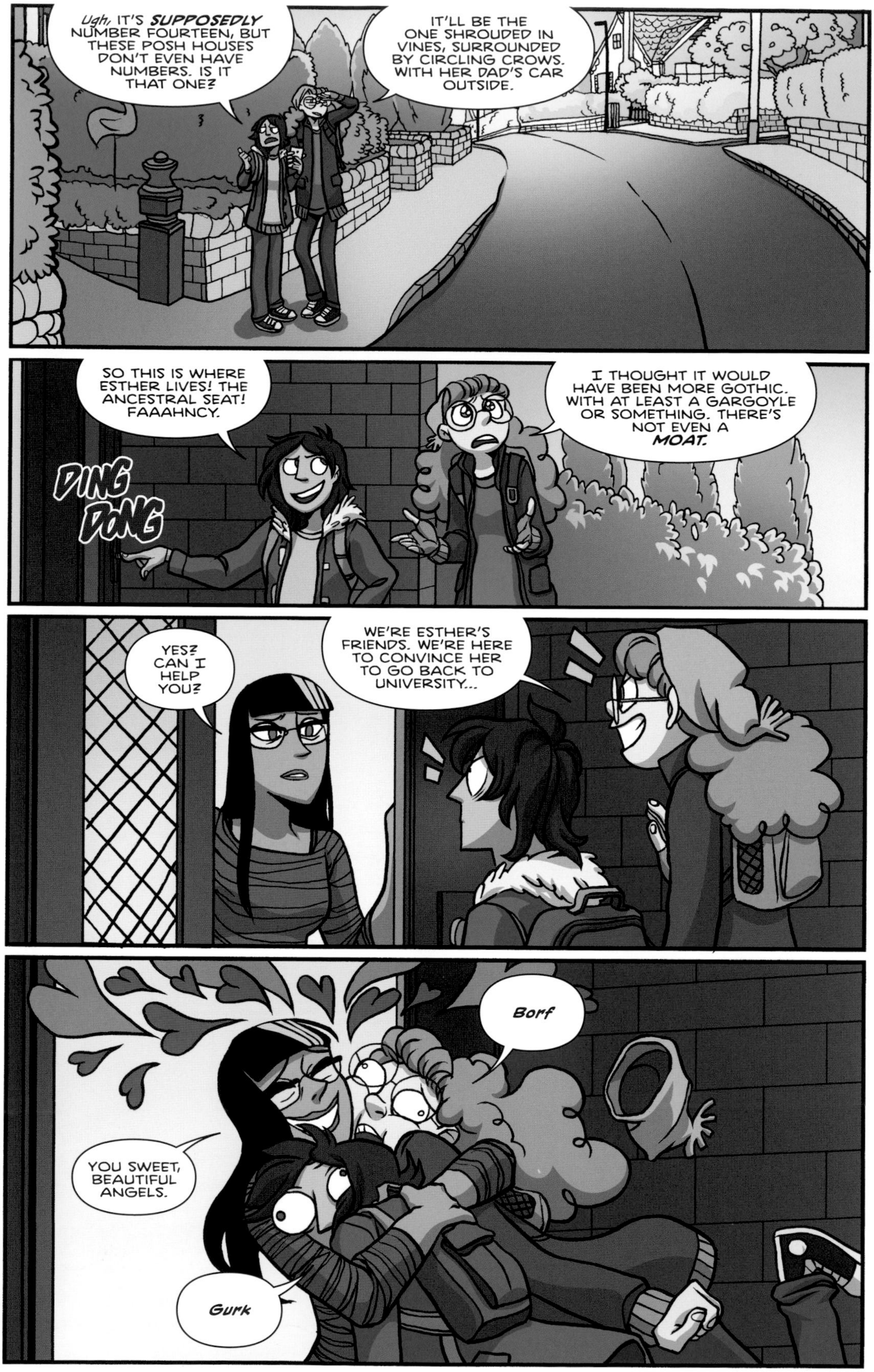
Ugh, IT'S SUPPOSEDLY NUMBER FOURTEEN, BUT THESE POSH HOUSES DON'T EVEN HAVE NUMBERS. IS IT THAT ONE?
IT'LL BE THE ONE SHROUDED IN VINES, SURROUNDED BY CIRCLING CROWS. WITH HER DAD'S CAR OUTSIDE.
SO THIS IS WHERE ESTHER LIVES! THE ANCESTRAL SEAT! FAAAHNCY.
I THOUGHT IT WOULD HAVE BEEN MORE GOTHIC. WITH AT LEAST A GARGOYLE OR SOMETHING. THERE'S NOT EVEN A MOAT.
DING DONG
YES? CAN I HELP YOU?
WE'RE ESTHER'S FRIENDS. WE'RE HERE TO CONVINCE HER TO GO BACK TO UNIVERSITY...
Borf
YOU SWEET, BEAUTIFUL ANGELS.
Gurk

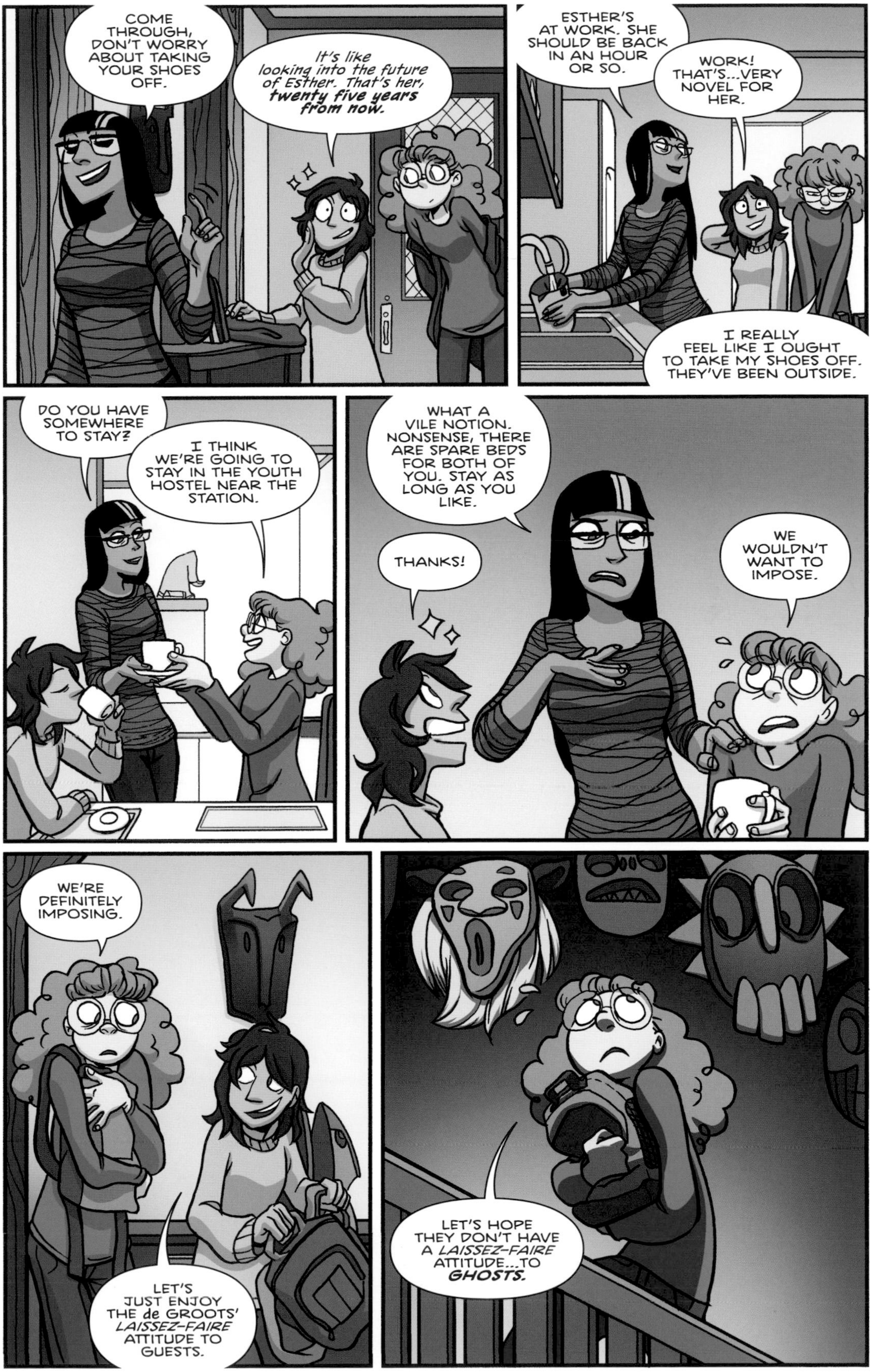
COME THROUGH, DON'T WORRY ABOUT TAKING YOUR SHOES OFF.
*It's like looking into the future of Esther. That's her,* ***twenty five years from now.***
ESTHER'S AT WORK. SHE SHOULD BE BACK IN AN HOUR OR SO.
WORK! THAT'S...VERY NOVEL FOR HER.
I REALLY FEEL LIKE I OUGHT TO TAKE MY SHOES OFF. THEY'VE BEEN OUTSIDE.
DO YOU HAVE SOMEWHERE TO STAY?
I THINK WE'RE GOING TO STAY IN THE YOUTH HOSTEL NEAR THE STATION.
WHAT A VILE NOTION. NONSENSE, THERE ARE SPARE BEDS FOR BOTH OF YOU. STAY AS LONG AS YOU LIKE.
THANKS!
WE WOULDN'T WANT TO IMPOSE.
WE'RE DEFINITELY IMPOSING.
LET'S JUST ENJOY THE de GROOTS' *LAISSEZ-FAIRE* ATTITUDE TO GUESTS.
LET'S HOPE THEY DON'T HAVE A *LAISSEZ-FAIRE* ATTITUDE...TO ***GHOSTS.***

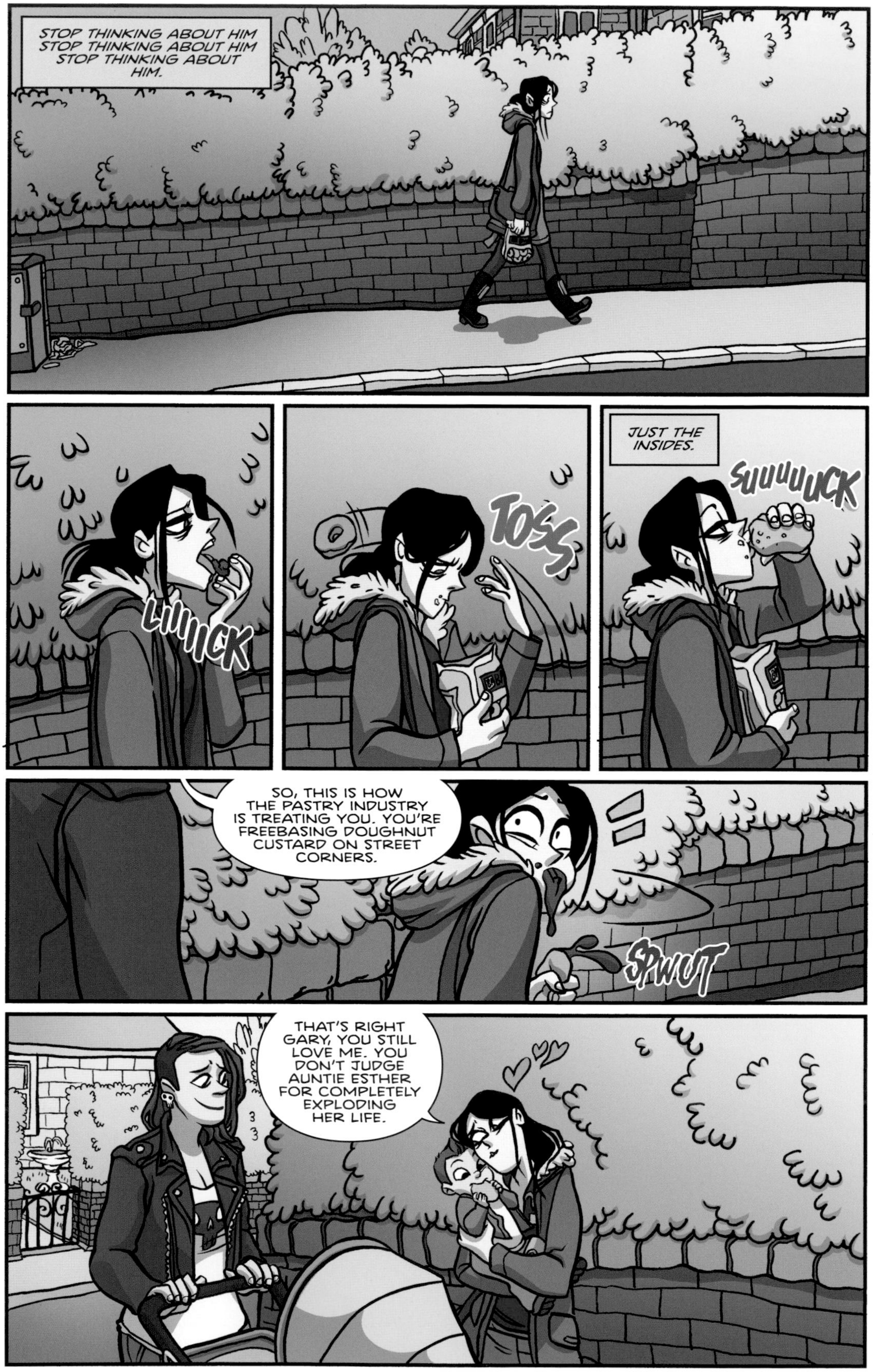
STOP THINKING ABOUT HIM STOP THINKING ABOUT HIM STOP THINKING ABOUT HIM.
LIIIIICK
TOSS
JUST THE INSIDES.
SUUUUUCK
SO, THIS IS HOW THE PASTRY INDUSTRY IS TREATING YOU. YOU'RE FREEBASING DOUGHNUT CUSTARD ON STREET CORNERS.
SPWUT
THAT'S RIGHT GARY, YOU STILL LOVE ME. YOU DON'T JUDGE AUNTIE ESTHER FOR COMPLETELY EXPLODING HER LIFE.

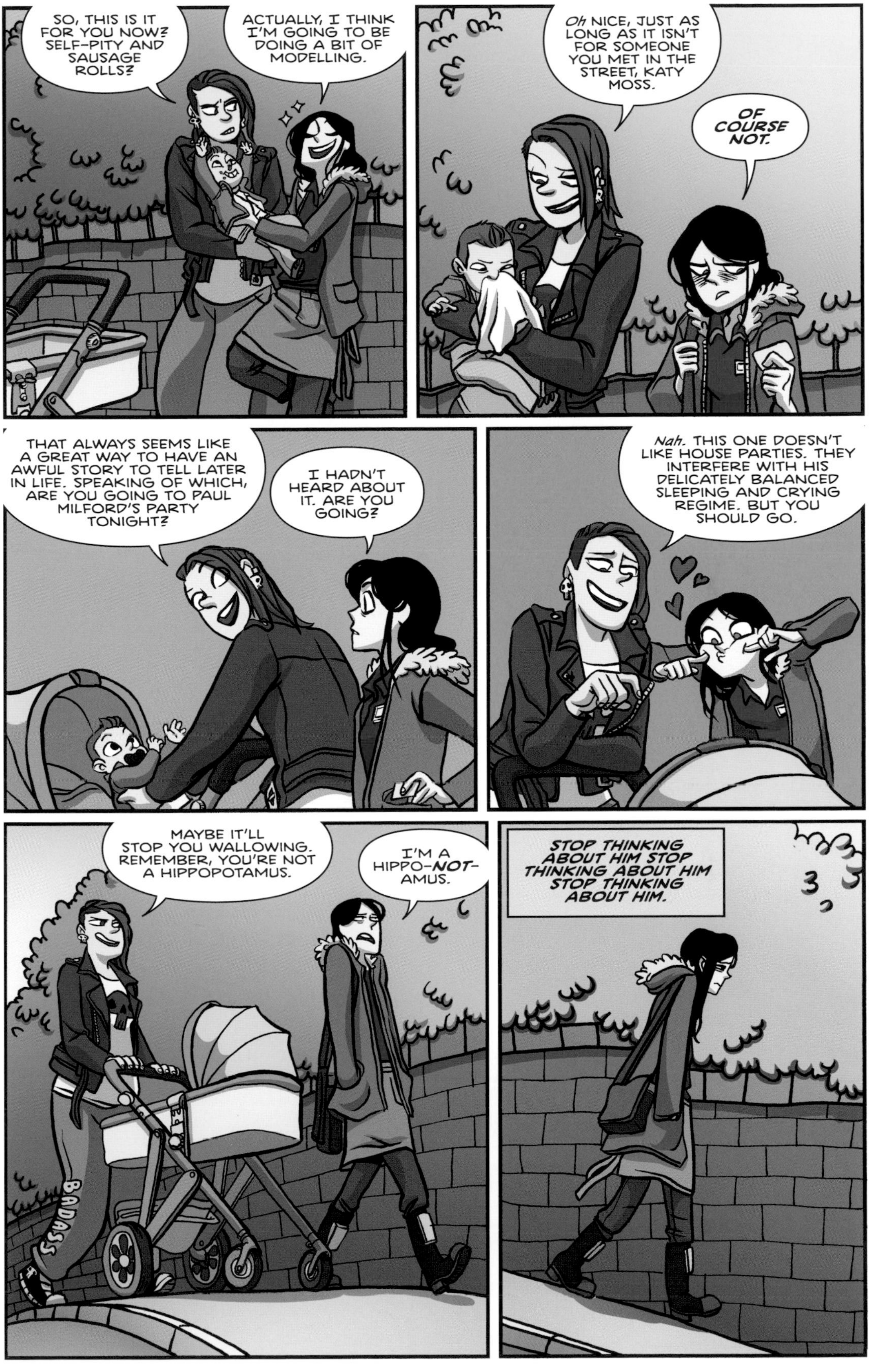
SO, THIS IS IT FOR YOU NOW? SELF-PITY AND SAUSAGE ROLLS?
ACTUALLY, I THINK I'M GOING TO BE DOING A BIT OF MODELLING.
*Oh* NICE, JUST AS LONG AS IT ISN'T FOR SOMEONE YOU MET IN THE STREET, KATY MOSS.
OF COURSE NOT.
THAT ALWAYS SEEMS LIKE A GREAT WAY TO HAVE AN AWFUL STORY TO TELL LATER IN LIFE. SPEAKING OF WHICH, ARE YOU GOING TO PAUL MILFORD'S PARTY TONIGHT?
I HADN'T HEARD ABOUT IT. ARE YOU GOING?
*Nah.* THIS ONE DOESN'T LIKE HOUSE PARTIES. THEY INTERFERE WITH HIS DELICATELY BALANCED SLEEPING AND CRYING REGIME. BUT YOU SHOULD GO.
MAYBE IT'LL STOP YOU WALLOWING. REMEMBER, YOU'RE NOT A HIPPOPOTAMUS.
I'M A HIPPO-**NOT**-AMUS.
BADASS
STOP THINKING ABOUT HIM STOP THINKING ABOUT HIM STOP THINKING ABOUT HIM.

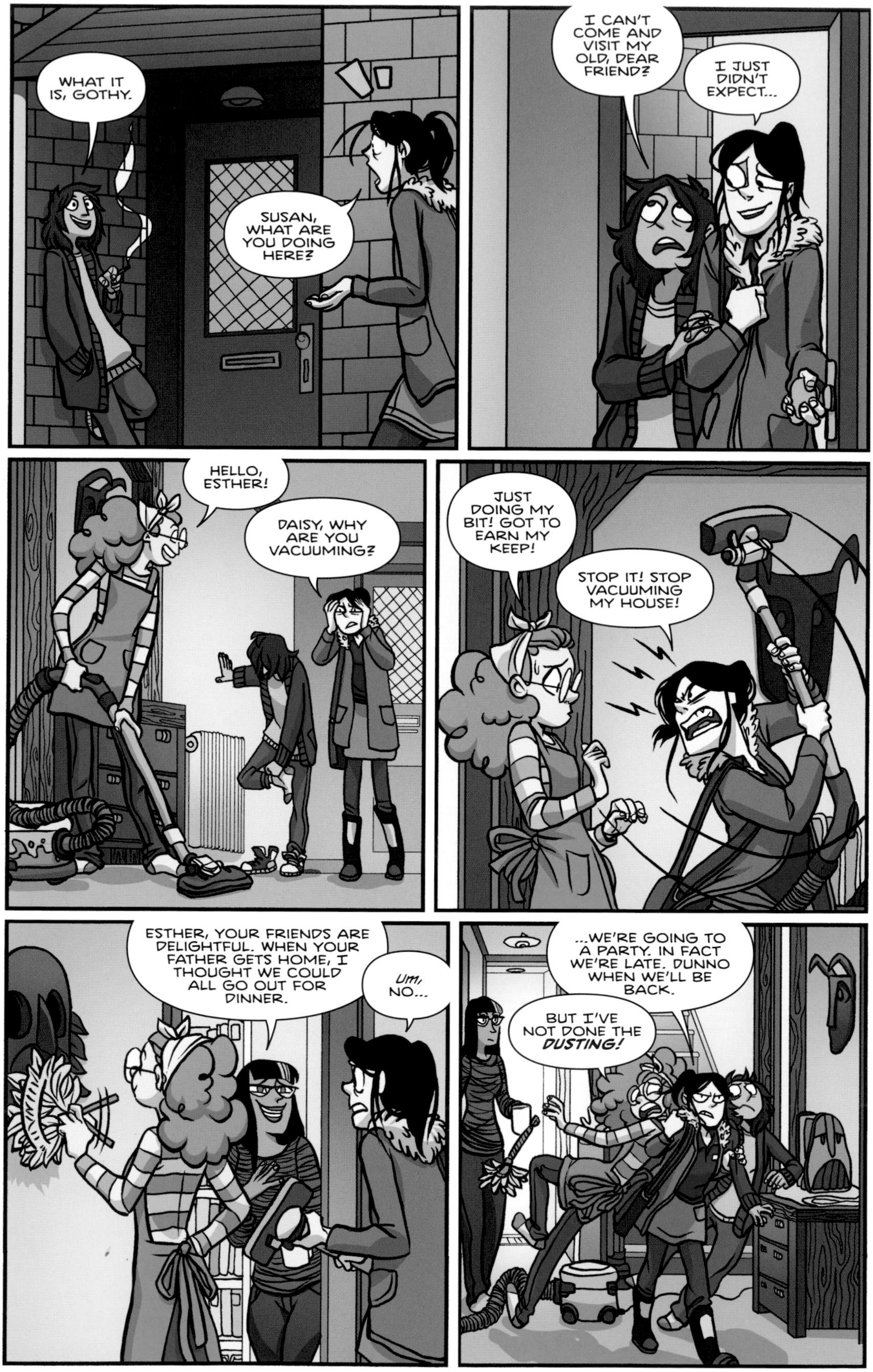
WHAT IT IS, GOTHY.
SUSAN, WHAT ARE YOU DOING HERE?
I CAN'T COME AND VISIT MY OLD, DEAR FRIEND?
I JUST DIDN'T EXPECT...
HELLO, ESTHER!
DAISY, WHY ARE YOU VACUUMING?
JUST DOING MY BIT! GOT TO EARN MY KEEP!
STOP IT! STOP VACUUMING MY HOUSE!
ESTHER, YOUR FRIENDS ARE DELIGHTFUL. WHEN YOUR FATHER GETS HOME, I THOUGHT WE COULD ALL GO OUT FOR DINNER.
UM, NO...
...WE'RE GOING TO A PARTY. IN FACT WE'RE LATE. DUNNO WHEN WE'LL BE BACK.
BUT I'VE NOT DONE THE DUSTING!

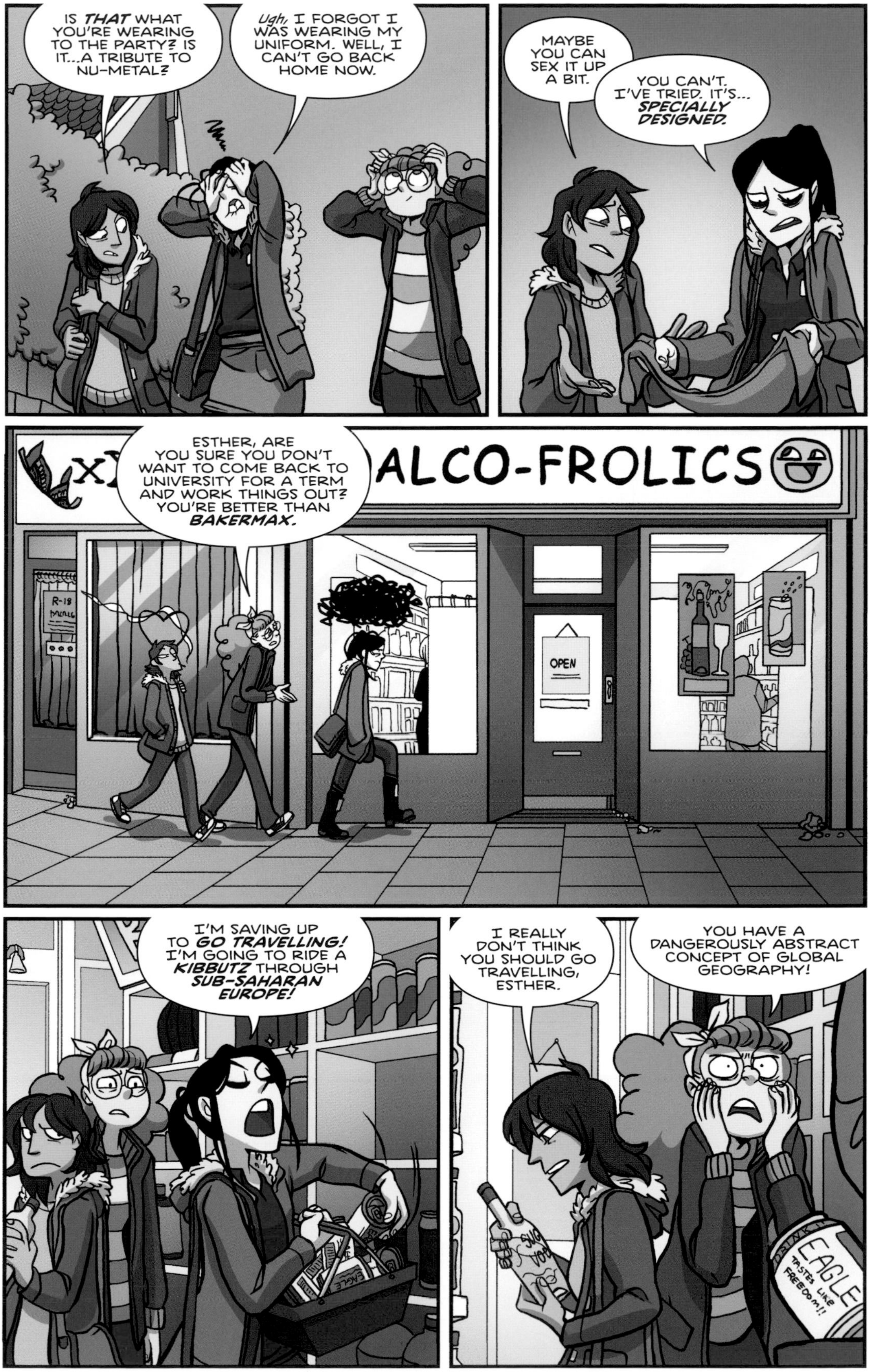

IS *THAT* WHAT YOU'RE WEARING TO THE PARTY? IS IT...A TRIBUTE TO NU-METAL?
*Ugh,* I FORGOT I WAS WEARING MY UNIFORM. WELL, I CAN'T GO BACK HOME NOW.
MAYBE YOU CAN SEX IT UP A BIT.
YOU CAN'T. I'VE TRIED. IT'S... ***SPECIALLY DESIGNED.***
ALCO-FROLICS
ESTHER, ARE YOU SURE YOU DON'T WANT TO COME BACK TO UNIVERSITY FOR A TERM AND WORK THINGS OUT? YOU'RE BETTER THAN ***BAKERMAX.***
R-18
OPEN
I'M SAVING UP TO ***GO TRAVELLING!*** I'M GOING TO RIDE A ***KIBBUTZ*** THROUGH ***SUB-SAHARAN EUROPE!***
I REALLY DON'T THINK YOU SHOULD GO TRAVELLING, ESTHER.
YOU HAVE A DANGEROUSLY ABSTRACT CONCEPT OF GLOBAL GEOGRAPHY!
EAGLE
TASTES LIKE FREEDOM!!

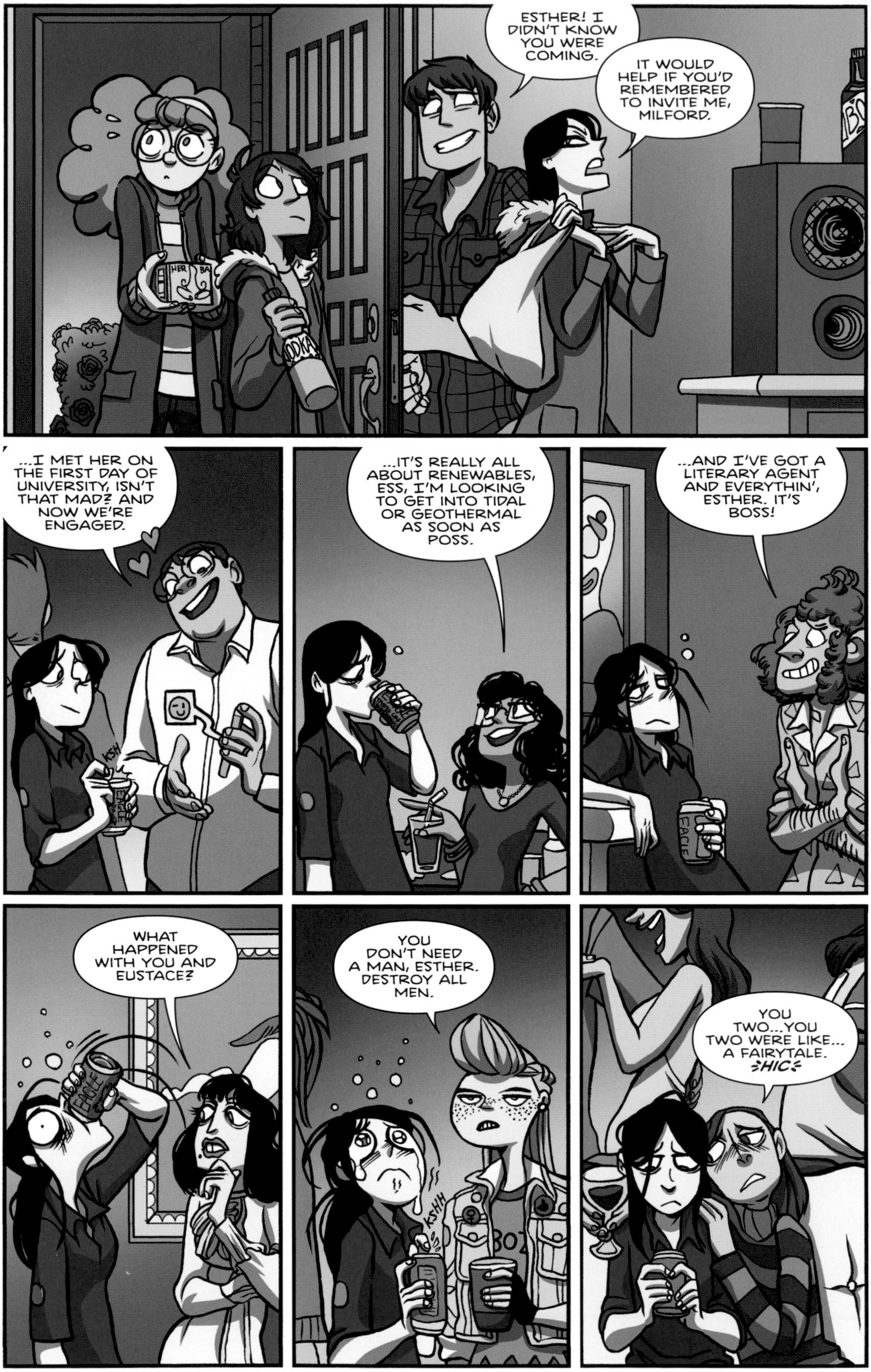
ESTHER! I DIDN'T KNOW YOU WERE COMING.
IT WOULD HELP IF YOU'D REMEMBERED TO INVITE ME, MILFORD.
VODKA
...I MET HER ON THE FIRST DAY OF UNIVERSITY, ISN'T THAT MAD? AND NOW WE'RE ENGAGED.
KSH
...IT'S REALLY ALL ABOUT RENEWABLES, ESS, I'M LOOKING TO GET INTO TIDAL OR GEOTHERMAL AS SOON AS POSS.
...AND I'VE GOT A LITERARY AGENT AND EVERYTHIN', ESTHER. IT'S BOSS!
WHAT HAPPENED WITH YOU AND EUSTACE?
EAGLE
YOU DON'T NEED A MAN, ESTHER. DESTROY ALL MEN.
KSHH
YOU TWO...YOU TWO WERE LIKE... A FAIRYTALE.
HIC

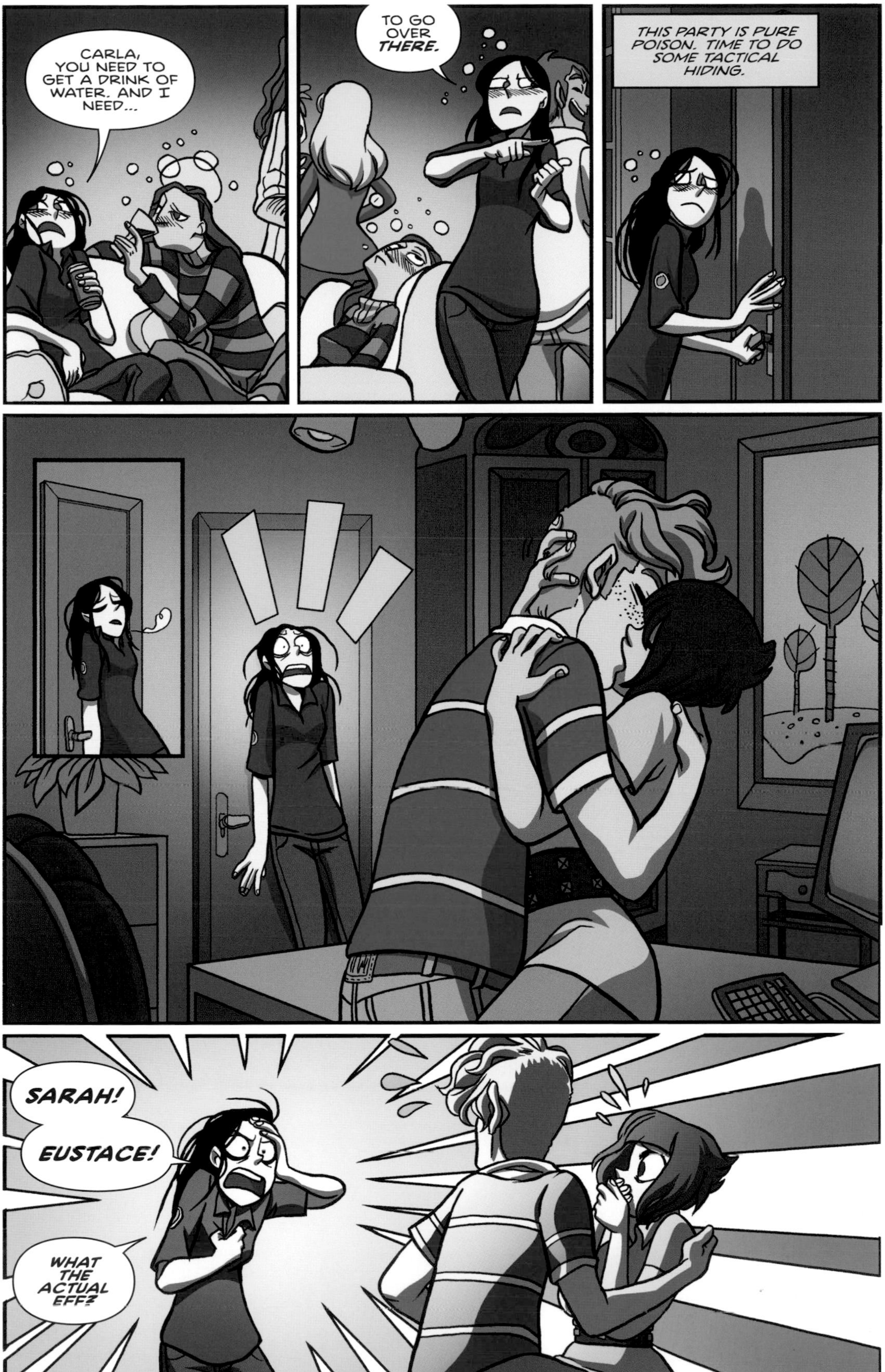
CARLA, YOU NEED TO GET A DRINK OF WATER. AND I NEED...
TO GO OVER *THERE.*
THIS PARTY IS PURE POISON. TIME TO DO SOME TACTICAL HIDING.
SARAH!
EUSTACE!
WHAT THE ACTUAL EFF?

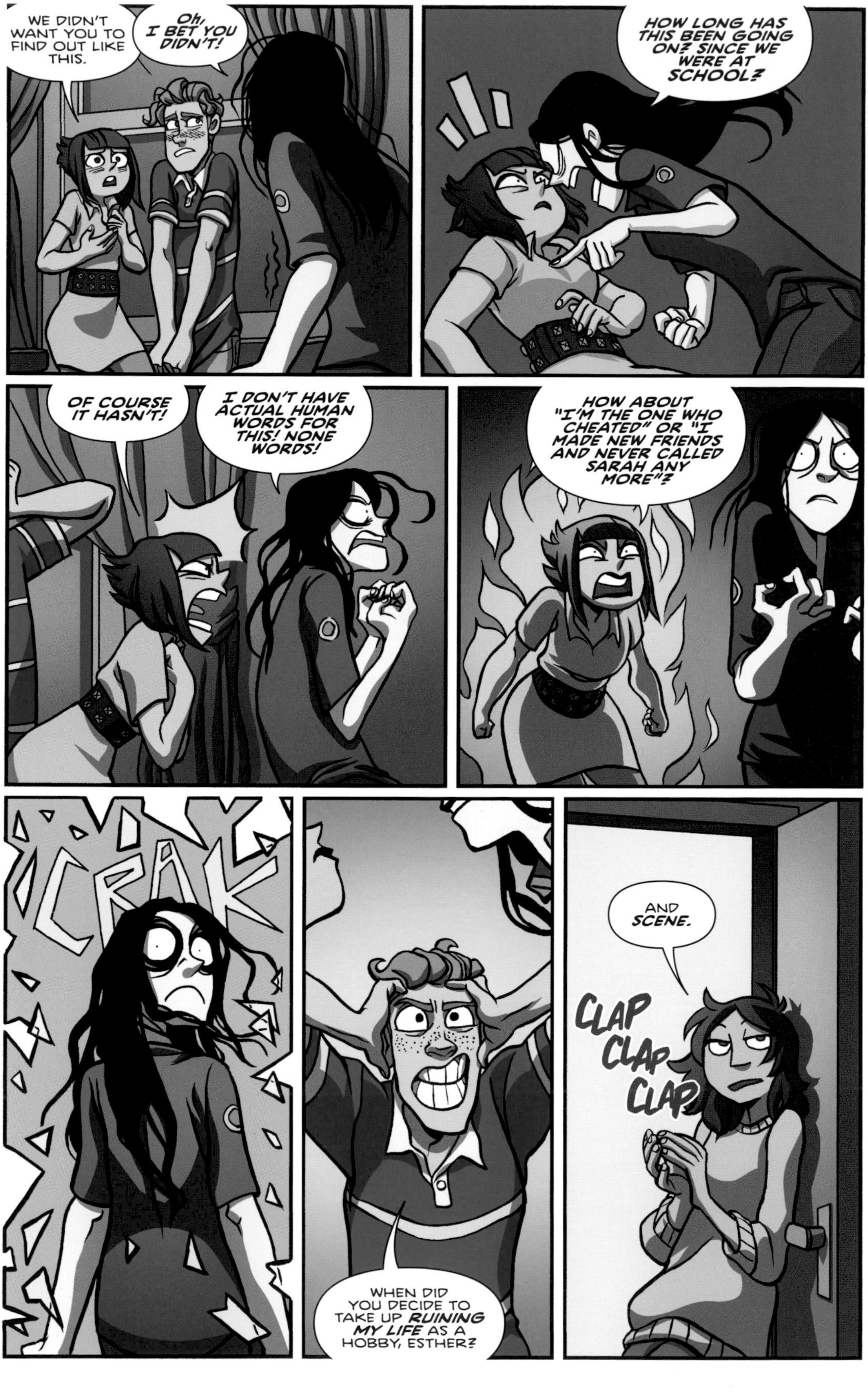
WE DIDN'T WANT YOU TO FIND OUT LIKE THIS.
Oh, I BET YOU DIDN'T!
HOW LONG HAS THIS BEEN GOING ON? SINCE WE WERE AT SCHOOL?
OF COURSE IT HASN'T!
I DON'T HAVE ACTUAL HUMAN WORDS FOR THIS! NONE WORDS!
HOW ABOUT "I'M THE ONE WHO CHEATED" OR "I MADE NEW FRIENDS AND NEVER CALLED SARAH ANY MORE"?
CRAK
WHEN DID YOU DECIDE TO TAKE UP RUINING MY LIFE AS A HOBBY, ESTHER?
AND SCENE.
CLAP CLAP CLAP

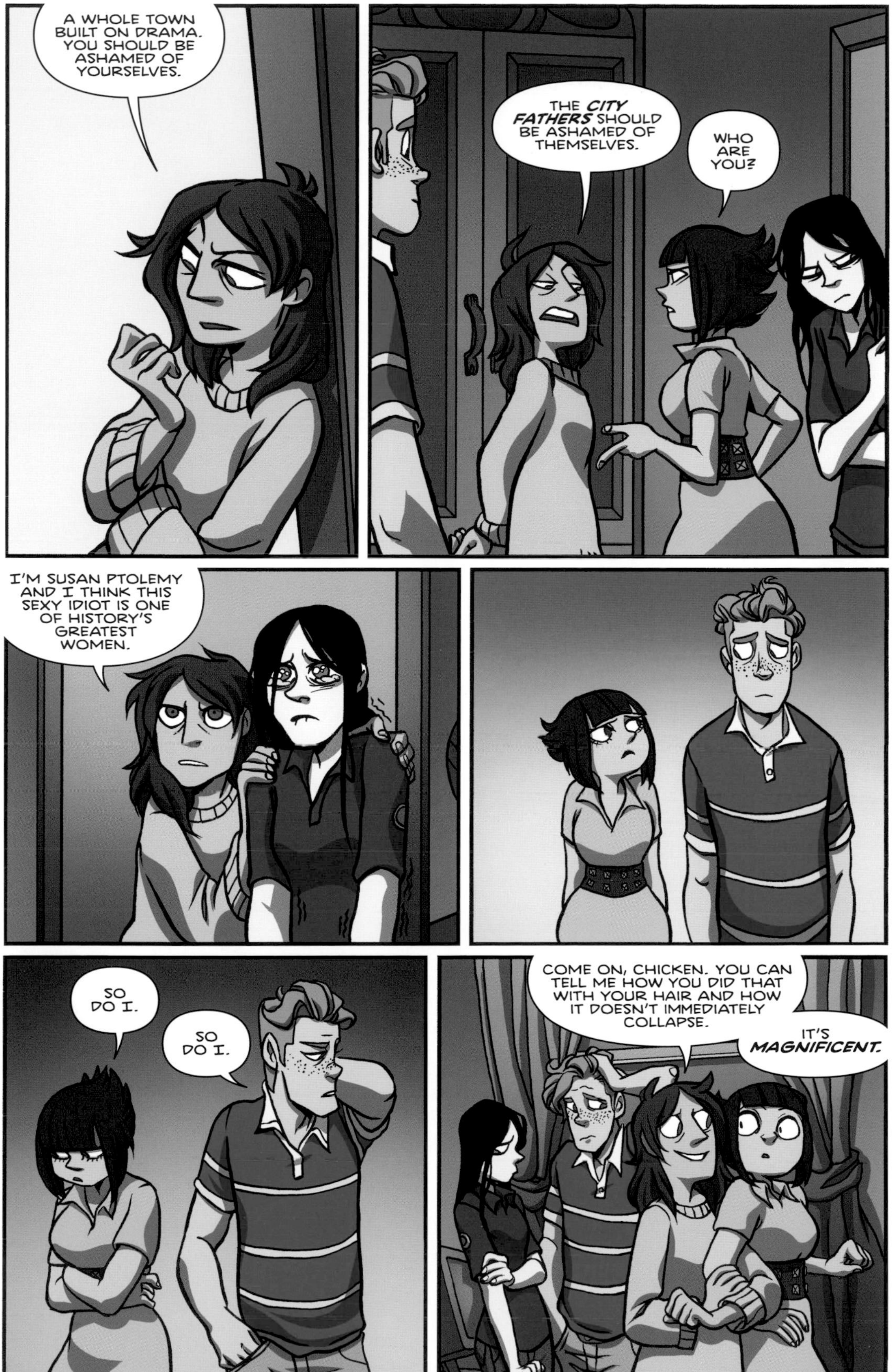
A WHOLE TOWN BUILT ON DRAMA. YOU SHOULD BE ASHAMED OF YOURSELVES.
THE CITY FATHERS SHOULD BE ASHAMED OF THEMSELVES.
WHO ARE YOU?
I'M SUSAN PTOLEMY AND I THINK THIS SEXY IDIOT IS ONE OF HISTORY'S GREATEST WOMEN.
SO DO I.
SO DO I.
COME ON, CHICKEN. YOU CAN TELL ME HOW YOU DID THAT WITH YOUR HAIR AND HOW IT DOESN'T IMMEDIATELY COLLAPSE.
IT'S MAGNIFICENT.

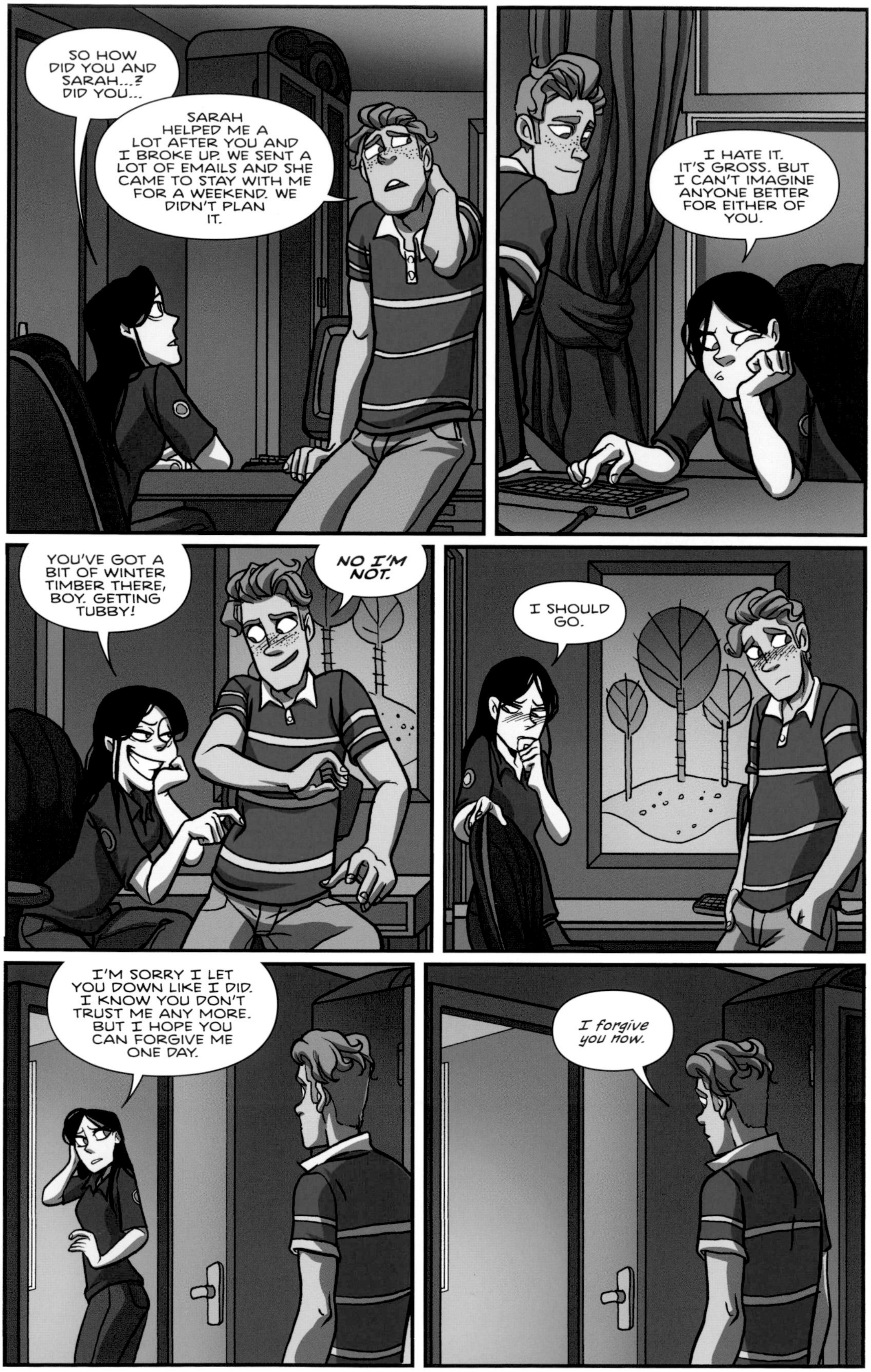
SO HOW DID YOU AND SARAH...? DID YOU...
SARAH HELPED ME A LOT AFTER YOU AND I BROKE UP. WE SENT A LOT OF EMAILS AND SHE CAME TO STAY WITH ME FOR A WEEKEND. WE DIDN'T PLAN IT.
I HATE IT. IT'S GROSS. BUT I CAN'T IMAGINE ANYONE BETTER FOR EITHER OF YOU.
YOU'VE GOT A BIT OF WINTER TIMBER THERE, BOY. GETTING TUBBY!
NO I'M NOT.
I SHOULD GO.
I'M SORRY I LET YOU DOWN LIKE I DID. I KNOW YOU DON'T TRUST ME ANY MORE. BUT I HOPE YOU CAN FORGIVE ME ONE DAY.
I forgive you now.

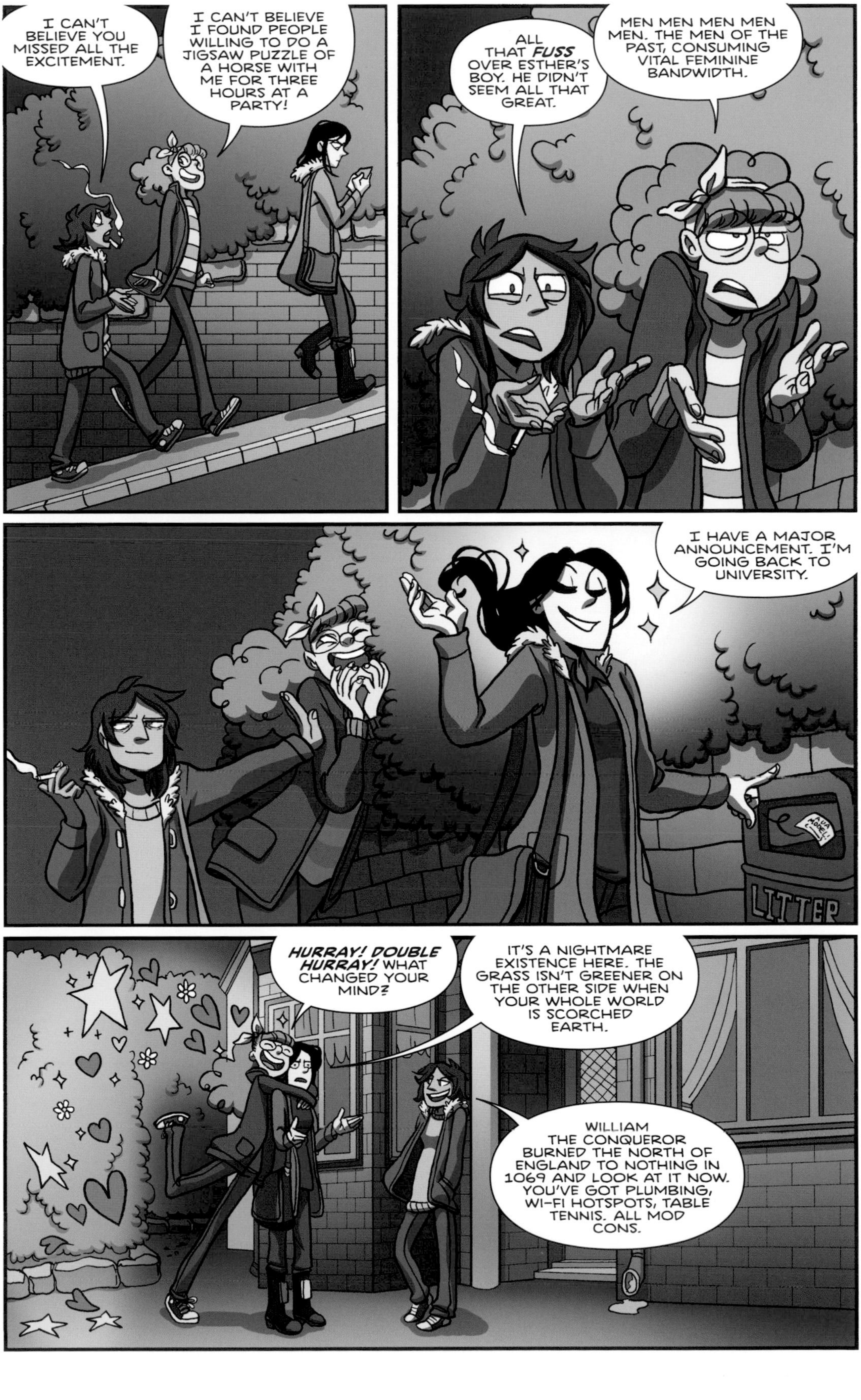
I CAN'T BELIEVE YOU MISSED ALL THE EXCITEMENT.
I CAN'T BELIEVE I FOUND PEOPLE WILLING TO DO A JIGSAW PUZZLE OF A HORSE WITH ME FOR THREE HOURS AT A PARTY!
ALL THAT FUSS OVER ESTHER'S BOY. HE DIDN'T SEEM ALL THAT GREAT.
MEN MEN MEN MEN MEN. THE MEN OF THE PAST, CONSUMING VITAL FEMININE BANDWIDTH.
I HAVE A MAJOR ANNOUNCEMENT. I'M GOING BACK TO UNIVERSITY.
LITTER
HURRAY! DOUBLE HURRAY! WHAT CHANGED YOUR MIND?
IT'S A NIGHTMARE EXISTENCE HERE. THE GRASS ISN'T GREENER ON THE OTHER SIDE WHEN YOUR WHOLE WORLD IS SCORCHED EARTH.
WILLIAM THE CONQUEROR BURNED THE NORTH OF ENGLAND TO NOTHING IN 1069 AND LOOK AT IT NOW. YOU'VE GOT PLUMBING, WI-FI HOTSPOTS, TABLE TENNIS. ALL MOD CONS.

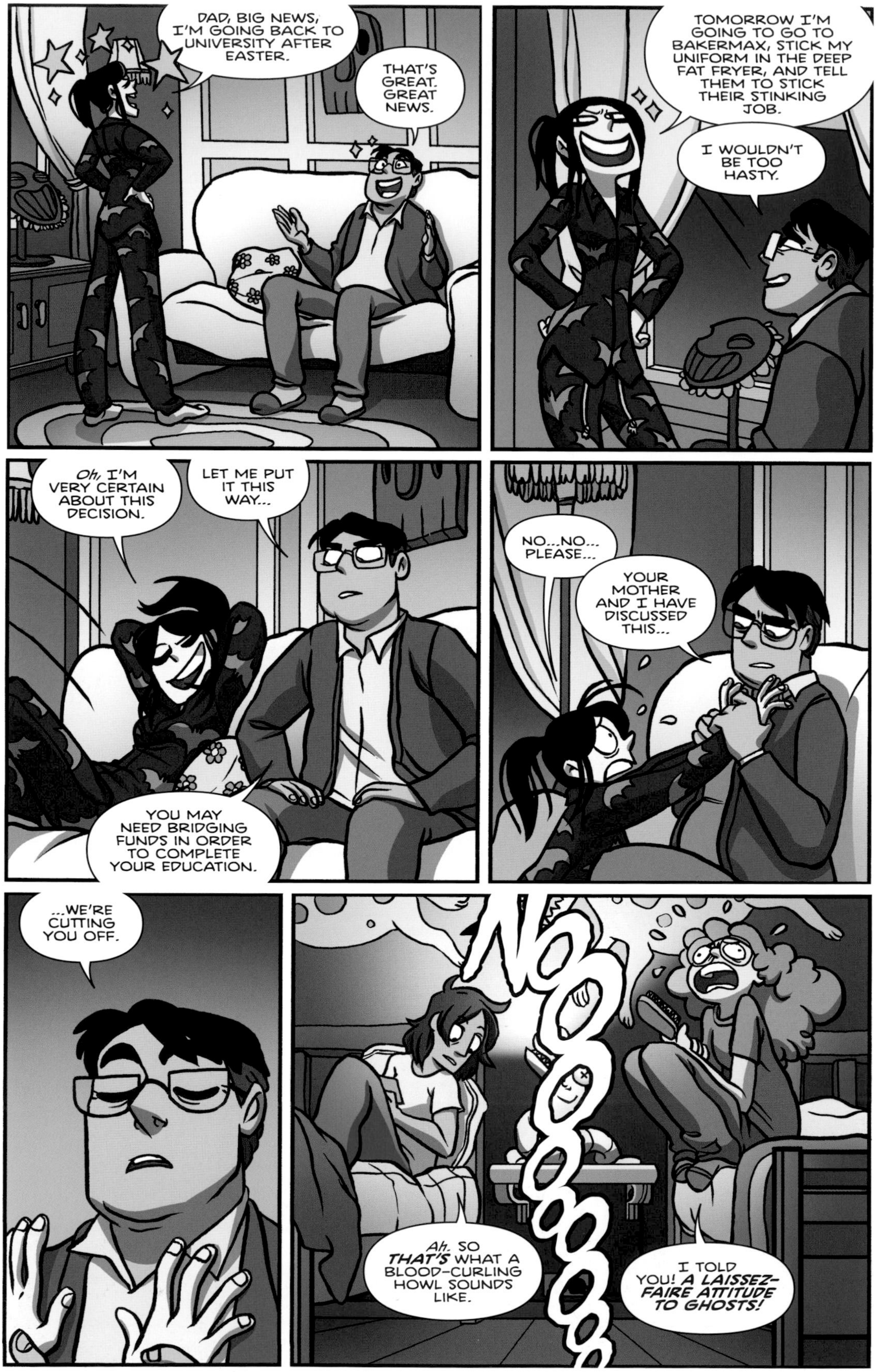
DAD, BIG NEWS, I'M GOING BACK TO UNIVERSITY AFTER EASTER.
THAT'S GREAT. GREAT NEWS.
TOMORROW I'M GOING TO GO TO BAKERMAX, STICK MY UNIFORM IN THE DEEP FAT FRYER, AND TELL THEM TO STICK THEIR STINKING JOB.
I WOULDN'T BE TOO HASTY.
*Oh,* I'M VERY CERTAIN ABOUT THIS DECISION.
LET ME PUT IT THIS WAY...
YOU MAY NEED BRIDGING FUNDS IN ORDER TO COMPLETE YOUR EDUCATION.
NO...NO... PLEASE...
YOUR MOTHER AND I HAVE DISCUSSED THIS...
...WE'RE CUTTING YOU OFF.
NOOOOOOOOOO
*Ah.* SO ***THAT'S*** WHAT A BLOOD-CURLING HOWL SOUNDS LIKE.
I TOLD YOU! ***A LAISSEZ-FAIRE ATTITUDE TO GHOSTS!***

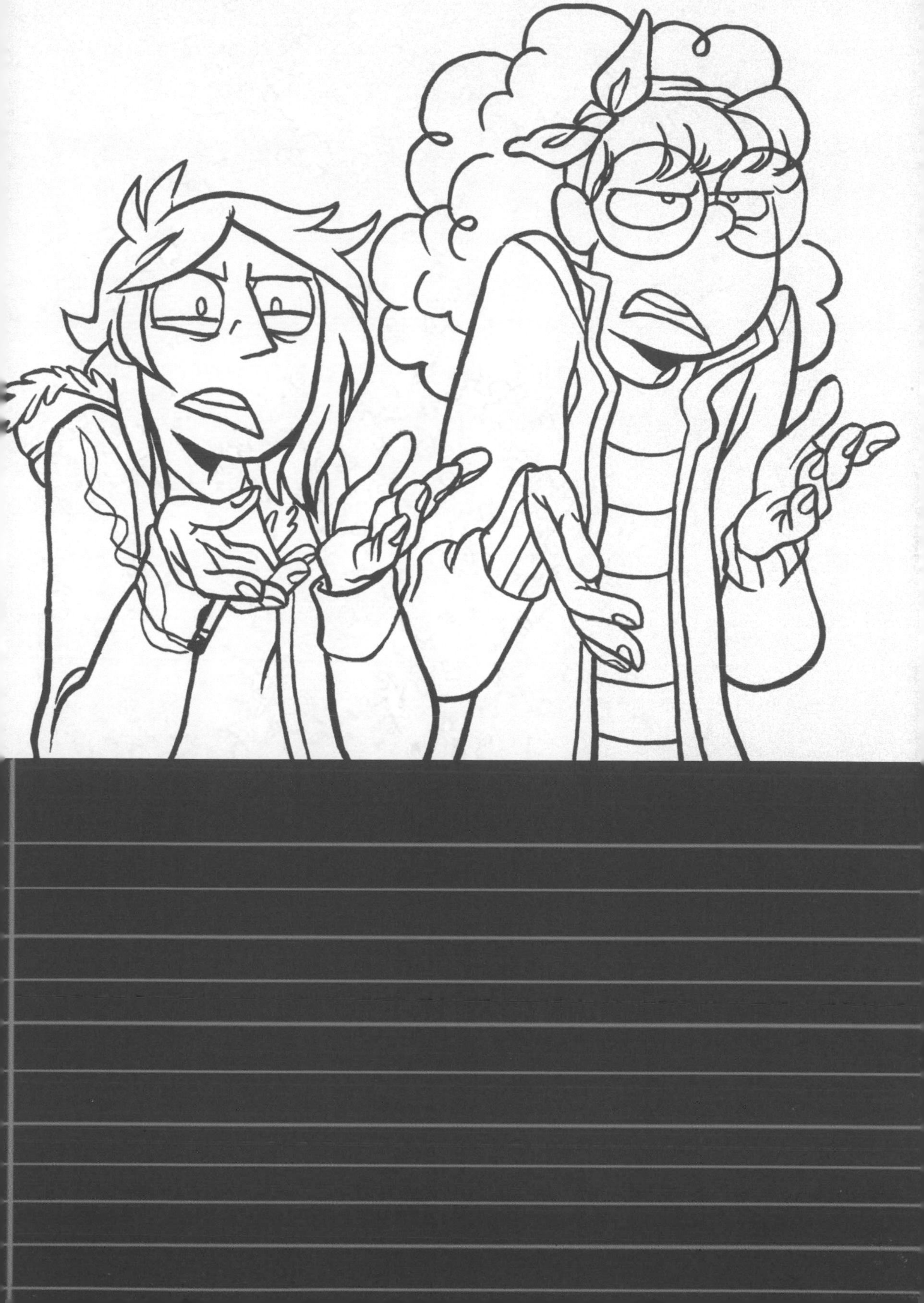

# CHAPTER
# FOURTEEN

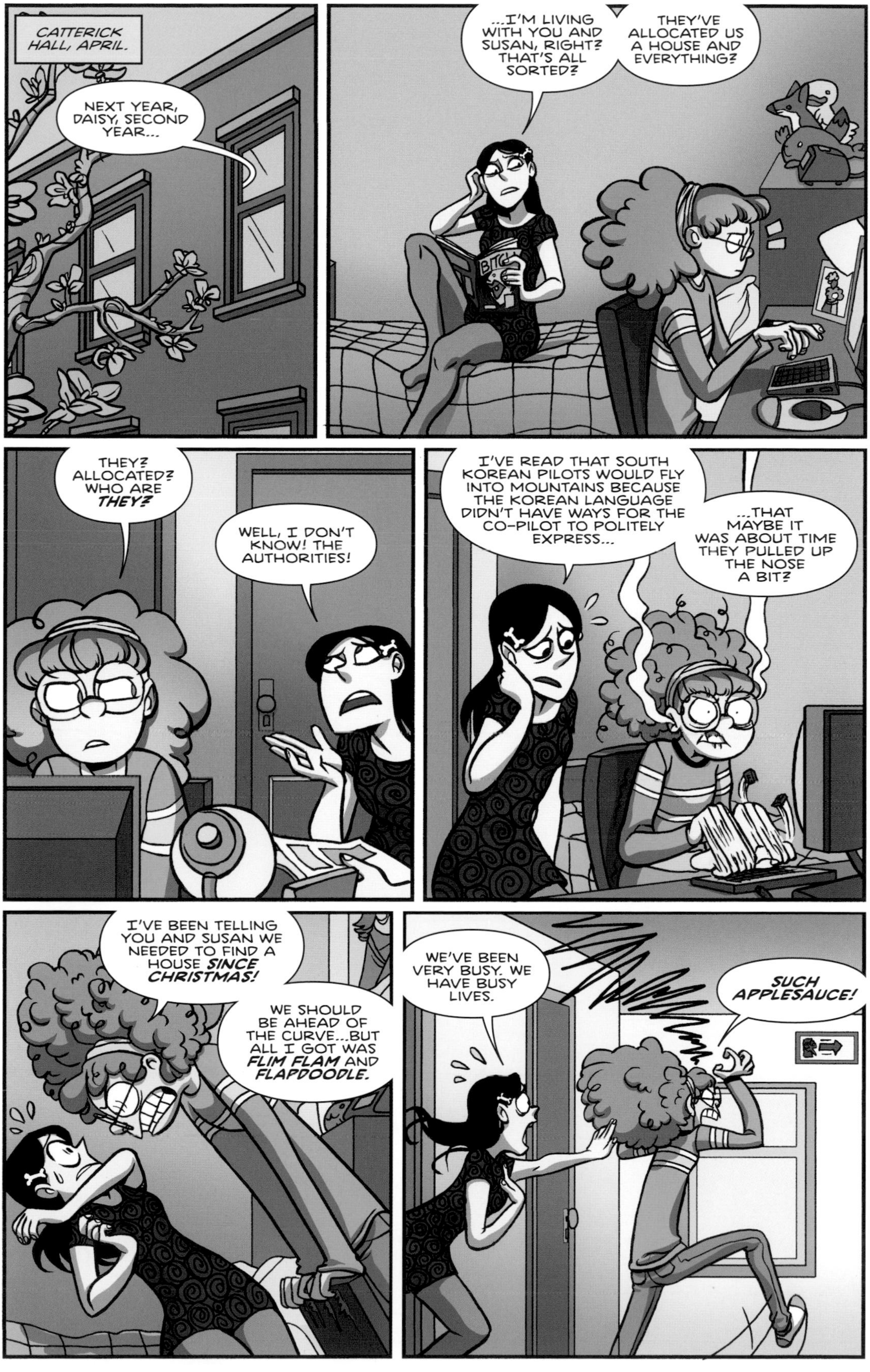
CATTERICK HALL, APRIL.
NEXT YEAR, DAISY, SECOND YEAR...
...I'M LIVING WITH YOU AND SUSAN, RIGHT? THAT'S ALL SORTED?
THEY'VE ALLOCATED US A HOUSE AND EVERYTHING?
THEY? ALLOCATED? WHO ARE *THEY?*
WELL, I DON'T KNOW! THE AUTHORITIES!
I'VE READ THAT SOUTH KOREAN PILOTS WOULD FLY INTO MOUNTAINS BECAUSE THE KOREAN LANGUAGE DIDN'T HAVE WAYS FOR THE CO-PILOT TO POLITELY EXPRESS...
...THAT MAYBE IT WAS ABOUT TIME THEY PULLED UP THE NOSE A BIT?
I'VE BEEN TELLING YOU AND SUSAN WE NEEDED TO FIND A HOUSE *SINCE CHRISTMAS!*
WE SHOULD BE AHEAD OF THE CURVE...BUT ALL I GOT WAS *FLIM FLAM* AND *FLAPDOODLE.*
WE'VE BEEN VERY BUSY. WE HAVE BUSY LIVES.
*SUCH APPLESAUCE!*

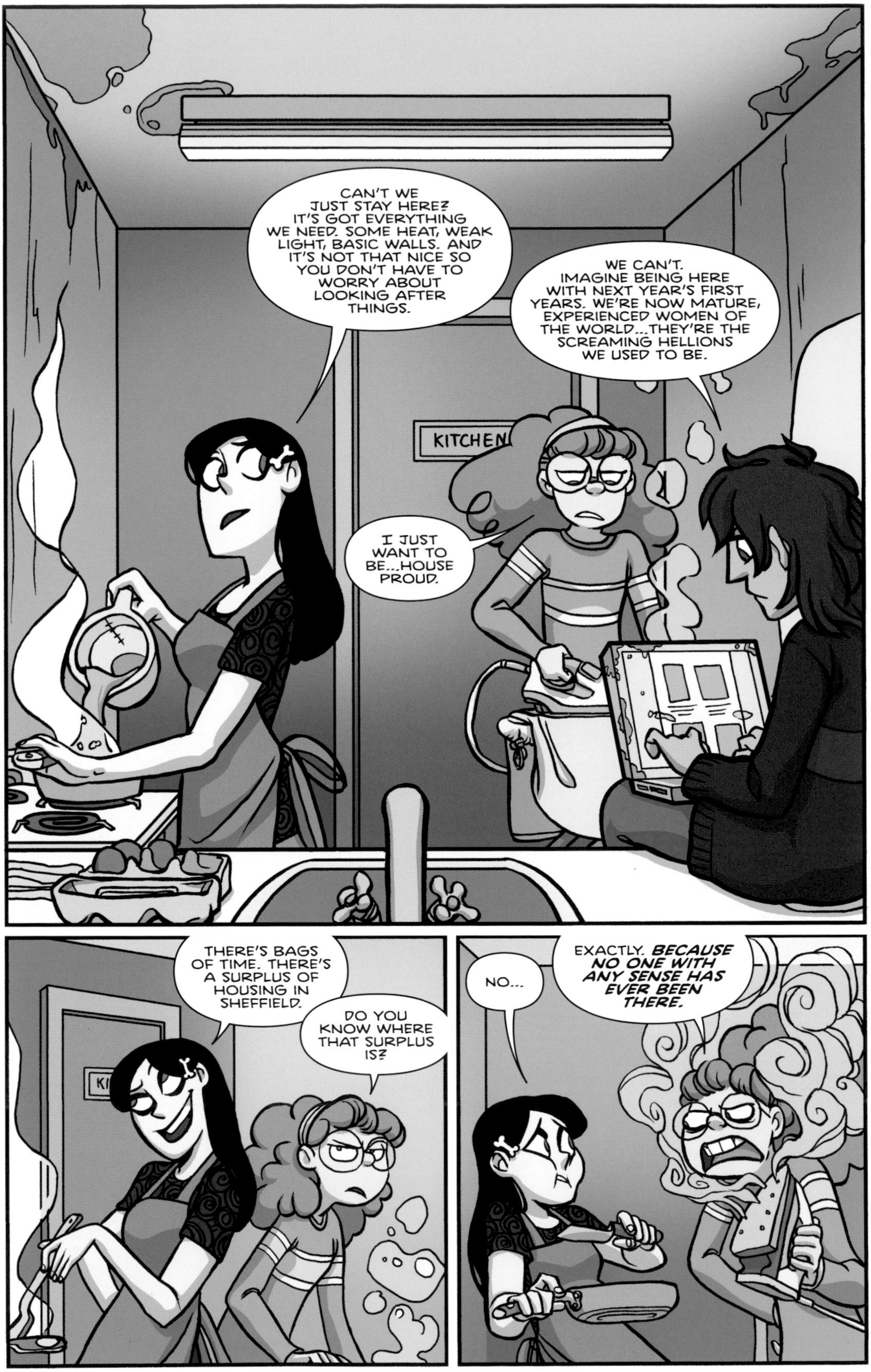
CAN'T WE JUST STAY HERE? IT'S GOT EVERYTHING WE NEED. SOME HEAT, WEAK LIGHT, BASIC WALLS. AND IT'S NOT THAT NICE SO YOU DON'T HAVE TO WORRY ABOUT LOOKING AFTER THINGS.
WE CAN'T. IMAGINE BEING HERE WITH NEXT YEAR'S FIRST YEARS. WE'RE NOW MATURE, EXPERIENCED WOMEN OF THE WORLD...THEY'RE THE SCREAMING HELLIONS WE USED TO BE.
KITCHEN
I JUST WANT TO BE...HOUSE PROUD.
THERE'S BAGS OF TIME. THERE'S A SURPLUS OF HOUSING IN SHEFFIELD.
DO YOU KNOW WHERE THAT SURPLUS IS?
NO...
EXACTLY. *BECAUSE NO ONE WITH ANY SENSE HAS EVER BEEN THERE.*

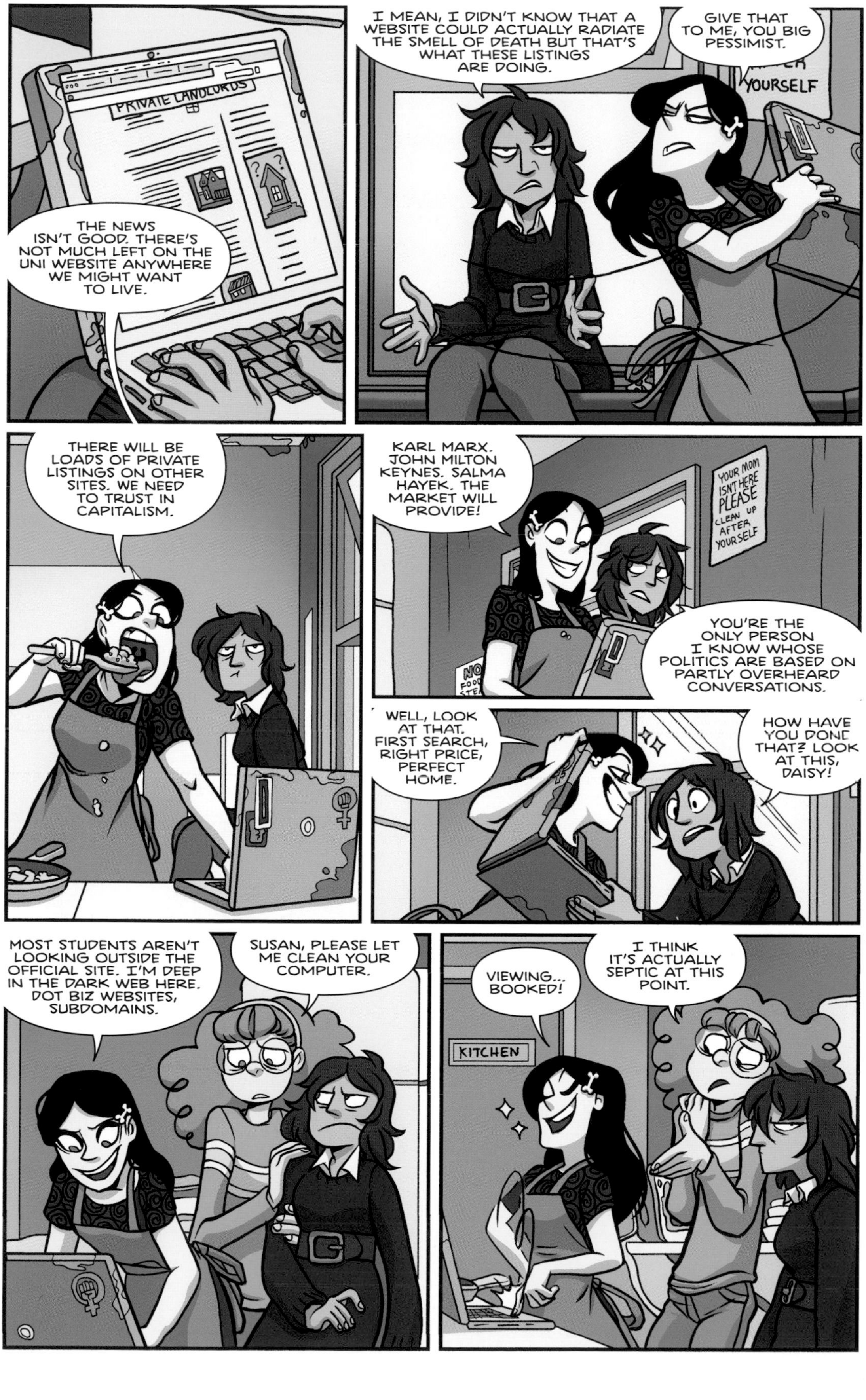
THE NEWS ISN'T GOOD. THERE'S NOT MUCH LEFT ON THE UNI WEBSITE ANYWHERE WE MIGHT WANT TO LIVE.
PRIVATE LANDLORDS
I MEAN, I DIDN'T KNOW THAT A WEBSITE COULD ACTUALLY RADIATE THE SMELL OF DEATH BUT THAT'S WHAT THESE LISTINGS ARE DOING.
GIVE THAT TO ME, YOU BIG PESSIMIST.
YOURSELF
THERE WILL BE LOADS OF PRIVATE LISTINGS ON OTHER SITES. WE NEED TO TRUST IN CAPITALISM.
KARL MARX. JOHN MILTON KEYNES. SALMA HAYEK. THE MARKET WILL PROVIDE!
YOUR MOM ISN'T HERE PLEASE CLEAN UP AFTER YOURSELF
YOU'RE THE ONLY PERSON I KNOW WHOSE POLITICS ARE BASED ON PARTLY OVERHEARD CONVERSATIONS.
WELL, LOOK AT THAT. FIRST SEARCH, RIGHT PRICE, PERFECT HOME.
HOW HAVE YOU DONE THAT? LOOK AT THIS, DAISY!
MOST STUDENTS AREN'T LOOKING OUTSIDE THE OFFICIAL SITE. I'M DEEP IN THE DARK WEB HERE. DOT BIZ WEBSITES, SUBDOMAINS.
SUSAN, PLEASE LET ME CLEAN YOUR COMPUTER.
KITCHEN
VIEWING... BOOKED!
I THINK IT'S ACTUALLY SEPTIC AT THIS POINT.

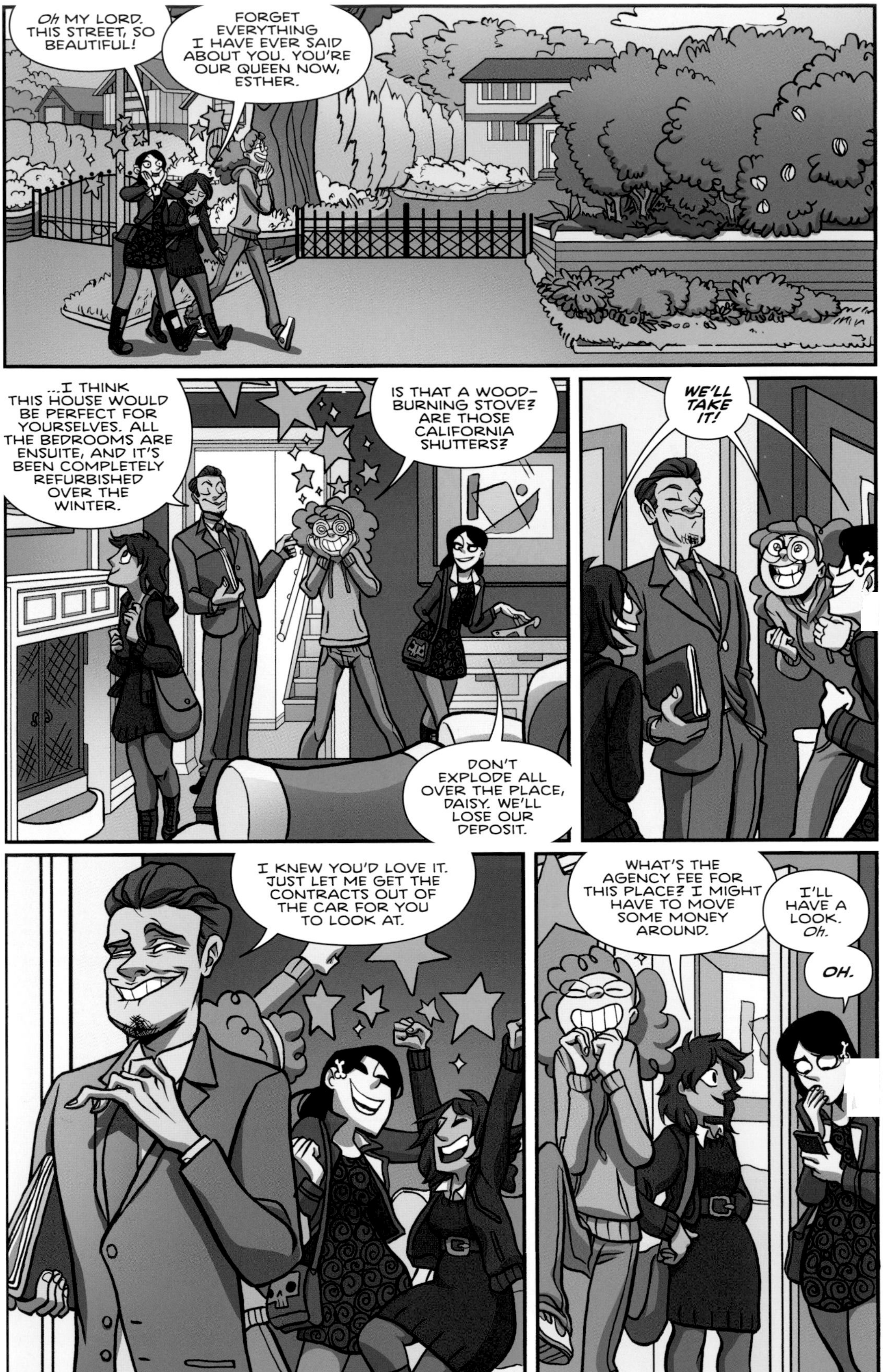

Oh MY LORD. THIS STREET, SO BEAUTIFUL!
FORGET EVERYTHING I HAVE EVER SAID ABOUT YOU. YOU'RE OUR QUEEN NOW, ESTHER.
...I THINK THIS HOUSE WOULD BE PERFECT FOR YOURSELVES. ALL THE BEDROOMS ARE ENSUITE, AND IT'S BEEN COMPLETELY REFURBISHED OVER THE WINTER.
IS THAT A WOOD-BURNING STOVE? ARE THOSE CALIFORNIA SHUTTERS?
DON'T EXPLODE ALL OVER THE PLACE, DAISY. WE'LL LOSE OUR DEPOSIT.
WE'LL TAKE IT!
I KNEW YOU'D LOVE IT. JUST LET ME GET THE CONTRACTS OUT OF THE CAR FOR YOU TO LOOK AT.
WHAT'S THE AGENCY FEE FOR THIS PLACE? I MIGHT HAVE TO MOVE SOME MONEY AROUND.
I'LL HAVE A LOOK. Oh.
OH.

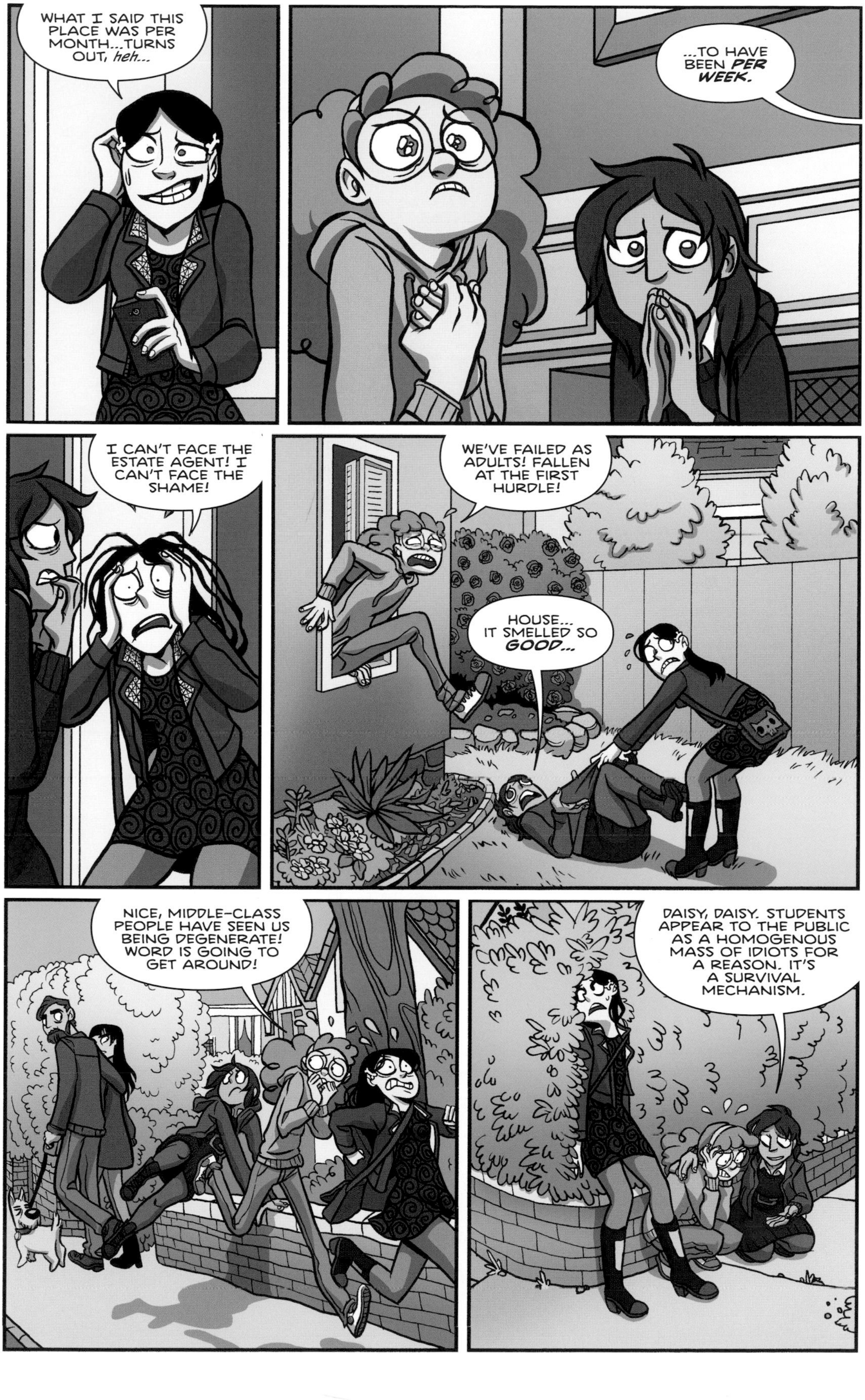
WHAT I SAID THIS PLACE WAS PER MONTH...TURNS OUT, heh...
...TO HAVE BEEN PER WEEK.
I CAN'T FACE THE ESTATE AGENT! I CAN'T FACE THE SHAME!
WE'VE FAILED AS ADULTS! FALLEN AT THE FIRST HURDLE!
HOUSE... IT SMELLED SO GOOD...
NICE, MIDDLE-CLASS PEOPLE HAVE SEEN US BEING DEGENERATE! WORD IS GOING TO GET AROUND!
DAISY, DAISY. STUDENTS APPEAR TO THE PUBLIC AS A HOMOGENOUS MASS OF IDIOTS FOR A REASON. IT'S A SURVIVAL MECHANISM.

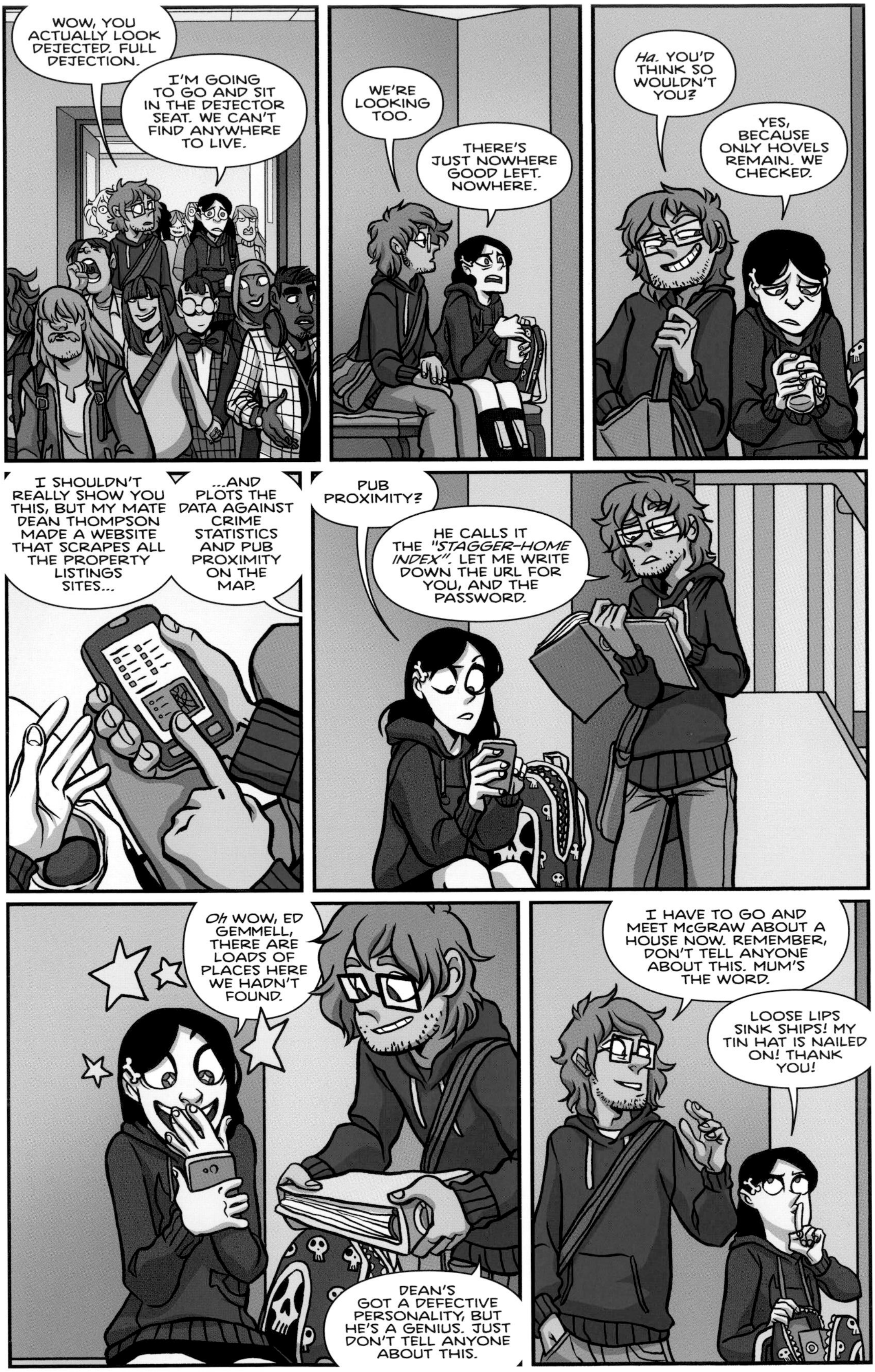

WOW, YOU ACTUALLY LOOK DEJECTED. FULL DEJECTION.
I'M GOING TO GO AND SIT IN THE DEJECTOR SEAT. WE CAN'T FIND ANYWHERE TO LIVE.
WE'RE LOOKING TOO.
THERE'S JUST NOWHERE GOOD LEFT. NOWHERE.
*Ha.* YOU'D THINK SO WOULDN'T YOU?
YES, BECAUSE ONLY HOVELS REMAIN. WE CHECKED.
I SHOULDN'T REALLY SHOW YOU THIS, BUT MY MATE DEAN THOMPSON MADE A WEBSITE THAT SCRAPES ALL THE PROPERTY LISTINGS SITES...
...AND PLOTS THE DATA AGAINST CRIME STATISTICS AND PUB PROXIMITY ON THE MAP.
PUB PROXIMITY?
HE CALLS IT THE *"STAGGER-HOME INDEX"*. LET ME WRITE DOWN THE URL FOR YOU, AND THE PASSWORD.
*Oh* WOW, ED GEMMELL, THERE ARE LOADS OF PLACES HERE WE HADN'T FOUND.
DEAN'S GOT A DEFECTIVE PERSONALITY, BUT HE'S A GENIUS. JUST DON'T TELL ANYONE ABOUT THIS.
I HAVE TO GO AND MEET McGRAW ABOUT A HOUSE NOW. REMEMBER, DON'T TELL ANYONE ABOUT THIS. MUM'S THE WORD.
LOOSE LIPS SINK SHIPS! MY TIN HAT IS NAILED ON! THANK YOU!

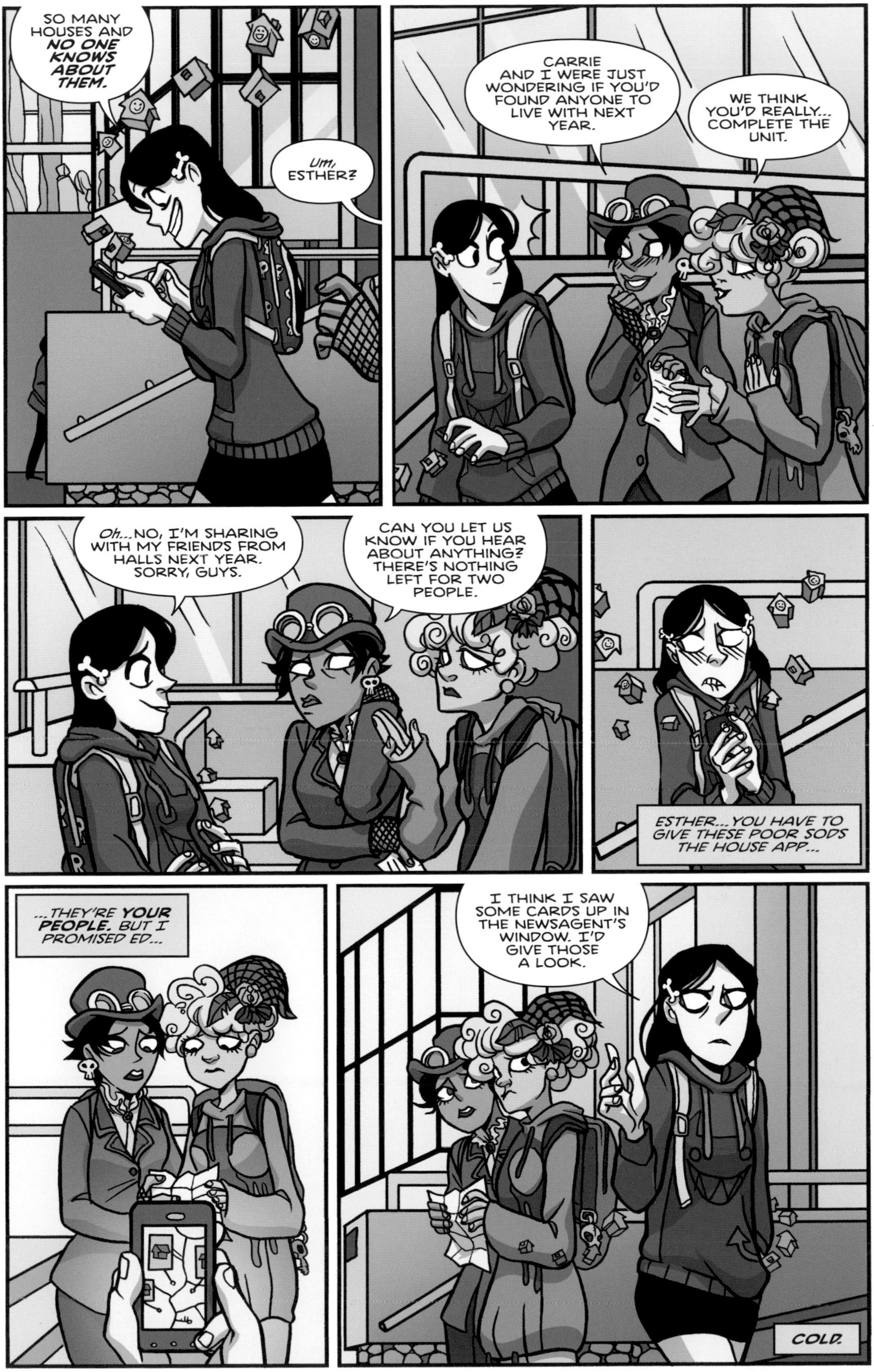
SO MANY HOUSES AND NO ONE KNOWS ABOUT THEM.
Um, ESTHER?
CARRIE AND I WERE JUST WONDERING IF YOU'D FOUND ANYONE TO LIVE WITH NEXT YEAR.
WE THINK YOU'D REALLY... COMPLETE THE UNIT.
Oh... NO, I'M SHARING WITH MY FRIENDS FROM HALLS NEXT YEAR. SORRY, GUYS.
CAN YOU LET US KNOW IF YOU HEAR ABOUT ANYTHING? THERE'S NOTHING LEFT FOR TWO PEOPLE.
ESTHER... YOU HAVE TO GIVE THESE POOR SODS THE HOUSE APP...
...THEY'RE YOUR PEOPLE. BUT I PROMISED ED...
I THINK I SAW SOME CARDS UP IN THE NEWSAGENT'S WINDOW. I'D GIVE THOSE A LOOK.
COLD.

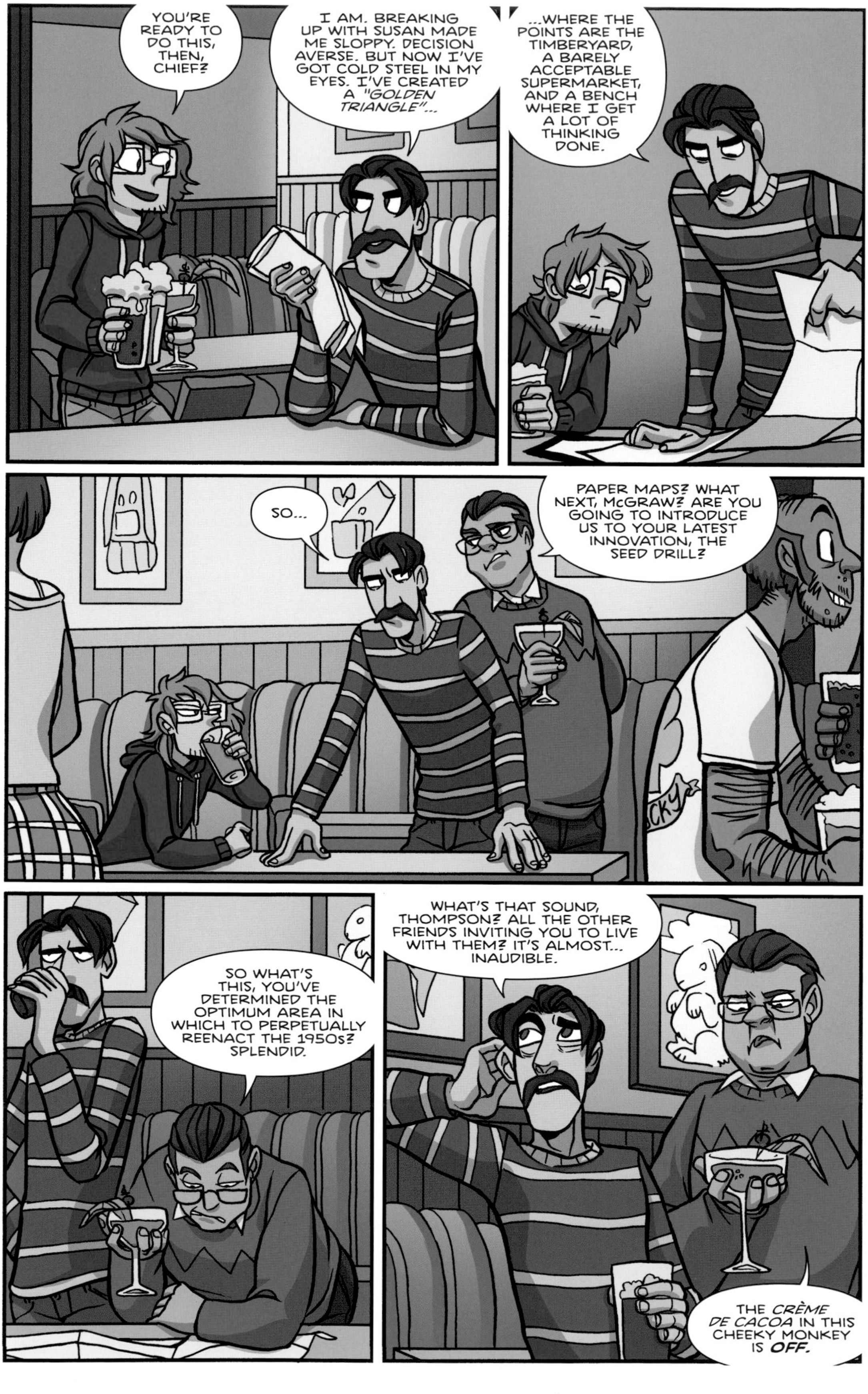
YOU'RE READY TO DO THIS, THEN, CHIEF?
I AM. BREAKING UP WITH SUSAN MADE ME SLOPPY. DECISION AVERSE. BUT NOW I'VE GOT COLD STEEL IN MY EYES. I'VE CREATED A *"GOLDEN TRIANGLE"*...
...WHERE THE POINTS ARE THE TIMBERYARD, A BARELY ACCEPTABLE SUPERMARKET, AND A BENCH WHERE I GET A LOT OF THINKING DONE.
SO...
PAPER MAPS? WHAT NEXT, McGRAW? ARE YOU GOING TO INTRODUCE US TO YOUR LATEST INNOVATION, THE SEED DRILL?
SO WHAT'S THIS, YOU'VE DETERMINED THE OPTIMUM AREA IN WHICH TO PERPETUALLY REENACT THE 1950s? SPLENDID.
WHAT'S THAT SOUND, THOMPSON? ALL THE OTHER FRIENDS INVITING YOU TO LIVE WITH THEM? IT'S ALMOST... INAUDIBLE.
THE *CRÈME DE CACOA* IN THIS CHEEKY MONKEY IS ***OFF.***

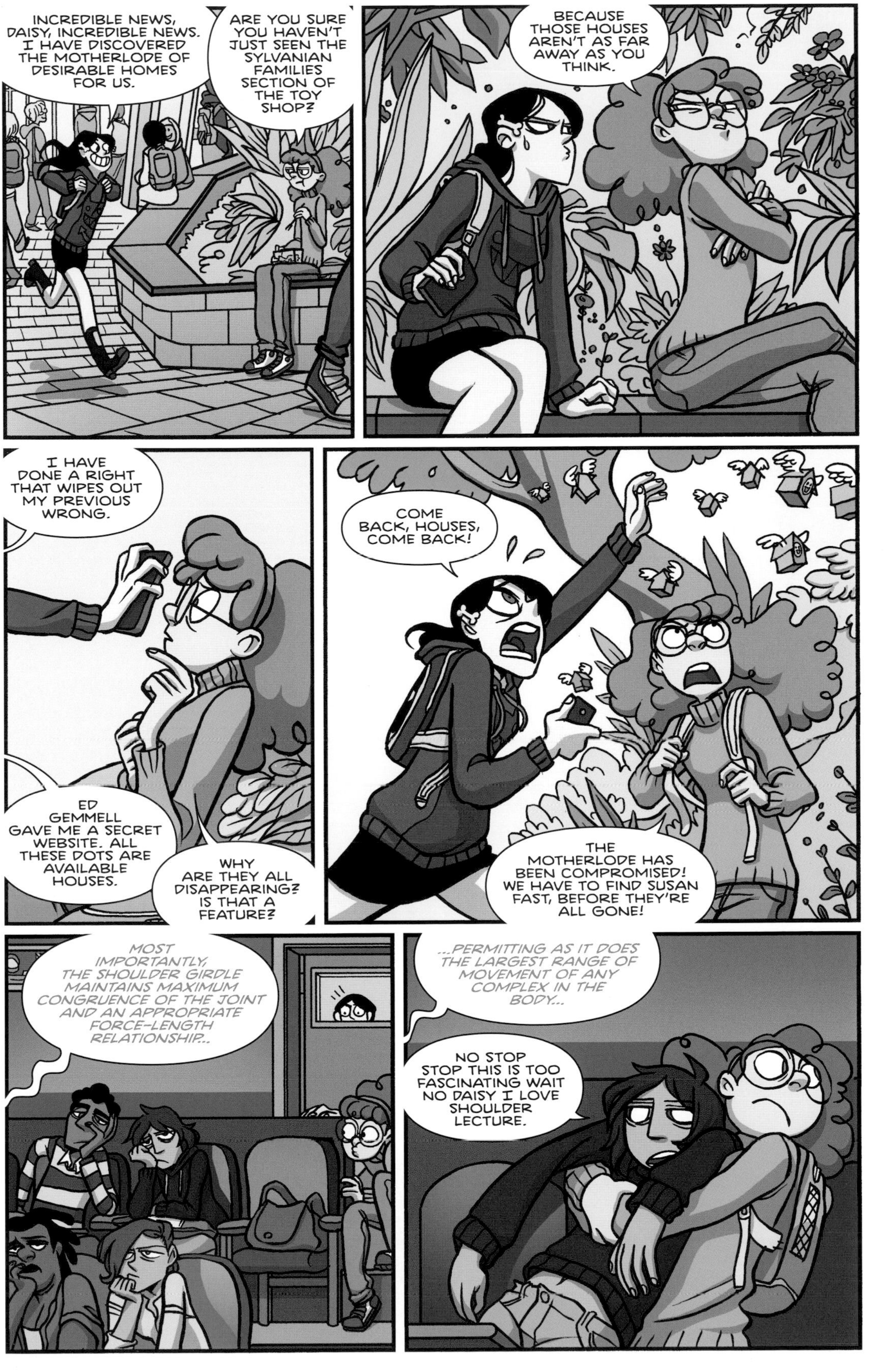
INCREDIBLE NEWS, DAISY, INCREDIBLE NEWS. I HAVE DISCOVERED THE MOTHERLODE OF DESIRABLE HOMES FOR US.
ARE YOU SURE YOU HAVEN'T JUST SEEN THE SYLVANIAN FAMILIES SECTION OF THE TOY SHOP?
BECAUSE THOSE HOUSES AREN'T AS FAR AWAY AS YOU THINK.
I HAVE DONE A RIGHT THAT WIPES OUT MY PREVIOUS WRONG.
ED GEMMELL GAVE ME A SECRET WEBSITE. ALL THESE DOTS ARE AVAILABLE HOUSES.
WHY ARE THEY ALL DISAPPEARING? IS THAT A FEATURE?
COME BACK, HOUSES, COME BACK!
THE MOTHERLODE HAS BEEN COMPROMISED! WE HAVE TO FIND SUSAN FAST, BEFORE THEY'RE ALL GONE!
MOST IMPORTANTLY, THE SHOULDER GIRDLE MAINTAINS MAXIMUM CONGRUENCE OF THE JOINT AND AN APPROPRIATE FORCE-LENGTH RELATIONSHIP...
...PERMITTING AS IT DOES THE LARGEST RANGE OF MOVEMENT OF ANY COMPLEX IN THE BODY...
NO STOP STOP THIS IS TOO FASCINATING WAIT NO DAISY I LOVE SHOULDER LECTURE.

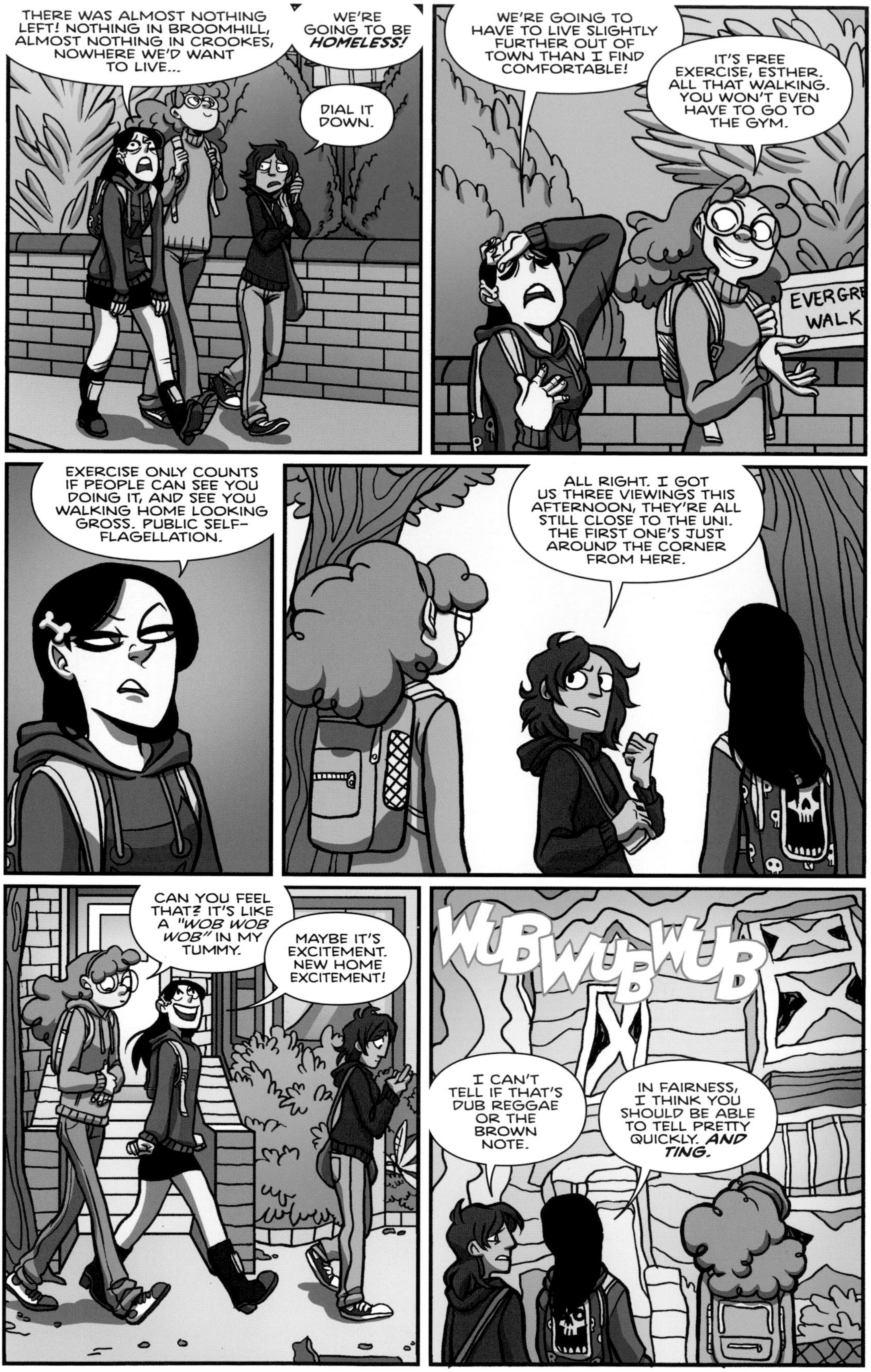
THERE WAS ALMOST NOTHING LEFT! NOTHING IN BROOMHILL, ALMOST NOTHING IN CROOKES, NOWHERE WE'D WANT TO LIVE...
WE'RE GOING TO BE *HOMELESS!*
DIAL IT DOWN.
WE'RE GOING TO HAVE TO LIVE SLIGHTLY FURTHER OUT OF TOWN THAN I FIND COMFORTABLE!
IT'S FREE EXERCISE, ESTHER. ALL THAT WALKING. YOU WON'T EVEN HAVE TO GO TO THE GYM.
EVERGRE
WALK
EXERCISE ONLY COUNTS IF PEOPLE CAN SEE YOU DOING IT, AND SEE YOU WALKING HOME LOOKING GROSS. PUBLIC SELF-FLAGELLATION.
ALL RIGHT. I GOT US THREE VIEWINGS THIS AFTERNOON, THEY'RE ALL STILL CLOSE TO THE UNI. THE FIRST ONE'S JUST AROUND THE CORNER FROM HERE.
CAN YOU FEEL THAT? IT'S LIKE A *"WOB WOB WOB"* IN MY TUMMY.
MAYBE IT'S EXCITEMENT. NEW HOME EXCITEMENT!
WUBWUBWUB
I CAN'T TELL IF THAT'S DUB REGGAE OR THE BROWN NOTE.
IN FAIRNESS, I THINK YOU SHOULD BE ABLE TO TELL PRETTY QUICKLY. ***AND TING.***

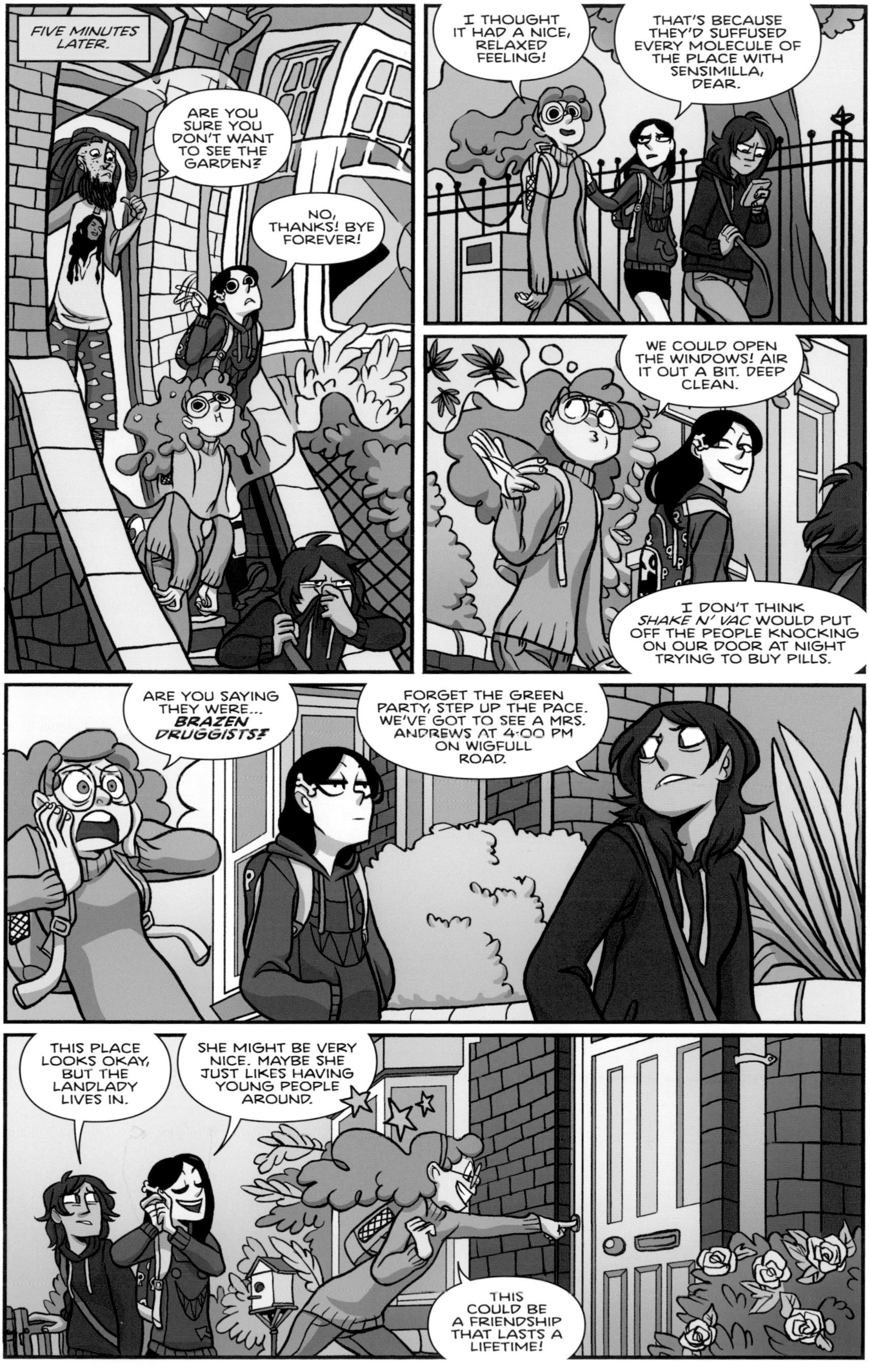
FIVE MINUTES LATER.
ARE YOU SURE YOU DON'T WANT TO SEE THE GARDEN?
NO, THANKS! BYE FOREVER!
I THOUGHT IT HAD A NICE, RELAXED FEELING!
THAT'S BECAUSE THEY'D SUFFUSED EVERY MOLECULE OF THE PLACE WITH SENSIMILLA, DEAR.
WE COULD OPEN THE WINDOWS! AIR IT OUT A BIT. DEEP CLEAN.
I DON'T THINK SHAKE N' VAC WOULD PUT OFF THE PEOPLE KNOCKING ON OUR DOOR AT NIGHT TRYING TO BUY PILLS.
ARE YOU SAYING THEY WERE... BRAZEN DRUGGISTS?
FORGET THE GREEN PARTY, STEP UP THE PACE. WE'VE GOT TO SEE A MRS. ANDREWS AT 4:00 PM ON WIGFULL ROAD.
THIS PLACE LOOKS OKAY, BUT THE LANDLADY LIVES IN.
SHE MIGHT BE VERY NICE. MAYBE SHE JUST LIKES HAVING YOUNG PEOPLE AROUND.
THIS COULD BE A FRIENDSHIP THAT LASTS A LIFETIME!

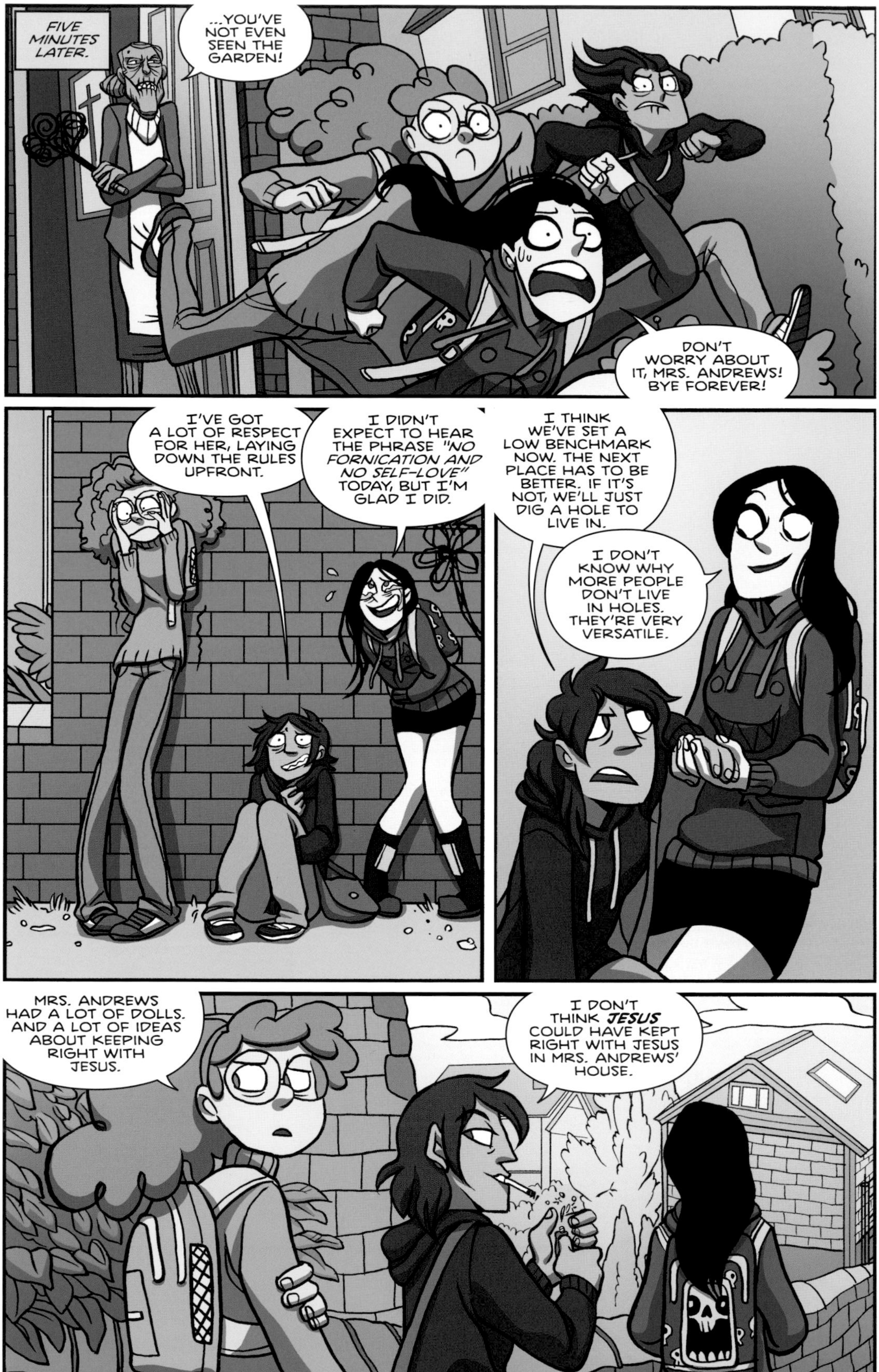
FIVE MINUTES LATER.
...YOU'VE NOT EVEN SEEN THE GARDEN!
DON'T WORRY ABOUT IT, MRS. ANDREWS! BYE FOREVER!
I'VE GOT A LOT OF RESPECT FOR HER, LAYING DOWN THE RULES UPFRONT.
I DIDN'T EXPECT TO HEAR THE PHRASE "NO FORNICATION AND NO SELF-LOVE" TODAY, BUT I'M GLAD I DID.
I THINK WE'VE SET A LOW BENCHMARK NOW. THE NEXT PLACE HAS TO BE BETTER. IF IT'S NOT, WE'LL JUST DIG A HOLE TO LIVE IN.
I DON'T KNOW WHY MORE PEOPLE DON'T LIVE IN HOLES. THEY'RE VERY VERSATILE.
MRS. ANDREWS HAD A LOT OF DOLLS. AND A LOT OF IDEAS ABOUT KEEPING RIGHT WITH JESUS.
I DON'T THINK JESUS COULD HAVE KEPT RIGHT WITH JESUS IN MRS. ANDREWS' HOUSE.

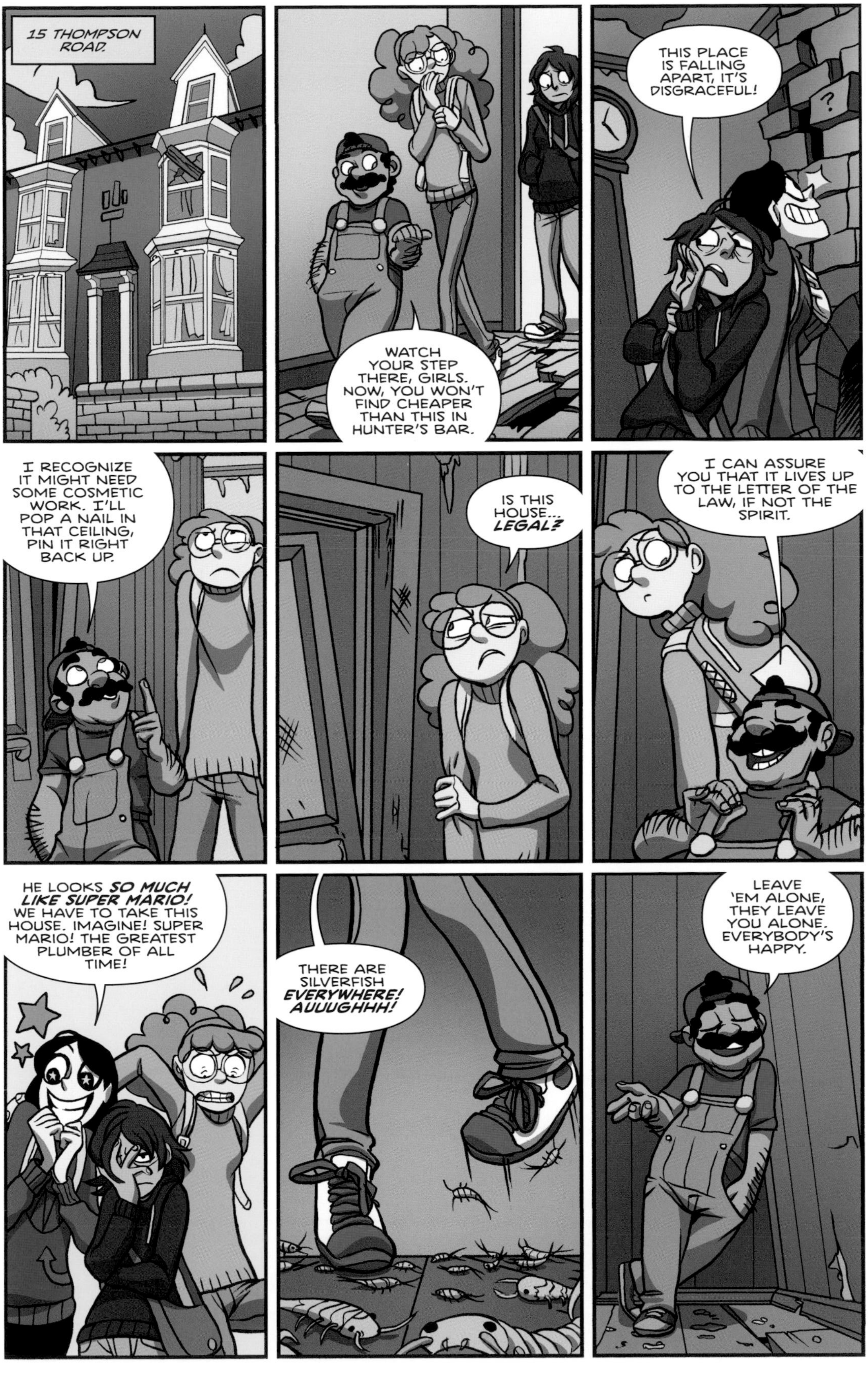
15 THOMPSON ROAD.
WATCH YOUR STEP THERE, GIRLS. NOW, YOU WON'T FIND CHEAPER THAN THIS IN HUNTER'S BAR.
THIS PLACE IS FALLING APART, IT'S DISGRACEFUL!
I RECOGNIZE IT MIGHT NEED SOME COSMETIC WORK. I'LL POP A NAIL IN THAT CEILING, PIN IT RIGHT BACK UP.
IS THIS HOUSE... *LEGAL?*
I CAN ASSURE YOU THAT IT LIVES UP TO THE LETTER OF THE LAW, IF NOT THE SPIRIT.
HE LOOKS *SO MUCH LIKE SUPER MARIO!* WE HAVE TO TAKE THIS HOUSE. IMAGINE! SUPER MARIO! THE GREATEST PLUMBER OF ALL TIME!
THERE ARE SILVERFISH *EVERYWHERE! AUUUGHHH!*
LEAVE 'EM ALONE, THEY LEAVE YOU ALONE. EVERYBODY'S HAPPY.

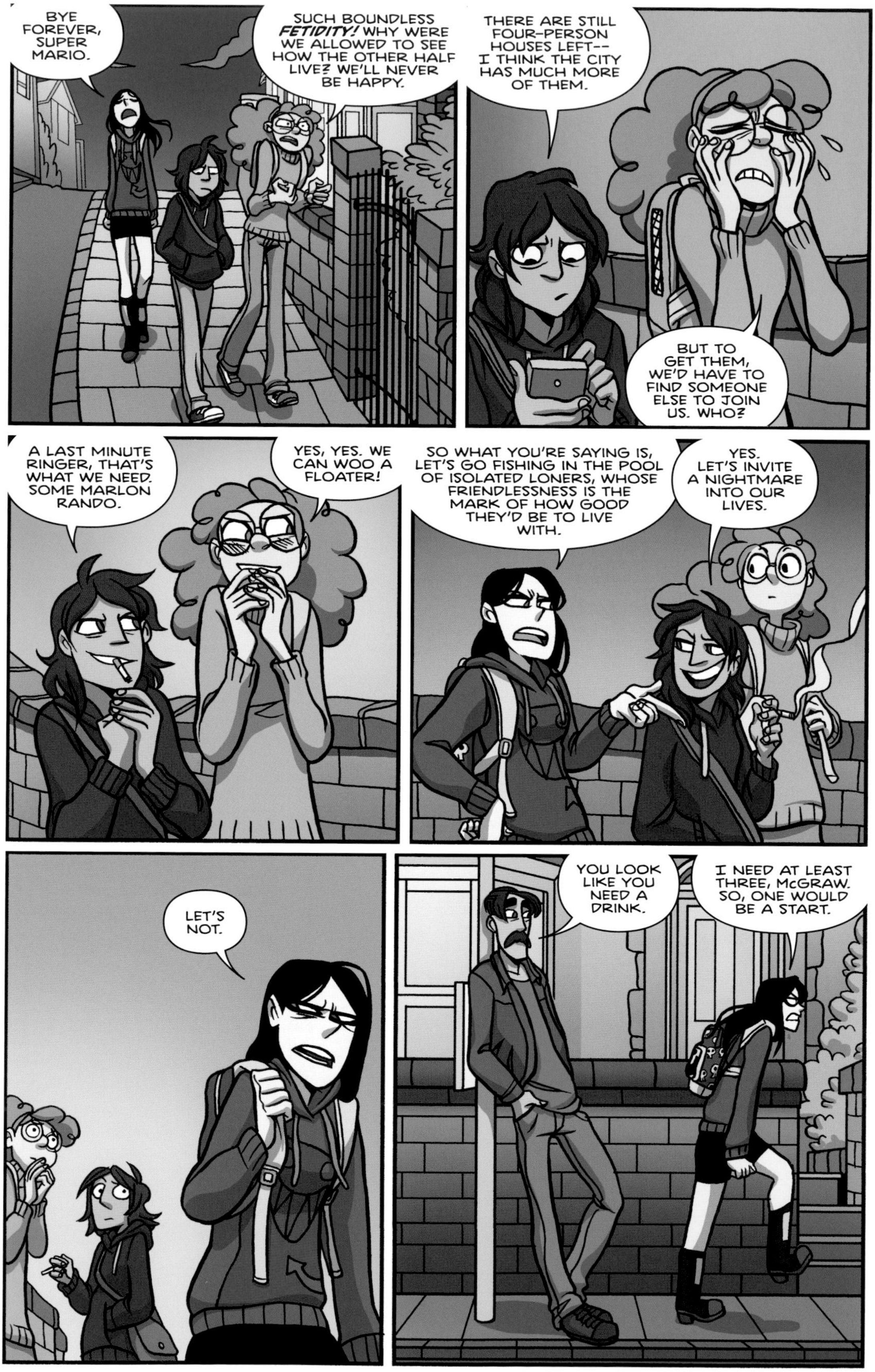
BYE FOREVER, SUPER MARIO.
SUCH BOUNDLESS **FETIDITY!** WHY WERE WE ALLOWED TO SEE HOW THE OTHER HALF LIVE? WE'LL NEVER BE HAPPY.
THERE ARE STILL FOUR-PERSON HOUSES LEFT-- I THINK THE CITY HAS MUCH MORE OF THEM.
BUT TO GET THEM, WE'D HAVE TO FIND SOMEONE ELSE TO JOIN US. WHO?
A LAST MINUTE RINGER, THAT'S WHAT WE NEED. SOME MARLON RANDO.
YES, YES. WE CAN WOO A FLOATER!
SO WHAT YOU'RE SAYING IS, LET'S GO FISHING IN THE POOL OF ISOLATED LONERS, WHOSE FRIENDLESSNESS IS THE MARK OF HOW GOOD THEY'D BE TO LIVE WITH.
YES. LET'S INVITE A NIGHTMARE INTO OUR LIVES.
LET'S NOT.
YOU LOOK LIKE YOU NEED A DRINK.
I NEED AT LEAST THREE, McGRAW. SO, ONE WOULD BE A START.

I'M SO SICK OF HORRIBLE HOUSES, THERE ARE NONE LEFT FOR THREE PEOPLE. IT'S *HORSE HOCKEY.*

WE'RE HAVING THE SAME PROBLEM.

*MORE FINE WINE! I'M SUCH A LUCKY LADY!*

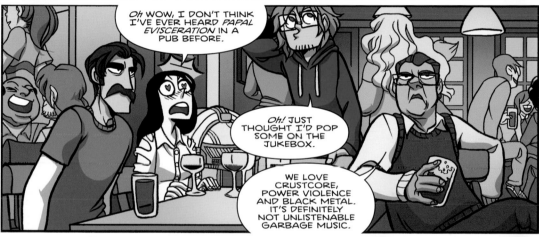

*Oh* WOW, I DON'T THINK I'VE EVER HEARD *PAPAL EVISCERATION* IN A PUB BEFORE.

*Oh!* JUST THOUGHT I'D POP SOME ON THE JUKEBOX.

WE LOVE CRUSTCORE, POWER VIOLENCE AND BLACK METAL. IT'S DEFINITELY NOT UNLISTENABLE GARBAGE MUSIC.

WE WANTED TO ASK YOU A QUESTION.

YOU WANT ME TO RESTYLE YOU. *Oh,* THANK GOD. I'VE BEEN WAITING ALL YEAR FOR THIS.

NO, WE WONDERED IF YOU...WOULD CONSIDER LIVING WITH US NEXT YEAR.

*Oh...oh!* THIS WINE IS GOING RIGHT THROUGH ME, GENTLEMEN. I WILL RETURN!

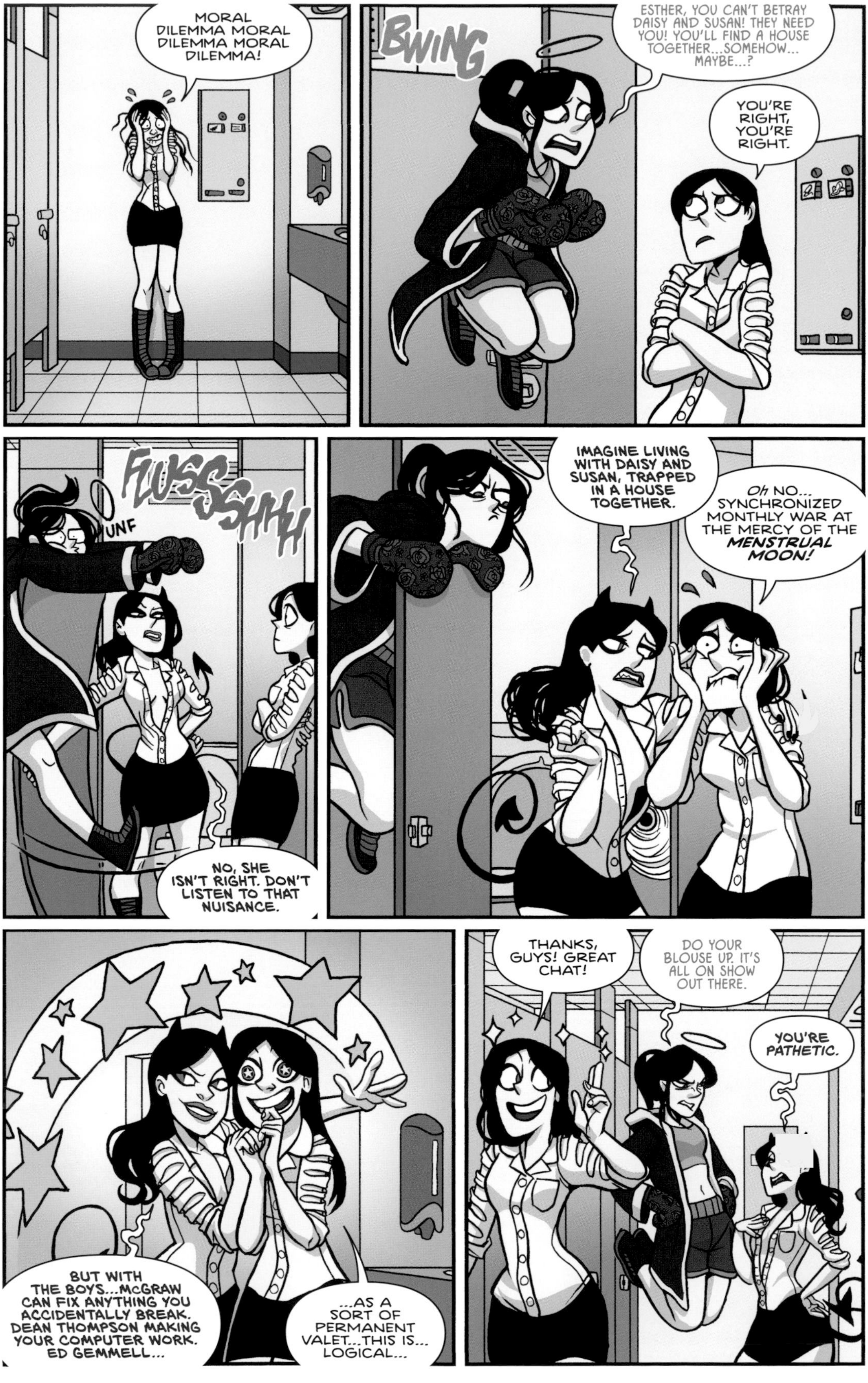
MORAL DILEMMA MORAL DILEMMA MORAL DILEMMA!
BWING
ESTHER, YOU CAN'T BETRAY DAISY AND SUSAN! THEY NEED YOU! YOU'LL FIND A HOUSE TOGETHER...SOMEHOW... MAYBE...?
YOU'RE RIGHT, YOU'RE RIGHT.
FLUSSSSHHH
UNF
NO, SHE ISN'T RIGHT. DON'T LISTEN TO THAT NUISANCE.
IMAGINE LIVING WITH DAISY AND SUSAN, TRAPPED IN A HOUSE TOGETHER.
Oh NO... SYNCHRONIZED MONTHLY WAR AT THE MERCY OF THE MENSTRUAL MOON!
BUT WITH THE BOYS...McGRAW CAN FIX ANYTHING YOU ACCIDENTALLY BREAK. DEAN THOMPSON MAKING YOUR COMPUTER WORK. ED GEMMELL...
...AS A SORT OF PERMANENT VALET...THIS IS... LOGICAL...
THANKS, GUYS! GREAT CHAT!
DO YOUR BLOUSE UP. IT'S ALL ON SHOW OUT THERE.
YOU'RE PATHETIC.

OKAY. IF YOU'LL HAVE ME, I'M IN.

ACTUALLY, YOU'RE OUT. YOU'VE BEEN GIVING THE PASSWORD TO MY WEBSITE TO EVERYBODY, YOU *PUFF ADDER.*

NO, I HAVEN'T! ED GEMMELL GAVE IT TO ME, BUT...

IF YOU ASKED THIS FEEBLE LIZARD FOR A KIDNEY, HE'D GIVE YOU TWO, YOU *BLACK MAMBA.*

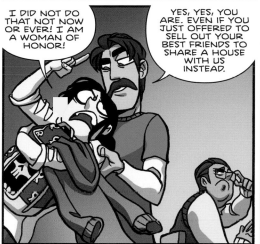

I DID NOT DO THAT NOT NOW OR EVER! I AM A WOMAN OF HONOR!

YES, YES, YOU ARE. EVEN IF YOU JUST OFFERED TO SELL OUT YOUR BEST FRIENDS TO SHARE A HOUSE WITH US INSTEAD.

*YOU INLAND TAIPAN!* THAT'S THE MOST VENOMOUS SNAKE THAT THERE IS!

IT'S NOT REPARTEE IF YOU HAVE TO READ IT OUT OF WIKIPEDIA.

*SISTERS BEFORE MISTERS,* ESTHER. BOYS STINK AND ARE GROSS. DON'T FALL FOR THEIR TRICKS.

BING

"WE'RE LOOKING AT A HOUSE AT 9:00 AM." SUSAN!

BING

Hmm. "LOWER YOUR EXPECTATIONS APPROPRIATELY."

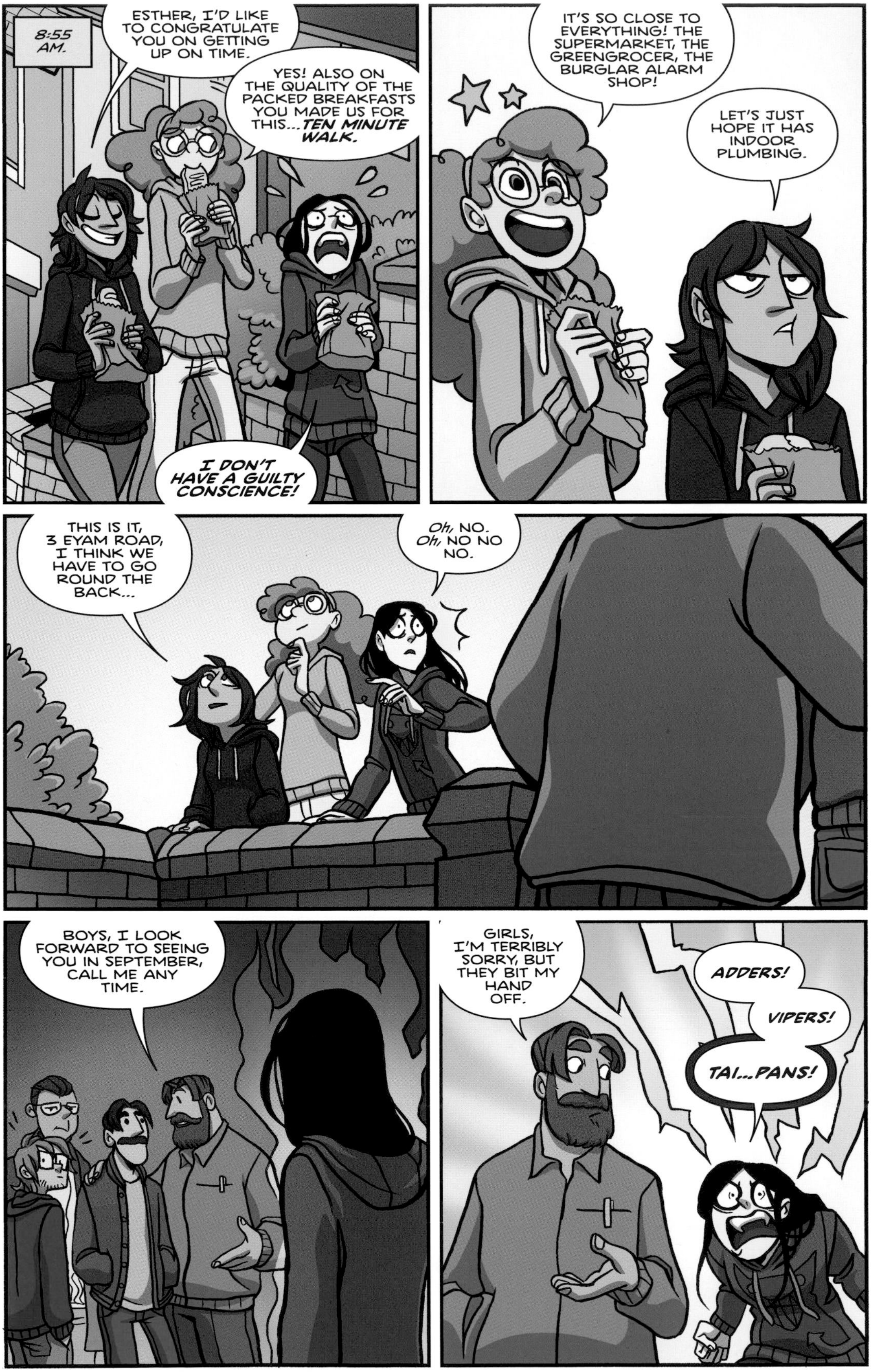
8:55 AM.
ESTHER, I'D LIKE TO CONGRATULATE YOU ON GETTING UP ON TIME.
YES! ALSO ON THE QUALITY OF THE PACKED BREAKFASTS YOU MADE US FOR THIS... TEN MINUTE WALK.
I DON'T HAVE A GUILTY CONSCIENCE!
IT'S SO CLOSE TO EVERYTHING! THE SUPERMARKET, THE GREENGROCER, THE BURGLAR ALARM SHOP!
LET'S JUST HOPE IT HAS INDOOR PLUMBING.
THIS IS IT, 3 EYAM ROAD, I THINK WE HAVE TO GO ROUND THE BACK...
Oh, NO. Oh, NO NO NO.
BOYS, I LOOK FORWARD TO SEEING YOU IN SEPTEMBER, CALL ME ANY TIME.
GIRLS, I'M TERRIBLY SORRY, BUT THEY BIT MY HAND OFF.
ADDERS!
VIPERS!
TAI...PANS!

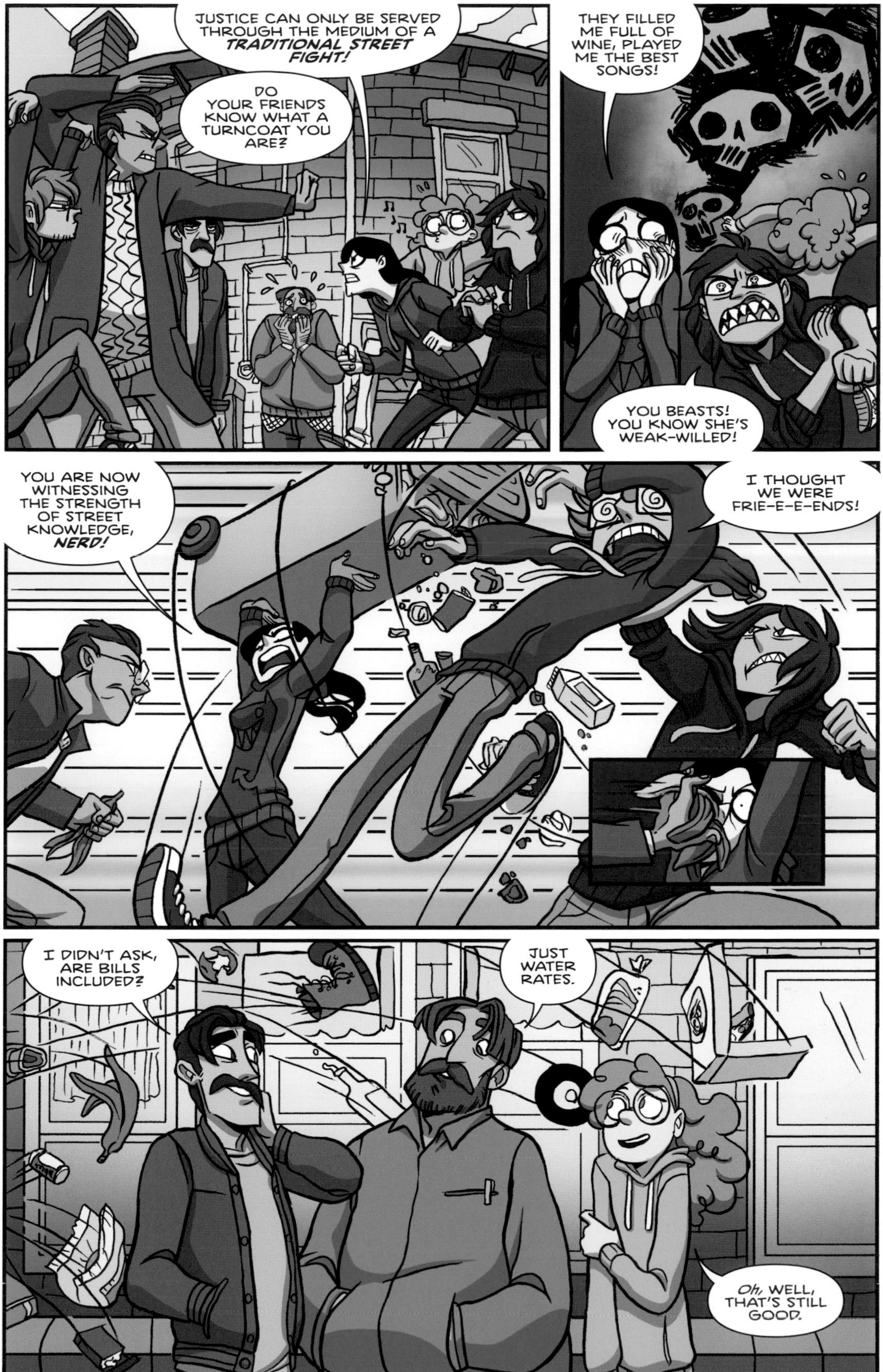
JUSTICE CAN ONLY BE SERVED THROUGH THE MEDIUM OF A *TRADITIONAL STREET FIGHT!*
DO YOUR FRIENDS KNOW WHAT A TURNCOAT YOU ARE?
THEY FILLED ME FULL OF WINE, PLAYED ME THE BEST SONGS!
YOU BEASTS! YOU KNOW SHE'S WEAK-WILLED!
YOU ARE NOW WITNESSING THE STRENGTH OF STREET KNOWLEDGE, *NERD!*
I THOUGHT WE WERE FRIE-E-E-ENDS!
I DIDN'T ASK, ARE BILLS INCLUDED?
JUST WATER RATES.
*Oh,* WELL, THAT'S STILL GOOD.

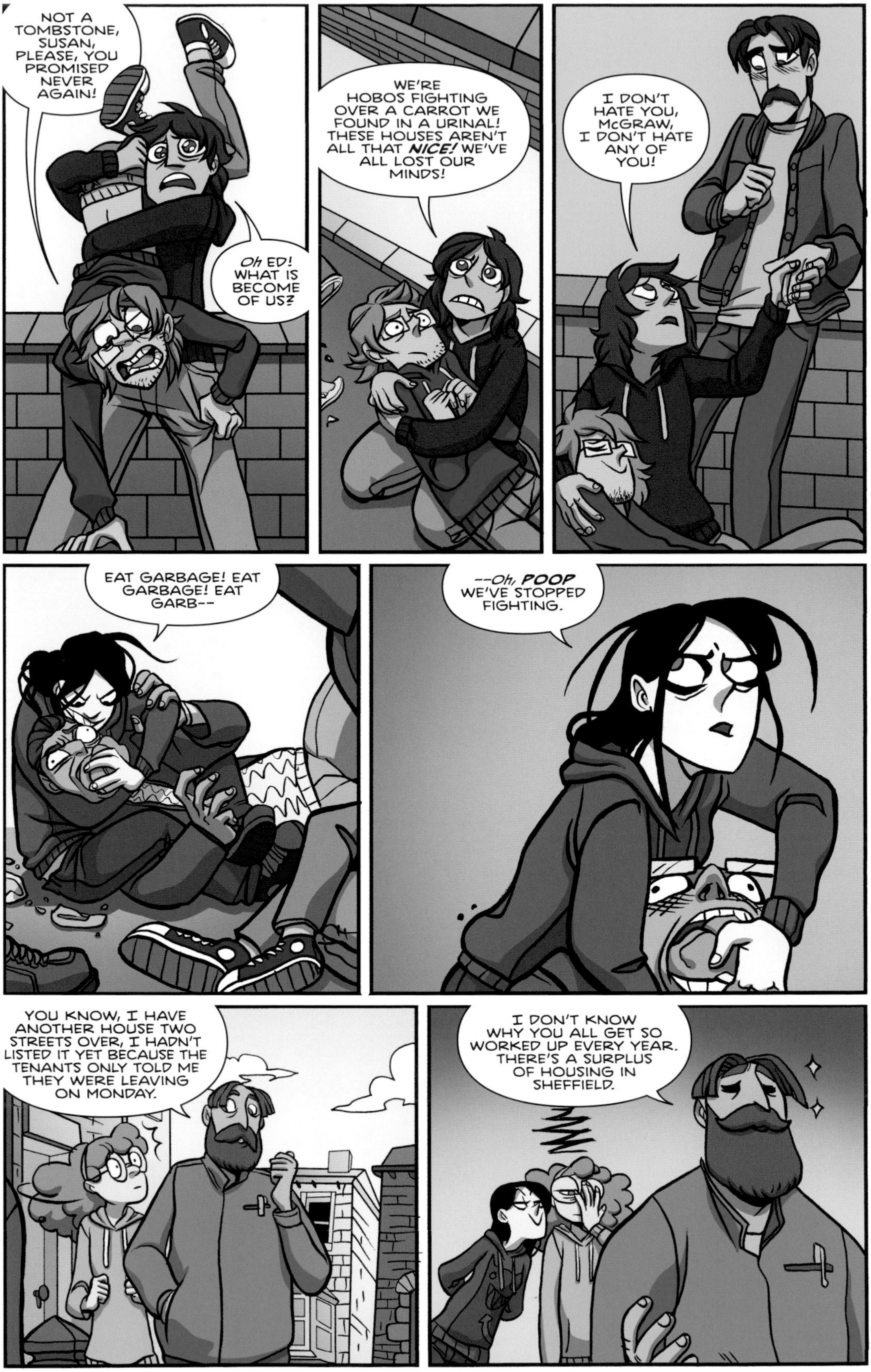
NOT A TOMBSTONE, SUSAN, PLEASE, YOU PROMISED NEVER AGAIN!
*Oh* ED! WHAT IS BECOME OF US?
WE'RE HOBOS FIGHTING OVER A CARROT WE FOUND IN A URINAL! THESE HOUSES AREN'T ALL THAT ***NICE!*** WE'VE ALL LOST OUR MINDS!
I DON'T HATE YOU, McGRAW, I DON'T HATE ANY OF YOU!
EAT GARBAGE! EAT GARBAGE! EAT GARB--
--*Oh,* ***POOP*** WE'VE STOPPED FIGHTING.
YOU KNOW, I HAVE ANOTHER HOUSE TWO STREETS OVER, I HADN'T LISTED IT YET BECAUSE THE TENANTS ONLY TOLD ME THEY WERE LEAVING ON MONDAY.
I DON'T KNOW WHY YOU ALL GET SO WORKED UP EVERY YEAR. THERE'S A SURPLUS OF HOUSING IN SHEFFIELD.

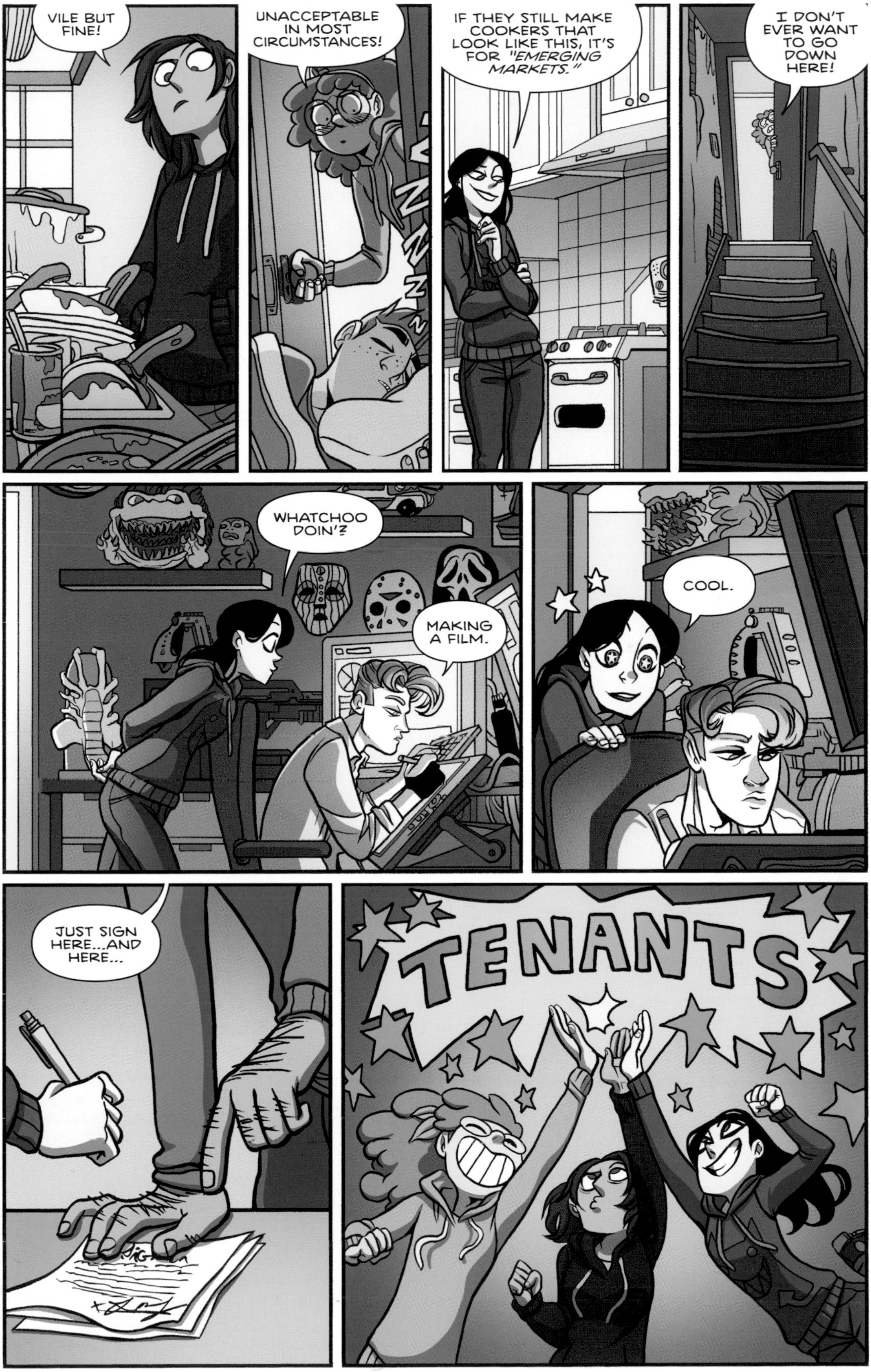
VILE BUT FINE!
UNACCEPTABLE IN MOST CIRCUMSTANCES!
IF THEY STILL MAKE COOKERS THAT LOOK LIKE THIS, IT'S FOR "EMERGING MARKETS."
I DON'T EVER WANT TO GO DOWN HERE!
WHATCHOO DOIN'?
MAKING A FILM.
COOL.
JUST SIGN HERE...AND HERE...
TENANTS

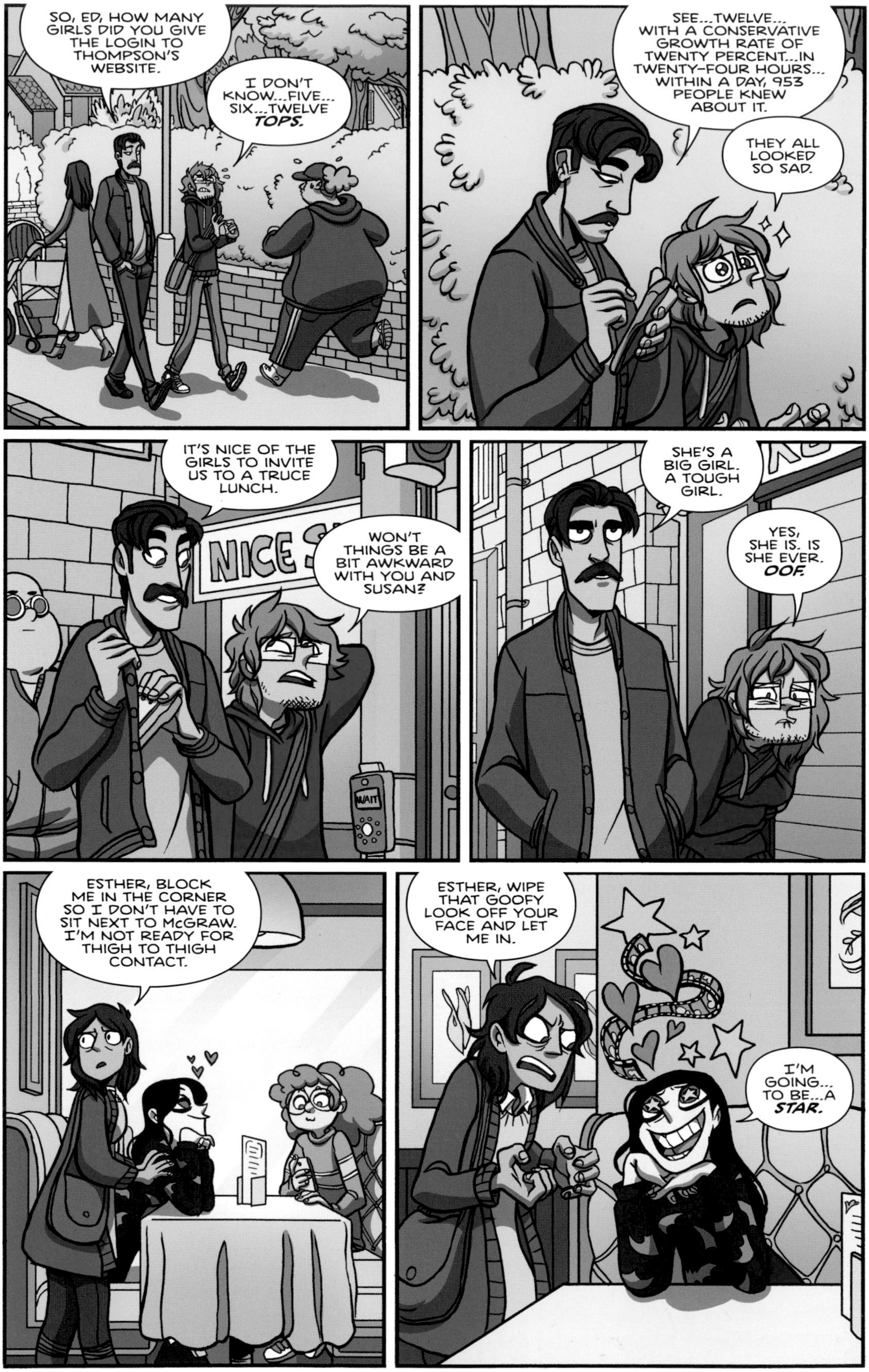
SO, ED, HOW MANY GIRLS DID YOU GIVE THE LOGIN TO THOMPSON'S WEBSITE.
I DON'T KNOW...FIVE... SIX...TWELVE *TOPS.*
SEE...TWELVE... WITH A CONSERVATIVE GROWTH RATE OF TWENTY PERCENT...IN TWENTY-FOUR HOURS... WITHIN A DAY, 953 PEOPLE KNEW ABOUT IT.
THEY ALL LOOKED SO SAD.
IT'S NICE OF THE GIRLS TO INVITE US TO A TRUCE LUNCH.
NICE S
WON'T THINGS BE A BIT AWKWARD WITH YOU AND SUSAN?
WAIT
SHE'S A BIG GIRL. A TOUGH GIRL.
YES, SHE IS. IS SHE EVER. *OOF.*
ESTHER, BLOCK ME IN THE CORNER SO I DON'T HAVE TO SIT NEXT TO McGRAW. I'M NOT READY FOR THIGH TO THIGH CONTACT.
ESTHER, WIPE THAT GOOFY LOOK OFF YOUR FACE AND LET ME IN.
I'M GOING... TO BE...A *STAR.*

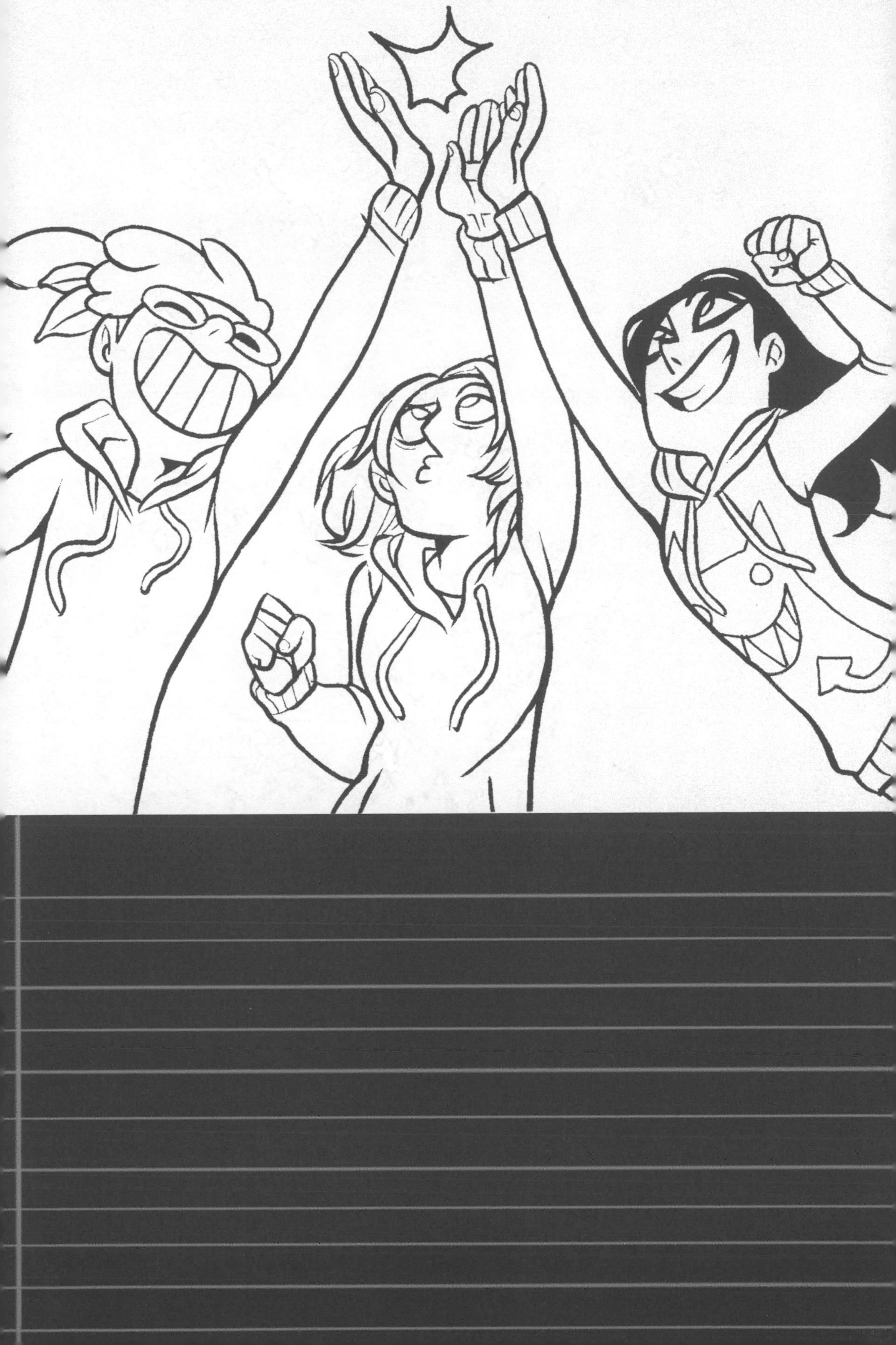

# CHAPTER FIFTEEN

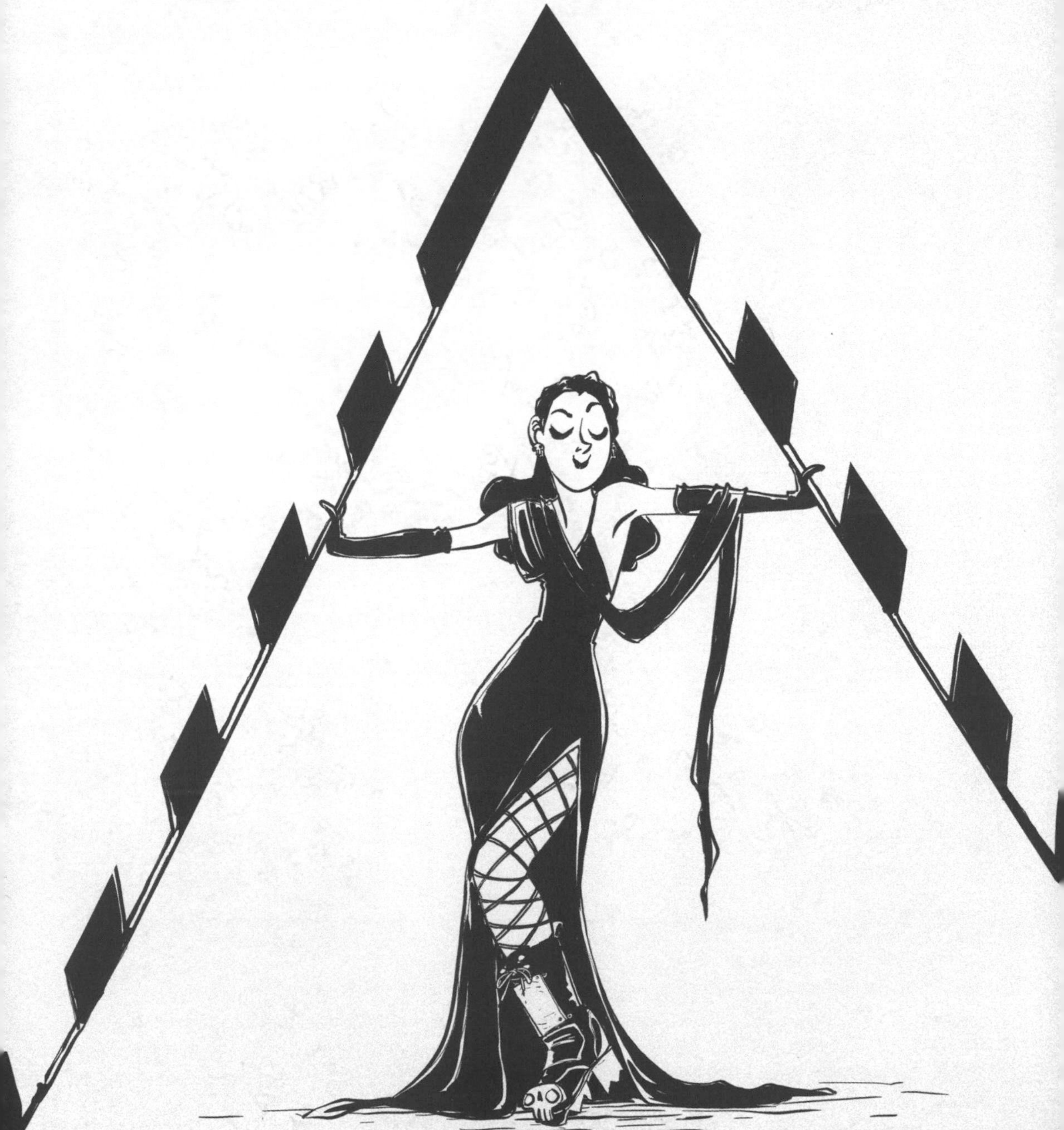

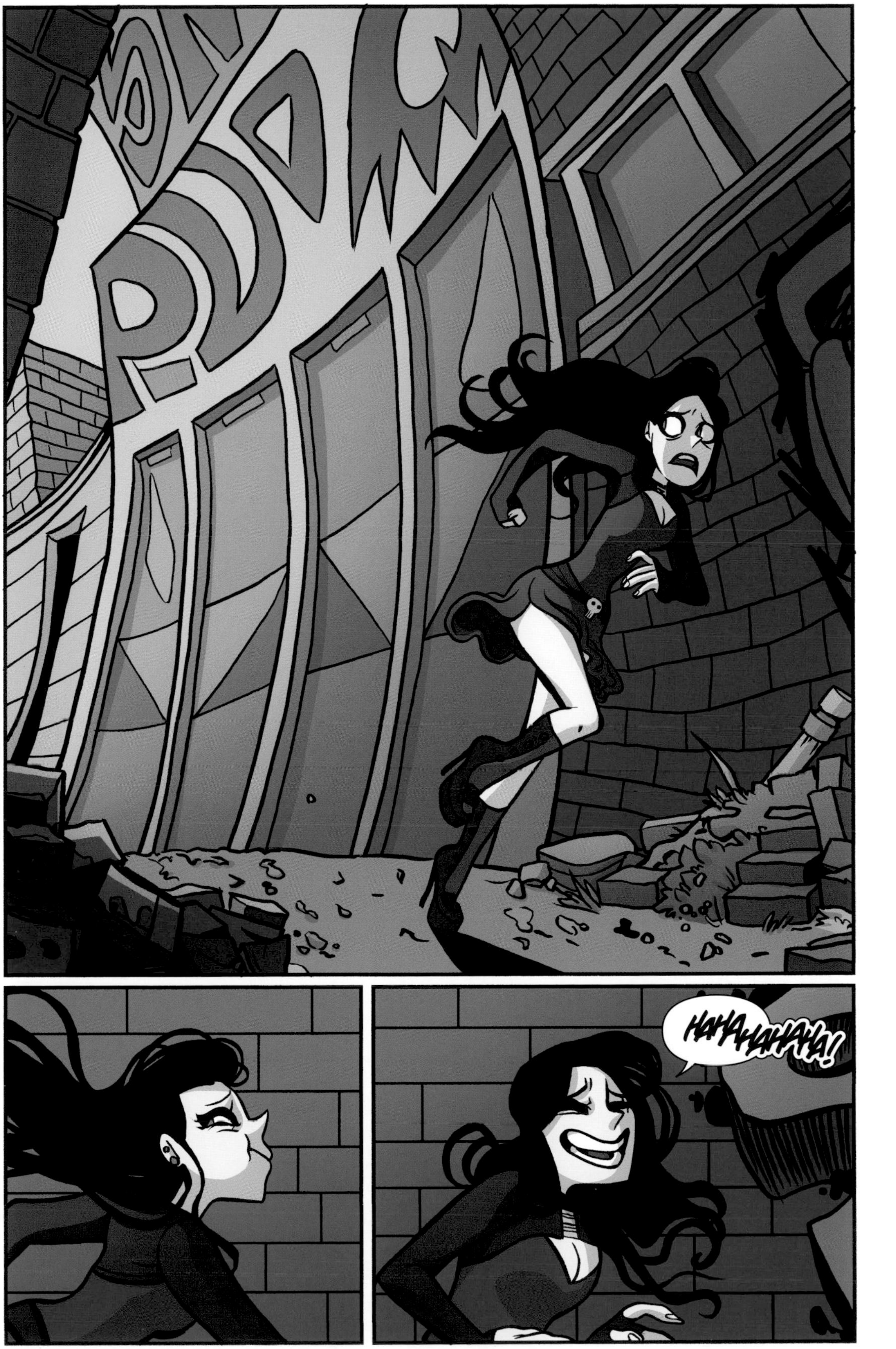
HAHAHAHAHAHA!

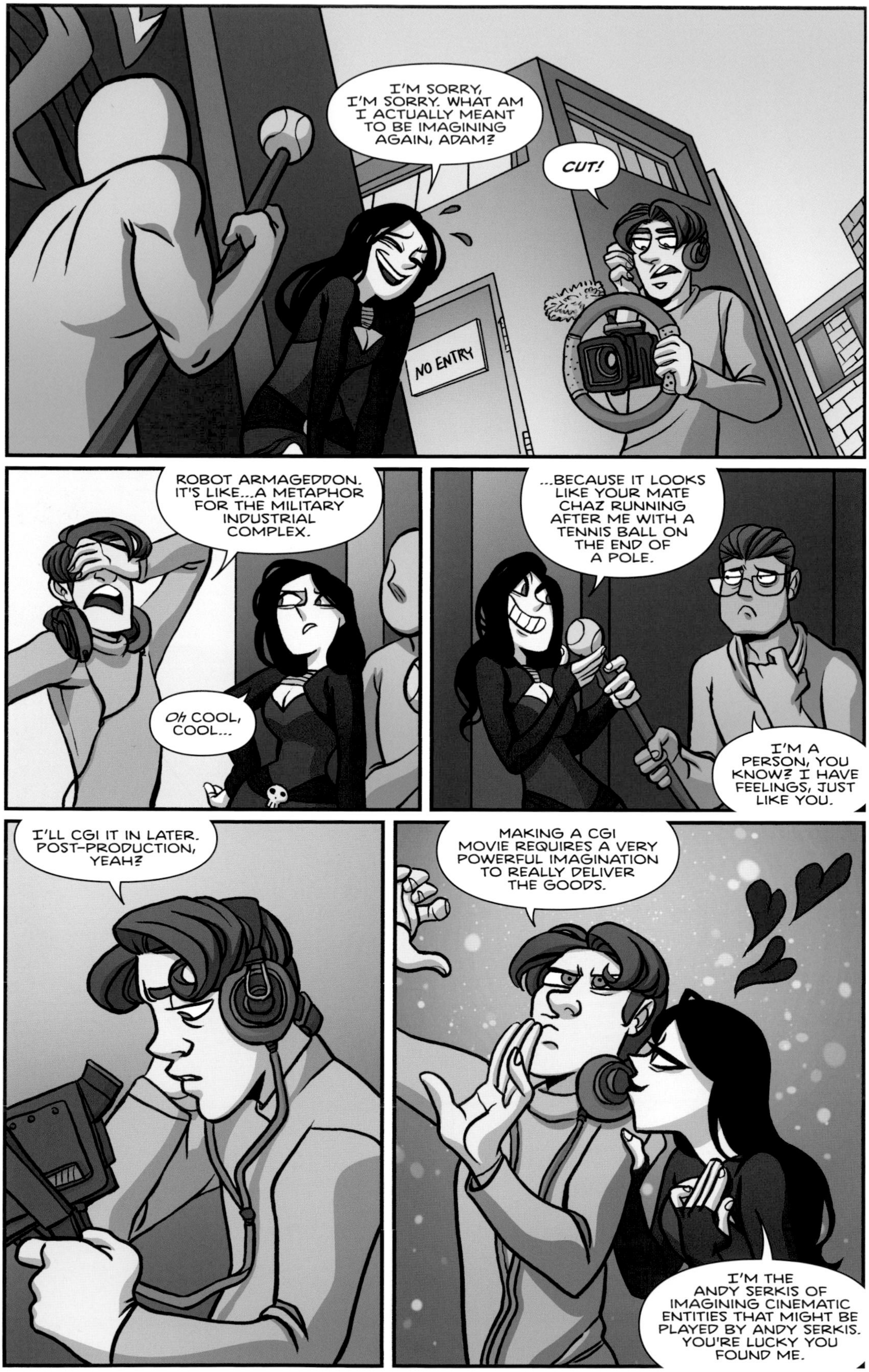
I'M SORRY, I'M SORRY. WHAT AM I ACTUALLY MEANT TO BE IMAGINING AGAIN, ADAM?
CUT!
NO ENTRY
ROBOT ARMAGEDDON. IT'S LIKE...A METAPHOR FOR THE MILITARY INDUSTRIAL COMPLEX.
Oh COOL, COOL...
...BECAUSE IT LOOKS LIKE YOUR MATE CHAZ RUNNING AFTER ME WITH A TENNIS BALL ON THE END OF A POLE.
I'M A PERSON, YOU KNOW? I HAVE FEELINGS, JUST LIKE YOU.
I'LL CGI IT IN LATER. POST-PRODUCTION, YEAH?
MAKING A CGI MOVIE REQUIRES A VERY POWERFUL IMAGINATION TO REALLY DELIVER THE GOODS.
I'M THE ANDY SERKIS OF IMAGINING CINEMATIC ENTITIES THAT MIGHT BE PLAYED BY ANDY SERKIS. YOU'RE LUCKY YOU FOUND ME.

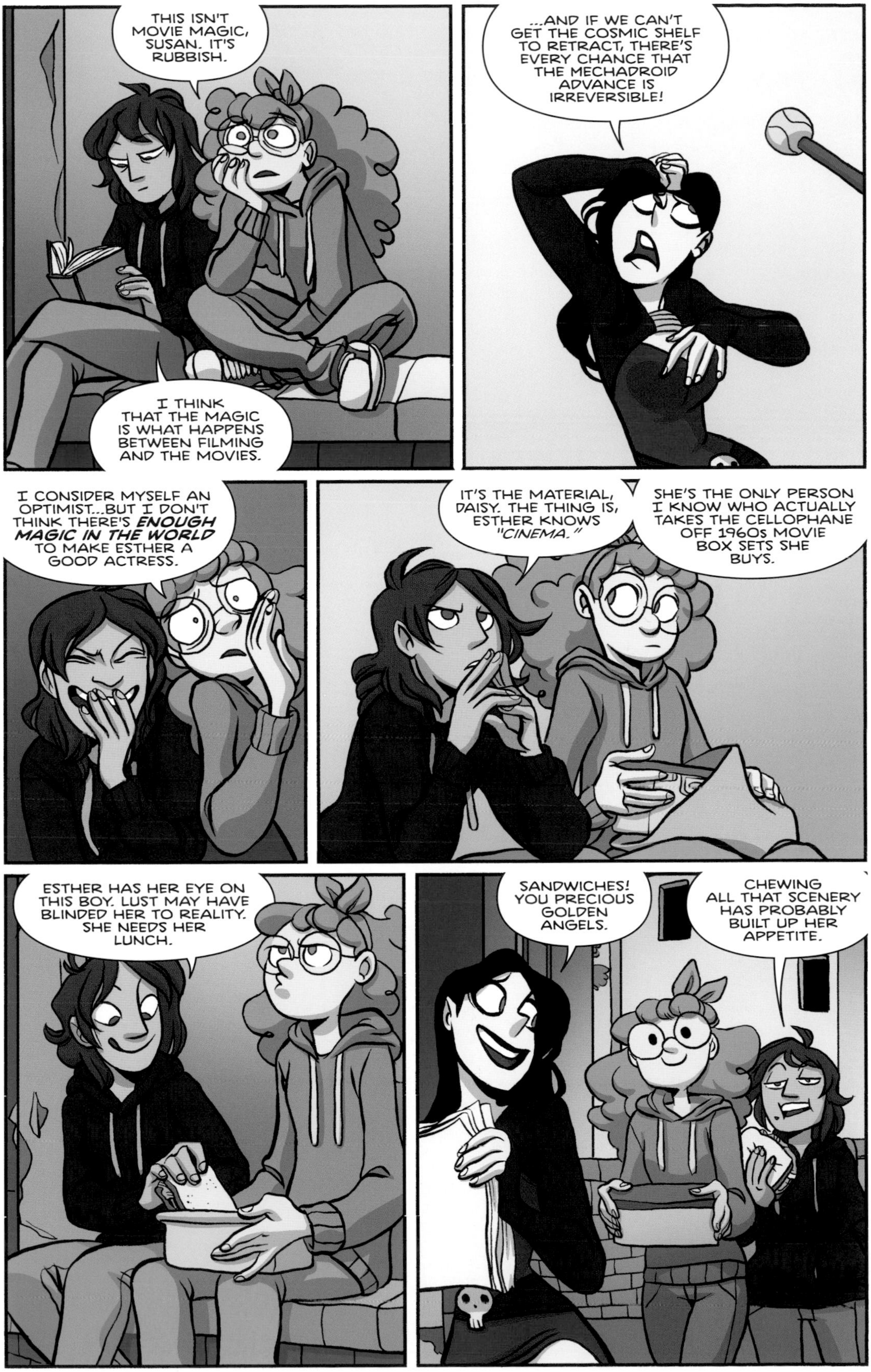
THIS ISN'T MOVIE MAGIC, SUSAN. IT'S RUBBISH.
I THINK THAT THE MAGIC IS WHAT HAPPENS BETWEEN FILMING AND THE MOVIES.
...AND IF WE CAN'T GET THE COSMIC SHELF TO RETRACT, THERE'S EVERY CHANCE THAT THE MECHADROID ADVANCE IS IRREVERSIBLE!
I CONSIDER MYSELF AN OPTIMIST...BUT I DON'T THINK THERE'S ***ENOUGH MAGIC IN THE WORLD*** TO MAKE ESTHER A GOOD ACTRESS.
IT'S THE MATERIAL, DAISY. THE THING IS, ESTHER KNOWS *"CINEMA."*
SHE'S THE ONLY PERSON I KNOW WHO ACTUALLY TAKES THE CELLOPHANE OFF 1960s MOVIE BOX SETS SHE BUYS.
ESTHER HAS HER EYE ON THIS BOY. LUST MAY HAVE BLINDED HER TO REALITY. SHE NEEDS HER LUNCH.
SANDWICHES! YOU PRECIOUS GOLDEN ANGELS.
CHEWING ALL THAT SCENERY HAS PROBABLY BUILT UP HER APPETITE.

SO WHAT DO YOU THINK SO FAR? PRETTY GOOD, RIGHT?

YOU'RE REALLY...DOING THE HEAVY LIFTING ON THIS THING. YOUR... *ENERGY*...IS OFF THE CHARTS.

OH, ADAM'S IN IT TOO! HE'S THE HERO!

OF COURSE HE IS. WHY WOULDN'T HE BE?

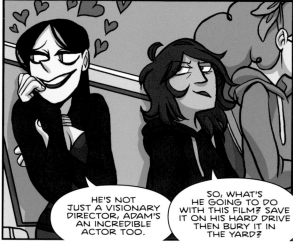

HE'S NOT JUST A VISIONARY DIRECTOR, ADAM'S AN INCREDIBLE ACTOR TOO.

SO, WHAT'S HE GOING TO DO WITH THIS FILM? SAVE IT ON HIS HARD DRIVE THEN BURY IT IN THE YARD?

HE'S ENTERING IT IN THE DON VALLEY FILM FESTIVAL! IT'S *PRESTIGIOUS.*

THERE'S A £5,000 PRIZE, ISN'T THERE?

WHY... WHY WOULD HE DO THAT?

H13-NOM

FIVE LARGE! I COULD BUY A SCOOTER WITH THAT, WRECK IT, THEN BUY *ANOTHER SCOOTER.*

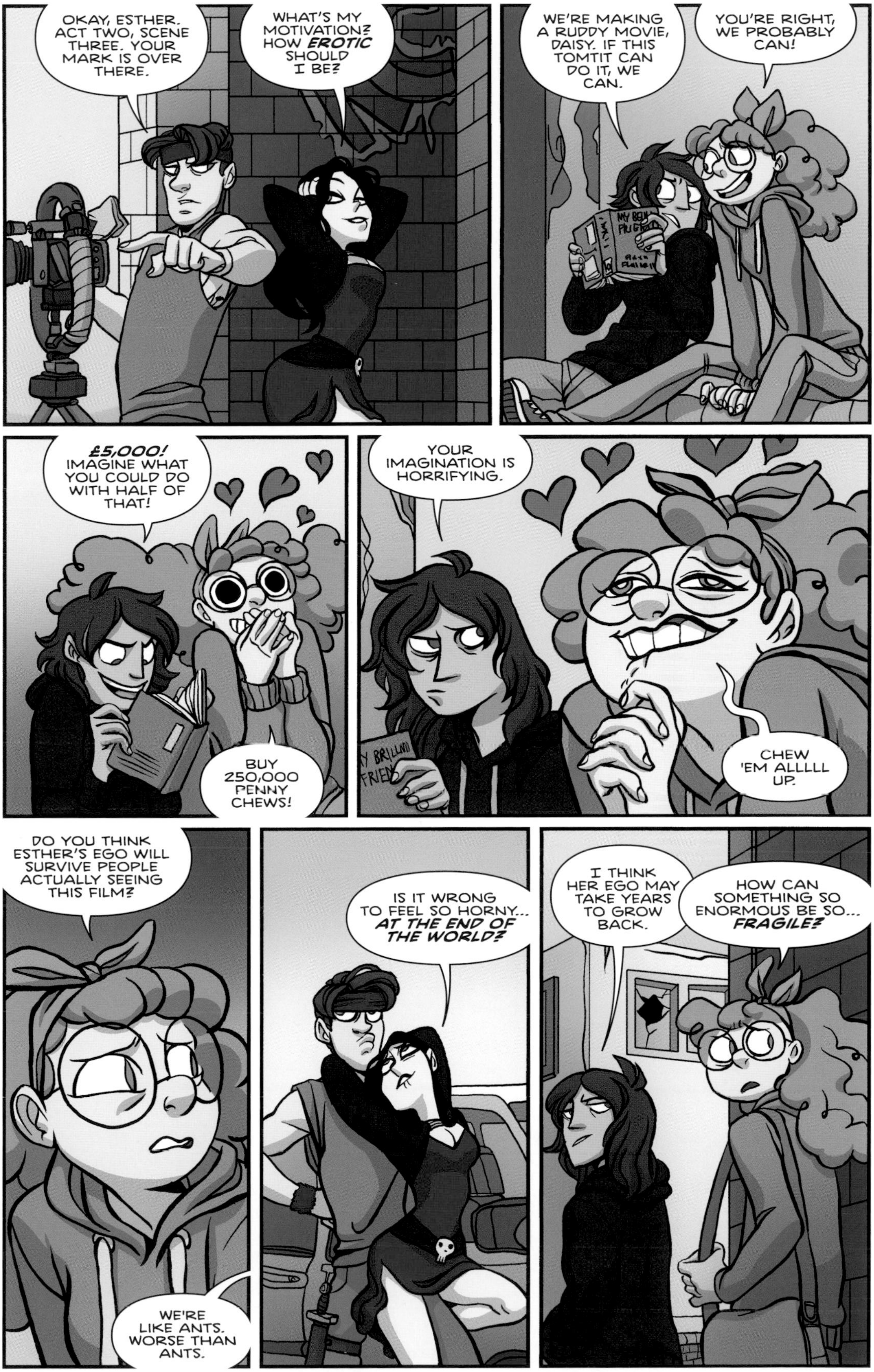
OKAY, ESTHER. ACT TWO, SCENE THREE. YOUR MARK IS OVER THERE.
WHAT'S MY MOTIVATION? HOW *EROTIC* SHOULD I BE?
WE'RE MAKING A RUDDY MOVIE, DAISY. IF THIS TOMTIT CAN DO IT, WE CAN.
YOU'RE RIGHT, WE PROBABLY CAN!
*£5,000!* IMAGINE WHAT YOU COULD DO WITH HALF OF THAT!
BUY 250,000 PENNY CHEWS!
YOUR IMAGINATION IS HORRIFYING.
CHEW 'EM ALLLLL UP.
DO YOU THINK ESTHER'S EGO WILL SURVIVE PEOPLE ACTUALLY SEEING THIS FILM?
WE'RE LIKE ANTS. WORSE THAN ANTS.
IS IT WRONG TO FEEL SO HORNY... *AT THE END OF THE WORLD?*
I THINK HER EGO MAY TAKE YEARS TO GROW BACK.
HOW CAN SOMETHING SO ENORMOUS BE SO... *FRAGILE?*

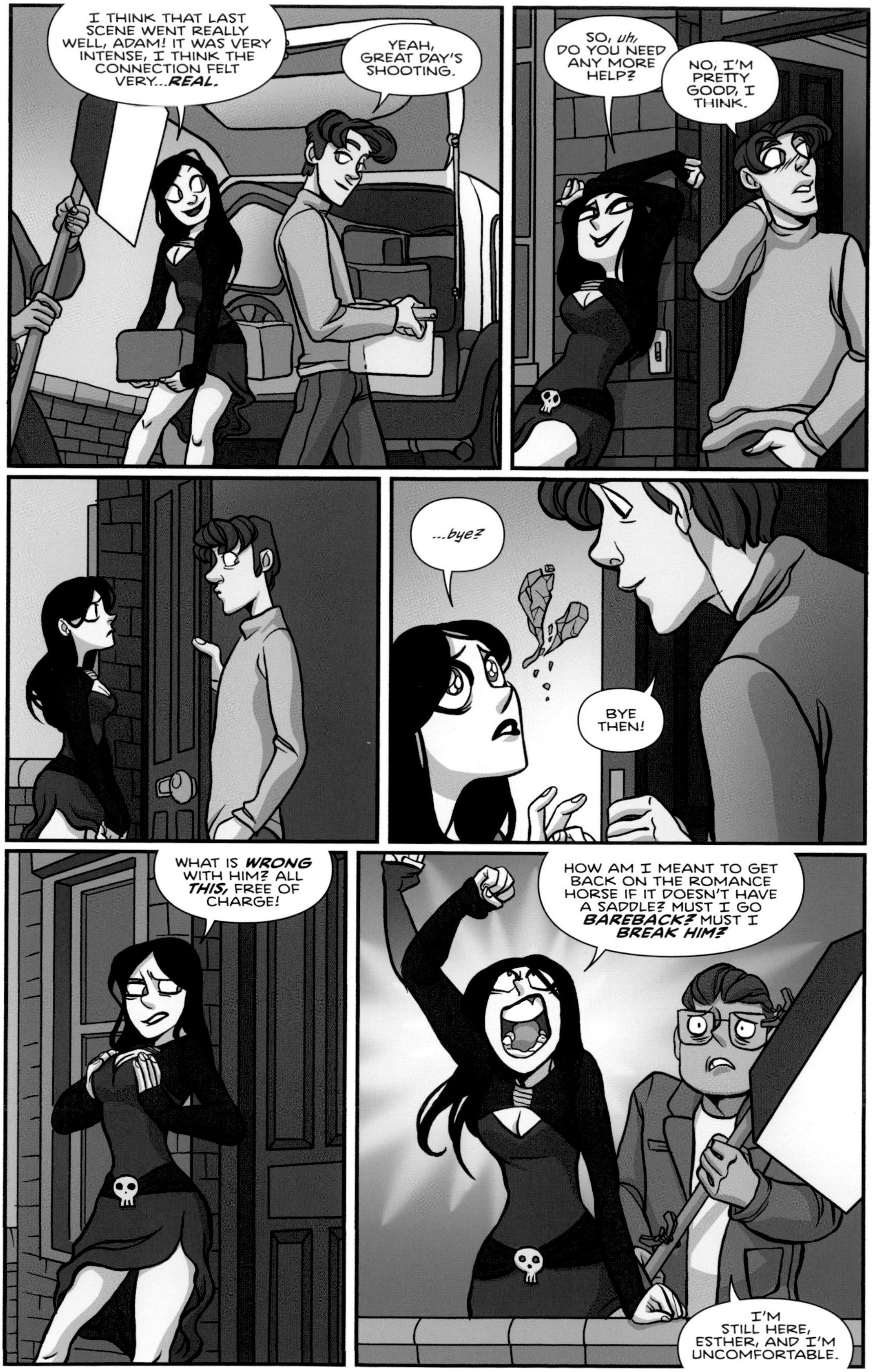
I THINK THAT LAST SCENE WENT REALLY WELL, ADAM! IT WAS VERY INTENSE, I THINK THE CONNECTION FELT VERY...**REAL.**
YEAH, GREAT DAY'S SHOOTING.
SO, *uh,* DO YOU NEED ANY MORE HELP?
NO, I'M PRETTY GOOD, I THINK.
*...bye?*
BYE THEN!
WHAT IS ***WRONG*** WITH HIM? ALL ***THIS,*** FREE OF CHARGE!
HOW AM I MEANT TO GET BACK ON THE ROMANCE HORSE IF IT DOESN'T HAVE A SADDLE? MUST I GO ***BAREBACK?*** MUST I ***BREAK HIM?***
I'M STILL HERE, ESTHER, AND I'M UNCOMFORTABLE.

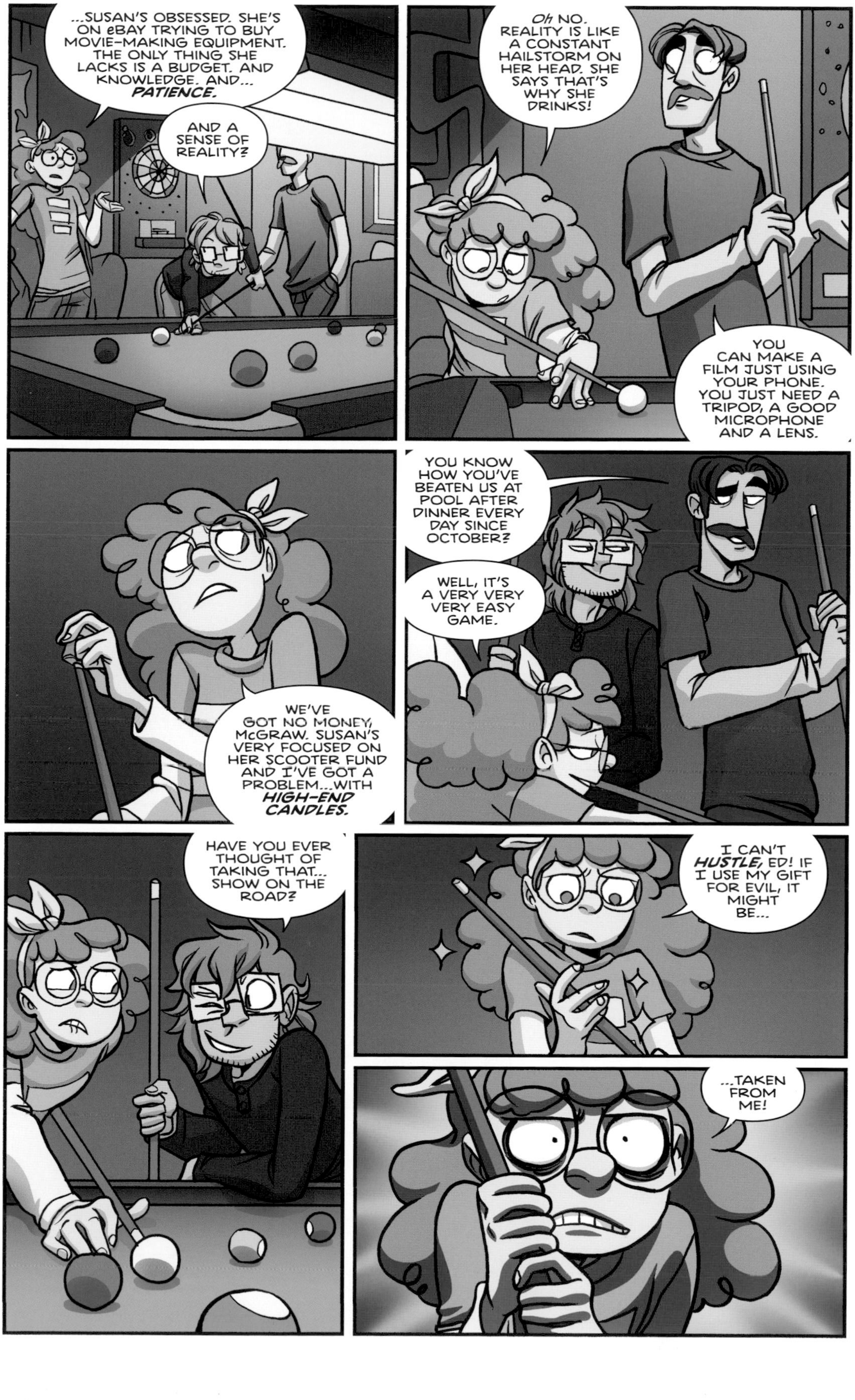
...SUSAN'S OBSESSED. SHE'S ON eBAY TRYING TO BUY MOVIE-MAKING EQUIPMENT. THE ONLY THING SHE LACKS IS A BUDGET. AND KNOWLEDGE. AND... PATIENCE.
AND A SENSE OF REALITY?
Oh NO. REALITY IS LIKE A CONSTANT HAILSTORM ON HER HEAD. SHE SAYS THAT'S WHY SHE DRINKS!
YOU CAN MAKE A FILM JUST USING YOUR PHONE. YOU JUST NEED A TRIPOD, A GOOD MICROPHONE AND A LENS.
WE'VE GOT NO MONEY, McGRAW. SUSAN'S VERY FOCUSED ON HER SCOOTER FUND AND I'VE GOT A PROBLEM...WITH HIGH-END CANDLES.
YOU KNOW HOW YOU'VE BEATEN US AT POOL AFTER DINNER EVERY DAY SINCE OCTOBER?
WELL, IT'S A VERY VERY VERY EASY GAME.
HAVE YOU EVER THOUGHT OF TAKING THAT... SHOW ON THE ROAD?
I CAN'T HUSTLE, ED! IF I USE MY GIFT FOR EVIL, IT MIGHT BE...
...TAKEN FROM ME!

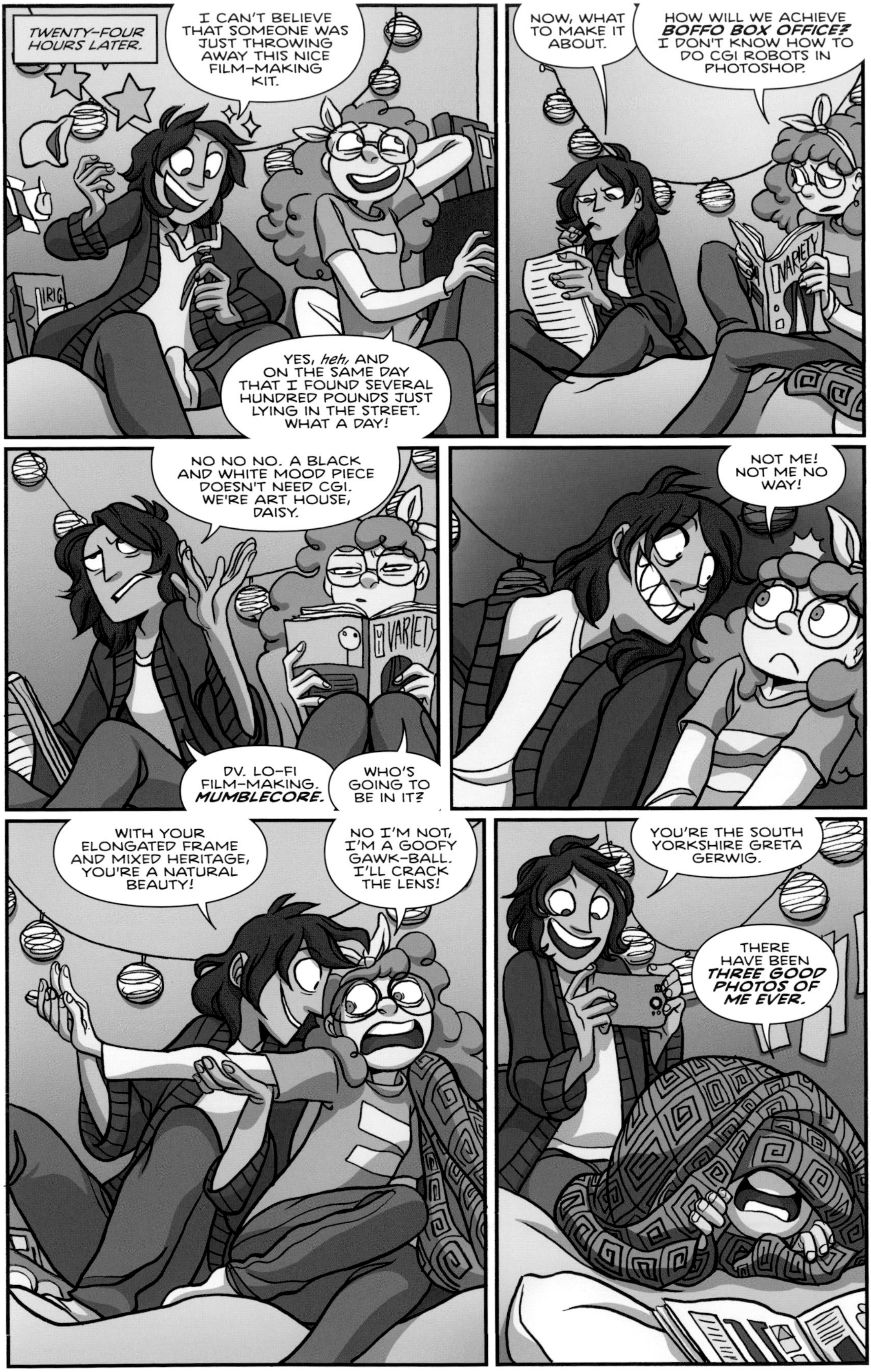

TWENTY-FOUR HOURS LATER.
I CAN'T BELIEVE THAT SOMEONE WAS JUST THROWING AWAY THIS NICE FILM-MAKING KIT.
YES, *heh*, AND ON THE SAME DAY THAT I FOUND SEVERAL HUNDRED POUNDS JUST LYING IN THE STREET. WHAT A DAY!
NOW, WHAT TO MAKE IT ABOUT.
HOW WILL WE ACHIEVE **BOFFO BOX OFFICE?** I DON'T KNOW HOW TO DO CGI ROBOTS IN PHOTOSHOP.
VARIETY
NO NO NO. A BLACK AND WHITE MOOD PIECE DOESN'T NEED CGI. WE'RE ART HOUSE, DAISY.
VARIETY
DV. LO-FI FILM-MAKING. ***MUMBLECORE.***
WHO'S GOING TO BE IN IT?
NOT ME! NOT ME NO WAY!
WITH YOUR ELONGATED FRAME AND MIXED HERITAGE, YOU'RE A NATURAL BEAUTY!
NO I'M NOT, I'M A GOOFY GAWK-BALL. I'LL CRACK THE LENS!
YOU'RE THE SOUTH YORKSHIRE GRETA GERWIG.
THERE HAVE BEEN ***THREE GOOD PHOTOS OF ME EVER.***

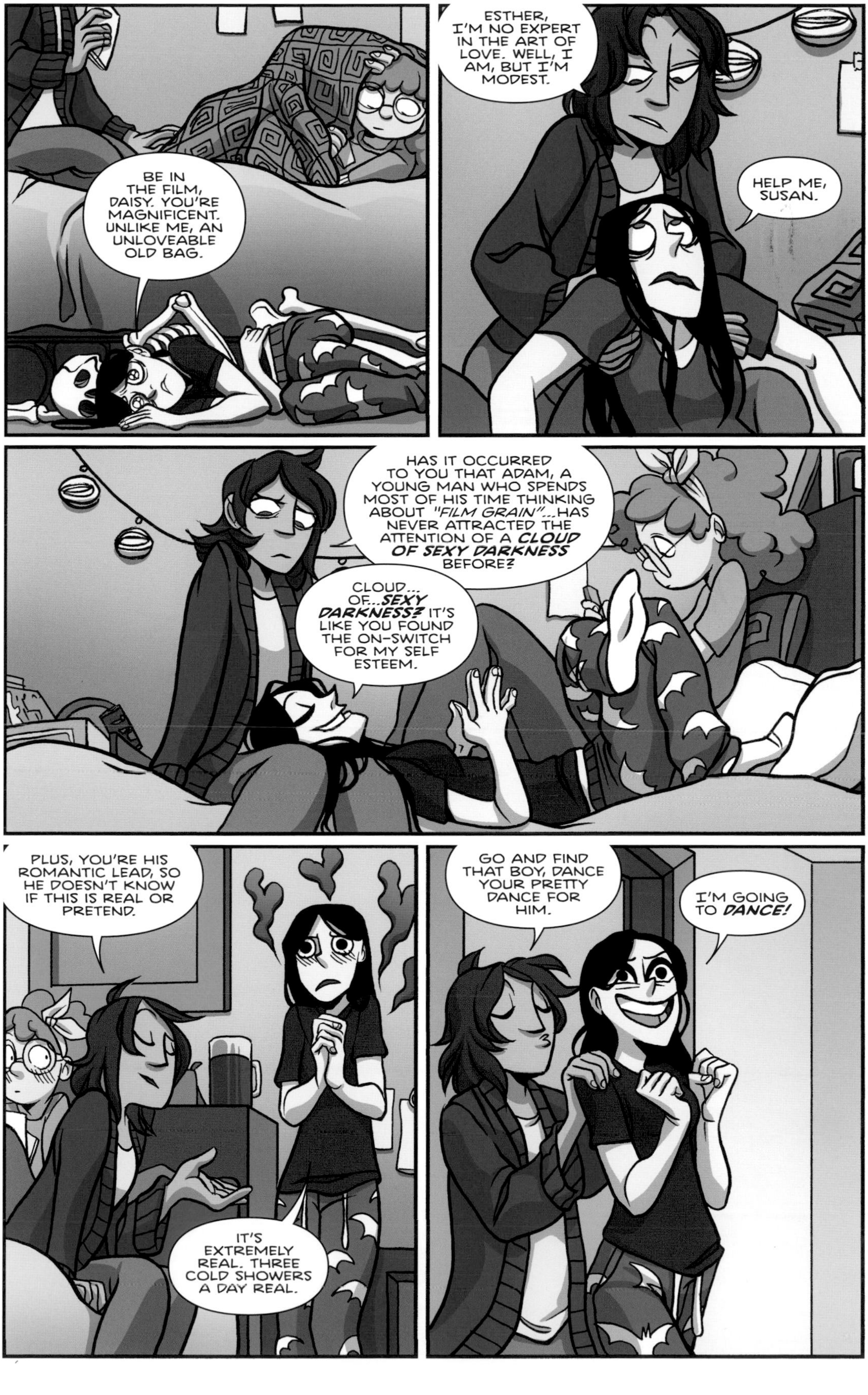
BE IN THE FILM, DAISY. YOU'RE MAGNIFICENT. UNLIKE ME, AN UNLOVEABLE OLD BAG.
ESTHER, I'M NO EXPERT IN THE ART OF LOVE. WELL, I AM, BUT I'M MODEST.
HELP ME, SUSAN.
HAS IT OCCURRED TO YOU THAT ADAM, A YOUNG MAN WHO SPENDS MOST OF HIS TIME THINKING ABOUT *"FILM GRAIN"*... HAS NEVER ATTRACTED THE ATTENTION OF A ***CLOUD OF SEXY DARKNESS*** BEFORE?
CLOUD... OF... ***SEXY DARKNESS?*** IT'S LIKE YOU FOUND THE ON-SWITCH FOR MY SELF ESTEEM.
PLUS, YOU'RE HIS ROMANTIC LEAD, SO HE DOESN'T KNOW IF THIS IS REAL OR PRETEND.
IT'S EXTREMELY REAL. THREE COLD SHOWERS A DAY REAL.
GO AND FIND THAT BOY, DANCE YOUR PRETTY DANCE FOR HIM.
I'M GOING TO ***DANCE!***

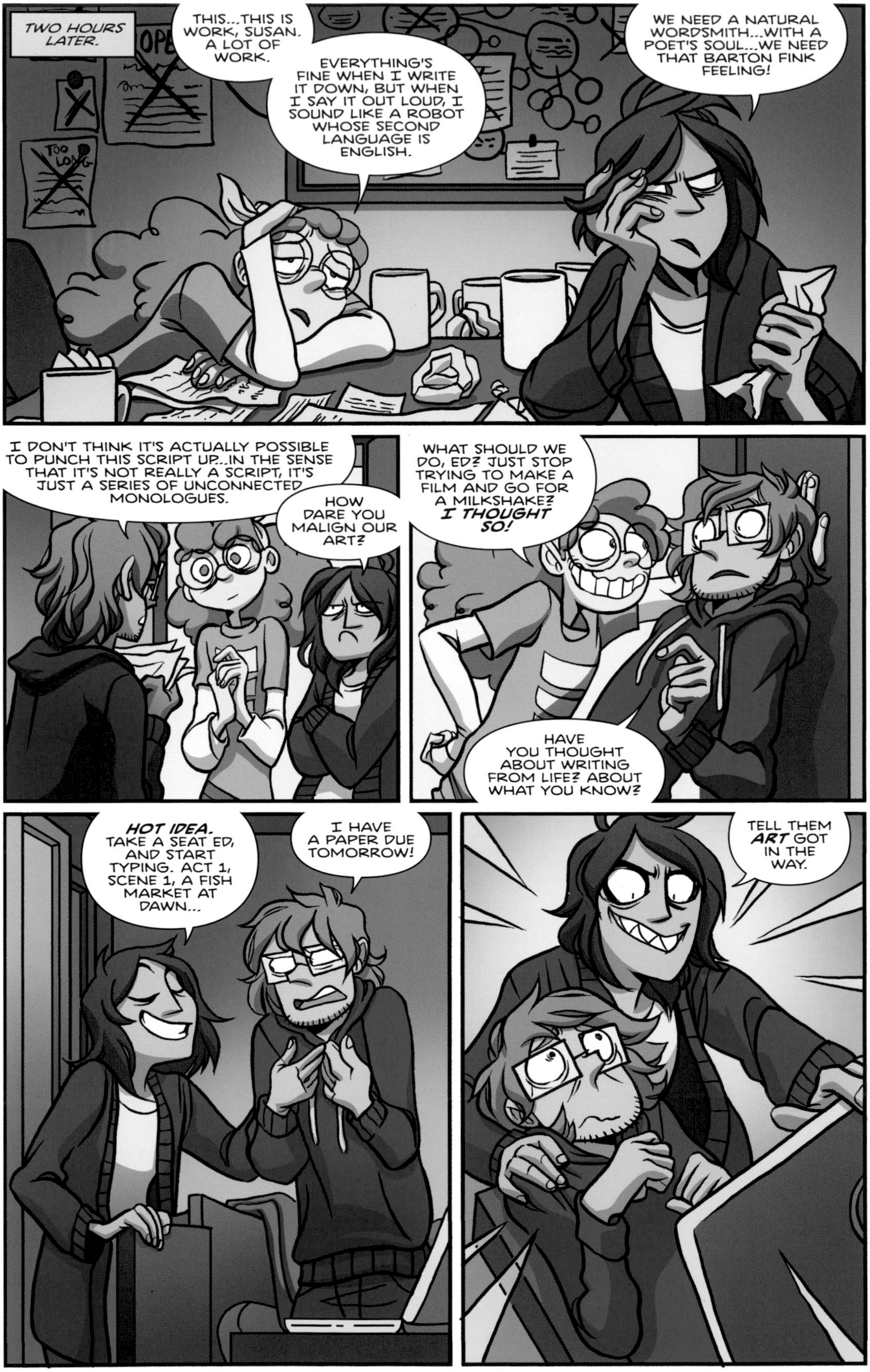
TWO HOURS LATER.
THIS...THIS IS WORK, SUSAN. A LOT OF WORK.
EVERYTHING'S FINE WHEN I WRITE IT DOWN, BUT WHEN I SAY IT OUT LOUD, I SOUND LIKE A ROBOT WHOSE SECOND LANGUAGE IS ENGLISH.
WE NEED A NATURAL WORDSMITH...WITH A POET'S SOUL...WE NEED THAT BARTON FINK FEELING!
I DON'T THINK IT'S ACTUALLY POSSIBLE TO PUNCH THIS SCRIPT UP...IN THE SENSE THAT IT'S NOT REALLY A SCRIPT, IT'S JUST A SERIES OF UNCONNECTED MONOLOGUES.
HOW DARE YOU MALIGN OUR ART?
WHAT SHOULD WE DO, ED? JUST STOP TRYING TO MAKE A FILM AND GO FOR A MILKSHAKE? *I THOUGHT SO!*
HAVE YOU THOUGHT ABOUT WRITING FROM LIFE? ABOUT WHAT YOU KNOW?
*HOT IDEA.* TAKE A SEAT ED, AND START TYPING. ACT 1, SCENE 1, A FISH MARKET AT DAWN...
I HAVE A PAPER DUE TOMORROW!
TELL THEM *ART* GOT IN THE WAY.

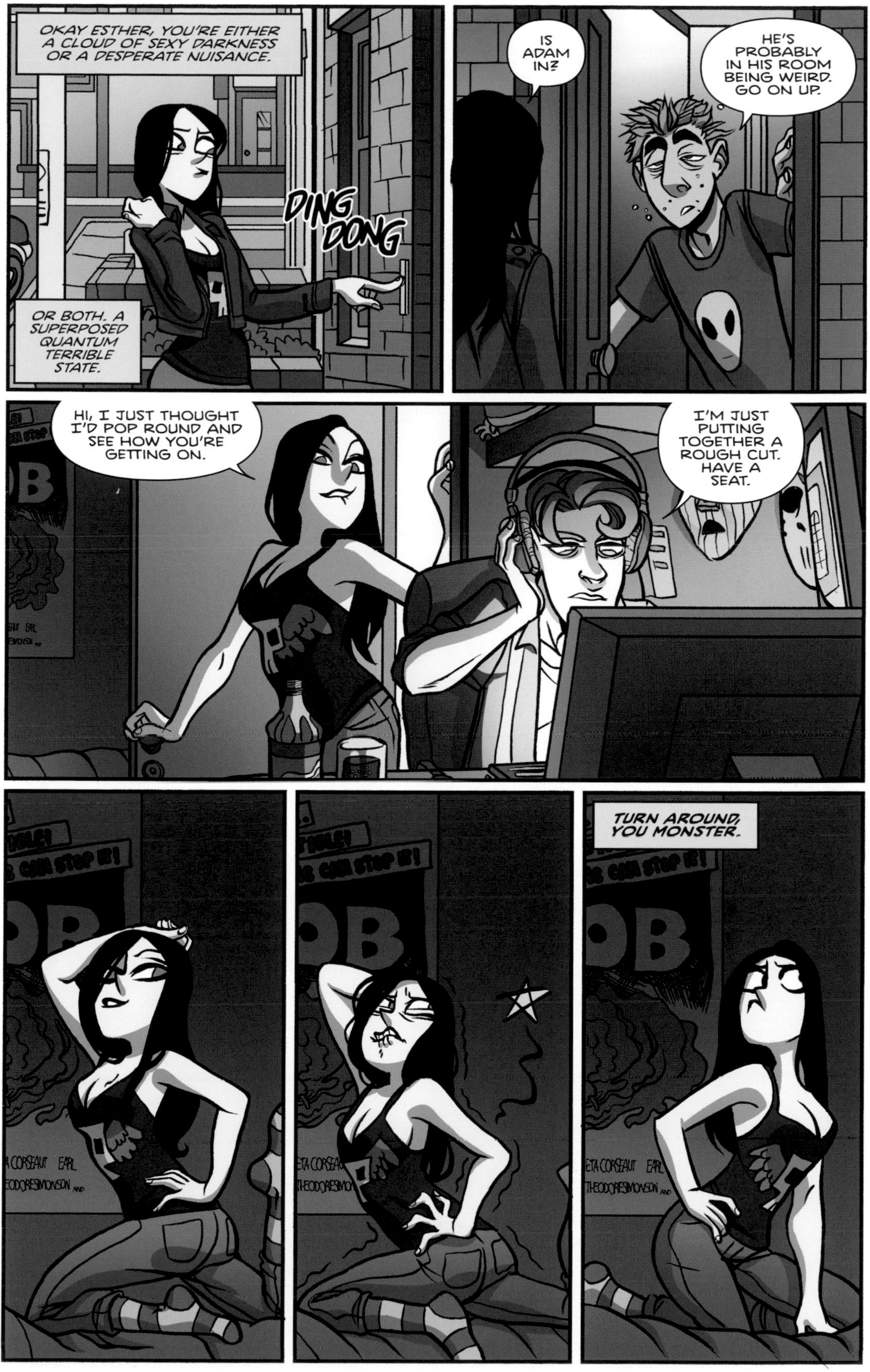
OKAY ESTHER, YOU'RE EITHER A CLOUD OF SEXY DARKNESS OR A DESPERATE NUISANCE.
DING DONG
OR BOTH. A SUPERPOSED QUANTUM TERRIBLE STATE.
IS ADAM IN?
HE'S PROBABLY IN HIS ROOM BEING WEIRD. GO ON UP.
HI, I JUST THOUGHT I'D POP ROUND AND SEE HOW YOU'RE GETTING ON.
I'M JUST PUTTING TOGETHER A ROUGH CUT. HAVE A SEAT.
TURN AROUND, YOU MONSTER.

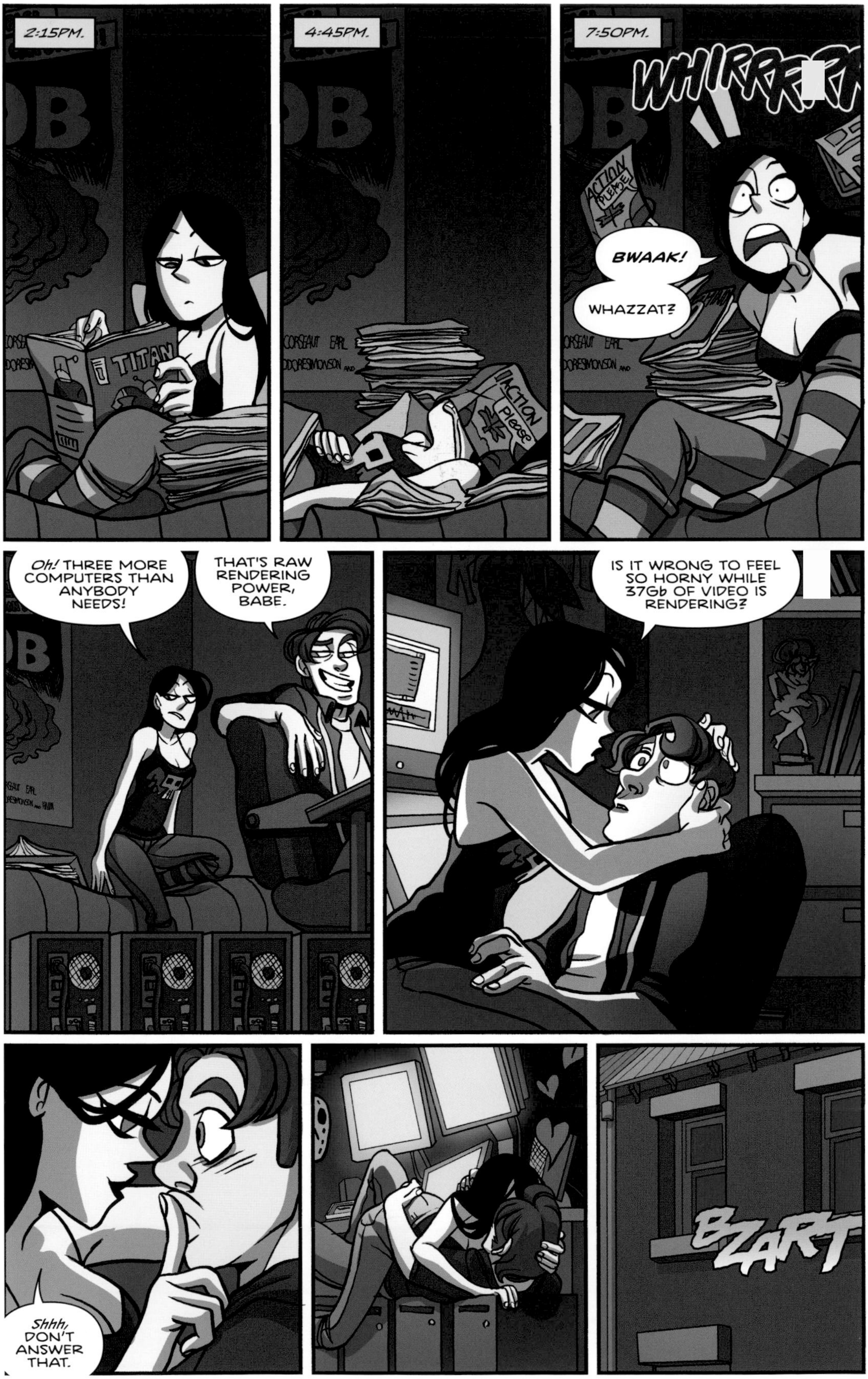
2:15PM.
4:45PM.
7:50PM.
WHIRRRR
BWAAK!
WHAZZAT?
Oh! THREE MORE COMPUTERS THAN ANYBODY NEEDS!
THAT'S RAW RENDERING POWER, BABE.
IS IT WRONG TO FEEL SO HORNY WHILE 37Gb OF VIDEO IS RENDERING?
Shhh, DON'T ANSWER THAT.
BZART

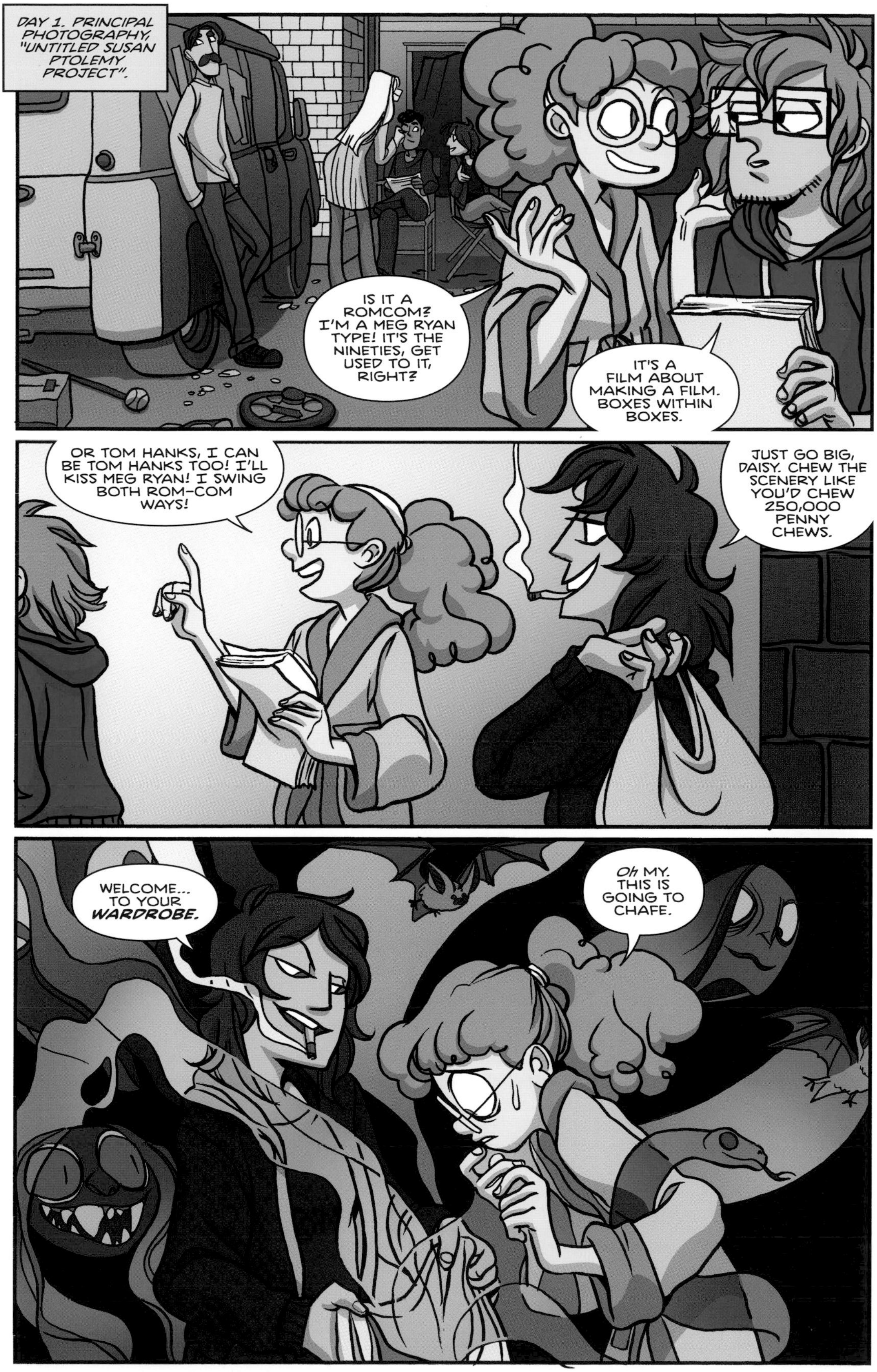
DAY 1. PRINCIPAL PHOTOGRAPHY, "UNTITLED SUSAN PTOLEMY PROJECT".
IS IT A ROMCOM? I'M A MEG RYAN TYPE! IT'S THE NINETIES, GET USED TO IT, RIGHT?
IT'S A FILM ABOUT MAKING A FILM. BOXES WITHIN BOXES.
OR TOM HANKS, I CAN BE TOM HANKS TOO! I'LL KISS MEG RYAN! I SWING BOTH ROM-COM WAYS!
JUST GO BIG, DAISY. CHEW THE SCENERY LIKE YOU'D CHEW 250,000 PENNY CHEWS.
WELCOME... TO YOUR WARDROBE.
Oh MY. THIS IS GOING TO CHAFE.

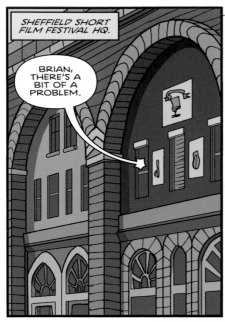

SHEFFIELD SHORT FILM FESTIVAL HQ.

BRIAN, THERE'S A BIT OF A PROBLEM.

YOU KNOW YOUR NEPHEW HARRY, WHO'S BEEN INTERNING WITH US?

LOVELY LAD, NEEDS A FIRM HAND IS ALL.

WELL, HE MAY HAVE WIPED ALL BUT *FIVE* OF THE HARD DRIVES WITH THE FESTIVAL FILMS ON THEM PLAYING WITH HIS BIG MAGNET.

I SEE. WELL, THIS INFORMATION MUST NEVER GET OUT. *YOU KNOW WHAT TO DO.*

OUR FILM WAS ACCEPTED FOR THE FILM FESTIVAL GRAND PRIZE!

SO WAS OURS! MAY THE BEST WOMAN WIN!

ARE YOU READY TO *OWN* THE RED CARPET, SUSIE PEE?

IF YOU MEAN, AM I READY TO RUN ALONG IT FASTER THAN ANY HUMAN EVER HAS? YES.

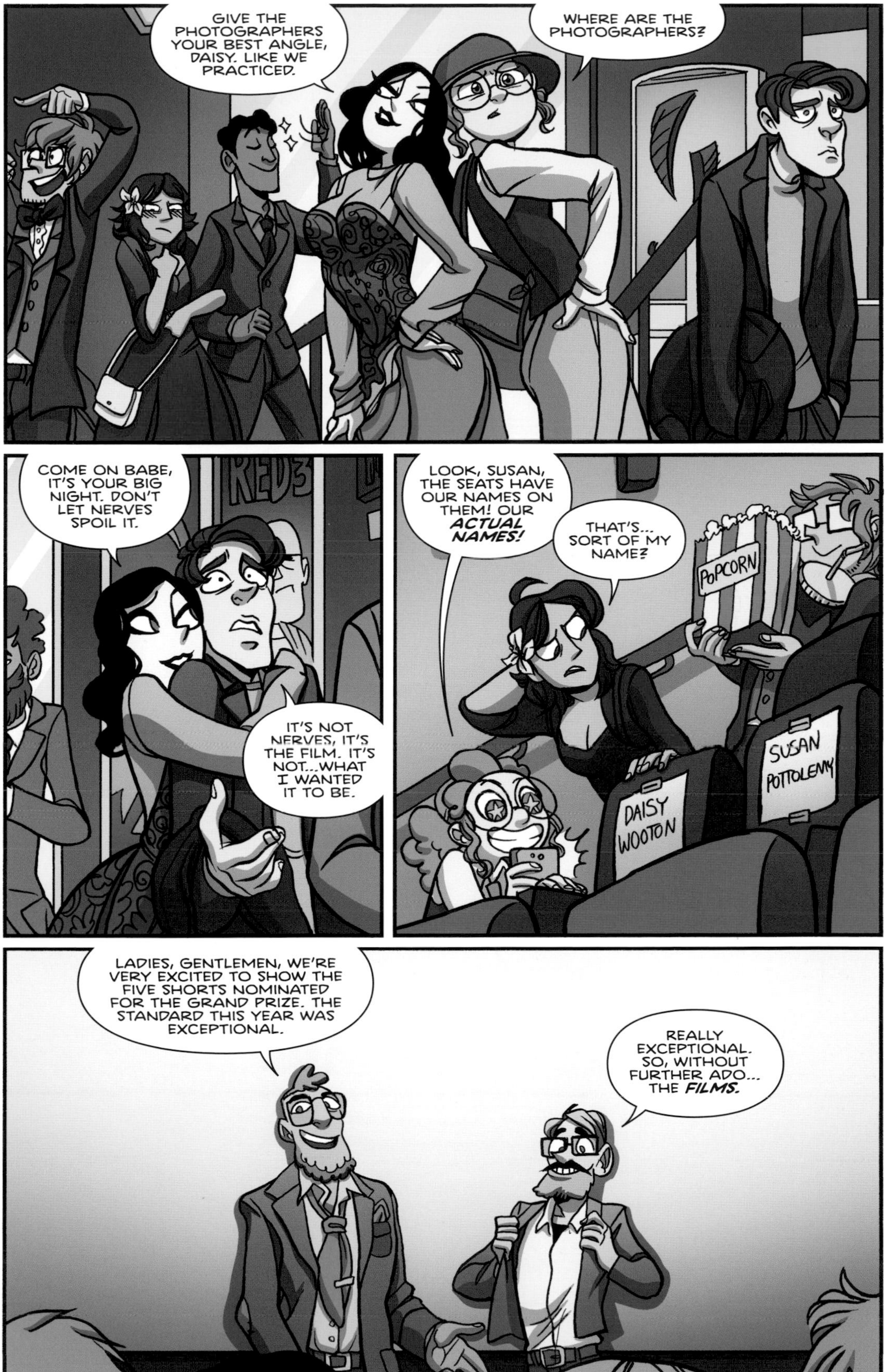
GIVE THE PHOTOGRAPHERS YOUR BEST ANGLE, DAISY. LIKE WE PRACTICED.
WHERE ARE THE PHOTOGRAPHERS?
COME ON BABE, IT'S YOUR BIG NIGHT. DON'T LET NERVES SPOIL IT.
IT'S NOT NERVES, IT'S THE FILM. IT'S NOT...WHAT I WANTED IT TO BE.
LOOK, SUSAN, THE SEATS HAVE OUR NAMES ON THEM! OUR *ACTUAL NAMES!*
THAT'S... SORT OF MY NAME?
POPCORN
DAISY WOOTON
SUSAN POTTOLENY
LADIES, GENTLEMEN, WE'RE VERY EXCITED TO SHOW THE FIVE SHORTS NOMINATED FOR THE GRAND PRIZE. THE STANDARD THIS YEAR WAS EXCEPTIONAL.
REALLY EXCEPTIONAL. SO, WITHOUT FURTHER ADO... THE *FILMS.*

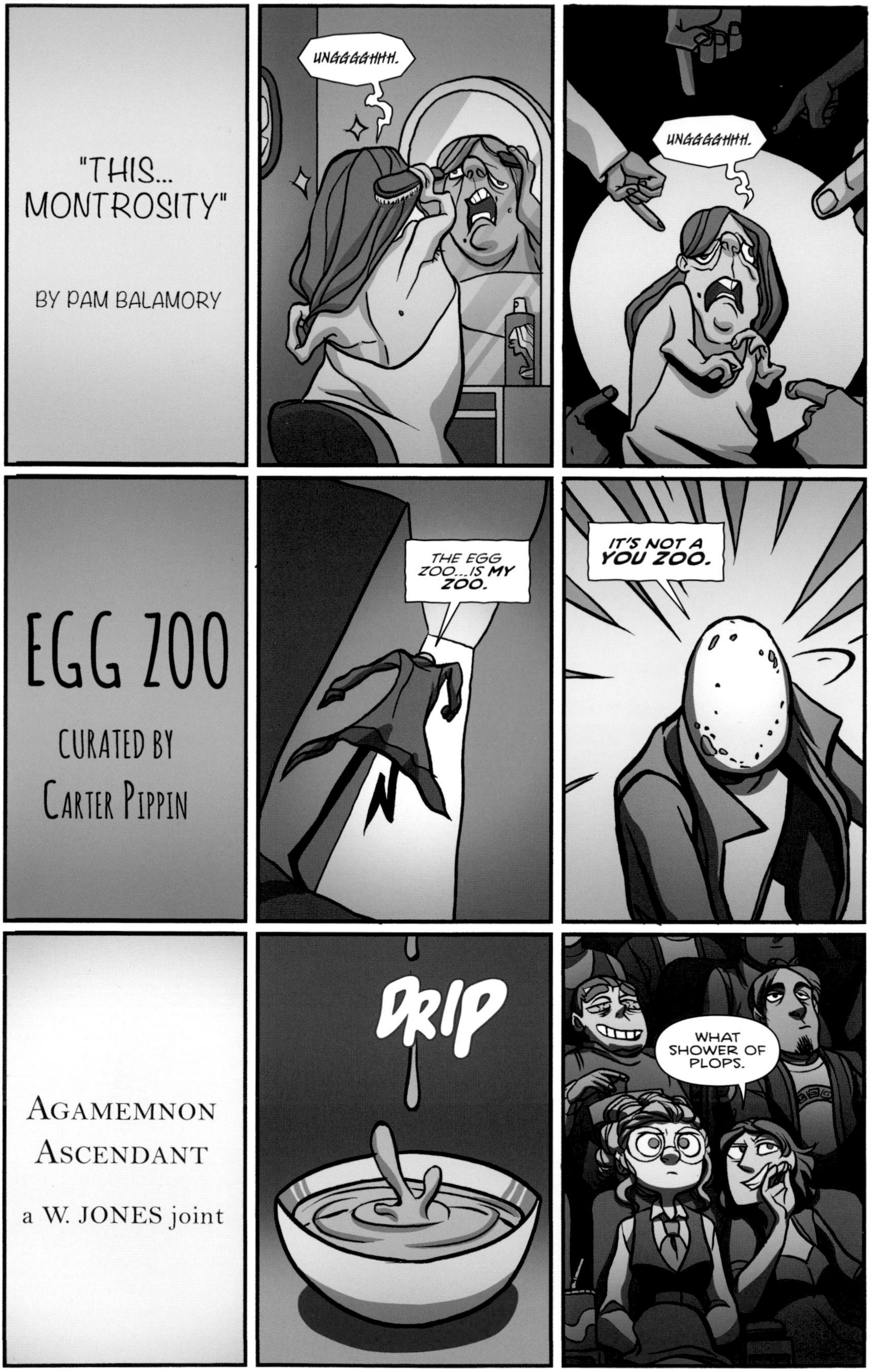
"THIS... MONTROSITY"
BY PAM BALAMORY
UNGGGGHHH.
UNGGGGHHH.
EGG ZOO
CURATED BY
CARTER PIPPIN
THE EGG ZOO... IS MY ZOO.
IT'S NOT A YOU ZOO.
AGAMEMNON
ASCENDANT
a W. JONES joint
DRIP
WHAT SHOWER OF PLOPS.

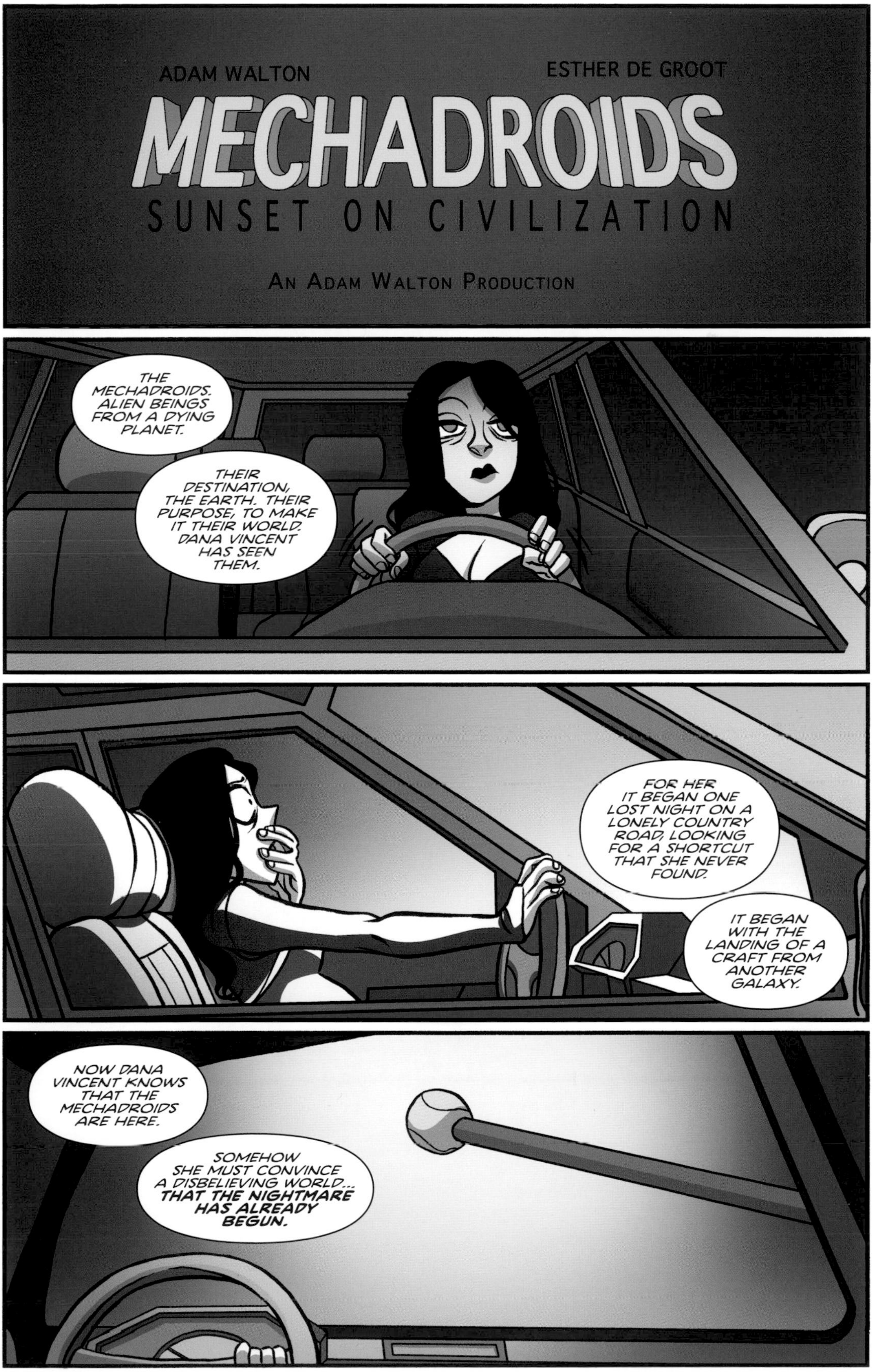
ADAM WALTON
ESTHER DE GROOT
MECHADROIDS
SUNSET ON CIVILIZATION
AN ADAM WALTON PRODUCTION
THE MECHADROIDS. ALIEN BEINGS FROM A DYING PLANET.
THEIR DESTINATION, THE EARTH. THEIR PURPOSE, TO MAKE IT THEIR WORLD. DANA VINCENT HAS SEEN THEM.
FOR HER IT BEGAN ONE LOST NIGHT ON A LONELY COUNTRY ROAD, LOOKING FOR A SHORTCUT THAT SHE NEVER FOUND.
IT BEGAN WITH THE LANDING OF A CRAFT FROM ANOTHER GALAXY.
NOW DANA VINCENT KNOWS THAT THE MECHADROIDS ARE HERE.
SOMEHOW SHE MUST CONVINCE A DISBELIEVING WORLD... THAT THE NIGHTMARE HAS ALREADY BEGUN.

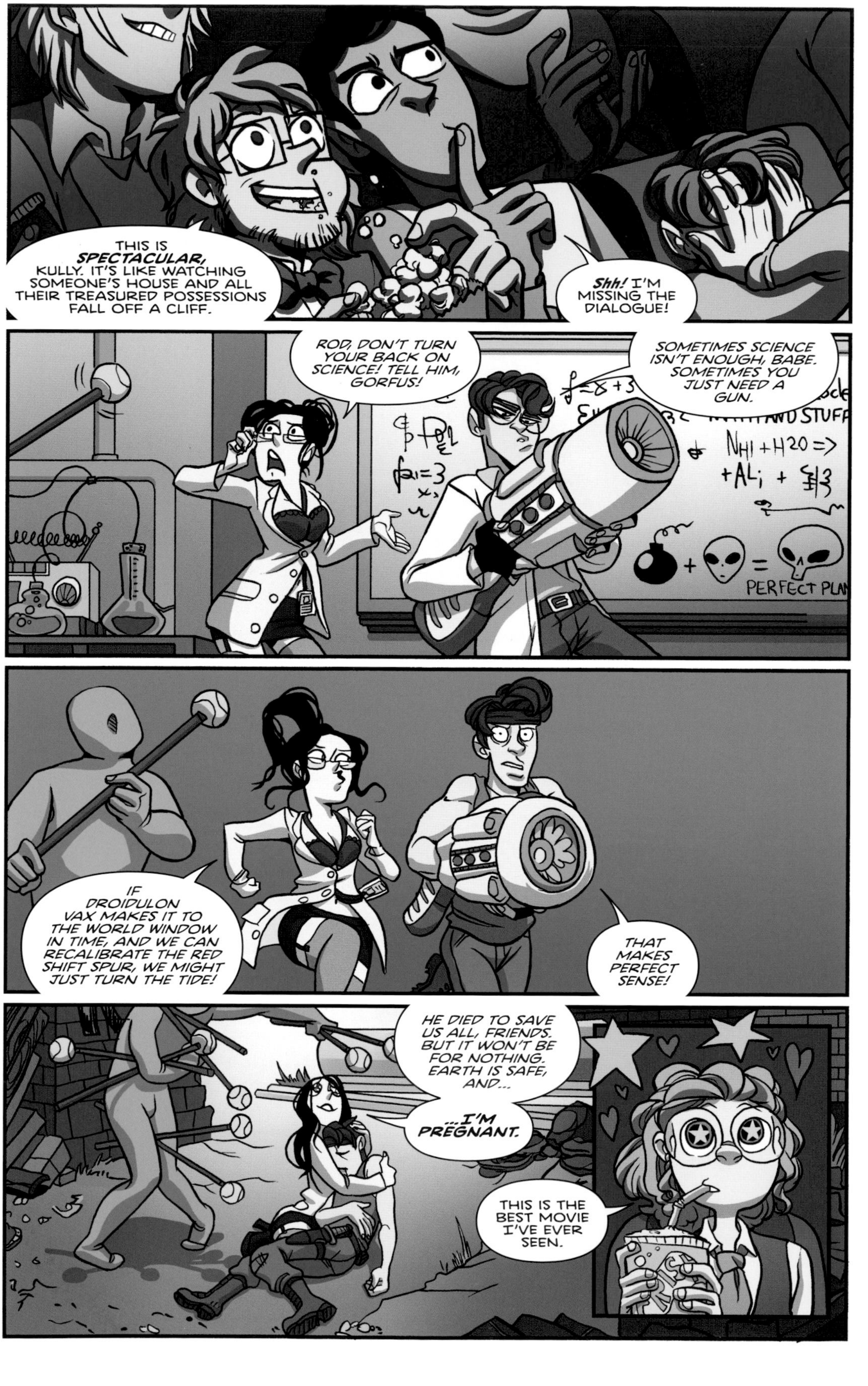
THIS IS **SPECTACULAR,** KULLY. IT'S LIKE WATCHING SOMEONE'S HOUSE AND ALL THEIR TREASURED POSSESSIONS FALL OFF A CLIFF.
**Shh!** I'M MISSING THE DIALOGUE!
ROD, DON'T TURN YOUR BACK ON SCIENCE! TELL HIM, GORFUS!
SOMETIMES SCIENCE ISN'T ENOUGH, BABE. SOMETIMES YOU JUST NEED A GUN.
MATH AND STUFF
PERFECT PLAN
IF DROIDULON VAX MAKES IT TO THE WORLD WINDOW IN TIME, AND WE CAN RECALIBRATE THE RED SHIFT SPUR, WE MIGHT JUST TURN THE TIDE!
THAT MAKES PERFECT SENSE!
HE DIED TO SAVE US ALL, FRIENDS. BUT IT WON'T BE FOR NOTHING. EARTH IS SAFE, AND...
**...I'M PREGNANT.**
THIS IS THE BEST MOVIE I'VE EVER SEEN.

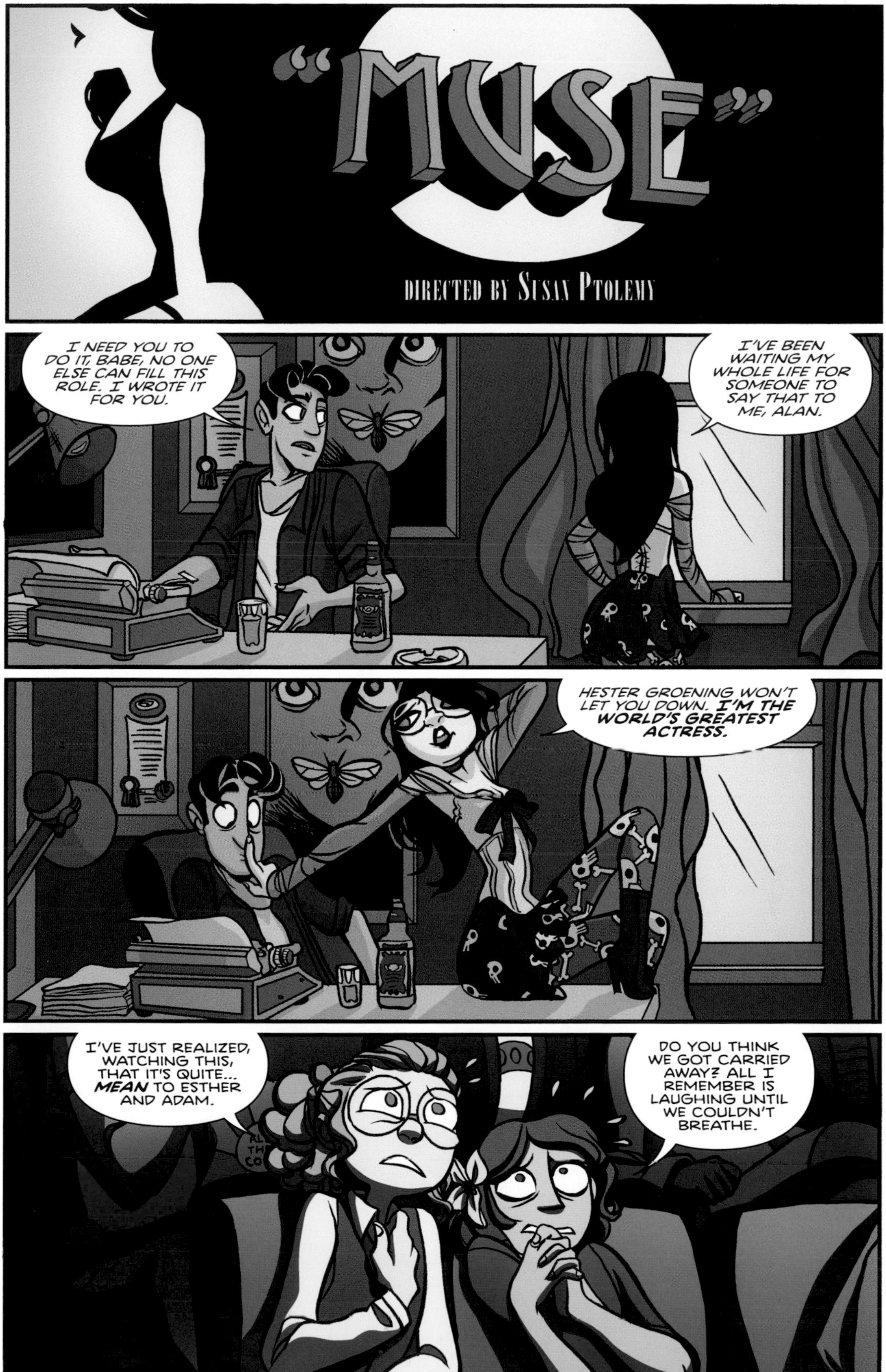
"MUSE"
DIRECTED BY SUSAN PTOLEMY
I NEED YOU TO DO IT, BABE, NO ONE ELSE CAN FILL THIS ROLE. I WROTE IT FOR YOU.
I'VE BEEN WAITING MY WHOLE LIFE FOR SOMEONE TO SAY THAT TO ME, ALAN.
HESTER GROENING WON'T LET YOU DOWN. I'M THE WORLD'S GREATEST ACTRESS.
I'VE JUST REALIZED, WATCHING THIS, THAT IT'S QUITE... MEAN TO ESTHER AND ADAM.
DO YOU THINK WE GOT CARRIED AWAY? ALL I REMEMBER IS LAUGHING UNTIL WE COULDN'T BREATHE.

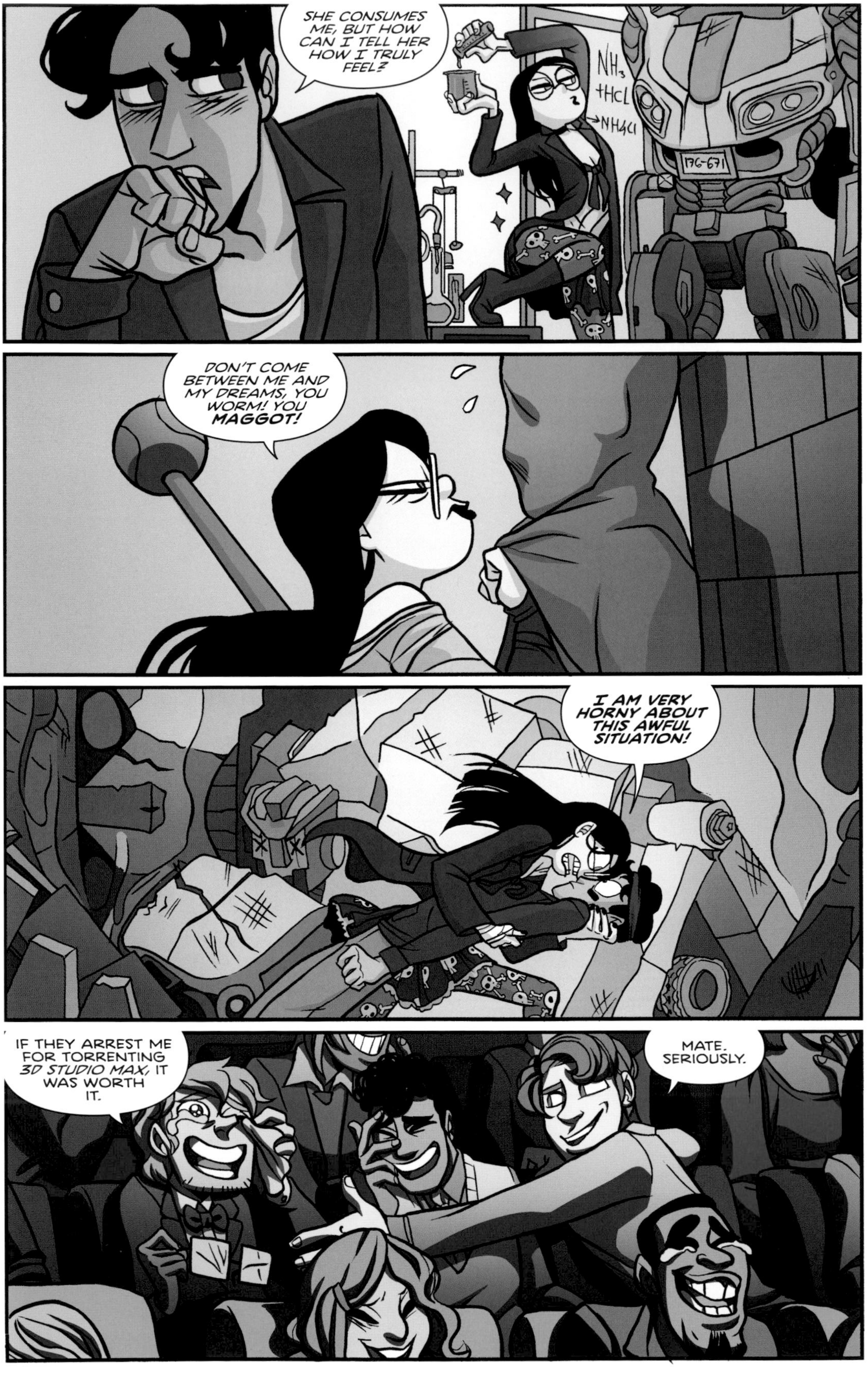
SHE CONSUMES ME, BUT HOW CAN I TELL HER HOW I TRULY FEEL?
DON'T COME BETWEEN ME AND MY DREAMS, YOU WORM! YOU MAGGOT!
I AM VERY HORNY ABOUT THIS AWFUL SITUATION!
IF THEY ARREST ME FOR TORRENTING 3D STUDIO MAX, IT WAS WORTH IT.
MATE. SERIOUSLY.

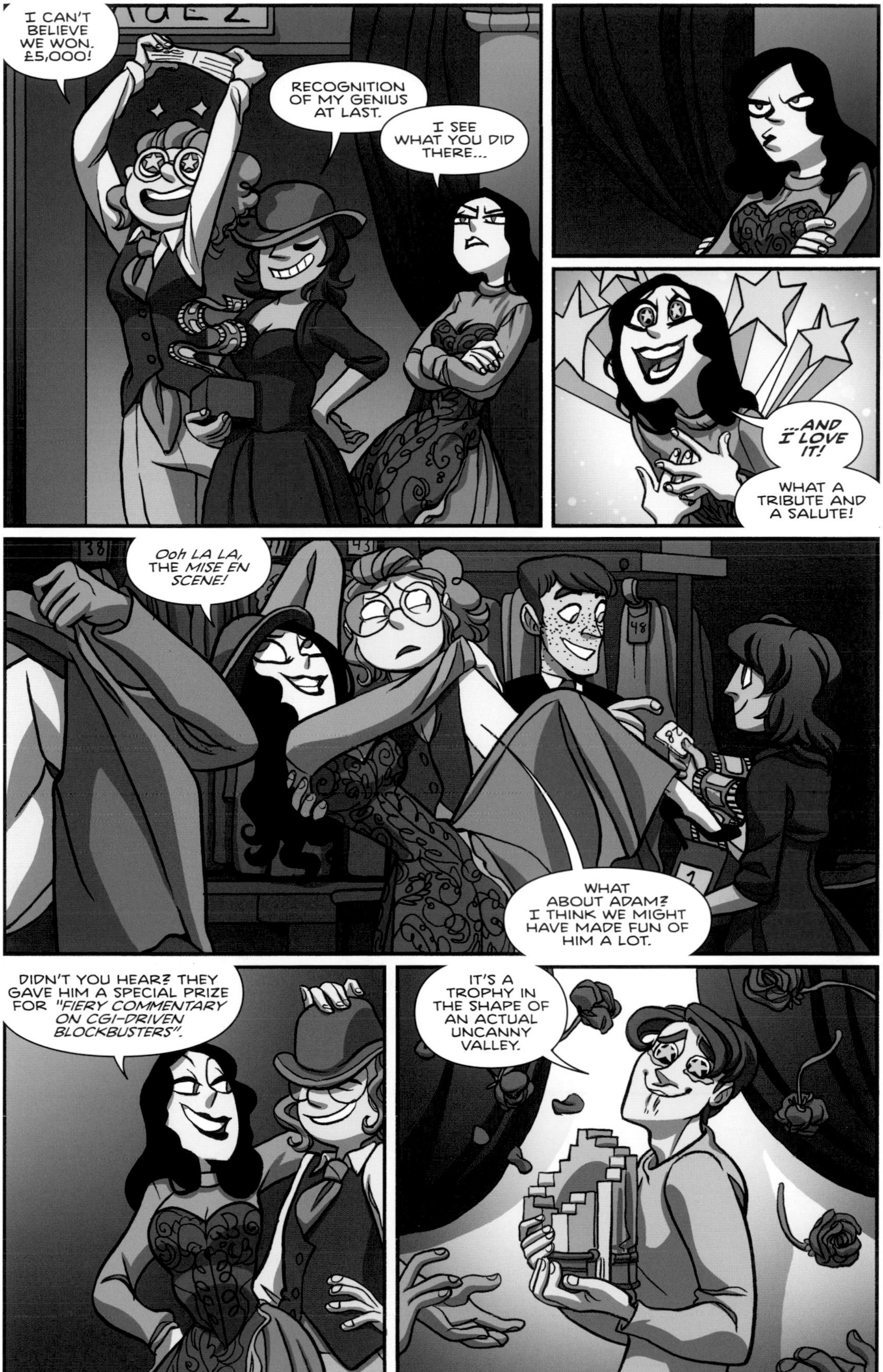
I CAN'T BELIEVE WE WON. £5,000!
RECOGNITION OF MY GENIUS AT LAST.
I SEE WHAT YOU DID THERE...
...AND I LOVE IT!
WHAT A TRIBUTE AND A SALUTE!
Ooh LA LA, THE MISE EN SCENE!
WHAT ABOUT ADAM? I THINK WE MIGHT HAVE MADE FUN OF HIM A LOT.
DIDN'T YOU HEAR? THEY GAVE HIM A SPECIAL PRIZE FOR "FIERY COMMENTARY ON CGI-DRIVEN BLOCKBUSTERS".
IT'S A TROPHY IN THE SHAPE OF AN ACTUAL UNCANNY VALLEY.

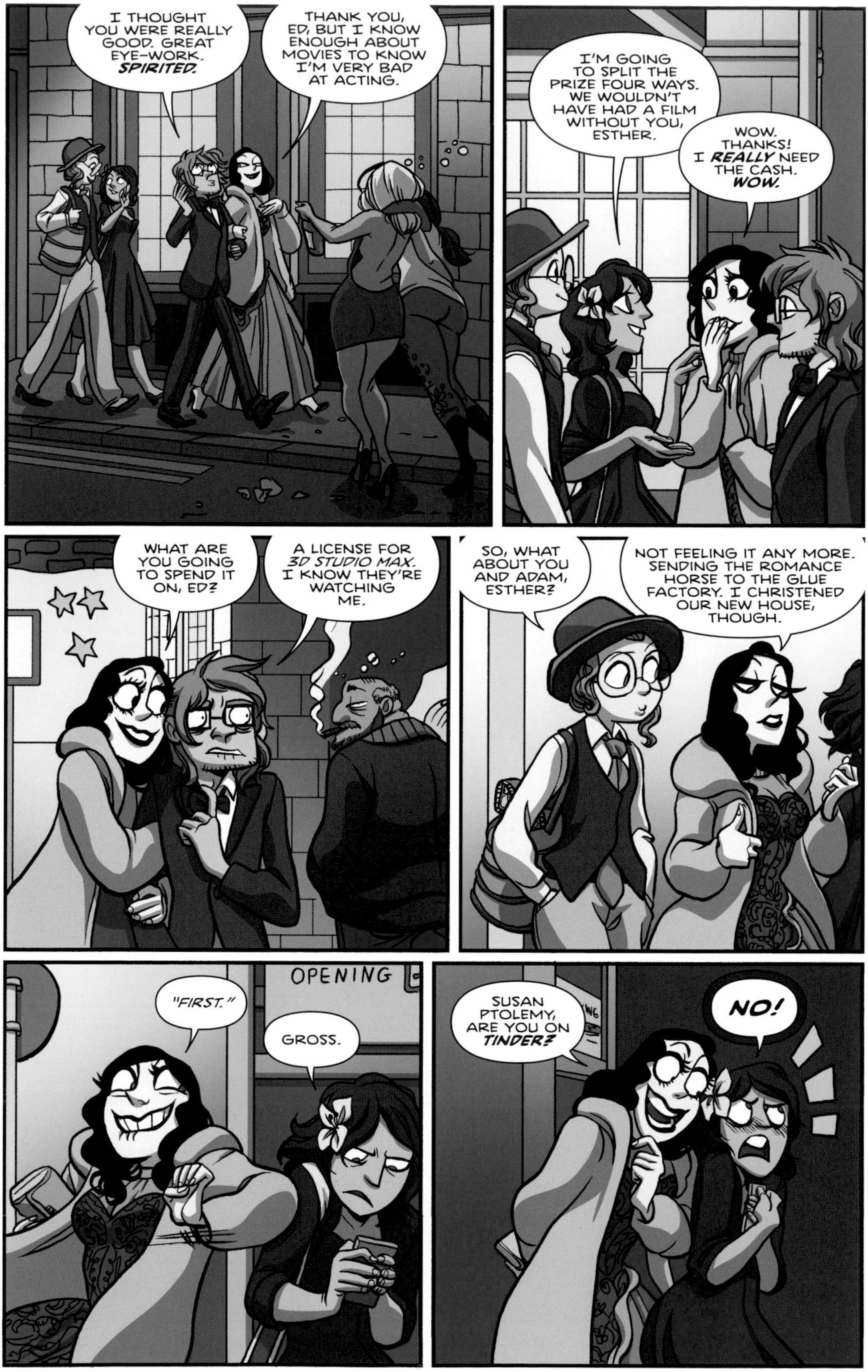
I THOUGHT YOU WERE REALLY GOOD. GREAT EYE-WORK. *SPIRITED.*
THANK YOU, ED, BUT I KNOW ENOUGH ABOUT MOVIES TO KNOW I'M VERY BAD AT ACTING.
I'M GOING TO SPLIT THE PRIZE FOUR WAYS. WE WOULDN'T HAVE HAD A FILM WITHOUT YOU, ESTHER.
WOW. THANKS! I *REALLY* NEED THE CASH. *WOW.*
WHAT ARE YOU GOING TO SPEND IT ON, ED?
A LICENSE FOR *3D STUDIO MAX.* I KNOW THEY'RE WATCHING ME.
SO, WHAT ABOUT YOU AND ADAM, ESTHER?
NOT FEELING IT ANY MORE. SENDING THE ROMANCE HORSE TO THE GLUE FACTORY. I CHRISTENED OUR NEW HOUSE, THOUGH.
OPENING
"*FIRST.*"
GROSS.
SUSAN PTOLEMY, ARE YOU ON *TINDER?*
*NO!*

# CHAPTER SIXTEEN

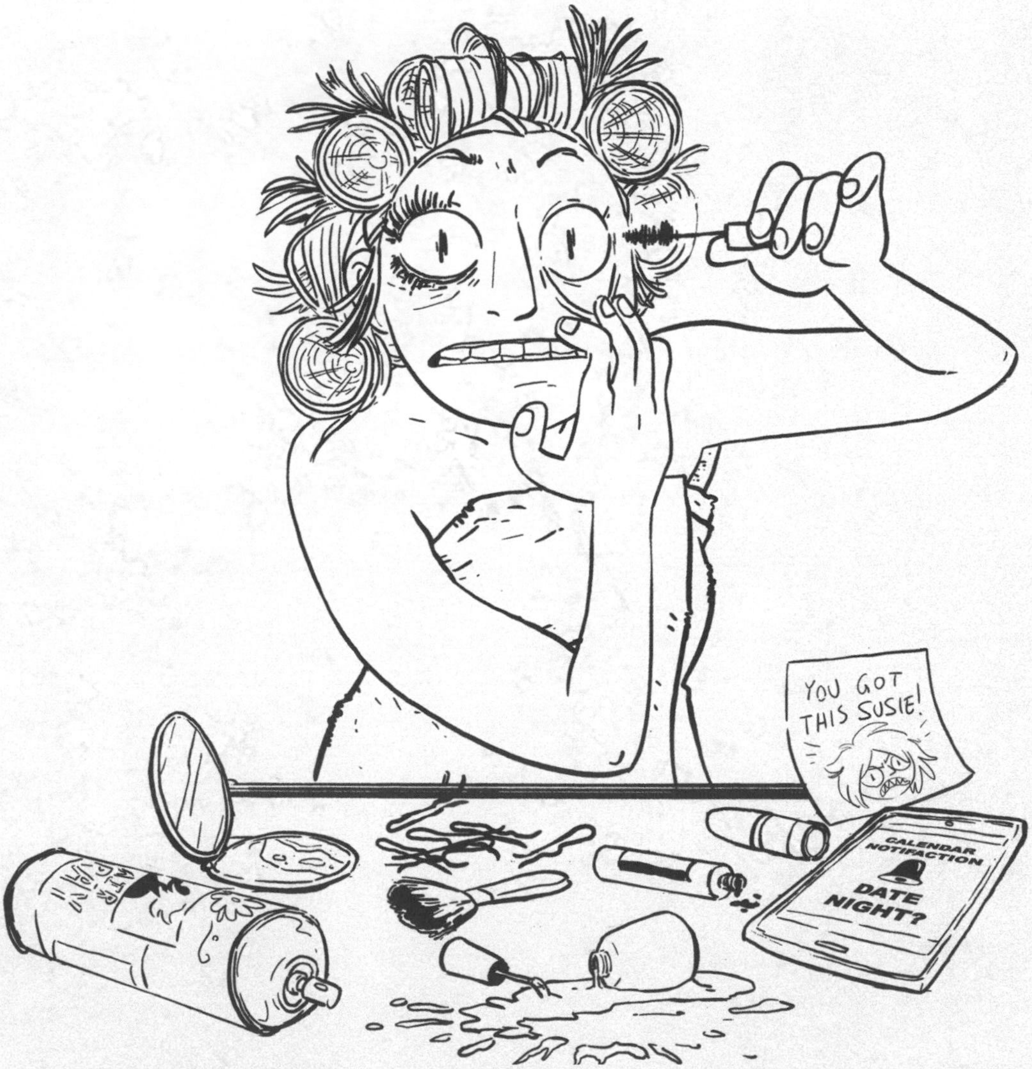
YOU GOT THIS SUSIE!
CALENDAR NOTIFACTION
DATE NIGHT?

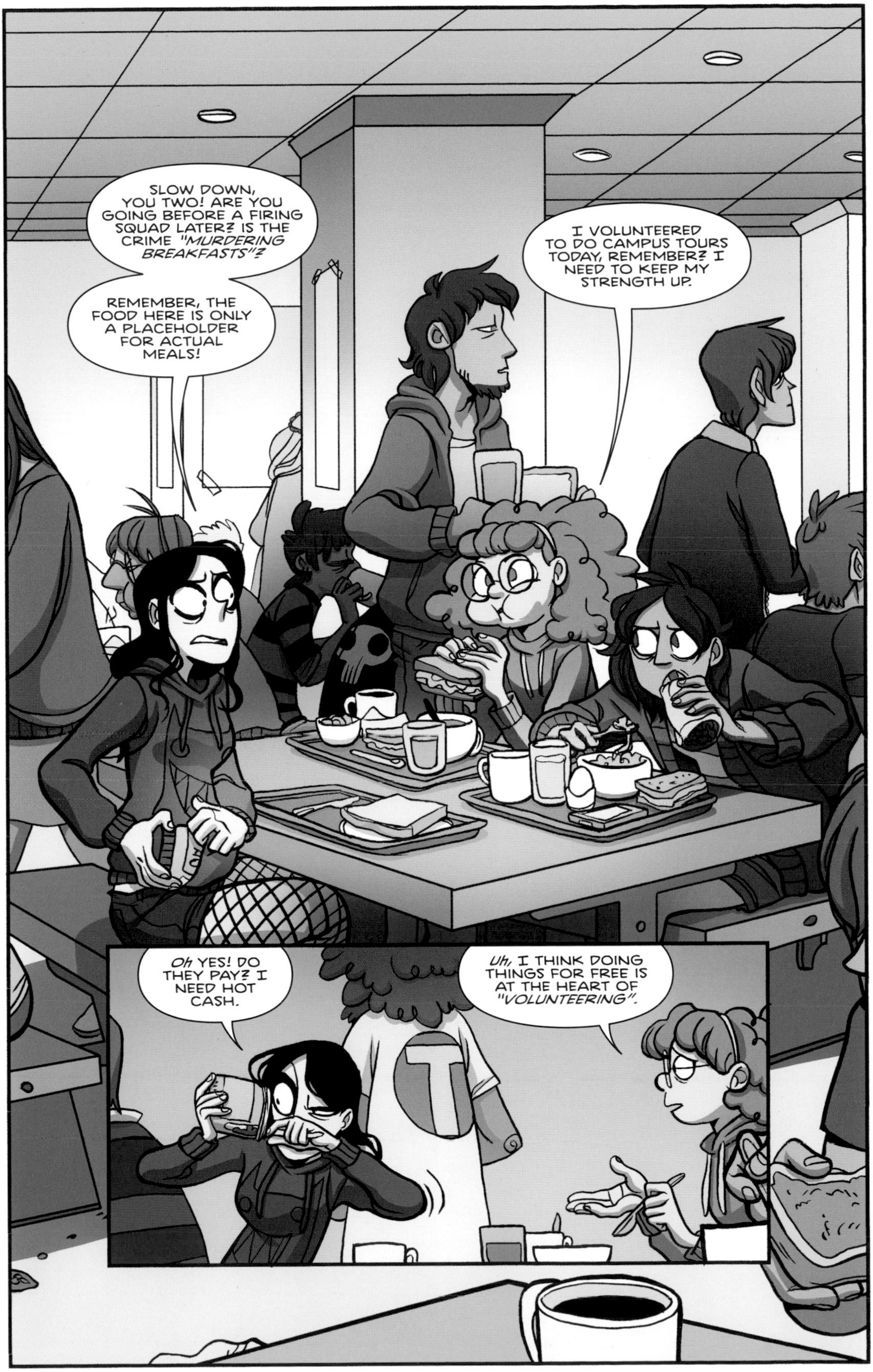
SLOW DOWN, YOU TWO! ARE YOU GOING BEFORE A FIRING SQUAD LATER? IS THE CRIME *"MURDERING BREAKFASTS"*?
REMEMBER, THE FOOD HERE IS ONLY A PLACEHOLDER FOR ACTUAL MEALS!
I VOLUNTEERED TO DO CAMPUS TOURS TODAY, REMEMBER? I NEED TO KEEP MY STRENGTH UP.
*Oh* YES! DO THEY PAY? I NEED HOT CASH.
*Uh*, I THINK DOING THINGS FOR FREE IS AT THE HEART OF *"VOLUNTEERING"*.

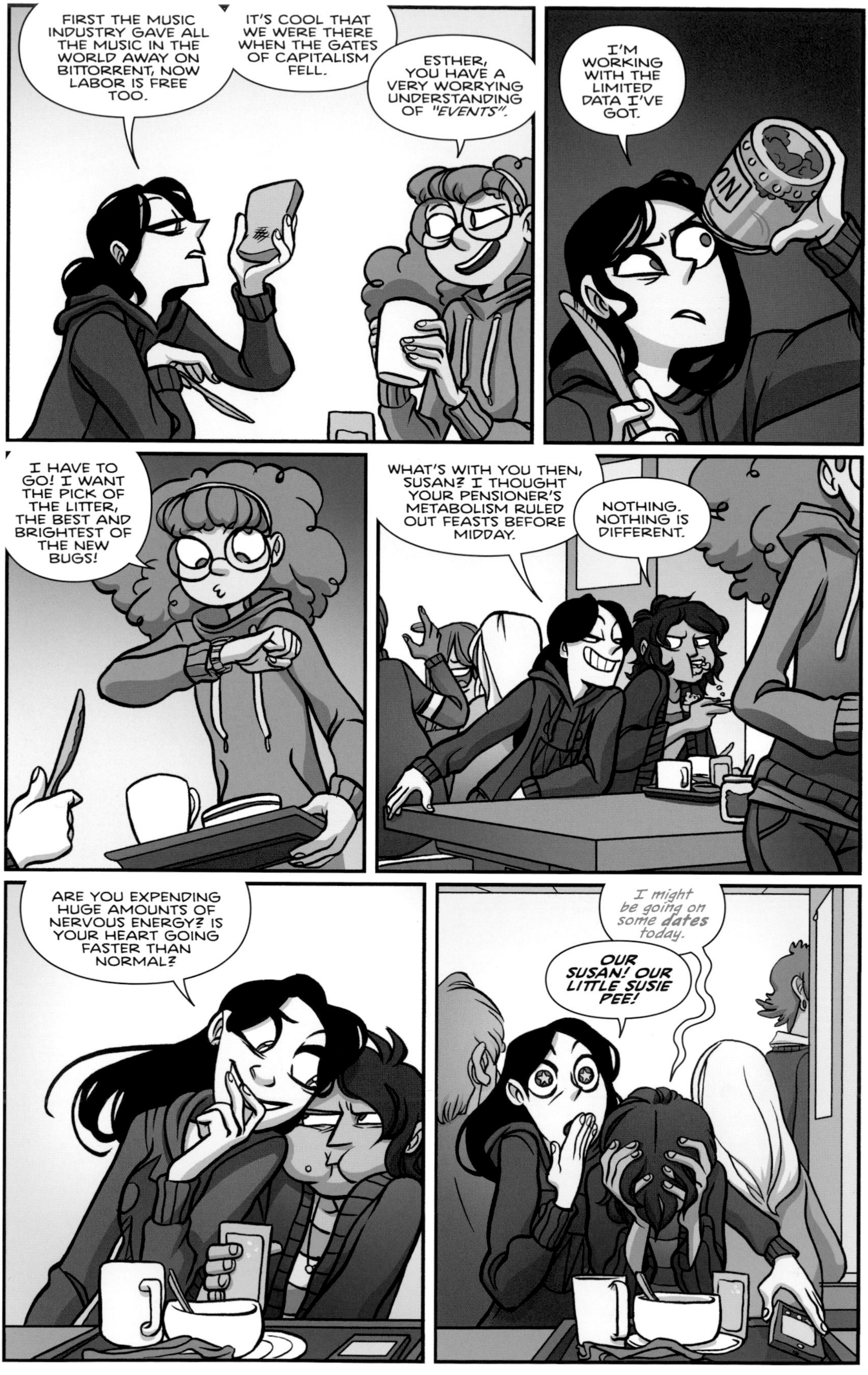
FIRST THE MUSIC INDUSTRY GAVE ALL THE MUSIC IN THE WORLD AWAY ON BITTORRENT, NOW LABOR IS FREE TOO.
IT'S COOL THAT WE WERE THERE WHEN THE GATES OF CAPITALISM FELL.
ESTHER, YOU HAVE A VERY WORRYING UNDERSTANDING OF "EVENTS".
I'M WORKING WITH THE LIMITED DATA I'VE GOT.
I HAVE TO GO! I WANT THE PICK OF THE LITTER, THE BEST AND BRIGHTEST OF THE NEW BUGS!
WHAT'S WITH YOU THEN, SUSAN? I THOUGHT YOUR PENSIONER'S METABOLISM RULED OUT FEASTS BEFORE MIDDAY.
NOTHING. NOTHING IS DIFFERENT.
ARE YOU EXPENDING HUGE AMOUNTS OF NERVOUS ENERGY? IS YOUR HEART GOING FASTER THAN NORMAL?
I might be going on some dates today.
OUR SUSAN! OUR LITTLE SUSIE PEE!

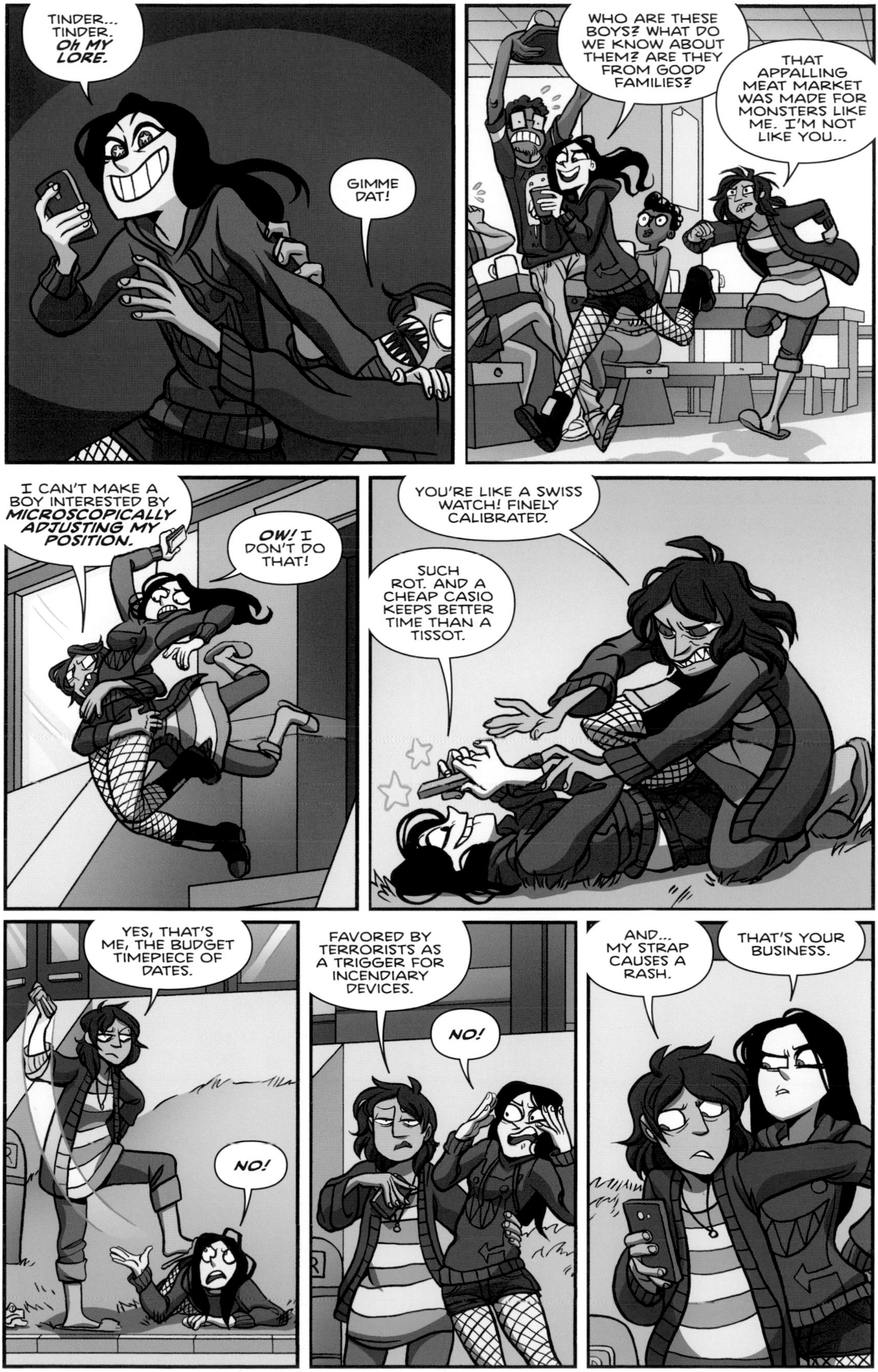
TINDER... TINDER. *OH MY LORE.*
GIMME DAT!
WHO ARE THESE BOYS? WHAT DO WE KNOW ABOUT THEM? ARE THEY FROM GOOD FAMILIES?
THAT APPALLING MEAT MARKET WAS MADE FOR MONSTERS LIKE ME. I'M NOT LIKE YOU...
I CAN'T MAKE A BOY INTERESTED BY ***MICROSCOPICALLY ADJUSTING MY POSITION.***
***OW!*** I DON'T DO THAT!
YOU'RE LIKE A SWISS WATCH! FINELY CALIBRATED.
SUCH ROT. AND A CHEAP CASIO KEEPS BETTER TIME THAN A TISSOT.
YES, THAT'S ME, THE BUDGET TIMEPIECE OF DATES.
***NO!***
FAVORED BY TERRORISTS AS A TRIGGER FOR INCENDIARY DEVICES.
***NO!***
AND... MY STRAP CAUSES A RASH.
THAT'S YOUR BUSINESS.

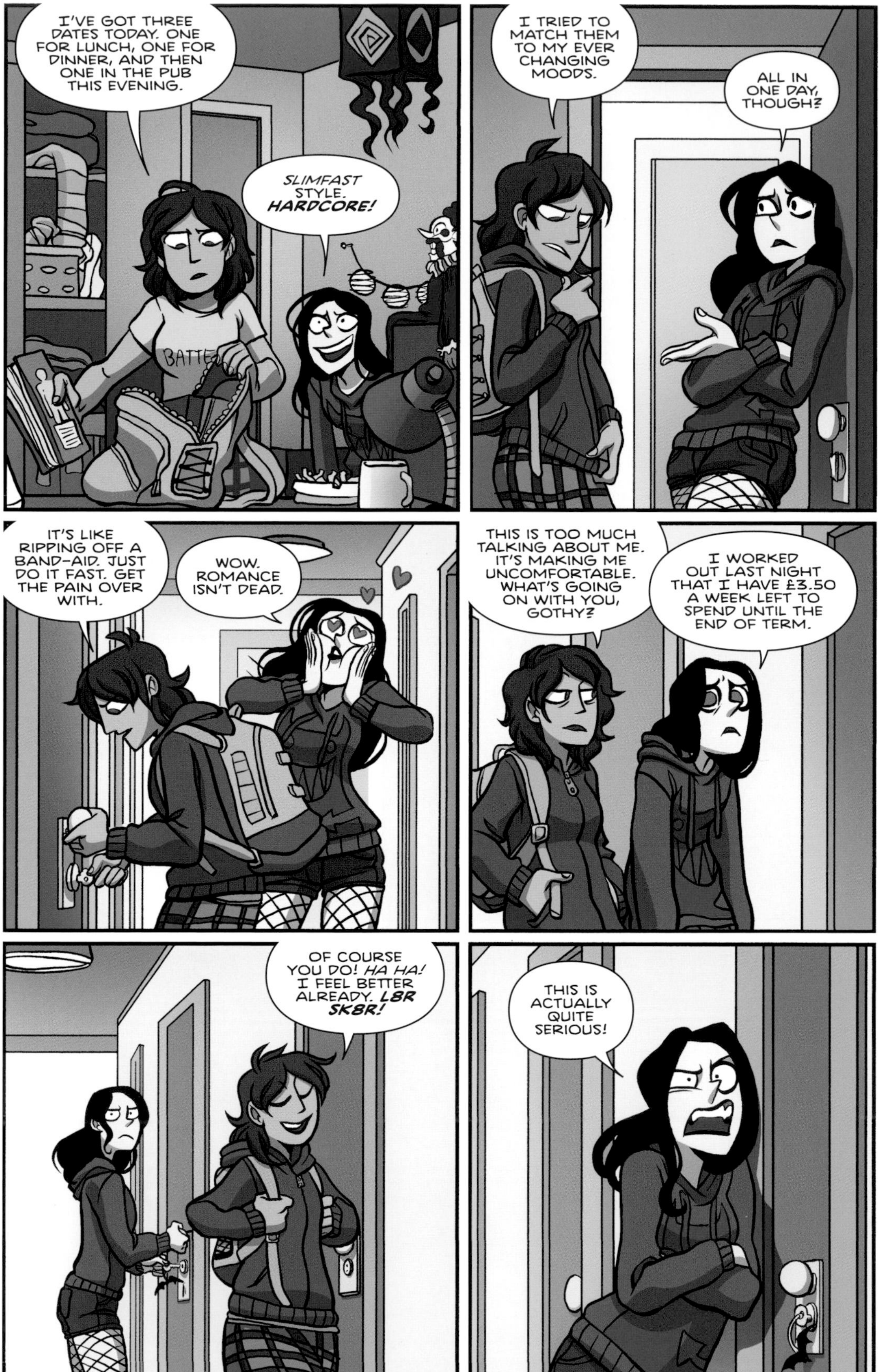
I'VE GOT THREE DATES TODAY. ONE FOR LUNCH, ONE FOR DINNER, AND THEN ONE IN THE PUB THIS EVENING.
SLIMFAST STYLE. HARDCORE!
BATTE
I TRIED TO MATCH THEM TO MY EVER CHANGING MOODS.
ALL IN ONE DAY, THOUGH?
IT'S LIKE RIPPING OFF A BAND-AID. JUST DO IT FAST. GET THE PAIN OVER WITH.
WOW. ROMANCE ISN'T DEAD.
THIS IS TOO MUCH TALKING ABOUT ME. IT'S MAKING ME UNCOMFORTABLE. WHAT'S GOING ON WITH YOU, GOTHY?
I WORKED OUT LAST NIGHT THAT I HAVE £3.50 A WEEK LEFT TO SPEND UNTIL THE END OF TERM.
OF COURSE YOU DO! HA HA! I FEEL BETTER ALREADY. L8R SK8R!
THIS IS ACTUALLY QUITE SERIOUS!

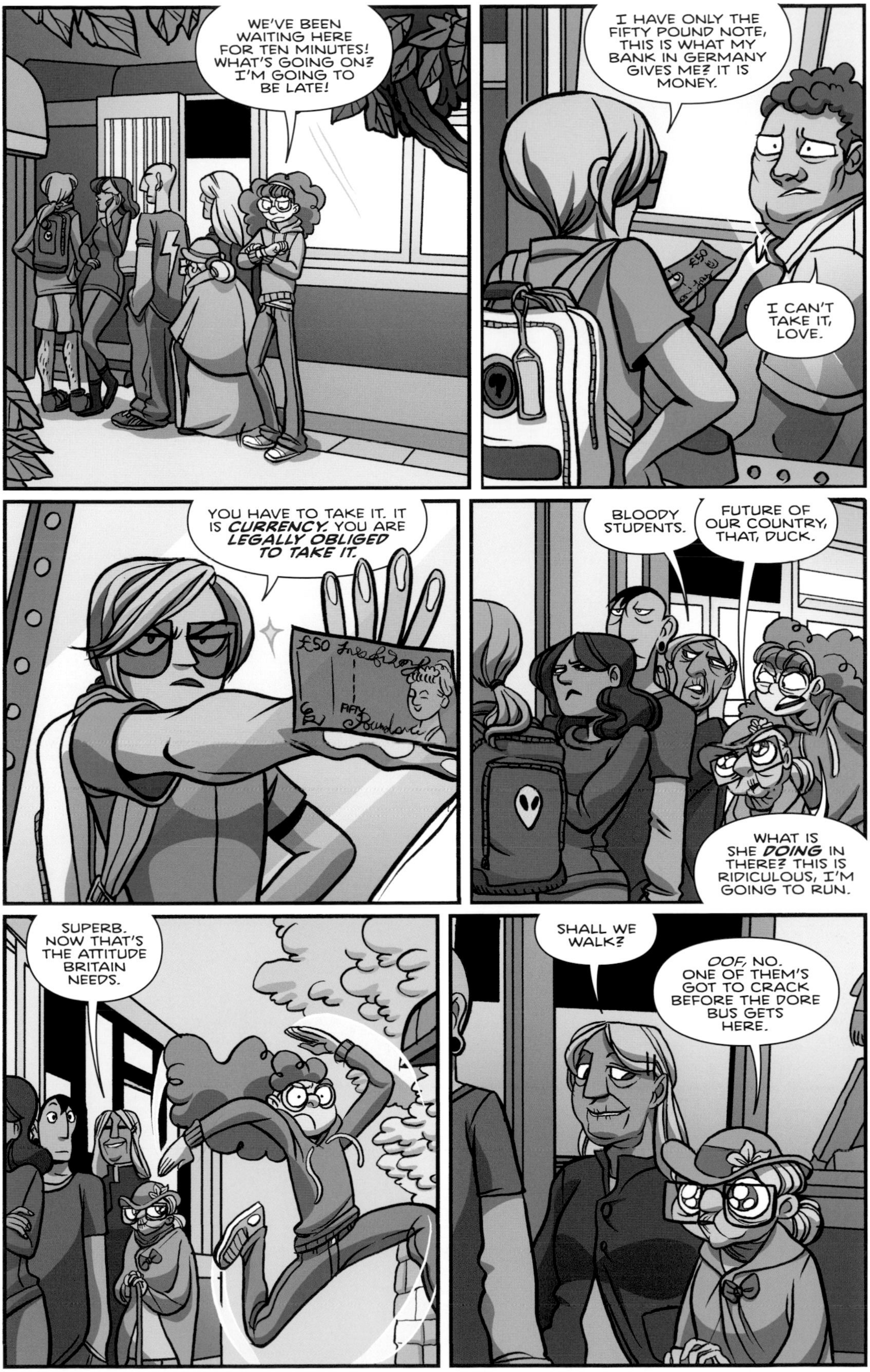
WE'VE BEEN WAITING HERE FOR TEN MINUTES! WHAT'S GOING ON? I'M GOING TO BE LATE!
I HAVE ONLY THE FIFTY POUND NOTE, THIS IS WHAT MY BANK IN GERMANY GIVES ME? IT IS MONEY.
I CAN'T TAKE IT, LOVE.
YOU HAVE TO TAKE IT. IT IS CURRENCY. YOU ARE LEGALLY OBLIGED TO TAKE IT.
BLOODY STUDENTS.
FUTURE OF OUR COUNTRY, THAT, DUCK.
WHAT IS SHE DOING IN THERE? THIS IS RIDICULOUS, I'M GOING TO RUN.
SUPERB. NOW THAT'S THE ATTITUDE BRITAIN NEEDS.
SHALL WE WALK?
OOF, NO. ONE OF THEM'S GOT TO CRACK BEFORE THE DORE BUS GETS HERE.

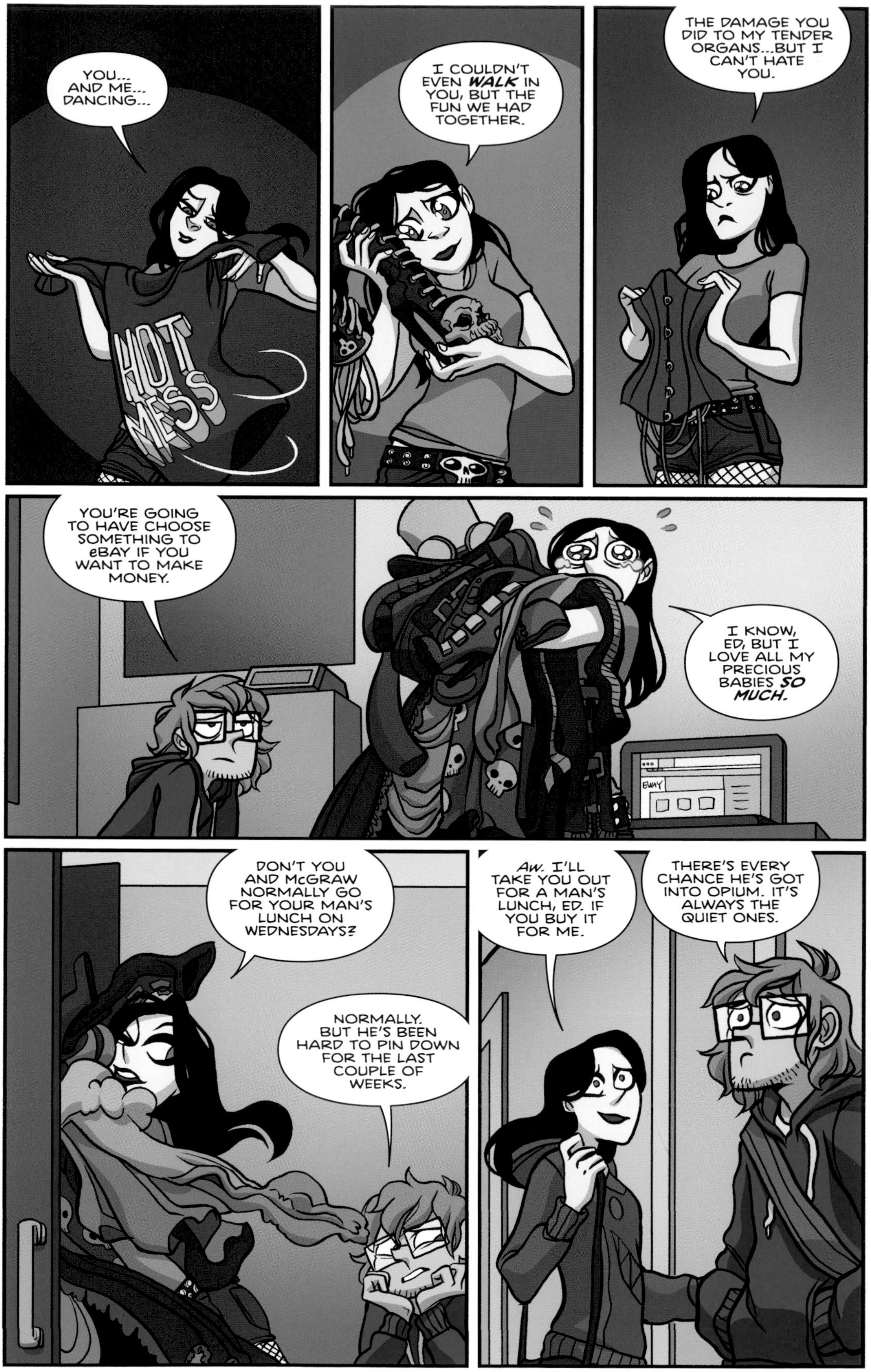
YOU... AND ME... DANCING...
HOT MESS
I COULDN'T EVEN WALK IN YOU, BUT THE FUN WE HAD TOGETHER.
THE DAMAGE YOU DID TO MY TENDER ORGANS...BUT I CAN'T HATE YOU.
YOU'RE GOING TO HAVE CHOOSE SOMETHING TO eBAY IF YOU WANT TO MAKE MONEY.
I KNOW, ED, BUT I LOVE ALL MY PRECIOUS BABIES SO MUCH.
EWAY
DON'T YOU AND McGRAW NORMALLY GO FOR YOUR MAN'S LUNCH ON WEDNESDAYS?
NORMALLY. BUT HE'S BEEN HARD TO PIN DOWN FOR THE LAST COUPLE OF WEEKS.
AW. I'LL TAKE YOU OUT FOR A MAN'S LUNCH, ED. IF YOU BUY IT FOR ME.
THERE'S EVERY CHANCE HE'S GOT INTO OPIUM. IT'S ALWAYS THE QUIET ONES.

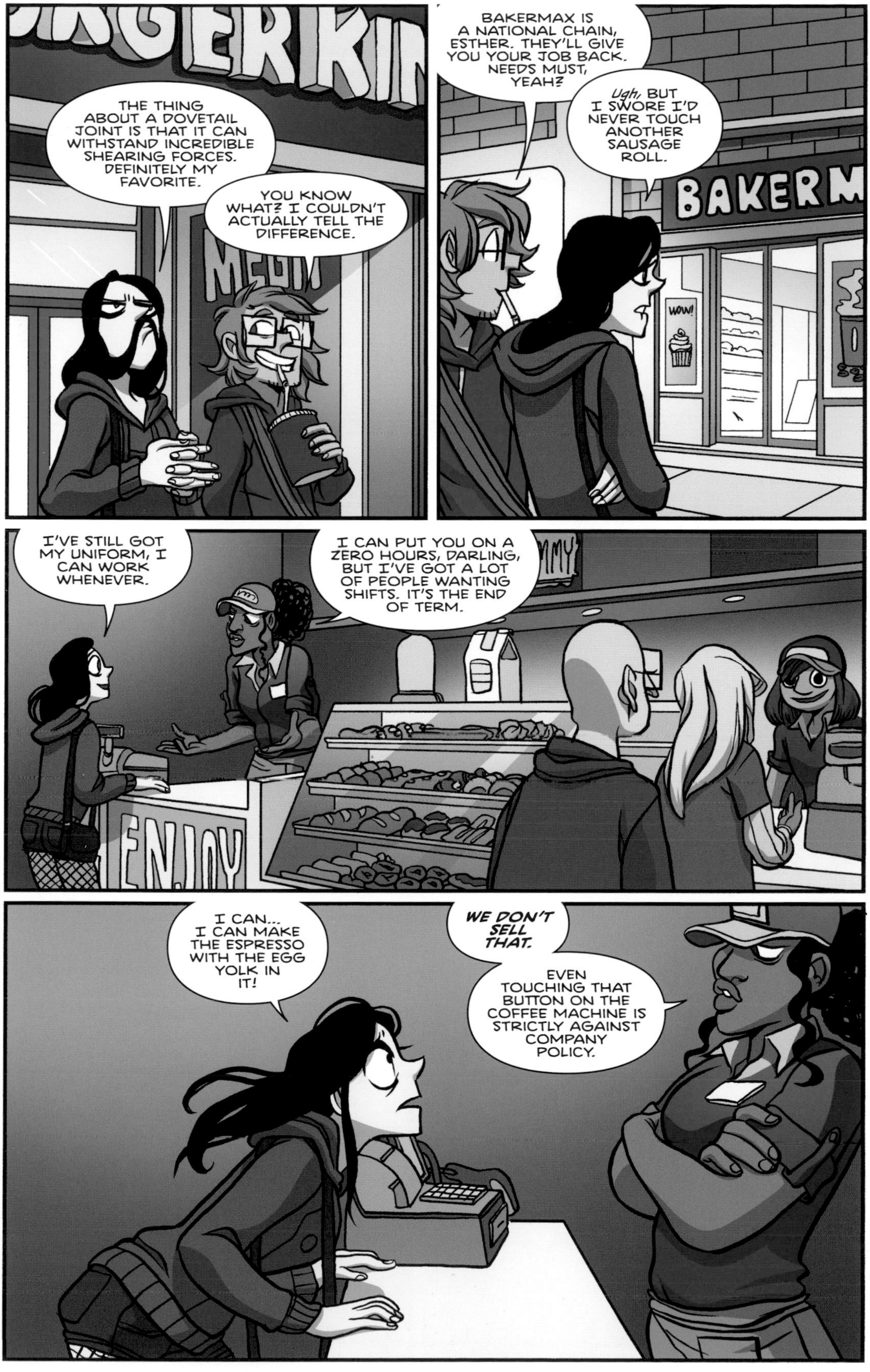

DGERKIN
THE THING ABOUT A DOVETAIL JOINT IS THAT IT CAN WITHSTAND INCREDIBLE SHEARING FORCES. DEFINITELY MY FAVORITE.
YOU KNOW WHAT? I COULDN'T ACTUALLY TELL THE DIFFERENCE.
MEOW
BAKERMAX IS A NATIONAL CHAIN, ESTHER. THEY'LL GIVE YOU YOUR JOB BACK. NEEDS MUST, YEAH?
*Ugh,* BUT I SWORE I'D NEVER TOUCH ANOTHER SAUSAGE ROLL.
BAKERM
WOW!
I'VE STILL GOT MY UNIFORM, I CAN WORK WHENEVER.
I CAN PUT YOU ON A ZERO HOURS, DARLING, BUT I'VE GOT A LOT OF PEOPLE WANTING SHIFTS. IT'S THE END OF TERM.
ENJOY
I CAN... I CAN MAKE THE ESPRESSO WITH THE EGG YOLK IN IT!
***WE DON'T SELL THAT.***
EVEN TOUCHING THAT BUTTON ON THE COFFEE MACHINE IS STRICTLY AGAINST COMPANY POLICY.

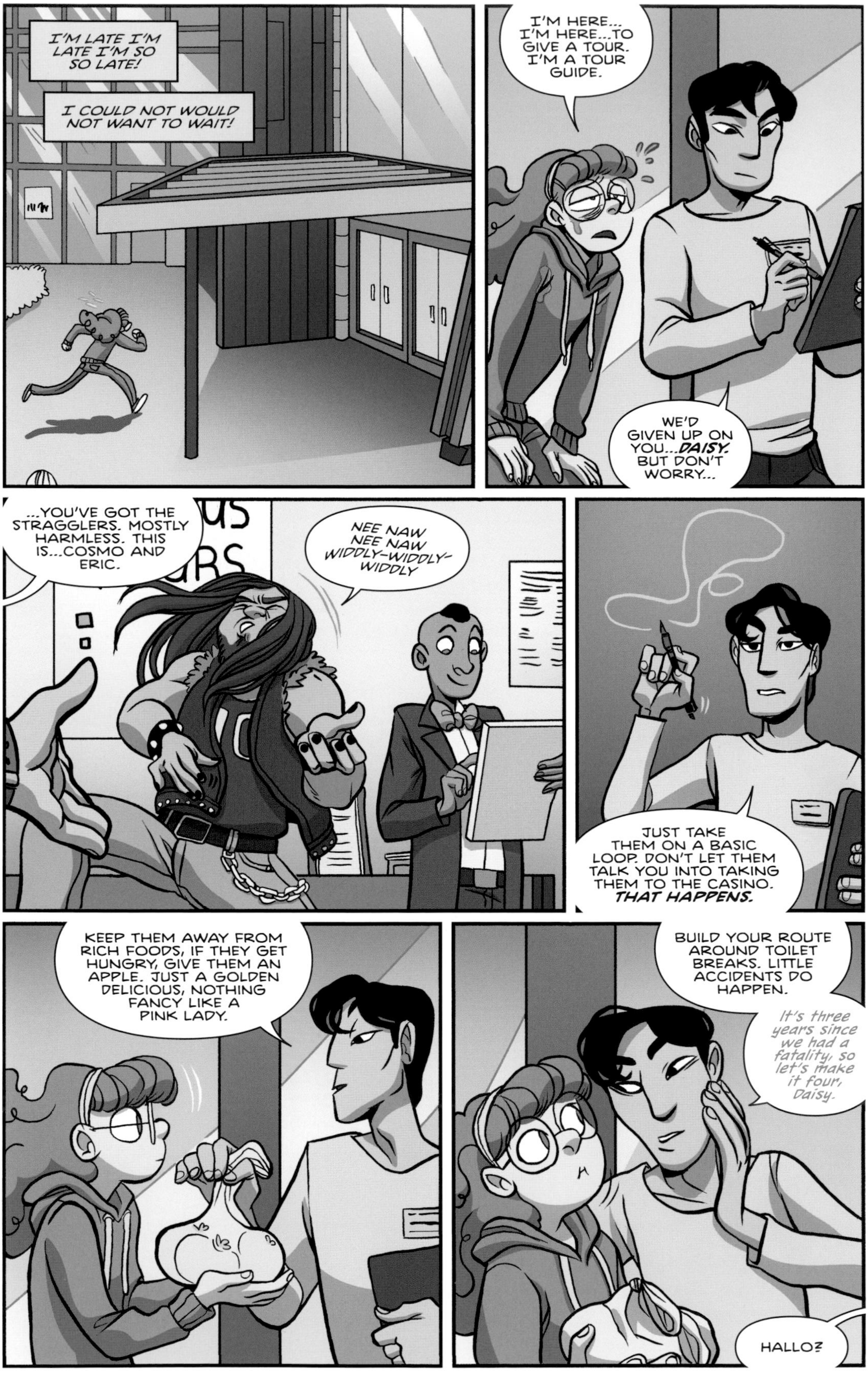
I'M LATE I'M LATE I'M SO SO LATE!
I COULD NOT WOULD NOT WANT TO WAIT!
I'M HERE... I'M HERE...TO GIVE A TOUR. I'M A TOUR GUIDE.
WE'D GIVEN UP ON YOU...DAISY. BUT DON'T WORRY...
...YOU'VE GOT THE STRAGGLERS. MOSTLY HARMLESS. THIS IS...COSMO AND ERIC.
NEE NAW NEE NAW WIDDLY-WIDDLY-WIDDLY
JUST TAKE THEM ON A BASIC LOOP. DON'T LET THEM TALK YOU INTO TAKING THEM TO THE CASINO. THAT HAPPENS.
KEEP THEM AWAY FROM RICH FOODS, IF THEY GET HUNGRY, GIVE THEM AN APPLE. JUST A GOLDEN DELICIOUS, NOTHING FANCY LIKE A PINK LADY.
BUILD YOUR ROUTE AROUND TOILET BREAKS. LITTLE ACCIDENTS DO HAPPEN.
It's three years since we had a fatality, so let's make it four, Daisy.
HALLO?

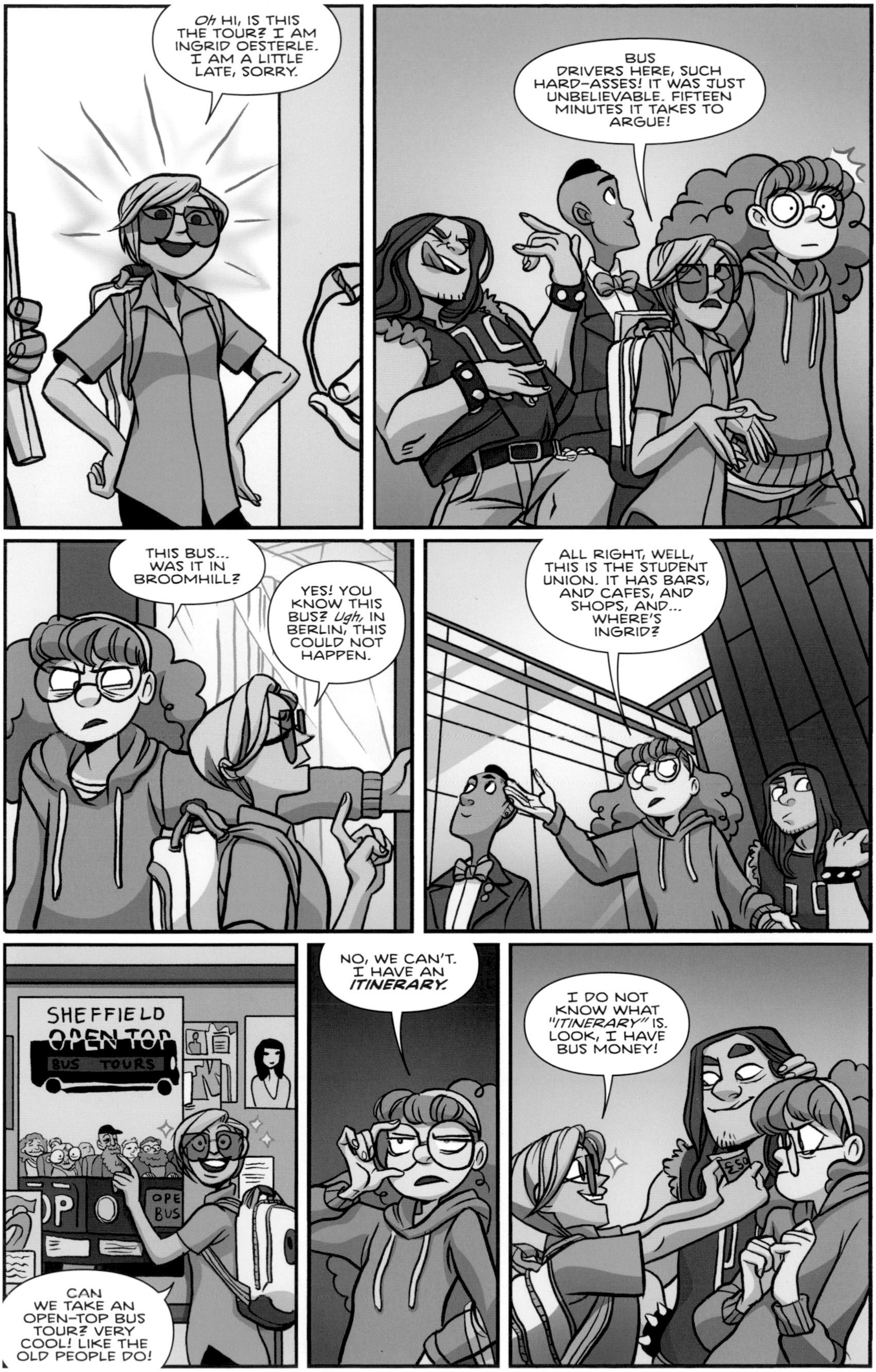

OH HI, IS THIS THE TOUR? I AM INGRID OESTERLE. I AM A LITTLE LATE, SORRY.
BUS DRIVERS HERE, SUCH HARD-ASSES! IT WAS JUST UNBELIEVABLE. FIFTEEN MINUTES IT TAKES TO ARGUE!
THIS BUS... WAS IT IN BROOMHILL?
YES! YOU KNOW THIS BUS? UGH, IN BERLIN, THIS COULD NOT HAPPEN.
ALL RIGHT, WELL, THIS IS THE STUDENT UNION. IT HAS BARS, AND CAFES, AND SHOPS, AND... WHERE'S INGRID?
SHEFFIELD OPEN TOP BUS TOURS
CAN WE TAKE AN OPEN-TOP BUS TOUR? VERY COOL! LIKE THE OLD PEOPLE DO!
NO, WE CAN'T. I HAVE AN ITINERARY.
I DO NOT KNOW WHAT "ITINERARY" IS. LOOK, I HAVE BUS MONEY!

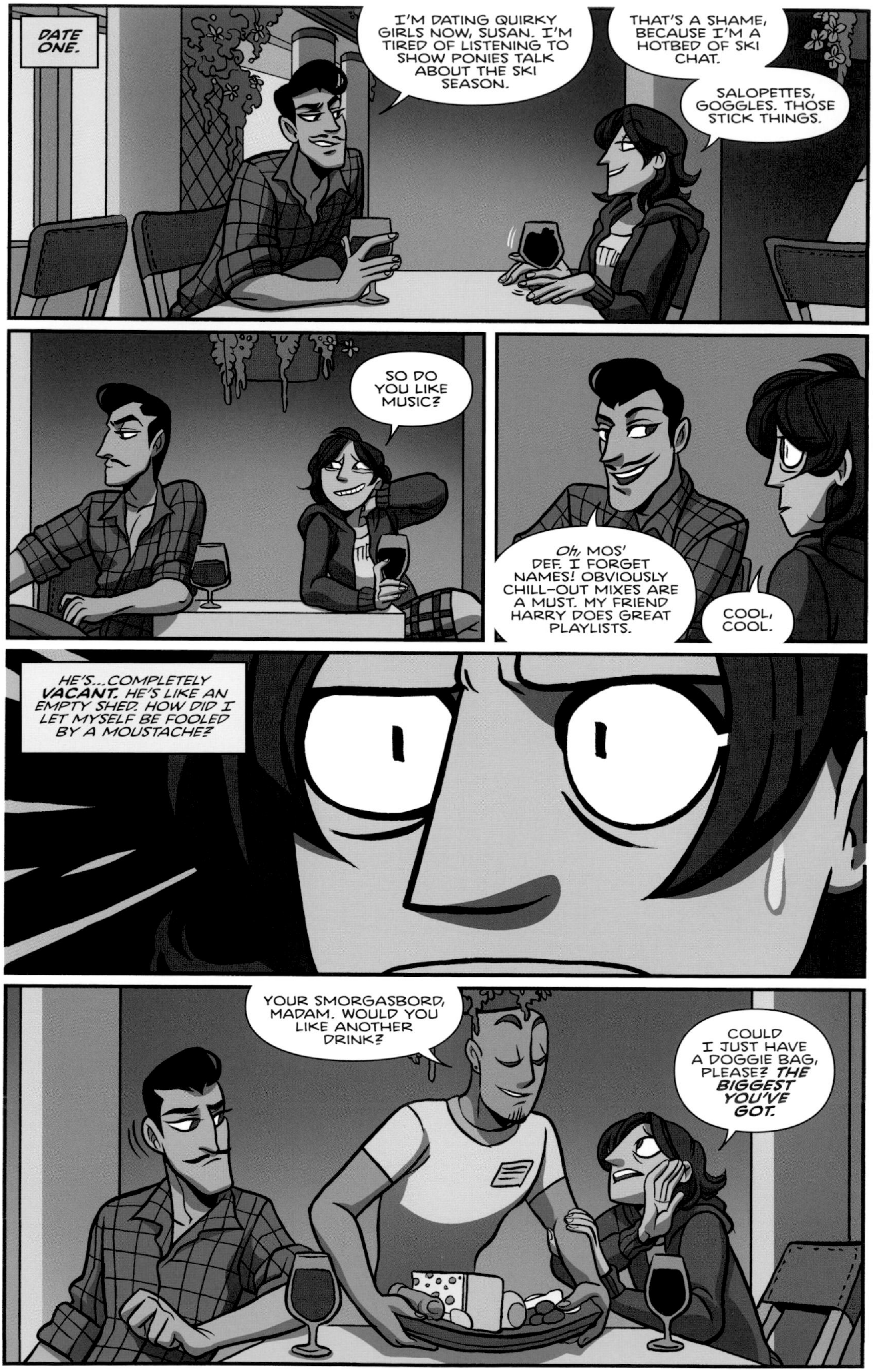
DATE ONE.
I'M DATING QUIRKY GIRLS NOW, SUSAN. I'M TIRED OF LISTENING TO SHOW PONIES TALK ABOUT THE SKI SEASON.
THAT'S A SHAME, BECAUSE I'M A HOTBED OF SKI CHAT.
SALOPETTES, GOGGLES. THOSE STICK THINGS.
SO DO YOU LIKE MUSIC?
*Oh,* MOS' DEF. I FORGET NAMES! OBVIOUSLY CHILL-OUT MIXES ARE A MUST. MY FRIEND HARRY DOES GREAT PLAYLISTS.
COOL, COOL.
HE'S...COMPLETELY **VACANT.** HE'S LIKE AN EMPTY SHED. HOW DID I LET MYSELF BE FOOLED BY A MOUSTACHE?
YOUR SMORGASBORD, MADAM. WOULD YOU LIKE ANOTHER DRINK?
COULD I JUST HAVE A DOGGIE BAG, PLEASE? ***THE BIGGEST YOU'VE GOT.***

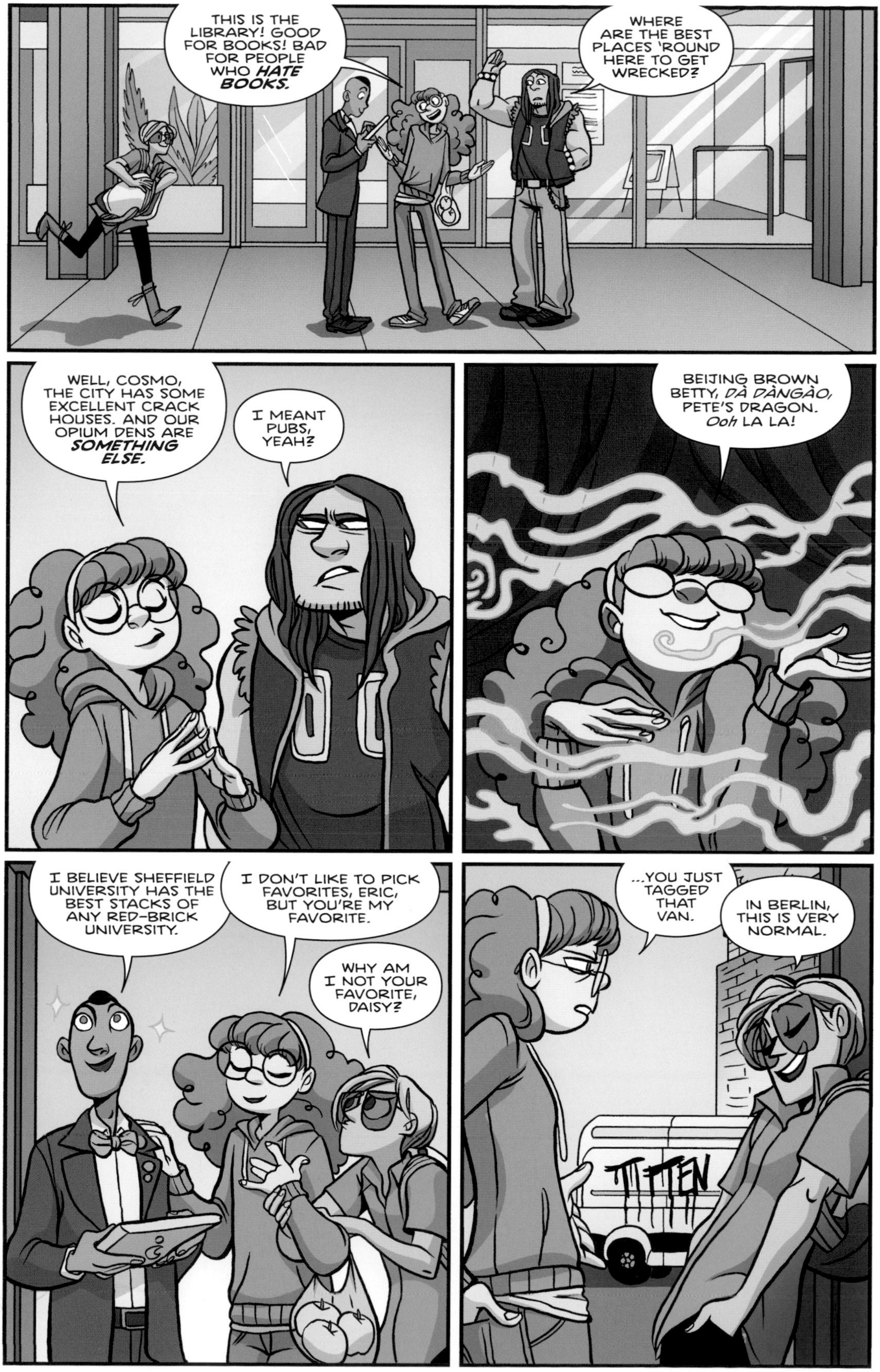
THIS IS THE LIBRARY! GOOD FOR BOOKS! BAD FOR PEOPLE WHO HATE BOOKS.
WHERE ARE THE BEST PLACES 'ROUND HERE TO GET WRECKED?
WELL, COSMO, THE CITY HAS SOME EXCELLENT CRACK HOUSES. AND OUR OPIUM DENS ARE SOMETHING ELSE.
I MEANT PUBS, YEAH?
BEIJING BROWN BETTY, DÀ DÀNGÀO, PETE'S DRAGON. Ooh LA LA!
I BELIEVE SHEFFIELD UNIVERSITY HAS THE BEST STACKS OF ANY RED-BRICK UNIVERSITY.
I DON'T LIKE TO PICK FAVORITES, ERIC, BUT YOU'RE MY FAVORITE.
WHY AM I NOT YOUR FAVORITE, DAISY?
...YOU JUST TAGGED THAT VAN.
IN BERLIN, THIS IS VERY NORMAL.
TITTEN

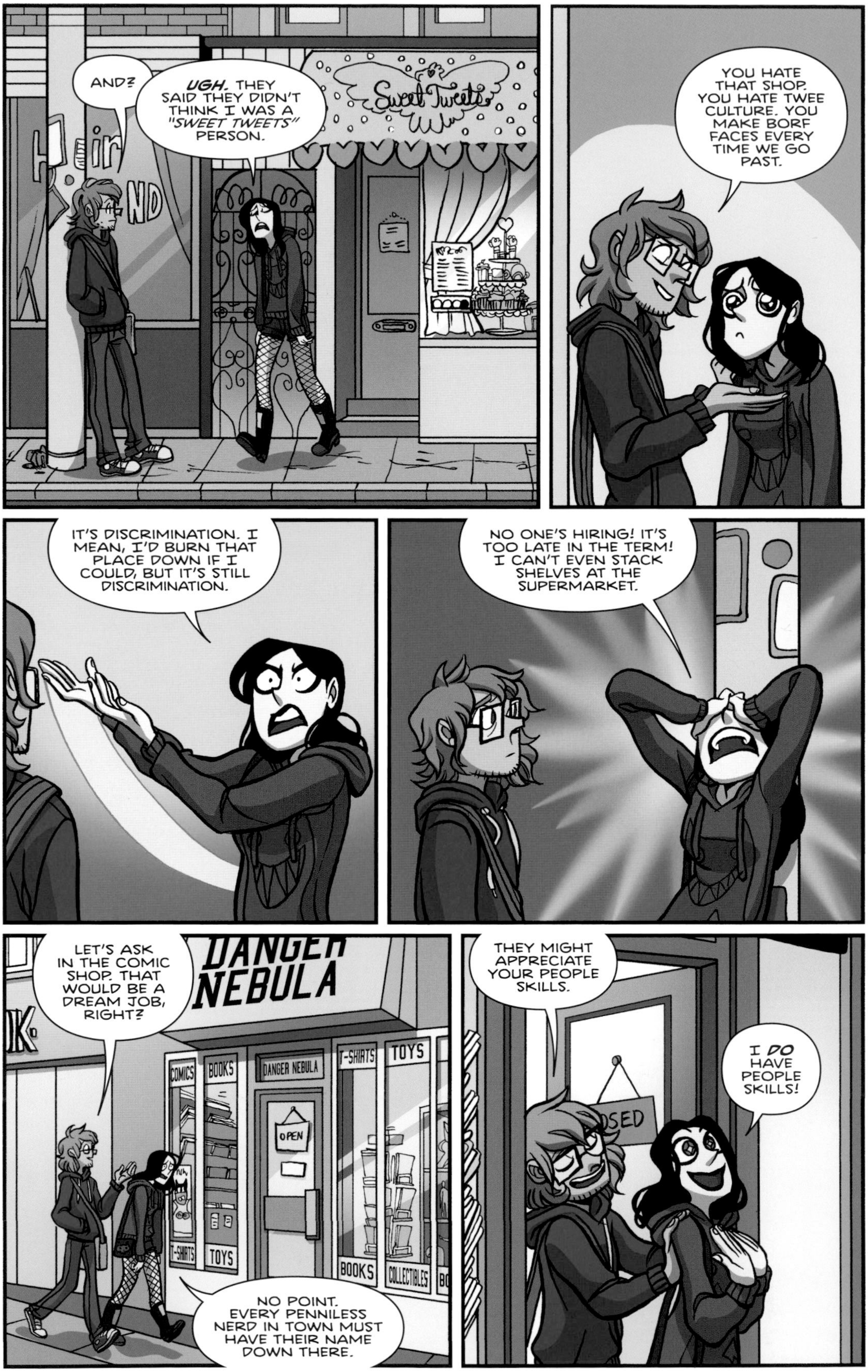
AND?
UGH. THEY SAID THEY DIDN'T THINK I WAS A "SWEET TWEETS" PERSON.
Sweet Tweets
YOU HATE THAT SHOP. YOU HATE TWEE CULTURE. YOU MAKE BORF FACES EVERY TIME WE GO PAST.
IT'S DISCRIMINATION. I MEAN, I'D BURN THAT PLACE DOWN IF I COULD, BUT IT'S STILL DISCRIMINATION.
NO ONE'S HIRING! IT'S TOO LATE IN THE TERM! I CAN'T EVEN STACK SHELVES AT THE SUPERMARKET.
LET'S ASK IN THE COMIC SHOP. THAT WOULD BE A DREAM JOB, RIGHT?
DANGER NEBULA
COMICS
BOOKS
DANGER NEBULA
T-SHIRTS
TOYS
OPEN
BOOKS
COLLECTIBLES
NO POINT. EVERY PENNILESS NERD IN TOWN MUST HAVE THEIR NAME DOWN THERE.
THEY MIGHT APPRECIATE YOUR PEOPLE SKILLS.
I DO HAVE PEOPLE SKILLS!

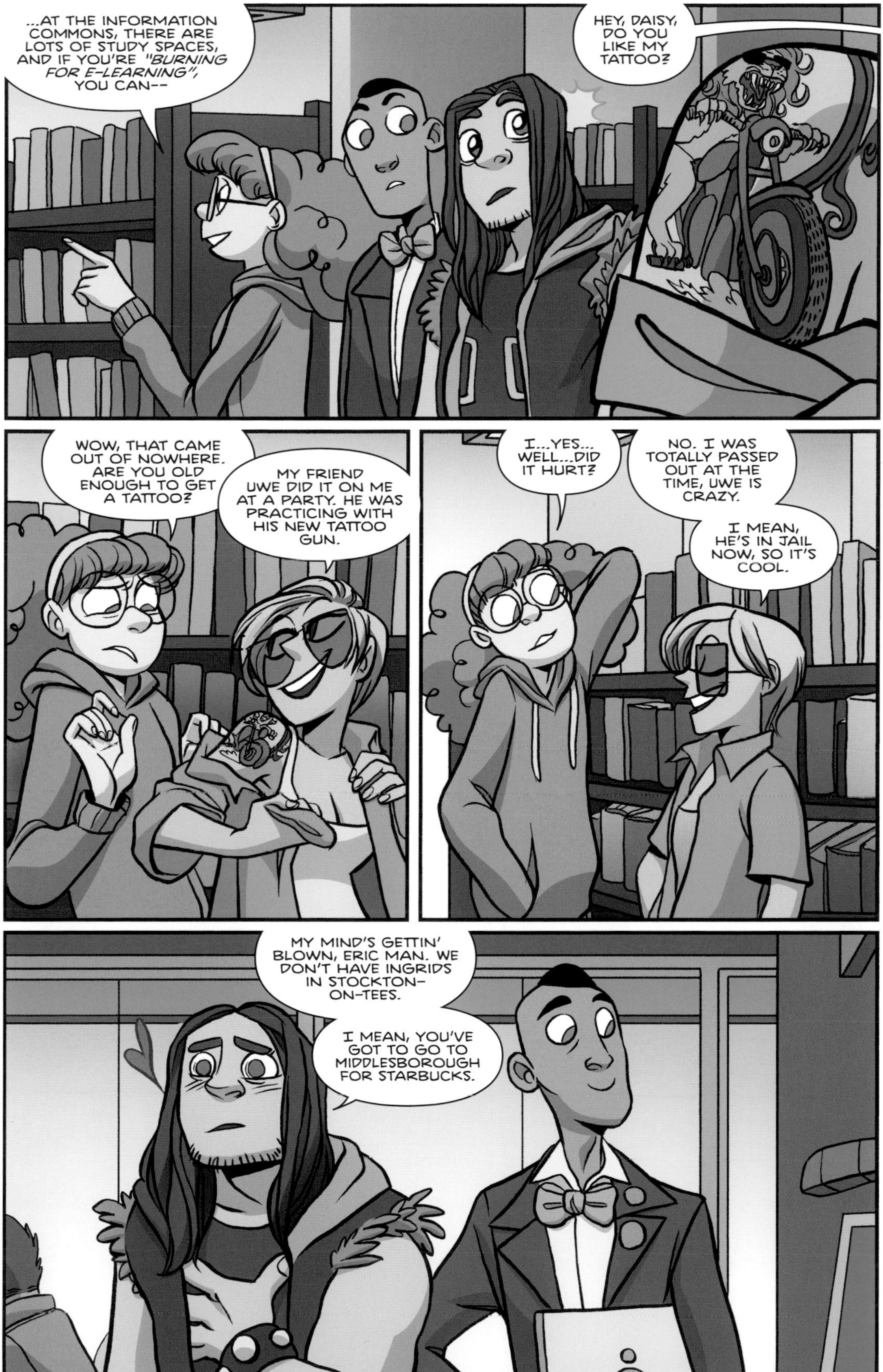
...AT THE INFORMATION COMMONS, THERE ARE LOTS OF STUDY SPACES, AND IF YOU'RE *"BURNING FOR E-LEARNING"*, YOU CAN--
HEY, DAISY, DO YOU LIKE MY TATTOO?
WOW, THAT CAME OUT OF NOWHERE. ARE YOU OLD ENOUGH TO GET A TATTOO?
MY FRIEND UWE DID IT ON ME AT A PARTY. HE WAS PRACTICING WITH HIS NEW TATTOO GUN.
I...YES... WELL...DID IT HURT?
NO. I WAS TOTALLY PASSED OUT AT THE TIME, UWE IS CRAZY.
I MEAN, HE'S IN JAIL NOW, SO IT'S COOL.
MY MIND'S GETTIN' BLOWN, ERIC MAN. WE DON'T HAVE INGRIDS IN STOCKTON-ON-TEES.
I MEAN, YOU'VE GOT TO GO TO MIDDLESBOROUGH FOR STARBUCKS.

4:00 PM.

...SO ON BEHALF OF THE UNIVERSITY, I'D LIKE TO OFFER YOU ALL AN APPLE AND WISH YOU THE BEST IN YOUR EXAMS.

PRAISE THE HEAVENS, IT'S OVER.

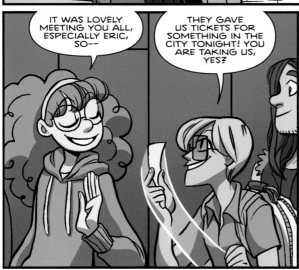

IT WAS LOVELY MEETING YOU ALL, ESPECIALLY ERIC, SO--

THEY GAVE US TICKETS FOR SOMETHING IN THE CITY TONIGHT! YOU ARE TAKING US, YES?

I SUPPOSE I AM.

WHAT ARE YOU DOING UNTIL THEN?

I HEAR SHEFFIELD HAS MANY HIDDEN TUNNELS, HARD TO ACCESS! WE ARE GOING TO INVESTIGATE, MAKE VIDEO WITH ERIC'S iPAD MAYBE!

NO, YOU AREN'T GOING TO DO THAT. YOU'RE ALL COMING HOME WITH ME.

Ugh, THANKS A LOT MUM.

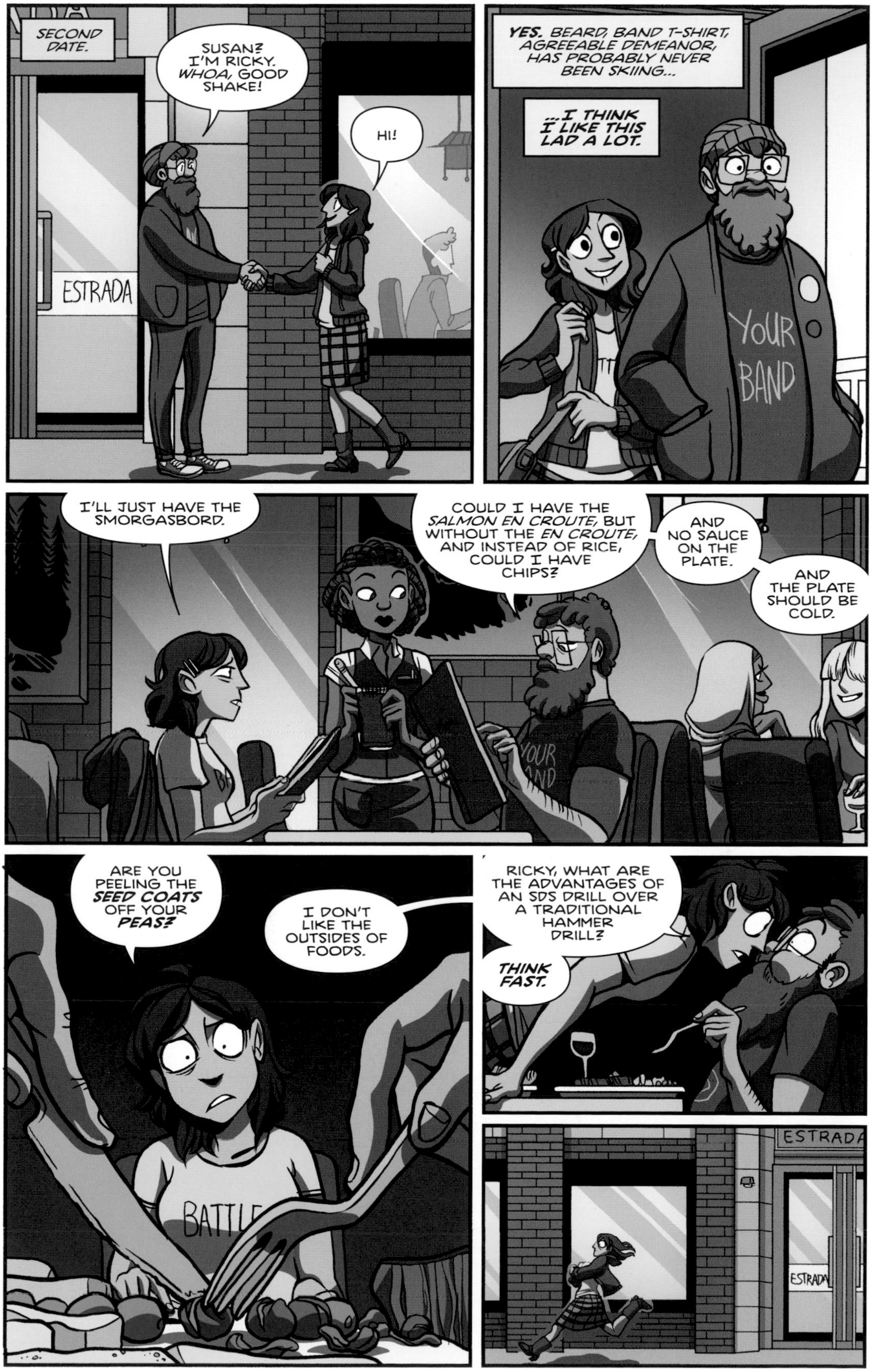
SECOND DATE.
SUSAN? I'M RICKY. WHOA, GOOD SHAKE!
HI!
ESTRADA
YES. BEARD, BAND T-SHIRT, AGREEABLE DEMEANOR, HAS PROBABLY NEVER BEEN SKIING...
...I THINK I LIKE THIS LAD A LOT.
YOUR BAND
I'LL JUST HAVE THE SMORGASBORD.
COULD I HAVE THE SALMON EN CROUTE, BUT WITHOUT THE EN CROUTE, AND INSTEAD OF RICE, COULD I HAVE CHIPS?
AND NO SAUCE ON THE PLATE.
AND THE PLATE SHOULD BE COLD.
ARE YOU PEELING THE SEED COATS OFF YOUR PEAS?
I DON'T LIKE THE OUTSIDES OF FOODS.
BATTLE
RICKY, WHAT ARE THE ADVANTAGES OF AN SDS DRILL OVER A TRADITIONAL HAMMER DRILL?
THINK FAST.
ESTRADA
ESTRADA

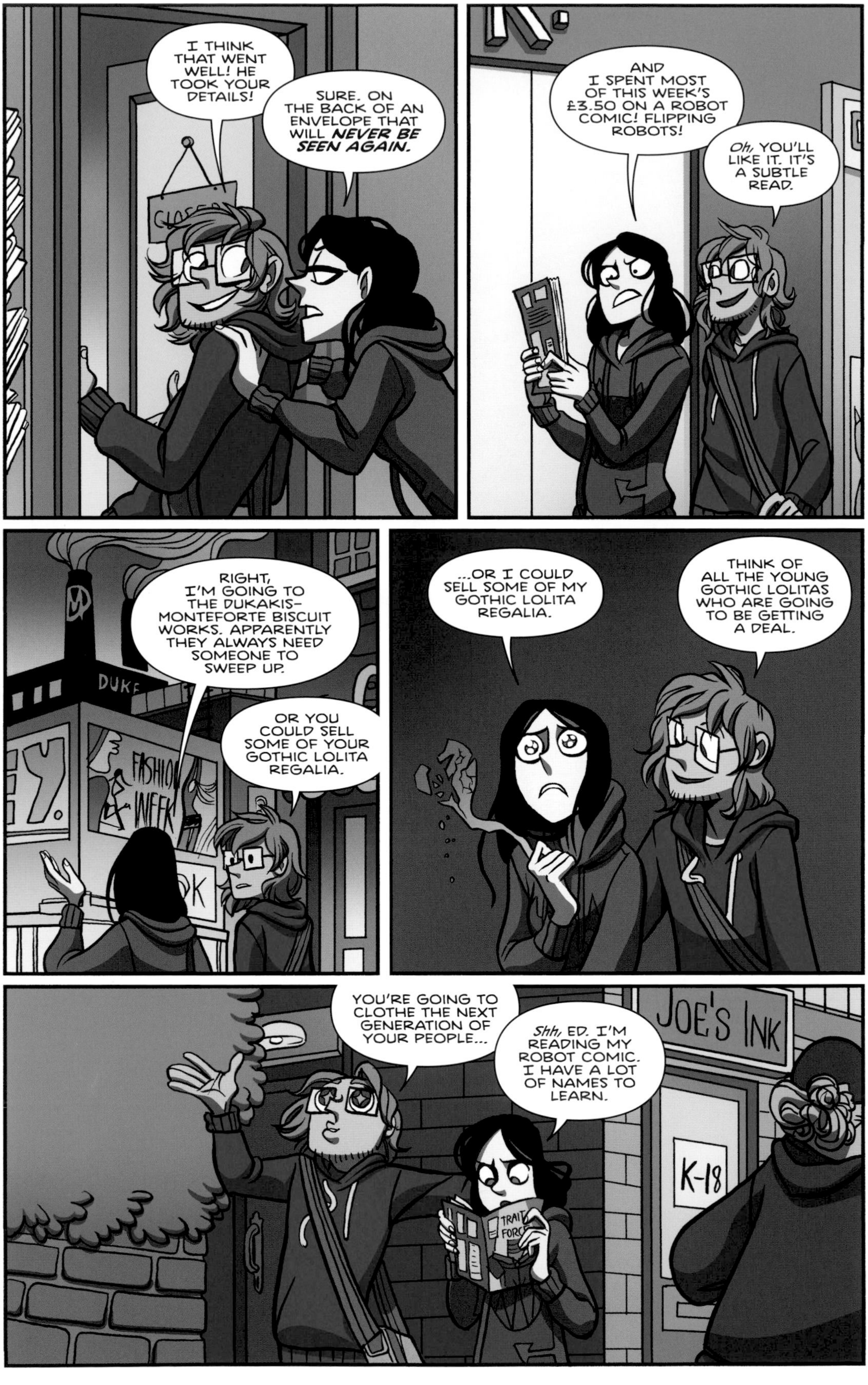
I THINK THAT WENT WELL! HE TOOK YOUR DETAILS!
SURE. ON THE BACK OF AN ENVELOPE THAT WILL **NEVER BE SEEN AGAIN.**
AND I SPENT MOST OF THIS WEEK'S £3.50 ON A ROBOT COMIC! FLIPPING ROBOTS!
*Oh,* YOU'LL LIKE IT. IT'S A SUBTLE READ.
RIGHT, I'M GOING TO THE DUKAKIS-MONTEFORTE BISCUIT WORKS. APPARENTLY THEY ALWAYS NEED SOMEONE TO SWEEP UP.
OR YOU COULD SELL SOME OF YOUR GOTHIC LOLITA REGALIA.
FASHION WEEK
...OR I COULD SELL SOME OF MY GOTHIC LOLITA REGALIA.
THINK OF ALL THE YOUNG GOTHIC LOLITAS WHO ARE GOING TO BE GETTING A DEAL.
YOU'RE GOING TO CLOTHE THE NEXT GENERATION OF YOUR PEOPLE...
*Shh,* ED. I'M READING MY ROBOT COMIC. I HAVE A LOT OF NAMES TO LEARN.
JOE'S INK
K-18

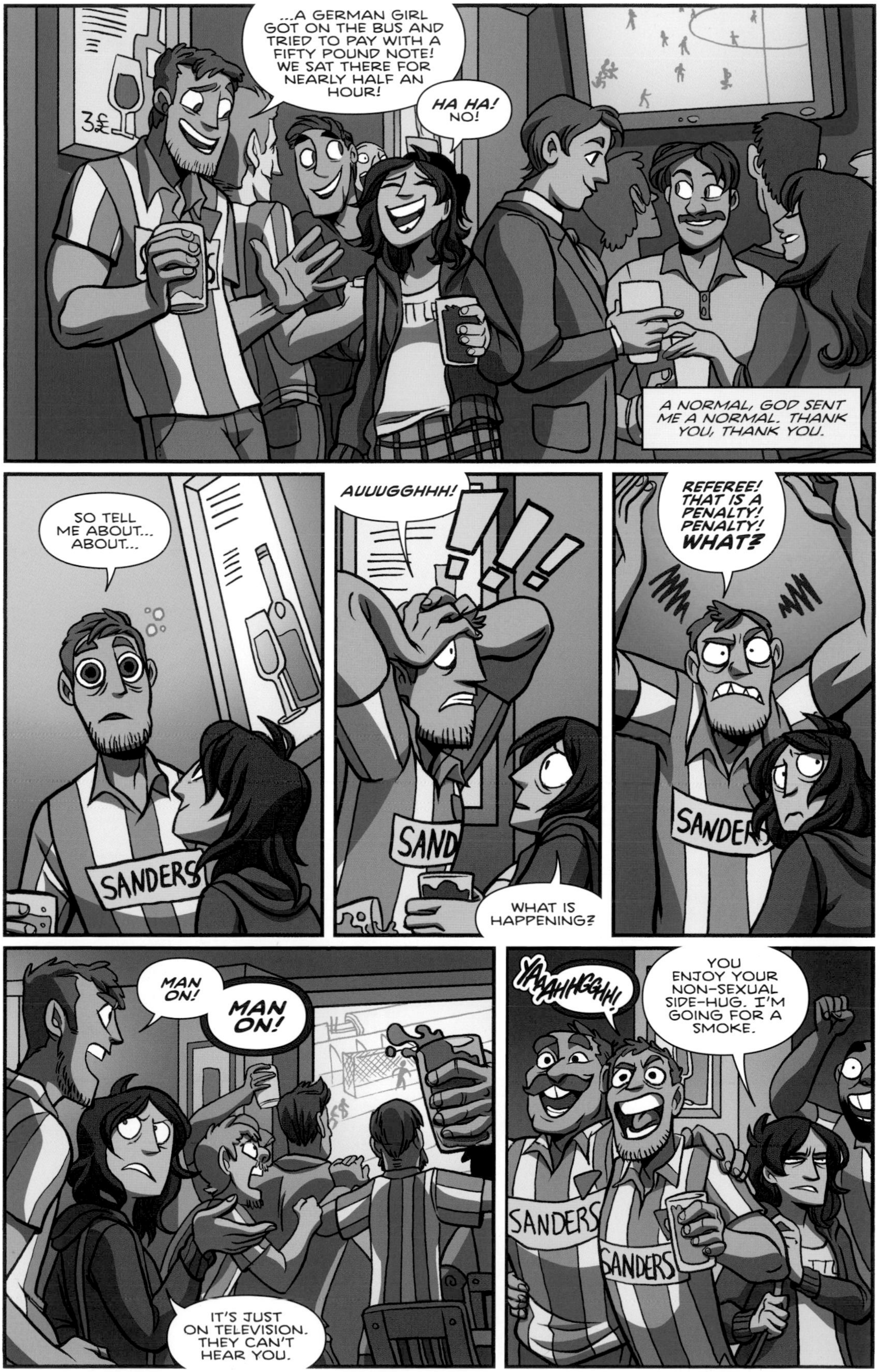
...A GERMAN GIRL GOT ON THE BUS AND TRIED TO PAY WITH A FIFTY POUND NOTE! WE SAT THERE FOR NEARLY HALF AN HOUR!
HA HA! NO!
A NORMAL, GOD SENT ME A NORMAL. THANK YOU, THANK YOU.
SO TELL ME ABOUT... ABOUT...
SANDERS
AUUUGHHH!
SAND
WHAT IS HAPPENING?
REFEREE! THAT IS A PENALTY! PENALTY! WHAT?
SANDERS
MAN ON!
MAN ON!
IT'S JUST ON TELEVISION. THEY CAN'T HEAR YOU.
YAAAHHGGHH!
YOU ENJOY YOUR NON-SEXUAL SIDE-HUG. I'M GOING FOR A SMOKE.
SANDERS
SANDERS

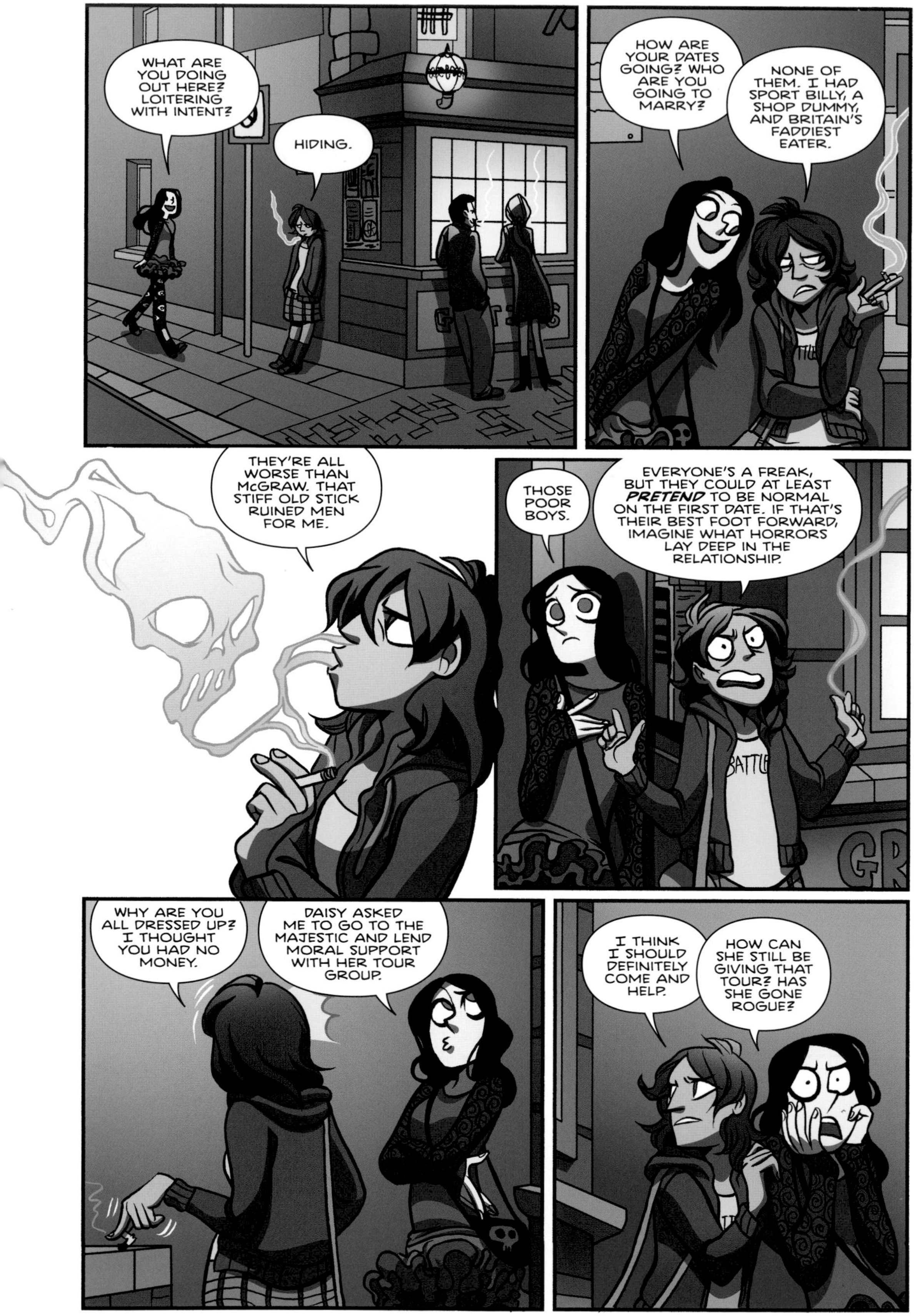
WHAT ARE YOU DOING OUT HERE? LOITERING WITH INTENT?
HIDING.
HOW ARE YOUR DATES GOING? WHO ARE YOU GOING TO MARRY?
NONE OF THEM. I HAD SPORT BILLY, A SHOP DUMMY, AND BRITAIN'S FADDIEST EATER.
THEY'RE ALL WORSE THAN McGRAW. THAT STIFF OLD STICK RUINED MEN FOR ME.
THOSE POOR BOYS.
EVERYONE'S A FREAK, BUT THEY COULD AT LEAST *PRETEND* TO BE NORMAL ON THE FIRST DATE. IF THAT'S THEIR BEST FOOT FORWARD, IMAGINE WHAT HORRORS LAY DEEP IN THE RELATIONSHIP.
WHY ARE YOU ALL DRESSED UP? I THOUGHT YOU HAD NO MONEY.
DAISY ASKED ME TO GO TO THE MAJESTIC AND LEND MORAL SUPPORT WITH HER TOUR GROUP.
I THINK I SHOULD DEFINITELY COME AND HELP.
HOW CAN SHE STILL BE GIVING THAT TOUR? HAS SHE GONE ROGUE?

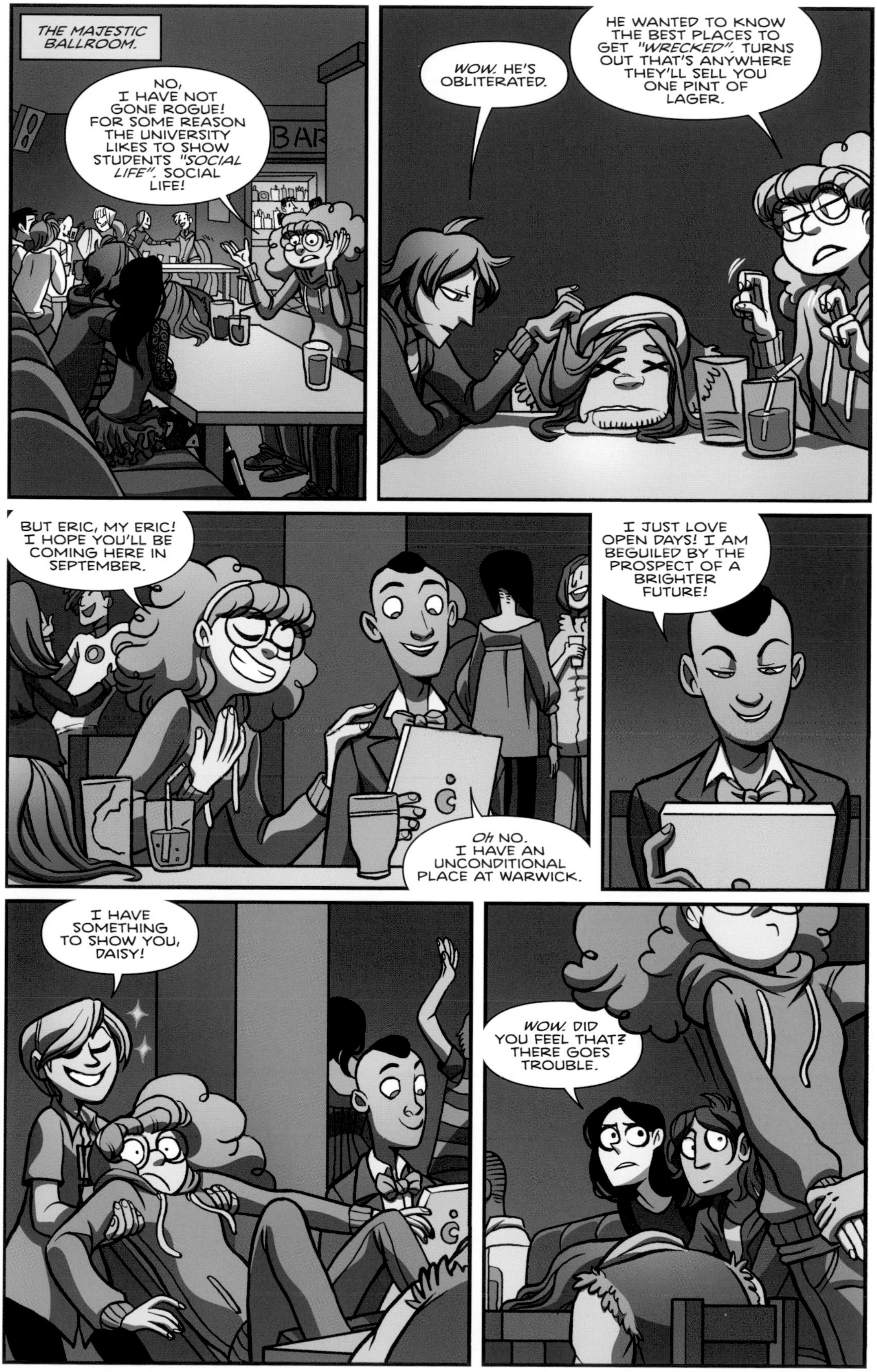
THE MAJESTIC BALLROOM.
BAR
NO, I HAVE NOT GONE ROGUE! FOR SOME REASON THE UNIVERSITY LIKES TO SHOW STUDENTS "SOCIAL LIFE". SOCIAL LIFE!
WOW. HE'S OBLITERATED.
HE WANTED TO KNOW THE BEST PLACES TO GET "WRECKED". TURNS OUT THAT'S ANYWHERE THEY'LL SELL YOU ONE PINT OF LAGER.
BUT ERIC, MY ERIC! I HOPE YOU'LL BE COMING HERE IN SEPTEMBER.
Oh NO. I HAVE AN UNCONDITIONAL PLACE AT WARWICK.
I JUST LOVE OPEN DAYS! I AM BEGUILED BY THE PROSPECT OF A BRIGHTER FUTURE!
I HAVE SOMETHING TO SHOW YOU, DAISY!
WOW. DID YOU FEEL THAT? THERE GOES TROUBLE.

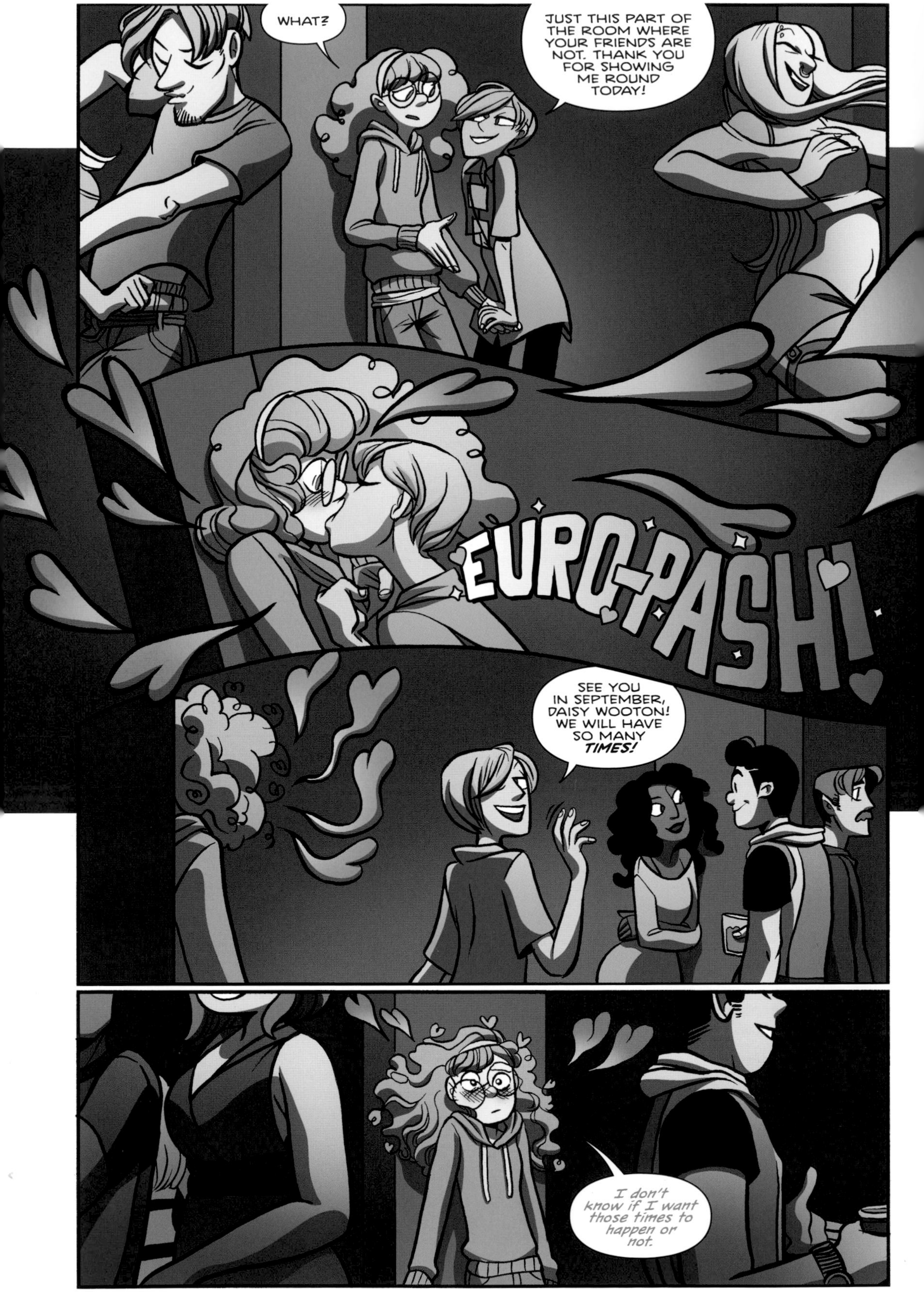
WHAT?
JUST THIS PART OF THE ROOM WHERE YOUR FRIENDS ARE NOT. THANK YOU FOR SHOWING ME ROUND TODAY!
EURO-PASH!
SEE YOU IN SEPTEMBER, DAISY WOOTON! WE WILL HAVE SO MANY *TIMES!*
*I don't know if I want those times to happen or not.*

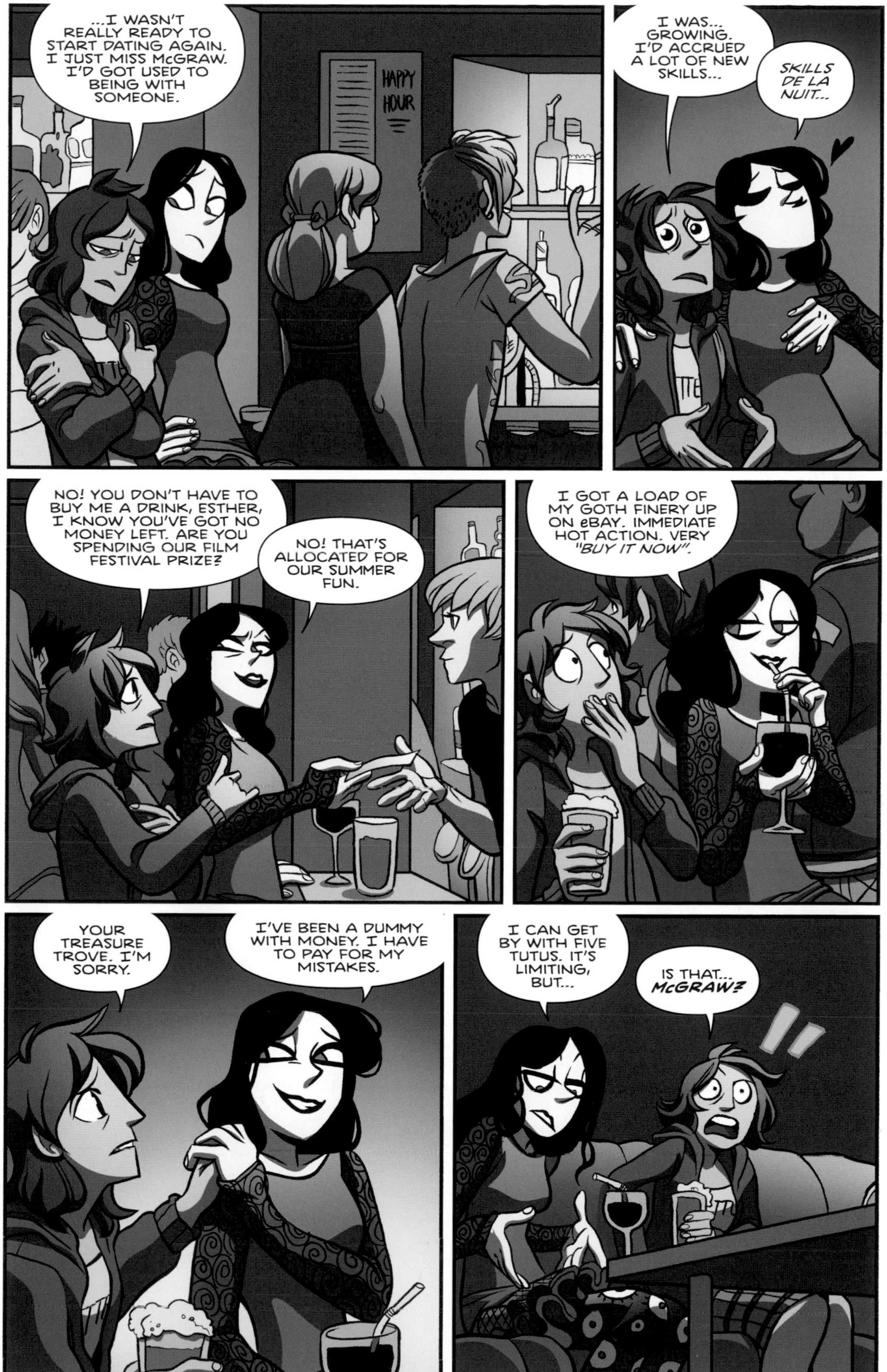
...I WASN'T REALLY READY TO START DATING AGAIN. I JUST MISS McGRAW. I'D GOT USED TO BEING WITH SOMEONE.
HAPPY HOUR
I WAS... GROWING. I'D ACCRUED A LOT OF NEW SKILLS...
SKILLS DE LA NUIT...
NO! YOU DON'T HAVE TO BUY ME A DRINK, ESTHER, I KNOW YOU'VE GOT NO MONEY LEFT. ARE YOU SPENDING OUR FILM FESTIVAL PRIZE?
NO! THAT'S ALLOCATED FOR OUR SUMMER FUN.
I GOT A LOAD OF MY GOTH FINERY UP ON eBAY. IMMEDIATE HOT ACTION. VERY "BUY IT NOW".
YOUR TREASURE TROVE. I'M SORRY.
I'VE BEEN A DUMMY WITH MONEY. I HAVE TO PAY FOR MY MISTAKES.
I CAN GET BY WITH FIVE TUTUS. IT'S LIMITING, BUT...
IS THAT... McGRAW?

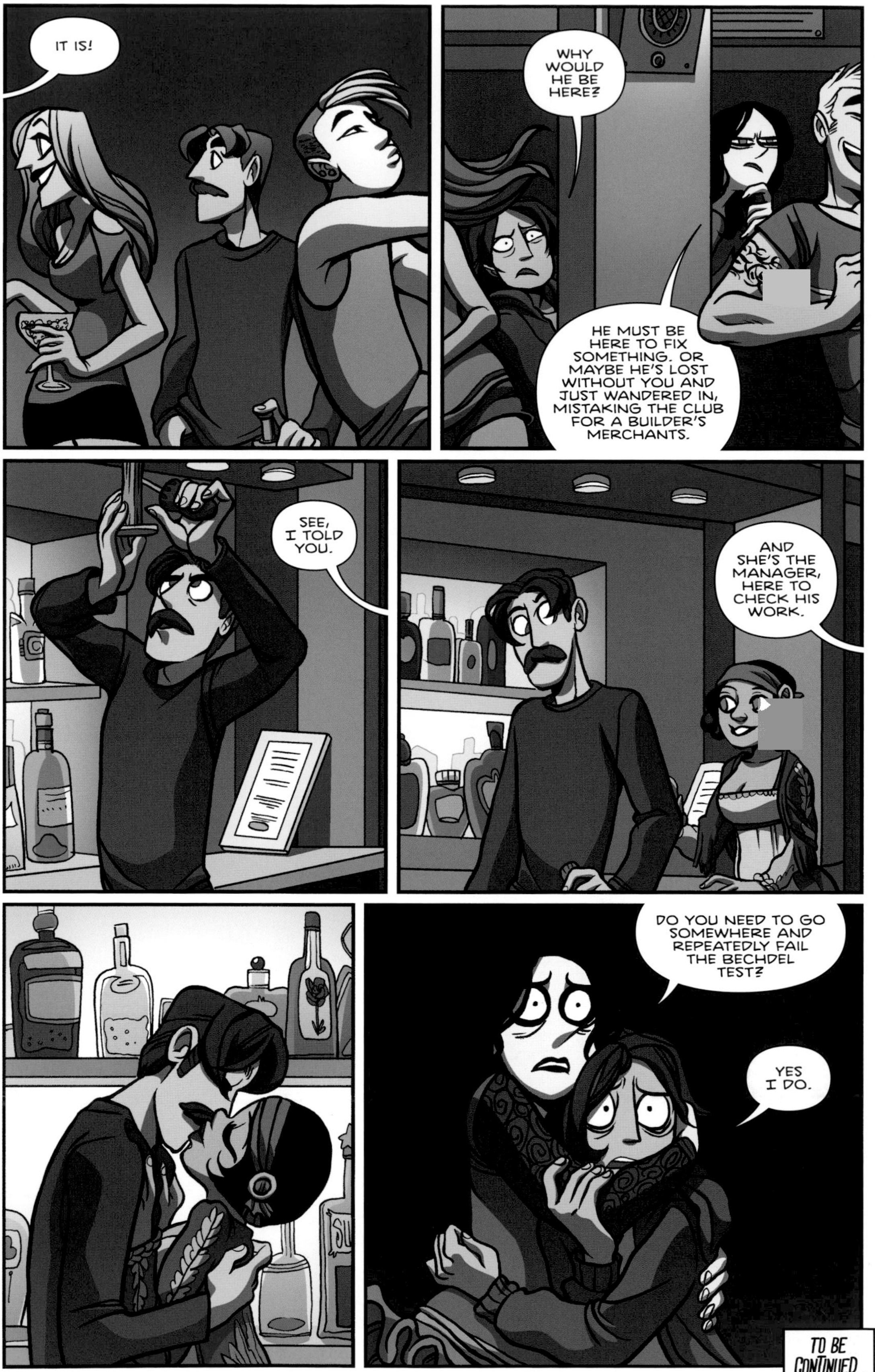
IT IS!
WHY WOULD HE BE HERE?
HE MUST BE HERE TO FIX SOMETHING. OR MAYBE HE'S LOST WITHOUT YOU AND JUST WANDERED IN, MISTAKING THE CLUB FOR A BUILDER'S MERCHANTS.
SEE, I TOLD YOU.
AND SHE'S THE MANAGER, HERE TO CHECK HIS WORK.
DO YOU NEED TO GO SOMEWHERE AND REPEATEDLY FAIL THE BECHDEL TEST?
YES I DO.
TO BE CONTINUED...

# GIANT DAYS:
## SELF-PUBLISHED
### PART II

**BY JOHN ALLISON**

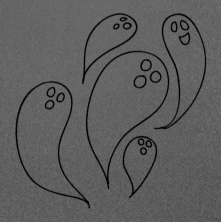

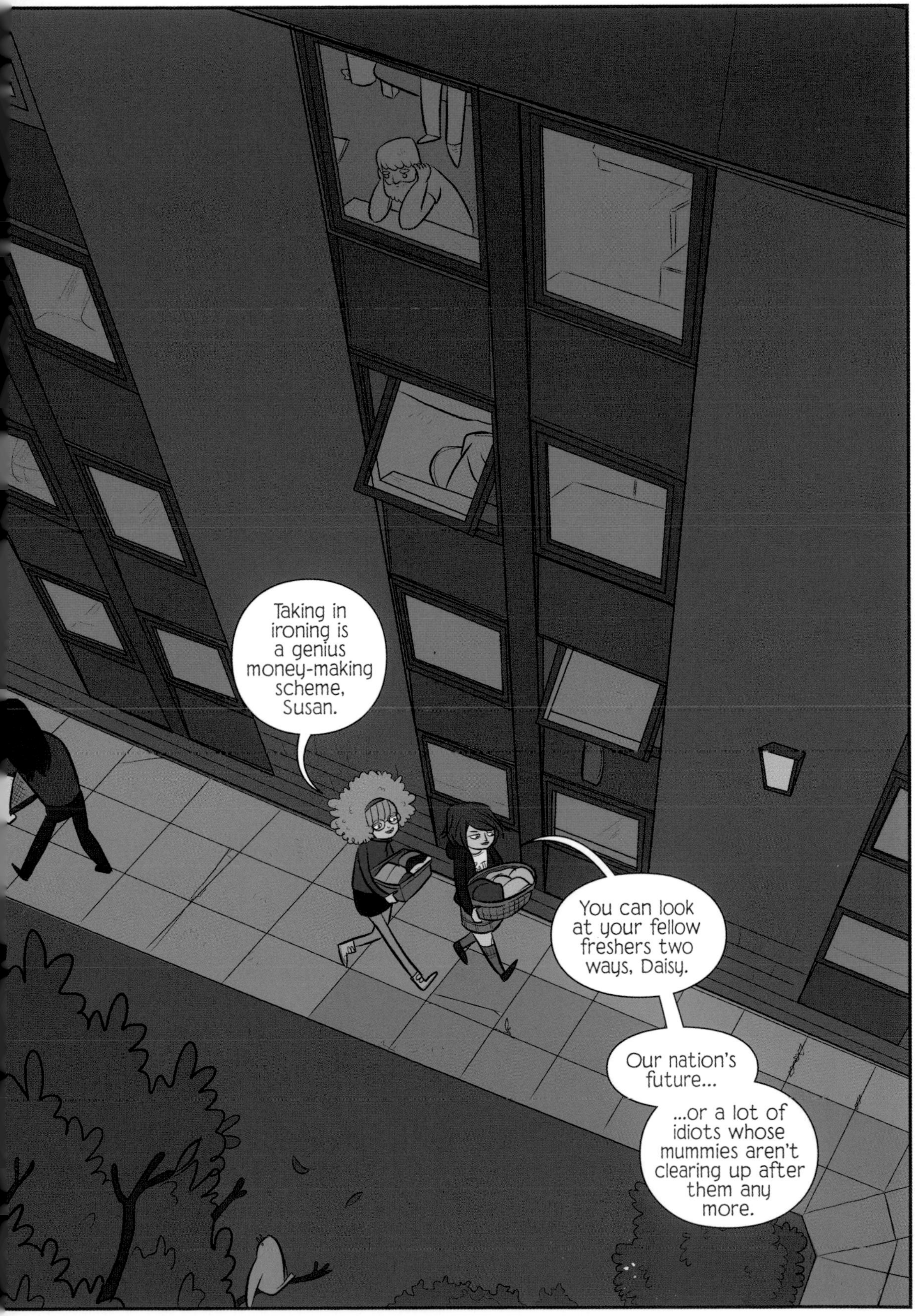
Taking in ironing is a genius money-making scheme, Susan.
You can look at your fellow freshers two ways, Daisy.
Our nation's future...
...or a lot of idiots whose mummies aren't clearing up after them any more.

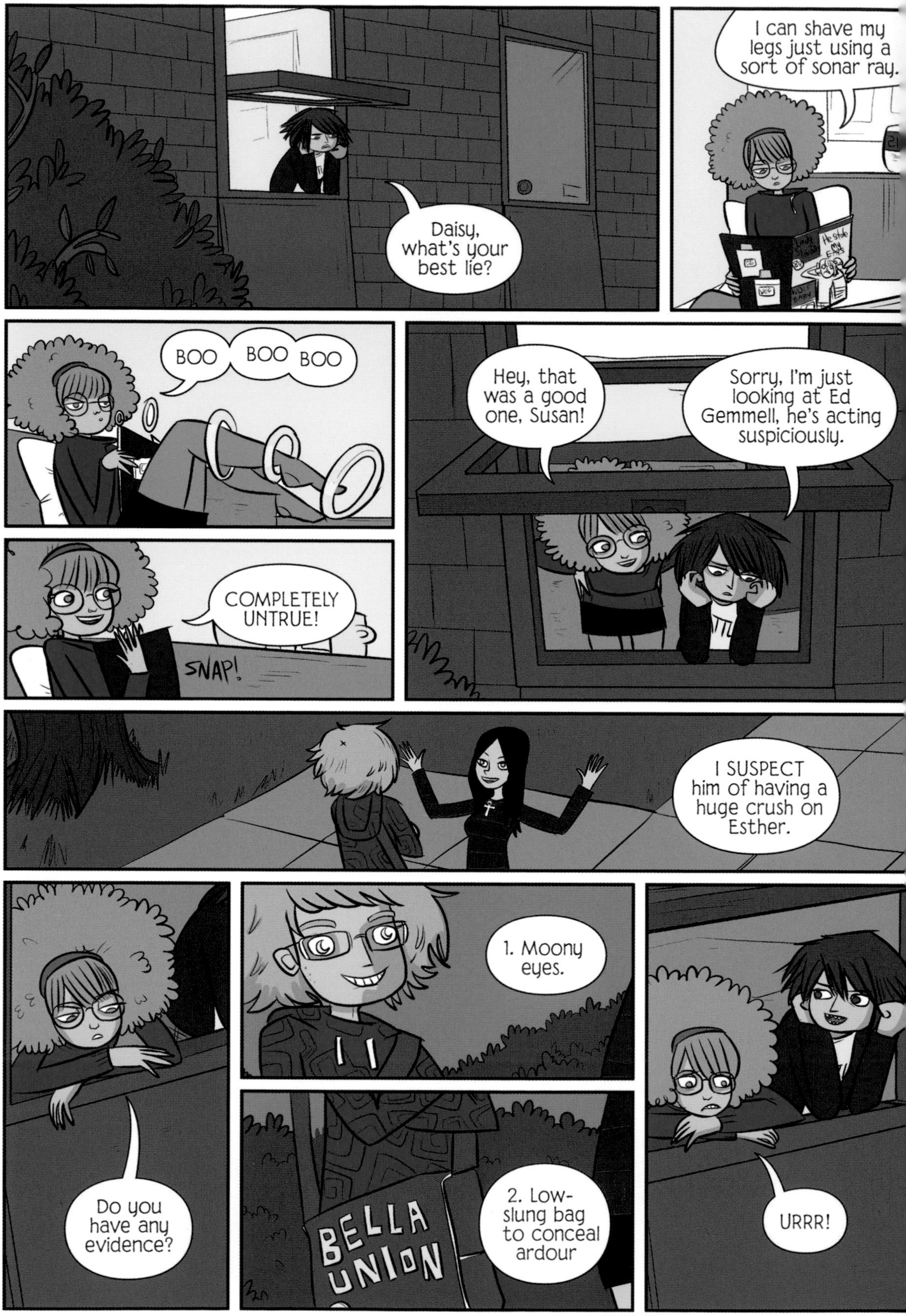
Daisy, what's your best lie?
I can shave my legs just using a sort of sonar ray.
BOO BOO BOO
COMPLETELY UNTRUE!
SNAP!
Hey, that was a good one, Susan!
Sorry, I'm just looking at Ed Gemmell, he's acting suspiciously.
I SUSPECT him of having a huge crush on Esther.
Do you have any evidence?
1. Moony eyes.
2. Low-slung bag to conceal ardour
BELLA UNION
URRR!

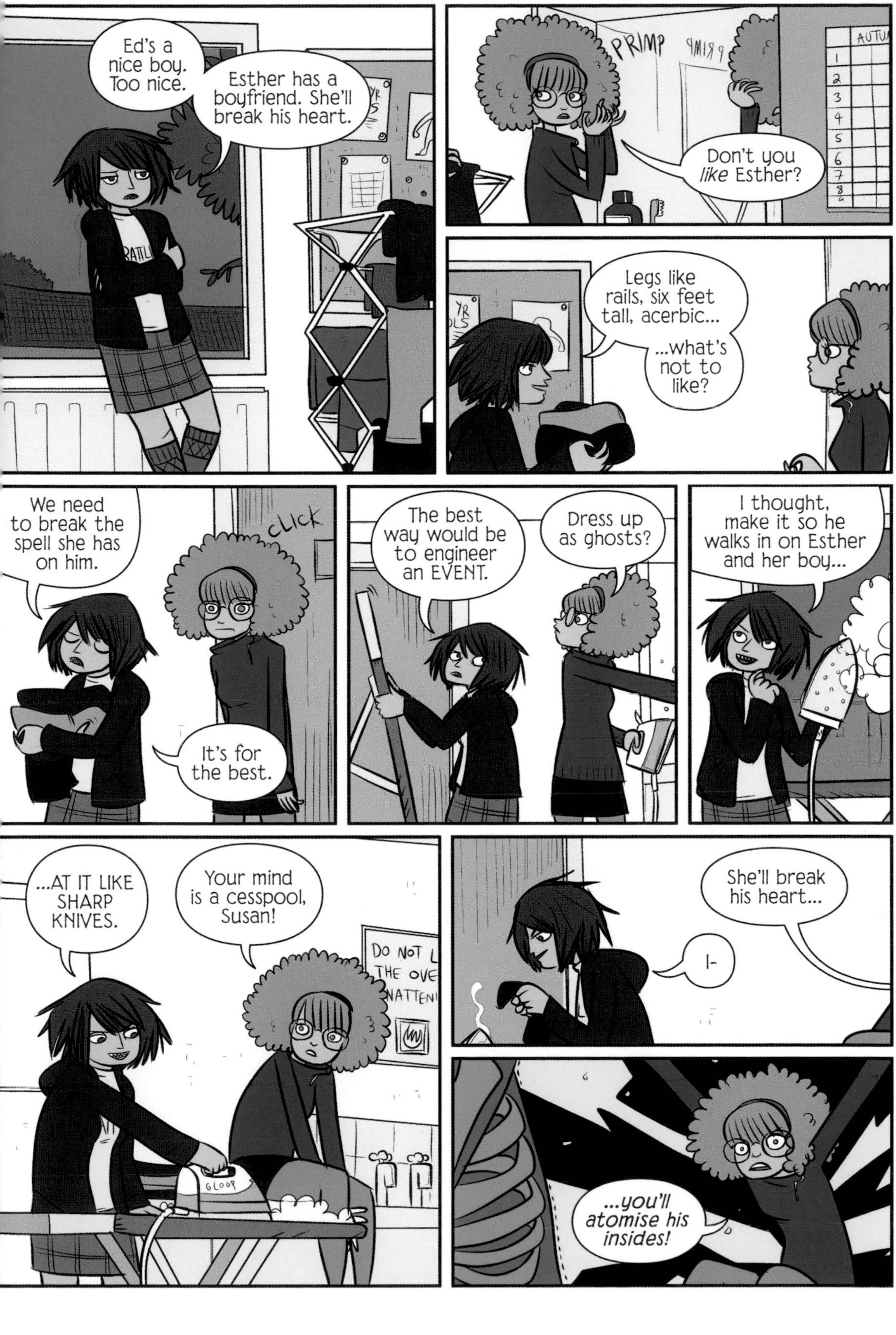
Ed's a nice boy. Too nice.
Esther has a boyfriend. She'll break his heart.
PRIMP
PRIMP
Don't you *like* Esther?
Legs like rails, six feet tall, acerbic...
...what's not to like?
We need to break the spell she has on him.
CLICK
It's for the best.
The best way would be to engineer an EVENT.
Dress up as ghosts?
I thought, make it so he walks in on Esther and her boy...
...AT IT LIKE SHARP KNIVES.
Your mind is a cesspool, Susan!
DO NOT
GLOOP
She'll break his heart...
I-
*...you'll atomise his insides!*

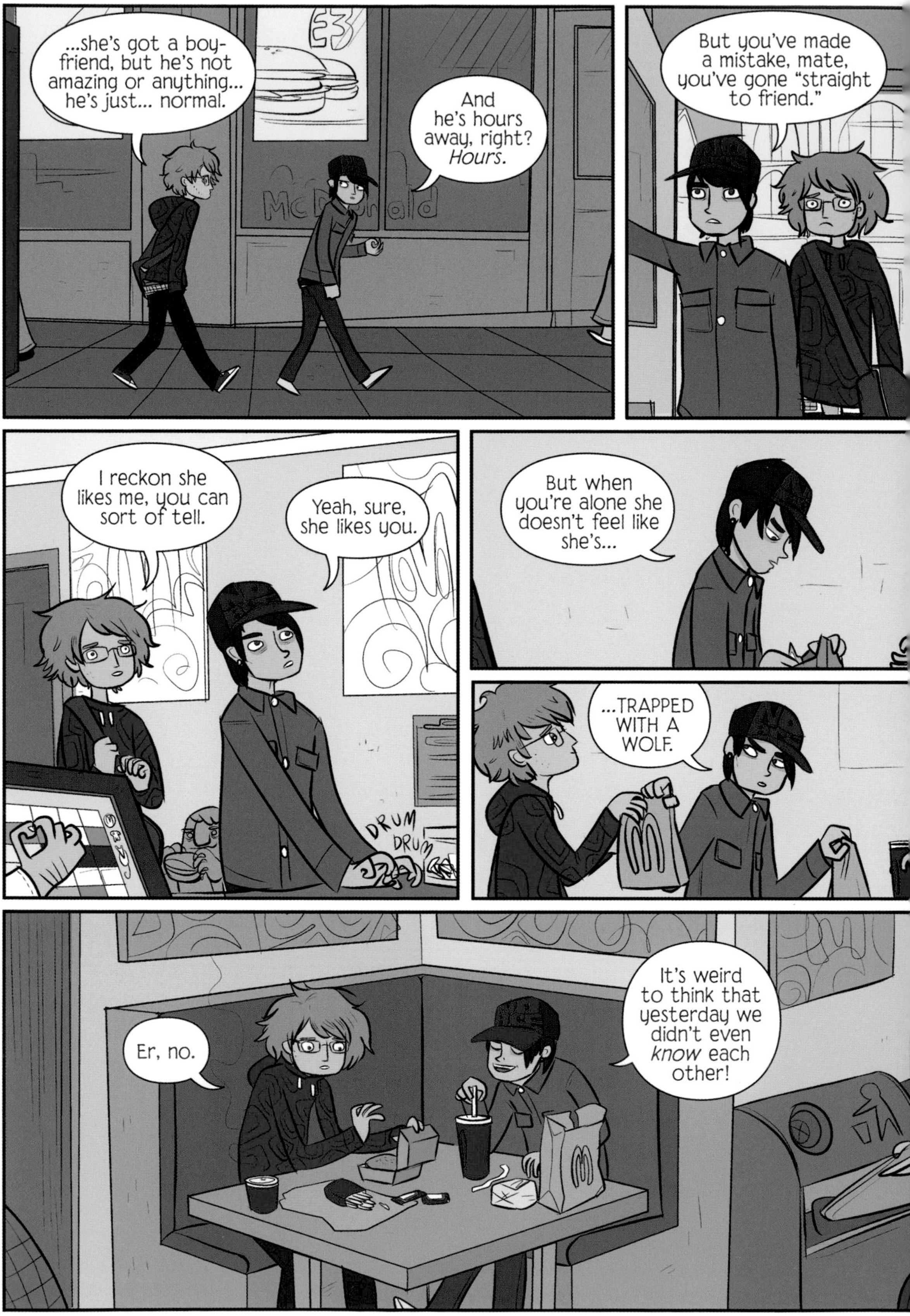
...she's got a boy-friend, but he's not amazing or anything... he's just... normal.
And he's hours away, right? *Hours.*
But you've made a mistake, mate, you've gone "straight to friend."
I reckon she likes me, you can sort of tell.
Yeah, sure, she likes you.
DRUM DRUM
But when you're alone she doesn't feel like she's...
...TRAPPED WITH A WOLF.
Er, no.
It's weird to think that yesterday we didn't even *know* each other!

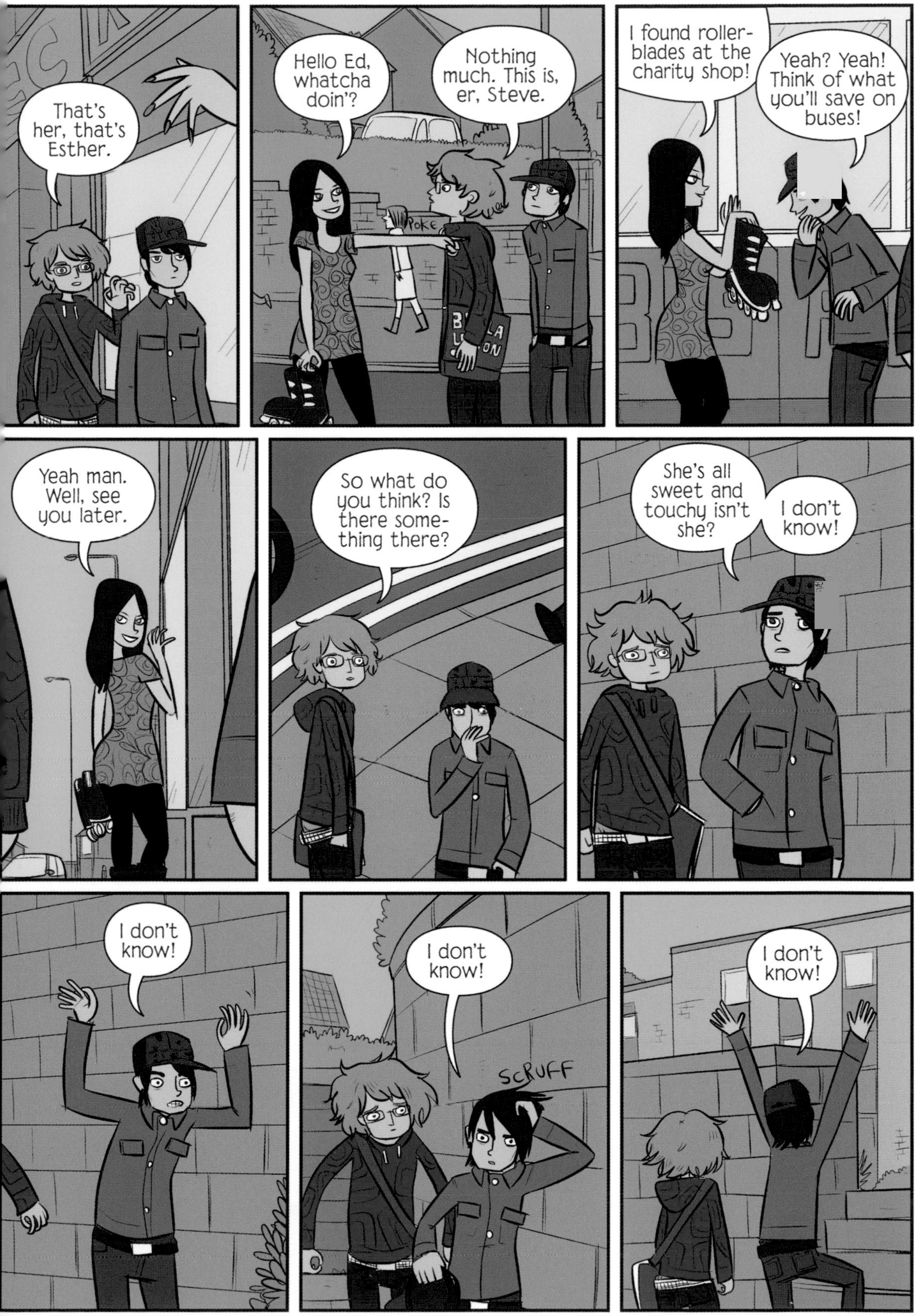
That's her, that's Esther.
Hello Ed, whatcha doin'?
Nothing much. This is, er, Steve.
POKE
I found roller-blades at the charity shop!
Yeah? Yeah! Think of what you'll save on buses!
Yeah man. Well, see you later.
So what do you think? Is there some-thing there?
She's all sweet and touchy isn't she?
I don't know!
I don't know!
I don't know!
SCRUFF
I don't know!

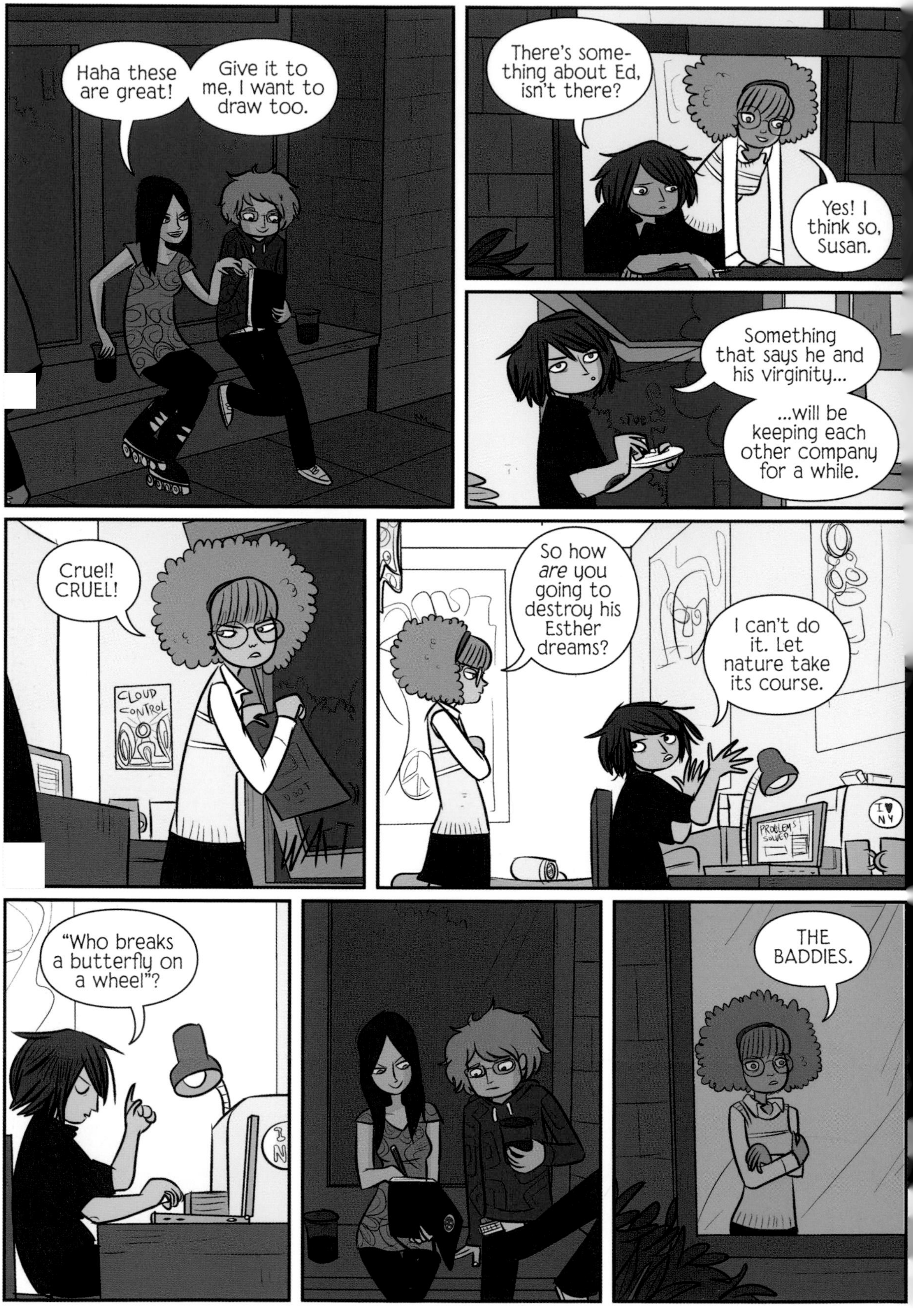
Haha these are great!
Give it to me, I want to draw too.
There's something about Ed, isn't there?
Yes! I think so, Susan.
Something that says he and his virginity...
...will be keeping each other company for a while.
Cruel! CRUEL!
CLOUD CONTROL
So how *are* you going to destroy his Esther dreams?
I can't do it. Let nature take its course.
PROBLEMS SOLVED
"Who breaks a butterfly on a wheel"?
THE BADDIES.

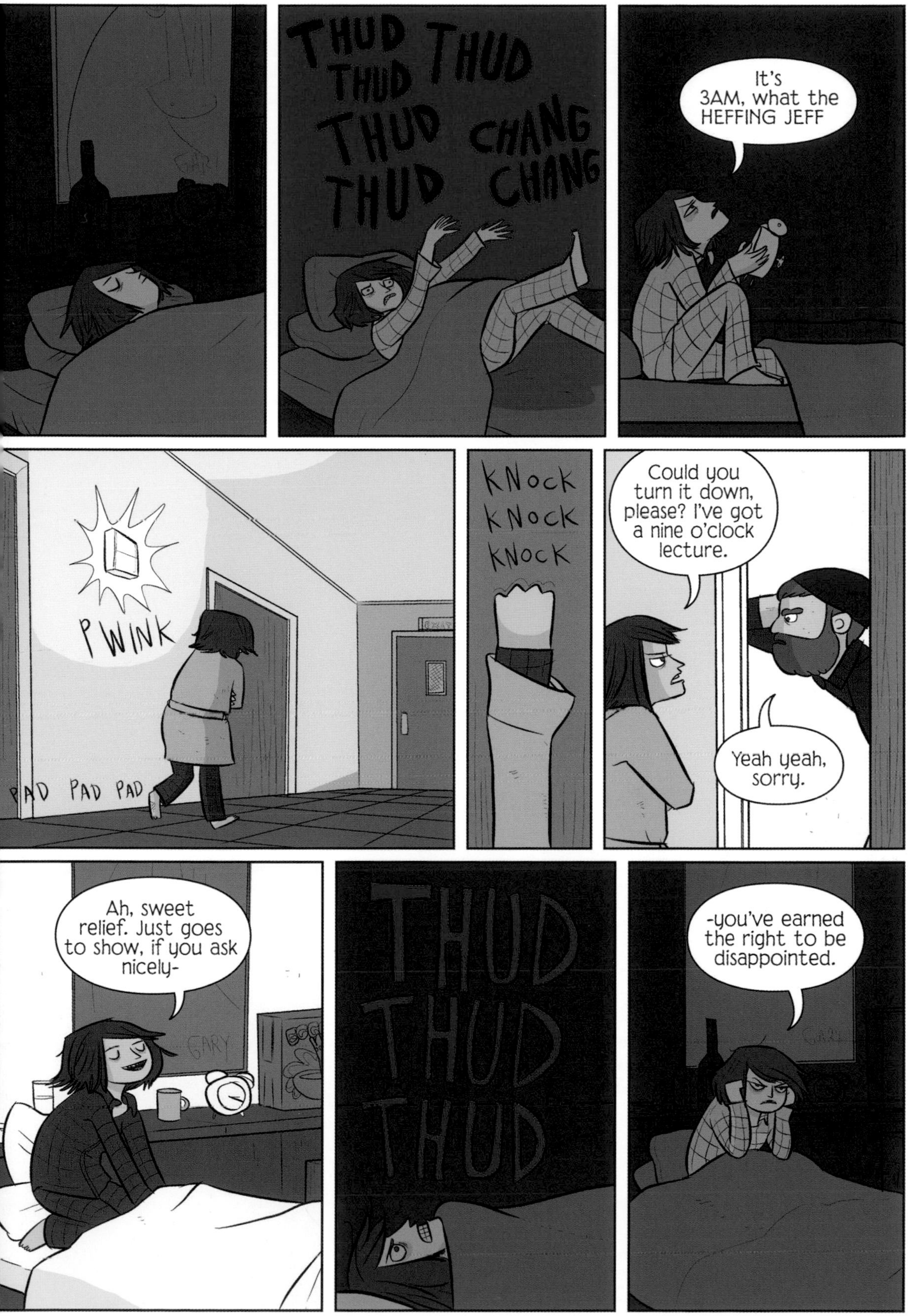
THUD THUD
THUD THUD
THUD CHANG
THUD CHANG
It's 3AM, what the HEFFING JEFF
PWINK
PAD PAD PAD
KNOCK
KNOCK
KNOCK
Could you turn it down, please? I've got a nine o'clock lecture.
Yeah yeah, sorry.
Ah, sweet relief. Just goes to show, if you ask nicely-
THUD
THUD
THUD
-you've earned the right to be disappointed.

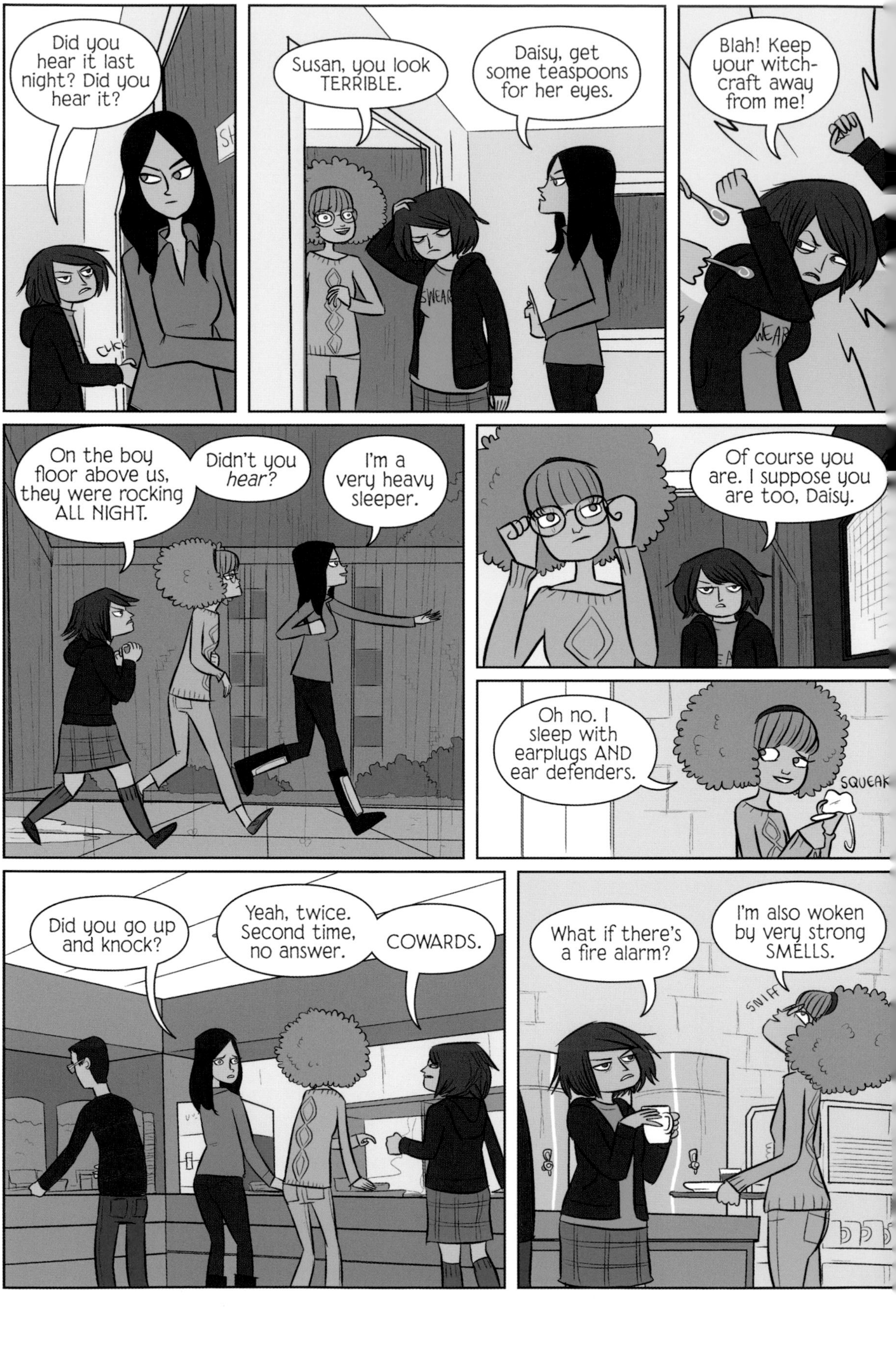
Did you hear it last night? Did you hear it?
CLICK
Susan, you look TERRIBLE.
Daisy, get some teaspoons for her eyes.
SWEAR
Blah! Keep your witch-craft away from me!
On the boy floor above us, they were rocking ALL NIGHT.
Didn't you *hear*?
I'm a very heavy sleeper.
Of course you are. I suppose you are too, Daisy.
Oh no. I sleep with earplugs AND ear defenders.
SQUEAK
Did you go up and knock?
Yeah, twice. Second time, no answer.
COWARDS.
What if there's a fire alarm?
I'm also woken by very strong SMELLS.
SNIFF

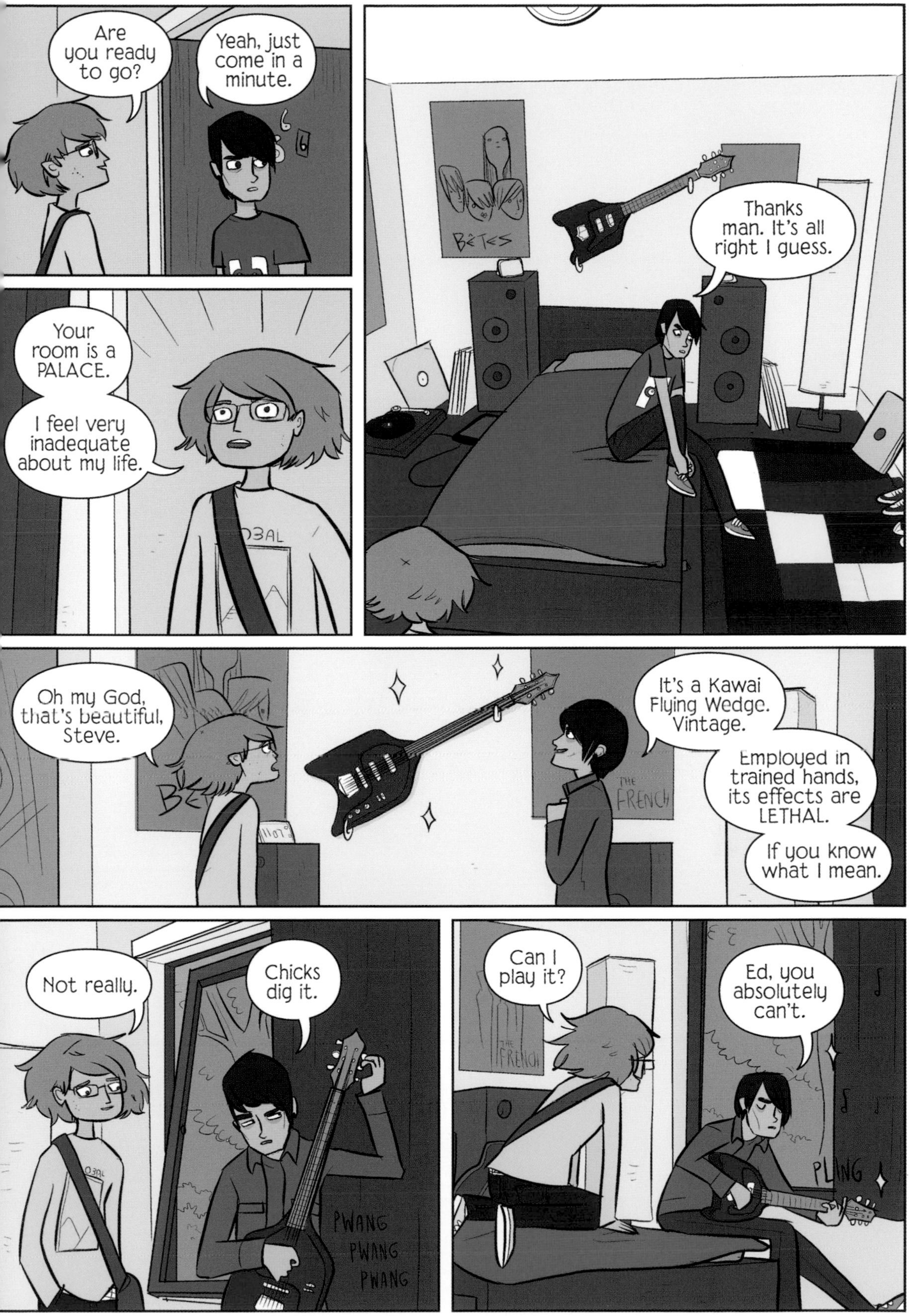
Are you ready to go?
Yeah, just come in a minute.
Thanks man. It's all right I guess.
Your room is a PALACE.
I feel very inadequate about my life.
Oh my God, that's beautiful, Steve.
It's a Kawai Flying Wedge. Vintage.
Employed in trained hands, its effects are LETHAL.
If you know what I mean.
Not really.
Chicks dig it.
PWANG
PWANG
PWANG
Can I play it?
Ed, you absolutely can't.
PLING

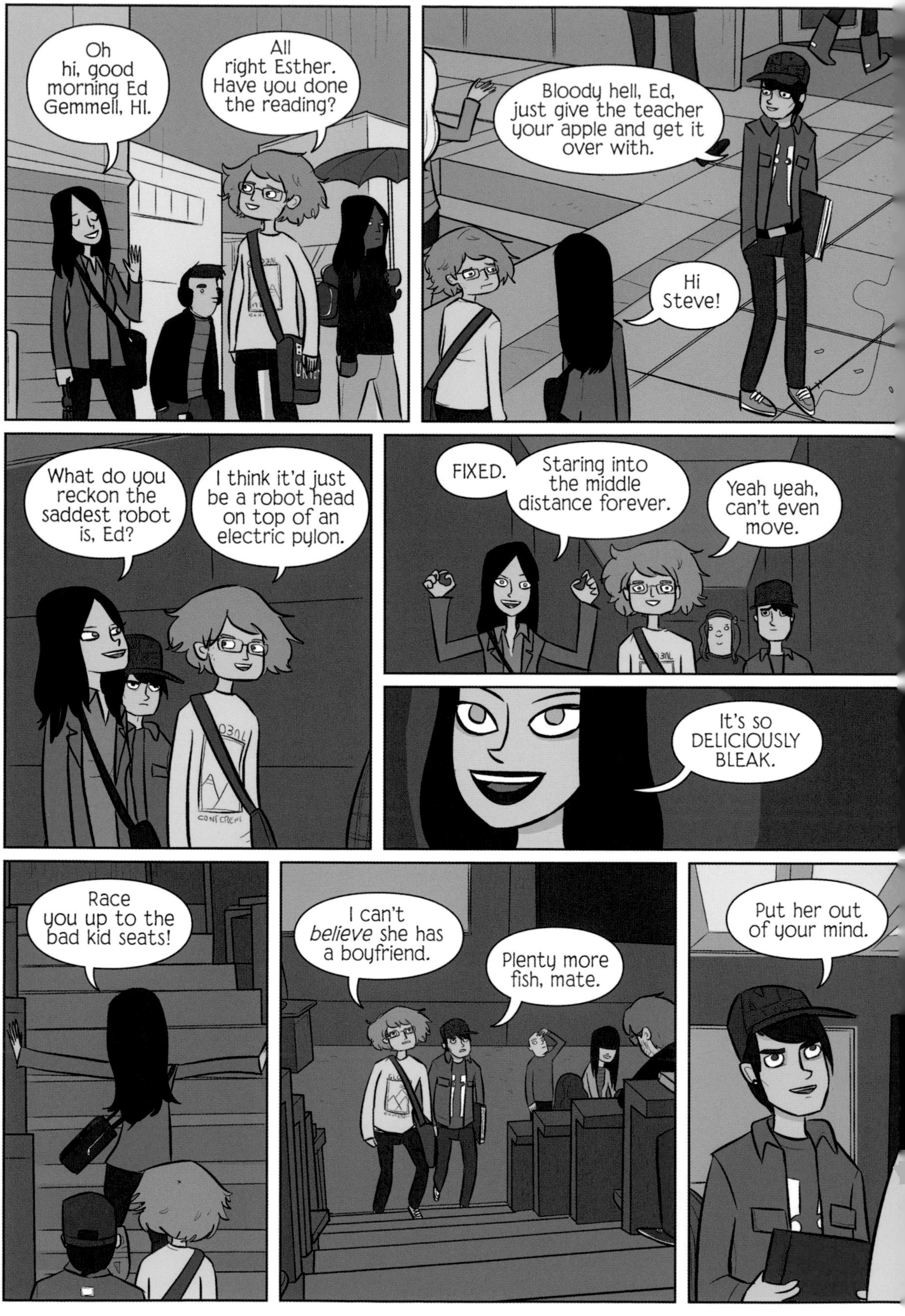
Oh hi, good morning Ed Gemmell, HI.
All right Esther. Have you done the reading?
Bloody hell, Ed, just give the teacher your apple and get it over with.
Hi Steve!
What do you reckon the saddest robot is, Ed?
I think it'd just be a robot head on top of an electric pylon.
FIXED.
Staring into the middle distance forever.
Yeah yeah, can't even move.
It's so DELICIOUSLY BLEAK.
Race you up to the bad kid seats!
I can't *believe* she has a boyfriend.
Plenty more fish, mate.
Put her out of your mind.

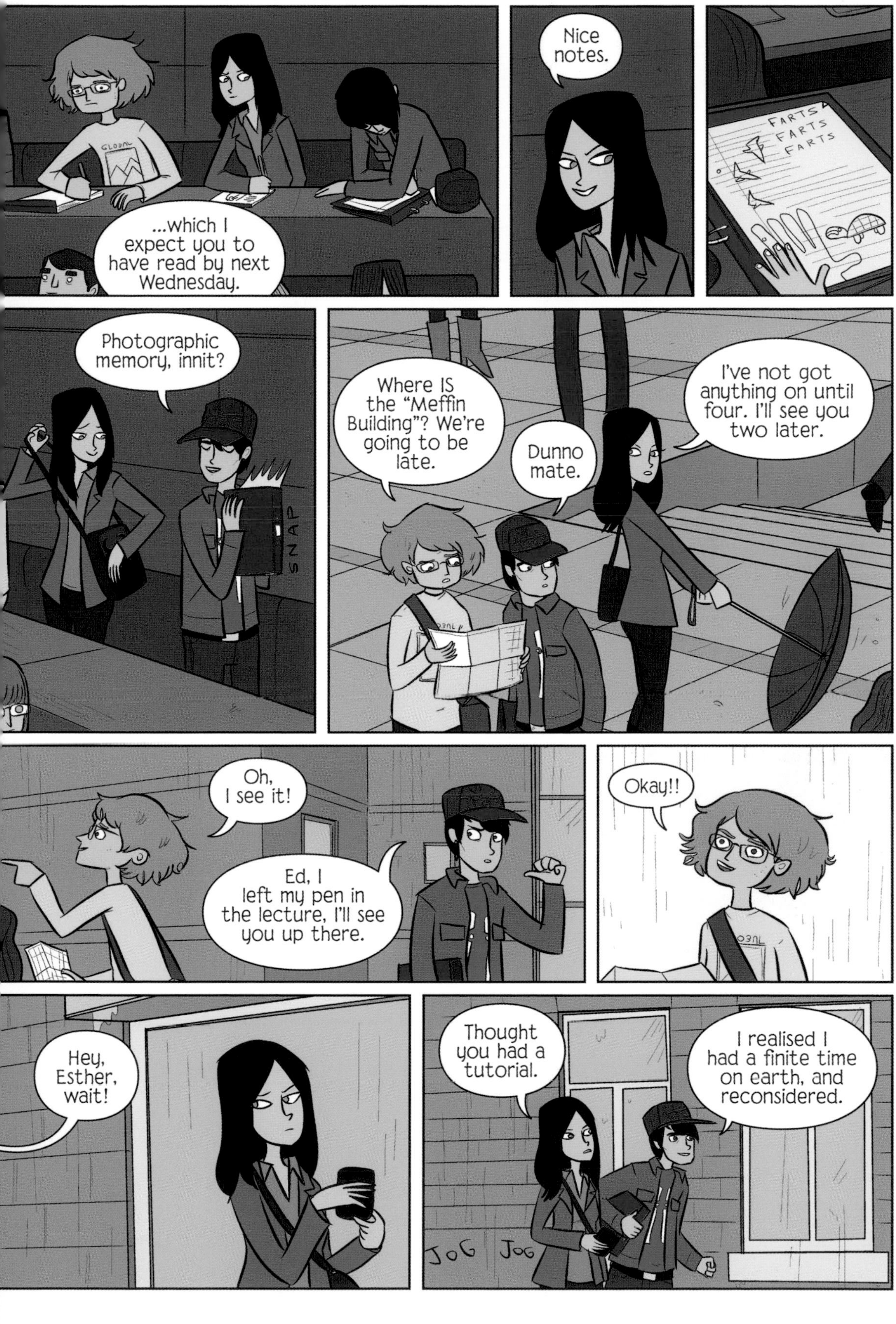
...which I expect you to have read by next Wednesday.
Nice notes.
FARTS FARTS FARTS
Photographic memory, innit?
SNAP
Where IS the "Meffin Building"? We're going to be late.
Dunno mate.
I've not got anything on until four. I'll see you two later.
Oh, I see it!
Ed, I left my pen in the lecture, I'll see you up there.
Okay!!
Hey, Esther, wait!
Thought you had a tutorial.
I realised I had a finite time on earth, and reconsidered.
JOG JOG

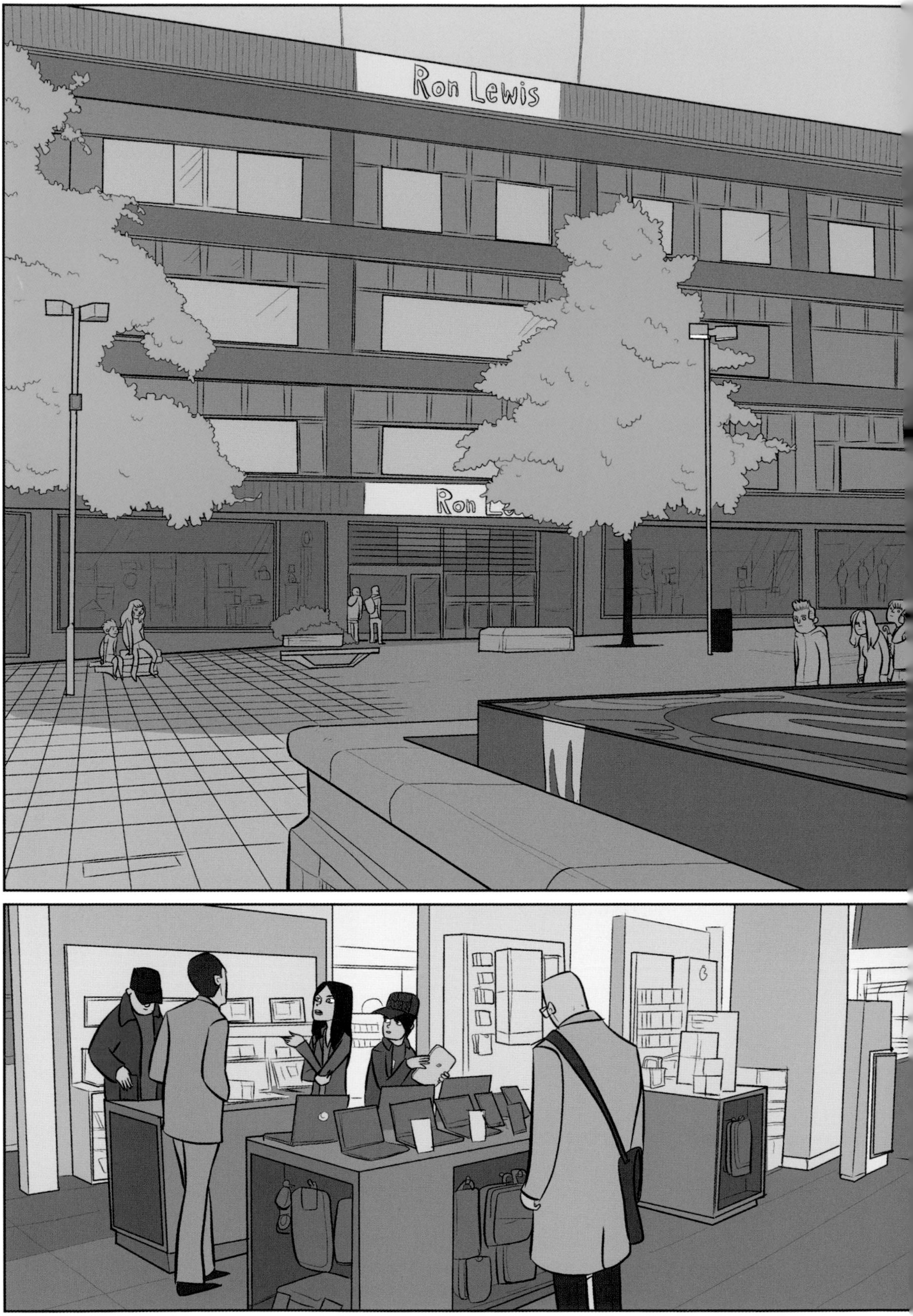
Ron Lewis

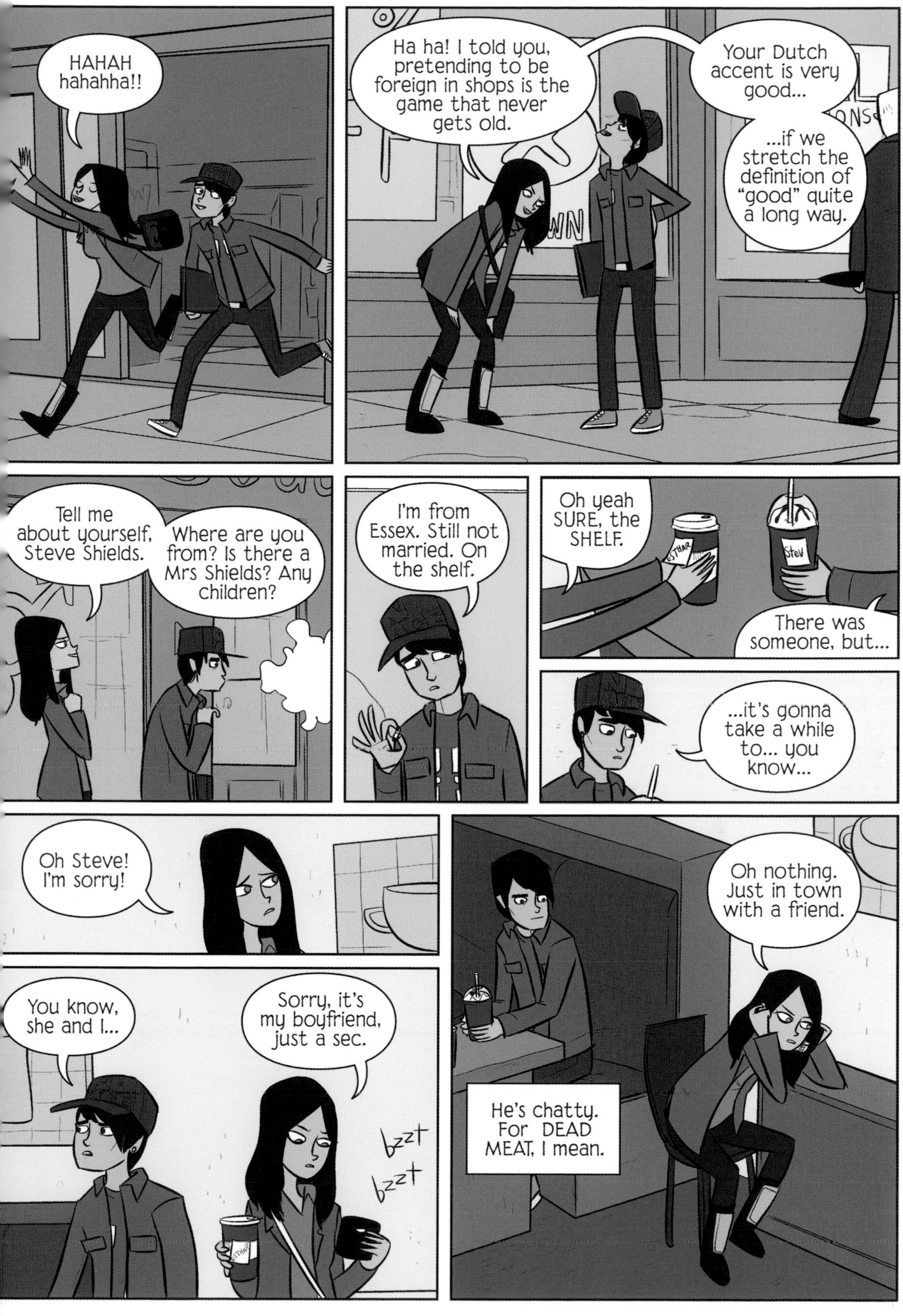
HAHAH hahahha!!
Ha ha! I told you, pretending to be foreign in shops is the game that never gets old.
Your Dutch accent is very good...
...if we stretch the definition of "good" quite a long way.
Tell me about yourself, Steve Shields.
Where are you from? Is there a Mrs Shields? Any children?
I'm from Essex. Still not married. On the shelf.
Oh yeah SURE, the SHELF.
ESTHAR
Stev
There was someone, but...
...it's gonna take a while to... you know...
Oh Steve! I'm sorry!
You know, she and I...
Sorry, it's my boyfriend, just a sec.
bzzt
bzzt
ESTHAR
Oh nothing. Just in town with a friend.
He's chatty. For DEAD MEAT, I mean.

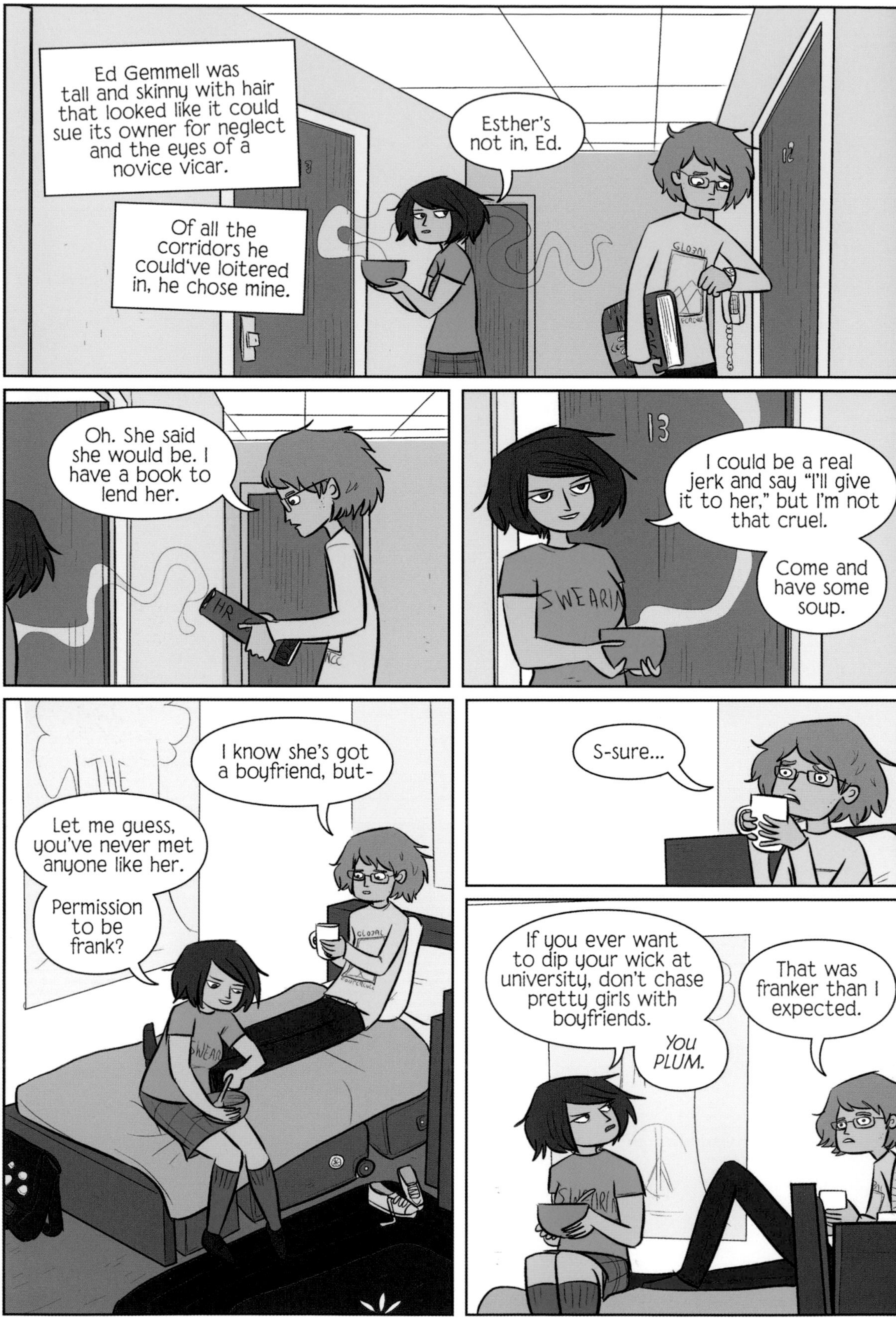
Ed Gemmell was tall and skinny with hair that looked like it could sue its owner for neglect and the eyes of a novice vicar.
Of all the corridors he could've loitered in, he chose mine.
Esther's not in, Ed.
Oh. She said she would be. I have a book to lend her.
13
I could be a real jerk and say "I'll give it to her," but I'm not that cruel.
Come and have some soup.
I know she's got a boyfriend, but-
Let me guess, you've never met anyone like her.
Permission to be frank?
S-sure...
If you ever want to dip your wick at university, don't chase pretty girls with boyfriends.
YOU PLUM.
That was franker than I expected.

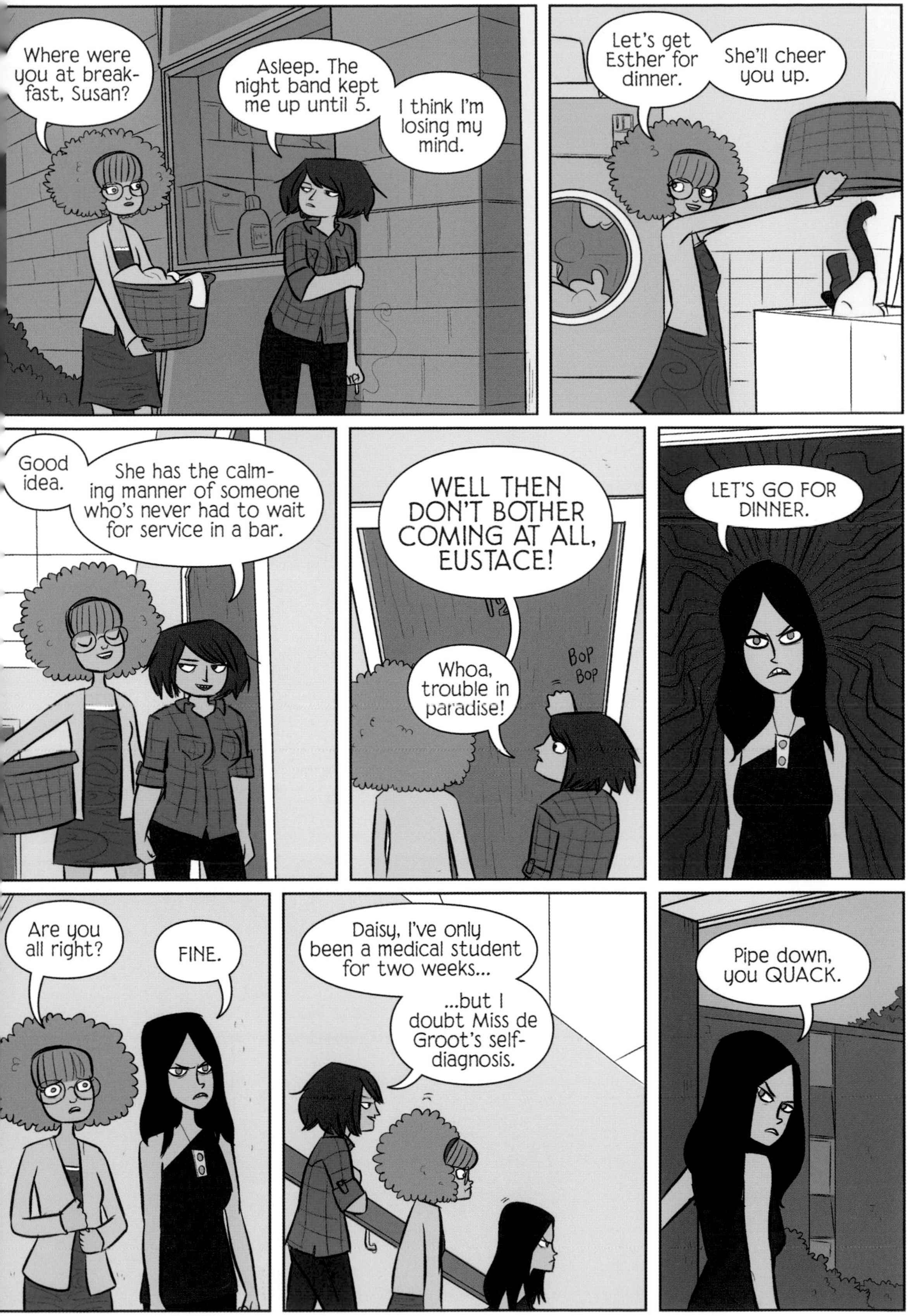
Where were you at breakfast, Susan?
Asleep. The night band kept me up until 5.
I think I'm losing my mind.
Let's get Esther for dinner.
She'll cheer you up.
Good idea.
She has the calming manner of someone who's never had to wait for service in a bar.
WELL THEN DON'T BOTHER COMING AT ALL, EUSTACE!
Whoa, trouble in paradise!
Bop Bop
LET'S GO FOR DINNER.
Are you all right?
FINE.
Daisy, I've only been a medical student for two weeks...
...but I doubt Miss de Groot's self-diagnosis.
Pipe down, you QUACK.

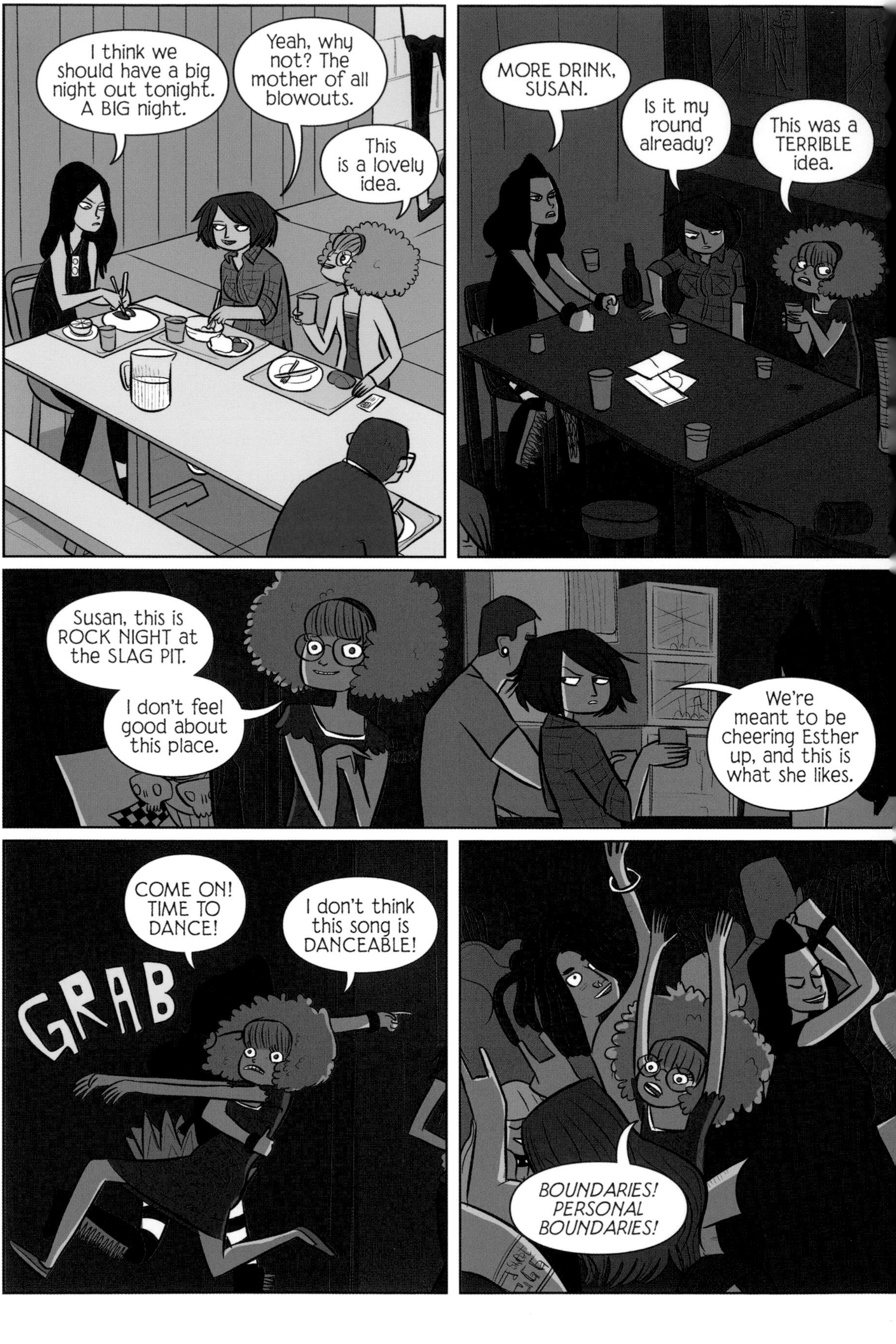
I think we should have a big night out tonight. A BIG night.
Yeah, why not? The mother of all blowouts.
This is a lovely idea.
MORE DRINK, SUSAN.
Is it my round already?
This was a TERRIBLE idea.
Susan, this is ROCK NIGHT at the SLAG PIT.
I don't feel good about this place.
We're meant to be cheering Esther up, and this is what she likes.
COME ON! TIME TO DANCE!
I don't think this song is DANCEABLE!
GRAB
*BOUNDARIES! PERSONAL BOUNDARIES!*

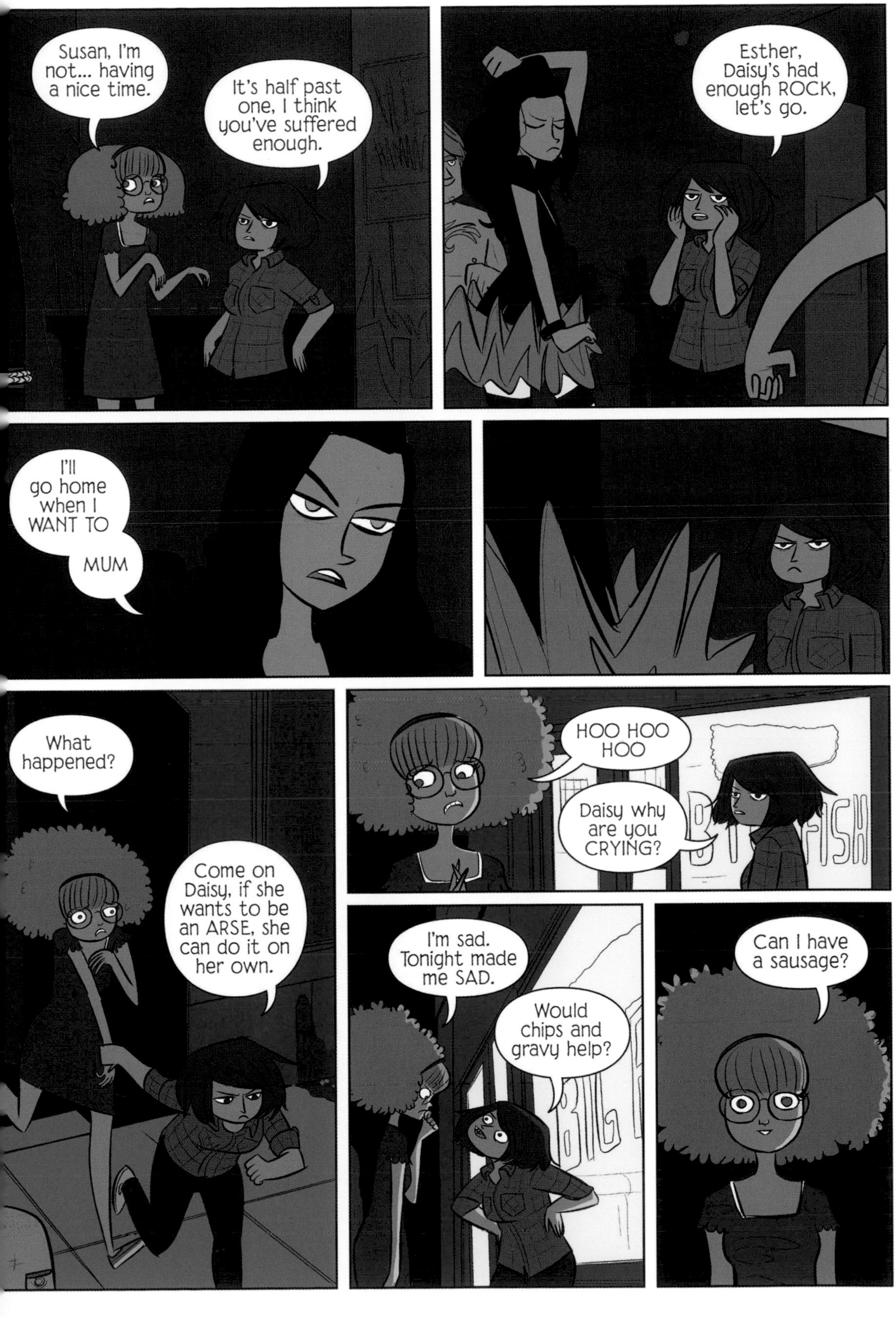
Susan, I'm not... having a nice time.
It's half past one, I think you've suffered enough.
Esther, Daisy's had enough ROCK, let's go.
I'll go home when I WANT TO
MUM
What happened?
Come on Daisy, if she wants to be an ARSE, she can do it on her own.
HOO HOO HOO
Daisy why are you CRYING?
I'm sad. Tonight made me SAD.
Would chips and gravy help?
Can I have a sausage?

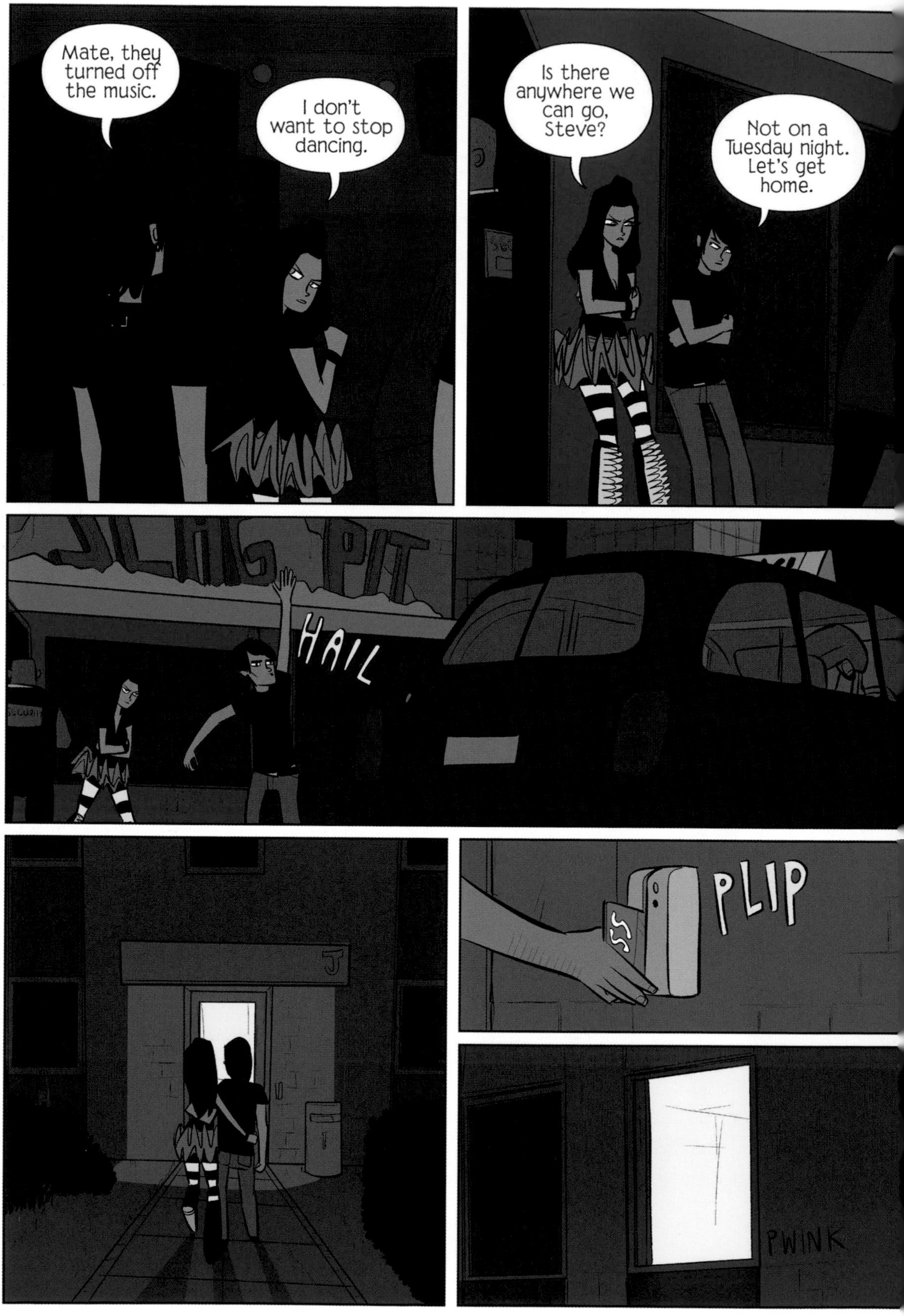
Mate, they turned off the music.
I don't want to stop dancing.
Is there anywhere we can go, Steve?
Not on a Tuesday night. Let's get home.
SLAG PIT
HAIL
PLIP
PWINK

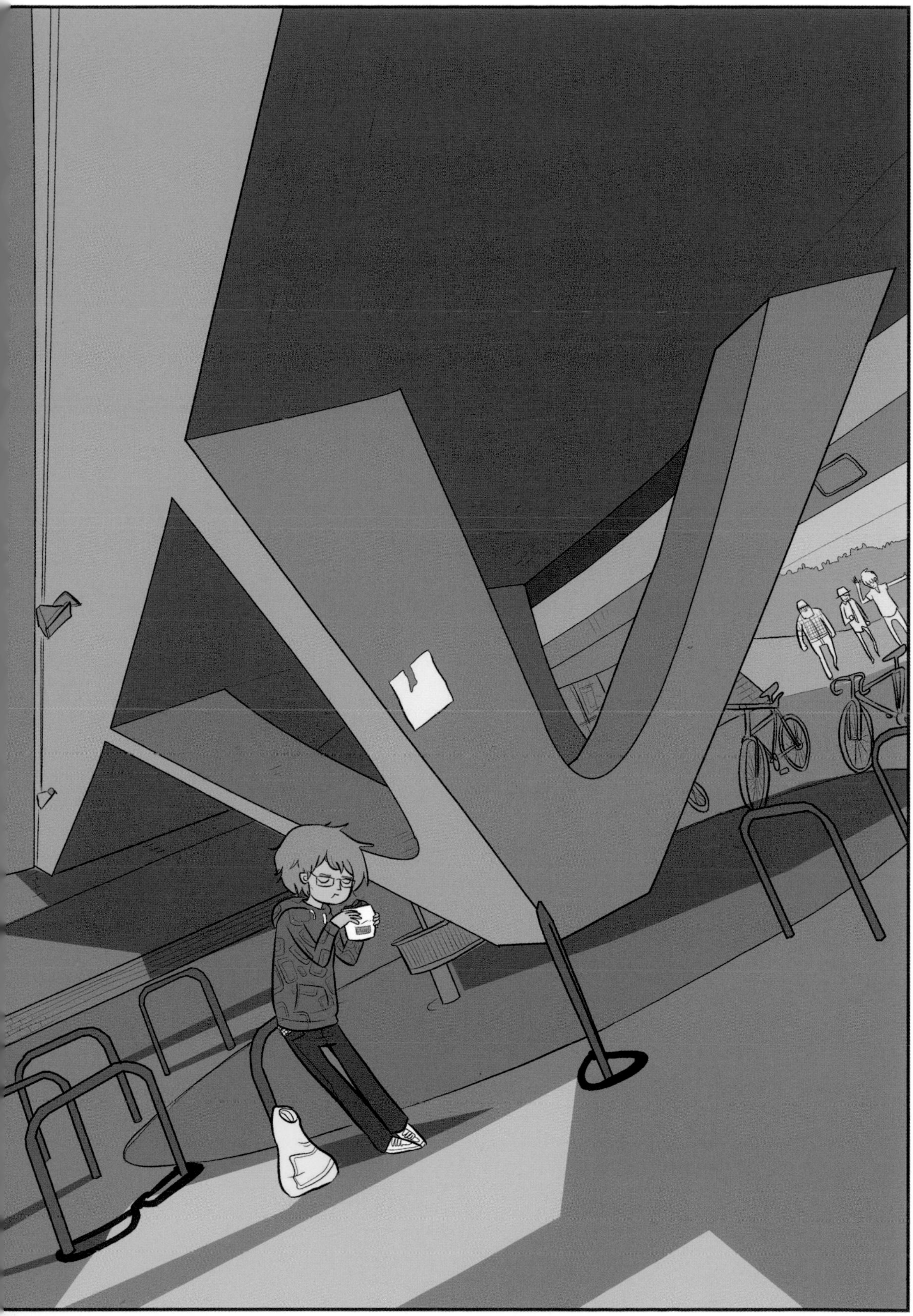

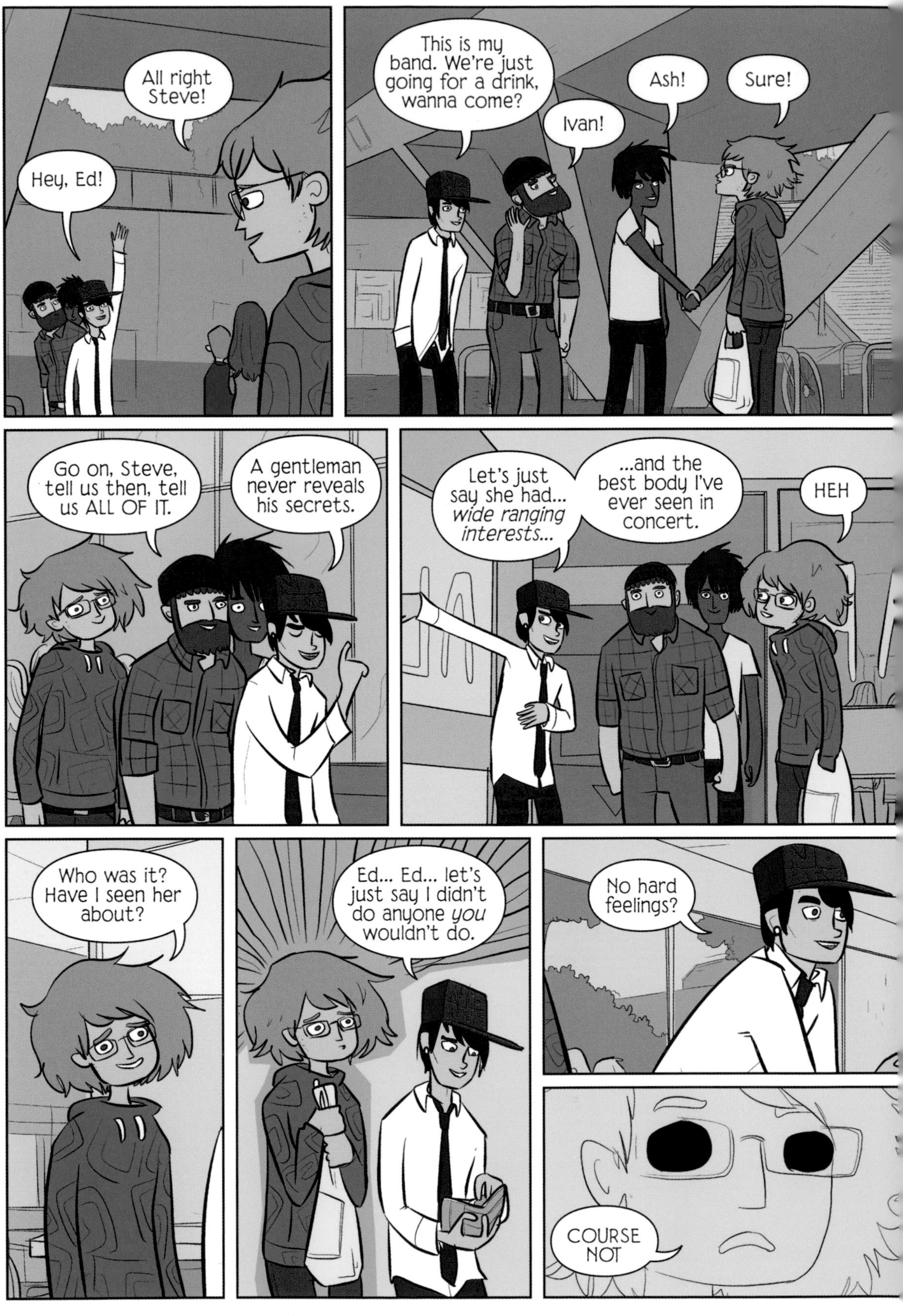
All right Steve!
Hey, Ed!
This is my band. We're just going for a drink, wanna come?
Ivan!
Ash!
Sure!
Go on, Steve, tell us then, tell us ALL OF IT.
A gentleman never reveals his secrets.
Let's just say she had... *wide ranging interests...*
...and the best body I've ever seen in concert.
HEH
Who was it? Have I seen her about?
Ed... Ed... let's just say I didn't do anyone *you* wouldn't do.
No hard feelings?
COURSE NOT

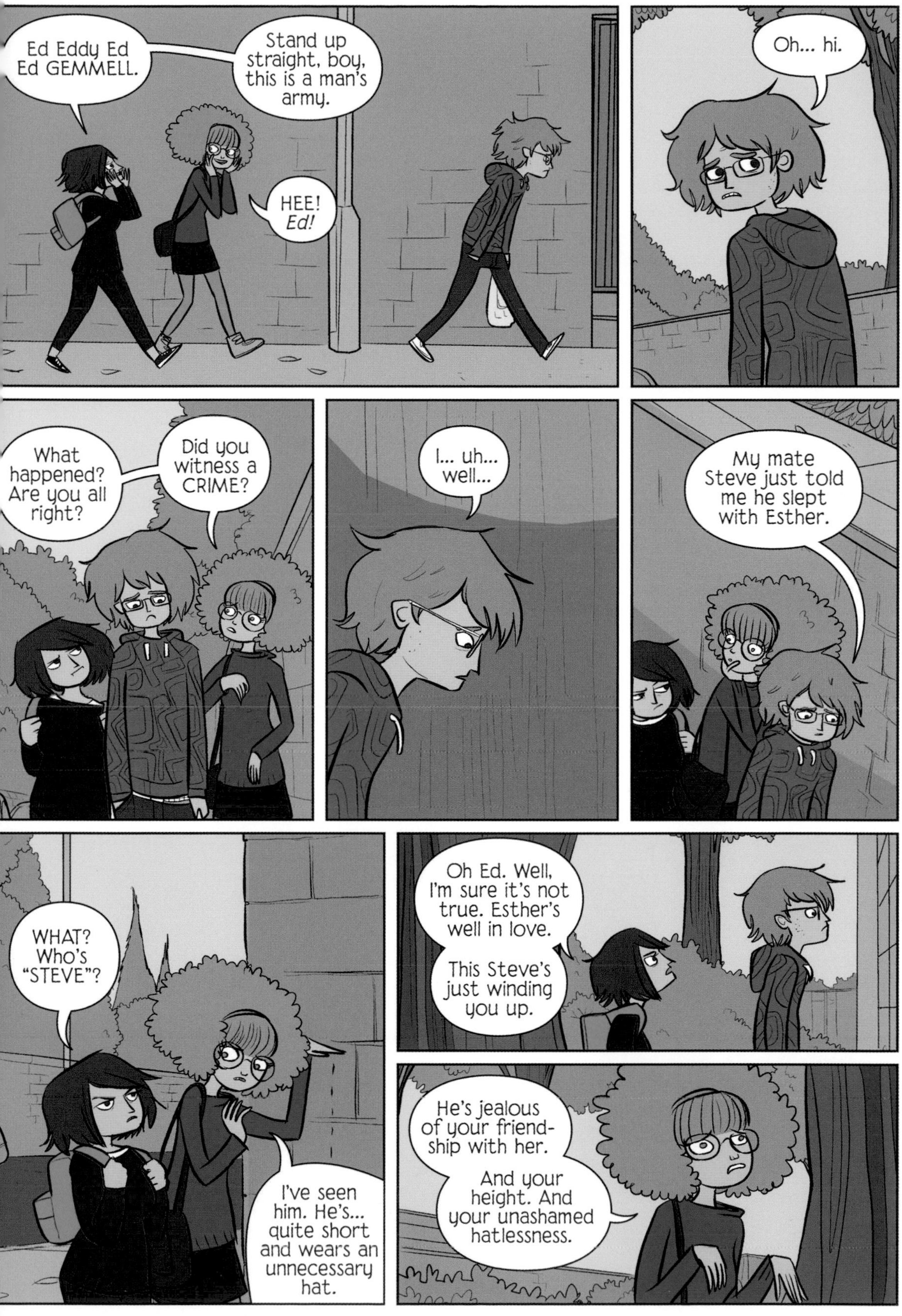
Ed Eddy Ed Ed GEMMELL.
Stand up straight, boy, this is a man's army.
HEE! Ed!
Oh... hi.
What happened? Are you all right?
Did you witness a CRIME?
I... uh... well...
My mate Steve just told me he slept with Esther.
WHAT? Who's "STEVE"?
I've seen him. He's... quite short and wears an unnecessary hat.
Oh Ed. Well, I'm sure it's not true. Esther's well in love.
This Steve's just winding you up.
He's jealous of your friendship with her.
And your height. And your unashamed hatlessness.

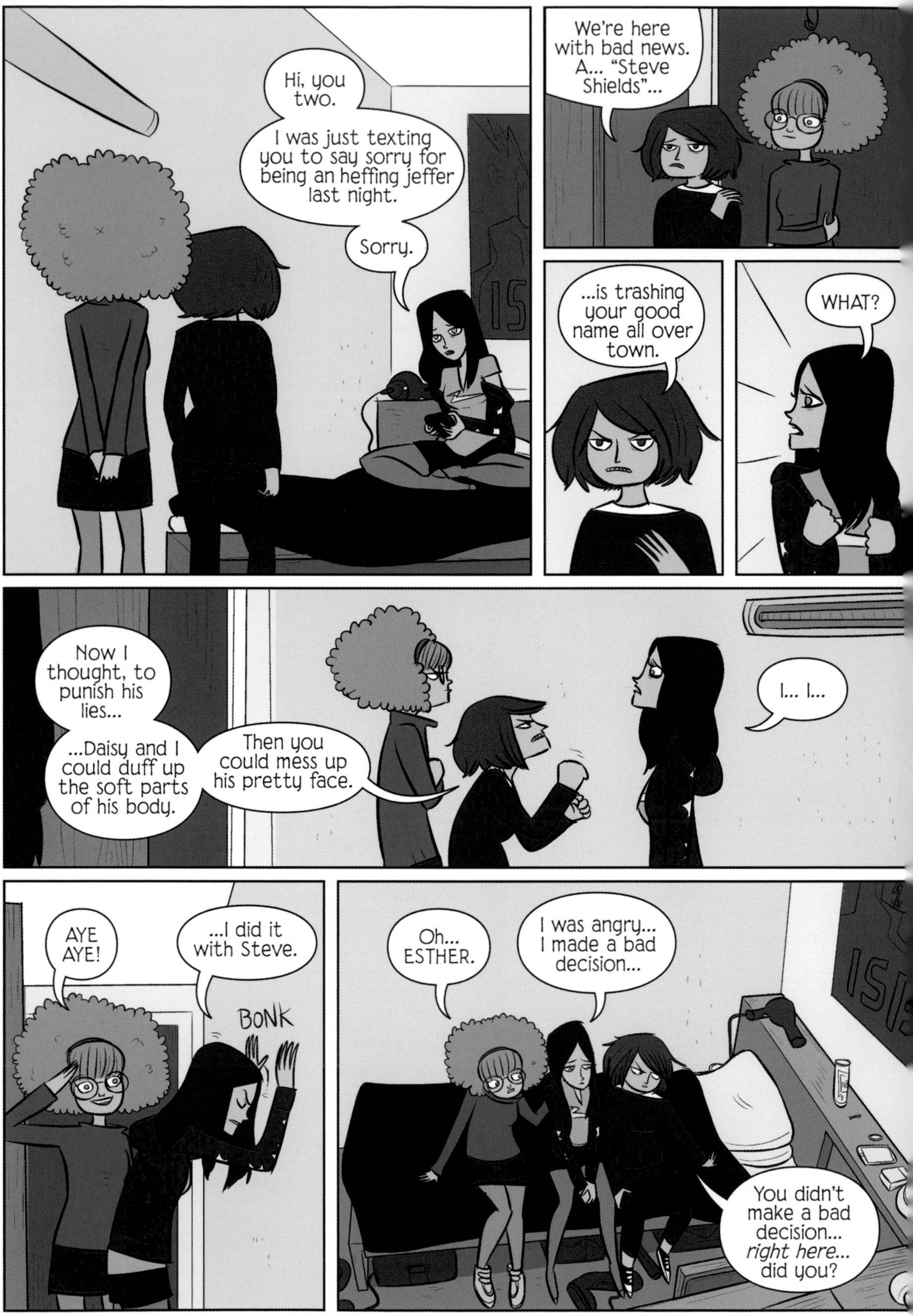
Hi, you two.
I was just texting you to say sorry for being an heffing jeffer last night.
Sorry.
We're here with bad news. A... "Steve Shields"...
...is trashing your good name all over town.
WHAT?
Now I thought, to punish his lies...
...Daisy and I could duff up the soft parts of his body.
Then you could mess up his pretty face.
I... I...
AYE AYE!
...I did it with Steve.
BONK
Oh... ESTHER.
I was angry... I made a bad decision...
You didn't make a bad decision... *right here...* did you?

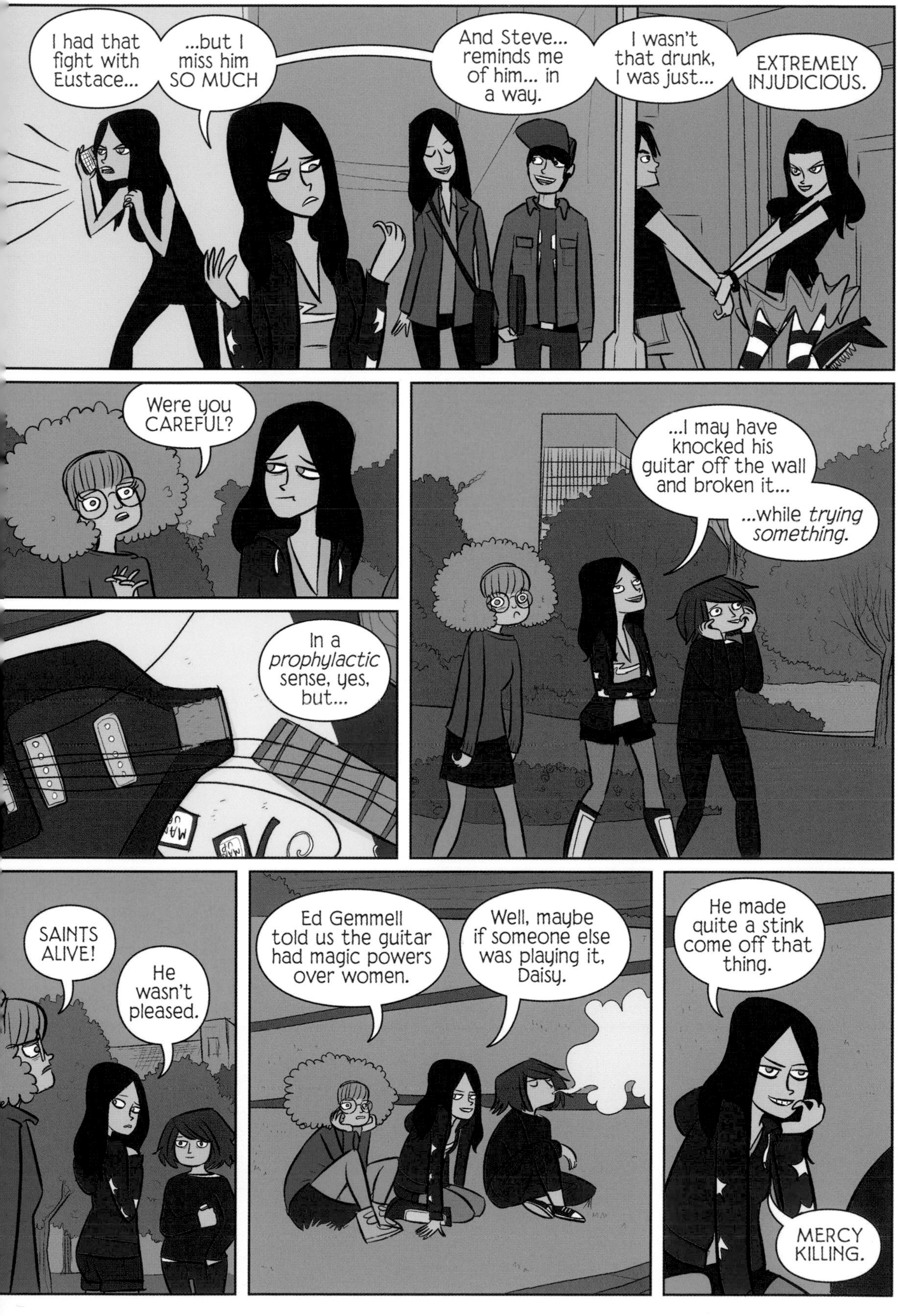
I had that fight with Eustace...
...but I miss him SO MUCH
And Steve... reminds me of him... in a way.
I wasn't that drunk, I was just...
EXTREMELY INJUDICIOUS.
Were you CAREFUL?
In a *prophylactic* sense, yes, but...
...I may have knocked his guitar off the wall and broken it...
...while *trying something.*
SAINTS ALIVE!
He wasn't pleased.
Ed Gemmell told us the guitar had magic powers over women.
Well, maybe if someone else was playing it, Daisy.
He made quite a stink come off that thing.
MERCY KILLING.

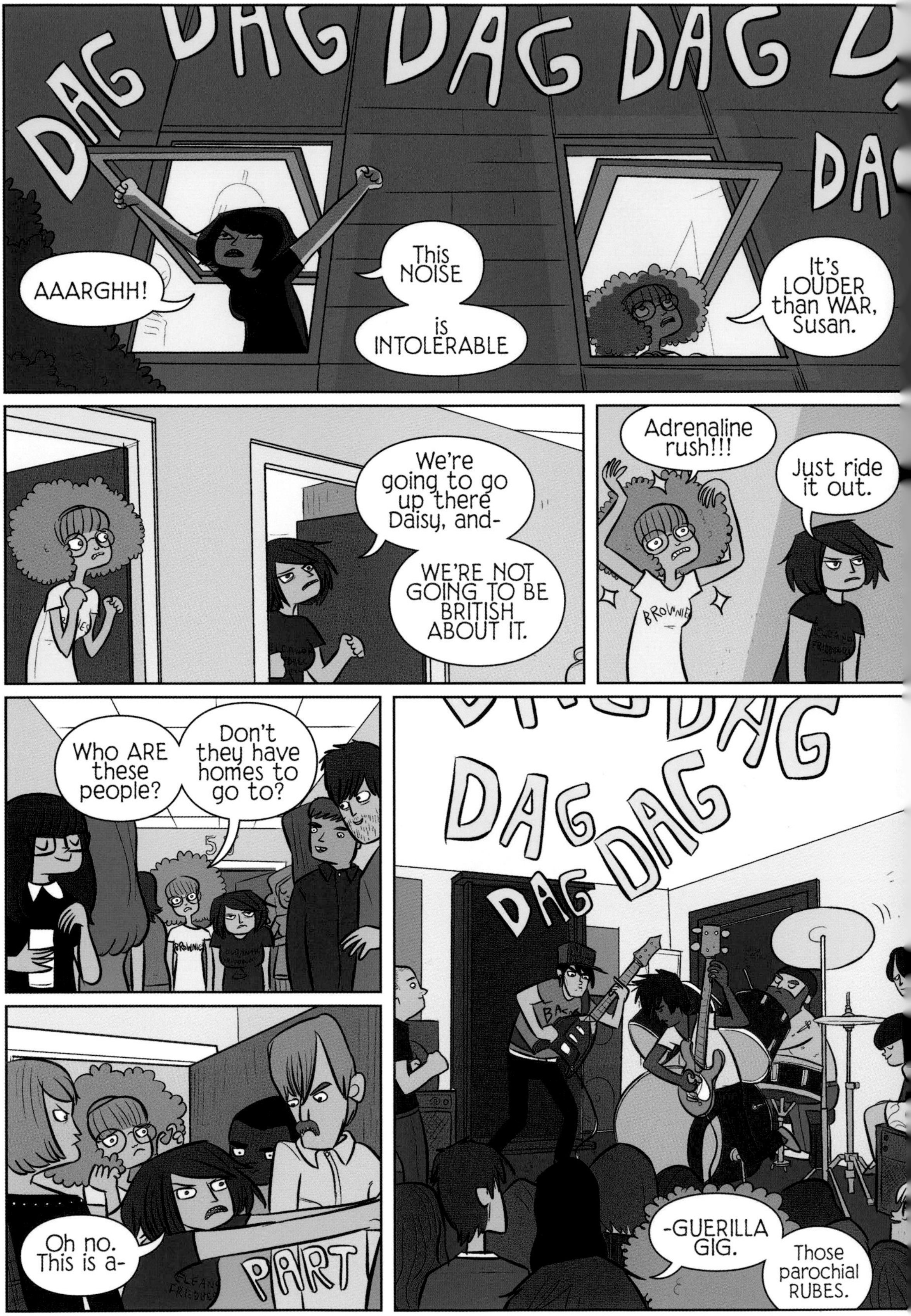
DAG DAG DAG DAG DAG D
DA
AAARGHH!
This NOISE
is INTOLERABLE
It's LOUDER than WAR, Susan.
We're going to go up there Daisy, and-
WE'RE NOT GOING TO BE BRITISH ABOUT IT.
Adrenaline rush!!!
Just ride it out.
Who ARE these people?
Don't they have homes to go to?
Oh no. This is a-
PART
DAG DAG DAG DAG
-GUERILLA GIG.
Those parochial RUBES.

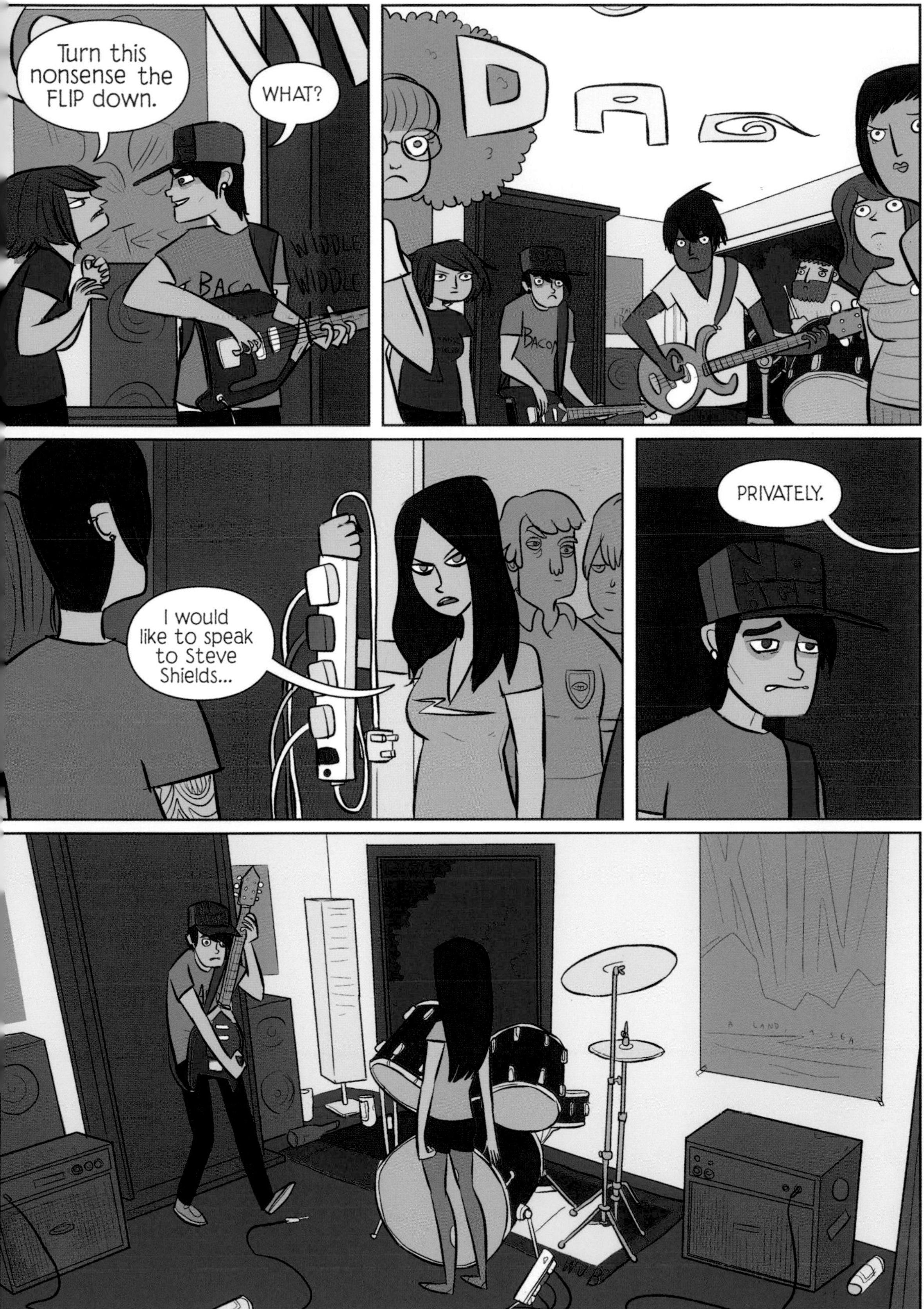
Turn this nonsense the FLIP down.
WHAT?
WIDDLE WIDDLE
BACON
D A G
I would like to speak to Steve Shields...
PRIVATELY.
A LAND, A SEA

Do you want us to stay?

Thanks Susan, but this is between me and Steve.

BEAST CASTLE
+ SPINAL EYE

I can't sleep now! I feel all CRAZY!

Let's have a night sandwich.

Or a NIGHT EGG!

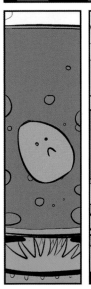

Ed, why are you wandering around like a ghost?

I couldn't sit still. Too many weird thoughts.

Thought I'd go for a walk.

I hope Esther's all right. Maybe we shouldn't have left her with Steve.

She's making

A TERRIBLE MISTAKE

Don't look at me like that! HE DIDN'T WAIT FOR THE CONTEXT!

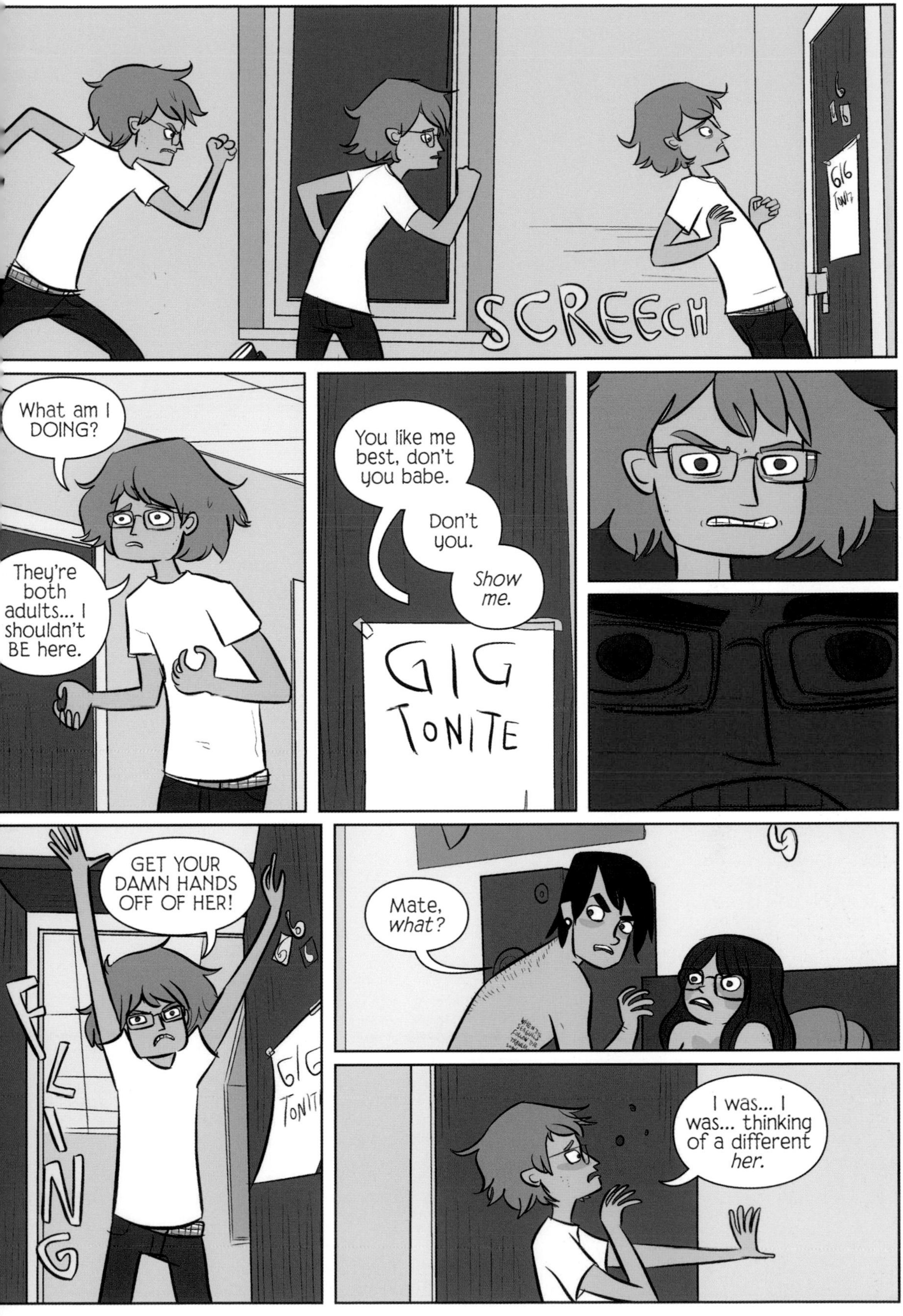
SCREECH
What am I DOING?
They're both adults... I shouldn't BE here.
You like me best, don't you babe.
Don't you.
*Show me.*
GIG TONITE
GET YOUR DAMN HANDS OFF OF HER!
FLING
Mate, *what?*
I was... I was... thinking of a different *her.*

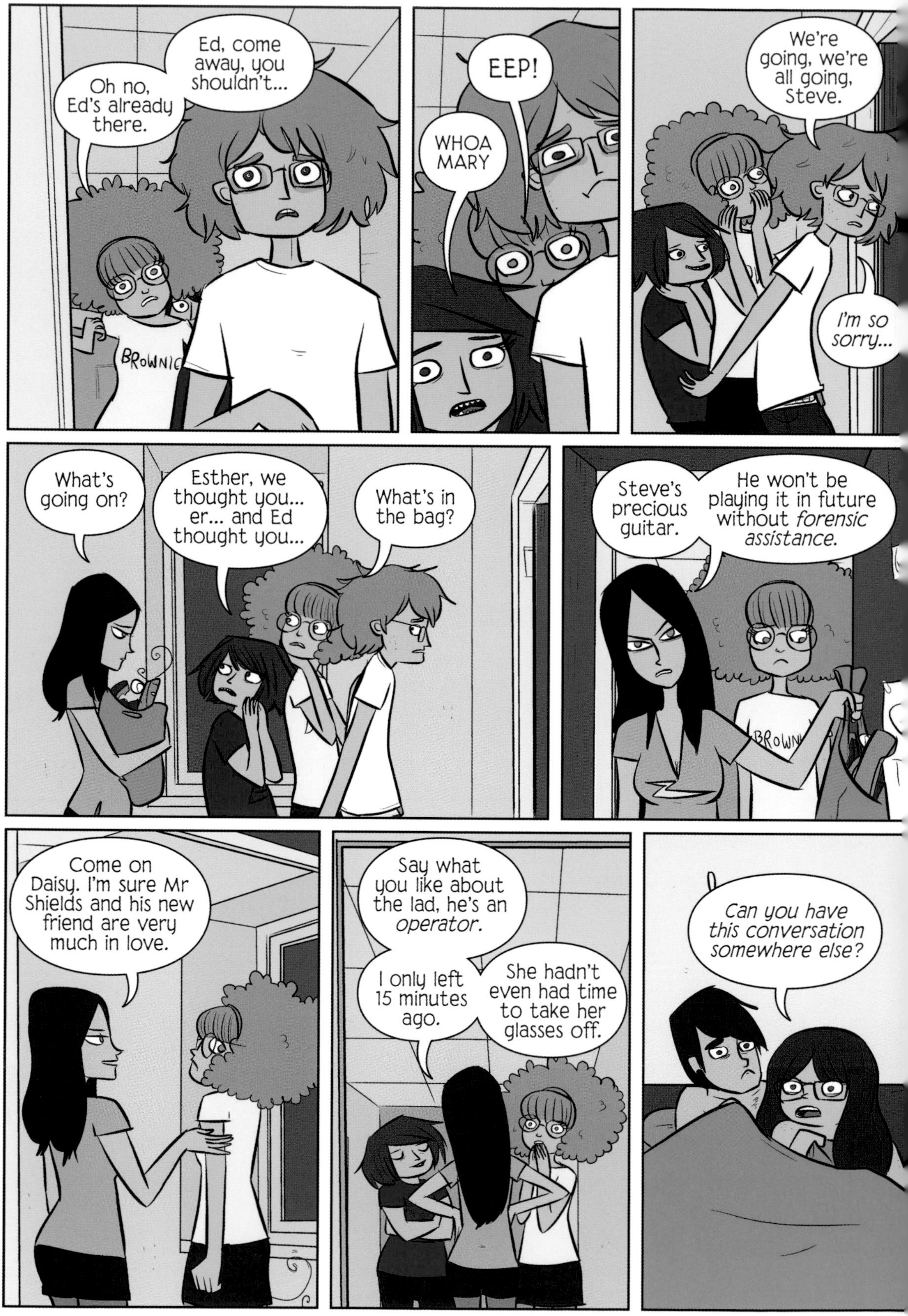

Oh no, Ed's already there.
Ed, come away, you shouldn't...
BROWNIE
WHOA MARY
EEP!
We're going, we're all going, Steve.
I'm so sorry...
What's going on?
Esther, we thought you... er... and Ed thought you...
What's in the bag?
Steve's precious guitar.
He won't be playing it in future without *forensic assistance.*
BROWNIE
Come on Daisy. I'm sure Mr Shields and his new friend are very much in love.
Say what you like about the lad, he's an *operator.*
I only left 15 minutes ago.
She hadn't even had time to take her glasses off.
*Can you have this conversation somewhere else?*

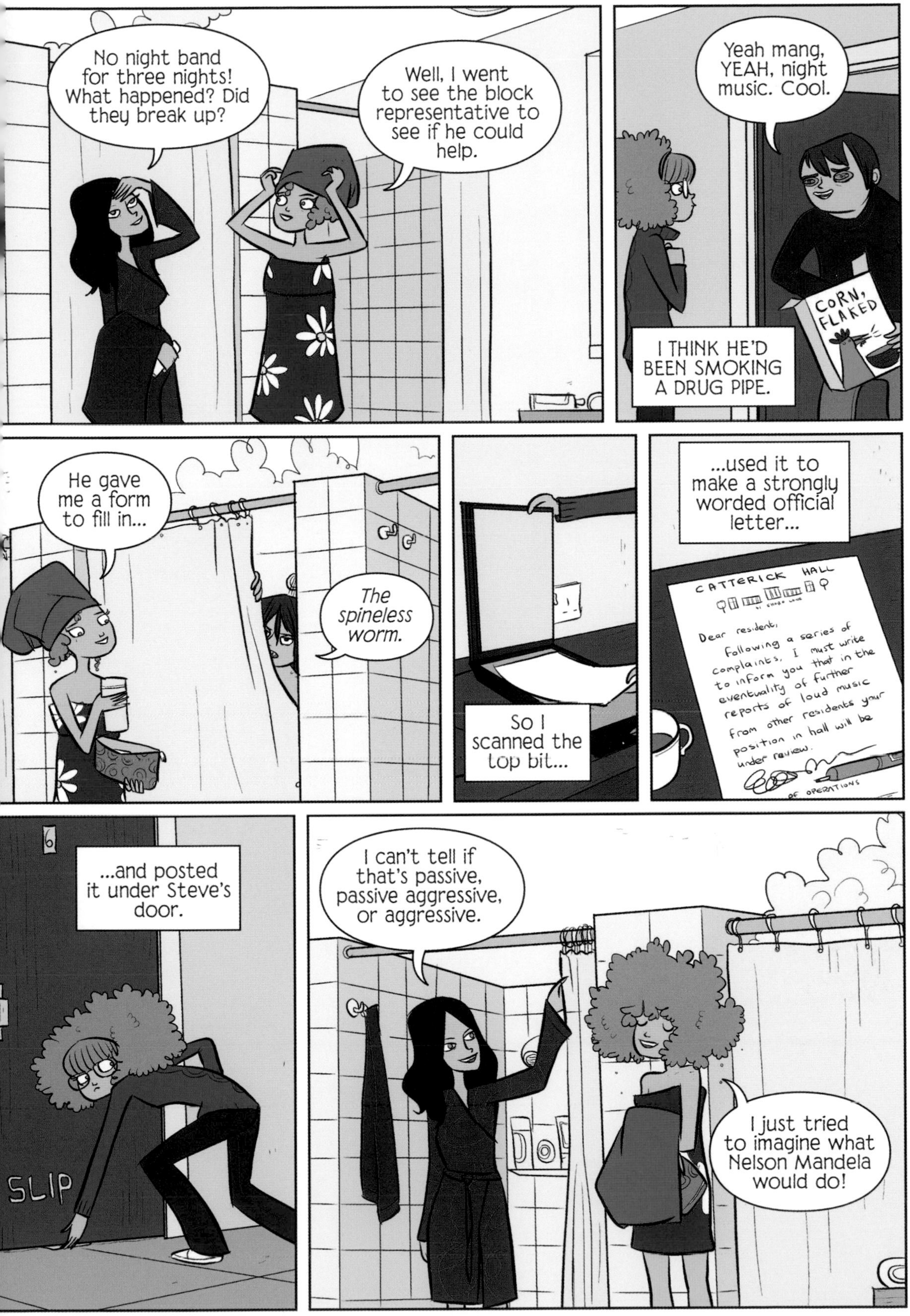
No night band for three nights! What happened? Did they break up?
Well, I went to see the block representative to see if he could help.
Yeah mang, YEAH, night music. Cool.
CORN, FLAKED
I THINK HE'D BEEN SMOKING A DRUG PIPE.
He gave me a form to fill in...
The spineless worm.
So I scanned the top bit...
...used it to make a strongly worded official letter...
CATTERICK HALL
Dear resident,
Following a series of complaints, I must write to inform you that in the eventuality of further reports of loud music from other residents your position in hall will be under review.
OF OPERATIONS
...and posted it under Steve's door.
SLIP
I can't tell if that's passive, passive aggressive, or aggressive.
I just tried to imagine what Nelson Mandela would do!

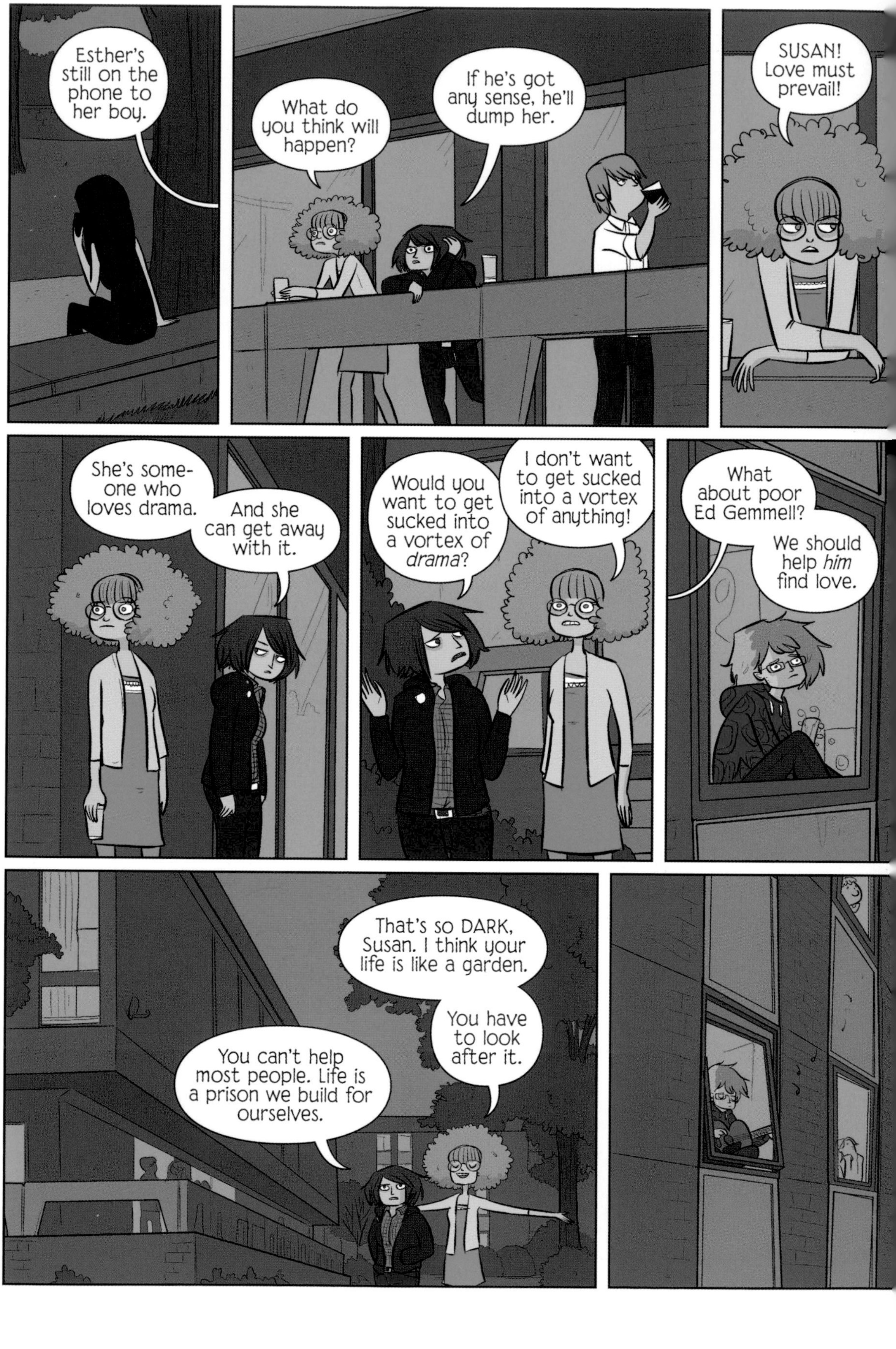
Esther's still on the phone to her boy.
What do you think will happen?
If he's got any sense, he'll dump her.
SUSAN! Love must prevail!
She's some-one who loves drama.
And she can get away with it.
Would you want to get sucked into a vortex of *drama*?
I don't want to get sucked into a vortex of anything!
What about poor Ed Gemmell?
We should help *him* find love.
That's so DARK, Susan. I think your life is like a garden.
You have to look after it.
You can't help most people. Life is a prison we build for ourselves.

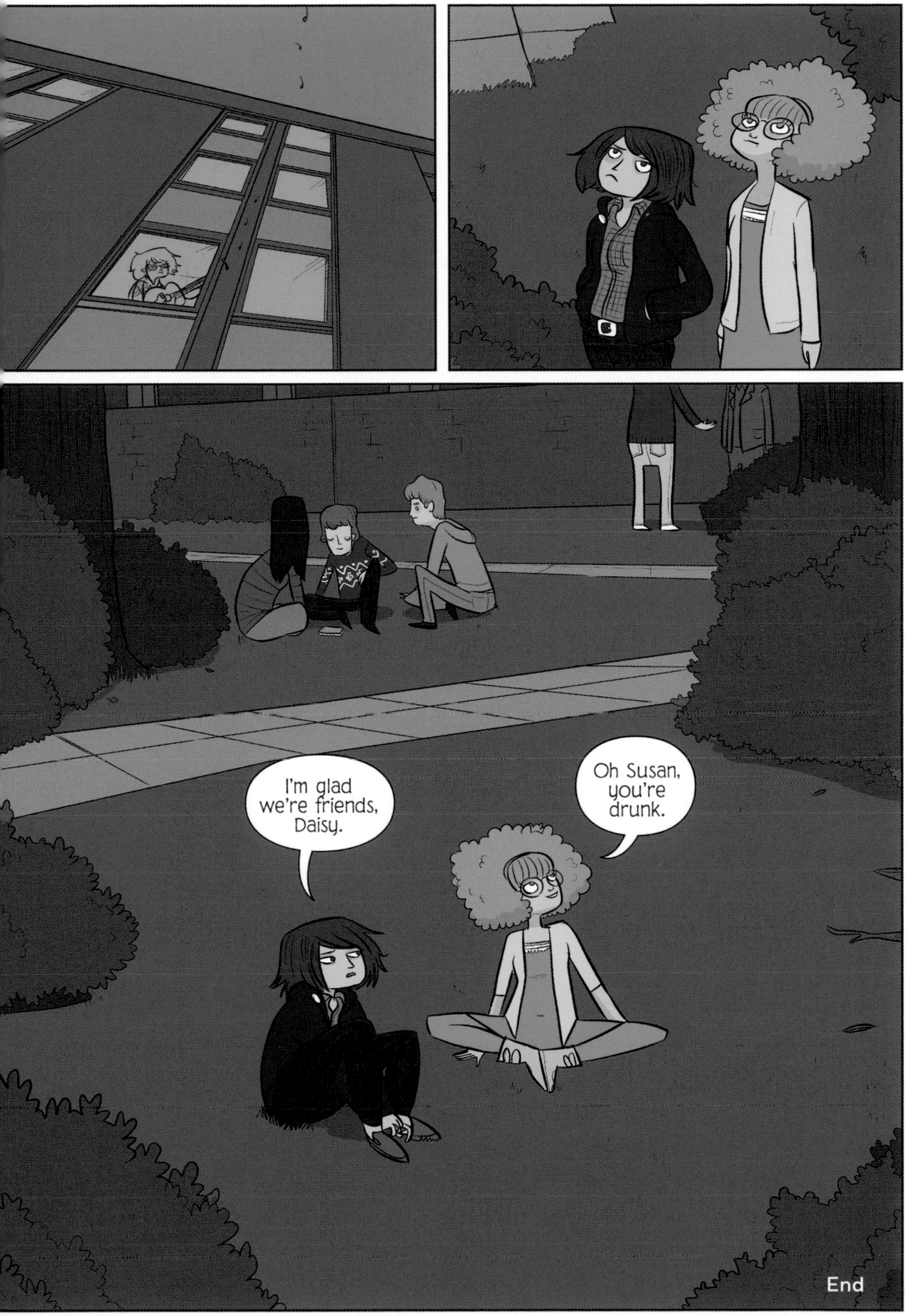
I'm glad we're friends, Daisy.
Oh Susan, you're drunk.
End

# GIANT DAYS:
## BOOM! BOX MIX TAPE
## 2016 SHORT

### BY JOHN ALLISON

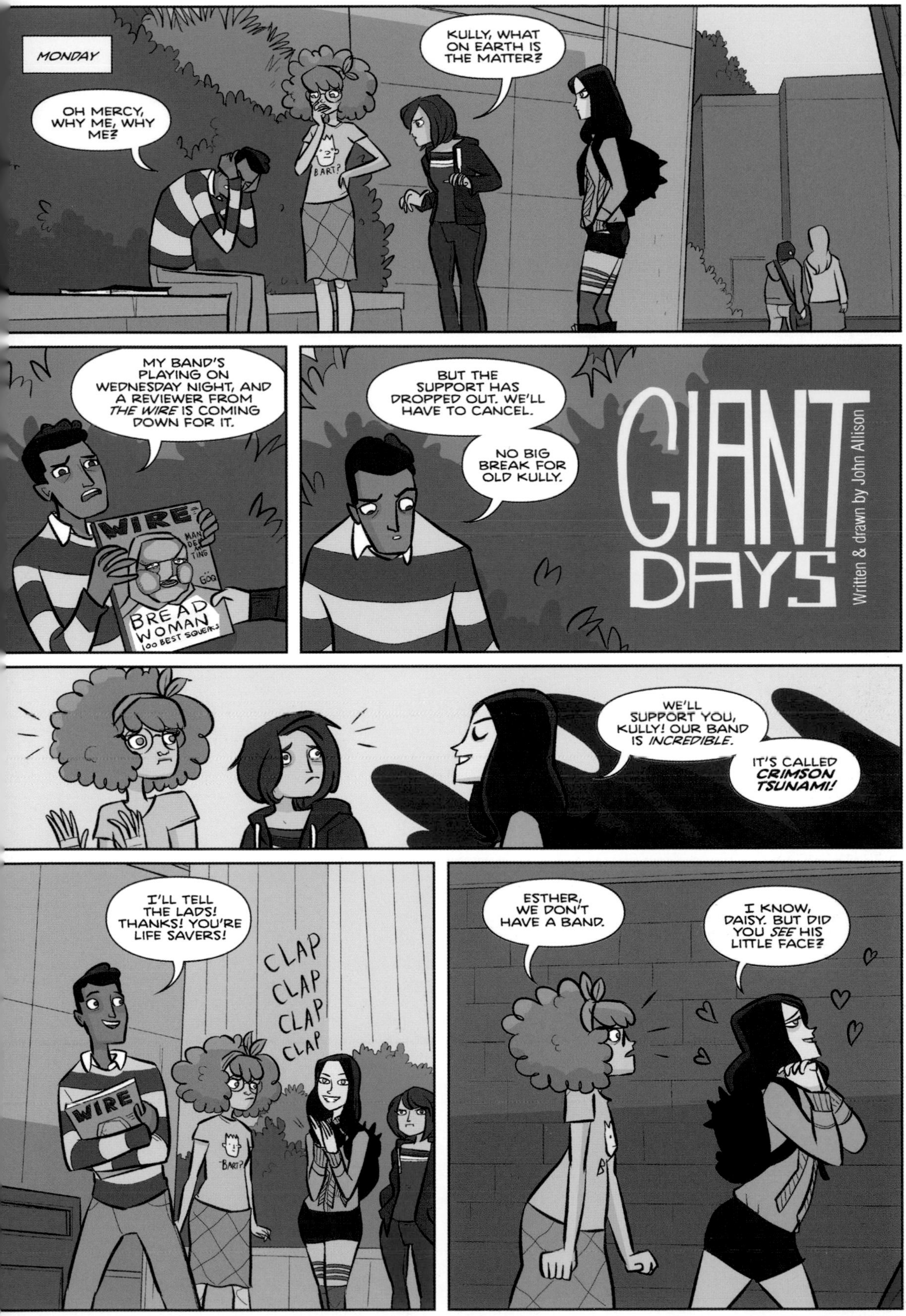
MONDAY
OH MERCY, WHY ME, WHY ME?
KULLY, WHAT ON EARTH IS THE MATTER?
BART?
MY BAND'S PLAYING ON WEDNESDAY NIGHT, AND A REVIEWER FROM *THE WIRE* IS COMING DOWN FOR IT.
WIRE
BREAD WOMAN
100 BEST SQUEAKS
BUT THE SUPPORT HAS DROPPED OUT. WE'LL HAVE TO CANCEL.
NO BIG BREAK FOR OLD KULLY.
GIANT DAYS
Written & drawn by John Allison
WE'LL SUPPORT YOU, KULLY! OUR BAND IS *INCREDIBLE*.
IT'S CALLED ***CRIMSON TSUNAMI!***
I'LL TELL THE LADS! THANKS! YOU'RE LIFE SAVERS!
CLAP CLAP CLAP CLAP
WIRE
BART?
ESTHER, WE DON'T HAVE A BAND.
I KNOW, DAISY. BUT DID YOU *SEE* HIS LITTLE FACE?

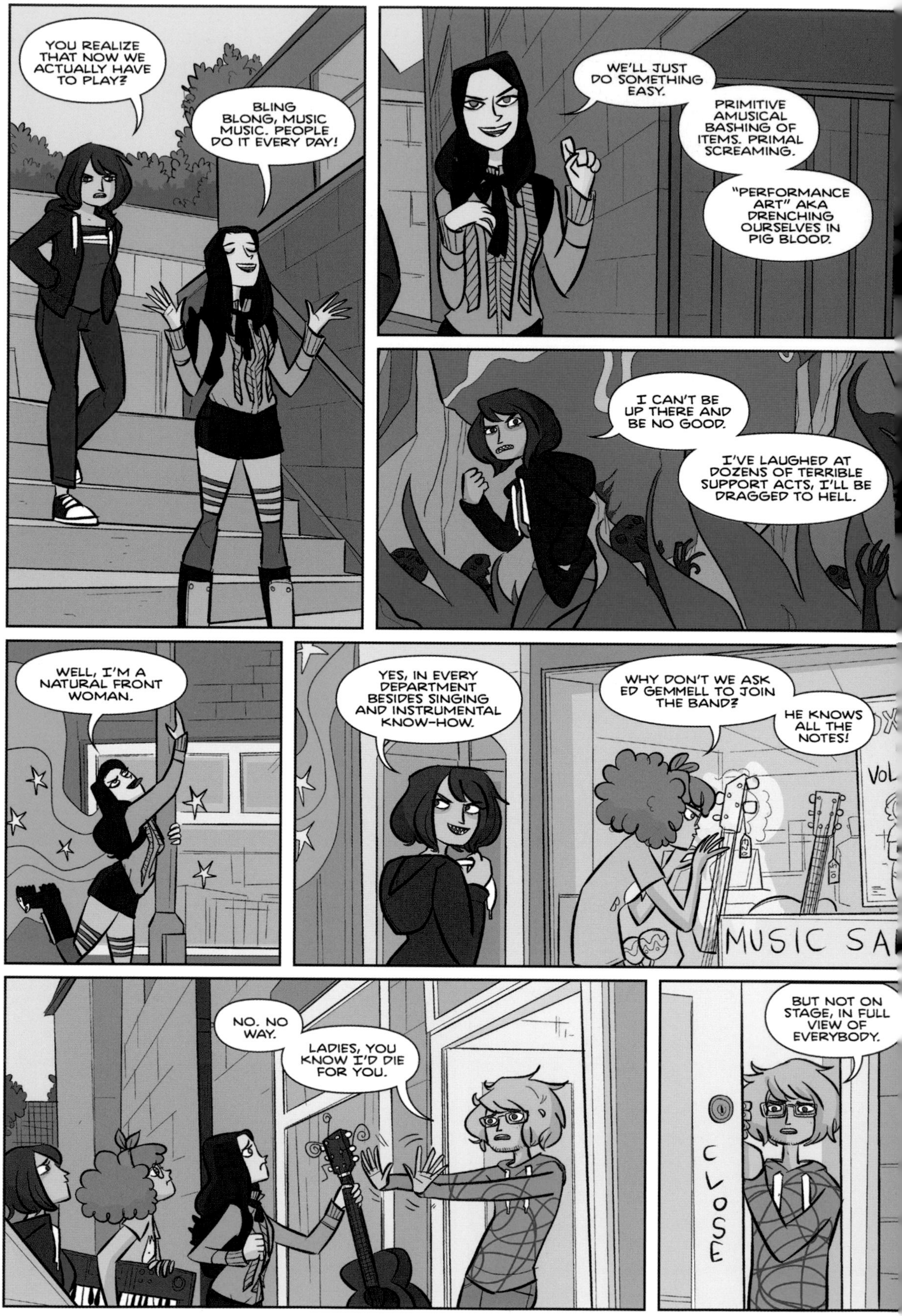
YOU REALIZE THAT NOW WE ACTUALLY HAVE TO PLAY?
BLING BLONG, MUSIC MUSIC. PEOPLE DO IT EVERY DAY!
WE'LL JUST DO SOMETHING EASY.
PRIMITIVE AMUSICAL BASHING OF ITEMS. PRIMAL SCREAMING.
"PERFORMANCE ART" AKA DRENCHING OURSELVES IN PIG BLOOD.
I CAN'T BE UP THERE AND BE NO GOOD.
I'VE LAUGHED AT DOZENS OF TERRIBLE SUPPORT ACTS, I'LL BE DRAGGED TO HELL.
WELL, I'M A NATURAL FRONT WOMAN.
YES, IN EVERY DEPARTMENT BESIDES SINGING AND INSTRUMENTAL KNOW-HOW.
WHY DON'T WE ASK ED GEMMELL TO JOIN THE BAND?
HE KNOWS ALL THE NOTES!
MUSIC SA
NO. NO WAY.
LADIES, YOU KNOW I'D DIE FOR YOU.
BUT NOT ON STAGE, IN FULL VIEW OF EVERYBODY.
CLOSE

24 WAKING HOURS LATER.

PRANG
PRANG
PRANG

BWONG

PLIP PLIP PLIP

...OHHHH BABY...

I'M CRUSHED BY THE KNOWLEDGE OF EVERY GREAT SONG I'VE **EVER** HEARD!

JUST WRITE A COUNTRY SONG, SUSAN!

I'VE WORKED OUT THE FORMULA!

"MY MAN"
FREEDOM
THE LORD
DOIN' WHAT'S RIGHT
USA
FAMILY
AMERICA
TRUCKS (PT 2)

SHUT UP!

OH, THAT SOUNDS GOOD!

STRESS

CREAK

IT'S "MORE THAN WORDS" BY EXTREME!

EVERYTHING I WRITE IS "MORE THAN WORDS" BY EXTREME!

ESTHER, COULD YOU MAYBE PUT YOUR HEAD-PHONES ON?

I DROPPED THEM IN THE BATH LAST WEEK.

MANN STEAM

PLIP
PLIP
PLIP
PLIP
PLIP
PWLIP

GOURANJA

I'M GOING TO WRITE IN MY ROOM.

PLIP

PLIP

*I'M GOING TO WRITE IN MY ROOM.*

URANJA

PLIP PLIP PLIP PLIP

SHE WAS JUST AN AMERICAN TRUCK...

TWO KIDS, AND A THIRD ON THE WAY...

PLINK

PWIP PWIP -IP PLIP PLIP PLIP!

GOURANJA

PLINK PLINK PLINK... PLINK!

The Last Days Of DISCO

STRUM STRUM

I'M A GENIUS!

MEET THE NEW MOZART!

I'M 80% SURE THIS ISN'T "MORE THAN WORDS"!

The Last Days Of DISCO

KULLY CERTAINLY DIDN'T SKIMP ON POSTERS.

HIS UNCLE OWNS A--

--A PRINT-SHOP?

A FOREST! ALTHOUGH IT'S PROBABLY MORE OF A CLEARING NOW.

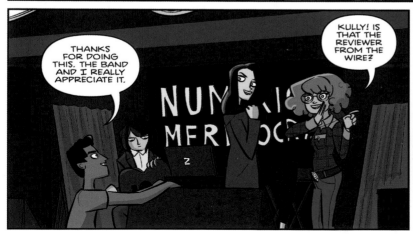

THANKS FOR DOING THIS. THE BAND AND I REALLY APPRECIATE IT.

KULLY! IS THAT THE REVIEWER FROM THE WIRE?

YES! IT'S ELTON WELSBY! HE HAS A COLUMN WHERE HE JUST REVIEWS SILENCE!

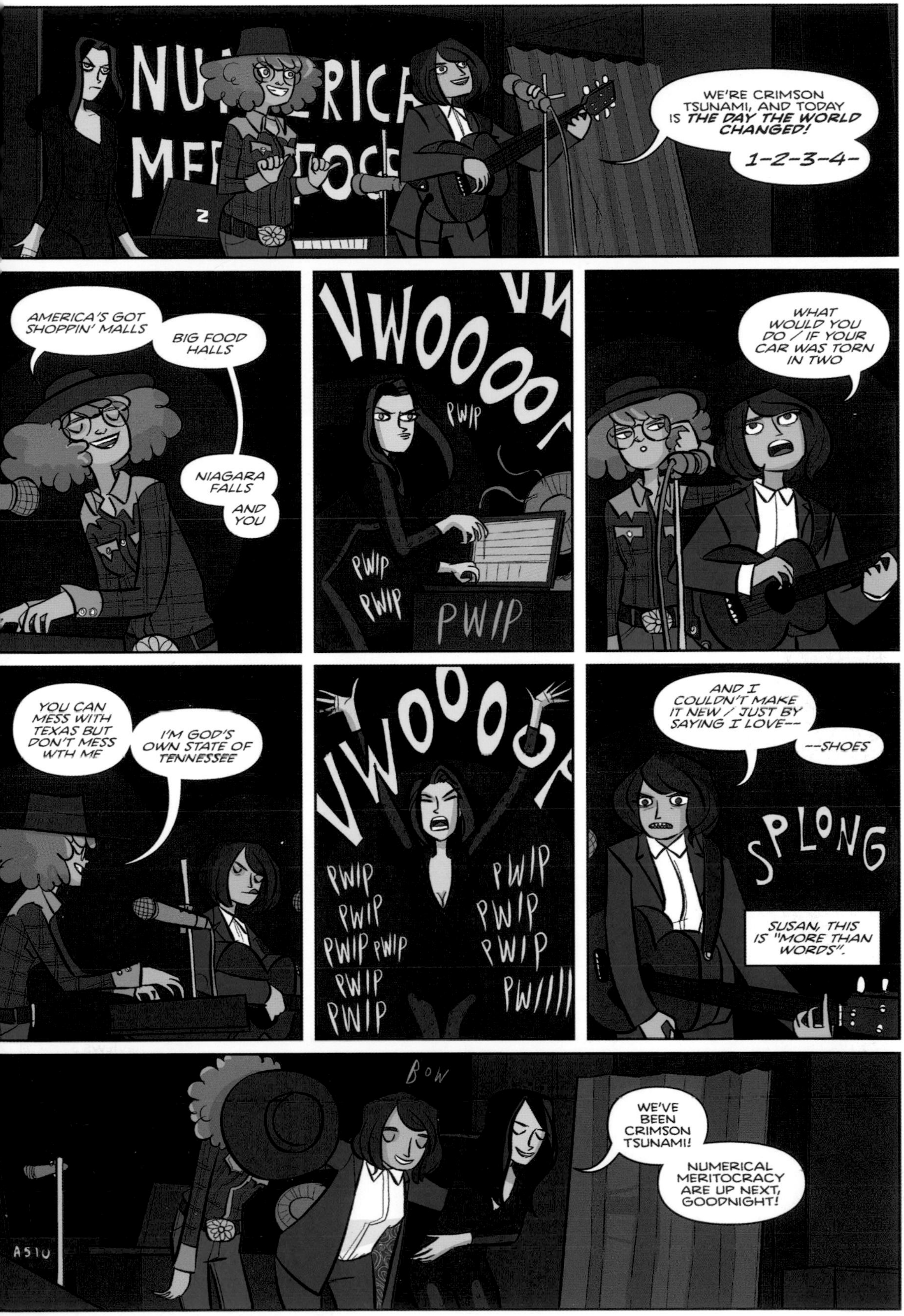
NU[...]ERICA MER[...]OC
WE'RE CRIMSON TSUNAMI, AND TODAY IS THE DAY THE WORLD CHANGED!
1-2-3-4-
AMERICA'S GOT SHOPPIN' MALLS
BIG FOOD HALLS
NIAGARA FALLS
AND YOU
VWOOOOR
PWIP
PWIP
PWIP
PWIP
WHAT WOULD YOU DO / IF YOUR CAR WAS TORN IN TWO
YOU CAN MESS WITH TEXAS BUT DON'T MESS WTH ME
I'M GOD'S OWN STATE OF TENNESSEE
VWOOOOR
PWIP PWIP PWIP PWIP PWIP PWIP
PWIP PWIP PWIP PWIIII
AND I COULDN'T MAKE IT NEW / JUST BY SAYING I LOVE--
--SHOES
SPLONG
SUSAN, THIS IS "MORE THAN WORDS".
BOW
WE'VE BEEN CRIMSON TSUNAMI!
NUMERICAL MERITOCRACY ARE UP NEXT, GOODNIGHT!

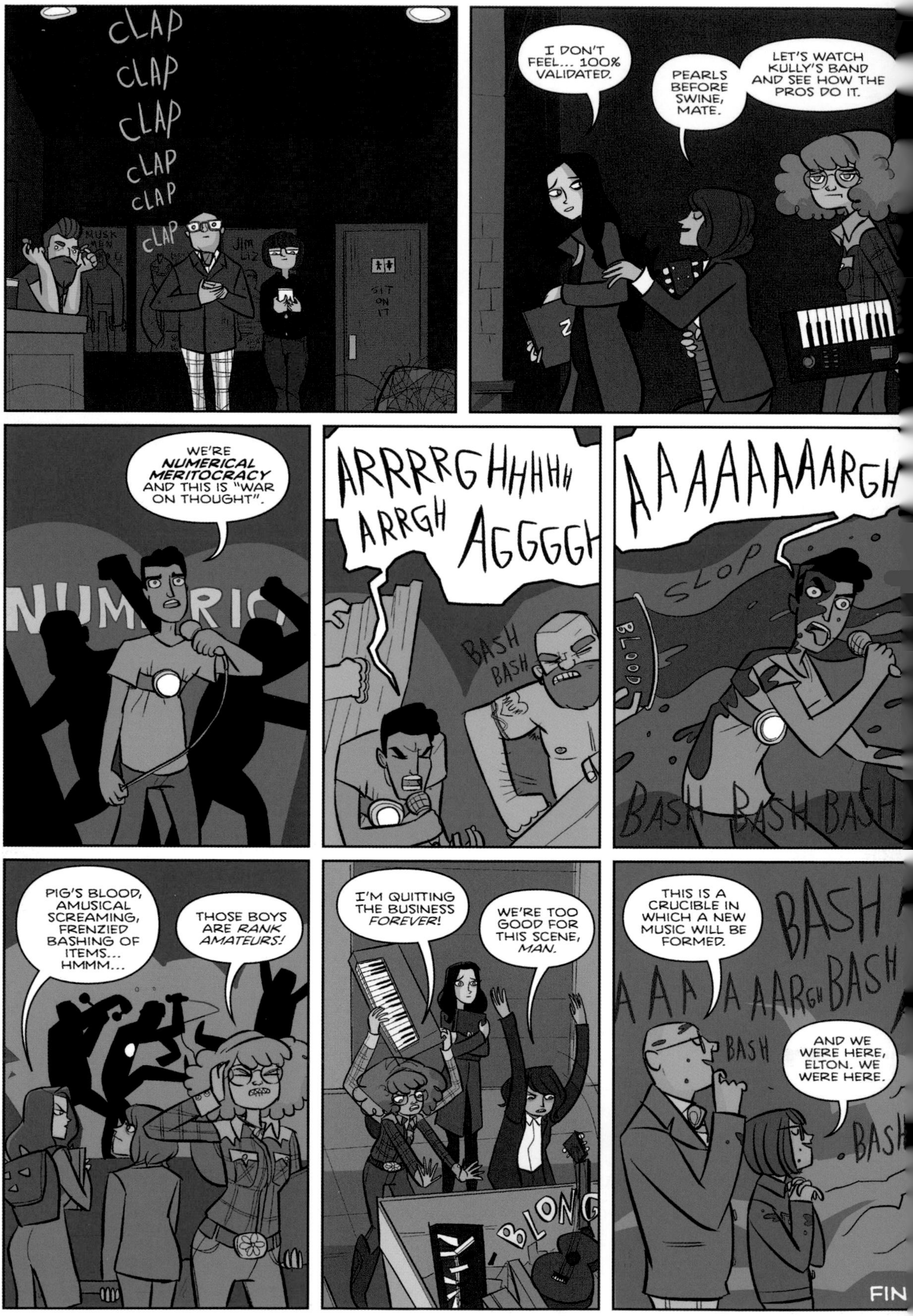
CLAP CLAP CLAP CLAP CLAP CLAP
I DON'T FEEL... 100% VALIDATED.
PEARLS BEFORE SWINE, MATE.
LET'S WATCH KULLY'S BAND AND SEE HOW THE PROS DO IT.
WE'RE NUMERICAL MERITOCRACY AND THIS IS "WAR ON THOUGHT".
ARRRRGHHHHH ARRGH AGGGGH
BASH BASH
AAAAAAAARGH
SLOP
BLOOD
BASH BASH BASH
PIG'S BLOOD, AMUSICAL SCREAMING, FRENZIED BASHING OF ITEMS... HMMM...
THOSE BOYS ARE RANK AMATEURS!
I'M QUITTING THE BUSINESS FOREVER!
WE'RE TOO GOOD FOR THIS SCENE, MAN.
BLONG
THIS IS A CRUCIBLE IN WHICH A NEW MUSIC WILL BE FORMED.
BASH
AAAAAARGH BASH
BASH
AND WE WERE HERE, ELTON. WE WERE HERE.
BASH
FIN

# GIANT DAYS:
## COVER GALLERY

**ISSUE #9 COVER A**
LISSA TREIMAN

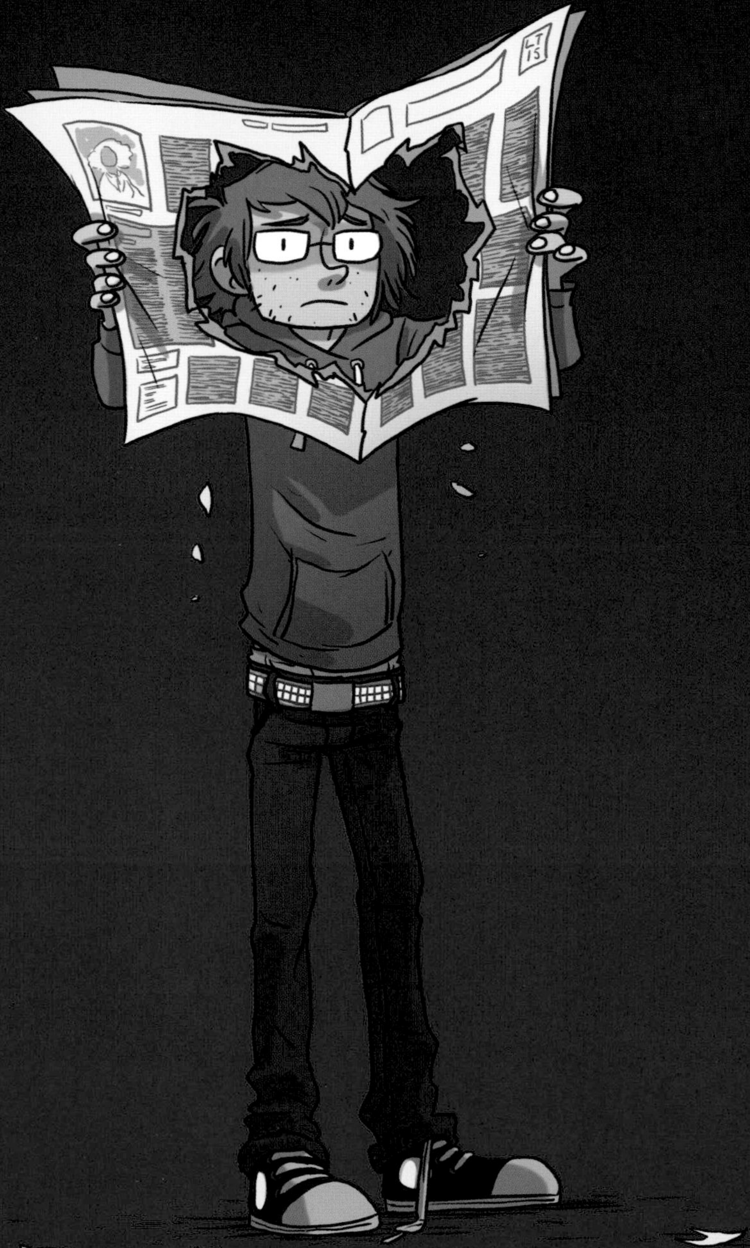

**ISSUE #10 COVER**
LISSA TREIMAN

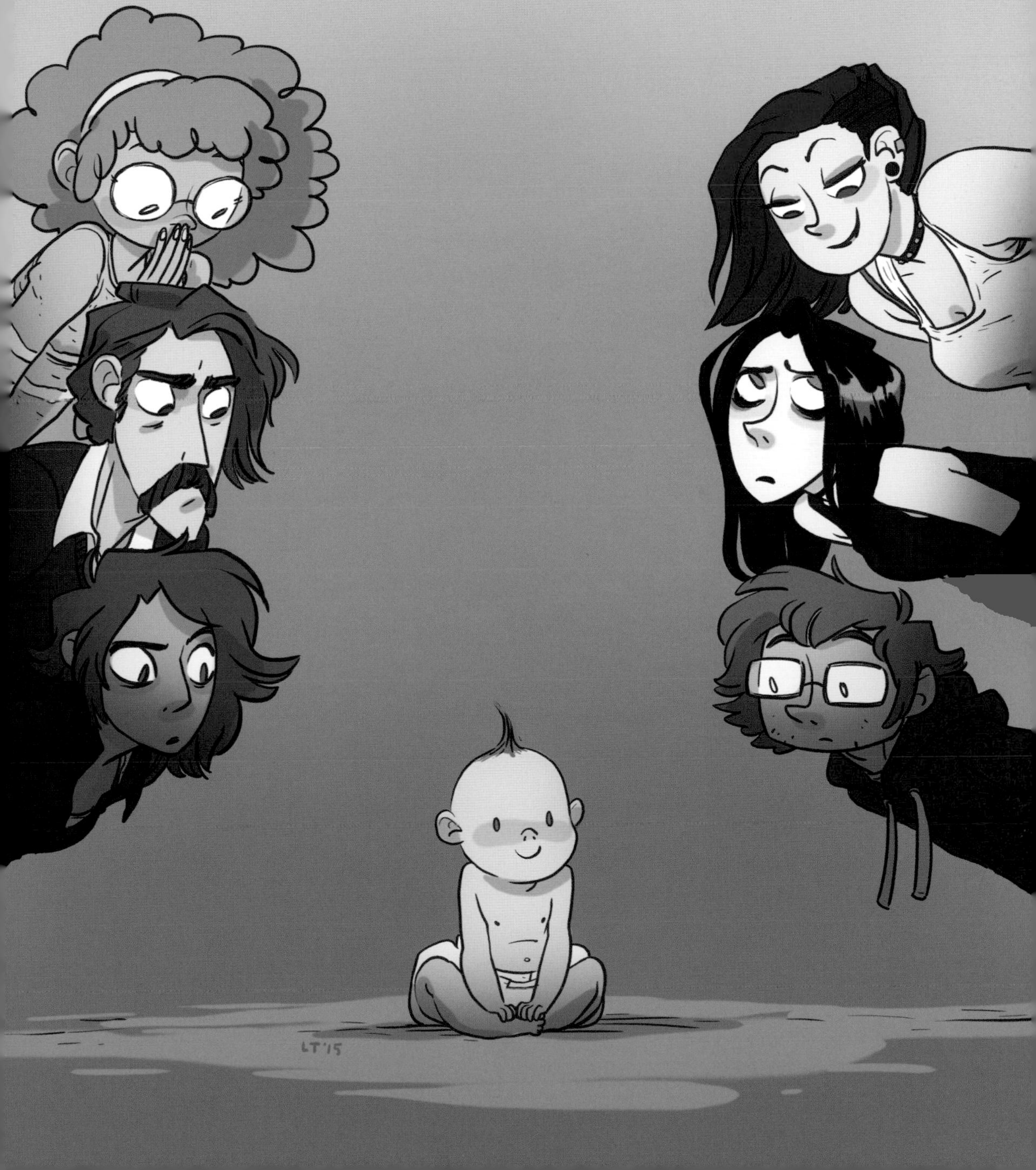
LT'15

**ISSUE #11 COVER**
LISSA TREIMAN

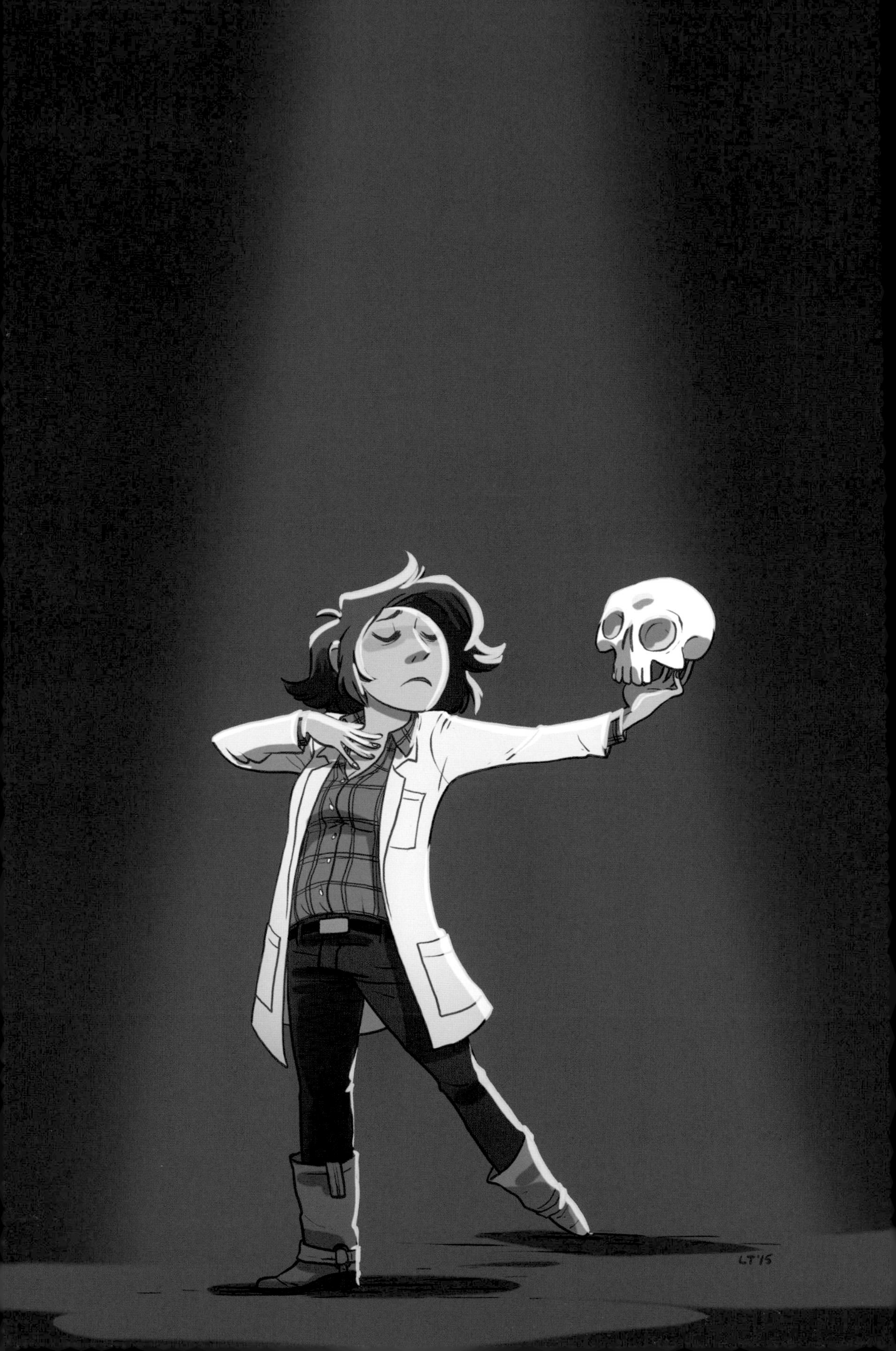
LT'15

**ISSUE #12 COVER**
LISSA TREIMAN

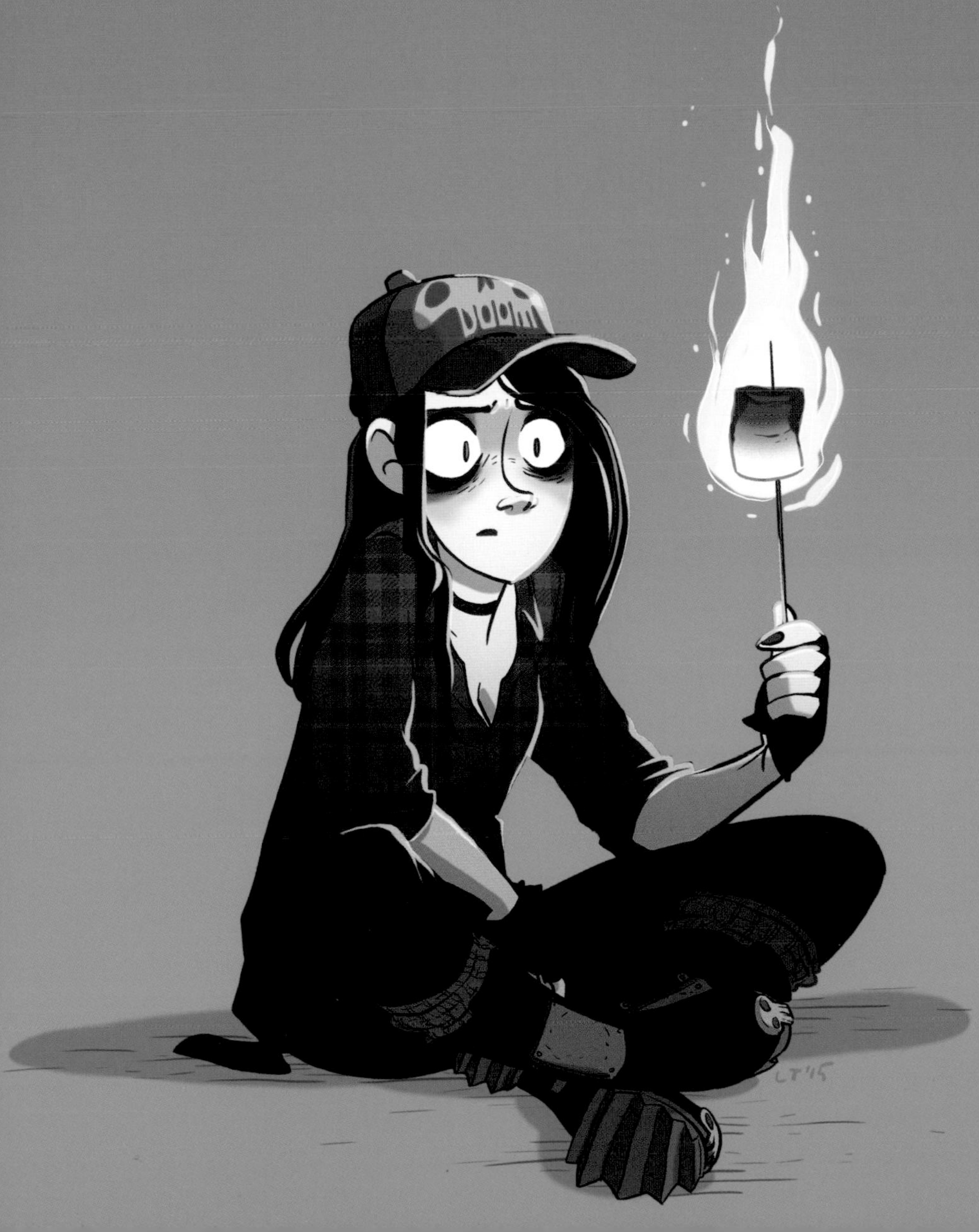
Doom
LT'15

**ISSUE #13 COVER**
LISSA TREIMAN

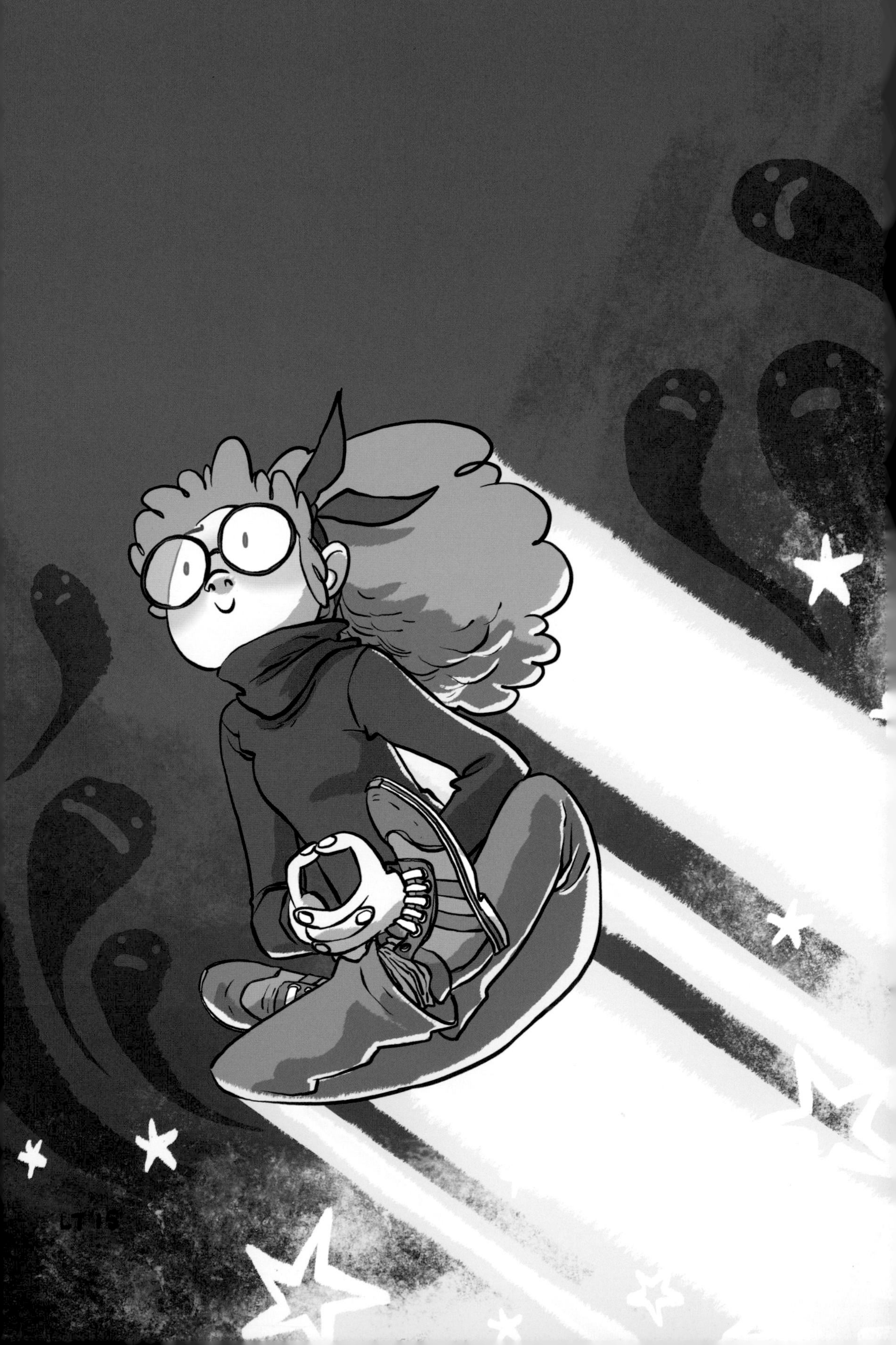
LT'15

**ISSUE #14 COVER**
LISSA TREIMAN

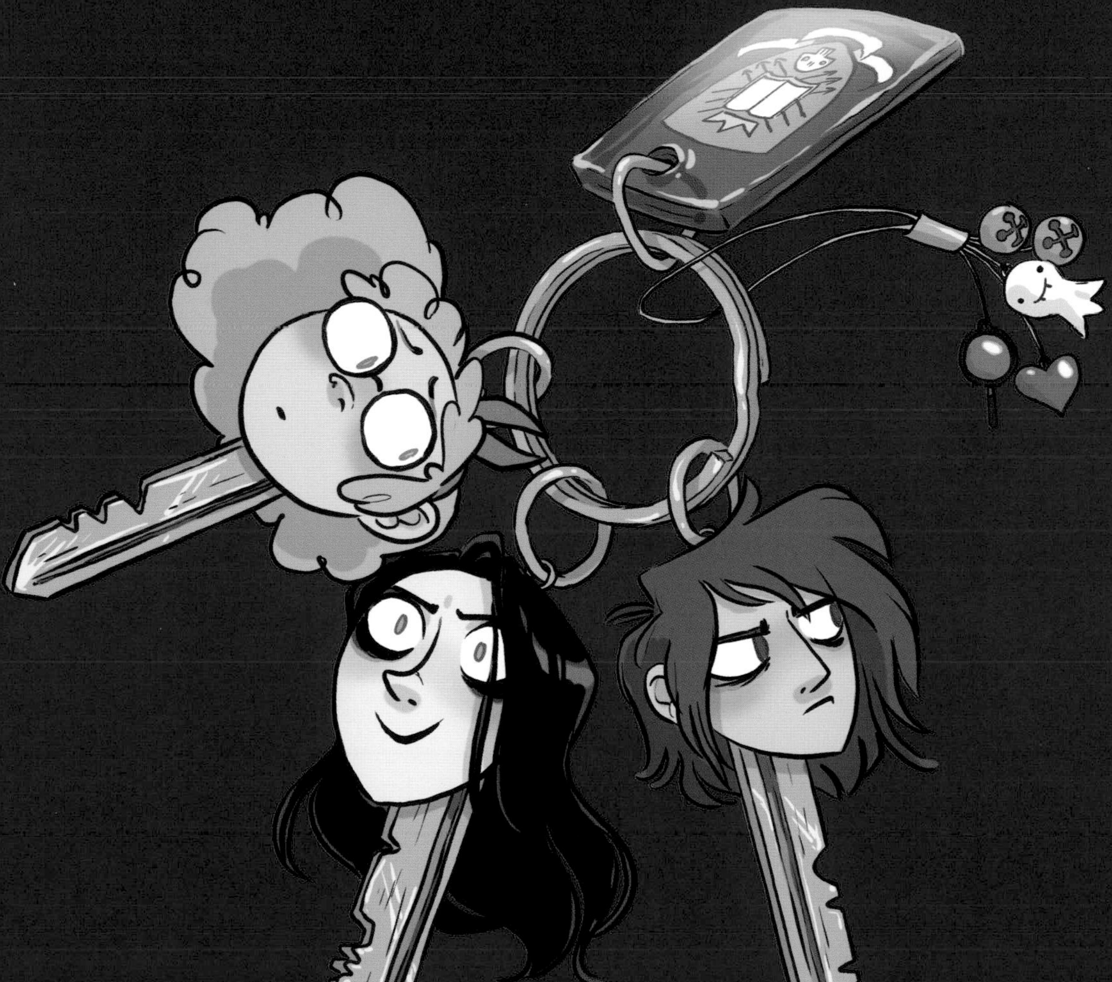

**ISSUE #15 COVER**
LISSA TREIMAN

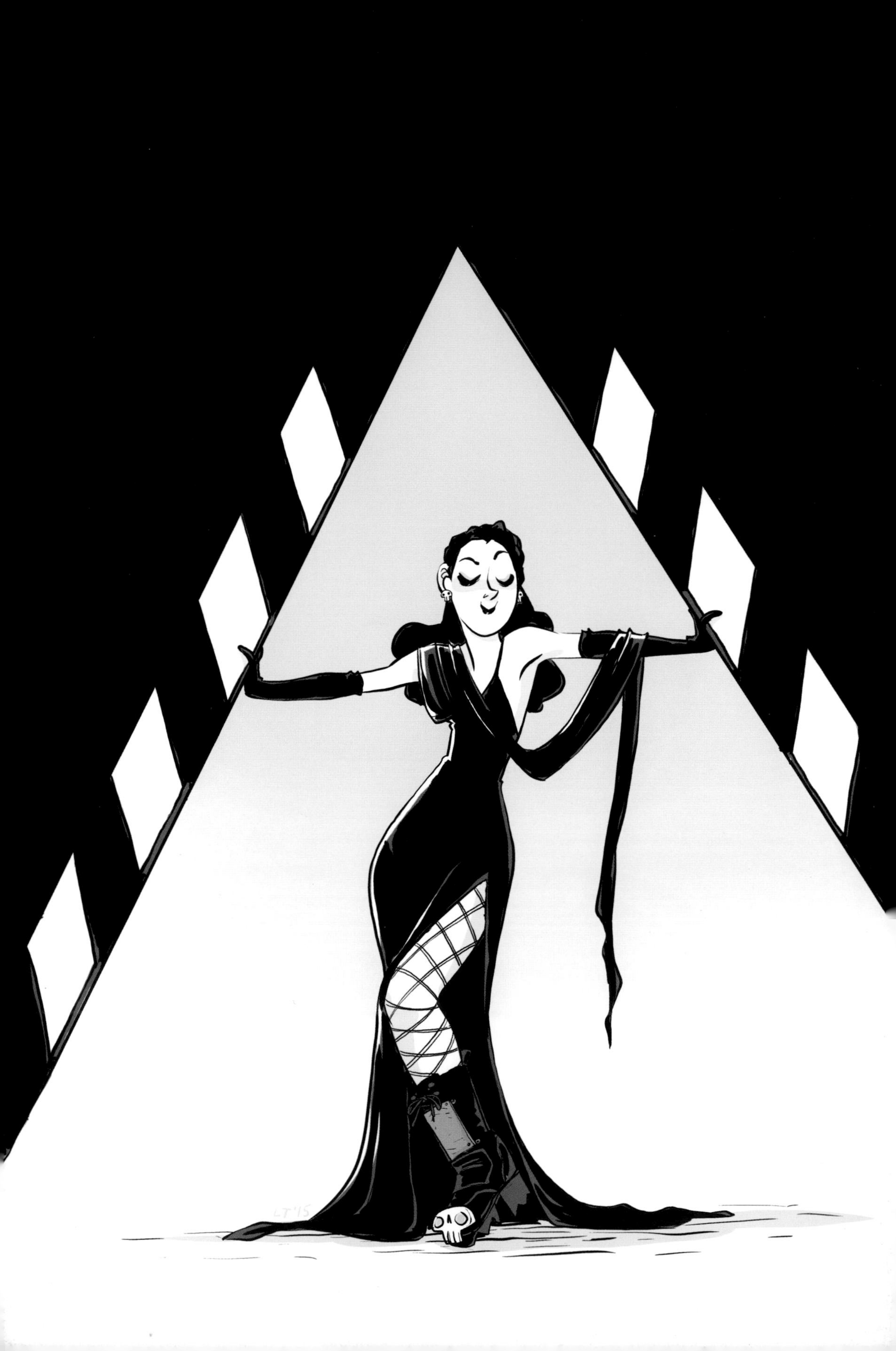
LT'15

**ISSUE #16 COVER**
LISSA TREIMAN

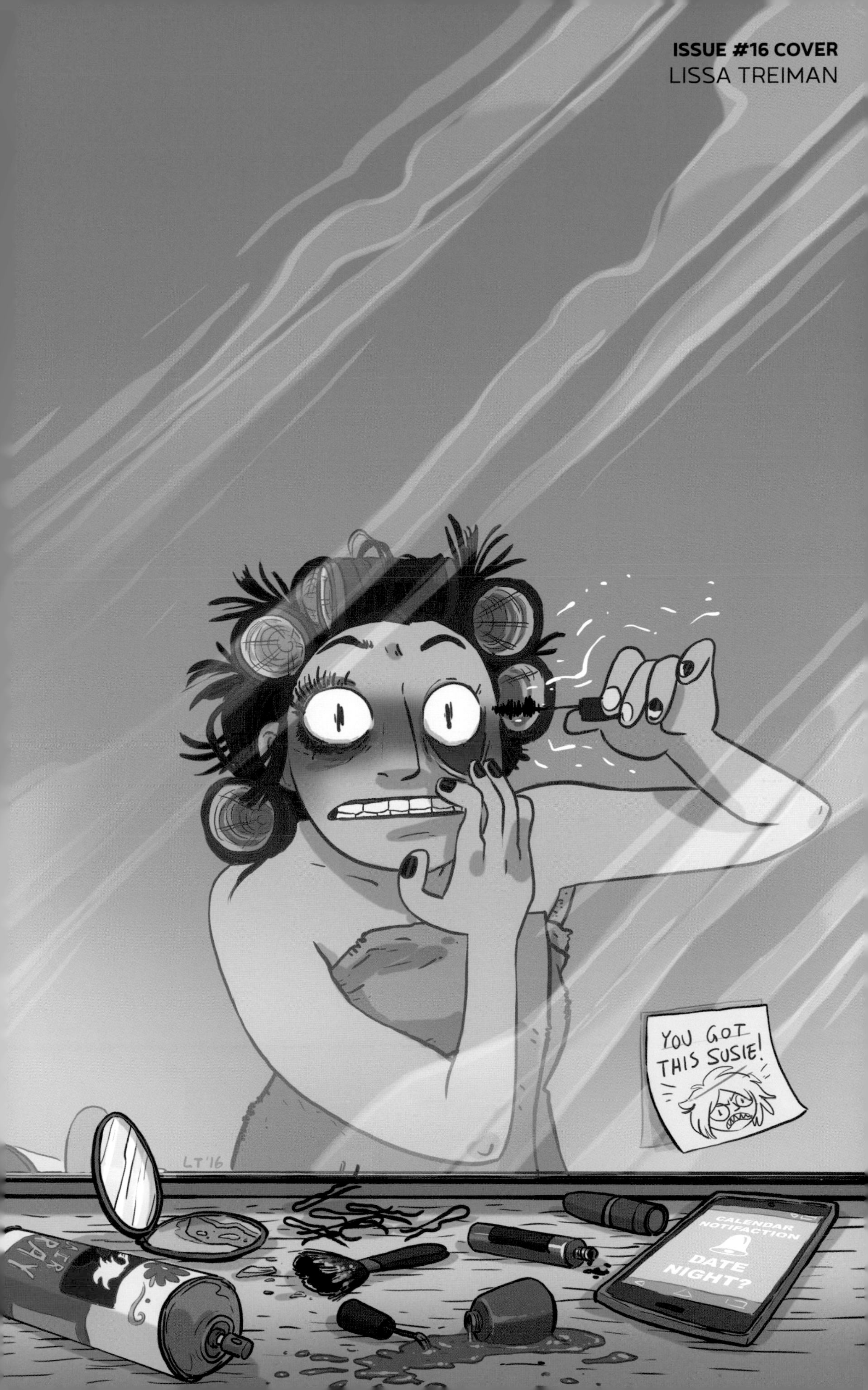
YOU GOT THIS SUSIE!
CALENDAR NOTIFACTION
DATE NIGHT?
LT '16

# GIANT DAYS:
## SKETCH GALLERY

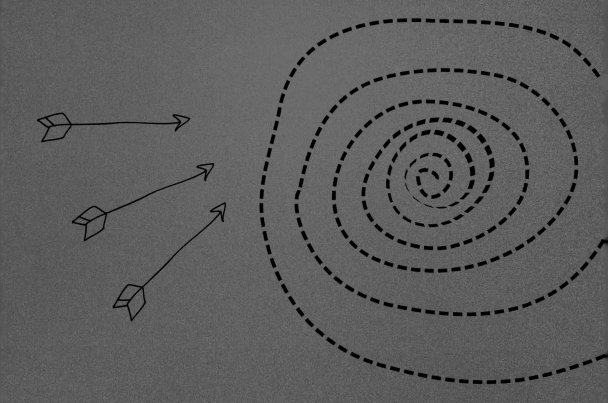

KETCHES BY **JOHN ALLISON**

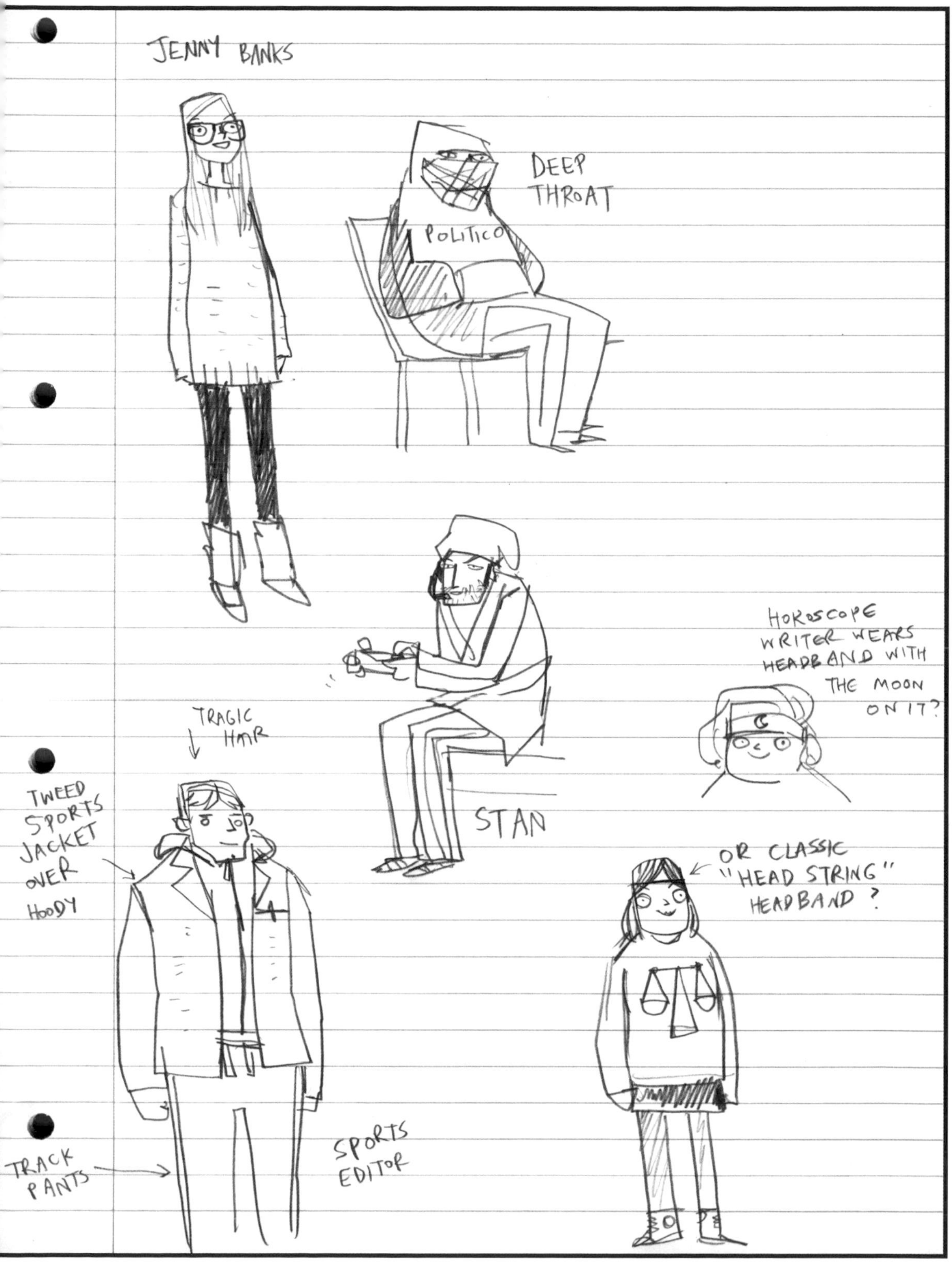
JENNY BANKS
DEEP THROAT
POLITICO
HOROSCOPE WRITER WEARS HEADBAND WITH THE MOON ON IT?
TRAGIC HAIR
STAN
TWEED SPORTS JACKET OVER HOODY
OR CLASSIC "HEAD STRING" HEADBAND?
SPORTS EDITOR
TRACK PANTS

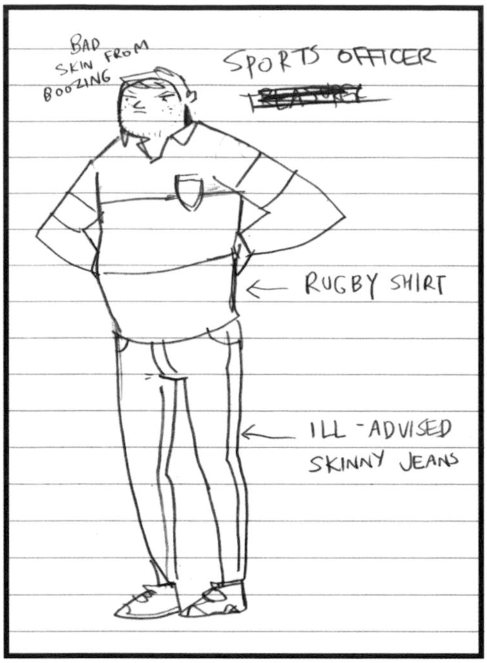
BAD SKIN FROM BOOZING
SPORTS OFFICER
RUGBY SHIRT
ILL-ADVISED SKINNY JEANS

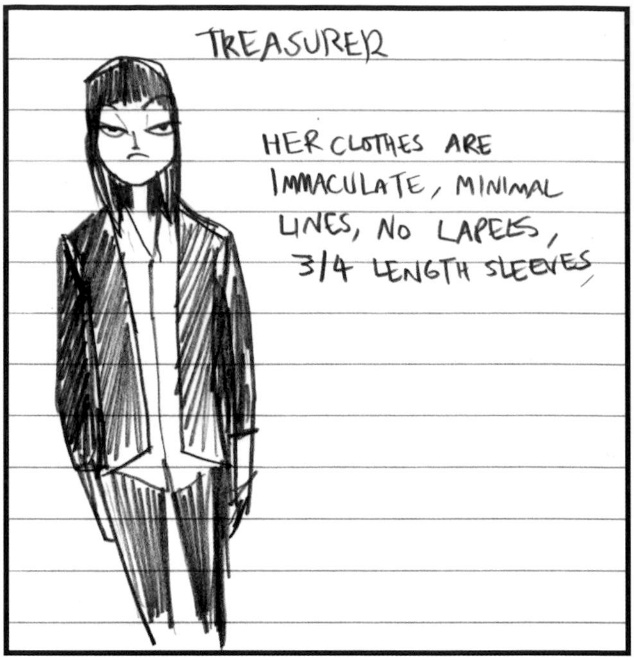
TREASURER
HER CLOTHES ARE IMMACULATE, MINIMAL LINES, NO LAPELS, 3/4 LENGTH SLEEVES

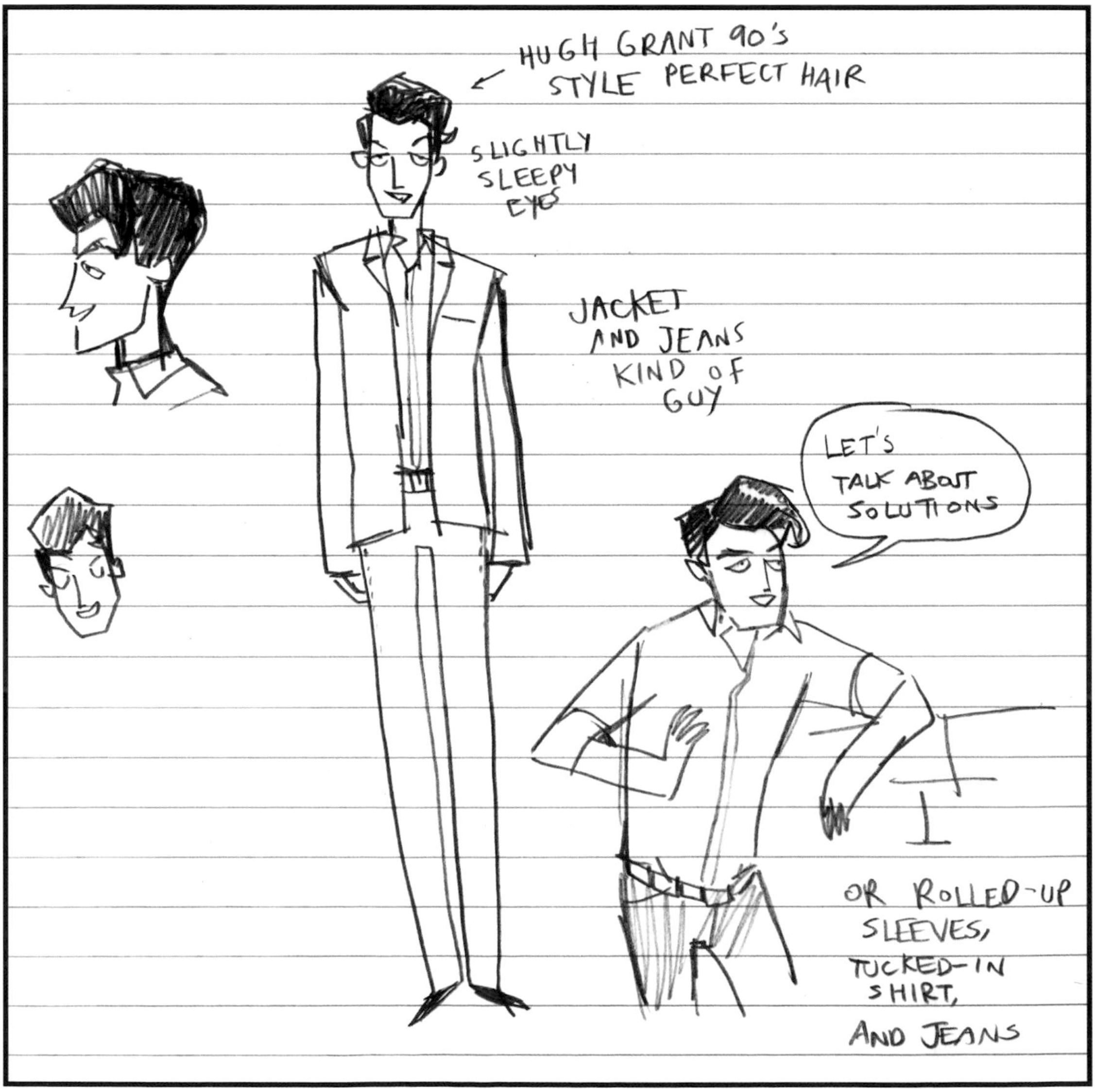
HUGH GRANT 90's STYLE PERFECT HAIR
SLIGHTLY SLEEPY EYES
JACKET AND JEANS KIND OF GUY
LET'S TALK ABOUT SOLUTIONS
OR ROLLED-UP SLEEVES, TUCKED-IN SHIRT, AND JEANS

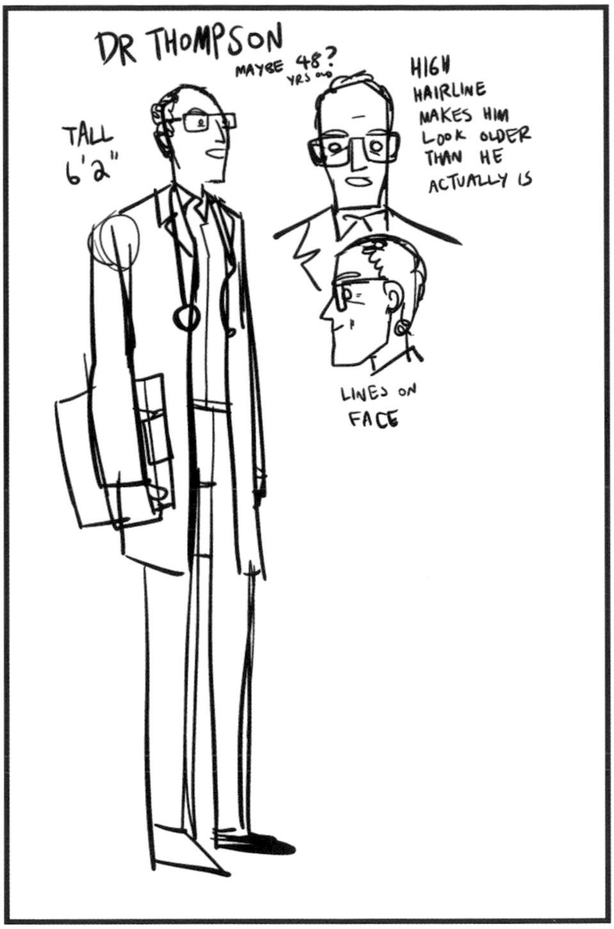
DR THOMPSON
MAYBE 48? YRS OLD
TALL 6'2"
HIGH HAIRLINE MAKES HIM LOOK OLDER THAN HE ACTUALLY IS
LINES ON FACE

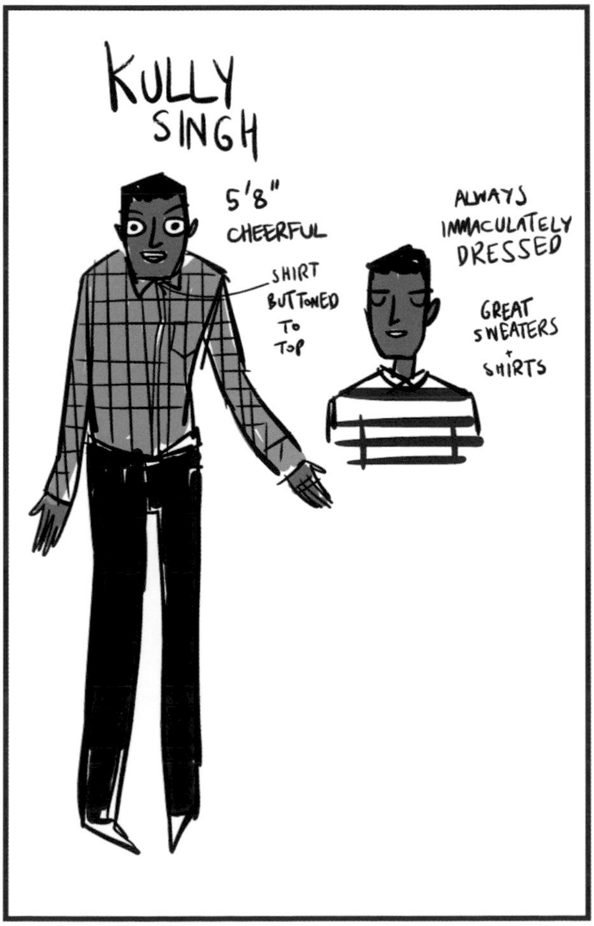
KULLY SINGH
5'8"
CHEERFUL
SHIRT BUTTONED TO TOP
ALWAYS IMMACULATELY DRESSED
GREAT SWEATERS + SHIRTS

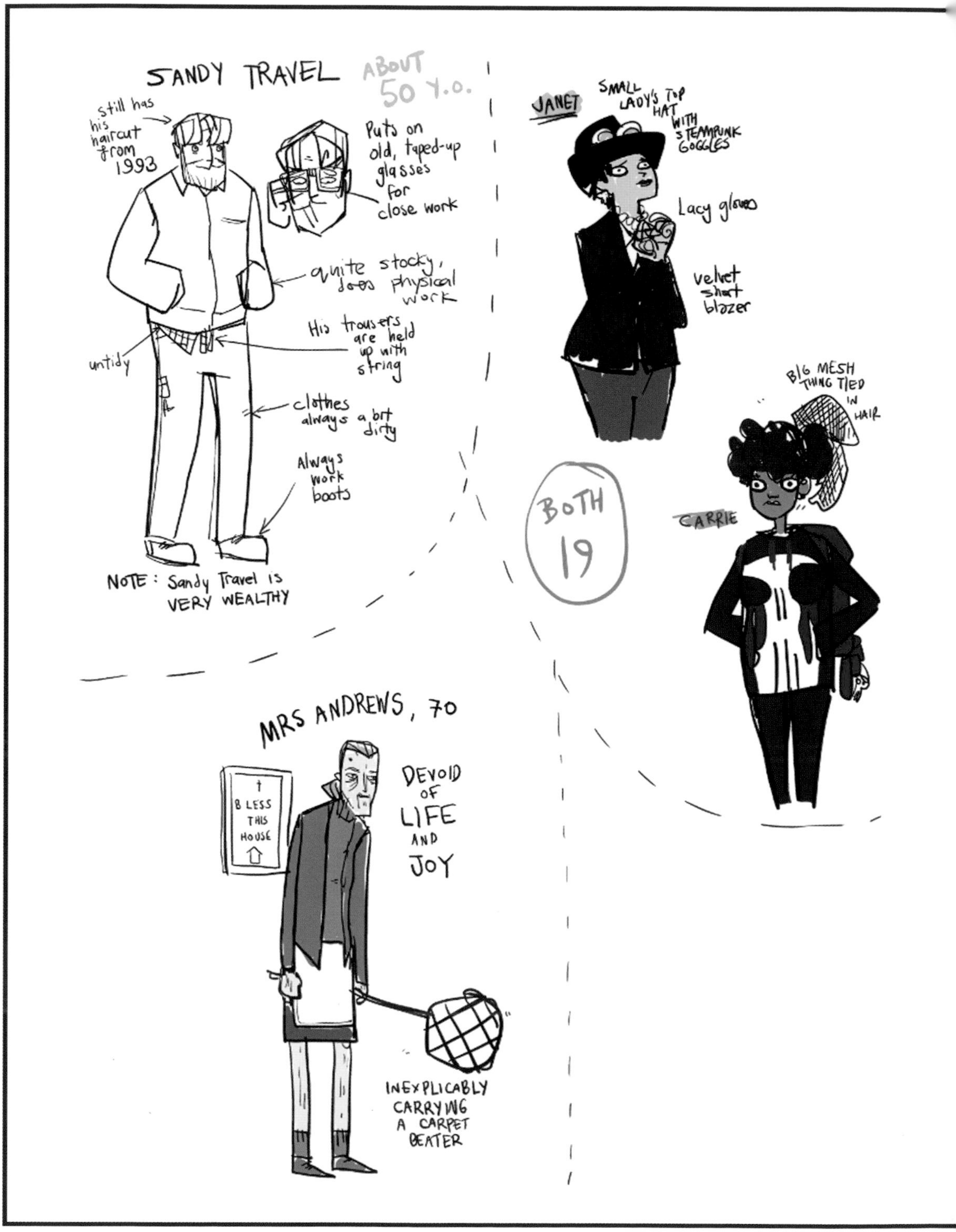
SANDY TRAVEL
ABOUT 50 Y.O.
still has his haircut from 1993
Puts on old, taped-up glasses for close work
quite stocky, does physical work
His trousers are held up with string
untidy
clothes always a bit dirty
Always work boots
NOTE: Sandy Travel is VERY WEALTHY
JANET
SMALL LADY'S TOP HAT WITH STEAMPUNK GOGGLES
Lacy gloves
velvet short blazer
BIG MESH THING TIED IN HAIR
BOTH 19
CARRIE
MRS ANDREWS, 70
BLESS THIS HOUSE
DEVOID OF LIFE AND JOY
INEXPLICABLY CARRYING A CARPET BEATER

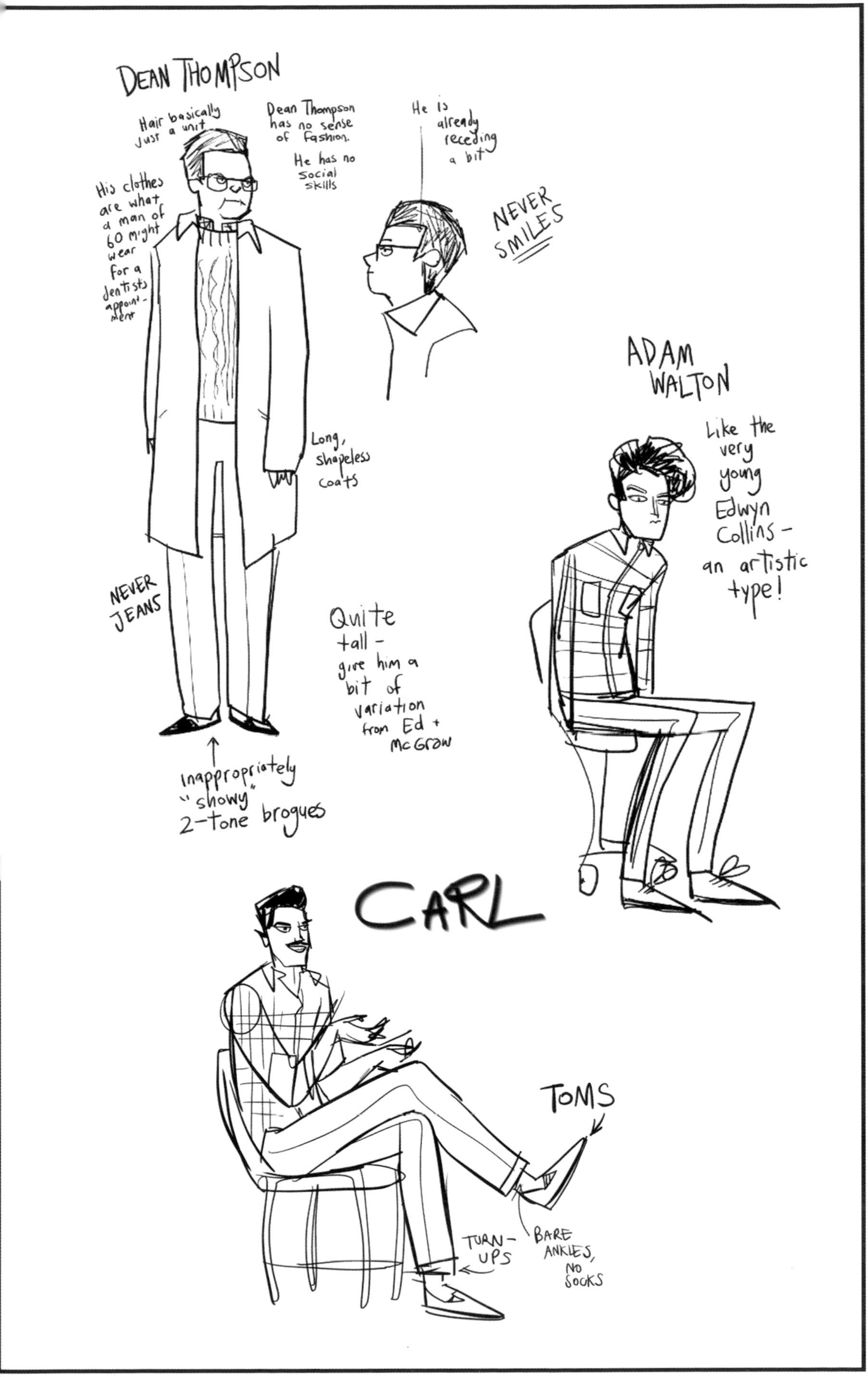
DEAN THOMPSON
Hair basically just a unit
Dean Thompson has no sense of fashion.
He has no social skills
He is already receding a bit
His clothes are what a man of 60 might wear for a dentist's appointment
NEVER SMILES
Long, shapeless coats
NEVER JEANS
Quite tall - give him a bit of variation from Ed + McGraw
Inappropriately "showy" 2-tone brogues
ADAM WALTON
Like the very young Edwyn Collins - an artistic type!
CARL
TOMS
TURN-UPS
BARE ANKLES, NO SOCKS

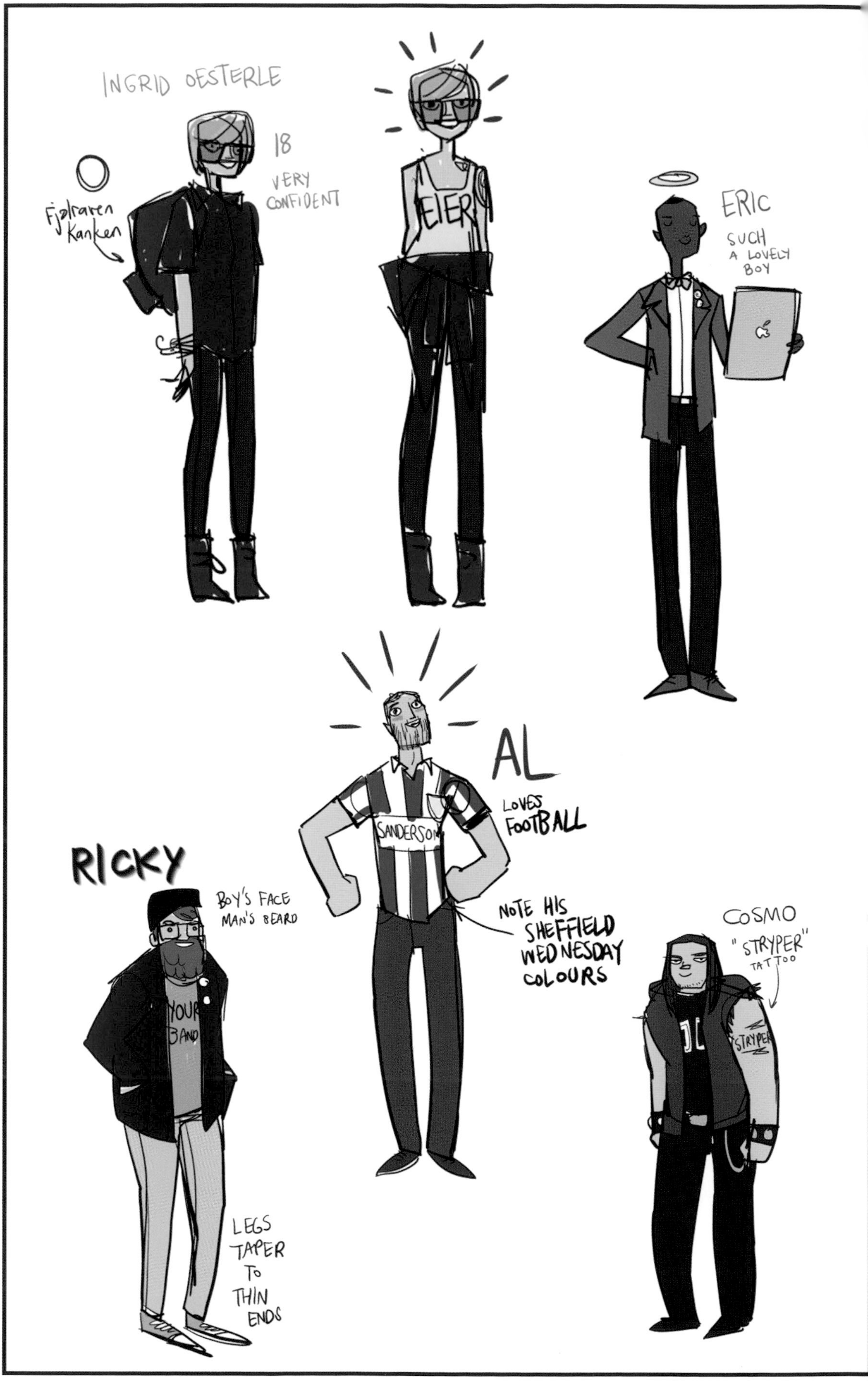
INGRID OESTERLE
18
VERY CONFIDENT
Fjalraven Kanken
EIER
ERIC
SUCH A LOVELY BOY
AL
LOVES FOOTBALL
SANDERSON
NOTE HIS SHEFFIELD WEDNESDAY COLOURS
RICKY
BOY'S FACE MAN'S BEARD
YOUR BAND
LEGS TAPER TO THIN ENDS
COSMO
"STRYPER" TATTOO
STRYPER

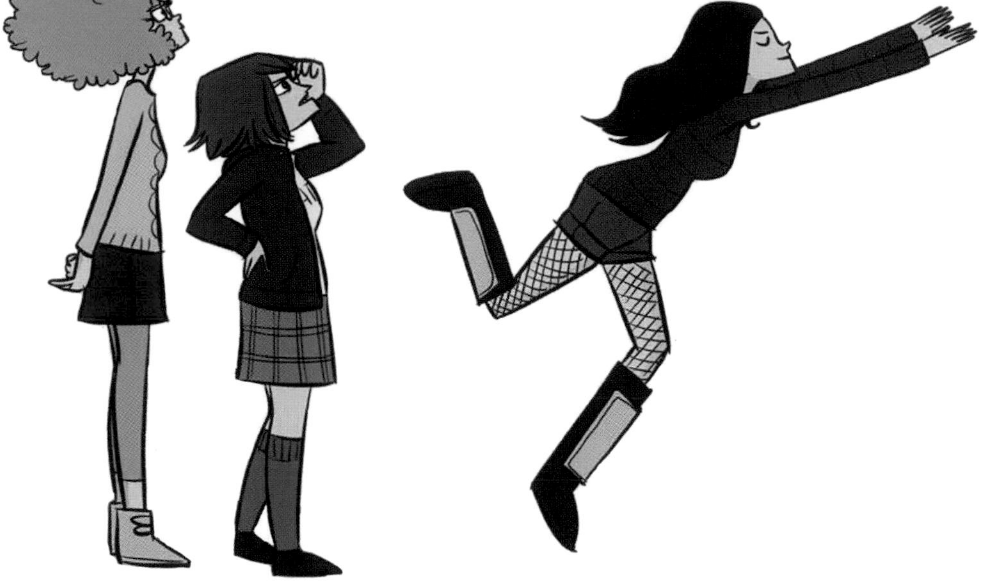

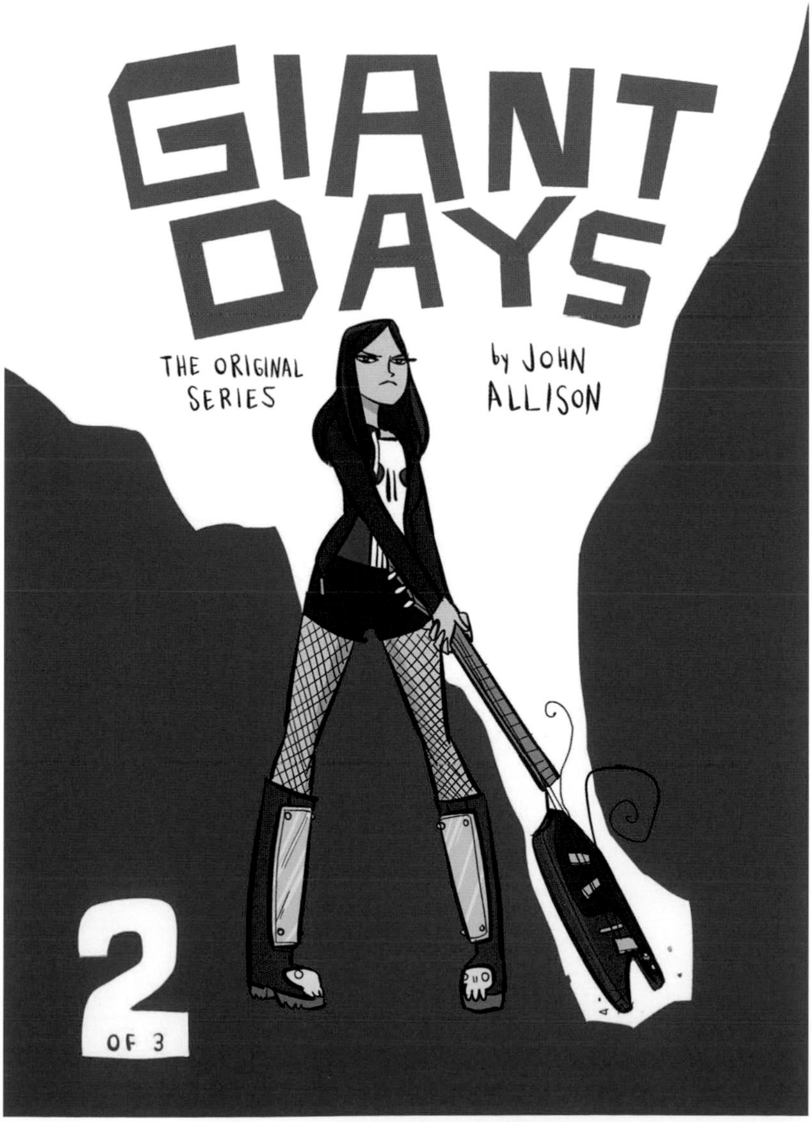
GIANT DAYS
THE ORIGINAL SERIES
by JOHN ALLISON
2
OF 3

# CREATOR BIOS

---

## JOHN ALLISON

John Allison is the artist and writer of the popular webcomics *Bobbins*, *Scary Go Round*, and most recently *Bad Machinery*, which won the British Comics Award for Best Comic in 2012 and is now collected by Oni Press. *Giant Days* is his first time writing for another artist. Raised in North and West Yorkshire, he now lives just north of London in Letchworth Garden City, where spends most of his spare time raking up leaves.

## LIZ FLEMING

Liz Fleming is a comic artist working out of Philadelphia. She graduated from the Savannah College of Art and Design and jumped right into the world of comics as a flatter for Lumberjanes. She's worked on dozens of BOOM! titles, such as *Regular Show*, *Steven Universe*, and *Bee and Puppycat*. In her spare time she works on her own personal comic projects and listens to a lot of Japanese rock music.